VOIC

As she and Nekaun left the balcony Auraya sought the Siyee priest's mind. It took some time to find him, and when she did she realised why. Teel was barely conscious and in terrible pain.

'What is wrong?' Nekaun asked.

The two Servants spoke at once, then the woman lapsed into silence. Auraya placed a hand on the Siyee's chest.

'He looked well enough this morning,' the male Servant confessed. 'It's strange. There is a—'

Nekaun raised a hand to silence the man. 'Auraya will want to make her own assessment,' he said. Looking at her, he nodded. 'Go on.'

She closed her eyes and quietened her mind as Mirar had taught her. It was not easy, but the distress of the body beneath her palm drew her in. She gasped at what she saw.

'He's dying,' she said.

'Can you do anything?' Nekaun asked.

She began to influence the body's processes, giving his heart strength, encouraging his lungs to work harder. Wherever she looked, organs were failing. Then she saw the cause. Something coursed through his veins. The source was his stomach.

Teel had been poisoned.

She reached for more magic . . . and was surprised and horrified when her efforts to heal the Siyee floundered. She reached out, trying to draw power to herself, but nothing came. In a rush, her awareness left the priest and flew outwards. She recognised the lack around her.

A void. I'm in a void. A big one, too. I should have detected it before but I was only concerned about Teel. He'll have to be moved. I wonder if Nekaun knows . . .

A chill ran through her body. Of course Nekaun knew about the void. How could he not? It was within the Sanctuary, the home of the Voices.

A trap. I fell right into it.

BY TRUDI CANAVAN

TRUDI CANAVAN

VOICE *of the* GODS

AGE OF THE FIVE: BOOK THREE

www.orbitbooks.net

ORBIT

First published in Australia in 2006 by Voyager
First published in Great Britain in 2007 by Orbit
This paperback edition published in 2008 by Orbit
Reprinted 2008 (three times)

Copyright © Trudi Canavan 2006

Excerpt from *The Magicians' Guild* copyright © 2001 by Trudi Canavan
Excerpt from *Wolfblade* copyright © 2004 by Jennifer Fallon

The moral right of the author has been asserted.

*All characters and events in this publication, other than those
clearly in the public domain, are fictitious and any resemblance
to real persons, living or dead, is purely coincidental.*

All rights reserved.
No part of this publication may be reproduced, stored in a
retrieval system, or transmitted, in any form or by any means,
without the prior permission in writing of the publisher, nor be
otherwise circulated in any form of binding or cover other than that
in which it is published and without a similar condition including
this condition being imposed on the subsequent purchaser.

A CIP catalogue record for this book is available from the British Library.

ISBN 978-1-84149-517-0

Typeset in Garamond 3 by Palimpsest Book Production Ltd,
Grangemouth, Stirlingshire
Printed and bound in Great Britain by Clays Ltd, St Ives plc

Papers used by Orbit are natural, renewable and recyclable
products made from wood grown in sustainable forests and certified
in accordance with the rules of the Forest Stewardship Council.

Mixed Sources
Product group from well-managed
forests and other controlled sources
www.fsc.org Cert no. SGS-COC-004081
© 1996 Forest Stewardship Council

FSC

Orbit
An imprint of
Little, Brown Book Group
100 Victoria Embankment
London EC4Y 0DY

An Hachette Livre UK Company
www.hachettelivre.co.uk

www.orbitbooks.net

TO MY PA, 'WINK' DAUNCEY,
WHO LOVED TO MAKE THINGS

ACKNOWLEDGEMENTS

Many thanks to:
'The Two Pauls' and Fran Bryson who read the roughest of the rough drafts. Also to Jennifer Fallon, Russell Kirkpatrick, Glenda Larke, Fiona McLennan, Kaaren Sutcliffe and Tessa Kum for their feedback. To all the readers, especially all my friends on Voyager Online. And, finally, to Stephanie Smith and the Voyager team.

JURAN

RIAN

MAIRAE

ARBEEM

MIRROR STRAIGHT

ALME

GENRIA

NORTHERN
ITHANIA

PORIN

TOREN

THE OPEN

SI

BORRA

PORTLESS

SOUTHERN
OCEAN

SOMREY

SEA OF CHAIA

IARIME

HANIA

CHON

DUNWAY

GULF OF LORE

SENNON

KARIENNE

SEA

SOUTHERN
ITHANIA

MUR

HANNAYA

GLYMMA

AVVEN

KAVE

DEKKAR

DYARA

AURAYA

PROLOGUE

The man staggering through the hospice door was covered in blood. It streaked his face and clothing, and leaked from between fingers pressed to his brow. As the occupants of the greeting hall saw him they fell silent, then the noise and activity resumed. Someone would take care of him.

Looks like that someone will be me this time, Priestess Ellareen thought as she glanced at the other healers. All priests, priestesses and Dreamweavers were occupied, though Dreamweaver Fareeh's bandaging of his patient's arm had quickened.

When the newcomer saw her approaching he looked relieved.

'Welcome to the hospice,' she said. 'What is your name?'

'Mal Toolmaker.'

'What happened to you?'

'Robbed.'

'Let me see that.' He reluctantly allowed her to lift his hand from his brow. A cut to the bone seeped more blood. She pressed his hand back over the wound. 'It needs some stitches.'

His gaze slid to the nearest Dreamweaver. 'You'll do it?'

She suppressed a sigh and indicated that he should follow her down the corridor. 'Yes. Come with me.'

It was not unheard of for a visitor to the hospice to request a Circlian healer, but it was unusual. Most who came here were

1

prepared to accept any help. Those who did not like or trust Dreamweavers went elsewhere.

Dreamweavers worked with Circlian priests and priestesses readily enough, and vice versa. They all knew they were healing many people who would not have received any help before. But a century of prejudice against Dreamweavers could not be erased in a few months. Ella had not expected it to be. Nor did she even want it to be. Dreamweavers did not worship the gods, so their souls died when their bodies did. She had great respect for them as healers – nobody who worked along-side them could deny being impressed by their knowledge and skill – but their dismissive, distrustful view of the gods irritated her.

I don't approve of blind intolerance either. The tendency in some people to fear those different from themselves to the point of irrational hatred disturbed her more than the common violence and miserable poverty that brought most patients to the hospice.

Recently a new group that called themselves 'true Circlians' had begun harassing the hospice workers. Their arrogant belief that their worship of the gods was more worthy than hers irritated her even more than the Dreamweavers' indifference. The only issue she agreed with them on was the Pentadrians. Unlike Pentadrians, Dreamweavers never claimed to follow gods – gods that didn't exist – or used that deception to convince a continent of people that Circlians were heathens and deserved to be exterminated.

At least this man isn't too proud to seek our help, she thought as she led him down the corridor into an unoccupied treatment room and directed him to sit on the end of a bench. Scooping water into a bowl from a trough of constantly flowing water at one end of the room, she warmed it with magic. She took some cloth from a basket, shook a few drops of wound-cleaning oil onto it, dipped it into the water and cleaned the man's face. Then she began stitching the cut.

A young priest, Naen, stepped into the doorway when she had nearly finished.

'Your mother just arrived, Priestess Ella.'

She frowned. 'Tell her I'll see her as soon as I'm finished with this patient.' *Yranna, make her stay put until I'm ready. And let her not be in one of her moods.*

:Naen will make sure she does not interrupt you, Ellareen, a voice assured her.

Ella straightened and looked around. There was no sign of the woman she had heard. *Am I hearing voices, like that crazy old man who comes in here all the time?*

:No, you're not crazy. You're as sane as most mortals. Saner, even. Even if you do talk to me all the time.

:Talk to . . . are you . . . Yranna?

:That's right.

:It can't be.

:Why not?

:Well . . . you're a god. A goddess. Why would you talk to me?

:I have a task for you.

A thrill of both excitement and fear ran down Ella's spine. At the same time she heard one of the priests in the greeting room raise his voice.

'There is a crowd blocking the street outside. They won't let us leave the hospice . . . no, we can't . . . best to wait it out.'

Not the 'true Circlians' again, she thought as she tied the last stitch.

:Yes. They have surrounded the hospice.

Ella sighed, then felt a chill of realisation.

:But . . . this blockade must be different to the others, or you wouldn't be asking me to perform a task for you.

:That's right.

3

:What is it?

:I want you to immobilise the man you are treating. Use magic, drugs – whatever it takes.

Ella froze and looked at the man sitting before her. He stared back at her, his pupils wide. It wasn't just the pain making him edgy, she realised. It was fear.

Her mouth went dry and her heart began to race. He might be more Gifted than her. He was certainly physically stronger than her. If this went wrong . . .

Don't think about it, she told herself. *When the gods ask for something to be done, I can only do my best to oblige them.*

The force of her magic knocked him against the wall, driving air from his lungs. Pushing him down onto the bench, she held him there, hoping that he was too caught up in fighting for air to use any Gifts he might have.

But he'll recover his wits soon enough. Yranna suggested drugs . . .

Grabbing a bottle of sleep vapour oil, she poured some onto a cloth and held it against his nose until his eyes glazed over. It would subdue him for several minutes, but what then? The blockade might last for hours.

I need a sleep inducer. She searched the room and found a nearly empty jar of sleepease powder. Mixing up a thin draught from the remnants, she carefully poured it down his throat. It roused him to a semi-conscious state; he coughed, then swallowed the mixture before subsiding into unconsciousness again.

She stood back to assess her handiwork, and realised she had no idea how long such a small dose of the drug would work for. A half-cupful induced a full night's sleep. The dose she'd given might last an hour, if she was lucky. She could find more sleepease, but it was dangerous and difficult to administer to a fully unconscious patient. It might get into his lungs. She looked down at the man.

Yranna said to immobilise you, she thought, *not kill you. What did you have planned, anyway, Mal Toolmaker?*

On impulse, she grabbed a few strips of bandages, tied his hands and feet and gagged him. To hide this, she took a blanket and covered the man, leaving only the top of his head showing.

But this would not stop him attracting attention when he woke up. *The others will want to know why I did this. What am I going to tell them?* She was not sure they would believe her if she told them the goddess had instructed her to immobilise a patient. *Well, they might eventually, but in the meantime they'll probably set him free to do whatever he intends to do.*

He'd suffered a blow to the head, so it would be plausible to say he'd experienced dizziness or disorientation. Sleep drugs were not the usual treatment, however. She would have to come up with other ways to explain that.

'Ella!' a familiar voice called from within the corridor.

Ella spun around. Her mother must have slipped away from Priest Naen. She hurried out of the room before the woman could discover her with a bound and gagged patient.

In the corridor a thin greying woman wrapped in a clean, well-made tawl of fine cloth, scowled disapprovingly as she saw Ella.

'Ella. At last. I need to have a little *talk* with you.'

'So long as it is little,' Ella said, keeping her attitude businesslike. 'Come back to the greeting hall.'

'You must stop working here,' her mother told her in a low voice as she followed Ella. 'It's too dangerous. It's bad enough knowing you're constantly under the influence of these heathens, but now it's worse. The rumours are all over the city. I'm surprised you haven't already had the sense to leave this—'

'Mother,' Ella interrupted. 'What are you talking about?'

'Mirar is back,' her mother replied. 'Or haven't you heard?'

'Obviously not,' Ella said.

'He was – is – the leader of the Dreamweavers. A Wild, you know. They say he wasn't killed a century ago; he survived. He's been in hiding and now he's returned.'

'Who says this?' Ella askèd, trying not to sound too sceptical.

'Everybody – and don't give me that look. He's been seen by many people. And the White aren't denying it.'

'Have they had a chance to?'

'Of course they have. Now, you listen to me. You can't work here any more. You have to stop!'

'I'm not abandoning people who need my help because of a rumour.'

'It's not rumour!' her mother exclaimed, forgetting that she had already called the claims of Mirar's return such. 'It is the truth! What if he comes here? Think what he might do to you! You might not even recognise him. He might be working here now, in disguise! He might *seduce* you!'

Ella managed, with difficulty, to keep the smile from her face. *Seduce indeed!* 'Dreamweavers do not interest me, Mother.'

But the woman wasn't listening. As the possible threats to Ella's person grew more preposterous, Ella steered her mother toward a bench in the greeting hall.

'And now look what's happened,' her mother said abruptly, sitting down. 'Because *he's* returned, *we're* stuck in here. Isn't there a back door to this place? Can't we—'

'No. When this happens there are always troublemakers waiting outside the back entrance.'

'If you were a high priestess they wouldn't dare.'

Ella smothered a sigh. *Tell me, Yranna, are all mothers like this? Are they ever satisfied with their offspring? If I managed to become a high priestess would she decide I ought to be a White? If by some miracle I became a White, would she start nagging me to become a god?*

She gave her mother the usual answer. 'If I were a high priestess I would have no time to see you at all.'

Her mother shrugged and turned away. 'We hardly see you anyway.'

Only every second or third day, Ella thought. *How neglectful I am. How deprived are my parents. If I ever get like this*, she thought, *please, Yranna, have someone kill me.*

'Have you heard who is going to replace Auraya?' her mother asked.

'No.'

'Surely you must have heard *something* by now.'

How is it she can make even that sound like a failing?

'As you've pointed out so many times before, I am only a lowly priestess, unworthy of notice or respect, or even the deepest of Circlian secrets,' Ella replied dryly, expecting to be scolded for her sarcasm.

But her mother wasn't listening. 'It'll be one of the high priests,' her mother said, mostly to herself. 'We need someone strong – not some frivolous young girl with a liking for heathens. The gods did right to kick that Auraya girl out of the White.'

'She wasn't kicked out. She resigned to help the Siyee.'

'That's not what *I* heard.' Her mother's eyes shone with glee at the gossip she was privy to. 'I heard she refused to do what the gods asked of her, and they took her powers from her.'

Ella gritted her teeth. 'Well, I talk to Yranna all the time, and she mentioned nothing about that. Besides, a good healer doesn't spend work hours gossiping.'

Her mother's eyes narrowed and her chin rose. Before she could speak, however, Ella heard her name called. She looked up and felt her stomach sink as she saw Priest Naen and Priest Kleven approaching. Both were frowning.

'What happened to the man with the cut brow, Ella?' Kleven asked.

'He . . . he became angry when he heard we were trapped here.'

'So you sedated him?'

Leaving her mother sitting on the bench, she rose and hurried over to Kleven, lowering her voice.

'Yes. He was . . . *very* angry. I used sleep vapour, and when he showed no ill effects I gave him a tiny dose of sleepease.'

'Sleepease? On a man suffering a head blow?' Kleven exclaimed quietly. He shook his head and started toward the corridor. Ella felt her heart skip a beat, and hurried after him.

'Anyone suffering a head injury who displays strange behaviour should be watched closely,' Kleven told her as he entered the room. He drew the blanket from Mal Toolmaker's head, exposing the gag.

'What is this?' he said. Pulling the blanket away, he exclaimed as the bandages tying the man's hands and feet were revealed.

'He attacked me,' she told him.

He looked at her sharply. 'Are you all right?'

She shrugged. 'Yes. He didn't touch me.'

'You should have told me about this.'

'I was going to but . . . Mother distracted me.'

He nodded, then turned back to the unconscious man. A chill ran down her back as he began to untie the bandages. 'Is that wise?' she asked hesitantly.

'Naen will watch him. How much sleepease did you give him?'

'Not much. A small spoon's worth.'

The man's eyes fluttered in reaction to Kleven's touch. He wasn't waking up, but he would soon.

'Stop,' she found herself saying. 'You can't let him wake up. You have to drug him again.'

Kleven turned to stare at her questioningly. 'Why?'

She sighed. 'It's incredible, but you have to believe me. I was warned about him and ordered to immobilise him by . . .' She grimaced. 'I know you'll find this hard to believe – by Yranna.'

Kleven's eyebrows rose. 'The goddess?'

'Yes. She spoke to me. In my mind. And no, I don't usually hear voices in my head.'

The priest considered her thoughtfully. She saw the doubts in his eyes, but could not tell whether he hesitated to believe her or to risk acting against a god's orders.

'How am I to know you're not making this up?'

'I can't prove it, if that is what you mean. But I can point out that I have never acted with anything but good sense before – or shown signs of madness.'

'You haven't,' Kleven agreed. 'But it does not make sense that Yranna would speak to you but not the rest of us. If this man is a danger to the hospice, we all need to know.'

'That puzzled me, too,' she admitted. 'Perhaps the danger has passed . . . but I'm not willing to take that risk. Are you?'

Kleven looked at the sleeping man dubiously.

'Can I offer any assistance?'

They turned to find Dreamweaver Fareeh standing in the doorway. Ella groaned inwardly. Kleven hadn't finished untying the bindings, and as the Dreamweaver noticed them his eyebrows rose.

'A troublesome patient?'

Kleven looked at Ella. 'In more ways than one.'

The Dreamweaver looked at the sleeping man, then at each of them, and nodded. He began to move away. Kleven sighed. 'Ella here says she was instructed by Yranna to immobilise him.'

Ella turned to stare at the priest in surprise.

'Ah,' was all Fareeh said.

Why would Kleven tell him that? Slowly the reason dawned on her. *If he doesn't, Fareeh would know we are keeping something from him. That might change how he deals with us.* She shook her head. *This balance of trust and distrust between our peoples is so easily tipped.*

'Do you believe her?' Kleven asked.

The Dreamweaver shrugged. 'I do not believe what I cannot confirm with my own senses, so belief is irrelevant. Either she is wrong, or she is right. Either situation is alarming. I can suggest only that you bring both patient and priestess to the greeting hall so that we can all help to watch and deal with any trouble that arises from this.'

The older priest nodded. 'Good advice.'

Ella watched anxiously as Kleven lifted the unconscious man with magic and carried him out into the hall. Visitors and healers alike, bored and eager for distraction, watched curiously as this stranger was laid upon a bench. But as time passed and the man did nothing but sleep, their attention soon strayed.

Watching the stranger, Ella wondered what he had planned to do. *Were you going to attack us? Were you going to slip out of the room while we were distracted and open the back door to let your people in?* Every time the man moved, Ella's heart lurched.

When the man's eyes finally fluttered open she rose, ready to face any kind of attack with magic.

'Sit down, Priestess Ella,' Kleven said calmly, but firmly. She obeyed.

The stranger struggled up onto his elbows, staring groggily about. His gaze fell on Ella, and he shuddered.

'Wha' hap'n'd?' he asked. 'Sh', she t'tack'd me.'

'Stay calm. You are not in any danger,' Kleven said soothingly. 'Take a moment to recollect yourself.'

The man's gaze roamed the room. 'Still here. Wh— . . . am I a pris'ner?'

'No.'

He began to struggle to his feet. Kleven stood and steadied the man.

'Let me go.'

'All in good time. You've had a small dose of a sleep drug. Just let it wear off.'

'Sleep . . . why'd you drug me?'

'One of us believed you intended us harm. Is that true?'

The expression that crossed the man's face sent shivers down Ella's spine. *Guilt!* she thought. *He was planning something.*

'No. I just came to . . .' He reached up and touched his brow, flinching as his fingers found the stitches. He drew in a deep breath and straightened his back, then stood up. He swayed a moment, then took a few steps. The drug was wearing off quickly, and nobody was moving to stop the man as he walked with growing confidence across the room and back.

'I'm right,' he said. 'Can I go now?'

Kleven shrugged and nodded. 'I can see no reason why we should keep you here . . . except that there's a hostile crowd outside. You'll get another one of those scratches, at the least, if you try to leave.'

The man looked at Ella pointedly. 'I'll risk it.'

Kleven shrugged. 'We won't stop you, we can only warn you. I will release the door.'

Nobody stirred as the man started toward the door. Ella frowned. She ought to be glad he was leaving, his plan foiled. But something nagged at her. Why would Yranna let this man go if he had threatened the hospice? Yranna had said . . .

Then she realised what it was.

'Stop!' she cried, jumping up. The man ignored her.

'Ella . . .' Kleven began.

As the man put his hand to the door Ella drew magic and sent out a barrier to stop him. He pressed the invisible shield and turned to glare at her angrily.

'Ella!' Kleven barked. 'Let him go!'

'No,' she replied calmly. 'Yranna told me to immobilise him. She didn't say why. Maybe it was to prevent him harming us. Maybe it was to prevent him leaving.'

The man backed away from the door and turned to face her, his face contorted with anger. She felt Kleven take hold of her arm.

'Ella. We can't . . .'

His voice faded and she heard him draw in a quick breath. A rapping came from the door. Kleven let her go.

'Drop your barrier, Ella,' he murmured. 'Rian of the White is here.'

She did as he asked. The door swung open. A man wearing an undecorated circ stepped over the threshold. Rian, the red-haired White, regarded the stranger with ancient eyes.

'You've led us quite a chase, Lemarn Shipmaker.'

The stranger backed away, his face pale. A high priestess stepped into the hospice. At a nod from Rian, she gestured at the man. He walked stiffly past her and through the door, obviously guided by an invisible force.

Rian turned to regard the hospice occupants. 'The trouble-makers have prudently found other places to be. You can leave safely now. Or stay and continue your work or treatment, as you wish.'

From around the room came several sighs of relief. Kleven stepped forward and made the formal two-handed sign of the circle.

'Thank you, Rian of the White.'

Rian nodded, then looked at Ella. 'Well done, Priestess Ellareen. We've been looking for this man for months. The gods are impressed with your loyalty and obedience. I would not be surprised if I heard you had been offered a timely high priestess position.'

She stared at him in astonishment. He turned away, obviously not expecting a reply, and stepped outside.

A timely high priestess position? Surely he isn't hinting that . . . no, he wouldn't.

But the Choosing Ceremony for the next White was only a month away. What other reason was there for a promotion to high priestess to be timely?

I have only to wait and see.

Feeling light-headed, she walked back into the hospice and returned to her work.

PART ONE

CHAPTER 1

The constant rush of cascading water echoed between the walls. As Emerahl moved further down the tunnel the noise diminished, but so did the light. She drew a little magic and created a spark, then sent it forward to the end of the tunnel and beyond.

Everything was as she had left it: the rough beds in the centre of the cave, made of logs lashed together and tough strips of bark woven into a tight net; the stone bowls Mirar had carved while stuck here last summer, waiting until he could master the skill of hiding his mind from the gods; the jars, boxes and bags of dried or preserved food and cures stacked against one wall, gathered over the months they had lived here.

Only one essential part of the cave could not be seen. Moving forward slowly, she felt the magic that imbued the world about her diminish to nothing and she smiled with satisfaction. Keeping her light burning with the magic she had gathered within herself, she continued to the centre of the room, where magic once more surrounded her. She was within the void.

Sighing, she sat down on one of the beds. When she had returned here last spring, she had noted that the space devoid of magic had shrunk since her last visit over a century ago. Slowly the magic of the world was seeping back to fill it. That suggested the original void had been even larger before she'd discovered it, and would eventually no longer exist.

For now it would suffice. She had travelled through the rough wild land of Si, a journey which involved a lot more climbing than walking, in order to reach this place. At every second step she had cursed Mirar, her fellow immortal and friend, for talking her into teaching Auraya. Every other step she had cursed The Twins, immortals even more ancient than herself and Mirar, who she had finally met for the first time a few months ago, for agreeing with him.

:We must know what Auraya is, Tamun had said to her in a dream link, the night after Mirar had made his request. *If she becomes an immortal she could also become a valuable ally.*

:What if she can't do it?

:She must still be a powerful sorceress, Surim had replied with uncharacteristic seriousness. *Remember, the gods do not like independent sorcerers any more than they like us immortals. If we do not help her they will kill her.*

:Will they? Just because she has quit the White doesn't mean she has turned against them, Emerahl had pointed out. *Auraya is still a priestess. She still serves the gods.*

:Her mind is full of doubts, Tamun said. *The gods' demand that she kill Mirar without trial weakened her regard for them.*

Emerahl nodded. She knew this herself. Once Auraya had removed the ring of the gods' power her mind had no longer been shielded. With help from The Twins, Emerahl had learned to mind-skim and had occasionally seen Auraya's thoughts.

The trouble is, while Auraya's loyalty toward some gods has been weakened she still feels a need to at least remain on good terms with them. If she discovers who I am, she will know the gods want me dead. And she doesn't have a prior friendship with me to make her reluctant to strike, as she had with Mirar.

Yet Emerahl didn't believe Auraya would kill her unless the

gods ordered it. She had seen enough of Auraya's mind to know the former White did not like killing. If their meeting went well the gods wouldn't even know Emerahl was here. She looked around the room again. The gods were beings of magic, and so could only exist where there was magic. They could not enter these rare, unexplained voids, nor could they see what lay within unless they looked through the eyes of humans standing outside it. Once Auraya was here the gods would not be able to read her mind.

There was still a good chance Emerahl had travelled halfway across the continent for nothing. She could not make Auraya learn anything. She would have to be careful what she told the woman, too. If Auraya left the void before learning to hide her thoughts, the gods would read her mind.

Emerahl shook her head and sighed again. *This is such a risk. It's all very well for The Twins, safely hidden away in the Red Caves in distant Sennon, or Mirar in Southern Ithania. They don't have to worry that Auraya will change her mind and decide killing immortals without due cause is acceptable.*

But The Twins' help was invaluable. Every day and night they reached out to minds across the continents, skimming thoughts, alert to the intentions and actions of powerful people. The pair had honed these skills over thousands of years. They knew mortals so well, they could predict their behaviour with uncanny accuracy.

Mirar had always said that the Wilds – or Immortals, as The Twins called them – each had an innate Gift. Emerahl's was her ability to change her age, Mirar's was his unsurpassed ability to heal. The Twins' was mind-skimming. The Gull's . . . she wasn't sure exactly what his was, but she was sure it had something to do with the sea.

And Auraya's, Mirar claimed, was her ability to fly. Emerahl felt a twinge of interest ease her annoyance at being here. *I*

19

wonder if she can teach it to others. Mirar taught me to heal, though I can't do it as well as he can. Perhaps I won't be able to fly as well as she can . . . actually, flying doesn't sound like an ability one can safely do less well at. Ineptitude could be fatal.

She snorted then. *It's worth a try, though. There has to be some benefit in this for me. It would be easier to like the idea of teaching this girl if I'm compensated for having to put off my search for the Scroll of the Gods.*

The Twins had told her that they'd picked up rumours of an artefact that described the War of the Gods from the viewpoint of a long-dead goddess. Emerahl had decided to find it. Such a record might contain information useful to the Immortals. Information that might help them evade the gods' notice, or survive if they failed. It might even give them the means to fight back.

According to The Twins, scholars in Southern Ithania had been searching for the Scroll for decades. They had made progress lately, but were still lacking enough information to discover the Scroll's location. The Twins had assured her that these scholars were not about to find it soon, however. She had time enough to teach Auraya.

She moved to the jars and pots and began looking over the cures and preserved food.

But first I need to gather some food. And then I have to figure out a way to get Auraya to come here, and persuade her to stay for a while, all without arousing the gods' suspicions.

The ship climbed steadily up one side of a wave, paused for a moment at the crest, then plunged down the other side. Mirar gripped the railing, half terrified, half exhilarated. Spray constantly wet him, but he didn't retreat below deck. The wind and water were a welcome relief from the heat in the small passenger compartment.

And the old man doesn't need me around to remind him that he's dying, Mirar told himself.

He'd treated Rikken in one of the small ports along the Avven coast. Tough and wiry, the old merchant had grown anxious at Mirar's assessment of his failing health. It was not the news that he was dying that bothered him, but that he might not expire in his homeland.

So he had asked Mirar to accompany him on his final journey home to Dekkar, in the hope that having a healer on hand would ensure he returned alive. Mirar had agreed out of restlessness and curiosity. He had encountered no hostility toward Dreamweavers in Avven, but the unending sameness of the towns he had passed through had begun to bore him. The buildings were made of mud-coated brick like those in Sennon, but did not vary in colour or design. The people, men and women, wore drab clothing and covered their faces with veils. Even their music was monotonous.

I'm not looking for trouble, he told himself, remembering Emerahl's accusation during their last dream link. *I like to travel and explore. It's been a long time since I was free to do so.* One of the crew hurried past Mirar, nodding and smiling as their eyes met. *And these southerners are friendly*, Mirar added, nodding in return.

He looked toward the coast again. A low rock face had appeared the day before and now it soared higher than the cliffs of Toren. Ahead its shadow abruptly ended, and he was beginning to make out the reason.

Time passed slowly, the ship only allowing a glimpse of the coast at the crest of each wave. Mirar waited patiently. Then, between one wave and another, the end of the cliff came into view.

The high rock face turned abruptly inland, its sheer sides dropping to a low, forested land fringed by gentle beaches. The change was extraordinary: bare rock to lush vegetation. The cliff continued to the east, folding back and forth into the distance, growing even higher than at the coast.

The sight was startling. It looked as if the land to the west had been levered up in an enormous slab, shifted forward and deposited on top of that of the east.

Is this natural? Mirar asked himself. *Or did some being – god or otherwise – heave up the land long ago?*

'Dreamweaver?'

Mirar looked for the source of the voice, and found the crewman standing nearby, a rope in one hand. The other hand pointed toward the forested land.

'Dekkar,' the man explained. Mirar nodded, and the crewman went back to his work with the speed of long practice.

So this was Rikken's homeland. Dekkar, southernmost of all countries, was famous for its jungle. The cliff was a natural barrier and border between it and Avven. As if obeying some local law, the seas had calmed. The crew put on more sail, and their pace quickened.

For the next few hours Mirar listened to the men talking, guessing at the meaning of their words. An unfamiliar language was a difficulty he hadn't needed to overcome in a millennium. The dialects of Southern Ithania were descended from a branch of languages far older than Mirar, and so there were few words recognisably related to those of the main continent. So far he had learned enough basic words of the Avven tongue to get by, and from the Dreamweavers he'd encountered he had gleaned most of what he needed to work as a healer.

His own people were more numerous here than in the north. They did not exist in the numbers they once had, but the general populace appeared to accept and respect them, as they did the followers of other 'cults'. Even so, he had avoided the few

Pentadrian Servants he had seen. Though local Dreamweavers assured him that Servants were tolerant of heathens, he was also a northerner. Those sick Pentadrians who had learned where he had come from had either refused his help, or reluctantly accepted it if he was in the company of local Dreamweavers. He did not expect the priests and priestesses of their religion to feel any differently.

The cliff that was the edge of Avven loomed over the forest like a great wave that threatened to crash down on Dekkar at any moment. As they sailed further south it withdrew slowly to become a bluish shadow as straight as the horizon. At intervals, buildings appeared along the coast. Standing on high stilts, they were constructed mainly of wood and connected by raised walkways, though here and there, usually in the midst of a town, a stone structure stood out. These stone edifices were painted black with the star symbol of the Five Gods outlined prominently in white.

The sun hung low on the horizon when the ship finally turned toward the shore. It tacked into a bay crowded with vessels and surrounded by the largest gathering of buildings Mirar had seen so far. The broad platforms the houses were built upon connected with neighbours via bridges of rope and slats or, occasionally, brightly painted wood.

Catching the talkative crewman's eye, Mirar glanced toward the town questioningly.

'Kave,' the man told him.

This was Dekkar's main city and Rikken's home. Mirar started toward the hold. The old merchant was being kept alive as much by his own determination as Mirar's help. Now that he was home, it was possible that his determination might fade too quickly to get him to shore.

So he stopped, surprised, when Rikken stepped out of the hold on wobbly legs. Yuri, the man's servant and constant companion, was supporting one arm. Mirar stepped forward to take the other.

The old man's eyes sought the town and he gave a small sigh.

'The Sanctuary of Kave,' he said. Mirar recognised the word 'sanctuary', but could only guess at the mumble that followed. Yuri was frowning, but he didn't speak as Rikken moved to the rail. From somewhere a crewman produced a stool, and Rikken lowered himself onto it to wait.

The ship worked its way into the bay, dropped anchor, then much fuss was made of lowering Rikken gently into a boat. Mirar collected his bag from the hold and joined the old man.

Crewmen swung down to pick up the oars, and the little boat began to move toward the city. When they reached the wharf, Mirar and Yuri helped Rikken disembark. Mirar noted that the stilts the houses were built upon were whole tree trunks and together they looked like a sturdy, leafless forest.

Yuri arranged for two of the sailors to carry Rikken up a staircase to the platform above. Two others lifted up a litter that had been stowed on the boat. Once they had reached the interconnected platforms of the city, Rikken slumped onto the litter and the four sailors lifted it up. Mirar watched as they started in the direction of the Sanctuary. He bade the old man a silent farewell.

As if hearing Mirar's thoughts, the old man looked back at him and frowned. He croaked something and the men stopped.

'You come with us,' Yuri explained.

Mirar hesitated, then nodded. *I'll accompany him as far as the Sanctuary*, he told himself. *After that I'll take my leave and seek out the local Dreamweaver House.* He followed as the crew carried Rikken from one house veranda to another, watched by the inhabitants of Kave.

A maze of verandas and bridges followed. The sailors could

not carry the litter across the less stable rope bridges, so they were forced to take a winding path. Over an hour passed before they reached the Sanctuary.

It was a massive stepped pyramid, rising from the muddy soil below. Though squat, it had a heavy, sober presence which made even the more robust wooden houses seem small and temporary. Several Servants hovered around the outside. Mirar moved closer to the litter.

'It has been an honour—' he began.

Rikken turned to look at Mirar. His face was deathly pale and glistened with sweat. Mirar's farewell died in his throat as he realised the old man was close to having another seizure. Yuri gave a low gasp and began urging the sailors to hurry.

As the group hastened toward the Sanctuary entrance, Mirar sighed and followed them. *I guess it's time to find out how these Pentadrian Servants are going to react to a northern Dreamweaver.*

Servants moved to intercept then guide the merchant into the Sanctuary. Once in the cool interior the litter was lowered to the floor. The old man was clutching his chest now. Yuri looked at Mirar expectantly.

Mirar crouched beside Rikken and took his hand. Sending his mind forth, he sensed that the man's heart was failing. Normally he would let the man die; his only malady was age. But he had been asked to ensure the man reached his home, and he was conscious that many black-robed men and women were watching him.

He drew magic and used it to strengthen the heart a little – enough to steady and restore its beat, but that was all. Rikken's face regained its colour and his pained expression eased. He took a few deep breaths, then nodded at Mirar gratefully.

'Thank you.'

Looking up, Mirar found a circle of Servants regarding him and Rikken curiously. Then an older male Servant stepped

25

through the others and smiled at the merchant. He spoke rapidly in Dekkan, and Rikken muttered a surly reply. The Servant laughed, then began ordering the other Servants about.

Clearly he's in charge around here, Mirar mused.

A chair was brought and Rikken helped into it. From the friendly manner of the old Servant and the merchant, Mirar guessed they knew each other well. He stepped back and looked around the room.

As he did, he could not help feeling a thrill of appreciation. The walls were covered in pictures made up of tiny fragments of glazed pottery, arranged so artfully that they suggested greater detail than they truly gave. The room was five-sided, each wall depicting one of the Pentadrian gods.

Sheyr, Hrun, Alor, Ranah and Sraal. Mirar had learned the names from the Dreamweavers he'd met. Unlike the Circlian gods, these preferred to keep to themselves, only appearing at momentous occasions. They let their followers run their own affairs, so long as they didn't stray too far from the central tenets of their religion.

Which makes one wonder how the Pentadrians came to invade Northern Ithania. Did they make that decision themselves, or is waging war one of those central tenets? They do train their priests in warfare, so I suppose the latter isn't impossible.

He frowned. *If that's true, then it doesn't bode well for Northern Ithania's future.*

'Dreamweaver,' Yuri called.

Mirar looked up and realised the old Servant was regarding him. The man began to speak, but Yuri interrupted him apologetically. The Servant listened, then his eyebrows rose and he looked at Mirar again.

'You from Northern Ithania?' he asked in Hanian.

Mirar blinked in surprise at the man's use of the northern language, then nodded. 'Yes.'

'How long you been in Southern Ithania?'

'A few months.'

'Do you like?'

Mirar smiled. How could any visitor to another land answer that question in any way but favourably?

'Yes. Your people are welcoming and friendly.'

The priest nodded. 'Dreamweavers not welcomed in north, I hear. Now it is more bad.' He looked at Rikken and smiled. 'Here we are not so fools.'

'No,' Mirar agreed. *More bad? Maybe I should contact Dreamweaver Elder Arleej tonight and ask if that's true – and why.*

'You do good work with this man. Thank you.'

Mirar inclined his head to acknowledge the thanks. As the priest turned to Rikken his expression became solemn. He spoke in the local tongue, then traced a star shape in the air. Rikken looked down like a chastised child and nodded with acceptance.

Taking a deep breath, Mirar let it out slowly. The Servant had been friendly and even respectful, despite knowing Mirar came from the north. Perhaps being a Dreamweaver was enough to make up for being a foreigner from an enemy land. Perhaps Servants were more sensible about these matters than ordinary Pentadrians.

Most likely there are just as many Servants inclined to be suspicious of me as ordinary Pentadrians. I've been lucky enough to meet one who isn't. He smiled grimly. *And the longer I stay in Southern Ithania, the better the chances I'll encounter one who is.*

CHAPTER 2

Snow still clung to the highest peaks in Si, but everywhere else the effects of warmer weather were plain to see. The forest was a riot of new growth and flowers. In narrow valleys and on natural tiers along the sides of mountains crops were green and thriving.

The last few days had been the hottest Auraya had endured. In the past she had visited Si during the cooler months of the year. Si experienced both warmer and cooler seasons than she was used to – colder because it was mostly mountainous, warmer because it lay further south than Hania, on the same latitude as the desert land of Sennon.

Flying could provide some relief. The air high up was always chilly. But today she flew low. Her Siyee companions could not tolerate flying for long in a cold wind. The chill stiffened their muscles and taxed their strength.

She looked at the man flying beside her. Though an adult, he was half her size. His chest was broad and his legs muscular. The bones of his last three fingers made up the frame of his wings, supporting a membrane that stretched to the sides of his body. She had spent so long with Siyee now that she had to consciously make herself notice the differences between them and herself. When she did she was amazed that they had offered her, a 'landwalker', a permanent home in their country.

Not that she didn't give them anything in return. The magical Gifts she had retained since resigning from the White were constantly in use for their benefit, most often flying and healing. She was just returning from a mission to heal a wounded girl in another Siyee village. And if not for those Gifts, many hundreds would have died from plague.

The pale stretch of exposed rock that was the Open – the main Siyee village – was visible ahead of her now. Auraya felt her heart lift. She could make out the Siyee's homes around the edge of the exposed rock face – bowers made of membranes stretched over a flexible wooden frame fixed to the trunk of a massive tree. She could also see two familiar figures standing on the highest rockshelf, looking up toward her and her companions: Speaker Sirri, the Siyee leader, and Sreil, her son.

Auraya swooped down and landed a few strides away, her companions following. Sirri smiled.

'You're back early,' she said. 'How did it go?'

'I was able to heal her arm,' Auraya replied.

'It was incredible!' the youngest of Auraya's companions exclaimed. 'The girl flew straight after!'

Auraya grimaced. 'Which I strongly warned against. I wouldn't be surprised if that girl's recklessness leads to worse than a broken arm in the future.'

'Her mother's a drunkard.'

Auraya glanced in surprise at the man who'd spoken. The Speaker for the girl's tribe had kept mostly silent until now. He met her eyes and shrugged. 'We try to teach the girl some discipline, but it is not easy when her mother allows her to do anything she wants.'

Auraya thought back to the hysterical woman who had hovered over the child protectively. 'Maybe that will change now.'

'I doubt it,' the man murmured. Then he shrugged. 'Maybe. I should not – what is that?'

She followed his gaze and smiled as she saw a small creature bounding toward her. His pointed ears were folded back and his fluffy tail furled out behind him like a banner.

'That is a veez. His name is Mischief.'

She bent down and let the veez scurry up her arms. Mischief sniffed her, then curled up around her shoulders.

'Owaya back,' he said contentedly.

The tribe leader stared at the veez in astonishment.

'It said your name. It can speak?'

'He can, though don't expect stirring conversation. His interests usually relate to food or grooming.' She scratched Mischief behind the ears and he proved her point by whispering: 'Scratch nice.'

Sirri chuckled. 'I'm afraid you'll have to leave that to his minder again soon. A messenger arrived from the North Forest tribe this morning. He says he encountered a sick landwalker woman a few days ago. She has requested you treat her.'

Auraya blinked in surprise. 'A landwalker?'

'Yes.' Sirri smiled grimly. 'I asked if he suspected she was a Pentadrian. He's sure she isn't. In fact, he says she's visited Si before in order to get out of harm's way when the war started. Would you like to question him yourself?'

'Yes.'

The Speaker looked at Sreil. 'Could you fetch him? Thank you. In the meantime,' she turned back to look at the Siyee who had accompanied Auraya to the Open, 'you are all welcome to join me for refreshments in my bower.'

As they began to walk toward Sirri's home, Auraya considered the possibility that this landwalker was a Pentadrian sorceress in disguise. It was likely that news of her resignation had reached Southern Ithania, and that one of their five sorcerers had come here seeking revenge for the death of their former leader, Kuar, whom Auraya had killed in the war.

She had retained her ability to fly and heal since resigning from the White, but she'd had no opportunity to test whether any of the fighting Gifts the gods had given her in order to defend Northern Ithania were still hers. *I have no idea how strong my Gifts are now, but so far they don't appear to have reduced by much. I guess I'll find out how much if this woman does prove to be a Pentadrian assassin!*

She could only assume she was no longer immortal. It would be a few years before signs of age confirmed that she had lost that Gift. Had it been worth it? She looked around the Open and nodded to herself. With her ability to fly rapidly from village to village, coupled with the healing Gift Mirar had taught her, she had prevented many hundreds of Siyee deaths during the spread of Hearteater through the country. Not all deaths, however. She could not be in two places at once, and when the plague had been at its worst there had been too many sick Siyee for her to reach.

Though the official reason for her resignation from the White – the plague in Si – had passed, she found she did not miss her former position. She was content to live out the rest of her life helping the Siyee. Juran had allowed her to remain a priestess and had even sent a priest ring and circs, brought to Si by one of two priests who had joined the pair already in the Open.

Juran was the only White who still communicated with her. She had heard nothing from the others. The gods no longer visited her either, though occasionally she had sensed something in the magic around her that suggested Chaia's presence.

I wonder if he's watching me. He must know whether this land-walker woman is a Pentadrian or not. I wonder if he'll warn me if she is.

31

She missed his visits. Sometimes at night she longed for his touch and the sublime pleasure he had brought her when they were lovers. But that had just been sensation, not affection. What she missed most was having someone to confide in. To share her worries with.

Even if that someone is the source of the worries, she mused.

Reaching the edge of the forest, Sirri led them to her bower. It was a little larger than the average bower, allowing her to host gatherings of visiting Siyee. Once inside they sat down and began to eat the bread, fruit and nuts Sirri laid out on the table for them. After several minutes Sreil returned with the messenger, a young man he introduced as Tyve, who looked familiar.

'We've met before, haven't we?' Auraya asked.

The Siyee nodded. 'Yes. I was helping Dreamweaver Wilar when you came to my village last year.'

Wilar. At the name Auraya felt a shiver run down her spine and a face flashed into her memory. Wilar was the name Mirar had been using while among the Siyee.

Wilar. Mirar. Leiard. I wonder if he goes by any other names. She had been appalled to discover that the man she had learned magic and cures from as a child, whom she had loved and trusted as an adult, was actually the famous Mirar, immortal founder of the Dreamweavers. The deception had angered her at first, but she hadn't been able to sustain her fury once he opened his mind to show her the truth about his past.

It was impossible to imagine what it had been like for him, crushed beneath a building then existing without a memory while his crippled body slowly healed over many, many years. He had invented the personality that was Leiard and suppressed his own in order to hide his true identity from the gods.

It is a miracle he survived, she thought. *I can't help admiring him for that.*

By the time she had encountered him in the North River

village, Mirar's true self had regained control, but only by somehow combining with the persona of Leiard.

I'd just started to like him again when the gods ordered me to kill him.

'Do you remember?' Tyve asked tentatively.

She dragged her attention back to him. 'Yes. I do. Sirri tells me you've met this landwalker woman before?'

He nodded. 'Yes, at the same place we first met Wilar. I think they know each other.'

Auraya's heart skipped a beat. Could this be the friend she had glimpsed in Mirar's mind when he had opened his thoughts to her?

'What does she look like?'

'Tall, hair the colour of bloodsap, but lighter. Pale skin. Green eyes.'

Auraya nodded. The woman in Mirar's memory had red hair. 'Did she give you her name?'

'Yes. Jade Dancer.'

'And what ails her?'

'She doesn't know. Something inside her belly.'

If the woman was Mirar's friend, why had she come to Si? Was she looking for Mirar? Had she come looking for his help only to find him gone? Auraya frowned. *Is the illness real or a deception to bring me to her? Why would she want to meet me?*

If the woman was Mirar's friend, the gods probably didn't approve of her. *Are any of them listening now?* She searched the magic around her but felt no sign of them. *The last thing I want is the gods asking me to kill someone again. The sooner I meet this woman and send her on her way, the better.*

'Will you help her?' Tyve asked. 'She's nice,' he added.

Auraya nodded. 'I will.' *Even if she isn't ill, I want to know how she came to be in Si. And perhaps she'll have news of Mirar.*

*　　*　　*

Faint scraping sounds and a clink of chains echoed in the stairwell as the cage Danjin stood within moved upward. He watched as the many levels of the White Tower passed. Sometimes it felt as if the cage was still, and the Tower was moving up or down around it. At those times he wondered if Auraya had the same impression when she was 'flying'. She had described her ability as moving herself in relation to the world. Did it sometimes feel as if she was moving the world in relation to herself?

The cage slowed and stopped level with a wide step in the staircase beyond. The door swivelled open, no doubt pushed with magic directed by the woman standing beside him.

He glanced at Dyara of the White, second-oldest and strongest of the Circlian leaders. Moving forward, Dyara led him out of the cage and across the staircase to a wooden door.

As she knocked, Danjin felt a twinge of apprehension. This had been Auraya's room. He had visited it many times as her adviser. Now it belonged to her replacement, Ellareen of the White.

Being Auraya's adviser had been a challenging task, but one made easier because he had liked and respected her. Was it too much to hope it would be the same with the newest of the White? At the same time as wondering if he would like her, he worried whether she would like him. *It won't help if I constantly compare her to Auraya*, he told himself. He knew he would not be able to help himself sometimes, and she would not be able to help reading it from his mind . . .

The door opened. A tall, slender woman stood in the opening. Her hair had been set in an elaborate style and she was wearing a white tunic and circ of the finest-quality cloth. She looked elegant and poised, yet she was not beautiful, he noted. Not unattractive, either. She appeared to be older than Auraya, but only by a few years.

'Ellareen,' Dyara said. 'This is Danjin Spear.'

'Come inside,' the new White responded, stepping back.

He watched her as she ushered them to chairs, then brought them glasses of water. His investigations had revealed that she was originally from Somrey. Her father had been employed by a wealthy trader and her family had moved to Jarime when he was chosen to manage the Hanian side of the business. Ella had joined the priesthood at twelve and eventually became a healer. She had worked at the hospice since it had opened. Something had happened at the hospice a short while before the Choosing Ceremony which had impressed the White enough to promote her to high priestess.

And she must have impressed the gods, too, because now she was a White.

She radiated a calm self-assurance despite the magnitude of the responsibilities she had suddenly been given. This surprised Danjin. Auraya had been a little overwhelmed by her Choosing the first time he had met her.

Dyara began praising Danjin's abilities and he pretended to deny all – just as they had each done when she had introduced him to Auraya, he remembered. Ellareen's mouth twitched up at one corner, then she lifted a hand to interrupt.

'I know Danjin Spear is the best man for the job,' she said, smiling at Dyara. Her eyes shifted to his. 'After all, he is the only one who can claim prior experience working with a new White.'

Dyara shifted in her seat slightly, perhaps a little annoyed at the interruption. 'That is definitely an advantage.'

'Indeed.' Ellareen turned to regard him. 'What was it like working with Auraya?'

He paused, surprised by the frank question. Naturally she would be curious about her predecessor, but he had expected the new White to avoid the subject. He wasn't sure why.

Perhaps only because of the rumours surrounding Auraya's resignation.

'Hard work, but enjoyable,' he replied.

'You liked her,' she stated.

He smiled. 'Yes.'

She raised her eyebrows, encouraging him to say more.

'She is able to empathise with others, though I think that made her work as difficult as it made it easy.'

Ellareen nodded. 'It would. As a healer, compassion can be a weakness as well as a strength.'

He smiled at this reminder that Ellareen had been a healer priestess. Perhaps that work had taught her to be composed no matter what the situation. 'What do you believe are your own strengths and weaknesses, Ellareen of the White?'

'Just call me Ella,' she said, then pursed her lips as she considered his question. 'I don't know . . . my faith in the gods, perhaps. When there is no obvious answer, I do what the gods tell me.'

That sounds like a personal mantra. Interesting. 'A wise policy.'

She glanced at Dyara, who smiled faintly, before looking at him again. 'Though the gods never told me to do anything until recently,' she told him, 'I always gave them a chance to – before sorting out my messes myself.'

He chuckled. 'They appreciated that, I'm sure. Not that I'm suggesting you're going to make any messes now.' He looked at Dyara. 'You have plenty of experienced helpers to call upon.'

'Yes. Including yourself. Dyara tells me you have spies all over Ithania.'

'Spies?' Danjin laughed. 'Hardly spies, just people I know in courts and old trading friends.'

'Tell me about them.'

Taking another sip of water, Danjin leaned back in his chair and began to regale her with stories of the people he knew, in both high and low places, as well as how they had helped him in the past and could do so again. She appeared to be genuinely amused at the more humorous of his anecdotes. That was a good sign. Her sense of humour was a good counterbalance to the almost unnerving confidence she exuded.

She'll make a good White, he decided. *Let's hope she lasts a little longer than Auraya did.*

CHAPTER 3

Auraya had glimpsed the waterfalls in the distance the few times she had flown to the North River tribe village. Now, as the young Siyee guide descended toward them, she saw that there were several falls, each plunging over a step in the land into a pool from which a shallow river flowed to the next fall.

Tyve swooped down to land beside one of the falls and Auraya dropped down beside him. The air hissed with the sound of falling water as Auraya looked around. It was a pretty place. She saw no sign of the landwalker woman.

Tyve gestured to the cascade. 'She lives in there, behind the water. You can get in from the side.'

Auraya nodded. 'Thank you, Tyve. You'd better go home. If I need anything I'll drop in to your village.'

He nodded, ran lightly across the exposed rocks at the river's edge, up onto a boulder, and leapt into the air. Watching him glide away, Auraya remembered something about the boy.

He wanted to become a Dreamweaver. She'd read it from his mind back when she had been helping Mirar treat his village. Mirar hadn't said he would teach the boy, but he hadn't refused either.

His dreams would have been dashed when Mirar fled Si. Still, it's for the best. If he turned from the gods to become a Dreamweaver his soul would be lost when he died.

The idea of Siyee becoming Dreamweavers disturbed her. It was ironic that while she had been setting up the hospice in Jarime – which might ultimately reduce numbers of Dreamweavers by drawing prospective students to the priesthood – a Siyee had been on his way to becoming a Dreamweaver.

It was almost a relief to no longer be responsible for the hospice. Juran had reported good progress. It was nice to know it continued to benefit the people of the city while improving Circlian healing knowledge. But she had never been comfortable knowing that, even though it saved souls by encouraging those who might have joined the Dreamweavers to join the Circlians instead, she had been working toward the demise of the Dreamweavers.

The Siyee were her only concern now. Putting all thoughts of the hospice out of her mind, she started toward the waterfall.

The rock face behind the fall formed an overhang, and she found that she could slip behind the water into a cave. While the water allowed enough light through to illuminate the front of the cave, the back was shrouded in darkness. She drew magic and created a light, revealing a tunnel, then started forward. A light appeared ahead leading her on, around a corner, to a larger cave. Pots and jars stood by one wall and some rudimentary furniture was arranged in the middle.

A woman was sitting on one of two rough beds with her back to Auraya. Her clothing was plain, but the hair that spilled over her shoulders was a rich red. Her arms moved at some hidden task.

'Are you Jade Dancer?' Auraya asked, using the Siyee language. The woman must be able to communicate with the sky people in order to send Auraya a message.

The woman looked up from her task, but didn't turn.

'Yes. Come in. I am making some hot maita. We have much to discuss.'

'Do we?' Auraya moved forward.

The woman chuckled. 'Yes.'

Something about this place made Auraya uneasy. She felt vulnerable, though she could see nothing threatening in the room. Stopping, she drew magic and created a barrier about herself.

The woman turned to look at Auraya curiously. 'Why so wary? I do not mean you any harm.'

Auraya stared back, looking for clues in the woman's expression. She had a beautiful face, but lines around the eyes and mouth indicated she was well into her middle years. They were lines of humour, but also of grief or bitterness.

'Why am I not convinced of that?'

Jade's eyes narrowed and she regarded Auraya thoughtfully. Then she beckoned. 'Come a few steps closer.'

Auraya hesitated, then obeyed. As she did her barrier faltered. She reached for more magic, but none came to her.

As she realised what her senses had been telling her all along, she felt a rush of terror. There was no magic around her. She was as vulnerable as any Giftless mortal. She backed away and found herself surrounded by magic again.

'What you are sensing is a void. It is only a few steps deep. See?' The woman waved a hand carelessly and a spark of light appeared before her. 'You can gather some magic first to protect yourself as you cross it.'

Auraya considered the woman. *If she wanted to take advantage of my moment of vulnerability she would have done so.* Drawing magic, she created another barrier and fed magic into it as she walked across the room. Now that her attention had been drawn to the void it was easy to sense. Still, she did not feel at ease until she was out of it again.

40

Jade regarded her with a knowing smile and gestured toward the other bed.

'Have a seat.'

Auraya sat down. Between the beds was a large rock with a smooth, round hole carved into it, filled with boiling water. Jade ladled out the water into a bowl. The grains in the bowl dissolved to make a dark red liquid, and the distinct smell of maita reached Auraya. The woman poured it into two small cups and handed one to Auraya.

'Mirar slept on that bed last year,' she said.

Auraya nodded slowly. 'So you're the friend. I suspected as much.'

'That was before you tried to kill him,' Jade continued, ignoring Auraya's comment. 'But you couldn't do it.' Her eyes narrowed. 'Why not?'

'I had my reasons.'

The woman's gaze was direct. 'He opened his mind to you, and showed you the truth. That's why. He risked a lot in order for you to know it.'

'Or simply to save himself.'

Jade's eyebrows rose. 'Is that what you think? Did you not consider he did it for love?'

Auraya met the woman's stare. 'Love had nothing to do with it. He wanted me to know the truth, but he would not have revealed it if I hadn't been about to kill him. He would have continued deceiving me.'

The woman nodded. 'But you must know he loves you. Do you love him?'

Auraya felt conflicting feelings returning and pushed them aside. Why was Jade asking these questions? Why did she want to know if Auraya loved Mirar? Was she jealous, or just a protective friend? Auraya considered different answers and how Jade might react to them. A denial might anger her, and Auraya did not want to risk that there were more surprises in this strange cave. An affirmation might be tested, however.

'I don't know,' she replied honestly. 'I doubt it, since I don't really know him – or rather, I know only a part of him. Do you love him?'

'As a friend.'

'You helped him regain his identity.'

'Yes.' Jade looked down at her cup and frowned. 'I brought him here after the battle. He was quite a mess. Wasn't sure who he was. Leiard one moment, Mirar the next.' She grimaced. 'He eventually sorted himself out. I thought he'd be safe here in Si, but he has a talent for getting himself in trouble. First you nearly kill him, then he narrowly avoided the White in Sennon, and now . . .' She shook her head.

Auraya looked at Jade sceptically. 'Since you so obviously want me to ask: where is he now?'

The woman's eyes flashed with amusement. 'Do I? But I can't tell you, or the gods will read it from your mind when you leave the void.'

'When I leave . . . ?' Auraya frowned and looked around the cave, though she didn't expect to see any visible clue to confirm her suspicions.

'The void surrounds us on all sides. The gods are beings of magic, so they can't reach us here.'

Auraya considered this news. If Jade told her where Mirar was . . . but if Jade knew then the gods could take the information from her mind when she left the void anyway. Unless . . . unless Jade could hide her thoughts, as Mirar could. Auraya resisted the urge to stare at the woman. *How powerful is she? Could she be another immortal?*

'When I leave they will know you are here,' she observed. 'They will read that from my mind, too.'

Jade spread her hands. 'Yes. But why would that concern them? I am just an old curer with dubious friends.'

'If Mirar feared revealing your existence, then you have reason to fear it.'

Jade's eyebrows rose. 'So you're not stupid. That's good.'

'How do you plan to stop me leaving?'

'By making you an offer too good to refuse.'

'And if I refuse it and leave?'

'You will never see me again.'

The woman sounded confident. *If she is an immortal, she has managed to evade the gods' notice for over a hundred years. Keeping away from me shouldn't be hard for her.*

'What is your offer?'

Jade smiled. 'To teach you how to hide your thoughts from the gods.'

So I was right. She can hide her mind. After all, she must be able to do it to be able to teach it.

'Why?'

'Why would I teach you or why would you agree to learn it?'

'Both.'

Jade leaned forward. 'What if I told you Mirar was in trouble? That he needed your help? What would you say to that?'

'I would tell you I cannot help him,' Auraya replied without hesitation. Huan's voice repeated in her mind: *If you set yourself against us or the White, or if you ally yourself with our enemies, you will be regarded as our enemy.* 'What sort of trouble is he in?'

'Mortal danger.'

Auraya's heart began to race. Was this woman testing her, or was he truly facing death? *What if he is?* She couldn't – *wouldn't* – help him if it meant making an enemy of the gods. Refusing to kill him had already cost her so much.

Abruptly, Jade stood up and moved away, walking to the pots by the wall.

'I'm glad I don't have such a choice to make,' she said. 'Though I never had a choice offered to me. I've always been despised by the gods.' She picked up a jar and turned to smile at Auraya. 'Mirar is in Mur, in a little seaside town called Bria, where Dreamweavers are accepted by the locals for all their skills. He is in no danger.'

Auraya sighed with relief, but suspicion quickly returned. 'You're lying, at least about his location. You wouldn't have told me where he was until I had agreed to learn to hide my thoughts.'

Jade unplugged the jar and sniffed the contents.

'Wouldn't I?' She set the jar down again. 'Are you willing to risk that it's true, and be the cause of his demise?'

Auraya shook her head. 'You haven't answered my questions. Why do you want me to learn this?'

'Mirar asked me to teach it to you. He believes you are in danger and I fear he will come here himself if I don't do it.'

'You risked exposing yourself on a whim of his?'

Jade's expression became serious. 'Not a whim, I'm afraid.' She walked back to the beds. 'You *are* in danger.'

'How so?'

'From the gods, you silly girl. You defied them. You are too powerful. The only reason they didn't kill you when you resigned was because you were still useful to them. Now that the Siyee are well they'll be looking for any excuse to get rid of you.'

Auraya thought of the conversation between the gods that she'd overheard after she'd announced her intention to resign.

:*Give her what she wants*, Saru had said. *Then we can get rid of her*.

:*Only if she turns against us*, Chaia had replied.

'Any excuse?' she said, standing up. 'Like learning to hide my thoughts from them. Like associating with yet another Wild.' She stepped around Jade and started toward the cave entrance. 'Tell Mirar the best he can do to protect me is stay away and stop meddling in my affairs.'

She heard Jade's footsteps behind her.

'Mirar is a besotted fool. That's why he taught you to heal, even though he knew you would eventually work out that it is the same Gift that makes us immortal. He gave you an escape route.'

Auraya caught her breath and slowed to a stop. If what Jade was telling her was true, Mirar had deliberately taught her something that could lead to her becoming immortal. No wonder the gods had forbidden Circlians to learn magical healing. Yet the gods had let her learn it . . .

'He saw the potential in you – and so did the gods,' Jade continued. 'Why do you think they gave you such impossible choices? They know your weaknesses. They manipulated you neatly into leaving the White, leaving their followers believing you sacrificed all for the Siyee. Now you can tragically die and nobody will question it.'

Auraya turned to stare at the woman. She shook her head. 'You're lying.' *She must be lying.*

Jade laughed. 'If only I was. Can you take that risk?'

Chaia's face rose in Auraya's memory. Even if Jade was right, she was only partly right. *Not all of the gods want me dead.*

If she refused Jade's help she risked that Huan and her allies would kill her, despite Chaia's opposition.

If she accepted she risked losing Chaia's support – if she still had it.

Auraya turned away. As she started toward the cave entrance again she expected Jade to follow. Instead the woman called after her.

'You're a Wild, Auraya. The gods know it. They're just waiting for the right moment to kill you.'

'I'm not immortal yet,' Auraya tossed over her shoulder. She sensed she was approaching the void and drew magic to maintain her barrier. 'I don't have to become immortal, even if I have the potential to.'

'You don't have to hide your thoughts either. But if you know how, then if Mirar's concerns prove valid you may find the Gift useful.'

Auraya slowed and stopped within the void, turned, then stepped back inside the barrier. Jade regarded her soberly.

If there is no crime in having knowledge that can lead to immortality, then there is no crime in knowing how to hide my thoughts, she thought. *And if Mirar returns because I refused to learn from Jade, it will cause all manner of trouble.*

'How long will it take?' she asked.

Jade's expression softened. 'A few weeks. Less, if you're a fast learner.'

'The Siyee will come looking for me.'

'We'll tell them you're staying only until you're sure I'm well.'

'Ah, yes. The mythical illness.' Auraya strode toward the woman. 'Expect to heal quickly, Jade Dancer, as I don't intend to be here any longer than necessary.'

The woman snorted. 'I assure you, neither do I.'

No matter how many times Reivan rode in a litter, she could never get used to the movement, especially when the carriers were jogging. Or was it the fact that the four slaves had her dignity and well being in their hands which made her uneasy? Like all slaves they were criminals, but these had been chosen for this task by the Servants of the Gods for their reliability, coordination and willing cooperation.

But whoever chose them probably assumed any Servant riding a litter has Skills to call upon if they ever need to defend themselves, or the slaves dropped the litter. She didn't even have enough Skill to stir up the still, hot air to cool herself. Usually one could only become a Servant if one had Skills, but she had been an exception. Being ordained as a Servant of the Gods had been Reivan's reward for saving the Pentadrian army from becoming lost in the mines of Sennon . . . was it really less than a year ago?

She sighed and tried not to look at the sweat running down the backs of the slaves. The signs of their discomfort only made her more uncomfortable. *And these black Servant robes don't help,* she added, plucking at the neckline.

The slaves turned onto the Parade and wound their way through the crowd toward the Sanctuary. The sprawl of buildings that made up the main Pentadrian Temple looked like a giant staircase. Imenja had ordered Reivan to return as quickly as possible, and the thought of ascending up through most of the Sanctuary to reach her wasn't a welcoming one.

At the wide stairs of the building, the slaves set the litter down. Reivan paused to nod in thanks to the slave master, then started her journey upward.

A wide, arched façade welcomed visitors to the largest Pentadrian building in all Ithania. Stepping through one of the openings, she entered a large, breezy hall. Servants hovered around, ready to greet visitors. Beyond the hall there was a courtyard, which she skirted so she could stay in the cool shadows.

A wide corridor followed, taking her through the Lower Sanctuary. Servants were everywhere, their black robes like ink stains against the white walls. The corridor split several times as it branched out into the Middle Sanctuary. As she hurried along the route to the Upper Sanctuary, Servants stepped out of her way and nodded politely.

Their respect roused a smug satisfaction within her. *They've been like this since Imenja and I returned from negotiating the agreement with the Elai.* There had been no protest when Imenja had made Reivan her Companion. *Even so, I can't help looking for signs that the Servants' acceptance of me is wearing off.*

The corridors in the Upper Sanctuary were wide and quiet. The walls were decorated with artworks, and mosaics covered the floors. Doors led to private courtyards, where fountains kept the air cool. She now had a suite of rooms decorated in the same austere but luxurious fashion the Voices enjoyed.

I suppose if you're going to spend eternity serving the gods you may as well be comfortable while doing so, she mused. *I may not be immortal, or need a suite of rooms all to myself, but I appreciate them as much for being an acknowledgement of all the work I do as for their comforts.*

:Are you far away? a familiar voice spoke into Reivan's mind.

It might have been Reivan's imagination, but Imenja's mental call seemed strained with anxiety. Reivan frowned.

:No. I've two corridors to go, she replied.

Now concern added to her discomfort. Small incidents and hints had led Reivan to suspect her mistress and Nekaun, the First Voice, had grown to dislike each other. She had noticed that Imenja frequently disagreed with Nekaun, and that the First Voice often overrode Imenja's decisions. Both did so while using the politest of language.

There were subtler signs, too. Whenever in the same room, Imenja never faced Nekaun directly. She often crossed her arms or leaned slightly away from him. He smiled at her frequently, but his eyes always expressed some other emotion than good humour. Sometimes anger; sometimes a challenge.

I'm probably just reading them badly, Reivan told herself. But

48

she could not help feeling disturbed. *Any sign of conflict between the Voices, no matter how small, is enough to make anyone uneasy. Even if one could forget the immense magical powers they could wield, there is the long-term welfare of the people to consider. The Voices have to put up with each other for eternity. It is better they get along.*

On a personal level it bothered her further. She liked Imenja. The Second Voice treated Reivan like a friend as well as a Companion. She also liked Nekaun, but in an entirely different way. He didn't treat her like a friend, though he *was* friendly. Whenever he turned his natural, habitual charm on her she couldn't help feeling a rush of hope and excitement.

Reivan had hoped a few months at sea would cure her of her attraction to Nekaun, but it hadn't. Yet the journey had boosted her confidence and determination not to make a fool of herself. She could not do her job and avoid him, so she had decided she simply had to ignore the fluttering in her stomach and the distracting thoughts he stirred until she had been around him so much that he was ordinary and unexciting.

Reaching the beginning of the corridor that gave access to the long balcony on which the Voices liked to meet, Reivan paused to catch her breath. She smoothed her robes, wiped her face, cleared her mind and set forth again.

The sound of chatter drew her to the end. Several woven reed chairs had been arranged where the view over the city was best. All Voices and their Companions were sitting except for Nekaun. As always, he stood leaning against the railing, looking down at his fellow rulers and their advisers.

Reivan made the sign of the star over her chest and nodded respectfully to all the Voices. The Fifth Voice, Shar, was sipping flavoured water. His pale skin and long pale hair was a stark contrast to Genza's warm brown skin and cropped hair. Vervel, the stocky Third Voice, was heavier and older in appearance than his companions. As always, Genza had brought one of her trained birds, and a vorn lay by Shar's feet. *On* Shar's feet, Reivan noted. The beast panted in the heat of the day.

Avoiding Nekaun's gaze, Reivan looked at Imenja, the Second Voice. Her mistress was slim and elegant, appearing to be in her late thirties. She smiled at Reivan and gestured to the empty chair beside her.

The conversation had stopped on Reivan's arrival, but attention had not shifted to her. All were regarding Nekaun expectantly.

He smiled. 'Now that we are all here, I'd like you to meet an old friend of mine, Heshema Guide. He has just returned from Northern Ithania, where he has been researching a little recent history for me.'

Glancing out of the corner of her eye, Reivan saw that Imenja was frowning. Her expression of disapproval vanished as footsteps echoed in the corridor. Reivan turned to see a middle-aged man enter the balcony.

She had expected someone with such a typical Sennon name to have the distinctive thin build and sun-browned skin of that race, but Heshema was an unimpressive-looking man. If she'd been asked to describe him, she would have been hard put to think of a feature that might single him out among others. *He is quite bland*, she mused. *But if he's been gathering information for Nekaun in Northern Ithania, that makes him a spy, and a spy hardly wants to stand out or be memorable.*

'An honour to meet you all,' Heshema said in a deep, melodious voice.

As the Voices murmured replies, Reivan smiled. *His voice is his distinctive feature*, she thought. *Though I expect he has learned to adopt a less memorable one when needed.*

'I have asked Heshema to tell you what he has learned,' Nekaun said. 'Some of you will already know part of it, but you should all learn something new.'

As the First Voice looked at Heshema expectantly, the man nodded.

'I arrived in Jarime in late winter,' the spy began. 'The cold there encourages the common people to meet at drinking houses to share the warmth of a fire and exchange gossip. Most of the talk was of Auraya the White's resignation. The official explanation is that she left in order to devote herself to helping the Siyee, who were suffering great losses to a plague.

'Many admired her for sacrificing immortality and great magical power for such a noble cause, but some questioned the truth of the explanation, speculating that perhaps their gods had banished Auraya from the White for some crime or mistake. The error they considered most likely was her sympathy to the Dreamweavers. She had arranged for Circlian healers and Dreamweavers to work together treating the needy in a building in the poor quarter they called a "hospice". It was an unpopular move, especially among the wealthy citizens.

'Other ideas circulating included an affair with a Dreamweaver, and that she had neglected her duties as a White in favour of helping the Siyee. There were even a few who thought she might have turned Pentadrian.'

The Voices chuckled and Heshema's lips thinned into a smile.

'There was also speculation that Auraya hadn't left the White at all,' he continued, 'and this was some ruse to lure us into battle. The rash of promotions among Circlians suggested otherwise to me. Only high priests and priestesses are eligible to become a White. Their gods apparently make the final choice, but the White ensure there are plenty of candidates.'

His voice was curiously devoid of scepticism, Reivan noted.

'Did you see anything to make you wonder if their gods are real?' Imenja asked.

Heshema glanced at Nekaun. 'Nothing to make me certain of it.'

'That is not what I sent Heshema to discover,' Nekaun interrupted.

'No?' Imenja turned to smile at Nekaun. 'Of course not, but he might have noticed something.' She looked at the spy. 'Go on with your tale, Heshema.'

The man inclined his head. 'I doubted the White would take kindly to me questioning them, so I sought other sources of information. I posed as a Genrian trader in order to meet Auraya's former adviser, Danjin Spear. He believed the official explanation to be the true one. According to him, the Siyee had stolen Auraya's heart the moment she first met them. I am sure he was keeping some secret about his former mistress, however. Something personal. He spoke as if something she had done had disappointed him.'

'An affair?' Genza asked.

Heshema shrugged. 'That is possible.'

'You said there were rumours of an affair with a Dreamweaver,' Vervel pointed out.

'Yes. I didn't give them much credence until I questioned the Siyee. I heard that there were a handful of the winged people in Jarime, some acting as ambassadors and others there in training to become priests and priestesses. They have a remarkably low tolerance for intoxicating liquor, and the pair of initiates I spoke to were only too happy to tell me of the rumours in Si concerning Auraya's last months there as a White.

'She returned to Si in response to your Servants landing there, but stayed due to the outbreak of a plague. When she arrived at the first village to succumb to the disease she found a Dreamweaver already there. She knew this Dreamweaver and those who observed the two of them together said it was clear there was a grudge between them, but they had settled their differences and were friendly by the time Auraya left the village.

'What happened afterwards is a mystery that the Siyee would dearly like to solve. The Dreamweaver left Si without explanation and Auraya returned to Jarime and quit the White. They believe both events are connected, but don't know how. When I suggested an affair, however, they were certain that couldn't be the reason.'

'Sounds like an affair to me,' Genza said.

'Sounds like the sort of gossip that would naturally arise in that situation, so we shouldn't assume it is true,' Imenja warned. 'Did the Dreamweaver return to Si after Auraya quit the White?'

'The Siyee initiates did not know,' Heshema replied. 'They were shocked by the hatred some Hanians felt toward the Dreamweavers. They might have decided to keep the return of the Dreamweaver a secret as a result.

'The Hanians' dislike and fear of Dreamweavers appeared to be getting worse while I was there. Their paranoia had grown so strong that a rumour that the Dreamweaver leader, Mirar, isn't dead and has returned to make mischief was circulating just before I left.'

Shar chuckled. 'If only he had. We could recruit him.'

'Dreamweavers abhor violence,' Imenja reminded him. 'But I expect a man of his Skills and experience could make a lot of trouble for the Circlians – if only he *was* alive.'

'These rumours are also circulating here,' Nekaun said. 'A few of my friends have sought the source of them, and it appears the rumours have originated among the Dreamweavers themselves, all over Avven, Dekkar and Mur, at about the same time.'

'Interesting,' Vervel murmured.

'Yes.'

'So the White are only four, and one of their former enemies may have returned,' Genza said. 'Can we take advantage of this?'

'No.' Nekaun's answer was firm and his expression serious. 'The rumours that Mirar is alive are just rumours, and our people in Jarime reported that a replacement for Auraya was chosen yesterday. Her name is Ellareen Spinner.'

The others absorbed this in silence for a moment, then Vervel made a low noise. He looked at Nekaun, then at the spy.

Nekaun nodded. 'Thank you, Heshema. We must now discuss this in private.'

The spy made the sign of the star, then left the balcony.

'So,' Vervel said when the man's footsteps had faded, 'if Auraya is still an ally of the White, they now have the advantage.'

'Yes.'

'Will they invade us, do you think?'

'We can't risk that they won't,' Nekaun replied. 'We must find a way to tip the balance in our favour again.'

'If only Mirar *had* returned,' Shar said wistfully.

'Even if he had, a sorcerer who will not kill is of no use to us,' Imenja said. 'Not when Auraya is willing to, as she so effectively demonstrated in the battle.'

'We must find another way,' Nekaun said – for once in agreement with Imenja, Reivan noted. 'I want you all to think about this carefully. My spies are gathering as much information as they can about the new White. I would like to know what Skills and strength Auraya has retained.'

The Voices and their Companions nodded. After a measured silence, Nekaun smiled and, without warning, looked at Reivan. A thrill ran through her body and she felt herself flush.

'Now, to other matters. Tell us, Reivan, how many raider ships have our Elai friends sunk this week?'

CHAPTER 4

Stopping before the bridge, Mirar looked up at the two-storey stilt house and smiled. He hadn't visited a Dreamweaver House in a century . . . if he didn't count his visit to the one in Somrey, when he had been Leiard. They had long ago disappeared from Northern Ithanian cities and towns so it had been a pleasant surprise to find they still existed in Southern Ithania.

He crossed the bridge, approached the door and knocked.

Footsteps sounded on a wooden floor inside, then the door opened and a middle-aged woman in Dreamweaver robes looked out. Mirar hesitated, sure that he had missed something, then realised he had been expecting to hear the rattle of a lock being opened.

The Dreamweavers in Southern Ithania don't even lock their doors!

'Greetings. I am Dreamweaver Tintel,' the woman said, smiling and opening the door wider. What she said afterwards was incomprehensible to him, but he sensed friendliness and her gesture told him she was welcoming him inside.

'Thank you. I am Dreamweaver Wilar.' He stepped into a small room. Pairs of sandals sat neatly at the edges. Removing shoes while indoors was a local custom. He could hear the sound of many voices somewhere beyond the walls.

Reaching into his bag, he took out the pouch of coins Rikken's assistant, Yuri, had given him. When Mirar had refused to take the large payment for his services, Yuri had told him to give the money to the Dreamweaver House instead.

'For the House,' Mirar said in the Avven tongue as he handed it to Tintel, hoping she understood.

The woman took the bag and looked inside. Her eyebrows rose. She said something he did not understand. When he frowned and shook his head, she stopped to consider him, and he saw comprehension dawn in her eyes.

'You are a foreigner?' she asked in Avven.

'Yes. From the north.'

'We do not often get visitors from there.'

That does not surprise me, he thought. He bent to remove his shoes. When he was done the hostess opened another door, revealing a much larger room. Tables ran the length of it and many of the chairs were occupied by Dreamweavers.

'We are near to eating dinner. Join us.'

He followed her in. Tintel spoke loudly and the Dreamweavers turned to regard her and Mirar. He guessed she was introducing them and made the formal gesture of touching heart, mouth and forehead. All smiled and a few spoke a greeting, but none returned the gesture. After Tintel had led him to a chair the Dreamweavers returned to their conversation.

The atmosphere was relaxed and though Mirar couldn't understand them he was reassured by their laughter. Servants brought a meal of flat toasted bread laid on top of bowls full of a spicy stew, and a milky drink that, to Mirar's relief, eased the burning of the spice. Most of the Dreamweavers were young, he noted. Their talk quietened and grew more serious as their bellies filled. Tintel had joined them when the food had been served, and now she looked at Mirar.

'What do you know of the trouble in Jarime, Wilar?' she asked in Avvenan.

He frowned. 'I know crowds of Circlians have gathered to speak out against the . . . the hospice.' He used the Hanian word, unable to think of an Avvenan equivalent.

Tintel grimaced. 'It is worse. Dreamweavers have been beaten. Killed. A Dreamweaver House was burned.'

'There is no . . .' Mirar stopped as he realised what she must mean. There were no Dreamweaver Houses in Jarime, but there were a few safehouses – homes of people who were sympathetic to Dreamweavers and offered them accommodation.

People like Millo and Tanara Baker. He felt a chill as he thought of the couple he had stayed with while in Jarime. *Only locals and friends had known their home was a safehouse – until I came along. Then I became Dreamweaver Adviser to the White and a lot more people would have known about the Bakers' safehouse. I hope it wasn't their house that was burned.*

'I had not heard about this,' he said. 'I will link with Northern Dreamweavers tonight to find out what I can of my friends there.'

'What brings you to Dekkar?' a young man asked.

Mirar shrugged. 'I like travelling. I wanted to see the south.'

'Not to escape the killings?'

Tintel made a warning sound and gave the man a disapproving look. Mirar smiled.

'It is a fair question,' he said. 'I did not know it would get so bad there so quickly. I am happy it is good here, but I wish I could help my friends.'

The men and women around the table nodded in sympathy.

'It is good here for Dreamweavers,' one of the young men said.

Mirar nodded. 'I found the Servants . . .' He searched for the right word. '. . . friendly.'

'They don't know healing like we do,' a young woman said. 'They pay well, too.'

'The Servants let you heal them?' he asked, surprised.

The Dreamweavers nodded.

'I heard linking is forbidden in the north. Is that true?' the young woman asked.

'It is.' As Mirar looked at her, she smiled. Something about the smile made him look closer. As he recognised the subtle messages in her posture and expression he felt his pulse quicken.

Ah. This one knows what she likes in a man and isn't afraid to seek it, he thought. He wouldn't be surprised if she sought him out later. The question was, what would he do if she did?

'Dreamweavers don't link at all?' someone asked.

He turned to nod at the young man. 'We do, but we don't tell Circlians about it.'

A murmur of amusement came from the Dreamweavers. The young woman continued to smile at him.

'You must not have many chances to link, if you travel a lot. We could link tonight.'

It's not mind *linking she means*, he found himself thinking. *But mind linking would be a great risk. I have too much to hide . . . though now that Emerahl has helped me regain the ability to shield my mind I should be able to listen to them without revealing myself. But not tonight.*

'Thank you, but I need sleep more,' he told her.

The others did not look offended. Instead, Tintel frowned at the young woman then grimaced apologetically at him, as if she was worried *he* might have taken offence.

'Forgive Dardel, she speaks too soon. You may join a link if you wish, but if you don't we will not question it. The north and south are enemies, and it may be that you know something that, should it spread through a link and reach the wrong people, could bring about conflict or war.'

Surprised by her perceptiveness, Mirar thanked her for her consideration. Attention moved from him and he tried to follow the conversation as the Dreamweavers talked of other things, slipping back into the local language. Finally they rose from the table and began to clear the plates.

'I will take you to your room,' Tintel offered. She led him into a corridor then up a steep flight of stairs. 'Tomorrow night, if you are still here, you are welcome to join us after dinner.'

'Thank you. I may not have much to say. There is still much of the Avven language I don't understand, and I am new to Dekkan.'

'How long are you planning to stay in Kave?'

'I don't know. How long should I allow to explore the city?'

She smiled. 'Some people say you need to stay a full year to know Kave well, others say an hour. If you have the time, stay as long as you want.' She stopped before an open door. 'This is for you. Sleep well.'

He thanked her again, then moved inside and closed the door. The room was narrow, containing only a bed, some shelving and a small table. He set his bag beside the shelves then sat down at the bottom of the bed. It was still early to be sleeping, but he wanted desperately to contact Arleej. She would know what was happening in Jarime.

Standing up again, he began to undress. He had removed only the vest when a knock came from the door.

Opening it, he smiled as he found Dardel standing outside.

She was not beautiful, yet she wasn't unattractive either. Some women were simply *appealing*. It was a combination of an honest and bold interest in sex and a curvaceous, womanly body that invited enjoyment. *You've got to like a woman who knows what she wants and knows how to ask for it.*

She was carrying a large bowl and a jug of water. 'For you,' she said. 'To wash off the travelling dirt.'

'Thank you.' He took them from her and turned to take them inside.

'If you need help . . . ?'

Help to wash myself? He smothered a laugh and turned to regard her. She was leaning against the door-frame now, arms crossed under ample breasts. A sly smile curled her lips.

I must talk to Arleej, he reminded himself. *I must find out if Tanara and Millo Baker are alive and unhurt.*

'I will be fine,' he told her.

Her smile faded, but only a little. 'I'll talk to you tomorrow,' she said, stepping away from the door. Somehow she made it sound like a promise. 'Sleep well.'

As the door clicked shut he drew in a deep breath and let it out slowly. *How can I be interested in this woman when . . . ? No. How can I be asking myself such a stupid question? I'm alive. I like women. Leiard is gone and can't stop me. Why should I turn this woman away because of Auraya?*

Yet he had. He wasn't *that* tired and he could have contacted Arleej later.

This is stupid. I love Auraya and I could ignore all other women for her, but I can't have her. I'm not even sure she loves me in return. She's had at least one other lover, too. So why shouldn't I?

He shook his head. *Because of the whore she saw me with after the battle. At the time it seemed justified, but I know it hurt her badly. I don't want to risk that in the future. If we ever manage to be together without the gods killing one or both of us, it would be ironic and annoying to find I've gone and spoiled it all again.*

Emerahl had expected Auraya to be difficult to teach. A former White ought to be full of her own importance, too proud to take orders from another – especially a Wild. But Auraya had followed every instruction without complaint, and her only questions had been sensible and reasonable.

I should be relieved, but instead I'm finding it irritating. The temptation to test Auraya's tolerance by asking her to do something ridiculous and humiliating was strong. It also disturbed Emerahl. She didn't like the thought that she might be capable of being such a tyrant.

Auraya sat cross-legged on the bed Mirar had once occupied. Her eyes were closed and her hands sat loosely in her lap, resting on the fabric of her white tunic. A priest ring encircled her finger; a priestess's circ hung from a screen nearby. Emerahl had never expected to find herself teaching a Circlian priestess, let alone a former White. The irony that she was teaching a priestess to hide her mind from the gods wasn't lost on her either.

Watching Auraya, she couldn't deny that the woman was attractive. Physically, Auraya could not have been more different to Emerahl. Her face was narrow and angular, whereas Emerahl's was broad. She was tall and slim; Emerahl was short and curvaceous. Her hair was straight and glossy brown; Emerahl's was red and curly.

If this is what Mirar likes . . . she began to think, then nearly laughed out loud. *Am I jealous? Is that why I find her so irritating?* She suppressed a sigh. *I've had good times with Mirar, we've been lovers, but I've never been in love with him. Not in the way normal people fall in love, become a 'couple' and all that. I've never been jealous of the women he sleeps with. Mirar and I are just friends.*

So why the resentment? Maybe it was simple protectiveness. Mirar had saved her, from others and herself, more than once. Would he do it again, if it came to a choice between her and Auraya?

He'd probably choose Auraya, she thought. *And then she'd kill him. She's still a follower of the gods. This is crazy! Why am I here, taking such risks?*

Because Mirar had asked her to, and The Twins had backed him up. Auraya was capable of becoming immortal. She might never take that step for fear the gods would reject her, but there was a chance something – or someone – would change her mind. If she became an ally the risks and gamble would pay off.

So I had better not make an enemy of her, Emerahl thought.

Auraya's breathing had been slow and regular for some time. She had surprised Emerahl by revealing that she knew how to enter a dream trance – to deliberately put herself into the mental state required to link with another via dreams – though she admitted she found it difficult sometimes. All mental links were forbidden to Circlians, but Auraya thought it an impractical law that few took seriously. She and Leiard had used dream links to communicate during their affair.

Closing her eyes, Emerahl slowed her breathing and gradually guided her mind into the dream state. When she was ready she called out Auraya's name.

:Jade? Auraya replied.

:Yes, it's me.

Emerahl sensed relief from the other woman and guessed it was at achieving the dream trance.

:In a dream link we can communicate with each other, she told Auraya, *but only if we're both in a trance or have slipped into a dream state from sleep. I am going to teach you to reach out to conscious minds. You won't be able to communicate with them, but you can see what they are thinking.*

:So Wilds can read minds?

:Yes, but only when in a trance. It requires concentration and practice and can be exhausting. The thoughts you detect are often incomprehensible at first, but you learn to interpret them. We call this 'mind-skimming'.

:So this isn't a lesson in hiding my mind?

:No, but it will help you comprehend the same concepts. Reach out with your mind to the left. It is both an advantage and disadvantage being in Si. There are fewer minds to skim, but those that exist stand out because of their isolation.

It took Auraya several long minutes to sense anything.

:I am sensing something . . . Ah. It's a Siyee. He's hunting.

:Good. I see him too. You can see that his thoughts aren't ordered like speech. They come in snatches, as much image as thought.

:Yes. This is just like mind-reading.

Emerahl felt a flash of irritation. *How could I have forgotten that she used to be able to read minds? She already knows how thoughts work.*

:Seek another mind.

Auraya paused only a moment before she responded again.

:I see Tyve. He's approaching the waterfall – he's carrying a message for me. I . . .

The link broke as Auraya's concentration faltered. Emerahl woke from the dream trance and wasn't surprised to find Auraya rising from the bed.

'Stay there,' Emerahl warned in a murmur. 'You must remain in the void. Tyve will have to come in and talk to you.'

Auraya sat back down. She looked at Emerahl. 'You had best pretend to be sick,' she replied.

Another flash of irritation went through Emerahl. She lay down and pulled a blanket over herself. Footsteps echoed from the passage and she turned to see a young Siyee step into the entrance of the cave.

'Tyve,' Auraya said, standing up and beckoning. 'Come in. What brings you here?'

His gaze shifted from her to Emerahl. 'I have a message for you.'

Auraya beckoned again and the boy approached. He smiled at Emerahl. 'How are you, Jade? Feeling better?'

'Yes,' she said. 'Thanks to Auraya.'

The boy moved closer to Auraya and murmured something. Auraya looked down at her priest ring then shrugged, and her reply was quiet. What were those two discussing that they didn't want Emerahl to hear?

Auraya's voice rose again as she thanked Tyve.

'Tell Speaker Sirri that I must stay and watch over Jade, but I will return soon. Fly safe, fly fast.'

The boy nodded, then said goodbye and hurried away. When his footsteps had faded Emerahl looked up at Auraya, who was frowning.

'What did he have to say?'

Auraya sighed and sat down. 'I think Sirri is surprised that I didn't just heal you and return.'

'How long until they grow suspicious?'

Auraya shrugged. 'A week. We can put them off for a while, but if something happens that they need me to attend to and I refuse to leave here . . .'

'Our cover will be as done as a whore with an empty purse,' Emerahl finished.

Both of Auraya's eyebrows rose in amusement, then she grew serious.

'If the gods were watching through Tyve, they will have seen us both when he entered the cave. They will also have been forced to leave him when he entered the void.'

Emerahl nodded. 'Yes. I suppose you could have prevented them discovering the void by speaking to him from the edge of it, but the gods would have still seen us both and not been able to read our minds and grown suspicious because of that.'

'Or they might not have been watching at all.'

'Do you think they were?'

'I don't know. They haven't visited me in months, but that

64

doesn't mean they're not watching.' She looked at Emerahl, her mouth set. 'Shall we return to the dream trance?'

Emerahl chuckled at her determination. 'Let's have some lunch first.'

CHAPTER 5

Ella was standing by the window when Danjin entered. He suppressed a shudder and tried not to think of the dizzying drop to the ground far, far below. The newest of the White took a step backwards from the window and turned to face him. There was something in her expression, a wildness about her eyes as she met his gaze. She smiled crookedly, and suddenly he understood what it was. He felt a wry pang of fellow feeling.

She, too, wasn't that fond of heights. Probably not as utterly terrified by them as he was, but still unsettled by them.

'Thank you for coming to visit me on such short notice,' she said, gesturing to a chair.

He sat down. 'No need to thank me. It's part of my job.'

She smiled again. 'That's no reason for me to be ungrateful.'

'How can I be of assistance?'

The smile faded. 'My fellow White and I met at the Altar today. Juran gave me my first task. It's a small one, but not an easy one, and I'd like your advice on how to approach it.' She frowned. 'He wants me to stop people attacking the hospice and Dreamweavers.'

Danjin nodded slowly. 'It makes sense that he gave you this task. You have worked at the hospice. You have dealt with Dreamweavers and protesters before.'

'Juran says the attacks on the hospice have lessened since I was Chosen,' she told him. 'But the attacks on Dreamweavers have increased.'

Danjin nodded. 'By choosing a healer from the hospice the gods suggest that they approve of it.'

'I doubt that is the only reason they chose me, or my usefulness would expire once the threat to the hospice ended.'

'Of course it isn't.' He smiled. 'But these are the sorts of conclusions the average mortal comes to about such matters.'

'And have some of them come to the conclusion that my Choosing justifies violence against Dreamweavers?'

'I can't see why they would have. No, I think there may be other factors at work, though I can't tell you what they are. That's what we must discover.'

'What would convince people to harm Dreamweavers, despite it being a crime? Do they pay us and our laws any attention at all?'

She looked genuinely distressed, though he wasn't sure if it was at the harming of Dreamweavers or the breaking of laws. 'There will always be people who think they know better, who believe laws don't apply to them. Or who twist the meaning of what the gods and White decree until it suits them better, so they can still believe they are working for the gods' benefit while doing what they want to.'

Ella sighed and looked away, her expression full of frustration. Following her gaze, he was surprised to see a spindle and a basket filled with fleece on a side table.

Her work? he wondered. *From the look on her face I'd say so.*

It seemed a ridiculously domestic task for one of the Gods' Chosen, but it was clear from her expression that she wished she was doing it. Perhaps it was a link to her past, work that kept her humble in the face of the fame, power and responsibility of her new position. She turned back to him, looking suddenly determined.

'What do you suggest I do to stop the violence?'

He considered the problem.

'Understand your adversary. If these people have always hated Dreamweavers, then why have they begun attacking them now?'

'Auraya's resignation? Are they blaming Dreamweavers for that?'

'I doubt it.' He looked at her closely. 'I can see no connection, though that doesn't mean others won't. Have you seen any in people's minds?'

She frowned. 'I should confront the next crowd of protesters at the hospice and try a bit of mind-reading.'

'Yes, but that won't necessarily help you understand your adversary. You need to read the mind of those inciting the protests, or planning to murder a Dreamweaver. Since the mind-reading abilities of the White are well known, I doubt the people you want to find are going to be at a protest.'

'So how can I find them?'

'They must visit the area around the hospice from time to time, or send someone else to scout the area and select victims. If you were there, watching, concealed from sight, you might catch them at it.'

She nodded slowly. 'Yes. Though . . . it will be time-consuming.' She sighed. 'I wish ordinary priests and priestesses could read minds. We'd find our murderers and conspirators faster if more of us were looking.'

'If mind-reading was a Gift that priests and priestesses could possess, it would also be a Gift non-Circlians could have – and use for great evil.'

She looked at him appraisingly. 'Yes. You're right. Any other advice?'

He nodded. 'There is a man in Jarime's prison who murdered a Dreamweaver a month ago. I believe Dyara read his mind to confirm his guilt. If you read his mind you may learn to recognise the mind of a killer more easily from among the general populace.'

Her eyes widened. 'Read a murderer? I . . . I hadn't thought of that.'

'Would you like me to come with you?' he offered.

'Do you want to? It could be unpleasant.'

He shrugged. 'I once accompanied Auraya on a similar visit.'

Ella's eyebrows rose. 'Why did Auraya visit the prison?'

'A Dreamweaver was accused of manipulating someone's dreams.' Ella watched him unblinkingly as he explained. Bemused by the sudden intensity of her interest, he considered and dismissed the possibility that it was the Dreamweaver's story that aroused such interest. No, he thought, *she's curious about Auraya.* 'She found him innocent,' he added.

She straightened abruptly, her manner suddenly composed.

'Could you arrange for me to visit this murderer?' she asked.

'Of course,' he said. 'Would you like me to do that now?'

'Yes.' She nodded, then rose to her feet and rubbed her hands together. Standing up, he followed her to the door. 'What time would be suitable for you?'

She considered. 'Tomorrow morning?'

'I will see what I can do.' He made the sign of the circle. 'Good day, Ellareen of the White.'

He stepped outside and started down the stairs. As he descended he considered Ella's interest in Auraya. There had been more than curiosity in her manner.

Perhaps jealousy, he thought. *But what does she have to envy? She has everything that Auraya had . . . except the ability to fly.* He smiled, remembering her obvious discomfort at the view from the Tower window. *I doubt she covets that.*

If it wasn't jealousy, what was it? She had been frowning. Surely it had not been disapproval. What reason did she have to disapprove of Auraya?

He shook his head. *Now I'm reading too much into her manner. If I start thinking in that direction I'll end up like the city gossips, believing every rumour of scandal in regard to Auraya.*

Ellareen was merely curious about her predecessor, that was all.

'That's it?'

Auraya stared at Jade in disbelief. The woman smiled, her green eyes glittering with amusement.

'What did you expect?'

'I thought you would teach it the same way Mirar taught me to heal – through a mind link.'

Jade laughed. 'If only that were possible. Unfortunately, it's not possible to see into a shielded mind, so I can't show you what I do to shield mine.'

'So I've just got to work it out for myself? I don't need anyone's help?' Auraya frowned. 'Then why am I here?'

'You need someone able to sense your thoughts to tell you if they're hidden or not.'

Auraya nodded. 'But you can only read my mind while mind-skimming. Are you planning to spend the entire time in a dream trance?'

'All immortals can sense emotions,' Jade told her. 'When I can no longer sense your emotions, I'll attempt to skim your mind.'

This was a new and interesting piece of information. Mirar must be able to sense emotions, too. He hadn't been able to sense hers when she was a White, but he would be able to now. And she couldn't read his mind any more.

How the tables have turned, she mused. *It's just as well he isn't here.*

'As I said,' Jade continued, 'imagine drawing a veil across your mind. You can see out but nobody can see in.'

Auraya tried. She pictured the veil over and over, even pictured a heavy sack over her head, but no matter what she did Jade could still sense her emotions.

Soon she was feeling such strong frustration she knew even a Giftless mortal would have detected it. The hours dragged past. Eventually Jade sighed and put down the basket she was weaving.

'That's enough for tonight. It is late. Get some sleep.'

Auraya smothered a smile at the woman's dismissive manner. She lay on her bed and listened as Jade walked to the back of the cave and began rustling among the supplies.

For a while she lay there, worrying. Tyve had told her that the priests in the Open had tried and failed to contact her through her priest ring. She had explained that hers was not working properly, though she didn't tell him that the void was the cause.

I have to hope that none of the White try to contact me, she thought. *The sooner I can leave here the better.*

So . . . a veil over my mind, she thought. *Sleep is sometimes described like that. So is it like falling asleep?* She closed her eyes and let her thoughts wander. Slowly she relaxed and felt the tension of striving with her mind fade away. *I'm more tired than I thought I was. It's so good just letting my mind rest.*

:Auraya.

The voice tugged her reluctantly back toward consciousness. For a moment she felt only annoyance, then she realised she knew the voice.

:Mirar?

There was a pause.

:How are you faring?

:You're dream linking . . . how is that possible? My priest ring doesn't work in the void.

:I don't know, but I guess the ring must require unbroken magic between itself and another. Or perhaps the ring relies on a link to the gods to work.

:So dream linking and mind-skimming don't require unbroken magic?

:No. So, how are you faring?

:If you mean at shielding my mind, then not well at all. I don't know how I'm supposed to just stumble upon it by myself in a few days. She felt the frustration of the day shift into anger. *Do you realise the risk you've forced me to take? The position you've put me in? The gods allowed me to resign and remain a priestess on the condition that I do not hamper them or ally myself with their enemies. It's quite clear they consider you an enemy. I should have left here as soon as I knew that Jade was your friend, even if that meant the gods would discover her, even if that meant the gods might find you.*

:But you didn't.

:No. You've both taken advantage of me. Forced me to learn to hide my thoughts in order to protect you.

:We've forced you to learn something that might save your life.

:Or end it.

:So you believe the gods will kill you if they can't read your thoughts?

Auraya paused. Anger and weariness were making her say illogical things.

:No. It will just make matters worse between us. Is this your way of avenging yourself? Are you punishing me or trying to force me to turn from the gods?

:Neither! I want to help you by teaching you to protect yourself. I want you to be all that you are meant to be — deserve to be! A powerful sorceress. An immortal. He paused. *Don't you want to be immortal?*

Auraya felt a shiver go through her. *Do I? Of course I do.*

But I don't want to be immortal if it means turning from the gods. I don't want to be a Wild, hunted and hated.

She felt anger deepen, but this time at the gods. *Why does it have to be like that? I can be immortal and still worship the gods. Why must they stop me from becoming all I can be, when it is of no threat to them?*

Perhaps Chaia would allow her that freedom, but Huan never would. Huan wanted unquestioning obedience from her worshippers. *I've already lost her regard by proving myself unworthy*, she thought. *Perhaps eventually she'll forgive me. In the meantime it would be better not to give the goddess any further reason to distrust me.*

:Jade says when you taught me to heal you taught me enough so that I could discover the secret of immortality for myself, she said to Mirar. *Perhaps one day I'll be in a position to try it without offending the gods. But for now it's pointless. What you call immortality isn't true immortality. I can still be killed. And I will be, if I defy the gods again.*

Mirar was silent for a long time before he replied.

:The gods can hold grudges for a very long time, Auraya. They might not use magic to kill you, but they can make sure age does it for them. And remember this: if I thought becoming immortal was the only reason the gods might kill you, I'd never have risked teaching you to heal.

And with that, he was gone.

CHAPTER 6

Older people are supposed to be the cautious ones, Ranaan thought as he followed Dreamweaver Fareeh down the dark alley. *Younger people are the ones that rush into danger. So what's wrong with us? Why is my teacher the one willing to take risks while I'm the one who's scared out of his wits?*

They reached the end of the alley and Fareeh stopped to peer around a building into the larger street.

Because I'm a coward, Ranaan told himself, *and Fareeh isn't. It's easier for him, too. He's Gifted and he's big. I'm a skinny runt, and I know I haven't even learned enough Gifts in six months to defend myself from an attack of dartflies.*

The big man stepped out into the street. Taking a deep breath, Ranaan forced himself to follow. They walked purposefully but kept to the shadows as much as possible. In this part of the city the only lamps that burned were those maintained by the occupants of the houses. The moon, however, was bright and round.

Ranaan glanced at his teacher. The Dreamweaver's quiet confidence reassured patients at the hospice. He was everything they liked about Dreamweavers: sturdy, calm, knowledgeable and patient. He made these trips out to visit sick people despite the dangers because he was a nice person.

I just wish he didn't insist I come with him.

Ranaan grimaced. *I am not a nice person. I'm a coward who'd rather let someone die than risk a beating. I don't deserve such a good teacher.*

A door opened ahead. Ranaan's heart began racing as three men stepped out, laughing. Fareeh did not even check his stride. He walked around them, Ranaan following.

The young Dreamweaver's legs were shaking as he and his teacher continued down the road. He strained his ears for sounds of pursuit. There were footsteps, growing quieter. Was that because the men were making an effort to make less noise?

He looked behind. The men were walking in the other direction.

'Nearly there,' Fareeh murmured.

Ranaan glanced at his teacher and caught a knowing smile. He felt his face warm and said nothing. They turned into a lane. Fareeh paused and created a spark of light to illuminate the directions on the slip of paper he carried. He nodded, extinguished the light, and continued down the lane.

The way turned around a protruding section of a building then ended. Fareeh slowed and began looking up at the buildings around them.

'It says they have left a light in the . . .'

His quiet words were lost behind the bang of a slammed door. Footsteps sounded behind them. Ranaan turned and felt his heart begin to race again. He counted eight, maybe nine figures fanning out to surround him and his teacher.

'What are you doing here, Dreamweaver?'

The accent was typical of the poor quarter, but there was something about it that sounded wrong to Ranaan.

Fareeh gave the windows of the buildings one more quick glance.

'Discovering that I am in the wrong place,' he replied. 'The directions I was given appear to be incorrect.'

'You're right about that,' another voice said. Ranaan looked at the speaker. The man's high voice did not match his heavy build.

'We will trouble you no longer,' Fareeh said. He took a step toward the gap between two of the men, then stopped. The men had moved closer together to block him.

Ranaan held back a groan of dismay and fear. His legs were shaking and he felt ill. He wondered if his heart could beat any faster. If it did, it might just leap out of his throat.

A spark of light appeared, illuminating the palm of Fareeh's hand. It brightened and Ranaan looked beyond to the faces of the men. His mouth went dry as he understood why the poor-quarter accent had sounded wrong.

This was no street gang of the area. The accents had been faked. Though the clothes the men wore were plain, they were well made – casual wear for outdoor sports. Their smiles revealed near-flawless teeth. The high-voiced man was not muscular, but wore the fat of one who lived an indulgent life.

One, a blond with immaculately trimmed hair, took a step forward.

'You're right,' he said. 'You're definitely not going to trouble us again.'

Then the lane contorted with magic. Ranaan heard Fareeh tell him to stay within his shield. He huddled against his teacher as attacks came from all sides.

All of them. They're all Gifted. How can this be? Are the rich buying magical training for those sons who do not become priests?

Fareeh gave a small grunt of anger. He reached behind and gripped Ranaan's arm. Pulling his student around, he leaned close.

'I'll hold them,' he murmured. 'You go. Go to the hospice. Get help.'

Ranaan staggered as Fareeh propelled him away. He saw the strangers turn to attack him and felt a rush of terror. His legs found their strength and he fled. Nothing stopped him. No one stepped out from the darkness to block his path. At the end of the street he threw himself around the corner and ran.

A few streets later he realised he wasn't being followed and the feeling of panic subsided. He stopped as his mind began to work again and he realised two things: Fareeh wouldn't have sent Ranaan for help if he'd thought he could free himself alone. He must be outnumbered.

Of course he's outnumbered. There were eight of them!

The hospice was several streets away. Fareeh couldn't possibly hold eight sorcerers off long enough for Ranaan to return with help.

I should go back and help him, he thought.

Don't be stupid. What can you do? Recite herb cures to them?

Indecision paralysed him. Suddenly he realised he could hear voices behind him. Laughter. Crows of delight. He recognised the high-pitched voice of the fat man and shuddered.

Realising he was standing right in the pool of light cast by a lamp he spun around, searching for a hiding place. The closest was the shallow alcove of a doorway. He dashed into it and pressed himself against the door-frame, trembling.

The voices grew louder. Words like 'easy' and 'pathetic' and 'good work' reached him. Then one of the men told the others to shut up.

They quietened. Urgent discussion followed, then footsteps. Ranaan held his breath as the men strode toward his hiding place.

'Hurry *up*!'

The steps quickened. Two men ran past Ranaan. They

disappeared down the end of the street. Other footsteps faded away as the men separated and headed in different directions.

Ranaan then listened to the sounds of the street: the tiny rustlings of what he hoped were animals, the faint voices of an argument somewhere inside the house he stood beside, the trickle of water or sewage somewhere below.

Caution and fear fought the need to discover Fareeh's fate. Finally, certain that the attackers were gone, he emerged from the doorway. He crept along the wall to the corner and peered into the lane. There were too many shadowed places there for him to be sure no one waited for him. With heart hammering, he forced himself to step into the lane.

His breathing seemed unnaturally loud. He reached the protruding building and peered around it. The lane was dark, but as he stared at the ground he began to make out a man-sized shape.

Fareeh . . .

Swallowing hard, he slowly made his way toward the shape. It was definitely a man, and the vest was a Dreamweaver's. Ranaan's boots made a small, wet sound as he reached the figure. He looked down and saw that the ground glistened faintly, and he recognised the tangy smell in the air. Blood.

The risk that the attackers might return suddenly did not matter. He concentrated and managed to produce a spark of light. The sight of Fareeh's blankly staring eyes, and the great red pool of blood spreading out from behind the man's head, shocked Ranaan so badly the light flickered out. He could not breathe properly. He found he was gasping out words as he stared at his dead teacher's face.

'No. Not Fareeh. It can't be.'

Then a hand touched his shoulder lightly. Ranaan jumped and spun around, terror suddenly returning. A man stepped back. Ranaan hadn't heard the stranger approach, hadn't even noticed the light from the spark hovering above the stranger's hand.

But the face of the stranger did not belong to one of the attackers. It was a strange face, but the expression on it was one of sympathy. The man glanced over his shoulder.

'Someone's coming. You'd best come with me.'

Ranaan hesitated and turned back to Fareeh.

'Nothing can help him now. Leave him, or you'll end up the same.'

Ranaan's legs obeyed him reluctantly. The stranger grasped his arm and drew him to a door. They moved down a long corridor and entered another lane.

A maze of lanes and passages followed. Time passed. Ranaan's awareness of their journey came and went. At one point he collected his thoughts enough to ask for his rescuer's name.

'Amli.'

'You're from Sennon, then?'

'The south.'

'Why are you helping me?'

'You need it. Where I come from people do not abandon their fellow mortals to thugs or killers, if they can help it.'

Ranaan winced. 'He told me to run and get help.'

'Ah. Sorry. I did not mean you, I meant myself. You could not have saved your friend. Neither could I, I must admit. There were too many of them.'

'He knew it. He knew I couldn't get back in time.'

'That is likely. It is also likely he sent you away to save your life.'

Ranaan shook his head. 'I should return to the hospice. I should tell them what happened.'

Amli stopped and placed a hand on his arm. 'Those thugs will be waiting for you there. I wouldn't be surprised if they were waiting outside wherever it is you stay when you're not at the hospice, too. You are a witness. Did you get a good look at them?'

'Yes.'

'Then you can't go back. They won't want to risk that you will identify them.'

Ranaan shuddered. 'Do you think the patient we came to see wasn't real? That it was an ambush?'

'Were you there to treat someone?'

'Yes. We had directions.'

Amli looked grim. 'Possibly. The sooner I get you off the streets the better.'

They started walking again. Ranaan could not help picturing Fareeh's body lying in the laneway, abandoned. He couldn't think beyond that image. When Amli stopped and opened a door, Ranaan let himself be ushered into the bright room beyond.

A middle-aged woman rose to greet Amli. He introduced her as his wife. She hummed with concern at Amli's story, guided Ranaan to a chair and pressed a mug into his hands. The drink within was unfamiliar and alcoholic, but it tasted sweet and brought a comforting warmth that soothed the ache inside enough so that he could think clearly again.

'Thank you,' he said belatedly. 'Both of you.'

The couple smiled. 'I'll put some bedding together for you,' the woman said, then disappeared up a staircase.

Ranaan looked around the narrow room. A brazier burned to one side, and benches were arranged around it, hinting that people gathered here from time to time. He guessed that there was a bedroom or two upstairs. It was a small house, but clean and tidy.

'How long have you been here?' he asked.

Amli filled another mug with the drink. 'Nearly a year. I have a stall in the main market. We import spices and pottery.'

A few strange ornaments adorned the walls. They looked out of place. Some of the pots near the brazier were oddly shaped. He examined the mug he was drinking from. The potter's mark on the base was a picture of one of these odd pots, with a star marked on the side.

A star. Ranaan felt his skin tingle as a possibility occurred to him. His eyes fell to Amli's neck. Beneath the collar of his tunic was a silver chain — a heavy chain for a heavy pendant.

'You said you're from the south?' Ranaan said.

'Yes.'

'You're Pentadrians?'

Amli did not reply straightaway. He regarded Ranaan solemnly, then took the mug from him.

'Why would you think that?'

'You don't hate Dreamweavers.'

Amli chuckled. 'So we can't be Circlians. Therefore we must be Pentadrians.'

'Fareeh used to say you could tell a Sennon from a southerner because while Sennons tolerate other religions, they still like to pretend they don't exist.'

'Not all Sennons are like that.'

'Which ones aren't?'

Amli smiled. 'The Sennonian Dreamweavers. And the Sennonian Pentadrians.' Amli refilled Ranaan's mug. 'We both know what it is like to be persecuted for our beliefs.'

'But you're not persecuted in your own land.'

Amli smiled. 'No.'

So he is a Pentadrian, Ranaan thought. He realised he was not bothered by that at all. Surprised, but not dismayed.

Amli handed Ranaan the refilled mug. 'When we first came here, jealous traders put about the rumour that we were Pentadrians so that people wouldn't buy from us. It convinced us we were right in claiming we were from Sennon.' He shook his head. 'That is nothing to what they do to Dreamweavers. The Circlians are an evil lot.'

'And Pentadrians aren't? Isn't invading another country an evil thing to do?'

'Yes,' Amli agreed. He looked away and sighed. 'It was wrong. Our gods had seen the evils of the Circlians and ordered us to stop them. We assumed war was the most effective way to achieve that, but we only ended up killing those we wished to save. And we paid the price for it with our own deaths.'

He looked terribly sad. Ranaan's thoughts turned to Fareeh and he felt his heart wrench painfully. His teacher hadn't been killed by Pentadrians, just thugs. Circlian thugs. Truly the Circlians were an evil lot.

'Tell me more about the Pentadrians. What are your gods like?'

Amli looked up and his gaze cleared. He smiled.

'What would you like to know?'

The roots Auraya was peeling were dyeing her skin orange. Jade hadn't asked Auraya to do the task, she had simply handed her the roots and said 'peel' in the tone of one who expected obedience. Auraya could see no point refusing; it kept her hands occupied while she tried to discover how to shield her mind.

At least Jade was willing to explain what the root was for. It was both a dye and a treatment for scalp disorders, though the latter worked best when the juice was applied fresh rather than as a powder mixed with water.

Other 'cures' that Jade had prepared included a potion to liven a lazy heart made from insect poison, bark which produced a stimulant similar to but more powerful than those Leiard had once taught Auraya about, and mushrooms that Jade admitted were useful only for 'recreational purposes'.

82

It was strangely logical to find that Mirar's friend was as learned in cures and healing as he was. Preparing the different substances brought back memories of Auraya's childhood, of helping and learning from Leiard. She felt a pang of regret. Things had been so much simpler then.

'Do you realise how much time you spend dwelling on regrets and worries?' Jade said suddenly. 'I don't know whether you're chewing over leaving the White, agonising over offending the gods or getting sentimental over your great lost love – or all three – but you certainly do a lot of it.'

Auraya looked up and managed a wry smile. Jade was constantly telling Auraya what she was feeling in order to let her know her attempts at hiding her mind were failing. 'There's not much else to do while peeling roots.'

'I must admit, self-pity wasn't something I expected to sense so much of from a former White.'

'No? What were you expecting?'

The woman pursed her lips. 'Arrogance. A self-righteous god-loving young woman with puffed-up notions of her own worth.'

'And that's not what you found?'

'No. I could have lived with that. Instead I get to put up with ingratitude and self-pity.'

Auraya blinked in surprise. 'Ingratitude?'

'Yes. I can sense your emotions, remember. There's been little gratitude.'

'Gratitude can't be forced. And it's hard to maintain when your teacher is trying to be as unpleasant a companion as possible.'

'You haven't done much to endear yourself to me so far either,' Jade retorted.

'Just proves your expectations were wrong. Though I think one was correct.'

'Oh?'

'I do love the gods.'

Jade stopped working and stared at Auraya, her expression unreadable.

'So I was wrong. Nice of you to point that out.' Her voice was flat, but Auraya could hear the suppressed anger and fear behind it.

'And you hate them,' she stated. 'Why?'

Jade scowled and the cuts of her knife became more aggressive. 'I could spend the whole day listing the reasons. I've had a thousand years to tally them up. But what point would there be in telling you? You won't believe me, and even if you did, you would still love the gods. Love is blind, whether it be for a lover, family or the gods.'

'I know there was much to hate about the gods in the Age of the Many. That's why the Circle fought the rest. You must have been pleased when so many were killed.'

Jade shrugged. 'Mostly. Not all the gods were bad, though.'

'The Circle?'

'Baddest of them all.'

'Before or after the war?'

'Both.'

'What did they do after the war that was bad?'

'They executed Mirar.'

'Is that all?'

'No.' Jade's expression darkened. 'They killed other immortals. They persecuted Dreamweavers.'

'Does knowing that Mirar survived diminish your hatred at all?'

The woman's eyes narrowed. 'No. They ordered him killed. That they failed doesn't change that. In fact, it makes it worse knowing the torment he went through afterwards, as he recovered.'

Auraya nodded. 'Why do you think they ordered him, and the other Wilds, killed?'

Looking at her knife, Jade ran her finger along the blade. 'Mirar actively worked against their control of mortals, as did some other immortals. The rest of us . . . they knew we hated them. We know what they were like before the war. If we told the world of their true natures, mortals might not be so willing to follow them.'

'What did the gods do that was so terrible?'

Jade stared at the cutting board, her eyes focused far beyond it.

'Enslaved people and nations, or wiped them out completely in revenge for a small slight in the distant past. They made whores out of their followers and sacrificed children. They changed mortals into monsters just to see if they could make them fly or breathe fire or grow to abnormal sizes.'

Auraya felt a shock. 'The Siyee? But they willingly allowed themselves to be changed by Huan.'

'Huan took advantage of them,' Jade said. 'She took the most gullible of her followers, those willing to do anything for her, to work on. They could not have known what it was going to do to them.' She made a noise of disgust. 'But when it came to seducing innocents, Chaia was the most gifted. He would select beautiful young women to be his lovers, and when they grew too old or they no longer adored him utterly, he would cast them aside. It was said the pleasure he gave them ruined them, as no mortal man could match it.'

Auraya stared at Jade. *The pleasure he gave . . . no mortal man could match . . .* She shivered. She thought of the nights she craved Chaia's touch. She hadn't attempted to lie with another man since. Was that because none interested her, or because she knew no man could? *Have I been ruined as well?*

Jade was watching her closely. Auraya made herself nod. 'You're right; I do find it hard to believe you.'

'Give it time,' Jade said. She put down her knife. 'I just need to . . . take care of something. I'll be back soon.'

As the woman rose and left the cave, Auraya picked up another root and began to peel it. She barely noticed what she was doing. Instead her mind returned to what Jade had told her of the gods.

When she had confronted Mirar, intending to kill him, he had argued that the gods had done terrible things. He hadn't described those deeds, but Huan had all but admitted that the gods had been guilty of something.

'*The Age of the Many ended long ago,*' Huan had said. '*The excesses of that time are forgotten.*'

She did not know what Huan had done to her followers in order to make the Siyee. It was hard to see their creation as a terrible thing, when the result was hardly a race of abominations.

But breathe fire? Abnormal sizes? Did Huan try to make races other than the Siyee and the Elai?

She shook her head. How could she judge the gods for things they had done so long ago? She hadn't witnessed them. She could not know the truth . . . unless Jade or Mirar agreed to show her their memories.

Mirar would, she guessed, but he was far away. Would Jade agree to it? *I don't think so. She likes to keep her thoughts to herself. Can't blame her, really. I wouldn't want to let anyone see my mind without good reason, either. I certainly wouldn't want her finding out about Chaia and me, for a start.*

Jade's story about Chaia had disturbed Auraya deeply. Had the nights she had shared with him damaged her in some way? Had he been trying to bind her to him through pleasure? Perhaps she had been wise to end the affair when she had.

:My, my. That took courage.

Auraya started and dropped the peeling knife. The voice in her mind had been faint, but familiar.

How can I be hearing Jade's thoughts? As the answer came she felt both anger and embarrassment. *She is mind-skimming! Is that what she wanted to take care of?* Looking into my mind? She felt herself mentally recoil, wishing there was a fog, or a haze of some kind, that could at least blur her mind.

Auraya stood up. She wanted to storm out of the cave, but she couldn't leave the void. Instead she paced around the beds.

'I was projecting.'

Spinning around, Auraya glared at Jade as the woman entered the cave.

'How dare y—'

'I wondered at first if you saw past my mind shield, but then I realised I was projecting my words as one automatically does in the dream trance. I didn't expect you to hear, because nobody can hear the thoughts of a mind-skimmer. Nobody but you. You've done it, by the way.'

'Done what?'

'Your mind is veiled. Can you sense what you have done?'

She stared at Jade, caught between wanting to voice her anger and the knowledge that she might be able to escape the void and Jade. Taking a deep breath, she concentrated and slowly came to see that she had created the haze she had wished for. *Not a veil, a fog.*

'Yes,' she said.

'Good. Well, that was an unexpected bonus. I was only looking for something I could use to persuade you to try harder. Now you just have to learn to keep your mind shield there, all the time, until you're not even aware of it – like breathing. I will provide distractions to test your concentration.' She sat down, wiped the knife clean and picked up a stone. Spitting on the stone, she began to sharpen the blade. 'You haven't finished,' she pointed out, nodding at the bucket of roots.

'I can't leave?'

'Not yet.'

Taking another deep breath, Auraya quelled her anger. She sat down, picked up the peeling knife and continued with her work.

'So Chaia was your other lover,' Jade said in a conversational tone.

As anger rose, Auraya felt the haze around her mind thin. She concentrated and was relieved when it thickened again.

Jade smiled slyly. 'You did say you loved the gods. I didn't realise you meant it so literally. I'm impressed – and I'm not easily impressed. So tell me: are the gods as good at love-making as the legends say?'

'I don't know,' Auraya replied. 'I couldn't say.'

Jade's eyebrows rose. 'I saw it all quite clearly, Auraya. You can't lie to me.'

'I didn't lie,' Auraya said. *There's no point denying it, so I may as well make the best of it.*

'Oh yes you did.'

'No, I didn't,' Auraya told her. 'I have no idea what the legends say.'

Jade looked at her questioningly, then threw back her head and laughed.

The night was warm, heralding the coming summer. Reivan could smell it in the air. Though she rose early to attend to her duties, she found it hard to sleep on nights like these. There was a tension in the air, a feeling of expectation and dread. Soon the sun would blaze down and the nights would be too hot for comfort.

Tonight she had tossed and turned until restlessness sent

her from her bed out onto the balcony. There the night breeze cooled her. She looked down at a city bathed in moonlight. Bright points of light outlined the main thoroughfares crisscrossing the city. Sanctuary lamps marked the edges of courtyards.

And in the courtyard directly below her room, a figure was strolling unhurriedly past. A familiar masculine figure. She held her breath, wondering if he had seen her, hoping he hadn't sensed the thrill that had run through her at the sight of him.

Her heart lurched as he looked up at her and smiled. She raised a hand in reply.

Gods, I hope he doesn't think I was watching him. Then she snorted quietly. *Well, of course he does. He can read my mind. Oh, no.*

He had changed direction and was now walking toward her. She forced herself to keep smiling, and to ignore the pounding of her heart. Stopping below her balcony, he looked up at her.

'The moonlight favours you, Reivan,' he said softly.

Her heart leapt into her throat, making it impossible to reply. *He's just being nice*, she told herself. *Flippant. Flirtatious.*

His smile faded a little.

'I hope you aren't allowing Imenja's and my differences of opinion to spoil our friendship.'

Friendship? What friendship? I lust after him and he rightly ignores it. Reivan's wry amusement eased the constriction around her throat.

'Of course not,' she replied, then impulsively added: 'I'm just not used to flattery.'

His smile broadened again. 'Then we shall have to amend that.'

She crossed her arms. 'And what impression would that give people?'

'The right impression. You are an admirable woman.'

Heat rushed to her cheeks, and hope sent her heart racing again.

'Don't tease me,' she said, then winced at the desperation in her voice. Embarrassed, she stepped back to hide her face.

'Forgive me.' His voice drifted up. 'I did not mean to anger you.'

Angry? I'm not angry, I'm ashamed. Surely he sees that. Of course he does! She peered warily over the balcony again, but he had moved. *Where is he now?* She moved to the railing and searched the courtyard.

He had gone.

Feeling as if she had said something wrong, she returned to her bed to toss and turn some more.

CHAPTER 7

Tyve had visited the cave twice more in the past week, apparently only to see if Auraya and Jade needed any food or help. Jade had thanked him politely and sent him away with a few of the cures she had made for people in his village.

We made, Auraya corrected as she continued grinding up the dried leaves Jade had left for her. Though Jade gathered the ingredients, venturing out for hours each day to find them, Auraya had spent much of her time preparing them. The woman was out foraging for cure ingredients now. Sometimes Auraya wondered if there was some special purpose for the growing supply of cures at the back of the room, or if Jade simply hated to be idle.

I wonder if she hesitates whenever she returns to the cave, trying not to imagine that I've betrayed her and one of the White is here waiting for her?

Auraya smiled, then sobered. Perhaps that was why Jade had skimmed her thoughts. Perhaps she had done it every time she was about to re-enter the cave, to ensure her student hadn't betrayed her.

It was impossible not to worry about what Jade might have read from mind. Having failed to extract a promise from Jade that she would not spy on Auraya's thoughts again, Auraya was determined to achieve a strong, stable mind shield as soon as possible. She was finding it easier to hold it in place now, sometimes even forgetting that it was there. Soon she would be able to leave.

Before she did, however, she wanted to ask Jade some questions.

The jar of ground leaves was nearly full by the time Jade returned. The woman said nothing as she set her buckets beside the bed and sat down. She took a lump of what looked like rock from one bucket and began to break off and scratch out areas of a whitish substance into a jar.

'What is that?'

'Poison,' Jade replied. 'At least in anything but the tiniest dose.'

'Do you often have a use for poison?'

'Surprisingly rarely. I've used poison only three times in the last thousand years. It's the kind of death you reserve for truly unpleasant people.'

The other woman spoke so lightly, Auraya wasn't sure if she was joking or not. She paused, then decided she didn't want to know.

'So you've lived a thousand years,' she asked instead.

'At least.'

'You don't know for certain?'

'No. I used to keep count, but after a while it became painfully obvious that the calendars people used to count the years were wrong, and then they made a great mess of recalculating. I moved around so much I lost count, but by then it didn't seem to matter any more.'

'What is it like, living that long?'

Jade looked up at Auraya and shrugged. 'Not as thrilling as you might think,' she said. 'Most of the time you don't think about it. Your thoughts are taken up with immediate concerns: what you will eat today, where you will sleep. You take the knowledge you've gathered over the years for granted. When you need it, it's there, and you don't often think back to when you learned it.

'Now and then something makes you stop and consider the past, and that's when you are most conscious of your age. You are aware of changes that no one else notices, not even historians. You also see that some things never change. People will always fall in and out of love. Ambitious men and women will always crave power. Greedy men and women will always hoard wealth. Mortals will be mortals.'

'So can immortals change in ways mortals can't?'

Jade looked thoughtful. 'Yes and no. Immortality doesn't make us smarter. Experience does. We try not to make the same mistake twice, but memories fade and some memories fade faster than others. And there are always new mistakes to make.' She grimaced. 'Sometimes we want to make the same mistakes. Love, for instance. In falling in love, mortals always risk great pain; for immortals that pain is guaranteed. Either love dies, or those you love do.'

A hint of bitterness had entered Jade's voice. Auraya felt a pang of sympathy.

'Is the pain worth enduring?'

Jade smiled humourlessly. 'Yes, so long as you don't suffer too often. I've borne children and watched them die as well. That was even more painful, yet I've done it more than once.'

'So immortals can have children?'

'Of course.' Jade frowned. 'Why wouldn't we?' Then her eyes widened in realisation. 'The gods made you unable to conceive while you were a White, didn't they?'

Auraya shrugged. 'We couldn't have devoted ourselves to our work if we were bearing and raising children.'

'The gods aren't ones for recreational time, are they? Still, children would have made you vulnerable. Believe me, I know how vulnerable children can make you, if they're used against you.'

'What happened?'

Jade shook her head. 'I would rather not speak of it. Some memories are best kept buried.'

Auraya nodded and considered how she could change the subject. 'Were your children sorcerers?'

'A few. Some had little Gifts at all. None became immortal. Not strong enough. I don't think any immortal has borne an immortal child.'

'Not even if both parents were immortal?'

'I've not heard of any who had such a parentage.'

'Perhaps that would make the difference.'

Jade shrugged, then she turned to stare at Auraya. 'Are you planning any such experiment soon? I had the impression you weren't that enamoured of Mirar.'

Auraya frowned at the woman, wondering at the sudden change in her mood.

'No.'

'Does Mirar know about you and Chaia?' Jade asked.

'Of course not.'

'Do you intend to tell him?'

'Do you?'

Jade put down her work. 'Yes.'

'I know you would, but Mirar deserves to know that you don't return his feelings.'

'He knows,' she told Jade.

'If you don't care for him, why would you care if he knew who your lover is?'

'Was,' Auraya corrected. 'Because that information is private.'

'For better or worse, it's no longer a secret. I may as well tell him before he finds some other stupid thing to do out of love for you.'

Auraya sighed. 'Tell him, then. I'd hate to take the blame for his habit of getting himself into trouble – again.'

Jade's eyes narrowed. 'You really don't care for him, do you?'

'I loved Leiard, not Mirar.'

'He *is* Leiard. Leiard is part of him.'

Auraya forced herself to meet Jade's eyes. 'Leiard was never real. I can't turn from the little I have left of my life for a made-up piece of a person buried somewhere within a man I don't know. And after all you've said about love being a mistake, I don't see why you expect me to feel any differently.'

Jade stared at Auraya for a long time, then she looked away. 'I think what infuriates me is that I agree with you,' she said in a fierce, quiet voice. 'I would do the same. I think I want you to love him simply to ease my fears. If you did, you wouldn't harm us. Instead I have to believe Mirar. He swears you will not. Fool that he is, he has never misjudged anyone in the past – not even when dazzled by love.' She raised a finger in warning. 'Don't prove him wrong.'

Auraya said nothing. Dropping her rock back into the bucket, Jade sealed the jar of white powder. She rose and placed it among her supplies, then turned to regard Auraya.

'I'm going to find us some dinner.'

After the woman had gone, the cave was oppressively silent. Auraya couldn't help feeling she had let Jade down somehow. *She is only disappointed that I don't love Mirar*, she thought. *And there's no reason I should feel guilty about that.*

Looking around the cave, she sighed. *I feel lonely*, she realised. *I wonder how Mischief is.* She missed his company, his unquestioning loyalty. *Why are veez like that? It's not like attaching themselves to humans is good for their kind . . . except, I suppose, that they don't have to hunt for food and have a good chance of a safe home and a warm bed . . . I think I just answered that question for myself.*

He'd never liked it when she went away. If only she could communicate with him somehow.

I wonder . . . would I be able to find him through mind-skimming?

It was worth a try. Lying down on the bed, she closed her eyes and slowly settled into a dream trance. When she judged herself ready, she reached out in the direction of the Open.

Some time later she found the minds of three Siyee making their way back to their village after a successful hunt. Next she found a village, and paused to skim the mind of a female Siyee cooking a complicated meal. The woman's hunger made Auraya notice her own.

She found several more Siyee and was relieved when she recognised the Open through a man's eyes. Finding Mischief among the multitude of Siyee minds wouldn't be easy. Eventually she saw her own bower through a Siyee child's eyes and that gave her the clue she needed to find him.

Reaching toward the structure, she concentrated hard, expecting that the mind of a little creature like a veez would be somehow smaller and fainter. She sensed an animal mind focused intently on a task. Fascinated, she watched as he drew magic as easily as he drew breath, and used it to move a mechanism of some sort, then she felt the animal's greedy satisfaction as he succeeded. He seized something edible, dragged it out of the container it had been sealed within, and began to eat.

I think Mischief may have just broken into some food container, she thought, amused. *I've never watched him use magic . . .*

Then something else caught at her attention. Something much closer. A voice spoke and she reeled as far stronger minds overwhelmed her senses and sent her rushing back to a place somewhere outside the cave.

: . . . *send one of the Siyee Watchers with orders for her to meet me at the Temple. If Chaia is right, she won't dare to disobey us.*

:*And if she does?*

:*We will all know Chaia is wrong.*

The first speaker was Huan; the second took Auraya longer to recognise. As he spoke a second time she realised the voice was Saru's.

:*And he can't stop us having her killed.*

Auraya felt her blood go cold. Were they talking about her?

:*He'll still try*, Huan said.

:*Yes. Why do you think he's so determined to keep her alive?*

:*Lust. She's just another one of his little infatuations.*

:*If she was he wouldn't think twice about casting her off as he did the others. This is different.*

:*In all the worst ways. She's not some pretty doll he wants to play with, like the other girls. She's too powerful.* Huan's voice darkened. *He must have plans for her.*

:*Too powerful to kill?*

:*Not yet. Not while she is ignorant of her true strength. Which is why I do not like her vanishing into the void to treat this woman. If my suspicions are correct, that woman is no mere curer. Auraya could be learning everything we don't want her to learn.*

:*You encouraged her by allowing her to learn to heal magically.*

:*That was meant to convince the others that she was too dangerous.*

:*It convinced me. What do you think would sway Lore and Yranna?*

Huan was silent a moment.

:*The confirmation of my suspicions. If she comes out of that void knowing what she shouldn't, only Chaia will be opposed to her death.*

:*He will be outvoted at last.*

:*Yes.*

:*And if she comes out knowing nothing?*

:*We will find some other way to persuade them. Eventually Auraya will defy us again. It is only a matter of time.*

:And her executors?

:Let's check . . .

With dizzying speed, the two minds flashed away, leaving Auraya dazed by her brief contact with them. She roused herself into full consciousness. Lying on her bed, she heard the gods' words repeating in her mind . . . *encouraged her by allowing her to learn to heal magically . . . meant to convince the others that she was too dangerous . . . only Chaia will be opposed to her death.*

Huan wants me dead, Auraya thought. *She has since before I refused to kill Mirar! She is so determined to kill me, she will even manipulate her fellow gods to achieve her aims.*

She felt a wave of nausea. *It doesn't matter that Chaia opposes her. The others will eventually outvote him.* Sitting up, she stared at the wall of the cave.

The knowledge made her head spin. They would outvote him soon, because the moment she left the void the gods would know she'd *learned* to hide her mind, whether she actually hid it or not. It didn't matter that she had never intended to hide her mind from *them*. Just learning such a thing had damned her.

Why? She felt a surge of curiosity and bitterness. *Because I'm too powerful? How powerful, I wonder?*

Powerful enough to frighten the gods.

She felt a thrill, but it quickly faded. *I may be powerful enough to worry them, but I doubt I'm powerful enough to survive if they decide I must be killed.*

Except that Mirar and Jade had both survived. If they could, she could too.

Standing up, she paced around the void and considered this. *I have two choices,* she decided eventually. *Either I submit to the gods' judgement and let them kill me, or I resist them. I doubt Huan or the others would take my soul when I die, but Chaia will. Would he still take it if I resist the others, and fail? Surely he wouldn't abandon it to fade out of existence. How much defiance would he be willing to forgive?*

Could she fight Huan and the other gods, and not Chaia?

I don't want to defy Chaia, she thought. *Then I must put this decision in his hands. I will fight the others or submit to death, according to his will.*

The decision brought relief, but it did not completely erase the fear. Could she really submit to execution if Chaia decided she must? *He won't.* And that brought her to another question. Who were the executioners Saru and Huan had spoken of?

The answer was painfully obvious: the White.

A noise interrupted her thoughts. She looked up to find Jade entering the cave carrying two girri. The woman lifted the birds high.

'We eat well tonight,' she said.

Auraya managed a smile. She wasn't hungry any more. Her stomach was twisted in knots. Jade gave her an odd look.

'You look as though you've just received bad news.'

Auraya looked away. 'Mind-skimming is much like mind-reading. Sometimes you find out things you wish you hadn't.'

'Ah.' Jade dropped the birds onto the cooking stone between the beds. 'Believe me, knowing too much is a familiar curse to us immortals.'

'Like knowing the secret of immortality?'

Jade's eyes rose to meet Auraya's, then narrowed. 'No, that's one piece of knowledge I don't regret having.' One of her eyebrows lifted. 'And it's one you have, too. You just need to spend a little time thinking about it.'

Jade was right. The gods already considered her knowledge of magical healing to be almost as damning as knowledge of immortality. And Huan had allowed Auraya to learn magical healing in order to persuade the other gods to kill her.

'Thinking time? That's all it takes?'

'Yes.' Jade smiled. 'Consider everything Mirar taught you about healing a body with magic. All you need do is apply it to your own. Begin a constant state of renewal and you need never age or die. Mirar said you learned to heal easily; this should come just as naturally. But don't think about it now,' she added, her tone suddenly practical. 'I need you to pluck and gut these feathered darlings while I fetch some vegetables.'

The house smelled faintly of stale sweat and mould beneath the tang of cleansing herbs. Danjin started up the stairs, trying not to breathe too deeply.

Ella had hired a few rooms in a house across the road from the hospice. The condition of it couldn't be helped. They needed to be in sight of the people passing the hospice and since the hospice was in the poor quarter most of the buildings were squalid. Ella didn't appear to be bothered by the smell. She didn't touch the food brought by the wife of the house's owner, however, and Danjin took that as a warning not to be ignored. If someone who could read minds avoided eating something, it was always wise to follow suit.

Ella had assured Danjin that the owner and his wife would not gossip about their guests. Having seen the mobs that gathered outside the hospice, and heard of Dreamweaver murders, their hosts weren't going to risk bringing any attention to themselves.

The alley behind the house was kept clear of the homeless and loiterers. Ella and Danjin arrived each day in an ordinary platten, entered the house via the rear door and for a few hours Ella sat by the window watching the people on the street below. She had seen a plan to block the hospice's entrance in someone's mind yesterday and managed to prevent it by stopping messages to supporters reaching their targets.

News of the most recent murder of a Dreamweaver and disappearance of his student had left her angry and disappointed. She had known and respected the Dreamweaver, though she did not remember much about his student. Danjin knew she was frustrated. They had hoped that by watching people around the hospice she would be able to prevent such crimes. Ella's expression while watching had grown more intense since the Dreamweaver's murder.

Reaching the top of the stairs, Danjin walked to the last door and knocked. There was a click and the door swung inward. Ella was sitting by the window as usual.

'Come in, Danjin Spear,' Ella said.

Closing the door, Danjin turned to find Ella rubbing her temples.

'You look pained, Ellareen of the White.'

She grimaced. 'All this mind-reading is disorientating.' She straightened. 'I have come to a few conclusions. Sit down and tell me what you think.'

He settled onto a chunky wooden chair made only slightly less uncomfortable by a few mean cushions. She looked out of the window again and her eyes narrowed. 'Remember how I said that the murderer we questioned not only hated Dreamweavers, but he feared them? I've been looking for what people fear about the Dreamweavers. It's been interesting. They don't fear individual Dreamweavers, nor Dreamweavers in general. Dreamweavers have always been too few in number and lacking in influence or ambition to be a threat. What people fear is that this will change.' She looked at Danjin. 'They fear that Mirar's return will make the Dreamweavers dangerous.'

'So when this rumour dies the hospice will be safe again.'

Ella shook her head. 'It won't die. Mirar *has* returned.'

He stared at her in shock. Mirar, the immortal leader of the Dreamweavers, *alive*? Now he could understand how those who believed the rumour must feel. Who would not feel a stirring of fear at the knowledge that the legendary immortal enemy of the gods still lived? To be immortal, a sorcerer must be immensely Gifted. Juran, the most powerful of the Gods' Chosen, had been given the task of executing Mirar. All believed he had succeeded. Had that been a lie, or had Juran been deceived?

'How did he survive?' he asked Ella.

'Mirar was buried and his body crushed, but with his healing magic he nurtured enough of himself that he was able to recover later. He suppressed his own knowledge of his true identity, and was able to hide from the gods.'

Hidden for a century. Waiting for his chance to . . . to what?

'Why reveal himself now?' Danjin asked, as much to himself as to Ella. 'Did he mean to?'

Ella smiled. 'No.'

'What happened?'

She looked away. 'I'm not free to tell you that. Yet.'

Danjin smiled and nodded. 'But there is more to tell.' He would consider that later. For now he could only give her advice based on the information she had given him. 'Most people will not be sure if the rumour is true or not,' he said, thinking aloud. 'Your concern is with those who believe it and hate the idea so passionately that they attack Dreamweavers and the hospice.'

She nodded. 'People fear Mirar deeply. Some even fear to seek Dreamweaver help in case the one they encounter turns out to be Mirar. Perhaps we could have artisans paint pictures of him so people know that the Dreamweaver they consult is just an ordinary man.'

'The people who visit the hospice are not the people you need to be concerned with,' he pointed out. 'I doubt the troublemakers would ever consider seeking Dreamweaver help. You said people feared a change in the Dreamweavers under Mirar's influence. That is the fear that drives them to kill.'

'How can I fight that?' she asked, frowning. 'I could tell them that we'll easily be able to stop the Dreamweavers if they turn on us, but why would they believe me? If they had any faith in us they wouldn't be attacking anyone now.'

'It helps, sometimes, to remind people they're safe. A little reassurance now and then never goes astray.'

Her frown faded and she looked thoughtful. 'Won't it seem as if we expect the Dreamweavers to turn on us if we say we're ready for it?'

'Maybe. Maybe it isn't a bad thing that they're becoming more suspicious of Dreamweavers. I might have suggested you find a way to reassure people that Mirar can't or won't influence Dreamweavers, but I fear that would be foolish. I expect Mirar *will* take control of his people again.'

Ella scowled. 'He won't live that long.'

Her confidence was both reassuring and disturbing. 'I'm glad to hear it.' He paused. 'And perhaps *this* is what people need to hear . . . unless there is a chance his execution will fail again.'

She looked at him, her eyes dark.

'It won't. Unless he can rejuvenate his body from ashes.' The corner of her mouth twitched. 'But we have to find him first, so we'd best not mention killing him just yet.'

CHAPTER 8

Outside the cave the tops of the trees glowed with the last rays of the sun. Emerahl set her back to the rock wall, far enough away from the waterfall that her clothes wouldn't end up saturated from the spray.

It was the same place she and Mirar had once rested and discussed their futures. At the time she had been full of optimism at the idea of searching out other immortals. Mirar had been struggling to acknowledge the part of him that was Leiard. The part that loved Auraya.

A good thing he hadn't known then that she doesn't return that love, Emerahl thought. *It would have made it much more difficult for him to accept the fragment of his personality he'd created. Why accept Leiard if it meant suffering a broken heart?*

He was whole now. Stronger. He could cope with the bad news that Chaia had been Auraya's lover. At least she hoped he could. There was a small danger he'd fragment into a split persona again.

Auraya probably hadn't considered that. Or maybe she had. Maybe this was why she was reluctant to tell Mirar.

Emerahl sighed. She had meant what she had said to Auraya. Put in the same situation, Emerahl would probably feel the same way about Mirar. She'd feel distrustful of any lingering feelings she had for someone who had turned out to not be who she thought he was. Even the prospect of meeting that man would make her wary. What else would prove to be untrue?

While Leiard was a part of Mirar, he would never again exist as the man Auraya had known. What had she said? *'I can't turn from the little I have left of my life for a made-up piece of a person buried somewhere within a man I don't know.'*

Beneath the defensiveness there had been something raw. Emerahl drew in a sharp breath as she realised what it was.

She's actually grieving for Leiard. To her he is dead. And she feels tricked and cheated for having fallen in love with an illusion. Why didn't I see that before?

It had turned into a big mess that did neither Auraya nor Mirar any good. Even without all this complication, the chances of Auraya and Mirar being happy together weren't great. Auraya was still loyal to the gods (and while Emerahl thought little of this, she had to allow the woman had the right to follow the gods if it pleased her). Mirar hated them and the feeling was mutual.

The sooner those two were relieved of the source of their misery, the better. It would hurt Mirar more, but he'd got over unrequited love plenty of times before. Auraya would recover from her grief for Leiard more easily without him reminding her of what she'd lost.

Emerahl sighed. *I was hoping Auraya felt something for Mirar so we immortals could feel a little safer.* She chuckled. *Making her hate me certainly isn't going to do us any good. I should be more sympathetic.*

She shifted into a more comfortable position. Closing her eyes, she let herself sink toward sleep. The pull toward full unconsciousness was strong, but she resisted.

:Mirar, she called.

There was no answer. It was early evening where he was

and he probably hadn't retired to bed yet. She turned her thoughts toward other minds.

:*Tamun. Surim.*

:*Yes, Emerahl?*

Sometimes The Twins spoke as one during links. It was disconcerting. The pair were so different in nature. The impression they gave when united like this was of a personality more complicated than an ordinary human. Something greater than human. Something inhuman.

At times like these she knew why they had been so revered in their time.

:*How are you two faring?*

:*As well as always*, Tamun replied. *Surim is getting all moon-eyed over a swamp girl again and I am endeavouring to put up with it.*

:*Tamun expects me to gather food and materials for her weaving, but she won't let me have some fun in the process*, Surim complained. *It's not fair and—*

:*How is Auraya doing?* Tamun asked.

Emerahl felt a wave of amusement at Tamun's sudden change of subject.

:*She's only let the shield around her mind slip once or twice since discovering how to raise it.*

:*Mirar did say she was a fast learner*, Tamun said. *Maybe it is because of her youth. She hasn't had time to become set in her ways of thinking.*

:*Maybe*, Surim agreed.

:*Something happened tonight*, Emerahl told them. *She saw something while mind-skimming that bothered her.*

:*She didn't tell you what it was?*

:*No. I don't think I should stay here much longer.*

:*But you have not taught her immortality.*

:*I will offer to, but I'm sure she'll refuse — and if she is as smart as Mirar says, she will work it out for herself.*

:You're right, Tamun said, *but that was what Mirar sent you there for. He may be disappointed.*

:He will have to live with that. I won't force her to learn it if she doesn't want to.

:If she does, will you teach her to change her age?

:Mirar says it is my innate Gift, and no other can learn it.

:Mirar may be wrong about innate Gifts. His is supposed to be magical healing, but he has taught it to others.

:But no other can use it as well as he. I wouldn't have been able to survive being crushed, as he did.

:You don't know that. But if an innate Gift is one that an immortal can do better than others perhaps Auraya will be able to change her age but not as well as you can. Perhaps you can learn to fly, but not as well as she.

:Flying is not a Gift you'd want to have less ability for. Failing could be painful or fatal. I'll hardly be able to take up the Quest for the Scroll again if I'm stuck in Si, healing from multiple bone fractures.

:True. What do you think Auraya will do once you leave?

:Return to the Open. Carry on as if nothing has happened.

:If she can do so will be up to the gods to decide, Surim said, suddenly serious. *They will not be able to kill her easily, but they may use her trust in them to trap her.*

:When they fail, Tamun continued, *she will have only us to turn to for help.*

:She will be a powerful ally, Surim finished.

:For all your claims the future can't be predicted, you two certainly like sounding as if you can do just that, Emerahl observed.

:I don't, Tamun said. *But when Surim gets all dramatic I feel I must support him.*

:You love it as much as I do, Surim told his sister. *Go on. Admit it.*

:I get no pleasure from unwarranted exaggeration or theatrics, Tamun declared. *But it would be—*

:Are you certain the gods will turn on Auraya? Emerahl interrupted. *No doubt in your minds?*

:There are always doubts, Surim admitted. *The future can't be predicted, only guessed. The gods have a habit of killing immortals, but there is always a chance they'll stay their hand for one of their followers.*

:Especially when that follower is one of Chaia's lovers, Emerahl pointed out.

:Ex-lover, Tamun corrected.

:I think it's time Mirar knew about that, Emerahl told them. *I think it's time he learned how Auraya regards him.*

The Twins were silent a moment.

:Yes. Tell him. He is among good people. They will support him, Tamun said.

:And one there is quite willing to provide comfort if he asks for it, Surim added.

Comfort? Emerahl thought, amused. The Twins regularly skimmed the minds of anyone near Emerahl and Mirar, keeping a watch for anyone intending harm. It hadn't occurred to Emerahl what else they might notice. *So Mirar has an admirer in the Dreamweaver House. How well timed,* she mused.

:I will tell him tonight, she said.

:Gently, Tamun advised.

:Of course. What do you think I am?

:Someone who has known him a long time. You have known him when he was made of tougher stuff. He is not the same person now. Remember that.

:I will, Emerahl assured her.

:Good. Good night. Travel well.

As The Twins' minds faded from Emerahl's perception, she turned her thoughts to that of an old friend.

:Mirar, she called.

There was no reply. She roused herself enough to open an

eye. The sky was dark, but still glowed where the sun had set. It was still too early.

Go to sleep, Mirar, she thought. *Don't you know how annoyingly suspenseful it is when you're waiting to deliver bad news?*

The dining hall of the Dreamweaver House had been full this night. Mirar had allowed himself to be recruited as a helper in the kitchen. He had listened to the constant chatter of the Dreamweavers there and during the meal, enjoying the relaxed, unworried mood of the house – and concentrating on trying to pick up more of the local language.

Being able to pick up emotions made it easier to understand these people, but it was a barrier as well as a boon when it came to learning the languages they spoke. It was easy, sometimes, to guess what they were saying from what he sensed rather than from the actual words they spoke. He must make himself note the words and work out what they meant.

It also helped that a fellow Northern Ithanian Dreamweaver with some knowledge of the southern languages had arrived the night before. Dreamweaver Moore was in Dekkar to collect or buy cures.

'Genrians have a crazy idea that the more exotic and distant the origin of a cure, the better it must be,' he had told Mirar. 'They'll pay us a lot of money for them, which we then put to good use providing perfectly adequate local cures for less affluent patients. There are many cures unique to Dekkar's jungle, though the last time I came here there was more of it. These people seem set on cutting the whole jungle down.'

There was a mood of anticipation among the Dreamweavers. Mirar had guessed that a ritual or celebration was going to take place. After the meal he helped clear the table and clean up. When all was in order, the Dreamweavers followed Tintel down a corridor and out onto a balcony. Tintel had shown

Mirar this place the morning after he had arrived. It was like a wooden courtyard, but was raised above the ground. Potted plants and low walls were arranged in a large circle in the centre, and the curved triangular spaces left by this formed small gardens with limited privacy.

The scent of flowers filled the humid air and the whir and creak of insect calls was so constant and powerful he could almost feel the heavy air vibrating. Mirar hadn't grown used to the heat: it made him sleepy during the day and unable to sleep during the night. The local Dreamweavers were affected by it, too, but not as much as he.

They formed a circle. Recognising the beginning of a link ceremony, he considered again the possibility that his mind shield might allow him to join a link without revealing his own thoughts. He wouldn't know until he tried, but if he failed his identity might be revealed.

The Dreamweavers linked hands and bowed their heads. Mirar felt a pang of frustration and longing. Except for the link he had joined in Somrey, it had been a long time since he had experienced the sense of belonging a link could bring.

It is a cruel irony that I, the man who invented this ritual, who founded these people's way of life, should now hesitate to join them, he thought. *But there is much I can learn from them, and about the people of Southern Ithania. It is worth the risk.*

He felt the grip of the man holding his right hand tighten, then the hand on his left twitched. Carefully, keeping the shield about his own mind strong, he sought the minds of those around him. Soon he could hear voices and see snatches of memories.

He saw the memory of a Dreamweaver who had examined a sick baby. The infant had underdeveloped and deformed organs, and could not be cured by any ordinary Dreamweaver. The father was a Pentadrian Servant, Mirar saw with a shock.

The Dreamweaver had given the man the bad news. The Pentadrian had accepted it, saying that if a Dreamweaver could not cure the child, nobody could . . .

. . . taxes were raised this year, probably to pay for the construction of the bridge. A Servant of the Gods had examined the House's records and was satisfied, and only asked for a small bribe. He was still grateful for the advice given to him and his wife about their marital troubles. Doesn't realise how common that . . .

. . . water lapped at the edges of the platform the Dreamweaver House was built upon. The flood had threatened to spill into the building last year. What would it be like this year . . .

. . . where there had been enormous trees there were now charred trunks surrounded by crops. Memories of the former forest and of the new fields overlaid each other. Shocking, but the locals need to eat. Trouble is, he hadn't been able to find that little plant with the pink flowers again. Hope that wasn't the only place it . . .

. . . *she is so beautiful*. Glimpse of naked body hastily pushed aside . . .

. . . *then where would he go? North up the gulf? Not likely. Back to the west? Doubt it. What if he went south? What if he's here somewhere? He could be in this very courtyard now* . . .

. . . *thinking about these stories that Mirar has returned. Not even sure I believe them. If Mirar's back, why haven't any of us seen him? No* . . .

Mirar suppressed the urge to laugh out loud. Even during a mind link, the Dreamweavers were still gossiping about his return. But then he sobered. They were watching for him. He must be careful.

Or must he? Would it be so bad if he allowed his identity to be known?

He listened and watched as the link continued. As always, one person's memories attracted the attention of the others. Advice was bestowed, or assurance given. At one point a Dreamweaver delved into memories of a recent festival in the city, and the others watched with interest. Nobody appeared to react to his own thoughts, and then he heard Tintel noting that he hadn't joined the link. *It worked*, he thought with relief.

Then Tintel called for the end of the link. Minds withdrew as Dreamweavers brought their awareness back to themselves, asserting their own identity as they did. Mirar opened his eyes and let go of the hands he had been holding. Dreamweavers around him did the same. He noticed one watching him.

Dardel. She smiled and winked at him, as subtle as ever. He smiled in reply. Something plucked at his thoughts. He sought it, but it was gone.

I think someone is trying to dream link with me.

Some Dreamweavers were lingering, talking in small groups. Others were saying their farewells. Mirar slipped away, made his way to his room and closed the door. In the relative silence, he felt the tug at his mind again.

Lying down on his bed, he guided his mind into a dream trance. There he drifted for several minutes. Just when he began to wonder if he had been wrong, a familiar voice spoke at the edge of his thoughts.

:Mirar?

:Emerahl.

:At last! What's keeping you up so late?

There was a hint of slyness to her tone. He found himself thinking of Dardel, then felt a twinge of guilt.

:A link ceremony, he told her.

:A link ceremony? I thought you were going to avoid them?

:Only joining in. I was able to listen to their thoughts.

:Learn anything useful?

:Perhaps. How is Auraya?

:A good friend would ask how I was first.

:I'm not a good friend. How are you?

:Better. I will be leaving soon.

:You've taught her the secret of immortality?

:Yes and no. I've told her, not taught her. I can't make her learn it if she doesn't want to. And she doesn't.

:I suppose not. He felt a nagging disappointment.

:I think she'll work it out for herself, if she ever changes her mind.

:She will. And she'll manage it easily.

:I'm sure she will, Emerahl agreed.

:So you've changed your mind about her?

:I never said she wasn't smart.

:But you like her better now.

:What makes you think that?

:You've stopped calling her 'god-loving' and 'self-pitying'.

:Have I? Maybe I'm sick of repeating myself. I should come up with some better insults.

:You should.

:Or maybe it's your turn. I have some bad news for you. I promised The Twins I'd break it to you gently, but I'm not sure how to do that.

He paused. It was hard to tell whether she was setting him up for some joke, or was serious.

:I'm used to your bluntness, Emerahl. What news do you have that is so terrible?

She didn't speak for a moment, then when she did it was quietly.

:Auraya doesn't love you, Mirar. She loved Leiard. Though she knows he is a part of you, that's not enough. You're a stranger to her and she doesn't trust you. I can't blame her. I'd feel the same.

He said nothing. There was no lie in Emerahl's words. No way he could have confused what she'd said. He felt suddenly empty. There was a hollow place now where there had been something wonderful and bright. A curl of smoke where a fire had been smothered . . .

Oh, listen to yourself! he thought. *So your heart is broken once more. Are you going to try your hand at poetry again? I'm not sure the world could survive that. Though it might be a fine way to torment the gods.*

But sarcasm and self-mockery didn't help. It never had in the past. This was something he would just have to endure for now. Eventually he would forget Auraya.

Though that might be a little hard if she's immortal. If every time I saw or heard about her I went through all the hope and pain again. And if—

:Mirar?

:Oh. Emerahl. Sorry.

:Are you all right?

:*Of course not. But I'm not about to throw myself out of the window either. Do you think there's a chance, in the future, if Auraya and I somehow spend some time getting to know each other again, she might—*

:*I wouldn't put your hopes on it. There is something else you need to know. She's had another lover.*

:*I know. I read that from her mind when I was teaching her to heal.*

:*Did you find out who it was?*

:*No.* A feeling of dread began to close in around Mirar. *Was it Juran? That would be understandable. I could accept that.*

:*It wasn't Juran.* She paused. As the silence lengthened Mirar grew impatient. Was she being theatrical, or was she truly reluctant to tell him?

:*It was Chaia.*

He felt his whole being go cold. A memory rose of helpless parents and a thin, wasted girl. It had been possible to

114

see hints of the beauty that had once been in that young woman's face, but there was madness in her eyes. She had been bound to her bed, because if freed she constantly rubbed and clawed at herself, most often at her breasts and between her legs.

In those times there were no laws against dream-healing. He had linked with her mind. He had expected to be confronted by something unpleasant. But what he saw had multiplied his hatred for the gods tenfold.

Chaia.

The god had chosen this girl as his lover, using magic in a way that generated exquisite pleasure. What he got from her in return Mirar had never been able to discover. When Chaia had tired of her he had left her like this, craving a pleasure she could never gain naturally from her own body.

Mirar had only been able to restore her sanity by blocking some of her memories. From then on she ate begrudgingly and never regained any sexual interest, and she was in a constant state of boredom. She became incapable of feeling any sort of pleasure. He had almost wished he'd let her die.

:*It's in the past*, Emerahl assured him. *She doesn't appear to have suffered any of the usual consequences.*

He had not detected any sign of madness when he had taught Auraya to heal back in Si. But then, not all Chaia's victims had lost their minds – just their ability to enjoy life, and sex.

Little wonder Auraya feels nothing . . .

:*Mirar? Are you all right?*

:*Of course I'm not*, he said, a little too sharply. *Sorry, Emerahl. I will talk to you later.*

He drew away from her mind, opened his eyes and stared at the wall before him.

Chaia. Of all the lovers she could have chosen . . . if she'd had any choice at all . . .

There was a light tap at the door.

He slowly looked up. The same hopeful tap had come every night. Quiet so as not to wake him. Never repeated, as if it was only to tell him she was still interested.

Dardel.

He should ignore it. But what alternative was there except to lie awake all night thinking? What good would that do?

He rose from the bed. When his hand touched the door handle he paused, but his conscience remained silent. Instead he found his thoughts returning where he didn't want them to go.

Chaia.

He opened the door and drew a smiling, pleasantly surprised Dardel into his room.

CHAPTER 9

*I**t was so easy.*
    Auraya paced the void. For the last hour she had walked
in circles, slowly making her way around the edge of the magic-
deficient boundary. Though her mind shield had become a
constant habit she rarely thought about any more, she did not
want to leave the void until Jade confirmed it was safe for her
to do so.

So easy. I can't believe it was that easy. And it hardly takes any
magic at all.

After Jade had left for the morning, Auraya had done what
the older woman had suggested: she had spent some time
thinking about magical healing and how it might be applied
to herself. Curiosity had led her to focus on her body, then
cautiously experiment. Within moments the logic of what Jade
had told her came to her.

A different reasoning had led her to take the next step and
apply the knowledge. If she was damned in the eyes of the
gods for just *knowing* how to become immortal, then she may
as well become immortal.

It had been unexpectedly easy.

The realisation that the same Gift could be used to heal
herself from almost any injury had helped her make that

decision. That Gift had enabled Mirar to survive being crushed under a building. If she was going to resist Huan, Chaia willing, she might need to do something similar.

The thought of ending up like Mirar, a hunted enemy of the gods, dismayed her, but she clung to the hope that she would remain Chaia's follower.

He will forgive me when he learns that Huan allowed me to learn to heal magically in order to persuade the others to let her kill me.

'Getting some exercise, are we?'

Auraya turned to see Jade striding into the cave carrying two buckets. She shrugged, then followed Jade to the beds, curious to see what the woman had found this time. Jade set the buckets down beside the cooking stone.

'You'll be happy to know you can leave the void now,' she said. 'I haven't sensed your emotions or been able to skim your thoughts in days.'

'I guessed it would be soon,' Auraya said. Both the buckets were full of clear water, but one had strange creatures swimming within it. 'What are they?'

'Shrimmi. They're hard to catch, but delicious. I thought we'd have a nice farewell dinner before I left.'

'When are you leaving?'

'Tomorrow.'

Auraya moved to her bed and sat down. She itched to tell Jade she had achieved immortality. There wasn't anyone else except Mirar who might congratulate her rather than be horrified. And Jade had wanted her to discover it.

Yet that was what made Auraya hesitate. What if Jade had a secret, malicious reason to lure Auraya into learning the Gift?

I don't know how much I can trust this woman. She says she has been helping me at Mirar's request, but there could be another reason I can't see.

It wasn't difficult to see that by helping one of the gods'

followers learn Gifts they disapproved of, Jade was striking a small blow against them. But if causing strife between the gods and a follower was Jade's intention, she had added little to a conflict that had already existed. Still, if that *was* Jade's purpose, it would be better to know it than suspect it.

And Auraya couldn't see any other way that immortality could be used against her. If there was, it would be better to know about it sooner rather than later.

'I had that long think you suggested I have,' Auraya told the woman.

Jade looked up, her eyebrows raised. 'You did? What did you discover?'

'You were right. It was easy.'

'Easy, eh?' Jade shook her head. 'One attempt. I've never known of anyone who learned so fast.' Her eyes narrowed. 'Are you sure?'

Auraya smiled, amused by the other woman's suspicion. 'Quite sure. But then, I already knew how to heal.'

Jade nodded and looked away. Picking up the bucket, she poured clear water into the hollow of the cooking stone.

'Are there other ways this Gift can be used?' Auraya asked.

The woman looked at her sharply. 'Like what?'

'It occurred to me that it could be used to change a person's appearance.'

Jade regarded Auraya thoughtfully. 'Do you want to change your appearance?'

'Me?' Auraya chuckled. 'One thing I learned from being able to read minds is that people are never satisfied with how they look. I'd like to fix a few things. I even considered trying it, but I didn't have a mirror and I thought I should ask you in case I did something permanent.'

'That's wise.'

'Then I thought, would I feel different if I changed how I

looked?' Auraya continued. 'If I *felt* different, would that mean I was a different person? And once I'd started, would it be tempting to keep changing things? Could I even turn myself into a Siyee?' She shook her head. 'More possibilities kept occurring to me then. Could a person change their physical age or their gender? Could they make themself smarter? So is it possible to make such changes?'

Jade smiled. 'You can change your appearance, but the rest . . . I don't know. You are wise to hesitate. Appearance does affect a person's identity, and Mirar is a good example of what can happen if you meddle with your own identity.'

Auraya nodded. 'Can I teach you something in return for what you've taught me?'

The woman looked amused. 'I ask only that you do not betray us to the gods.'

'That is reasonable. By "us" you mean yourself and Mirar?'

Jade hesitated. 'Yes.'

'So you wouldn't be interested in learning how to fly?'

The woman regarded Auraya with an unreadable expression. 'You would teach me that?'

'Yes. I'm curious to know if anyone else can do it.'

Jade looked down at the shrimmi, then back at Auraya.

'I suppose I could stay one more day.'

Dardel opened her eyes and experienced a moment of disorientation. The furniture in her room had been arranged differently. Things were missing. Then she saw the man sitting on the chair by the window and she smiled as she remembered she was in Dreamweaver Wilar's room.

Wilar was watching her. He still had that haunted look about his eyes, but as he noticed she was awake his mouth twitched into a crooked smile.

'Tintel was looking for you before,' he told her.

She looked toward the window. From the angle of the sunlight, she guessed it was late morning. She stretched, enjoying the feeling of cloth against her bare skin. 'I was wondering if I was going to get any sleep at all last night.'

'You didn't seem to mind.'

'Not at all.' She sat up, drawing the bedding up around herself, and looked for her clothes. They were on the floor next to the bed. 'In fact,' she found herself saying, 'I've never encountered a man with such stamina. And I'm surprised at my own. I ought to feel worn out, literally, but I don't.' She picked up her clothes, then paused and looked up at him. 'Was this a once-only thing?'

His mouth twitched with amusement. 'It is temporary, but how temporary depends on how long I stay here, and if we grow bored with each other.'

She chuckled. 'I don't think I'll tire of you. In fact, I think I'll be fussy who I bed from now on. You've given me higher expectations.' She shot him a mock glare. 'You've probably ruined me for any other man.'

All amusement fled from his face and he actually winced. She immediately regretted her words. There was no doubt a reason for that haunted look, and she had obviously reminded him of it. A past lover, perhaps? It would explain his initial hesitation.

She let the bedding fall. His eyes dropped to her breasts and the strained look in his eyes disappeared. 'Of course, if I found someone willing to learn, I'm sure I could teach him some of what you showed me,' she said as she began to dress.

That brought a smile. Good.

She lost herself in memories as she dressed. How could a man come to be such a good lover? At times he had almost seemed to read her mind. He obviously understood women's bodies. Better than the average Dreamweaver male, who needed to understand more than the average male because he must treat women's illnesses. Maybe better than she did, which had been disconcerting.

Obviously he had known many women. There could be no other explanation. Who would have thought this reserved, quiet Dreamweaver had such a past?

She glanced at him. He was looking out the window again, his expression distant. Now he looked old and sad. Sometimes he looked a little lost, but that was understandable. He was far from home.

Had he ever explained why he was here? She couldn't remember. There was definitely something mysterious about him. But to her, having spent all her life in this city, every foreigner seemed exciting and mysterious.

He is also strangely familiar. Like a friend I haven't seen since I was a child. There's something about him . . .

As she slipped her Dreamweaver vest on over her tunic, she looked at him again.

'Shall I come by tonight?'

He smiled. 'Let's wait and see how we feel tonight. You may prefer to catch up on sleep.'

'Unlikely.' Winking, she turned and walked to the door. When she looked back before closing the door, he was looking out of the window again, smiling faintly. A strange, secretive smile.

Humming as she made her way to her room, she passed Nirnel and Teiwen, a young Dreamweaver couple. Both looked at her crumpled clothes and she gave them a smug smile.

'So the new Dreamweaver finally gave in, did he?' Nirnel asked.

'That took longer than usual,' Teiwen said. 'You're losing your touch, Dardel.'

'You're quite right,' she replied. 'It did take longer than usual. He lasted all night, in fact.'

The pair rolled their eyes. Dardel continued on, chuckling to herself. Wilar was exactly what she had always imagined Mirar to have been like. Knowledgeable, powerfully Gifted (she knew Wilar was – she'd heard Tintel's stories), not too young, not too old and a good lover. Everything that had attracted her to Dreamweavers in the first place.

Halfway to her room she slowed as a possibility suddenly occurred to her.

What if he is Mirar? The younger Dreamweavers have been saying Mirar might have come south. What if he had, and is here pretending to be a traveller?

The idea set her pulse racing. Even if it wasn't true, what harm was there in indulging a little fantasy?

Formal dinners of the Voices had an undercurrent of tension that never eased, though their guest, the Sennonian ambassador and nephew of the Sennonian emperor, appeared not to have noticed. Reivan took another piece of crystallised spice root and chewed slowly, listening to the idle chatter. Genza was relating an amusing piece of town gossip, with occasional injections of dry humour from her Companion, Vilvan.

When the others laughed, Imenja only smiled. If the ambassador had noticed that she and Nekaun had not exchanged a word, he didn't show it. Imenja did occasionally join in conversations, but Reivan knew her mistress was participating only enough to show she was listening. She was the image of a polite guest, when she ought to be behaving like a host. Or matriarch. Or at least like someone who had a say in matters.

Nekaun laughed at the conclusion of the story and Reivan felt a shiver run down her spine at the sound of his voice. She resolutely forced her mind from considering why. Taking her glass, she drained the last of her water.

It's late, she thought. *And it doesn't look like we'll be turning in soon. Sometimes these dinners feel like they'll never end.*

Abruptly, Nekaun stood. 'It is late,' he said, 'and our guest has travelled far. He must be tired, and I know we,' he looked at Imenja and then the other Voices, 'have much to do tomorrow. Let us retire for the night.'

Is that relief on Imenja's face? Reivan wondered. She moved her chair back and stood, then waited her turn to bid the ambassador good night. When the young man had left, Reivan followed Imenja out of the room.

'Is there anything you need from me tonight?' she asked.

Imenja looked at Reivan and smiled, and this time it was a warm, genuine smile.

'No. There's one small matter I have to attend to, but I shouldn't need you for that. Go to bed, Reivan. You look tired.'

Reivan made the sign of the star. 'Good night.'

'Good night.'

Reivan turned back and walked to her rooms. Warm nights had made her sleep restless. Though she was eager to get to bed, she doubted she would rest any easier tonight.

Her doubts proved well founded. As soon as she lay down on her bed she knew sleep wasn't going to come soon or easily. Sighing, she let her mind run over the work of the day and list the tasks for tomorrow.

Then a voice called her name.

It was a male voice. A little louder than a whisper, and coming from the direction of the balcony. She knew at once who it was.

I should ignore it, she thought. *If I do he'll go away.*

But she didn't want him to go away. And besides, he was the First Voice. You didn't ignore the leader of the Pentadrians and the gods' highest servant.

Standing up, she moved to the balcony and looked down. A figure stood in the shadows, barely visible.

Nekaun.

'Good evening, Reivan.'

'First Voice.'

'There is no need for formality now.'

'Isn't there?'

'No. There is nobody here but the two of us. I'd prefer for you to call me Nekaun in private. Will you, for me?'

'If you wish.'

'I do.'

'Then I will, Nekaun.'

He tilted his head to one side. 'You are so beautiful, Reivan.'

Her heart did something she knew to be physically impossible. She found she had pressed a hand over it unconsciously.

'Do you find me attractive, Reivan?'

What a ridiculous question, she thought. *Anyone that good-looking* knows *that everyone finds them attractive, whether they can read minds or not. And he can read minds.*

So why did he want her to say it?

'Sometimes, from the right person, hearing them say such a thing is . . .' He sighed. '. . . more real. Somehow it means more.'

She felt her heart twist. 'I do, Nekaun. I find you attractive. Too attractive.'

His eyebrows rose. 'Why "too"?'

'It is . . . it is awkward. I am Imenja's Companion.'

'So you are. That does not mean we cannot be . . . friends.'

'No. But it is still awkward.'

'Let it be. There is nothing wrong with us being together. As friends. Or even something more.'

Something more. She found she could not speak.

'Reivan?'

'Yes?' Her voice was thin and breathless.

'Would you welcome me in, if I came to your door?'

She took several deep breaths.

'I would not turn you away.'

He moved away. Her breath caught in her throat, and her heart was racing. *What am I doing? I just invited him in. There was nothing subtle about what he just said. I'm no fool. I know it's not just my room he wants me to invite him into.*

Footsteps were fading away. She backed into her room and stopped. *He's coming to the door. Now.*

This is a bad idea. What about Imenja? She won't be happy about this. I know it. She cast about, then hurried out of the bedroom. The main door of her suite was a few strides away. She stared at it, heart hammering.

I have to turn him away. I'll . . . I'll tell him I changed my mind. Surely he'll understand. I can't do this.

He'll know I'm lying.

The knock made her jump even though she was expecting it. Swallowing hard, she made herself walk to the door. She took hold of the handle, drew in a deep breath, and pulled.

He moved into the room like a gust of warm air. The smell of him enveloped her senses. He moved close and warm hands pressed against the sides of her jaw. She stared at his face, unable to believe this intense expression of desire was directed at her.

'I . . .' she began.

A frown of concern creased his forehead. 'What is it?' he asked gently.

'I . . . haven't done this before,' she said weakly.

He smiled. 'Then it's about time you did,' he said. 'I can think of no better teacher than the former Head Servant of the Temple of Hrun.'

With those words echoing in her head, she could not gather

her thoughts enough to protest any more. She did manage to laugh when he picked her up, just like in the silly romantic tales some women liked to read, and carried her into the bedroom.

I'm going to regret this, she thought as he shrugged off his robes and she hesitantly slipped off her nightdress. Then a little while later, as his lips and tongue descended to her nipples and his fingers trailed down over her belly, she began to change her mind.

No, I'm not going to regret this at all. Not one bit.

CHAPTER 10

Emerahl watched Auraya's face as they stepped out from behind the waterfall into the sunlight. The former White's frown disappeared and she stopped to take a deep, appreciative breath of fresh air. Catching Emerahl watching her, she smiled.

'It's good to be outside again,' she said. She stepped up onto a boulder and stretched. 'I feel like I haven't flown for months.'

'You enjoy it, then?'

Auraya grinned. 'Yes. It's so . . . unrestrained. I feel unbound. Free.'

As the younger woman jumped back down again, Emerahl chuckled. 'That's how sailing feels. Just me and a boat, and nothing to worry about but the weather.'

'Ah. Yes. The weather. It's best to avoid flying in storms. There's not just the cold and rain, but the risk you'll be struck by lightning or fly into a mountain hidden in the clouds.'

'Sounds just as dangerous as sailing in a storm,' Emerahl noted wryly.

Auraya looked thoughtful, and nodded. 'How shall we start these flying lessons, then?'

'I have no idea. You're the one teaching, this time.'

'So I am.' Auraya looked around, then started toward a flat, clear area a little downstream. 'And I have no idea how to teach this. The other White couldn't do it, but I don't know if that was because they were incapable or I'm a bad teacher.'

'I'd suggest you teach it by putting your pupil in the same situation you were in, except Mirar told me you discovered the Gift after falling off a cliff.'

Auraya looked back at Emerahl, her face serious. 'We could do that.'

Emerahl gave her a level look. 'Let's consider it a method of last resort.'

'It wouldn't be as dangerous as it sounds,' Auraya continued. 'We'd need higher cliffs than those around us, though. You need time in the fall for the initial shock to pass, then to figure it out, then to apply magic to—'

'Actually, let's consider it out of the question.'

'I'd catch you if it didn't work. You'd be quite safe.'

Emerahl decided not to respond to that. She wasn't sure she trusted Auraya *that* much. 'How did you go about trying to teach the White? Did they throw themselves off the Tower?'

'No, they tried to lift themselves off the ground.' Auraya stopped as they reached the flat area.

'Then that's what I'll do.' Emerahl turned to face her. 'Tell me what to do.'

'Can you sense the magic around you?'

'Of course.' Emerahl let her senses touch the energy all around them.

'Can you sense the world around you? It's a similar feeling.'

'The world?'

'Yes. I find it easier when I'm moving. Then my position is changing in relation to it. That's why falling was so useful. The world was rushing past me, or I past it, so I noticed the change in my position.'

Emerahl took a few steps while searching for a sense of her

surroundings other than what she could see and hear. She paced around Auraya in a circle.

'I don't sense anything.'

'It's similar to sensing the magic around you.'

Circling Auraya again, Emerahl felt nothing like what Auraya had described. She shook her head.

Auraya frowned and looked around them. 'Perhaps you're not moving far or fast enough. If you jump off a boulder you'd move faster. The fall is short, so you'll have to be concentrating.'

'I'll give it a try.'

They moved toward the stream. Choosing a boulder as high as her shoulder, Emerahl clambered up. From the top it seemed higher than it had from the ground.

Auraya stepped back, giving Emerahl plenty of room.

'Concentrate,' she said.

Taking a deep breath, Emerahl made herself jump down to the ground. She landed off balance and staggered forward. Auraya caught her shoulders and steadied her.

'Sense anything?'

Emerahl shook her head. 'Too busy thinking about how hard the ground was going to be.'

'Try again. Maybe if you do it often enough, you'll forget about the ground.'

Forget to be scared, you mean, Emerahl thought wryly. She climbed up and forced herself to jump again. Before Auraya could ask anything, she turned and climbed the boulder once more.

After twenty jumps, Emerahl could land with practised grace. She could even manage to remember to concentrate on 'the world around her' as she fell. But she still sensed nothing.

'What happens next?' she asked, more for the opportunity to rest than any confidence in her readiness to move on.

Auraya's eyes brightened. 'You *change* your position in relation to the world. Using magic.'

Emerahl stared at Auraya, knowing her face expressed utter incomprehension but not caring. The woman's expression changed to disappointment.

'The cliff might be the only way. It might just take rapid motion for a certain length of time in order for the mind to com—'

'I'll keep trying,' Emerahl told her.

A while later Emerahl stopped. Her knees and ankles were hurting. Her body told her that hours had passed, but the world she was failing to sense somehow kept up the illusion of it still being early morning.

'This isn't working,' she muttered to herself. 'There's got to be another way.'

'Maybe if we found a steep slope, we could carve out a gully for you to slide down,' Auraya suggested. 'That would be almost like a fall.'

A fall? Emerahl felt her skin tingle with sudden excitement as an idea came to her. Turning, she regarded the waterfall. The pool was deep beneath the cascade. As a child she had loved to dive into the ocean . . .

'It'll be cold,' Auraya warned, guessing Emerahl's intentions.

'If I can stand the ocean in winter, I can put up with this chilly puddle,' Emerahl told her.

She retrieved a rope from the cave. The climb up to the top of the fall was not easy. Moisture had encouraged moss to form in cracks, which made handholds slippery. At the top, Emerahl secured the rope to a tree, then tied loops along the length for hand- and footholds.

Moving to the edge of the stream, she stepped out into the water. The flow pulled at her legs, trying to tug her off balance. At the edge of the fall the force of the water was insistent, working hard to convince her there was no way to go but over the edge.

This first time I'll just concentrate on getting the dive right – and not knocking myself senseless on the bottom of the pool.

She closed her eyes and sent her mind back to a time when she was younger – much younger – and the imagined monsters living in the dark corners of her home had been more frightening than throwing herself off a cliff into the churning ocean.

Opening her eyes, she bent her knees, let herself fall forward, and sprang out into the spray-filled air.

The pool rushed up and slapped her with shocking cold. As the chill water surrounded her she instinctively curved her body forward and upward to shorten her dive. Her knees knocked against the pool floor.

Then she was swimming up to the surface. Sodden sandals dragged at her feet as she waded out. She drew magic and directed it to heat the air about her.

Auraya was sitting on top of a boulder nearby. She smiled and raised an eyebrow.

'Didn't even try,' Emerahl told her. 'Wanted to get the dive right first.'

Auraya looked at the rope hanging down the cliff. She opened her mouth, then closed it again and shrugged.

Feeling warmer and not a little exhilarated by her dive, Emerahl kicked off her sandals and started toward her makeshift ladder.

If I have to jump off cliffs to learn this, she thought, I may as well have some fun at the same time.

Danjin opened the door and hesitated. The hair and clothes of the two Dreamweavers glistened with droplets of rain, and water was beginning to puddle around their boots. Raeli followed his gaze and smiled faintly.

A warm breeze touched Danjin's skin. The Dreamweavers' clothes began to steam. In a moment both were dry.

'We are here at Ellareen the White's request,' Raeli said. 'This is Dreamweaver Kyn, Dreamweaver Fareeh's replacement.'

'Welcome,' he said. 'Ellareen of the White is waiting for you.'

Danjin ushered the Dreamweavers in. Ella was standing beside the table, a few steps from what she had affectionately dubbed her 'spying chair'. For a moment he saw her as these Dreamweavers must: a young Circlian healer they had once known and worked with, transformed by undecorated white robes, elegantly arranged hair and the gods' favour into an imposing, powerful woman.

'Dreamweaver Adviser to the White, Raeli,' Danjin said by way of introduction. 'And Dreamweaver Kyn. This is Ellareen of the White.'

Ella smiled at the pair. 'Thank you for coming here. I apologise for the humble surroundings. Be seated, if you wish.'

As the pair settled into the chairs, Ella sat down on her seat beside the window. The room contained no other seats so Danjin remained standing.

The Dreamweavers looked calm and relaxed. He hadn't seen Raeli much since Auraya's resignation, not even in passing at the Tower. The male Dreamweaver with her was middle-aged, thin-faced and wore a short beard. He reminded Danjin a little of Leiard.

'What can we help you with, Ellareen of the White?' Raeli asked.

Ella smiled. 'I was hoping I might be able to help you. A few weeks ago I was given the task of finding a way to end the violence against Dreamweavers and the hospice.' If this news pleased the pair, Danjin noted, they showed no sign of it. 'At the advice of my adviser, Danjin Spear, I have been examining the reasons people might wish you and the hospice harm. That is why I have been using this room.' She glanced at the window. 'To watch the thoughts of those passing the hospice.'

The eyebrows of the two Dreamweavers rose.

'Did you discover anything of use?' Raeli asked.

'I did. I don't need to point out to you that some people of this city have an irrational dislike of Dreamweavers.' Ella's expression was serious now. 'That has been so for a long time and doesn't explain the recent attacks. I suspected that something happened a few months ago that changed people's opinion.' She paused, looking from one Dreamweaver to the other. 'I believe the cause was the news that Mirar is alive.'

Raeli's gaze sharpened. 'A rumour,' she said. 'That is all.'

Ella nodded. 'A rumour some believe enough to start killing Dreamweavers.'

'You want us to deny the rumour?' Kyn asked. 'They won't believe us.'

'No,' Ella agreed. 'Some people will never believe anything but what they want to. Most, however, are simply followers, as easily led astray into lawlessness as back to lawfulness. We must find the leaders, but also woo back their followers. To do so . . .' Ella paused and glanced at the window. She frowned and turned her attention back to the Dreamweavers. 'To do that, we must assuage their fears. What they fear, I have learned, is what will happen if Mirar begins to influence the Dreamweavers again. They fear he will make Dreamweavers dangerous.'

Raeli pursed her lips as she considered Ella's words. She looked at Kyn, who was frowning.

'You want us to assure people otherwise?' he asked. 'They won't believe that either.'

Danjin expected Ella to deny that, but she did not speak. He looked at her and found she was staring out the window again. When she turned back she wore a distracted expression. It quickly disappeared.

'No,' she said, meeting Kyn's eyes. 'I want you to declare that you won't have anything to do with Mirar. That the Dreamweavers have got along without him for a hundred years and will continue to do so.' She turned to Raeli, who had opened her mouth to protest. 'Have you found that missing Dreamweaver student yet?'

Raeli closed her mouth, then shook her head. 'We believe he is dead.'

Ella grimaced. 'Poor Ranaan.' She sighed. 'I know my suggestion angers you, but I ask you: what is more important, the lives of your people or your loyalty to a man who abandoned you for a hundred years and now cannot be here to help you fight the violence his return has . . . Excuse me a moment.' Her eyes widened and she rose and turned to the window in one movement, then whirled about, strode to the door and left the room.

The two Dreamweavers looked at Danjin questioningly. He shrugged to indicate he hadn't any idea what she was up to, then hurried after her.

She was already at the base of the stairs. As he started down she paused and looked up at him.

'Stay here, Danjin.'

Then she was gone. He returned to the room reluctantly. Raeli had moved to the window and was peering down at the street.

'I see nothing unusual,' she said.

As Danjin moved to her side she glanced at him and stepped away. Looking outside, he drew in a quick breath. Ella had emerged on the street. People were stopping and staring at her in surprise, but she ignored them. She walked up to a bread-seller lounging against his cart. As he realised she was approaching him he straightened and glanced to either side as if looking for an escape. Then he turned to face her, keeping his eyes to the ground.

Whatever she said to him brought a look of terror to his face. She turned and walked away. The young man hesitated, again glancing around. Ella looked over her shoulder and spoke again. The bread-seller's shoulders slumped and he shuffled after her.

As the pair moved out of sight, Danjin stepped back. *She must have caught some of his thoughts and seen in them something important. Something very important. Nothing else would make her risk revealing that she has been secretly spying on people outside the hospice.*

The silence in the room was rapidly growing awkward. Danjin began to make polite enquiries of the two Dreamweavers. How had Raeli been since the war? Where was Kyn born? The male Dreamweaver was from Dunway, as his name suggested, but his mother was Genrian. It was an unusual heritage, and Danjin guessed that becoming a Dreamweaver had earned the man an acceptance and respect that his half-breed status would never have in Dunway or Genria.

When the sound of a door closing echoed through the house, Danjin paused to listen. He heard distant voices but could not discern what was said. Then a single set of footsteps drew closer.

The door opened and Ella stepped inside.

'Please excuse my abrupt departure,' she said. 'I just found someone I've been looking for and couldn't risk that he might move on before I had a chance to talk to him.' She sat down and adjusted her circ. 'Now . . . well, I asked you to come here so I could tell you the results of my research.' Her expression

became earnest. 'I hope you'll take my advice, but I'll understand if you don't. It is no easy thing to do. You can contact
Mirar, if you choose to take my advice, and explain that it is
necessary – and temporary.'

She smiled and regarded the two Dreamweavers expectantly.
The pair glanced at each other, then Raeli looked at Ella.

'Thank you for giving us this information. It is reassuring
to know the White are so concerned for our welfare. I will
communicate your advice to Dreamweaver Elder Arleej and
let you know what she decides.'

Ella nodded. She stood up. 'Let me know if you need anything
from us.'

The Dreamweavers rose and Danjin ushered them out. When
he returned, Ella was standing at the top of the stairs.

'Someone you were looking for?' he prompted.

She smiled grimly. 'Yes.' Crossing her arms, she drummed
her fingers against her sleeve. 'In a moment our guests will
be out of the alley . . . there they go. Come on, Danjin. We're
going back to the White Tower.'

He followed her down the stairs and out into the alley, to
the tired old covered platten they always arrived in. As she
reached out to the door flap she paused and held a finger to
his lips, before gesturing for him to enter.

Someone was in there, he realised. Two people. He climbed
in slowly and cautiously. One of the men was the driver.
The other was the bread-seller, bound, gagged, and looking
terrified.

There was something disturbing about that. Danjin found
himself imagining what had happened after Ella and the bread-
seller had moved out of sight. Had she forced the man into
the platten? Had she bound him? *No, the driver must have done
that for her.*

Ella climbed in after Danjin. Her expression was grim as

she regarded the prisoner. She gave the driver a nod, and he got out. The platten swayed as he stepped up onto the driver's seat and urged the arem into motion.

'Bagem here has been paid to watch the hospice,' Ella told Danjin. 'He was to note the movements of Dreamweavers in particular, and follow them if he could.'

And kill them? Danjin thought, giving the young man a speculative look. Though the bread-seller looked completely intimidated, that might simply be because he'd been caught by one of the White.

'He wasn't to harm them himself,' Ella said. 'But he knew it was likely his information would lead to more Dreamweaver murders. He can identify his employer, and others involved in the game. I think the other White need to see what I've seen in his mind, too.' She turned to look at Danjin, her eyes wide with distress. 'Because if the men who paid Bagem weren't in disguise, they must be priests.'

CHAPTER 11

If Reivan's assistant, Kikarn, had been puzzled by her behaviour this morning he hadn't given any sign. She had asked him to list all of the possible matters she could attend to until he came up with one that would take her away from the Sanctuary for the day. The way he had taken her break of routine in his stride had been almost unnerving.

Perhaps he simply understands that a person has to get away from the Sanctuary now and then to preserve their sanity, she mused.

Reivan had managed to keep her mind occupied on her chosen task for most of the day. Only occasionally did she find herself thinking back to the previous night, and then it felt more like a dream than a memory. Those moments of distraction were pleasant, but were soon spoiled when she found herself worrying about what Imenja would think. Or say. Or do.

Like dismiss me, Reivan thought. *Send me away to be an unSkilled Servant in some remote place, spending the rest of my days translating scrolls. No, translating scrolls would be too enjoyable. More likely I'd end up doing unpleasant menial work or some boring administration job.*

Avoiding Imenja all day had been a futile, childish thing to do, and had only gained her a few extra, anxiety-filled hours before the inevitable confrontation. When her task had been complete, and shadows had begun to envelop the city, she had dragged herself back to the Sanctuary.

All was quiet as she reached the stairway that would take her up to her rooms. She paused and looked through an archway to the courtyard outside. Everything was blue with the twilight, except where lamps cast orange pools on the pavement.

Will Nekaun visit me again tonight? she wondered. Her heartbeat quickened. *I hope so but . . . I'm tired.* Moving to the archway, she leaned against one side. It was so peaceful here. She felt the knots of tension inside her loosen.

Maybe Imenja won't mind, she thought. *Maybe this will prompt her and Nekaun to reconcile their differences. I could be the one who, inadvertently, makes peace between the First and Second Voice.*

She snorted softly.

Not likely! What do I know of reconciling differences or making peace? I had a hard enough time convincing the Thinkers to even notice I existed, and they kicked me out at the first opportunity. The way the Servants reacted to me when I first came here made it clear they didn't think I belonged. I still don't even have any friends, so what chance is there that I can mend rifts between others?

'You have one friend,' a familiar voice said from behind Reivan.

Looking back, she grimaced apologetically at Imenja.

'Second Voice. I . . . ah . . . I . . . I'm sorry for—'

Imenja put two fingers to her lips, then beckoned and moved out into the courtyard. She turned to regard one of the pools. The water rippled, then a spout formed and droplets arched through the air. The courtyard echoed with the sound. Imenja sat on one of the benches nearby.

'There. A small measure of privacy. I would advise against raising your voice, however.'

Reivan nodded. Imenja patted the bench.

'Sit. As you know, we need to talk.' When Reivan obeyed, Imenja smiled. 'What are you sorry for?'

'For . . . for hiding from you.'

'It was silly of you, but I see you know that. You don't need to feel guilty about taking Nekaun to bed, Reivan. It's hardly something to be ashamed of.'

'I know, but . . .'

'But?'

'You and he . . .'

Imenja's nose wrinkled. 'We haven't been agreeing on much lately.' Her shoulders lifted. 'That is between us, and shouldn't stop you taking pleasure whenever you find it. Pleasure doesn't happen along as often as it should.'

'There's a "however" coming,' Reivan found herself saying. 'I can hear it in your voice.'

Imenja laughed, low and quiet. 'Yes, there is.' She drew in a deep breath, and all humour vanished from her face. 'It is possible that Nekaun does regard you affectionately. I don't want to dash your hopes there. There is also the possibility that he is simply using you.'

'Well, it's not like we can get married. I don't expect that.'

Imenja shook her head. 'Think politically, Reivan. You didn't avoid me all day just because you thought I wouldn't approve of you having a little fun.'

'Do you think he's using me to hurt you?'

'I have to consider it a possibility. So do you.'

Reivan looked at the pavement. If Nekaun thought Imenja would object to him bedding her Companion, it would be a way to strike at her. It was a low and petty thing to do, with no purpose other than to annoy someone who was supposed to be one of his closest allies.

'Surely not. It wouldn't gain him anything.'

Imenja sighed. 'Nothing but to weaken me a little more.'

Looking at the Second Voice, Reivan saw a resignation in the woman's face that had never been there before. She felt a pang of concern. What had happened to make her mistress distrustful of Nekaun? How could such a powerful woman look so defeated?

Imenja straightened and turned to regard Reivan. 'If his intentions are harmful, he'll find me tougher than he expects,' she said. 'It is you I worry about, Reivan. Could you stand being humiliated and manipulated? Are you strong enough to endure a broken heart? It could be unpleasant for you, if Nekaun's intentions are ill.'

Reivan stared at her.

'Do you think he could be that cruel?'

Imenja sighed. 'Do I think he is capable of low, immoral tactics? Yes. I know it to be so. Do I think he truly regards you with the deepest of affection?' She smiled and shrugged. 'You're an attractive woman. Not beautiful, but you have a sharp wit and a good sense of humour that more than makes up for that. There's much to love. So maybe he does.'

Reivan felt her mouth stretching into a smile, and tried unsuccessfully to stop it.

'I would never want to rob you of any chance of love or pleasure,' Imenja said. 'But if it turns sour, remember I am your friend. If you need to talk to someone, I will listen. If you need to get away from him, I will send you wherever you wish to go. I will do all I can to prevent you from coming to harm, but I can't save you from hurt feelings. You must be strong, too.'

'I will be,' Reivan promised.

'Good.'

Imenja stood up. 'Now, I have a meeting to attend, so I'd best move on.'

'Need my help?'

'No. I'll speak to you tomorrow. Sleep well.'

Reivan smiled. 'You too.'

As the Second Voice disappeared into the archway, the fountain dwindled to a stop. Reivan drew in a deep breath, yawned, and headed for her rooms, feeling better than she had all day.

The sun hung just above the top of the trees, as if preparing itself to dive within them. Auraya looked up at the rope. She had strung it from the top of the cliff to the branches of the trees below, then made a sliding seat out of wood and more rope. It was a rough copy of the system Mirar had used to get from platform to platform of the tree-bound Siyee village she had found him in months before. She felt a sudden anger and clenched her fists.

What did he get in return for helping the Siyee fight the plague? she thought. *An executioner. And now Huan wants to send one to me.* She took a deep breath and slowly let it out, while pushing anger aside. For the last few days she had found herself brooding over Huan and Saru's conversation often. Too often. She lay awake at night, alternately furious at the gods' distrust and betrayal and fighting a lurking, will-sapping fear that one of the White – probably Rian – would step into the cave and kill her and Jade.

'Here.'

Auraya roused herself from her thoughts and accepted the steaming cup of maita from Jade. Taking a sip, she sighed in appreciation as the hot liquid warmed her.

Jade sat down beside her and looked up at the swing. It had carried her swiftly and safely to the ground many times, but she still hadn't succeeded in sensing her position in the world around her. Still, it wasn't a particularly high cliff.

'We could probably find a higher cliff and make a longer rope,' Auraya began.

Jade shook her head. 'No. I think it's pretty clear I haven't got this ability to sense the world that you have. I need to be on my way, as well.'

'You're just going to give up? After only one day?'

The woman chuckled. 'Yes, I am. Maybe I'll have the misfortune of falling off a cliff some day. If that happens, I'll remember your instructions and try again. For now I'm happy to have my feet firmly on the ground.'

Auraya smiled. 'We could still try the cliff jump. It might work.'

'And it might not.'

'I'd catch you.'

'It's not that I don't trust you . . .'

Auraya lifted her eyebrows.

'Well, yes, you're right,' Jade admitted. 'I don't trust you enough for that. Even so, all my good sense tells me jumping off a cliff is a bad idea. Logic tells me that if I need to move in order to learn to sense my position in the world, moving horizontally should be just as effective as vertically. If I was capable of learning this, I would have discovered this sense of the world you describe by now.'

'You're probably right.' Auraya sighed. 'Or else I'm a terrible teacher. Or maybe Mirar is right. He keeps insisting this is my innate Gift.'

Jade looked at Auraya closely. 'How often do you speak to him?'

'We've talked a few times in dream links.'

'You talk to him? I thought you didn't like him.'

Auraya smiled. 'I never said I didn't like him.'

Jade frowned, then looked away. All was subdued, as if the creatures of the forest must wait for darkness before they could gain the courage to make their calls. Auraya listened with her other senses, paying attention to what she usually ignored unless she was flying: the magic around her, the feeling of where she was placed in the world. Her senses had grown clearer since she had come here.

A faint whisper or vibration caught her attention. She focused on it and realised it was a mind. A Siyee was flying toward them. It was Tyve.

I'll just make a quick visit before it gets too dark, he thought.

'You may as well take that down,' Jade said, apparently unaware of the approaching Siyee.

The rope! Tyve might fly into it. Auraya set her cup aside and jumped up. Drawing magic, she sent a thread of heat out to the end fastened at the top of the cliff. Fibres burst into flame as the heat quickly scorched through them. The rope fell to the ground, some of it sinking into the stream.

'It's good to know you agree with me so heartily,' Jade said wryly.

'Tyve is coming. He might not see it.'

'Tyve? How do you know?'

'I saw his . . .' Auraya felt a shock as she realised what she was about to say. She concentrated on Tyve's mind. To her surprise, his thoughts were clear. She looked at Jade.

'I can read minds again.'

The woman stared at her, then turned to look in the direction of the approaching Siyee. 'I can sense anticipation and haste. Why has he come here?'

'Just to check on us.'

Auraya frowned. A feeling of anticipation and suspicion overlapped Tyve's weariness and wish to be home. This duality of thought was strange.

:She's emerged at last. Finally we'll know what she's been up to in there and if that woman with the hidden mind is who I suspect . . .

The thought ended abruptly and suddenly all she sensed of

145

Tyve was tiredness. Something else came toward her. Something without form, rushing at her at incredible speed.

Huan.

The goddess rushed past her, followed by another. Auraya rocked back on her heels. The second god was Saru. They were behind her, searching . . .

:Where is she? I can't see her!

'What is it?' she heard Jade ask.

I ought to let the shield around my mind drop to prove that I'm trustworthy, Auraya thought. *But I don't trust them.*

Huan flashed back toward Tyve. The boy didn't notice as the god's mind connected with his. He was concentrating on descending and choosing a place to land.

:I cannot see her! Her mind is hidden!

Then the gods were gone, shooting away faster than Auraya could follow.

That's done it, she thought. *They know now. I wonder if this is the excuse Huan needs to kill me.*

'What is wrong, Auraya?' Jade hissed.

Auraya shook her head, trying to think how she could possibly explain what had just happened. 'Tyve wasn't alone for a moment. Huan was with him, watching us through Tyve's eyes.'

'Huan?' Jade's eyes widened. 'Here? Watching us?'

'Not any more,' Auraya assured her quickly. 'They – Saru was with her – left to tell the others that my mind is shielded.'

Jade stared at her. 'In all my years,' she murmured, 'I've never encountered *anyone* who could sense the gods. Do the gods know you can?'

'Yes, but not like this. Before I could only do so when they were close.'

'And when did this change?'

'After you taught me to skim minds.'

Jade nodded. 'Don't let them know. Former White or not, they will kill you if they learn that you can spy on them. Don't even tell Chaia.'

Auraya opened her mouth to protest that Chaia meant her no harm, then closed it again as Tyve landed. Jade gave her a meaningful look, then turned to greet the Siyee.

CHAPTER 12

It took several seconds for Kalen to realise he was awake, then several more to remember where he was and why.

The Pentadrians' house. Warm. Not hungry. Going to make me a Servant.

Waking up no longer brought a nagging dread over what the day might serve up to him. Not since he'd attempted to pick a man's pockets and somehow found himself having a discussion with his intended victim about religion over a few drinks. The man had made him an offer too good to refuse: food and shelter in exchange for learning about his people.

A full stomach and safe, warm sleeping arrangements had been worth a few boring lectures, but Kalen found he got a buzz of excitement from being part of these secret followers of the forbidden cult of the Pentadrians. He'd been surprised to find himself learning beside, and being accepted as an equal by, people from all kinds of backgrounds. Like the young man sleeping on the next pallet, Ranaan, who used to be a Dreamweaver.

Who was breathing quickly as if he'd just had a fright.

'Nightmare?' Kalen asked.

A faint grunt of affirmation came in reply.

Talking helped after a nightmare, Kalen knew. *It's close to morning, I reckon. I'll never get to sleep again, so I may as well talk.*

'Ranaan?'

He heard the sound of the young man rolling over to face him.

'Yes?'

'Were you really a Dreamweaver?'

'Yes.'

'Why'd you join the Pentadrians?'

Ranaan sighed. 'After my teacher was killed, Amli helped me get away. Amli saved my life and gave me a place to stay until it was safe to go back.' He paused. 'But it'll never be safe to go back. Fareeh's murderers know I can identify them. They'll kill me.'

'Is that why you became a Pentadrian?'

'It's too dangerous being a Dreamweaver.'

'And being a Pentadrian isn't dangerous?'

'Not as dangerous. Not for me, anyway. I . . . I like what Amli teaches. Their gods don't make them kill Dreamweavers.'

'That doesn't matter to you now. You're not a Dreamweaver any more.'

'Just because I'm not a Dreamweaver doesn't mean I don't care what happens to them. Amli says that is the Pentadrian way. Dreamweavers don't deserve what the Circlians do to them.' He paused. 'Why did *you* come here?'

Kalen chuckled. 'They feed me. I've got a warm place to sleep. I'm thinking all these boring lessons are worth sitting through if we end up joining in an orgy now and then.'

Ranaan burst out laughing. 'Sorry to kill your hopes, Kalen, but they don't have orgies.'

'They do so. Everybody knows they do.'

'It's just a rumour the Circlians invented. Pentadrians have

149

special rites for married couples that help them conceive children, but not orgies.'

'Amli might be telling you that in case you get offended.'

'Dreamweavers have known this for years, Kalen. There are Dreamweavers in Southern Ithania too, remember.'

'Oh.' Kalen cursed under his breath. 'That's the second bit of bad news I've had today.'

'Sorry.' Ranaan chuckled. 'What was the first?'

'That they can't make Giftless people Gifted.'

'Nobody can make their Gifts stronger,' Ranaan agreed.

'The Circlians would never make me a priest, but these Pentadrians don't mind if I don't have Gifts.'

'Do you think their gods are real?'

'Amli's stories make them sound like they are.'

'Yes. They do. What's that noise?'

They both lay silent, listening. The faint sound of hurried footsteps reached them, coming from above, below and beyond the wall that separated them from the alley outside. There was a cry of alarm, cut short. Kalen felt his heart start racing. He stood up and tiptoed to the window. Something was happening. Something bad.

'What are you doing?' Ranaan asked fuzzily.

He's actually falling asleep again! Kalen shook his head. *He might be Gifted, but he has no instinct for survival.* Looking out of the window, Kalen noted movement in the shadows. The noises grew louder.

'What's going on?' Ranaan sat up, fully awake now.

'I don't know, but I don't intend to wait around to find out,' Kalen told him. 'There are people in the alley outside. From the sound of it, they're upstairs, too. There must be another way out. Amli probably has a secret exit somewhere.' He started for the door.

A shout rang out, muffled by the floorboards.

'That's Amli,' Ranaan said.

A bright pinpoint of light appeared, illuminating the room. Below it hovered Ranaan's palm.

'Put that out!' Kalen hissed. 'They'll—'

Footsteps pounded outside their door. Kalen cursed and dived for the window. He felt hands clamp about his leg and pull him back.

'Don't be an idiot,' Ranaan said, standing up. 'You could kill yourself falling from there. Or at least break a limb.'

'Worth the risk,' Kalen said. He looked past Ranaan's shoulder. The door was open and two Circlian priests were striding toward them. One grasped Ranaan's shoulder. The other took Kalen's arm. Kalen sagged with resignation.

What's the point of having an instinct for survival when it kicks in too late? he thought.

The priests escorted them out of the room and down the stairs. In the main room several of the Pentadrian converts stood in a huddle, surrounded by priests and priestesses. Amli and his wife faced another priestess, who was glaring at the couple.

'You disguised your men as priests and had them hire others to track Dreamweavers,' the priestess said. She spoke so confidently her words were more a statement than an accusation. 'Then you had your men murder those Dreamweavers. You tried to make Circlians look bad in order to make Pentadrians appear better, when the truth was the opposite.' She shook her head. 'I was told Pentadrians respected Dreamweavers. Was I told a lie?'

Ranaan made a small, strangled noise. Amli said nothing, just looked at the ground. The priestess stared at him, then shook her head. 'If you found it so distasteful, why did you do it?' She paused. 'Ah. Such loyalty is admirable, but it comes at a cost.'

'I am prepared to face the consequences,' Amli replied.

'I see that. Did you ever question whether a man with such low and dishonourable methods deserved your loyalty?'

'Ultimately it is the gods I serve,' Amli said, in a voice so quiet Kalen could only just hear him.

The priestess crossed her arms. 'If your gods are real and as worthy of your loyalty as you think, would they allow such a man to rule your people? I think – ah! There he is, watching through your eyes from the safety of his home.' Her eyes flashed and she leaned closer. 'You are a liar and a coward, First Voice Nekaun. Wherever your people are in the north, we will find them. And we will make sure everyone in the world knows of what you arranged here in Jarime. How will your people react when they know how low you've stooped?'

She blinked, then smiled and stepped back. Turning to another priest, she gestured at the Pentadrians. 'Take them all to the Temple.'

As the priests began to herd everyone out, the priestess's eyes moved around the room. Her eyes reached Ranaan and widened. Kalen's heart sank as she walked over to his new friend.

'Ranaan,' she said quietly. 'Why didn't you come back to the hospice?'

Ranaan kept his eyes lowered. 'I was afraid to, Priestess Ellareen – I mean Ellareen of the White.'

Her expression softened. 'That's understandable. You couldn't have known you were saved by the people who had arranged your teacher's murder.'

Ellareen of the White? As it dawned on Kalen that he was in the presence of one of the Gods' Chosen he felt a rush of fear. *The White are the Pentadrians' enemies. She's supposed to be my enemy, too.*

The woman's gaze shifted to Kalen and his stomach sank

to the floor. *I only joined them for some food and a bed*, he thought at her. *And for the thrill of it*, he admitted. *I'm so stupid. What was I thinking? They don't even have orgies.*

Ellareen's lips twitched.

'Is it true?' Ranaan asked in a thin voice. 'Did they kill Fareeh?'

The White turned back to him, her expression grave and sympathetic. 'Yes. If you don't believe me, I can introduce you to someone you will.'

'But . . . why would they do that?'

'To make Circlians look bad. To make becoming a Pentadrian more appealing.' She glanced around the room. Most of the Pentadrian converts had been taken out and the remaining priests were regarding her expectantly. 'I will know more when I've had the chance to question everybody. I'm afraid you and your friend will have to come as well, but I'll see you're well treated.'

'Will . . . will we be locked up for this?' Ranaan asked.

She smiled. 'Probably only for one night. Tomorrow we will know who has committed a crime and who hasn't. You'll be released then – and it will be safe for you to rejoin your people.'

Ranaan looked relieved. As the White stepped back and the priests began to usher them out, Kalen patted Ranaan on the shoulder.

'Don't worry, my friend. Even if the food isn't as good, at least we'll get a bed for the night.'

The flat bread Jade usually made each morning, of a local root pulped and flavoured with spices, was surprisingly tasty. She had taught Auraya how to make it, and this morning Auraya had prepared the meal while Jade readied herself to leave. The bread baking on the heated cooking stone was nearly ready, so she busied herself making hot drinks.

Jade packed slowly and carefully, taking out and replacing several jars and bags along the back wall before deciding which to take. She had made many small pouches and tough clay jars that she fired to hardness with magic. These she filled with powders, dried leaves, fungi, roots, hardened resins, sticky gums and thick oils. Auraya realised she knew the uses most of these substances could be put to. During the preparation of her cures, Jade had explained what each was for, freely giving a little of what Auraya suspected was a great wealth of healing knowledge.

The bread was beginning to smoke as its crust toasted. Auraya removed it and poured hot water into two cups.

'Breakfast is ready,' she announced.

Jade straightened, then breathed deeply. 'Ah, the smell of maita is so good in the morning.' She walked over to the beds and took the cup Auraya offered. Taking a sip, she sighed appreciatively.

'Will you come back here?' Auraya asked, breaking the bread in half and giving a portion to Jade.

'Eventually.' Jade looked at all the pots and bags. 'Can't let all that go to waste. You're welcome to use it, too. No point in letting it go stale.'

'Thank you.'

Jade took a bite, chewed, swallowed and then sipped from her cup. 'You still plan to go back to the Open?'

Auraya nodded. 'My place is with the Siyee.'

'Well then, remember this: if you find the gods don't agree, you have a place among us immortals, if you need it.'

'I'll keep that in mind.'

'You do that.' Jade chuckled. 'You do realise we'll be watching closely to see what the gods will do. They've claimed all immortals are evil for a century. If they accept you, they prove themselves wrong.'

Auraya smiled. 'Assuming I'm not evil.'

Jade laughed. 'Yes.' She turned away and moved back to her pack. Putting her cup down, she held the bread between her teeth and stowed a few more items with quick, decisive movements. Then she picked up the pack and returned to the beds.

'Good luck, Auraya the immortal,' she said.

Auraya rose. 'Thank you, Jade. You took a risk coming here. I do appreciate it.'

The woman shrugged. 'I did it for Mirar, remember. He's the one you should thank.'

'Maybe I will, next time he interrupts my dreams.'

Jade's eyebrows rose. 'Dreams, eh? Like that, is it?'

Auraya laughed. 'Not for a long time. Go on, then. The sooner you leave, the sooner I can return to the Siyee.'

The woman turned away and strode toward the cave entrance. She paused and looked back once, then disappeared into the shadows. Auraya regarded the entrance for a long time after the woman had gone.

She's a strange one, she thought. *Cranky, cynical, but also strong and determined. I imagine that's what living so long does to a person. Will I get like that? I suppose there's worse I could be. Underneath all the moodiness, there's an optimism in Jade that reassures me. She can still laugh at things. Maybe that's because she's been through so much that she knows it's only a matter of time before bad situations sort themselves out.*

She had agreed to give Jade three days' head start before leaving the cave herself. Auraya had no idea how far a landbound person could travel in three days. Hopefully far enough to evade any Siyee scouts the gods might send after her.

She's lived this long, Auraya told herself. *I'm sure she can take care of herself.*

Picking up her half of the bread, she began to eat.

*   *   *

Tintel was silent as she led Mirar from platform to platform. He sensed that her mind was occupied with planning and worrying, and he felt a pang of sympathy. A city Dreamweaver House was always a busy place, and the more Dreamweavers there were to organise, the more organising there was to do. He couldn't help her with that, only with the sorts of healing emergencies they had dealt with tonight.

If she hadn't worked out that he was powerfully Gifted before, she knew it now. They had visited a woman bleeding profusely after bearing a child, and the only way Mirar had been able to save her was to heal her magically. Tintel had clearly been impressed, but hadn't said anything.

She had also tried a method he had never encountered before in an attempt to stem the bleeding. He had noted a few other improvements in the local Dreamweavers' knowledge since coming here, as well. Advances and discoveries ought to filter through to Dreamweavers everywhere through mind links, but clearly the restrictions and intolerance in the north had prevented or slowed the transferral of knowledge there.

They crossed the bridge to the Dreamweaver House. He opened the door for Tintel, and she smiled in gratitude.

'I wish the men of Dekkar had the manners of those of the north,' she said wryly. 'Thank you for your help, Wilar.'

He shrugged and followed her inside. The smell of food filled the hall and his stomach grumbled.

'I'll get someone to bring you some food,' he said, guessing that Tintel would go straight to her room to work.

'Thank you.' She nodded. 'Don't forget yourself.'

He smiled. 'I won't.'

A few servants and Dreamweavers remained in the kitchen. One Dreamweaver woman was preparing a meal for her infant daughter, while another was complaining about her husband's snoring. There was soup and the local doughy bread left over from dinner. He asked the complaining wife to take Tintel a serving of both, then took a portion out to the hall.

Several of the younger Dreamweavers were sitting around the table. They all looked up as he arrived, then quickly down at their meals. An awkward silence followed and Mirar sensed a mix of suppressed amusement and speculation from them.

He set his plate on the table, sat down and began to eat.

The silence continued, now imbued with embarrassment. When one of the Dreamweavers cleared his throat to speak, relief spread among the rest.

'Forgive our silence, Wilar,' the Dreamweaver said. 'Your arrival made us see we were gossiping.'

Mirar smiled. 'People gossip. It is in their . . .' He searched for the right word for 'nature' and one of the Dreamweavers supplied it. 'What did I miss?'

They smiled and exchanged glances. His question had eased some of their embarrassment, but not the tension in the room.

'The newest talk is that you are Mirar,' the youngest Dreamweaver said in Avvenan.

The others frowned at the young man disapprovingly. He spread his hands. 'He should know. What if someone takes it seriously? It could be awkward.'

Mirar laughed and shook his head. 'Mirar? Me? Why? Is it because I am foreign?'

They nodded.

'Mirar came south,' another added. 'He must be here somewhere.'

'We don't know that for sure,' the older Dreamweaver pointed out.

'We don't know anything for sure.'

They began to talk over each other, making it difficult for Mirar to understand them. Suddenly one of the Dreamweavers who had remained silent turned to him.

'So you're not Mirar?'

Mirar paused. If he denied a direct question, then in the future, if he needed to reveal his identity, he would also reveal that he had lied to them. It was never good to lie. People resented it, even when they knew it was justified.

So instead he smiled coyly. 'I am for someone here, and I don't want to, er, spoil the illusion for her.'

There were laughs all around. One of the men rolled his eyes.

'Dardel, I bet.'

'But she was the one that suggested it to me,' said another.

'That explains *everything*.'

They laughed again.

The Dreamweaver next to Mirar leaned closer. 'Lucky you,' he murmured.

'We should all tell her she's right about Wilar, but let everyone else know she's wrong,' the youngest suggested. 'How long do you think we could keep the truth from her?'

'Tintel would tell her.'

'Don't tell Tintel either.'

'She'd work it out.'

Mirar smiled and listened as they plotted their teasing of Dardel. They didn't appear to be serious about carrying it out, which was a relief.

What would they do if they found out that she was right? he wondered. These Dreamweavers would probably welcome him with enthusiasm. More than enthusiasm. That was the trouble. It had been so long since he had moved among his own people, they now regarded him with awe.

It's ironic. For a century the gods have spread the lie that we immortals encouraged people to worship us as gods, and now it appears that in my absence my people have begun to do just that.

They'd get over it, he thought. *It is not my people I'd need to worry about, it is the Pentadrians. So far what I've seen has been encouraging. No Dreamweavers here have been able to think of more than a few conflicts between Dreamweavers and Pentadrians in the last few decades, and those were only about money.*

Discovering that a powerful sorcerer with influence over the Dreamweavers had settled here might make the local Pentadrians feel threatened, however. He needed to know what they would do in response, and there was a way he could find out.

Dream linking was not banned in Southern Ithania. Even so, he would have to ensure he wasn't detected. He would hardly endear himself to the Pentadrians if they discovered their dreams were being spied upon and manipulated.

Rising, he took his empty plate to the kitchen then ascended to his room. Before he could undress there was a familiar knock on his door. He smiled.

Dardel. I could ignore her, he thought, *but she'll be disappointed and I'm not in that much of a hurry to go dream hunting.*

Hours later, as Mirar sank into the dream state, he let his awareness of Dardel's weight and warmth slip away. Sending his mind forth, he found other dreaming minds. He sought their identities then planted the idea of his return into their thoughts.

Their responses were varied, but generally favourable. Some were suspicious of anyone who had power, but none imagined themselves taking action to get rid of him. Most others didn't care what happened so long as their lives weren't adversely affected. A few found the idea heartening. They appreciated the Dreamweavers' skills and thought the return of Mirar could only improve them even further.

Hours passed and he felt excitement growing. He could do it. He could stop hiding and guide his people again. Yet one night of searching dreamers' minds wasn't enough. He must do this every night for . . . weeks? Months?

Then he remembered The Twins. They skimmed the minds of people everywhere, every day. They might already know how Southern Ithanians would greet the news that he had established himself in one of their lands.

He'd linked with The Twins only a few times before. Since he hadn't met them, he had a more formal relationship with them than Emerahl had. He only contacted them when he had something important to discuss, and he suspected they treated him like the rulers, wisdom seekers and academics who had once sought their advice, long ago – with polite interest.

While he'd found their advice sensible and insightful, he was not as trusting of them as Emerahl was. Just because they were fellow immortals didn't mean they would always be allies. There was one small oddity that bothered him. All of the joined twins he had ever encountered had been identical. Clearly Surim and Tamun weren't. They weren't even of the same gender. Emerahl had dismissed this, pointing out that immortality and the ability to skim minds were just as uncommon. Still, it bothered him that The Twins might have been lying to her.

:*Tamun? Surim?* he called.

:*Mirar.*

It was Tamun. Her response was disturbingly prompt, as if she had been close by.

:*How are you both?* he asked.

:*The same. Little changes here. I am skimming alone today. Surim is out hunting again.* Her mind-voice always brought an image of a sharp-witted, wiry old woman to mind, despite Emerahl's assurances that Tamun looked like a young woman.

:*I have a question to ask.*

:*Wait a moment. I'll see if I can get Surim's attention.*

:*Isn't he hunting?*

:It's more the sort of hunting you were just indulging in. He always falls asleep straight after . . . ah, there he is.

:Are you watching me again? Surim accused.

:Of course not. Mirar has a question for us, Tamun replied.

:Mirar! Surim exclaimed. *How is life in Dekkar?*

:It is good here, Mirar told them. *Better than I expected.*

:Yes, Pentadrians are a more tolerant people in some respects than those in the north, Tamun agreed.

:I'm tempted to reveal myself – to reclaim my position among the Dreamweavers again. How do you think the Pentadrians will react?

:If you're expecting a parade, you'll be disappointed, Surim said. *Although I doubt the Voices will come after you with execution in mind either, though they will probably want to meet you just to make sure you're not a threat to them.*

:So long as you don't challenge their authority or start converting Pentadrians, they'll leave you alone, Tamun added. *But you aren't known for keeping silent when you disagree with those in power, Mirar. Could you stand by and not protest if you did not like the way they ruled their people? Or your people?*

:I've just spent a hundred years being someone who did. I've learned caution and patience.

:You learned to run when you used to fight. That is not the same, Surim pointed out.

:No, he agreed. *I'll be aiming for somewhere between run and fight.*

:You'll compromise and negotiate? Surim sounded amused.

:If I have to.

:It is a risk to yourself and your people, and a change that you cannot easily reverse. What will you gain from it? What will the Dreamweavers gain? Tamun asked.

:They will have my knowledge to call upon and I think my return will give them hope and courage, especially in the north.

:They may expect too much of you. They may think your return

will bring about the empowerment of Dreamweavers everywhere, Tamun warned.

:Dreamweavers do not seek power, and from what I have seen, they still don't.

:We agree. There is another matter you should consider, Surim said.

:Yes?

:While we believe the Pentadrians will not object to you establishing yourself there, they are still not to be trusted. Have you heard from your own people regarding the attacks in Jarime and the Pentadrian involvement?

:No. What happened?

:Some of the Dreamweaver attacks and murders were organised by a Pentadrian group. They knew Circlians would be blamed for the violence, and took advantage of people's disillusionment to recruit new followers.

:That is alarming.

:Yes, but the Pentadrians were not motivated by hatred of Dreamweavers but a ruthless practicality. In Southern Ithania there is no need for Pentadrians to harm Dreamweavers in order to find converts, but that does not discount the possibility they may use your people in other ways.

:That would always be a risk.

:And there is one more matter you should consider, Tamun added.

:What is it?

:If you have the Pentadrians' good will, you may gain Auraya's enmity.

Mirar paused to consider that.

:I already have it, he replied. *So long as she follows the gods, she must regard me as her enemy. Even if that weren't true, I cannot let Auraya's regard for me influence my decisions in regard to the Dreamweavers.*

:No. Surim and I do not agree about this. Auraya may not share

162

the gods' hatred of immortals, but she has little regard for the Pentadrians. Settling here may make a difference.

:I can't help that. These people do not deserve her contempt. I won't reject them for fear of offending Auraya. He paused. How is she? I haven't heard from Emerahl for days.

:Emerahl has been waiting for you to contact her.

:Because she's worried I will rebuff her for delivering bad news last time we spoke?

:Yes.

:Silly woman. She knows I wouldn't do that.

:No, but we can't help retaining old fears and habits, despite the years. It would be tactful for—

:Auraya has made herself immortal, Surim interrupted.

Mirar felt his heart leap.

:Emerahl thought she wouldn't do it!

:Something changed her mind. She also revealed two unexpected Gifts. Firstly, she has regained the ability to read minds.

:But . . . no immortals have ever been able to . . . have they?

:Not in our lifetime, Tamun confirmed. The second Gift she revealed is the ability to sense and hear the gods. Apparently she can see them when she is mind-skimming, too.

:Emerahl wisely advised her to keep this from the gods, Surim added. I can't imagine they'd be thrilled to know they can be spied upon.

:Auraya said the gods already knew she could sense them when they were close by, Tamun continued.

:That's . . . Mirar shivered. That's not just another innate Gift.

:No, Tamun agreed. It seems Auraya is no ordinary immortal. Perhaps it is the consequence of her being a White first. The powers the gods gave her imprinted themselves on her somehow.

:Except that they wouldn't have given her the power to sense and hear them when she was a White. That is entirely new.

:No. It may be an unintended side-effect of her being linked to them previously, Surim suggested.

:Whatever the reason, she would be wise to keep it a secret. In a few days she will return to the Open. Then we will see how well the gods take the news that their former favourite has learned to hide her mind – and whatever else she allows them to know she has learned. We'll let you know what happens.

Mirar felt a pang of anxiety. He had tried to tell himself it didn't matter. Auraya was out of reach and had no regard for him anyway. Trouble was, the part of him that couldn't help worrying wasn't inclined to listen to the part with a grasp of logic and practicality.

:Thank you for the news, he said. *And your advice.*

:Use it well, The Twins replied together. Then their twinned voices fell silent and he let himself drift off into his usual troubled sleep.

CHAPTER 13

'O waya!'

As a small fluffy blur streaked across the bower, Auraya crouched down and held out her arms. Mischief bounded up onto her shoulders and rubbed his whiskered cheek against her ear.

The female Siyee who usually looked after the veez, Tytee, stepped out of the side room Mischief had bounded out from.

'Welcome back, Priestess Auraya,' she said, smiling.

Auraya sensed relief from the woman. Mischief was making small whimpering noises as Auraya scratched him.

'Owaya back. Owaya back,' he murmured over and over.

'Thank you, Tytee. Anyone would think I'd been away for months,' Auraya said, surprised. She hadn't seen him so emotional since after he had been snatched from her tent before the battle with the Pentadrians. 'Has something happened to him?'

'No. He was fine until a day after you left,' Tytee told her. 'He suddenly became distressed, saying "Auraya gone" over and over. Then he became very sad. It was as though you had died and he was grieving. I carried him around with me, concerned he would pine away like old people sometimes do when their spouse dies.'

Auraya lifted Mischief down and looked at him closely. 'I

wonder.' She let the shield around her mind thin. At once a small, familiar voice spoke in her mind.

Owaya back! There was a fading sadness and puzzlement behind the delight of his words.

She felt a pang of guilt. Somehow Mischief must have forged a link to her mind. Once she had entered the void that link had broken. The only explanation he could have come up with was that she had died.

'Poor Mischief,' she said, hugging him close. At once his delight changed to irritation and he wriggled free. The veez climbed up to his basket and curled up inside.

'Msstf sleep.'

Tytee laughed. 'If only we were all so easily satisfied,' she said.

'And forgiven,' Auraya agreed. 'Thank you for looking after him while I was gone.'

The woman shrugged. 'I don't mind. He's always amusing, and a lot less demanding than the children I look after. I must—'

'Priestess Auraya?'

They both turned to see Speaker Sirri standing in the doorway.

'Come in,' Auraya said, beckoning. As the Speaker entered, Tytee excused herself and slipped outside.

'Welcome back,' Sirri said.

'Thank you.' Sensing tension in the Siyee leader, Auraya looked closer. She saw that Sirri had grown concerned as Auraya's absence had lengthened. The presence of an uninvited landwalker in Si had bothered her, too.

'How did it go?' Sirri asked.

'Very well,' Auraya told her. 'Jade has left for home. I learned a great deal while I was with her. She has quite a knowledge of healing and cures.' Auraya gestured to the bag she had brought with her.

'Yet she was unable to treat her own illness?'

Auraya shook her head. 'She sent for me because she couldn't manage what she needed to do by herself.'

'So she's better now?'

'Yes.'

Sirri nodded. 'Good.' She smiled. 'We have you all to ourselves again.'

'Did anything happen while I was gone?'

'Nothing drastic. Just a bit of an argument between tribe leaders.' Sirri sighed. 'I'm afraid I can't stop and explain. I was at a meeting between the leaders when the news of your arrival came. I called for a break, but I can't stay away long. I must go back and try to knock some sense into the two of them.'

'What is the argument about?'

Sirri grimaced. 'Mines. The Fire Mountain tribe claim that once the mines pass beyond the ridge that divides their territory then everything cut from them is theirs to sell.'

'Ah. That won't be an easy one to settle. You have my sympathies.'

'Thanks,' Sirri said dryly. She moved toward the entrance.

'Come and tell me about it later, if you have time.'

'I will.'

Sirri slipped out through the door-hanging and hurried away. Alone at last, Auraya moved to a chair and sat down.

Everything's back to normal, she mused. Then she shook her head. *No, it just seems that way on the surface. My mind is shielded and my body is no longer aging. As far as the gods are concerned, nothing is as it was — or should be.*

She had sensed nothing of the gods since Huan and Saru's last visit. After the pair had sped away to find the other gods, Auraya had expected Yranna, Lore and Chaia to visit, even if just to confirm what Huan claimed.

Perhaps Huan didn't tell Chaia, she thought. *So much depends on Chaia. I need to talk to him. I need to know if he will accept what I've done.*

She briefly considered calling to him, but that hadn't always got his attention in the past. Instead she decided to try finding him through mind-skimming.

Closing her eyes, she slowed her breathing and let herself sink into a dream trance. At first she skimmed the minds of the Siyee around her, finding men and women engaged in domestic tasks and a group of children playing a game. Stretching out further, she let herself be aware of the minds in the world as points of thought, like tiny lights, and sought bigger, brighter presences.

She found an unfamiliar feminine presence and guessed she'd found Yranna, sure that she would have recognised Huan instantly. The goddess was not conversing with anyone else, and Auraya could not hear her thoughts. Confirming that she couldn't actually read the gods' minds was reassuring. Moving on, she found a masculine presence. It was not Chaia and she continued searching.

I'm doing this to find Chaia, not to eavesdrop, she told herself.

Finally she sensed a buzz like the sound of someone speaking just within hearing. Drawing closer, she felt a thrill of triumph as she recognised Chaia's voice.

: . . . are in place. What do you think they'll do next?

:Depends if they've heard about what happened in Jarime. They'd be fools to try the same thing. The second voice belonged to Lore.

:They're not that stupid.

:No, but if they're given orders what choice do they have?

:None, Chaia replied. *It will be interesting to watch.*

:Yes. Anyway, I came to tell you your favourite has returned to the Open.

:Ah.

:Huan will want us to decide now.

:Of course. You know how much Huan likes complications, dull bitch that she is.

Auraya felt amused surprise. She doubted Chaia would have spoken of Huan that way if he knew Auraya was listening in.

:There are interesting complications and there are dangerous ones, Lore warned.

:Auraya is not dangerous – or she won't be if Huan stops manipulating her, Chaia replied.

:How will you know if Auraya is dangerous if you can't see her mind?

:Because I took the time to get to know her. She won't betray us unless we make her.

:She won't betray you.

:No. Ironically, I have Huan to thank for that.

:So what will you do? Lore asked.

:I won't let the bitch kill her.

:Even if the others outvote you?

:Especially not then. Things are only just getting interesting. Consider this: there are other ways of redressing the balance. I've always favoured recruitment over extermination.

:I'm finding I agree with you more and more. I wonder if I could persuade Yranna . . .

:You'd have a better chance than I.

:I will try.

As Lore flashed away, Auraya began to pull her mind back. She had found answers to more than what she had sought.

:Before you sneak away, Auraya . . .

She froze.

:Chaia?

:Yes, I can sense you there, though you're keeping quiet. How often have you spied on us like this?

:Only twice. The first time it was an accident. This time I came to ask you a question.

:Then ask away.

Chaia did not sound angry, only amused.

:Will you . . . How long have you known I was listening?

:From the moment you arrived.

:And Lore?

:Oblivious. He doesn't know what you're capable of, so he doesn't watch for spies.

:But you knew, she pointed out.

:I suspected your abilities would develop, under the right circumstances. What made you decide to learn to hide your mind?

:What I heard the first time I, er, eavesdropped.

:Ah. And have you become immortal?

She paused. If she didn't trust Chaia, she may as well abandon her loyalty to the gods completely.

:Yes. Huan said I was doomed anyway just for knowing how.

:I'm a little disappointed you didn't consult me first.

:I would have, she said honestly, *if you'd been around to ask. Do you forgive me?*

:For becoming immortal or not consulting me?

:Both.

:We'll see. You have not lost my love and support. I know I can't stop you growing into your powers any more than a parent can stop their child growing up. Stay loyal to me, and I will stay loyal to you.

Auraya felt a wave of relief.

:I will.

:Don't think it will be easy, he warned. *Huan may like the world to be simple and straightforward, but her traps and schemes are not. The more powerful you get, Auraya, the harder she will try to destroy you. And the easier it will be for you to thwart her.* He paused. *Never forget that while she may not be able to harm you easily, she can harm those you love.*

Auraya found herself thinking of Mirar. Though she did not

care for him as she had cared for Leiard, she did not want him harmed because Huan *thought* she did. Fortunately he was out of Huan's reach in Southern Ithania.

Who else might Huan harm? Mischief? That would be a low and petty thing to do. Danjin? Auraya *liked* him, but he wasn't her adviser any more. Her father? She hadn't seen him in years . . .

:How can I protect them? Huan can see their minds. She can find them.

:You can't, Chaia said. *You can only try not to give Huan anything which she can use to persuade the other gods to act against you. I will . . . He* stopped abruptly. *Go back, Auraya. And do not seek to speak to me this way again. Just as you can hear us talking, we can hear you talking, and it would not take much for your new ability to be noticed.*

Abruptly he moved away, flitting out of reach of her senses. She withdrew to her own body again. Opening her eyes, she looked around the bower and felt a pang of loneliness.

So this is the price of learning what the gods did not want me to learn — instead of bringing harm to myself, I must ensure I don't start to love anyone, for fear Huan will strike at them to get at me.

She stood up and began pacing. *This isn't fair!* she thought. Then she let out a bitter laugh. *Listen to me; I sound like a child.*

But it *wasn't* fair. And if Huan was willing to harm innocent people just to hurt Auraya, she was every bit as despicable as Mirar claimed she was. And if the other gods agreed with her? She let out an explosive sigh of dismay. *Then I'm doomed. Ithania is doomed.*

A whimper broke Auraya's train of thought. Looking up, she saw that Mischief was watching her, his eyes wide and dark and his whiskers trembling. She sensed fear and concern. Her frustration and anger faded and she walked over to pat him and murmur reassuring words.

171

Lies, she couldn't help thinking. *I'm afraid everything isn't all right, Mischief. But one thing is true: I won't let anyone harm you.*

The screech of birds echoed over the town and Servant Teroan cursed under his breath. He was late again. Though it was possible that the bird trainers had misjudged the release time for their charges' exercise flight, it was unlikely.

About as likely as the sun misjudging the time to rise, he told himself. *Dedicated Servant Cherinor has more sundials than anyone else in Avven.*

It was said the man in charge of the town and the birds had even trained his favourite to squawk on the hour. And that his assistant Servant kept a schedule for Cherinor that was planned to the minute. And that Cherinor didn't sleep.

I doubt he appreciates the pleasure of a long bath and conversation, Teroan thought sourly. *If he does, I bet every minute is choreographed to ensure no time is wasted.*

The path to the Baths was steep and he was panting by the time he reached the entrance. He paused to catch his breath. The view here was good and it was a shame the Baths had so few windows. They had to keep the warm air inside from escaping, he supposed.

From the doorway he could see most of the town. Klaff's houses were the same colour as the cliffs. The main road wound out of the town, through the valley, then straightened and thinned into the distance. Somewhere at its end was Glymma and the Sanctuary.

He'd cursed his luck when he'd been sent here. The capital cities of Mur and Dekkar were villages compared to Avven's, and in comparison to them Klaff was a one-house hamlet. The troupes of actors he used to enjoy watching never came here. He had to order wine or any delicacy or luxury he craved from

Glymma, at great expense, and his wife constantly complained about the noise of the birds. The only consolation was the Baths. They were as good as, if not better, than those at Glymma's Sanctuary.

The hills around the town were riddled with caves and some contained springs. The water was not as pure as that at the Sanctuary but the locals claimed the red-brown colouring was from a mineral that was good for one's health. The mineral was filtered out of the drinking water and sold throughout Southern Ithania as a rejuvenating mud that could be painted onto the skin.

Birds wheeled not far above, their screeching deafening. He winced and turned back to the door. Sometimes he couldn't help agreeing with his wife. It was not a pleasant sound.

A domestic greeted Teroan, tracing the sign of the gods over his chest, and ushered him down a familiar corridor. Most of the doors they passed were curtained with hangings, but a few were uncovered. He glimpsed slaves in these, near naked, scrubbing the walls. A sharp smell stung his nostrils and made his eyes water. He wondered how the slaves endured it.

The domestic stopped at a door and waved Teroan inside. The room he walked into had been recently cleaned. Teroan thought it a shame, as the patterns that the green mould formed had made it easy for him to imagine he was soaking in some natural pool in the middle of a forest somewhere.

Still, the mould had smelled bad. The room now smelled like the ocean. He chuckled as he approached the room's only other occupant.

'Sea salts again, Dameen?'

The man looked up and grinned. 'Reminds me of home.'

Teroan peeled off the layers of his Servant robes and tossed them on a bench next to Dameen's neatly folded ones. He stepped down into the tepid water, then lowered himself onto one of the ledges. The red-brown murk of the water did not quite hide his rolls of fat or the absence of his friend's legs below the knees. Somehow Dameen had managed to keep his muscular good looks despite his injury. Teroan suspected the man maintained a routine of exercise out of habit, unable to completely put aside his warrior training.

They sat in silence for some time, content to relax in each other's company.

'I had a strange dream last night,' Dameen said eventually.

'Oh?'

'I dreamed the leader of the Dreamweavers came to Southern Ithania.'

Teroan looked at his friend in surprise. 'I dreamed of the same man last night. I suppose the rumours of his return are working on our minds. What happened in your dream?'

'I asked myself what I'd do if I was one of the Voices . . .' He paused and frowned. 'Or maybe someone else asked me . . . I can't remember.'

'The same happened in my dream. What did you decide?'

'That I'd do nothing, so long as he didn't cause trouble.'

Teroan nodded. 'Me, too. It could only be a good thing, if he returned. He made the Dreamweavers good at healing; he might make them even better. We owe them a lot for the help they gave us after the battle, too.'

'Yes.' Dameen looked down at the stumps of his legs and shrugged. 'But then I'm biased. This morning I found myself thinking about it again. The Voices might not see it that way. They'd see a powerful sorcerer who might turn people against them.'

'What do you think they'd do?'

'Kuar would have made him an ally.' He frowned. 'I don't know Nekaun. I have no idea what he'd do.'

Teroan smiled. The warrior couldn't help himself. He was

supposed to have left his past behind him, but while his body might no longer be whole his mind was as lively as ever.

A waste, he thought. *He couldn't accept anyone in place of Kuar, so he wound up here, his potential as an adviser lost.*

For that Teroan was selfishly grateful. If Dameen left Klaff, who else around here was interesting and intelligent enough to talk to? Certainly not the bird breeders. Or his wife.

'Do you think it strange that we had the same dream on the same night?' Teroan asked.

Dameen's sharp eyes narrowed. 'You suspect Dreamweavers of meddling in our dreams?'

Teroan shrugged. 'Two people dreaming the same dream on the same night is only coincidence. If we find anyone else has had the same dream, perhaps there is more to it.'

'And if Mirar does appear in Southern Ithania?'

Teroan nodded. 'Yes. That might convince me, too.'

Glowing coals were all that was left in the brazier. Cushions had been scattered before the hearth, and a woman lay sleeping upon them. Beside her was an empty cup and a jug. Danjin paused to admire the curve of her hip and fine angles of her face before walking toward her. He felt a warm affection. Truly he was lucky to have Silava as a wife.

There had been times he thought himself cursed, but they were long ago and best forgotten.

She stirred, probably at the sound of his sandals on the floor. Her eyes opened and she blinked at him, then smiled.

'Danjin,' she said.

'Silava. You weren't waiting for me, were you?'

'Yes and no. I was having a private celebration. If you happened to turn up to join me, all the better.'

'What are you celebrating?'

'We,' she corrected, 'are celebrating the birth of another grandchild. A granddaughter.'

He looked at her in surprise. 'She arrived early?'

'Yes.' Silava hesitated. 'I want to stay with Tivela a while.'

He nodded. 'Yes. Help with the baby. When will you leave?'

Silava narrowed her eyes at him. 'You aren't displaying nearly enough reluctance or disappointment at the prospect of my absence for my satisfaction.'

'No,' he agreed, chuckling. 'Though I have been led to believe that would go against all laws of nature and the gods.'

Her eyes narrowed further.

'I have some news of my own,' he told her quickly. 'You may wish to hear it before you flay the skin from my body.'

'Oh?'

'Ellareen is going to Dunway and she wants me with her.'

'Oh.' She looked downcast, then she smiled and regarded him triumphantly as she rose to her feet. 'See. That's how one shows disappointment. It's quite simple, and should be well within the abilities of an adviser. Why Dunway?'

'Hania is not the only county the Pentadrians have tried converting. They sent their Servants all over Northern Ithania – except Si, for some reason. Maybe because Auraya is there, though I have no idea why that would deter them.'

'They did send people into Si,' Silava said. 'It was the reason Auraya went back there.'

He smacked his palm against his forehead. 'Of course! I forgot about that. It seems like so long ago.'

Silava linked her arm in his and nudged him toward the door. 'You miss her, don't you?'

Danjin frowned. 'I suppose I do.'

'You don't like Ella as much, do you?'

He looked at her in surprise. 'Why do you say that?'

'You don't talk about her in the same way. Do you like her?'

He shrugged. 'Ella's likeable but . . . With Auraya I knew there were things she couldn't tell me but it was easy to forget that. With Ella I'm reminded of it all the time.'

'Maybe she has more secrets than Auraya did.'

Danjin laughed. 'More than Auraya? I hope not!' Or at least not such scandalous secrets. He couldn't imagine Ella taking a Dreamweaver as a lover. He couldn't imagine Ella taking *anyone* as a lover. Though as passionate about her work as Auraya, she was somehow colder and more distant.

But maybe that was only because it was taking longer for him to relax around her. Auraya hadn't broken his trust, but he had been disappointed with her for having an affair with Leiard. He had never forgiven himself for not noticing something was going on. He hadn't even had a chance to advise her against such foolishness. Now he couldn't help watching Ella closely, ready to offer a sensible viewpoint if she faced a similar dilemma.

They reached the doorway and stepped out into the corridor. Silava yawned. 'Or maybe Auraya is one of Ella's secrets.'

He considered his wife. 'You think there's more to Auraya's resignation, then?'

'Maybe.' She shrugged. 'Not that it would matter to anyone now. She's gone. Ella's taken her place. Hmm, you still haven't told me why Ella's going to Dunway.'

'The Pentadrians are up to something there.'

'Not murdering more Dreamweavers, are they?'

He shook his head. 'We're not sure what, which is why we're going.' The shocking revelations about the Pentadrians' plot in Jarime had spread through the city quickly, and the protests against the hospice and attacks on Dreamweavers had stopped. At the same time, dozens of people had been either dragged to the Temple, beaten, driven out of their homes or even murdered, at sometimes the mere suspicion of being

Pentadrian. Ella had not been as dismayed by this as he had expected.

'People like having something to direct their hate at,' Ella had said. 'The Pentadrians are far more deserving of it than the Dreamweavers.'

'But some of the people who have been attacked aren't Pentadrians,' he'd pointed out.

'Yes, and we've compensated them – after we confirmed their innocence, of course.'

'Once this plot is forgotten, people will start worrying about Dreamweavers again,' he'd warned.

'Then we'll have to keep reminding them who the true enemy is.'

Silava squeezed his arm, drawing his attention back from his thoughts. 'I meant, why is Ella going, not one of the other White? She's a bit new to her role to be given such a task.'

Danjin shrugged. 'They must consider her capable enough. And the sooner she gains some experience of other lands the better.'

'How long will you be gone?'

'I don't know. Months, probably.'

Silava sighed. 'At least you're not going to war. A warrior nation, but not a war.' She yawned again. 'I'm too tired to think about it. Let's get some sleep.'

He gave in to a yawn of his own as they went upstairs. News upon news. 'Another grandchild,' he murmured. 'A man could start feeling old.'

Silava's eyebrows rose, but she said nothing. Her silence came as a surprise.

No teasing? She really must be tired.

He took that as a hint to hold his tongue and followed her into the bedroom. Despite his weariness he lay awake, his mind too full of matters he must take care of before leaving.

'Yes. The counters set. That'll do,' Silava murmured suddenly.

'What?'

'Oh.' He heard her turn her head toward him. 'Are you still awake?'

'Yes.'

'Sorry.'

'What were you thinking about?'

'Packing,' she said. 'I have two lots of packing to do now.'

'You don't have to pack for me.'

She laughed. 'Since when have you packed for yourself? Go to sleep. And don't worry. I'll arrange everything.'

CHAPTER 14

Shadows sat below Tintel's eyes. The woman looked older than her years as she regarded Mirar with weary patience.

'What is it, Wilar?'

He took a step back. 'You're tired. I will return tomorrow.'

'No, come in.' She beckoned and turned away, giving him no chance to retreat.

'I'll be brief then,' he said, stepping into the room and closing the door.

She collapsed into a chair and waved toward another. 'You wouldn't have come here if you didn't have something you needed to discuss. Have the boys been gossiping again?'

He smiled. 'I don't know. Probably.'

'If it bothers you I will tell them to stop.'

'Which would make no difference at all,' he told her. 'They respect and admire you greatly, Dreamweaver Tintel, but trying to stop gossip is like trying to stop the tide.' He shook his head. 'No, the only ill effect is that it will make what I have to tell you harder to believe.'

Her eyebrows rose. 'Will it? What unbelievable news do you have, then?'

He looked at her and considered what he was about to do.

It was a risk. There were benefits to remaining anonymous. None of the hassles of trying to please everyone, for a start.

Yet where would that leave his people? They were strong in this place, but not in others. Perhaps he was wrong in thinking he could help them, but when he looked at Tintel's worn and weary face he felt a pang of affection and knew he had to try.

'They're right,' he told her. 'I am Mirar.'

She blinked with surprise, opened her mouth to speak, then paused and frowned at him thoughtfully.

'It is hard to believe,' she said. 'Yet I find I can't dismiss it completely.' She pursed her lips. 'Nor can I accept it completely.'

He shrugged. 'That is what I expected.'

'I need proof.'

'Of course.'

'And something else.'

'Oh?'

'Your forgiveness for doubting, if you do prove to be Mirar.'

He laughed. 'I could hardly begrudge you that.'

She did not smile. 'If you're not Mirar . . .'

'You'll give me a thorough spanking?' he suggested.

'This is not a matter to joke about.'

'No?' He sobered. 'No, it isn't. I have done all I can to ensure I do not endanger myself or my people by revealing my identity today, but it is still a risk.'

'A risk worth taking?'

'Obviously.' He leaned forward and held out his hand. 'Link with me.'

Her frown vanished. She stared at him for a moment, then took his hand. He watched her close her eyes, then shut his own and reached out with his mind.

As her thoughts came clearly to his senses, he drew up memories for her. Old memories of the formation of the Dreamweavers. Memories of healing discoveries and memories of Dreamweavers long dead. Memories of civilisations that had dwindled to nothing long ago and of those that still existed.

He did not show her the gods or their work, his own 'death' or his life as Leiard. This should be a moment of joy, not one of relived terror or pain. Drawing away from her mind, he opened his eyes and released her hand. Her eyelids fluttered open. She stared at him, then lowered her eyes.

'I . . . I don't know what to say. Or what to do. How should I address you?'

'Just call me Mirar,' he told her firmly, disturbed by her almost subservient behaviour. 'I am a Dreamweaver, not a god or a king or even a second cousin of the nephew of a prince. I have never led my people by force, only guided them with experience and wisdom – though I have to admit to having failed in the latter more than a few times. Look at me.'

She obeyed. He hadn't expected her to be so overwhelmed. Reaching forward, he took her hand again.

'You are the leader here, Tintel. That is how I arranged things. One Dreamweaver is chosen to maintain each House and lead those who stay there. They are the authority in that place, and all travelling Dreamweavers should obey them or move on. I am a travelling Dreamweaver. That means you have to order me around, or I've got to leave.'

The corner of her mouth twitched and he sensed her amusement.

'That could be a little difficult,' she said. 'And the others . . . they will be in awe of you. They will worship you.'

'Then we're both going to have to discourage them. My safety – our safety – relies on the Pentadrians thinking I am no threat to them. If I am worshipped like a god, they will consider me a threat.'

She shook her head. 'Pentadrians are not Circlians, Wi—Mirar. They do not resent other religions.'

'Only because the gods of those religions do not exist. The one religion they do resent is the Circlians', whose gods do exist.'

She frowned and he sensed her growing anxious. He squeezed her hand.

'I never wanted to be worshipped and I still don't. It would be better if the Dreamweavers here regarded me more like a teacher than a god. I think, between us, we can manage that.'

She looked at him and nodded. 'I'll try.'

'I know you will.' He grinned. 'This is like announcing an engagement, isn't it? Who shall we tell first?'

Tintel snorted softly. 'If you don't want to be worshipped, why are you revealing your identity?'

'I want to be among my people again,' he told her seriously. 'As myself.'

She nodded, extracted her hands from his and rose. Facing the door, she took a deep breath and let it out slowly.

'Then wait here. I'll gather everyone in the hall and call you down when they're ready.'

He smiled. 'Thank you, Tintel.'

She walked to the door and opened it. Pausing to look back at him, she shook her head in wonder. Then, without saying a word, she left the room.

Mirar smiled to himself. Once they got over their surprise and awe, it would be just like the old days again. He could travel around Southern Ithania like he had once travelled around the north, meeting Dreamweavers and sharing knowledge.

And maybe this time he wouldn't mess it all up.

* * *

Blowing out her lamp, Reivan stretched out on her bed and considered the day that had just passed. The news that the High Chieftain of Dekkar had died suddenly of a fever had rushed through the Sanctuary and stirred up Servants, ambassadors and other dignitaries as if they were leaves in a dozen whirlwinds. It left the inhabitants of the Sanctuary subdued and expectant.

One of the lesser Voices was to leave the next morning for the Dekkan city. He or she would lead the funeral rites and, once the official mourning time was over, arrange trials to select a new High Chieftain. The Trials were an old tradition. Any man or woman could enter them but, apart from a few occasions, they were always won by a man of 'royal' bloodline. The entrants were tested on their strength and fitness, intelligence and knowledge, organisational and leadership skills, and dedication to the gods. Reivan assumed a mixture of privileged access to training and customising the tests to the candidates of 'royal' blood explained the predictable outcome.

A flood of important personages, and those who merely thought they were important personages, had come to the Sanctuary to ask if they, or their messages of sympathy, might travel south with the Voice. All this had kept Imenja and Reivan occupied late into the night. Too late, Reivan had told herself, for any nocturnal visits by a certain First Voice. And besides, he was probably even busier than Imenja.

Maybe he'll visit me tomorrow night, she thought.

Maybe he'd satisfied his curiosity, and had no intention of returning. *If it meant nothing to him, he won't visit a second time.* And a second visit didn't mean he was going to see her a third or fourth time, and so on. It didn't mean he loved her.

Curse it! I've started thinking about him again. I'm never going to get to sleep at this rate.

Rolling over, she discovered she had tossed and turned herself into a tight tangle with the bedding. As she began to unwind the sheet from around herself she heard a quiet tapping from the other room.

From the main door to her apartment.

Freeing herself suddenly became more difficult than before. When she had finally unwound the sheet, she donned her Servant robes hastily and hurried out of the bedroom.

Finally reaching the door, she hesitated. There had been no second tapping. If it was Nekaun, surely he would have read from her mind that she was coming to answer the door. Surely he wouldn't leave just because she hadn't responded fast enough.

If it wasn't Nekaun, or any of the Voices, the visitor might have given up and left.

Sighing, she grabbed the handle and pulled open the door.

Nekaun smiled at her. She felt her heart flip over.

'Good evening, Reivan,' he said, stepping into the room. 'It has been an eventful day, hasn't it?'

'Yes,' she replied.

He had stepped past her and moved into the centre of the main room. Looking back at her, he beckoned.

'I have a serious question for you,' he told her.

A serious question! As he sat down she tried unsuccessfully to avoid thinking of what he might wish to ask. Was it about their relationship? Was it about Imenja? She moved to the chair opposite him. He rubbed his hands together, his gaze distant.

'The gods visited me tonight,' he told her.

She felt both disappointment and a thrill of amazement. This wasn't about their relationship. Still, the gods had spoken to him and he had chosen to tell *her*.

'They said that the Thinkers are searching for an ancient artefact called the Scroll of the Gods. Have you heard of this?'

Reivan frowned. 'No. I know there is a group of Thinkers

in Hannaya that study and search for objects of antiquity. It sounds like the sort of thing they'd look for.'

Nekaun nodded. 'The gods are concerned that if these Thinkers found this scroll – if it even still exists – they would remove it from its place of safekeeping or even damage it. They want me to ensure that doesn't happen.'

She grimaced. 'Telling the Thinkers to stop searching for it will probably only encourage them to continue.'

'Then I can see only one course of action. I will have to place a spy among them.' He looked at her. 'Is there anyone here you would recommend?'

Reivan looked away. 'I don't really know that many people here. Not well enough to suggest anyone, that is.'

'Then what sort of person would you advise me to send?'

She paused. Helping Nekaun spy on the people she had once belonged among felt a little like betrayal. Then another thought occurred to her and she frowned.

'Why do the gods need you to send a spy? Couldn't they watch the Thinkers themselves?'

He laughed quietly. 'The gods can't be everywhere at once, Reivan, nor would they want to be. This is the sort of chore best given to a mortal.'

'Ah.' There was no getting out of this. *But what loyalty do I owe the Thinkers, anyway?* she asked herself. *They never accepted me. I never truly belonged. My loyalty is with the gods now. And Nekaun.*

'Your spy will have to be intelligent,' she told him. 'And show little or no Skills, because most Thinkers don't have any and are jealous of those that do. He needs to be opinionated, too.'

'"He"? Why not a "she"?'

'Most Thinkers are male. Female Thinkers are ignored.'

'Being ignored would be good, for a spy.'

'They are also excluded from important work.'

'Ah.'

'Why didn't you ask your Companion, Turaan?'

'I did.' He smiled. 'The more advice the better. It gave me a good excuse to visit you.'

Her heart jumped and began to race. She looked up and met his eyes.

'You don't need an excuse, Nekaun.'

His smile widened. 'Old or young?'

She frowned, then realised he was talking about the spy again.

'I'm not sure. A young Thinker might gain a place among the searchers by being willing to do boring work. An old Thinker would need to offer something valuable. Useful expertise, perhaps. Something that would persuade the others to allow him to join them.'

'What nationality?'

'Probably doesn't matter. If he is to bring useful information, there should be a good reason they haven't found it yet. They are jealous of their knowledge and suspicious of convenient coincidences. Some see plots everywhere.'

'What if this spy was from the north? Would that make them even more suspicious?'

'No. Most Thinkers don't hold the sort of grudges ordinary people hold against other races. Knowledge is everywhere, regardless of landscape or race. Instead, they look down on those less intelligent. They're fond of saying, "Wisdom and knowledge is everywhere, but so is stupidity".'

Nekaun chuckled. 'Everyone needs someone to despise,' he quoted.

. . . *and someone to love*, Reivan finished silently.

He stood up. She slowly followed suit. Moving closer, he reached toward her. As his hand slid about her waist and he drew her against him she felt her pulse racing . . . and a whole lot of sensations his previous visit had introduced her to.

'Does my plan to spy on the group you used to belong to bother you?'

She shook her head. 'No.'

He smiled, then kissed her, and all thoughts of the Thinkers slipped from her mind.

CHAPTER 15

Returning from the priests' bower, Auraya noticed Speaker Sirri sitting among some children, laughing. The Siyee woman looked up at her and beckoned.

Walking over, Auraya dodged as several of the children suddenly dashed away, shrieking. Tiny missiles were streaking back and forth. At Sirri's feet was a large basket full of berries. The Siyee leader's mouth was stained dark red from the juice – and so were the faces of the children.

Sirri looked down at Auraya's clothes and put a hand over her mouth. Following her gaze, Auraya realised that her white circ and tunic were splattered with red spots. Sirri stood up abruptly and called out to the children.

'That's enough!' she said firmly. The children skittered to a halt and then gathered into a group, their eyes on the ground. 'Don't waste them,' Sirri urged, her voice gentle again. 'Take a handful each and be on your way.'

The children obeyed, breaking into a run as soon as they were twenty paces from Sirri. The Siyee leader looked at Auraya and sighed.

'I'm sorry.'

Auraya shrugged and sat down beside the woman. 'I have a spare.'

'Not any more. That'll never come out.'

Examining the spots, Auraya shrugged again. 'If magic doesn't work I'll just have to order new clothes – and I'm sure the Priests here have a few spares in reserve. How did your meeting with the tribe leaders go?'

Sirri grimaced. 'Not well. Who'd have thought trade with landwalkers would make some of us turn greedy.'

Auraya said nothing. The difficulties the Siyee had endured in the past had forced them to look after each other or perish. The lands returned to them by the Torens had been developed in ways the Siyee hadn't had the numbers or knowledge to try, and now they found themselves arguing over sudden and unevenly distributed wealth. It was not landwalkers that had made some turn greedy.

'I've been wondering if we should consult the gods on the matter,' Sirri continued. 'Leave the decision in their hands.'

'Better to sort it out yourselves,' Auraya replied.

Sirri's eyebrows rose. 'Why is that?'

Auraya frowned as she realised she could not provide an answer Sirri would accept. *Have I come to distrust the gods so much I would warn others to have nothing to do with them? I'm starting to sound like a Wild.*

'The gods would expect you to do all you could before consulting them,' she replied. She looked at Sirri. 'But I guess you're telling me you have.'

Sirri smiled. 'Yes. But maybe you're right. Maybe we should try harder. Have some berries. They've just come in season.'

They both scooped up a handful and began eating. Auraya thought of Jade. *She would have liked these berries. I suppose she is still making her way out of Si.*

She was surprised to find she missed the woman's company. Though domineering and moody, Jade had been full of interesting anecdotes and knowledge. Auraya smiled. Jade might have been immensely old, but Auraya had managed to surprise her a few times.

'*I wonder if there's a way to remove the void,*' Auraya remembered saying one night. '*Perhaps if magic was drawn from another place and released here it could be filled in.*'

Jade had stared at her in surprise. '*I hadn't thought of that.*'

Finishing her handful of berries, Sirri began talking about the tribes fighting over the mines. Though she had heard it all the previous night, Auraya let the woman talk through it again, knowing Sirri simply needed to air her frustration.

:Auraya.

She jumped at the voice in her mind, then looked down at her priest ring. Juran was calling her through it. *Well, I no longer have to wonder if shielding my mind prevents it working.*

:Juran? she replied.

:Yes. Where are you?

:In the Open.

:Is Speaker Sirri with you?

:She is.

:I have something to request of her. Will you speak for me?

:Of course.

'Speaker Sirri,' Auraya interrupted. 'Juran of the White wishes me to communicate a request to you.'

Sirri froze, mouth open. Then, as she recovered from the surprise, she straightened, smiled and nodded. 'Tell him I'm listening – and give him my greetings and good wishes.'

:Give her my thanks, Juran said. *Recently we have discovered a Pentadrian plot in Jarime in which citizens of our city were murdered and others tricked into converting to the Pentadrian religion.*

Auraya relayed this to Sirri.

:We have unearthed Pentadrian plots in Toren and Genria, and are investigating other reports of their operations. Their aim has been to quietly subvert the rule of these lands, while luring Circlians into

abandoning the gods and worshipping theirs by offering positions of power to those without Gifts. Have Pentadrians or suspicious foreigners been seen in Si recently?

'Not recently,' Sirri replied. 'Not since last spring, when we requested Auraya's help. We have kept a watch on our shores ever since. The only visitors have been Elai.'

:I hope you are right. We have long debated what action would be appropriate in response to the Pentadrian attacks in our cities. If we ignore them, they may grow bolder. They may attempt to reenter your land. They will certainly try to subvert others again. We must let them know they can't attack us without retaliation. Will you help us?

'Of course,' Sirri replied. 'What can we do?'

:Huan herself suggested we attack them in their own land. Speed and surprise will be essential, so your Siyee warriors came to mind straightaway. The target was then obvious: the breeding stock of the black birds.

Sirri's eyes widened. 'That would be a risky and . . . daring attack. I trust you know where the breeding stock are?'

:In an isolated town, far from major Pentadrian cities. We will send maps and information about the town, the daily routine of the breeders and their birds – everything your warriors will need.

Auraya realised her heart was racing. Juran was asking the Siyee to take a great risk. They would enter enemy lands. If they failed, nobody could help them.

'I will go with them,' she said.

Sirri frowned. 'Juran will . . . oh! Of course. You were speaking for yourself, Auraya. Thank you.'

:You may go with them if you wish, Juran said. *But the gods forbid you to use your Gifts to help the Siyee or hinder the enemy. This must be a strike made by the Siyee, not by a White or even an ex-White.*

Auraya gave a gasp of disbelief.

192

:Do you really expect me to let them die if they are attacked? she asked silently.

:The gods do, Juran replied. *This strike is as much a symbolic act as it is an attempt to hurt the enemy. If you cannot obey the gods in this you should not accompany the Siyee.*

:Can I heal them if they're injured?

Juran paused.

:I suppose that would not negate the symbolism of the attack.

Auraya scowled.

:I suppose it would be an even better symbolic gesture if the Siyee all died in the attack. A noble sacrifice, and all that.

:Of course it wouldn't be better. To strike and escape would be much stronger proof of our ability to retaliate.

'Well?' Sirri asked.

Realising she hadn't relayed Juran's words since he had revealed that she was forbidden to use her Gifts, Auraya grimaced in apology. 'Sorry. The gods have decided I can heal the Siyee, but do nothing else. I can't fight the Pentadrians.'

'Well,' Sirri said grimly, 'that is better than nothing.'

:Will the Siyee go? Juran asked.

'As always I must consult the Speakers of the tribes,' Sirri replied. 'Though I doubt they would refuse something we agreed to in our alliance. When will this attack take place?'

:Not for some months. We must get the maps and instructions to you first.

'I will let you know as soon as a decision is made,' Sirri promised.

:Thank you. Goodbye, Speaker Sirri, Auraya.

As his mind faded away, Auraya felt anger seething inside. Clearly the gods wanted her to stay behind. She felt a light touch and looked down to find Sirri's small hand resting on her own.

'I'm sure you'll find a way around their restrictions,' the Speaker said.

Auraya met Sirri's eyes and nodded, though she could see the questions in the woman's mind and longed to answer them.

Why are the gods testing her like this? Sirri wondered.

Because some of them hate me, Auraya replied silently, though she knew the woman couldn't hear her. Then she smothered a curse. *When Chaia said Huan might try to hurt those I loved, I never thought of the Siyee.*

But surely the goddess wouldn't harm the people she had created?

Sunlight filtered through the trees. Emerahl's bag was full and heavy and she was fighting the temptation to lighten it by removing a few cures. She hadn't been to Southern Ithania before, however, and wasn't familiar with local ingredients. If she was going to pay her way she would need to bring her own supplies.

The distance between herself and her destination seemed immense. It would take her a month to get out of the mountains, then she had to cross the Plains of Gold to another range. Once through the pass she must cross the northern edge of the Sennon desert. At the coast she would buy passage on a ship sailing to the Murian capital, Hannaya. It would be a long journey.

According to The Twins, the Thinkers in search of the Scroll of the Gods based themselves there. She had two choices: try to find the Scroll on her own or attempt to join them. Both choices presented her with difficulties.

If she chose to search for the Scroll herself, The Twins would skim the Thinkers' minds and pass on everything they learned. The Twins had more than just the Thinkers to watch. They were keeping an eye on people around Mirar as well as keeping up their usual skimming of minds in Ithania. Added to that,

Emerahl couldn't stay in a constant trance linked to The Twins. She would only find out what they had learned whenever she found time to communicate with them, so she might receive important information up to a day later.

If she joined the Thinkers she would find out what they discovered as they discovered it. The only problem was, they were notoriously jealous of their knowledge and disdainful of women.

The Twins doubted she would ever gain their trust. Instead, she would have to prove herself useful to them. She could read most ancient scripts. She knew a lot about history. She spoke ancient languages.

Coming around a curve of the steep mountain slope she was traversing, she stopped and cursed. The narrow fold in the rock she had been following abruptly ended a few steps ahead under a loose covering of boulders and stones. There had been a landslide further up the mountain.

Crossing that would be foolish, she thought. *It's likely to start sliding down the mountain all over again.* She would have to go back and find a new route.

She cursed Auraya and Mirar under her breath. *I might have already found this Scroll by now, if Mirar hadn't insisted I come here and teach Auraya.*

But he owed Emerahl a big favour now. She smiled at the thought. *And it wasn't so bad, anyway, teaching Auraya. The girl is likeable enough – if one ignores her loyalty to the gods. It would be a pity if that loyalty proves her downfall.*

She had to admit The Twins were right. If Auraya did join the rest of the immortals, she would be a powerful ally. With the ability to sense and hear the gods, and read the minds of mortals, she could help them all survive.

It doesn't hurt to have someone that powerful owe you a favour, either.

Thinking back, she considered how Auraya's manner had changed once she was able to leave the cave. The woman appeared to relish being in the forest. *She was relaxed in that way people are when they feel at home*, Emerahl thought.

How could an ex-White feel at home in the Si mountains, with no luxuries, no servants, nothing to rule over?

Suddenly she saw Auraya in a different light. *She likes wild places*, Emerahl thought. *Places untouched by humans. Oh, she is happy enough to be around people, and the Siyee clearly have a place in her heart, but I think it is more than just the Siyee that calls her to the mountains.* Emerahl laughed quietly to herself. *She might not be so comfortable if she had to climb up and down cliffs, tramp through mud and cut her way through dense undergrowth, however.*

Was Mirar aware of this? He had always been attracted to cities — to the bustle of crowds. A memory rose of a conversation she'd had with Auraya.

'*I thought you didn't like him.*'

Auraya had smiled. '*I never said I didn't like him.*'

Emerahl sighed. She knew there was always a chance that like could become love. She'd seen it happen often enough. Not that it *would*, but Emerahl was always going to wonder if she had ruined that chance for Mirar by telling him about Auraya's affair with Chaia. *And now that I've met Auraya I'm no longer opposed to the idea of Mirar and her together.*

What was done was done. Mirar was resilient. Better for him to know the quick pain of truth than the ongoing pain of a long-held false hope. Turning around, she retraced her steps and began searching for a safer route.

PART TWO

CHAPTER 16

When the horizon had taken on the form of an undulating shadow the previous day, Auraya had assumed she and the Siyee were headed toward low hills. Now it appeared the smooth, gentle lines of these landforms were much larger than she had first thought. Used to the jagged peaks of Si, she did not realise these were the mountains of western Sennon until their scale became apparent.

She could feel the excitement of the Siyee. They were looking forward to leaving the desert and just as their water carrier was burdened with a heavy load, so was she. Extra skins were tied to her back and, with Mischief safely curled up in her pack, she felt as if she was covered by a heavy, lumpy blanket.

The desert had served up more difficulties than they had imagined it could. At first they had flown directly across it, but a dust storm had blown them back toward the coast. Since the Siyee could not carry much, they relied on finding water along the way. Mischief had shown them where to dig for water a few times and they encountered a lonely well once, but these had not been enough.

They dared not land at any landwalker settlements. The Sennon emperor's policy of allowing the practice of any religion in his country meant that Pentadrians could be living in the desert villages. If they were, a group of Siyee warriors seen heading south was sure to be noted and reported to the Pentadrian leaders. Even if there were no Pentadrians in the villages, it was still possible that an ordinary Sennon villager would decide there was profit to be gained in delivering the news to the nearest Pentadrian.

Most settlements were on the coast, so the Siyee kept inland. They had expected to find the occasional river but had encountered only one thread of muddy, near-undrinkable water. It probably flowed cleanly at other times, but in the middle of summer it had dwindled to a sluggish stream. Auraya hadn't visited Sennon before, so she could not advise them. All she could do was fly back to the closest water source each morning to refill their skins.

The mountains ahead gave the Siyee hope, but Auraya wasn't so optimistic. They associated mountains with water, but that was not always true. These peaks were well eroded, yet it looked as if rain hadn't fallen here in centuries. The sparse vegetation was bleached a pale yellow. There wasn't a hint of green anywhere.

The group had begun to descend, though no order had been given, toward the closest of these sprawling mountains. At the base was the winding indentation of a dead river, heading toward the ocean to their right. Between it and the mountain, the land had eroded into terraces.

Then Auraya felt amazement from one of the Siyee. Seeking his mind, she read that he thought the terraces were not natural. She looked closer and realised that he was right. There were roads as well, and tiny shapes that might be the remains of ruined buildings. The spread of them across the side of the mountain suggested a city. A long-dead city.

Other Siyee noticed the ancient metropolis and pointed it out to fellow warriors. To her amusement, the sight made them intensely curious. They wanted to land and explore. She watched Sreil consider.

Exploration of ruins isn't the purpose of our journey, he thought, *but if a city once stood here then there must have been water about. Perhaps only the river, but those terraces look like they might have been fields and how would they have brought water up to them? Perhaps there once was a spring up higher . . . well, there's just as much chance of finding water here as anywhere else . . .*

At his order to head for the city, the mood of the other Siyee brightened. While the desert tested their bodies, it offered little to occupy their minds. The whistling games they had played at the beginning of the journey had been abandoned when their mouths had dried out with thirst.

Auraya looked at the Siyee priest, Teel. He did not wear the circ as it hampered flying, but instead wore a smaller circle of white material tied closely about his throat. In her opinion, he had been prematurely ordained. He was inexperienced and had less grasp of magic than an initiate. Yet the gods had given him the task of reporting to Juran every day, not Auraya. She felt vaguely irritated by that. She was a former White and the Siyee's protector. But he was a Siyee and she a landwalker, and that must matter more.

Of course it doesn't, she thought. *It's just another way the gods are demonstrating their distrust of me.*

Searching the magic around her, she was relieved to see none of the gods were present. Though Teel hadn't been given specific orders, she suspected the only reason this young man had been ordained early was so that a priest could keep an eye on her during this mission.

Yesterday Auraya had heard a Siyee wonder aloud why the gods hadn't ensured there would be clean water for them. Another had muttered annoyance that the gods didn't at least guide them to sources. A third had observed that they probably would have died here if Auraya hadn't accompanied them.

Teel had overheard and quietly told them the gods were not their servants. Auraya had smiled at that, but she suspected the gods simply couldn't do either. They weren't aware of anything in the world that wasn't observed by a human or an animal, so if no human or animal was aware of sources of water nearby, or how to get to them, then neither were the gods.

The only humans who could have given the Siyee guidance, Sennon guides, couldn't fly. Even if the White had trusted one enough to send him or her to meet and advise the Siyee, he would not have arrived in time to help them. The distance was too great.

One of the Siyee whistled their signal for 'Tracks!' and Auraya followed the direction of his gaze. A line of stirred sand led from the city to the river then along the dry watercourse toward the sea. Or in the other direction. Perhaps the city was already host to passing visitors.

It was a good sign, though. No traveller would ascend into those terraces unless there was a good reason, and water was a likely good reason.

She caught up with Sreil.

'Shall I check if they're still there?'

He whistled an assent. Auraya propelled herself into a dive, heading through the dry air toward the tracks. She felt Mischief stir awake.

The footprints wound along the river through strange pinnacles of rock that turned out to be buried towers, then up to the beginning of a road. There they grew difficult to follow, as the roads were not always covered in sand. She flew about slowly as if searching.

Which was all for show. She could sense no minds in the city, but she couldn't tell the Siyee that without revealing to the gods that she had developed the telepathic Gift they had previously given to her when she was a White.

Flying back to the Siyee, she whistled the signal that all was safe. The Siyee circled around the city before landing, a cautious habit rather than any distrust of her assessment. Once on the ground, Sreil ordered them to set out in pairs to explore and search for water. Auraya shrugged off her pack and opened it. Mischief blinked in the sudden bright light.

She hadn't wanted to take him on this journey, but couldn't bring herself to force him to stay behind. Since she had returned to the Open he was constantly by her side, and had grown distressed whenever she made him stay behind in the bower. No longer able to sense her mind, being near her was the only way he could reassure himself that she was still alive. Fortunately he was content to remain curled up in the pack during flight, and he had proved himself both useful and entertaining to the Siyee.

Whispering in his ear, she sent him a mental impression of water. His nose twitched and when she set him down he trotted away. She followed.

The sunlight beat down relentlessly and reflected off stone to assail her with heat from all directions. She realised after a few turns that Teel had chosen to follow her, and she resigned herself to the inevitability of being followed everywhere by the priest.

'How old do you think this place is?' he asked after a while.

She shrugged. 'I have no idea.'

'Look.' He walked up to a large stone in a wall and pointed to markings. 'Can you read this?'

'No.'

'You understand many languages, don't you?'

'Yes. That doesn't mean I can read them, though.'

'I should copy this,' he said. 'If the priests in the Open don't know what it says they might know someone who does.'

As he drew a scrap of leather out of a pouch she smiled, but her amusement quickly faded. He was a scholar at heart, not a warrior. She would not find it easy to forgive herself if he died in this attack, though she couldn't be completely sure he was only here because of her.

Mischief had disappeared, not caring whether the priest followed or not. Auraya hurried around a corner and came upon a large archway that looked as if it had been carved into solid rock. The sound of her footsteps in the entrance echoed in a way that suggested a large space inside.

'Owaya?'

'I'm coming, Mischief,' she replied.

As she stepped out of the sunlight her eyes began to adjust. A short corridor led to a huge hall. At the far end an enormous figure was just visible in the gloom. A statue. She shivered at the size of it.

Drawing magic, she created a spark of light and sent it up toward the ceiling. Brightening it, she felt a thrill of wonder as the statue was illuminated. It had a muscular male body, but the face was a flat disk with one enormous lidless eye. Mischief stared up at it with wide eyes.

One of the old gods, she thought. *Long dead*.

She heard a gasp behind her and turned to see Teel gazing at the statue in horror. A look of disgust crossed his face.

'Things like that should be destroyed,' he said.

She stared at him, disturbed. The god was long dead. What threat did the statue hold now? To destroy something so amazing would be spiteful and pointless.

'Perhaps,' she said slowly, 'such things should be kept to remind us of the Age of the Many, and of the chaos that enslaved mortal man until the Circle saved us.'

He looked at her blankly, then became thoughtful. 'If the gods willed it to remain, I suppose it could be used to shock those with rebellious hearts.'

Auraya suppressed a sigh. There were zealots and fanatics in any race. It looked as if the gods had found one among the Siyee.

The buzz of thoughts at the edge of her mind suddenly grew louder. Other Siyee had found water – a great pool of it deep within another hall like this one. She let her light die and called to Mischief. A little shadow bounded out of the darkness into her arms and climbed up onto her shoulders. Auraya walked past the priest into the sunlight.

'Let's see how the others have fared, shall we?' she tossed over her shoulder.

Rising from his seat, Danjin walked to the narrow window and looked out at what served as Dunwayan cosmopolitan life. Below him servants and traders hurried to finish their tasks before the night curfew, while warriors strode about with the confidence and arrogance of men who considered their position of power in society as their natural right. The stone houses they lived among were built in an orderly pattern between rings of high walls. Beyond the last wall he could see the Dey River winding away toward the distant ocean.

Chon was a fortress, but as the largest fortress in Dunway it also had the role of administrative capital. To get there, Danjin and Ella had sailed to the mouth of the Dey River where they were transported by barge to the fortress. Reaching Chon, they had been greeted with typical Dunwayan formality – brief and efficient – and were taken to the quarters the White always occupied during visits: a wing of the innermost part of the fortress.

The rooms were small and the walls bare stone. Furniture

was simple and heavy, yet the rugs on the floors and walls were colourful and finely made, if a bit crude in design. Most depicted famous battles and Dunwayan leaders and warriors, always watched over by the god Lore.

I-Portak, the Dunwayan ruler, was neither hereditary king or elected counsellor. Danjin had never met anyone who knew all the complexities of the Dunwayan method of selecting their ruler. It seemed that anyone could declare themselves ruler, but holding the position depended on the agreement of important warrior clans. The claimant could be challenged by a warrior willing to fight for the position, yet if the challenger won and the warrior clans didn't approve of him, he could not keep the position.

Despite this, when the last ruler had died the process of selecting a replacement had been free of challenge or argument. I-Orm's son had taken his father's place without a murmur of dissent from his people. At least, Danjin hadn't heard of any. The Dunwayans were not ones to complain loudly. When the likely response to rebellion was a challenge to the death, one tended to keep one's opinions to oneself unless sure of winning.

'The light is dimming,' Ella said. He turned to see her sigh and reluctantly put her spindle aside. 'Another day gone and still no progress. How long do you think it will take before they let me do my job?'

'Subtract their respect for the gods and the White from the depth of their pride, add their eagerness for us to leave, and take some lingering resentment for the White's attempt to dissolve the sorcerer Scalar over a decade ago, and you'll have the moment they offer their reluctant cooperation.'

Ella chuckled ruefully. 'You told me they were a straight-forward and economical people.'

'Compared to other Northern Ithanian peoples, they are.

You have to let the clans try to find the culprits for you. It's a matter of honour.' Danjin moved away from the window. The air was quickly growing chilly. The Dunwayans believed heating and window coverings made one weak, that sickness was caused by too little action, food, sex, or either sleeping too much or too little.

Hmm. Maybe we can use that to our advantage, he thought. *We could say Ella doesn't want to remain cooped up and inactive too long lest she fall sick. But they might decide the solution to that is to send her out to one of the female warrior clans for a few bouts of fighting practice. I doubt she'd appreciate that.*

'Well, at least I'm getting something done,' Ella murmured, looking at the basket beside her. Most of the fleece was gone, and the thread she had produced had been twisted together into yarn and wound into neat balls. Danjin had found the deft movements of her spinning and twirling a little hypnotic to watch. He had no idea what she would do with it next.

During the day they were mostly left to themselves, but every night they visited local clan leaders or dignitaries of other countries. Ella took the opportunity to read the minds of everyone she encountered, including the servants.

'They're more like slaves than servants,' she had told Danjin. 'All they get for their work is food and a roof over their heads. They can't marry and raise a family without their master's approval, and their children work from the moment they can be put to use. Nobody taught me about this when I learned about Dunway as a priestess.'

He had to agree about the servants' lives, but reminded her that the Dunwayans had lived this way since the god Lore had adopted them as his own people. 'And how servants live is hardly a subject likely to capture the attention of a class of young initiates,' he had added.

She had shaken her head at that. 'Injustice always captures

the attention of the young,' she said. 'But as we get older we discover how difficult it is to change the world, and we learn to turn our eyes away from what we can't fix until we no longer see injustice at all.'

'Not all of us,' he told her. 'Some of us still look for ways to make improvements.'

Ella rose and moved to the window. 'The man we'll be seeing tonight is well known for his cruelty toward his servants.'

She stared out silently, her eyebrows knitted together. He suspected she was scanning the minds of those below and said nothing, not wanting to distract her.

A knock came at the door.

'Gillen Shieldarm, Ambassador of Hania, has come to fetch Ellareen of the White and Danjin Spear, Adviser to Ellareen of the White, and take them to the house of Gim, Talm of Rommel, Ka-Lem of the Nimler clan,' a voice bellowed.

Danjin smiled and walked to the door. The habit of yelling such a greeting from behind a door was Dunwayan, but the greeting had been spoken in Hanian. He opened the door to find Gillen grinning widely.

'You can just knock,' Danjin said. 'We won't think less of you.'

'Ah, but that wouldn't be as amusing,' the ambassador replied. He looked over Danjin's shoulder. 'Good evening, Ellareen of the White.'

'Good evening, Fa-Shieldarm,' she replied. 'We have been waiting for you.'

He gestured to the corridor behind him. 'I would be most honoured to guide you to the abode of our guest.'

'Thank you.'

She stepped past Danjin. Closing the door, Danjin followed as she and Gillen started down the corridor.

Soon they had left the wing and emerged into the chill

evening air. Each section of the city was separated by a well-guarded gate. Each time they reached one of these Gillen produced an amulet which the guards examined before they ordered muscular servants to haul open the gates. After passing through three gates, they arrived at a stone house distinguished from its neighbours by a large shield carved into the door, painted in bright colours.

'The house of Gim, Talm of Rommel, Ka-Lem of the Nimler clan,' Gillen told them. He knocked, then bellowed their names and purpose.

The door creaked open. A servant bowed then silently gestured into the room. Ella stepped inside, followed by Danjin and Gillen.

They entered a large hall furnished with a huge wooden table already crowded with men, women and children. If it were not for their smiles and laughter, the tattooed faces might have made it a ghoulish scene. The patterns accentuated their expressions, so that a frown looked like a scowl, and a smile a grin.

Danjin recognised a few of the people and guessed that most present were of Gim's clan. The servant hurried away to speak to a large Dunwayan man at the head of the table. This was Gim, a proud and arrogant man even by Dunwayan standards.

The man stood and beckoned to them with expansive gestures.

'Ellareen of the White. Welcome to my home. Come join me.'

Gim waved at the people sitting around him. At once they shuffled along the bench seats to make room. Ella sat down with dignity and accepted a goblet of fwa, the local liquor. Danjin squeezed in beside her.

Danjin sipped his own drink only enough to, hopefully, satisfy his host. He listened as Ella and Gim talked, recalling details about the clan that he had learned before and after they had arrived in Chon. He also kept his eyes on the other people at the table, aware that he was an extra pair of eyes to Ella.

At some signal from Gim, servants began to bring plates of food out to the table. Gim sliced a haunch off a roasted yern with a knife shaped like a miniature sword, and then the other guests began to help themselves and chatter. An argument broke out between two boys, one of whom had taken an entire girri for himself. When the boys began to shove each other one of the men got up, hauled them both out of a door and told a servant not to let them in until they'd fought it out. Returning to the table, he took the girri for himself.

Danjin then felt Ella's elbow press against his arm. He realised he'd lost track of her conversation with Gim.

'. . . know the Pentadrian way of life appeals to many of your people,' she said.

Gim's eyebrows rose. 'What is so appealing about the way they live?'

'Only criminals are enslaved there.'

The clan leader frowned at her. She shrugged.

'That is how they see it.'

'Are you saying we may have spies among our servants?'

'Probably.'

He glared at the servants in the room. 'I shall question them all.'

She waved a hand dismissively. 'That would disrupt your household unnecessarily. A clever spy deflects attention from himself to others when he knows there's a hunt on, and you could end up executing innocent and useful people. Better to set a trap.'

Gim grunted his reluctant agreement. 'What do you suggest?'

'Obviously we can't discuss the details here,' she said,

smiling. 'Someone who knows your household well would be better able to suggest an effective trap than I. You must have a few servants that you trust?'

The clan leader scowled, then changed the subject. As the night grew older, Danjin was sure he detected a change in Ella. She seemed more genuinely cheerful than she usually was during these dinners.

:I am, her familiar voice said in his mind. *I'd never give Gim the satisfaction of knowing this, but his habit of treating his servants badly has worked in our favour. There are plenty of Pentadrian sympathisers here, and more than one of them has decided it's time to make his escape. Tomorrow we shall see who aids them.*

Progress at last, he thought. *No wonder she looks happier.*

Gim belched loudly, then called for more fwa.

:Yes. And I have to admit, I'm finding Gim more entertaining than I thought. He's every bit the clichéd warrior brute Dunwayans are made out to be. Eating with his hands, talking with his mouth full, making crude jokes and drinking too much. What next?

He'll probably call in the dancing girls, or some wench to fondle.

:I don't think even he would . . . oh.

Danjin smiled as two men walked into the room playing pipes and drums, followed by four Dunwayan women wearing a lot of jewellery, but not much more.

At least that answers one question that's been on my mind, Danjin thought wryly. *Their tattoos really do go all the way down.*

This time Ella's elbow somehow managed to reach his ribs, and with considerably more force than before.

CHAPTER 17

The rosy light of dawn tinted the sky beyond Reivan's window when she woke. She felt a mingled relief and disappointment. Relief that she hadn't slept late again, but disappointment that she didn't have cause to.

Rising, she went to the basin of water and washed herself down. The moisture on her skin was pleasantly cool, but dried quickly. Soon she would be sweating in the heat of another midsummer day, but at least she would stink of fresh sweat rather than stale. She wished she could say the same of the merchants and courtiers that she had to deal with.

Dressing in her robe, she left her rooms and started for her office, pausing only to tell a domestic to have food brought to her. Several Servants were about. They nodded respectfully at Reivan as she passed.

Suddenly her sandal loosened and nearly tripped her. She stopped and steadied herself with one hand on a wall while she inspected it. A strap had come apart from the sole.

'. . . why he chose her. She's not beautiful, or even pretty,' a voice said.

Realising that the voice belonged to one of two female Servants she had just passed, she paused to listen.

'She's supposed to be smart. Former Thinker, they say. Maybe they play mind games while they're . . . you know.'

'I don't want to think about it.'

Reivan found herself smiling. So the other Servants had heard about Nekaun's nocturnal visits to her rooms. Were these two jealous?

'From what I hear, his attention is hard to keep. He gets bored easily.'

'She's wise to keep it quiet, then. It'll be humiliating enough when he moves on. Wouldn't want the whole Sanctuary to know, if I were her.'

'The whole Sanctuary does know.'

Reivan felt her stomach sink. She drew off the sandal and took a few steps, no longer wanting to eavesdrop. But with only one sandal, walking was awkward and ungainly. She stopped to take off the other.

'. . . rather have him for a little while than never,' one of the Servants said.

'Me, too.'

That ought to have cheered her, but it didn't. Her stomach sank further. *He's been visiting me for months now,* she thought. *If he was only doing it for entertainment, surely he would have grown bored after a few nights? I'm not exactly a goddess of the bedroom.*

Days. Weeks. Months. Years. What did it matter? He was immortal, powerful and beautiful. She knew she could not expect to hold his attention forever, yet she could not imagine life being any different than how it was now. Sometimes she struggled to comprehend how she had existed before.

I've never been this happy. Or this anxious. I must be in love.

With sandals in one hand, she continued on. When the next domestic appeared she stopped him, gave him the sandals and told him to arrange for someone to bring her a new pair. He made the sign of the star and hurried away.

Though she tried to turn her thoughts to the work ahead, the words of the Servants kept creeping into her mind.

'He gets bored easily.'

Maybe Nekaun was growing bored with her. He hadn't visited last night and the previous evening his visit had been brief.

Too brief, she thought. *He seemed distracted, as if his mind was elsewhere and only his body was present.*

'Companion Reivan.'

She stopped and turned, surprised to see Imenja striding toward her.

'Second Voice,' she replied, making the sign of the star.

Imenja smiled. 'Come with me. I want to ask you something.'

They were only a short distance from Reivan's office, yet Imenja walked to a stairwell and began to climb. Reivan followed, conscious that her feet were still bare.

They climbed up into one of the towers in the lower levels of the Sanctuary. The stairs led through a hole in the floor of the topmost room. Open arches gave a view all around.

Imenja moved to the side facing the city.

'We shouldn't be overheard here,' she murmured. She turned to face Reivan. 'Nekaun left early this morning.'

'Left?' Reivan repeated. 'To go where?'

'I don't know,' Imenja replied. 'Nobody does. I was hoping you would.'

Reivan shook her head. 'I haven't seen him since the night before last.'

The Second Voice smiled and turned to regard the view.

'Well then. He's gone and left us all wondering.'

'The other Voices?'

Imenja shook her head. 'They're just as perplexed as I am.'

Reivan looked away. 'He was a bit distracted the night before last.' As she said it, she felt her face warming. 'He didn't tell me he was planning to leave.' She felt a stab of hurt. Surely he could have confided in her. Didn't he know he could trust her?

But he couldn't tell her anything he didn't want the other Voices to read from her mind.

Imenja sighed. 'I guess we'll find out what this is about when he's ready to tell us.' She shrugged and moved away from the arches. 'I have to go, but I'll see you this afternoon.'

'Yes.' Reivan managed a smile. 'Hopefully I won't have too many matters to bother you with.'

Imenja's nose wrinkled. 'I think that's what annoys me most. He's off having some adventure while we're stuck here doing the boring work.' She started to descend the stairs.

When she had gone, Reivan looked out over the city.

So he's left, she thought. *He could have left me a message. Even a cryptic one. Just . . . something..*

And nobody knows how long he'll be gone. She felt a pang of longing and fear. *That's just what having a Voice as a lover entails*, she told herself. *There'll always be secrets and mysteries. Unexplained disappearances.*

Distracted lovemaking.

She sighed and turned away from the view. Nothing but the return of Nekaun was going to make her feel better, so she may as well lose herself in work.

Spice Merchant Chem, also known as Servant Chemalya, counted up the tally on his clay tablet and marked in the total. Sitting back in his chair, he smiled. Business was good. Dunwayans had taken to the hotter spices of his homeland like all competitive, pain-loving warriors should. His spiced version of the local brew, fwa, had brought him profits far higher than his expectations. Every day the door of his shop squeaked continually with clan servants come to buy more wares.

It had taken a while for the Dunwayans to take to the spices. Chemalya had made no secret of the fact they were from Southern Ithania. That made them 'Pentadrian' goods, which gave them the taint of the enemy. It was said Dunwayan warriors loved their god, Lore, more than their own fathers. This was not surprising, since the god had apparently arranged for every aspect of Dunwayan life to favour them. They would not touch anything associated with the enemy.

At least, they didn't at first. Then the allure of exotic goods with dangerous associations brought the first customers. The heat of the spices took those first young Dunwayans by surprise. Soon they were daring their friends to try it. When one spiked a mug of fwa with the spice, they discovered that the two substances complemented each other perfectly.

So Chemalya began selling pre-spiced fwa. It gained popularity so quickly he began to run out of spice. He ordered more and raised his prices. When two servants had bid on the last jar of his first shipment, the loser had looked so dismayed at his defeat Chemalya had offered the man a consolatory drink. Soon he was regaled with tales of the brutal treatment of servants.

Listening patiently, he realised his secret task was going to be easier than he had first thought. His future converts were all around him, and their masters had prepared them for their new faith better than any Pentadrian could have.

He had sent the servant away with a small jar of spice he'd been keeping for himself in the hope this would fend off the beating the man was expecting. From then on, he was generous to all the servants who came to buy wares. He told them the tale of half-truths that had allowed him to set up shop in Dunway – that his mother had been a Dunwayan servant woman who had run away to Sennon (true) and married a Murian trader (false – she'd become a whore), who had employed their son as an assistant (delivery boy). Taking over the business when the Murian died (true – but it had been arranged by the Pentadrians), Chemalya had come to Dunway out of a curiosity to see his mother's homeland (false – his mother's hatred for her people had killed all curiosity years ago).

To his surprise, he had enjoyed his time in Dunway so far. Not all warriors were cruel and stupid. Some treated their servants as if they were family. There was a tradition of poetry of surprising beauty and their honest and open attitude toward physical lust was refreshing compared to the coyness and embarrassment of Southern Ithanians.

He wasn't going to be as glad to leave as he'd thought he'd be, and now that one of the White was here he was expecting that moment to arrive any day now. The thought filled him with sadness and a little resentment.

He looked down at the tablet.

Maybe that's more to do with the profit I'm making. At times like these I have to remind myself that I'm here to serve the gods. Riches will not get me a place with them, when my soul is released from my body.

The door creaked. Chemalya looked up and smiled as he saw it was one of his latest recruits: Ton, a servant of the Nimler clan. It would not be long before he helped this one 'escape' to the south.

Chemalya put his tablet under the bench, out of sight. Ton stepped forward hesitantly, wringing his hands.

'That arrangement you talked about,' the man said, his voice quivering. 'Can it happen today?'

Surprised, Chemalya looked at the man closely. Ton always looked a little strained and anxious. Had he finally been pushed too far by his master, or was it something more serious?

'It can,' Chemalya told the man. 'What has happened?'

'The White. She was at dinner last night. Said there were spies in the household and that Gim should set a trap.' He reached across the bench and gripped Chemalya's arm. 'If I go back he'll find me. He'll kill me. I have to go.'

Chemalya patted the man's shoulder. 'And you will. What did you come here for, and what else are you buying today?'

'Spiced fwa. Grain. Oil.' The man let go of Chemalya's arm and drew a pouch of coins out of his shirt.

'Good. Tell me the names of the shops and I'll send someone to meet you. He will take you out of the city.'

'Where?'

'I don't know. My friends and I took the precaution of knowing only as much as we needed, in case our minds were read. You have to trust me.'

Ton nodded and shrugged. 'It's a risk. I have to take it.'

'You will be the last for a while,' Chemalya told him.

The man looked stricken. 'But . . . my wife and children? You said they—'

'Will escape later. They will, once the White has left and we can set things up again.' He paused. 'I may need your help with that.'

Ton straightened. 'You'll have it.'

'Thank you. Now you had better tell me which shops you plan to visit.'

After Ton had left, Chemalya called one of the street boys into the shop and paid him a coin to deliver an order for five and a half barrels of fwa. He scratched Ton's name and the shops he planned to visit onto a scrap of parchment and gave it to the boy.

Then he locked the shop door and sat down behind the bench. Closing his eyes, he pressed a hand to the star pendant under his tunic and sent out a call.

:Deekan.

After a moment the Dedicated Servant that had trained Chemalya replied.

:*Chemalya? What is it?*

He told her what Ton had said.

:*Should I close the shop and leave?*

:*I will seek permission.*

There was a long silence in which Chemalya heard knocking on the shop door. He ignored it.

:*No*, Deekan's reply came. *Continue sending converts south.*

:*And if the White finds me?*

:*She will not learn any more than you know.* Deekan paused. *I'm sorry, Chemalya. Those are Nekaun's orders. He must have good reason to want you there.*

Chemalya sighed and tried to suppress a feeling of rising panic.

:*And I will obey them*, he replied.

:*Good luck.*

Opening his eyes, Chemalya looked around the shop. When the White found him – and he was not foolish enough to think she wouldn't – he would go from rich trader to imprisoned enemy. He doubted prisoners survived long in Dunwayan jails.

For a moment he considered running away. But the price of survival would be to betray the gods. He would not gamble that losing one's soul was less terrible than capture by the White.

Another knock came from the door. He sighed and hauled himself to his feet.

At least I saved a few poor souls along the way. He smiled. *And mother will be proud of that.*

The wide, interconnected wooden porches of Kave were crowded but quiet. People sat on reed chairs in the shade, fanning themselves. Decorated fans were the height of fashion this year.

Mirar had noted some truly gaudy ones in the hands of women dressed with equal flamboyance.

The men, women and children of this wealthy district of the city fell silent as he strode past and he sensed intense curiosity. Though he still dressed in the same worn Dreamweaver clothing, somehow they always recognised him. Kave was not a large city. Just as all the houses were connected so were the people, and gossip travelled as quickly as traffic. Within a few days of revealing his true identity to Tintel and the Kave Dreamweavers, the news had spread throughout the city.

Dreamweavers were even more effectively linked. The news spread much faster by dream links and he had been contacted by Dreamweaver Elder Arleej, in Sennon, the next night. She had demanded to know why he hadn't warned her of his intentions.

He smiled. *I like her. She's not intimidated by me at all. Pity the local Dreamweavers can't see that. They might get over their awe of me a little faster.*

Tintel was the exception, though he still had to stop her from deferring to him on occasion. The only time he accepted it was at times like this, when she called upon him to deal with seriously ill or injured patients.

The murmur of many subdued voices reached him from somewhere ahead. Turning a corner, he saw a house and the porches around it crowded with people. They fell silent and turned to stare at him. The servant that had fetched and guided him through the city hurried across an ornately carved bridge and disappeared among the crowd.

Mirar strode after him, the people moving back as he passed. Stepping through a door into a sparsely furnished room, he stopped to take in the scene within. A boy lay on the floor, unconscious. His parents knelt beside him, weeping and clinging to each other. Tintel stood over them. She looked up at Mirar as he entered, and beckoned.

'What happened?' he asked as he moved to the boy's side and crouched down.

'A fall,' Tintel said. 'His spine is broken and his ribs and skull are cracked.'

'They laid bets on who could leap across the gap,' the mother said in a small voice. 'He didn't make it.'

Mirar guessed the gap was the space between the house and a neighbour's. Yet another foolish game between boys. He laid a hand on the boy's throat and sent his mind into the young body. Tintel's assessment was right, but didn't describe the full damage. Organs had been torn and bruised and the boy was bleeding internally. He was fortunate he was not already dead.

Drawing magic, Mirar set to work.

He lost himself in the binding of flesh and bone. Time ceased to matter. It was good to be able to do this without pretending to take longer, and use more effort. As the restoration drew close to finishing he began to catch flashes of memory from the boy's mind. He saw a familiar story forming. The wager had been an imitation of the father's many bets, as well as an attempt to gain money, spurred by the recent selling of the family's furniture to meet debts.

Completely healing an injury caused by foolishness sometimes did more harm than good. He had seen people, convinced they could recover from any injury, court danger over and over again until they harmed themselves once more, or worse.

In this case, the parents would benefit as much from the boy spending a few weeks healing as the boy would. *Who says we Dreamweavers don't make judgements?* Mirar thought. He felt a quiet amusement. *I did.*

But no ordinary Dreamweaver could do what he had just

done. They didn't have to face the consequences of perfect healing. He left the boy with enough bruising and soreness to give him cause to rethink any future wagers, then drew his mind away.

As Mirar leaned back the boy's mother called her son's name. The boy's eyes opened and he began to grumble about his hurts. Mirar advised rest and gentle exercise. He accepted the parents' grateful thanks, but when the father offered money Mirar gave the man a direct stare. The father flushed and looked away.

It was dark outside when he and Tintel walked back to the Dreamweaver House. The porches and bridges were alight with lamps, turning Kave into a glittering, suspended city. Tintel said nothing and he sensed she was not bothered by his silence. She was content.

And me? He considered. *I am not unhappy.* Abruptly he thought of Auraya and felt a small pang of sadness. *No point mourning what could have been. Besides, I caused her enough grief by simply being someone I wasn't, even if I didn't mean to.*

Now he was himself again. Completely. As they arrived at the Dreamweaver House he stepped forward to open the door for Tintel. She smiled crookedly at his manners.

'Thank you. Smells like we're just in time for dinner,' she said.

The hall was full of voices and the aroma of cooking. The chatter diminished as he entered, but as he took a seat beside Tintel it returned to a normal level. Despite this, he felt the Dreamweavers' suppressed excitement and nervousness. A particularly strong emotion of mixed fear and longing drew his attention to one side. His eyes met Dardel's. He smiled and she quickly looked down at her plate.

She had stopped visiting his room the night she had learned who he was, too overwhelmed by the revelation that her fantasy was real to even speak to him. He had hesitated to tell her that she was still welcome in case she thought she had no choice but to accept his invitation. It was a disadvantage of reclaiming his identity that Emerahl had found immensely amusing.

The door to the House opened and a group of young Dreamweavers arrived. The room quietened again as attention shifted to the newcomers.

'I have news,' one of the young men announced. 'The Trials for the new High Chieftain will begin tomorrow.'

At once the mood of the room changed to one of anticipation. Mirar had heard of the ritual for choosing a new leader, a spectacle that came once or twice in a lifetime. It seemed all Dekkans wanted to see it. Everyone turned to regard Tintel expectantly.

Good, Mirar thought. *They're looking to her for leadership at last.*

'I wouldn't dream of stopping anyone from attending,' Tintel said, rolling her eyes. 'But I would appreciate it if a few of you volunteered to remain here, in case our services are needed.'

Heads nodded, and one or two offered to stay. Talk turned to the likely contestants. Mirar listened closely, intrigued by this method of making a great game out of the selection of a ruler.

'You'll be going?' Tintel asked him quietly.

He smiled. 'Yes – unless you have other uses for me tomorrow?'

'No,' she said. 'I can't help but think of it as your first public appearance. How will the Voice attending the Trials react to you, I wonder?'

'I doubt he or she will notice me at all,' he said, chuckling. 'I have no intention of dressing up for the occasion or strutting about asserting myself.'

The corner of her mouth twitched into a half smile. 'No, I don't imagine you have. I have to admit, I'm relieved to hear it. You announcing your presence here when Dekkar was leaderless did give a few people cause for concern.'

Mirar sobered. He hadn't thought of that. *It's always the way. You think you've considered all the possible problems an action might cause, but miss the most obvious one.*

'They have nothing to fear,' he told her. 'From what I've heard, the contestants have to run around Kave seven times. I'm a little old for . . .'

The table fell abruptly silent. People had turned to look at the main door. Following the gaze of his fellow Dreamweavers, Mirar saw a man in a fancy uniform standing at the end of the hall.

The man cleared his throat.

'Is the sorcerer known as Mirar here?'

All heads turned to Mirar. He rose. 'I am he.'

The man strode around the table and bowed formally. 'I bring an invitation to you from Fourth Voice Genza, Holy Servant of the Five, to join her in witnessing the Chieftain Trials tomorrow. I am to ask if you are free to attend.'

Mirar felt a muscle in his belly tighten. *A meeting with one of the Voices. I should have expected this.* He could sense nothing but nervousness and curiosity from the messenger.

'I will be honoured to attend,' he said.

'A servant will come here at an hour past dawn to escort you to the ceremony.' The messenger bowed again, then strode out of the room, leaving it quiet but full of both excitement and fear.

CHAPTER 18

The caravan leader, Korikana – known as Kori to the cara-
vaneers – was a small man. One of his legs was shorter
than the other, so he walked with a jerky, pronounced limp.
He was more at home on his arem than on his feet, and doted
on the creature so much it was clear he regarded it as a
companion as much as a beast of burden.

During the day Kori travelled up and down the line of
carts and platten, checking that passengers and goods were
in order. Two days ago he had pulled up beside the platten
Emerahl had bought a seat on and pointed to a dark line that
had appeared on the horizon.

'Hannaya!' he had declared before riding on.

Now she witnessed the same scene repeated. This time,
however, his finger directed her attention toward what the
dark line had become: a high cliff. Or, more specifically, a
section of the rock wall.

She hadn't had more than the occasional glimpse of it in
the last day and she couldn't see much now. The country she
travelled through was covered in strange trees. They varied
in size and also appeared to come in a few similar types. The
largest had either a single or several trunks springing from
its base. Sometimes they were straight, sometimes they twisted

sinuously. Their bark could be smooth or rough, pale or dark. All were remarkable in that they had no branches. At the top of each trunk was mop of large, stringy leaves of varying colours. Some bore odd fruit that was popular with the locals. Its flesh was sweet and dense. Others bore richly flavoured berries that could be eaten fresh or dried. Another smaller variety produced spicy seeds. Emerahl could see potential for cures in the seeds and berries.

Another common variety of local plants were the ones with sharp prickles. They grew in all kinds of bulbous shapes, from tiny stone-like ones that quickly discouraged any traveller from walking barefoot or sitting down without first checking the ground, to enormous spheres twice as tall as a man with spines as long as her arm. Most varieties were edible, apparently, and Kori had demonstrated this once by slicing open a head-sized plant with a sword and scooping out the surprisingly sweet, watery contents for them to taste.

The platten turned and Emerahl realised the road they had been following since the coast had met a wider thoroughfare. People, animals and vehicles travelled back and forth on this new road. Looking up, she caught her breath.

So that's what Kori's all excited about, she thought.

The cliff was now in full view, and the sight was like nothing she'd ever seen. The high rock face had been carved with tier upon tier of windows and balconies. Near the centre, enormous arched windows suggested grand halls within. Toward the edges, smaller ones hinted at more humble abodes. Smoke wisped from what looked like horizontal chimneys and water cascaded out of the mouths of carved faces.

'The palace!' Kori said to her as he rode past, gesturing grandly.

It was both fantastic and ridiculous. In one place the face of the cliff had collapsed, revealing abandoned rooms within.

Emerahl wondered how far the tunnelling went into the rock face and if any other collapses were hidden within. She knew she wouldn't feel completely at ease in this city; she would always be expecting the ceiling to fall on her, or the floor to drop away.

As the caravan drew closer to the cliff face, Emerahl was relieved to see plenty of buildings at the palace's base. The citizens of Hannaya didn't just live in the rock wall. More buildings filled the gap between the rock wall and the river.

She regarded the boats on the river wistfully; she had wanted to buy a place on one, but the fee had been too expensive. Kori halted the caravan in an area alongside the river where several other collections of carts and platten had camped. She paid him the final quarter of his fee and asked where she should look for accommodation. He drew a symbol in the dust, a star inside a circle, then gave her directions. When she was sure she had memorised the instructions well enough, she bade him farewell and set off in the direction he'd indicated.

She found the accommodation easily and was amused to discover it was a place for women travellers run by Pentadrian Servants. They gave her a bed in a room with three other middle-aged women, who appeared to be travelling together. The women tried to strike up a conversation, but Emerahl pretended she didn't know the local language well enough to hold one. Which was partly true. Though The Twins had taught her Murian during her long journey, the speed at which the locals spoke made it difficult to understand at times.

She set a shield of magic about her bag and lay down on her bed. It didn't take long before she was sliding into sleep – it was more of a struggle stopping herself lapsing into full unconsciousness. She had been travelling continually for months and craved a good long rest.

No time for that yet, she thought. *But I don't think I'll bother mind-skimming. The Twins should be able to tell me what I need to know.*

:Surim. Tamun.

:Emerahl, they replied.

:I've arrived. I'm in Hannaya. Are the Thinkers still here?

:Yes. They are in the library, deep within the palace, Surim told her. *Are you going there next?*

:No. I'm tired. I'll need a fresh mind if I'm to convince them to let me join them. I hope they don't realise the parchment is a fake.

With The Twins' help she had located some old parchment and made a fake fragment of a scroll. It had the same pronouncement written in two languages, one in the script the Thinkers were trying to decode and another in a slightly younger language that they understood. It didn't give them the entire key to the unknown language, however.

Once the Thinkers knew she could read the older script they would want her to translate the artefacts they had been studying. She had wondered, at first, why The Twins needed her to translate them.

:We can only see what is in the minds we read, they had said. *Since the Thinkers do not understand it, neither do we. Only when they study the shapes of the script are we able to identify them. But they rarely do that, so it is slow work. It will be much faster if you read them for us.*

:Why don't we send them a fake parchment with the complete key to the language and let them work it out for themselves? We can read the location of the Scroll of the Gods from their minds and I can go fetch it.

:If the gods are watching and learn of the Scroll's location through the Thinkers, they may send someone to destroy it.

It was logical to assume that both Circlian and Pentadrian gods wouldn't want any scroll containing their secrets to be found.

:You followed our instructions on making the parchment appear genuine, Surim now said. *Without looking at it ourselves, we can't tell you how convincing it is, but we trust you've done a good job. Still, it would be wise for you to avoid leaving it with them.*

:We have other news, Tamun said. *One of the Thinkers has been offered a large sum of money for the Scroll. The other Thinkers won't want to sell it, so he knows he would have to betray them. He's not sure he wants to.*

:Which of the Thinkers is it?

:Raynora. You will like him, I think. He is good-looking and devious.

:I'm not sure which to be most disturbed by – that you think I'll like him because he's good-looking or because he's devious. Do you think he'll take the offer?

:Perhaps if the price is raised. We will watch him closely.

:Good. I've been too busy for much mind-skimming, and I doubt that's going to change. For now, the Scroll and the Thinkers can wait until tomorrow, she told them. *I need a good long sleep.*

:Good night, they both chimed, then their minds faded from her senses.

To the left hunkered the mountains of south-western Sennon that the Siyee had flown over the previous day. Their lower slopes folded into root-like shapes that sank into a wide, sandy strip of land caught between mountains and sea. On the other side, across the water, the dusty shadow of the southern continent could be seen. A haze obscured the land and made it impossible to tell if the distant shapes were hills or mountains.

In front was a thin strip of land linking the two continents.

The Isthmus of Grya, Auraya recalled. *It looks so fragile, as if the sea ought to have washed it away centuries ago. Maybe it was wider once and the tide has slowly worn it into this narrow land bridge.*

Danjin had once said, just before the war, that the Isthmus would have been an effective defensive position to hold against the Pentadrian invaders, if only the Sennons hadn't agreed to help the enemy. Auraya wasn't sure she agreed with him now. The lack of water or food in the Sennon desert would make holding such a position difficult. Supplies could be transported to the Isthmus, but only with great effort.

Which meant it might be a better defensive position for the Pentadrians, if they had a supply of food and water on the other side. She knew their main city, Glymma, was not far from the Isthmus, so both resources must be available in large enough quantities to keep a big city thriving.

Sreil turned toward the southern continent and the rest of the Siyee followed. They were flying high, hoping that any human that chanced to look up would dismiss them as a flight of birds. The haze of dust ahead would also hide them.

Sennon slowly retreated behind them and Auraya began to make out details of the land ahead. A road extended from the Isthmus into the haze. The darker shapes proved to be low hills in the distance. The sun glinted off water at the turns of a wide, ropey river.

Then slowly the lines and structures of a city began to appear.

The road curved to meet it, turning into a paved street wider than any Auraya had seen. On either side, smaller streets spread in an ordered grid. Houses were sturdy structures of brick with tiled roofs. They stretched in all directions, from the wharves at the sea's edge out to where green fields began. Here and there gardens of green vegetation and pools of reflected sky caught the eye like jewels in a fantastic necklace.

It was a city as large as Jarime. Perhaps larger. It had none of the labyrinthine disorder of the Hanian capital, however. Signs of intelligent pre-planning continued to the city edge and beyond. Impressively large aqueducts carried water far out from the mountains, and canals from the river were spanned by bridges of strange and beautiful shapes.

At the centre of the city, where the wide main road ended, a hill broke the urban order. On this was built a complicated series of structures: a muddle of roofs and courtyards. Auraya wondered why this place was so chaotic when the rest of the city was not.

If this is Glymma, is that the Temple of the Pentadrians?

There was no other building or set of buildings so grand. She decided it must be. Looking around the city, she wondered what it was like to live there. To her surprise she found herself thinking of Mirar. Had he visited Glymma? He could have passed through on the way to the town Jade had said he was in. A town in Mur, in the north, if Jade hadn't lied to protect him. *In fact, Mirar could be down there right now.*

Her musings were interrupted by a whistle from Sreil. He changed course again, heading away from the city.

Auraya sensed the mood of the Siyee shift. They had been even more impressed by Glymma than she, most of them having never seen a landwalker city. Now that their fascination had been broken, a gloom was settling over them. If the enemy was this powerful, how could the Siyee ever hope to fight them?

She wished she could reassure them. None of the whistles of the Siyee could communicate her confidence in them and any words she spoke would be difficult to hear over the wind. *And I have no idea if this place they're going to attack is well*

231

defended, she thought. *I can't promise them that they'll succeed*. Sometimes it was better to remain silent.

The aqueducts and fields stretched a long way from the city. Weariness began to nag at the Siyee. Sreil was leading them toward the low hills, where he hoped they could find a safe place to rest for the night. The sun dropped until all was stained the colour of gold.

They reached the hills as the sun touched the horizon. All were relieved to see the dry valleys and ridges were uninhabited. Sreil gave the signal to descend and circled down into a gully.

A dim light still remained as they landed, but within moments it had died and left them in impenetrable darkness. Auraya felt the Siyee standing around her, uncertain and a little frightened.

'Shall I create a light?' she suggested.

'Yes,' Sreil replied quietly. 'It is worth the risk, I think. The hills around us should hide it.'

She drew magic and channelled it into a tiny spark that barely lit the faces around her. The Siyee crowded around anxiously.

'Snack?' a small voice at Auraya's shoulder said hopefully.

Chuckles broke out all around. Auraya smiled as the Siyee relaxed a little. She reached back to scratch Mischief's head.

'Yes, I think it's time for a snack.'

The Siyee began to settle in for the night. Food was unpacked and Auraya's burden as water carrier lessened. Watchers were chosen and patches of ground were swept free of stones. Although the Siyee were used to sleeping in hammocks, not the hard ground, their exhaustion would ensure they got some rest.

As quiet settled over the camp, Auraya's stomach sank as she felt a familiar approaching presence. She knew it was Huan by the way the hairs rose on the back of her neck.

Huan moved to priest Teel and spoke into his mind. First she asked how the Siyee had fared, then, as always, she asked what Auraya had done. Teel reported Auraya's every movement faithfully.

:She is not to fight in this battle, Huan told him.

:Even if we are losing? Teel asked.

:Even then. This is to be a warning to the Pentadrians that every time they strike at Circlians there will be retribution. It needs to be delivered by Circlian fighters. If Auraya fights, it will appear to come from her.

:But she is a Circlian, too.

:But not our chosen weapon of retribution. How will the Pentadrians learn to respect ordinary Circlians if ordinary Circlians do not stand up and fight?

:I see.

:Yes. You are a good example for your people, Teel. You are loyal and obedient.

Auraya felt Teel's pride swell.

:I will do whatever you want me to.

:I know you will, Teel. Your heart is true. Of the Siyee priests, you show the most promise. I know you will not fail me.

Auraya rolled her eyes. The young man was already stuffed full of his own importance. He did not need Huan boosting his confidence and pride any further. As the flattery and declarations of loyalty continued, she found herself feeling faintly nauseous.

This is one of the gods I used to love unreservedly? she asked herself. *It was terrible discovering that Huan hates me and wants me dead, but this is sickening. She's turning him into a blind fanatic. He'll probably be so sure she will protect her little favourite that he'll rush into the battle and get himself killed.*

Sighing, she rolled over. *I don't love the gods equally any more. When I die Chaia had better be the one to take my soul. I think if*

233

it was a choice of being taken by Huan or fading out of existence, I'd choose the latter.

This was a terrible blasphemy, she knew, but for once it didn't send a shiver of fear down her spine.

CHAPTER 19

Ella's circ lay beside her, neatly folded. On top of her white dress she wore the travelling wrap local women favoured. She wore it in the usual fashion: slung around the shoulders. It could also be lifted to cover the head during rain, or wrapped about the torso for warmth, but Danjin hadn't seen her try either yet. They'd had only dry summer days since leaving Chon.

Sitting opposite Ella in the platten was Yem, the eldest son of the Dregger clan leader. The young man was as lean and muscular as most warriors were, and he was intelligent and politically astute. Danjin had also noticed that Yem was unusually sympathetic toward servants and for that reason he was a strange choice of guide for them.

Dunwayan warriors expected loyalty from their servants. There was no law preventing a servant leaving a household; he or she could even try to find employment elsewhere, though doing so was difficult since most clans had plenty of servants and few warriors would accept a servant who had already proven disloyal by leaving the service of another.

What the Pentadrians had done by arranging the 'escape' of servants could rouse a general rebellion of servants against the warriors. Danjin had expected I-Portak to choose someone less sympathetic to the servants to be Ella's guide. Someone more like Gim, their last dinner host.

The other occupant of the covered platten was Gillen Shieldarm, the Hanian ambassador. During the long hours that Danjin and Ella had spent waiting in Chon, Gillen had visited at least once a day, keeping them entertained with stories or games of counters. Now, on the road, he did the same using the small set that Silava had packed for Danjin. Sometimes it seemed the only conversation in the platten was between Danjin and Gillen, and about counters.

Danjin suspected Gillen had offered to accompany them because he was bored in Chon. Ella had accepted Gillen's offer because he had a deeper understanding of Dunwayan customs and recent politics than Danjin. Ella spent most of her time staring into the distance, listening to the minds of the men they were tracking. Yem remained quiet, only speaking when addressed. Danjin was sure Yem's silence had nothing to do with snobbery, but was either a sign the young man was unsure of himself, intimidated by Ella, or was simply the sort who preferred to listen rather than talk.

Yem and Gillen didn't know as much as Danjin did about the reason for this journey. During the dinner at Gim's household, Ella had caught the nervous thoughts of Ton, a servant planning to leave his master's service. For some time now the man had been meeting a Sennonian spice seller. The seller had told him that Dunwayan servants were little more than slaves, and spoke of a place where all people were equal and all work was shared. A place in the south of Dunway.

A visit to the market confirmed Ella's suspicions. One of the spice sellers was a Sennonian Pentadrian with orders to send potential Dunwayan converts out of Chon. He did not know where he was sending them, unfortunately, but through him Ella found the mind of the escaping servant, Ton.

As she'd hoped, Ton had just begun the journey to the haven for servants. From that day he passed in and out of the care of various men and women — none of whom knew where this haven was or more than one other guide. It was a carefully planned system designed to make tracing the Pentadrians difficult.

Difficult, but not impossible, Ella had said. All she had to do was follow the servant. Though he did not know where he was most of the time, she was able to learn his location from the people around him.

Looking out of the open door flap, Danjin found himself looking into the tops of tall trees. The road had been hewn out of the steep sides of the mountains south of Chon. If he looked down, which he preferred not to do, he would see the edge of the road and a slope that was too close to vertical for comfort.

Ella made a small, frustrated sound, drawing his attention away. She was shaking her head.

'What is it?' he asked.

'They've sent him on alone. He has no idea where he's going.' She frowned and looked at Yem. 'Let's consult the map.'

The young man drew out a wooden cylinder and unstoppered it. From it he took a roll of thin leather covered in tattooed pictures and lines. He had told them it was human skin. The warrior who had created it had travelled around Dunway for years, carefully etching his map into the back of his most devoted servant. Since hearing the tale, Danjin had done all he could to avoid touching the map.

Small blurred pictures of fortresses were spread evenly across the country. The roads were inaccurately straight, showing none of the winding turns the platten had taken. Lines in a faded red showed the boundaries of land owned by different clans.

'He's here,' Ella said, pointing to a group of symbols that indicated the houses of land servants. 'His instructions are to walk along this road until he sees a big rock shaped like an arem, then take the next left turn. Then he's to look for a large tree and cut across fields.'

Danjin suddenly understood her frustration. These instructions couldn't be followed on a map. The man had no idea where he was, or where he was going, and had no companions or guides who did.

These Pentadrians are clever, Danjin thought. *But they won't evade us. It's just a matter of time.*

'Eventually he will see a landmark I know,' Yem assured her.

'And by then we will have fallen behind,' Ella said, clearly not happy.

'We could travel to the place he just left,' Gillen suggested. 'Then follow the instructions.' Their platten was taking a parallel route to the servant's along roads to his east, in case the Pentadrians and helpers on the route saw them and suspected pursuit.

'No,' she said. 'It is better we wait than take the risk they will discover us.'

Yem rolled up the map and slid it back in its case. As Ella's gaze shifted to the distance again, Gillen raised his eyebrows at Danjin. Smiling, Danjin brought out his counters set. It was a finely crafted set for travellers. Each piece had a peg at the base which slotted into holes in the board – but the drawer in which the pieces were stored had warped and would no longer open fully.

'Care for a game?'

Gillen nodded. 'I thought you'd never ask.'

The town of the bird breeders was nestled high in a steep-sided valley and was surrounded by caves. It was called Klaff.

Auraya had read the name from the mind of an inhabitant, but she couldn't tell the Siyee without risking the gods guessing how she had learned it.

It was getting close to the hottest part of the day and the Siyee scouts that had watched the town yesterday had noticed that the inhabitants were quietest at this time. Locals were inclined to retreat inside their houses or nap in a shady place. The birds were safely caged. Hours had passed since their morning flight and more would pass before their late afternoon one.

Mischief was huddled in the shade of a boulder, panting. Auraya's pack was not a pleasant place to be in the heat of the day. She poured water into a small depression in a rock and he lapped it up thirstily.

The Siyee were waiting just over the ridge on one side of the valley. A few were keeping watch on the town while Sreil addressed the others.

'The birds are kept inside caves,' Sreil told them, 'with only iron bars holding them there, so we can shoot them with arrows and darts without even going inside or letting them out. There's an empty space in front, surrounded by buildings, where we'll land. There weren't any guards there yesterday, but they may have been inside. If we are quiet we may get out of there without anyone noticing, though I doubt the birds will stay silent.

'I want six warriors to land in a half-circle and ready their bows. They will deal with any landwalkers that emerge.' He paused, looking expectantly around until six hands rose. 'The rest of us will land between them and the wall. We'll go to the cages and kill all of the birds. If there are eggs, smash them too.'

Auraya had suggested she provide some sort of distraction for the townsfolk, but Sreil had decided against it. He wanted to take advantage of the inhabitants' sleepiness; any distraction she arranged would make them more alert.

Sreil straightened and looked around at his force of Siyee warriors. 'We must work fast. Don't stay any longer than you must. We are not landwalker fighters. If we meet any resistance we must leave. We'll meet back here.'

The Siyee whistled an acknowledgement. Auraya bade them good hunting, bringing a few grins to otherwise grim faces. Then Sreil flexed his arms, sprang into a run down the steep slope and leapt into the air, and the rest of the Siyee went surging after him.

Auraya watched them swoop away and then wheel toward the town. She climbed to the top of the ridge, finding a boulder to crouch next to that would prevent her silhouette being visible against the sky. Her heart was beating quickly and as the Siyee began their descent she felt her stomach clench with anxiety.

Looking around the town, she searched for anyone who might have noticed their approach. The streets were empty.

Heat radiated from the boulder. She hoped the citizens of Klaff were soundly asleep.

The Siyee were a swarm of distant figures just above the town now. They abruptly dived downward into a courtyard. Buildings surrounded three sides and on the other was a rock wall dotted with dark holes, just as Sreil had described. Auraya held her breath as they landed, but no figures rushed out to attack them.

. . . *must still be asleep*, she heard Sreil think smugly. She felt his pride in his warriors as they took their places as he'd ordered. Then from all the Siyee came a jolt of surprise and fear.

From her vantage point, Auraya saw something dark spray out of one of the holes to cover the Siyee. She leapt to her feet as she sensed the Siyee's surprise and confusion. Their thoughts were an incoherent jumble of terror and dismay. She could not work out what was happening.

Looking down, she realised the ground was far below her. She had lifted herself into the sky without intending to. Now she deliberately flew out over the town until she was above the courtyard. Understanding finally came as she made out Siyee struggling to free themselves from under a heavy net.

A net?

Cold rushed through her as she realised the Pentadrians must have known the Siyee were coming.

How? Did someone betray us? Who?

Some of the Siyee were thrashing about out of sheer panic but others had brought out knives and were sawing at the thick cords. Auraya felt her stomach sink as she saw men and women in black robes hurrying out of the buildings to stand on the edges of the net, preventing Siyee escaping. A couple of Siyee scrambled clear. The escapees darted toward the cages, leapt up onto the rock wall and used their momentum to help them scramble higher. Springing out into the air and flapping hard, they managed to pass over the tops of the buildings and swoop away across the town.

At the same time, other Siyee had given up the struggle and Auraya felt a surge of pride as they used their pipes and harnesses to shoot poisoned darts at the landwalkers. A few of the Servants slowly collapsed onto the net, but their weight only served to hold the Siyee more firmly. The rest were unaffected.

They're shielding themselves with magic, Auraya realised, her heart sinking. *The Siyee can't hope to fight off Servants.*

:Auraya!

Her heart skipped as she recognised Juran.

241

:Yes?

:What is going on? I can't make any sense out of what Teel is showing me.

:The Siyee attack failed. The Pentadrians knew they were coming, and have captured them.

Auraya felt a pang of hope from someone below and realised that one Siyee, held down by the net, was staring up at her.

Help me, he thought at her.

She felt guilt, frustration and then anger. *I can't*, she thought at the trapped Siyee. She clenched her fists. The gods had forbidden her to fight. There was no way she could help the Siyee without fighting.

:What do you want me to do? she asked Juran.

:The Pentadrians aren't killing the Siyee?

:No.

He fell silent – probably deliberating. At his question an idea had come to Auraya. If the Pentadrians had known about the attack and intended to kill the Siyee, they wouldn't have used the net. They *intended* to capture them.

And a captive could always be freed. *Perhaps I won't have to fight the Pentadrians in order to free the Siyee.*

Looking into the minds of the Pentadrians, she saw both triumph and surprise. Yesterday she had seen nothing in the thoughts of the townsfolk to suggest they were expecting an attack or planning an ambush. Now she saw that they had been ignorant of the ambush until moments ago, when they had been called here for a meeting only to witness First Voice Nekaun net the flying people.

First Voice Nekaun? Auraya felt her heart sink even further as she saw that one of the Pentadrians was looking up at her. She searched for his thoughts and sensed nothing.

Memories rose of Kuar, the former First Voice, holding her imprisoned with magic. She pushed them aside. *Kuar is dead,* she reminded herself. *Still, this new First Voice may be as powerful as he was.*

He could probably blast her out of the sky if he wanted to. She drew back hastily, but he made no move to stop her.

:Juran.

:Yes?

:The enemy leader is here. I have to leave. But I will stay close. I'll take any opportunity to free the Siyee, without fighting.

:Yes. Do that. I will discuss the situation with the others and let you know what we decide.

As she moved further and further away from the scene she felt the despair of the Siyee. They were running out of darts and the enemy were now tackling them one by one, extracting weapons and binding wrists together. Auraya reached the ridge she had begun watching from and set herself down.

She felt awful, as if she had abandoned them. *But I can't do anything yet. I have to think of a way to free them.*

'Owaya?'

A relieved and frightened Mischief bounded up to her. He climbed onto her shoulders and sat quietly, trembling slightly. As she scratched his head she realised her hands were shaking.

'They're alive,' she told him. 'At least they're alive.'

The sound of air on wings drew her attention away. The two Siyee who had escaped landed beside her. Their expressions were terrible.

'Are they dead?' one asked.

She shook her head and their relief washed over her.

'Prisoners, then?' the other asked.

'Yes.'

'What will you do now?'

Auraya sighed. 'Whatever I can do without disobeying the gods. They said I must not fight. They did not say I couldn't sneak up to a prison and set anyone free.'

They fell silent, staring down at the village. The magic around her roiled and she almost hissed out loud as two strong presences suddenly shot out of the town and into the two Siyee beside her. Her skin crawled as she recognised Huan, then she relaxed a little as she realised the other was Chaia.

:*So what will your pet sorceress do next?* Huan asked.

:*Make a choice*, Chaia replied. *That is what you mean to accomplish, isn't it?*

:*From this? No, this was merely retribution for the murders in Jarime and the attempts to convert Circlians*, Huan said.

:*For the murders of Dreamweavers? I didn't think you liked them that much.*

:*I don't dislike them as much as you do*, she retorted. Besides, the White have decided to encourage tolerance of Dreamweavers for now. It makes sense to avenge Dreamweaver deaths.

:*Yet you arranged for the Siyee to fail. How does that avenge anyone?*

:*It doesn't matter. What matters is that the Pentadrians know the White are upset with them.*

:*You're taking unnecessary risks, Huan. Juran considered this attack a gamble. He's not surprised it failed. Now he'll wonder why you ordered it. He will doubt the wisdom of following your orders.*

:*A small test of his loyalty.*

:*Was it really? And why didn't you consult the rest of us before you arranged it?*

:*I consulted. I didn't need to consult you since all the others agreed.*

:*Lore would not have agreed to this.*

:*He did. You forget his fondness for war games.*

:*So why did you have the Siyee captured, not killed? That would stir the world into war more effectively.*

:*It is more interesting this way.*

:*Interesting? You're not interested in war*, Chaia said. *You're only interested in getting rid of Auraya. If this ambush of yours leads to Auraya turning from us, you will regret it.*

:Is that a threat? Huan laughed. *You can harm me no more than I can harm you.*

With that she moved away, speeding toward the town. Auraya sighed with relief.

:That's where she's wrong, Chaia said to himself. He chuckled. *Did you hear all that, Auraya? I hope so.*

And then he too was gone, leaving her blinking in surprise. He knew she could hear the gods talking. Had he encouraged Huan to discuss the ambush with him?

Perhaps only to show me he wasn't responsible . . . and that Huan was.

She felt her stomach turn over as she realised what that meant. Huan had betrayed the Siyee. She had not just arranged this mission as a test of Auraya's loyalty, but she had ensured the *failure* of it as well.

Then she remembered Chaia's warning. Huan would seek to hurt her by hurting those she loved. It seemed that Huan *was* willing to harm the people she had created.

She felt a hand on her arm.

'How can we help?'

Auraya turned to blink at the Siyee in surprise, then dragged her mind back to the dilemma she faced. At once she realised that if Huan wanted to harm the Siyee in order to hurt her, then it was better to get them as far away from here as possible.

'Go back to our last camp,' she told them. 'I will meet you shortly. I'm going to get some food and water for you. You should leave some at the camp, and in the places we stopped on our way here, for any of the others that manage to escape.'

'You want us to go home?' one of the Siyee asked doubtfully.

'Yes.' She met the Siyee's eyes. 'This was a trap. They were expecting you. I will do what I can to free the others. You must ensure they survive the journey home.'

The two Siyee nodded. They knew she was right, but they were reluctant to leave their companions behind.

'Go,' Auraya told them. 'Get yourselves home, at least. Speaker Sirri and your fellow warriors' families should know what happened here.'

At that they bowed their heads in agreement. She watched them fly away, then turned her attention back to Klaff. There were quite a few public wells, and she had noted a small market on the edge of town. Even if Nekaun had been reading the Siyee's minds as she had told them her intentions, she doubted he would get to the market in time to catch her.

Lifting Mischief off her shoulders, she put him on the ground.

'Stay,' she ordered.

His head drooped, but he obediently walked to a patch of shade and curled up to wait.

Satisfied, she stepped out into the air and propelled herself back to the town.

CHAPTER 20

Heavy rain and fierce winds had roused Mirar from sleep several times during the night, but when he woke in the morning all was quiet. He looked outside his window. Cloud covered the sky, but in places it had parted to reveal patches of blue. Despite the rain it was still warm.

Though it was barely past dawn there was a smell of baking bread coming from the kitchen and Tintel was already in the hall, delicately slicing and eating fruit. She looked up at him and nodded in greeting. As he sat down in the hall to eat, the sound of heavy rain suddenly resumed.

'Not a pleasant day for the Trials,' Tintel said, joining him at the table. 'I'd have thought the gods would arrange better.'

'I guess that depends on their own interpretation of the word "trial".'

She chuckled. 'Yes, I guess it does. Would you like me to accompany you today?'

He smiled and shook his head. 'No – but thank you for offering.'

She nodded. He could sense her anxiety, though he could not tell if it were for his safety or that of all Dreamweavers – or both. If this meeting between him and Fourth Voice Genza went badly, would it affect the good relationship between Southern Ithanian Dreamweavers and Pentadrians?

I will just have to ensure it does not go badly, Mirar told himself.

A knock came from the main entrance. Tintel rose to answer it and returned with a man and a teenage boy. Both wore ribbons of blue and white sewn all over clothing of the same colours, but neither looked as cheerful as their costume. The boy was supported by the older man, hopping in order to avoid putting weight on one leg.

Tintel called to one of the Dreamweavers in the kitchen, who emerged, took one look at the colourful pair, and led them away. Tintel returned to her seat.

'We'll be seeing plenty of broken bones and twisted ankles today,' she said.

Mirar looked at her questioningly.

'Wet platforms can be dangerously slippery,' she explained. 'During an exciting public event, people – particularly young people – have a habit of rushing about carelessly. Ah. Here's your escort.'

Mirar turned to see a middle-aged woman dressed in Servant robes standing on the threshold of the room. The woman was red-faced and sweating. As Mirar rose, her gaze slid to his.

'You are Mirar, founder of the Dreamweavers?' she asked.

'I am,' he replied.

Her eyebrows rose. 'I am Servant Minga. I am to take you to meet Fourth Voice Genza.'

Mirar turned to Tintel. 'Good luck.'

'You too,' she replied quietly. 'Watch your step out there today.'

He smiled, sure that she was not referring to wet platforms, and walked over to greet the Servant. The woman was short but her bearing was proud. She was used to being respected and obeyed, Mirar guessed.

He gestured to the door. 'Please lead the way.'

She nodded to Tintel before turning away. Mirar couldn't help marvelling at the little gesture of respect. A Circlian priestess would never have done such a thing.

I could really come to love this country.

They stepped outside into fat, soaking drops of rain, and Mirar's enthusiasm was quickly dampened! He drew a little magic and shielded them both, earning a small smile of gratitude from his guide. Despite the rain it didn't seem much cooler, but the upper level of Kave was gleaming with moisture and smelled of wet timber.

They walked slowly, making their way from platform to platform. Dekkans lounged in chairs under wide verandas, fanning themselves. They smiled and nodded as Mirar passed, and he took that to be a good sign. If the people of Dekkar liked him being here perhaps the Voices would, too.

After a few minutes, however, he heard the patter of several footsteps behind him and his heart sank as he imagined a mob of supporters following him to the Hall of Chieftains. That would only give the Voice the impression he had a strong influence over them – which she could hardly be expected to like.

He stopped and looked over his shoulder, then smothered a laugh. The crowd was a group of children, their eyes wide with curiosity. They grinned at him.

'Hello,' he said. 'Why are you following me?'

'We like you,' a boy said.

'You healed Pinpin,' a girl told him.

'And Mimi.'

'And Doridori's mother.'

'Are you going to the Trials?'

He nodded.

'We are too!' The children cheered, then as one they ran away, their feet pounding on the boards. Smiling, Mirar turned to find the Servant regarding him curiously. He shrugged and they continued on their way.

As they crossed a bridge Mirar caught a movement below and looked down. Tiny temporary shelters had been constructed on the ground below the platforms, on either side of a creek. He caught the smell of refuse and sewage. This was where the poorer residents of Kave lived, gathering what the affluent ones discarded. Those above complained about the smell from below, yet if the poor didn't gather the garbage dropped from above and keep the creeks flowing freely the whole city would have smelled far worse.

Tintel had told Mirar that the poor lashed the walls of their shelters together to form rafts when the floods came. They tethered these to trees or platforms to prevent them being washed out to sea. Pentadrians had condemned to slavery three rich young men who had loosed several rafts as a prank the year before. A few of the families had been rescued by ships and had identified the men, but most were never found.

The closer they came to the Hall of the Chieftains, the more crowded the porches of Kave became. Everyone wore bright clothing decorated with ribbons or flowers. More blossoms bedecked the houses and platforms, though those unprotected from the rain were drooping with moisture.

The rain ended suddenly, but water continued to drip from rooftops. Sometimes the crowd was so thick the Servant had to clear her throat or ask loftily that people stand aside. At last the Hall of the Chieftains came in sight. Like Kave's Sanctuary, it was made of stone. It was a squat pyramid of three levels, rising up from the muddy ground below. The sloped sides were of enormous staggered stone bricks, like an oversized staircase. In the centre of the structure was a section of normal-sized stairs leading to the topmost level. A visitor must literally climb the walls to get there.

A pavilion had been erected on the first level. Several men and a few women sat on reed chairs beneath this. Servants stirred the air in the room with large fans. Their efforts were directed mainly at a dark-skinned woman in black robes sitting on a reed couch at the centre of the pavilion.

Mirar's guide led him across the bridge. She stopped by one of the corner poles of the pavilion and he waited beside her. The dark-skinned woman was talking to one of her companions. As he finished she looked up at Mirar and smiled, then rose and walked forward to meet him.

She's tall, he noted. *And she walks with the grace of someone who is fit. But she is lean rather than muscular, and her face is quite beautiful.*

'I am Genza, Fourth Voice of the Gods,' she said in Dekkan. 'You are Mirar, immortal leader of the Dreamweavers?'

'I am,' he replied. He felt a small shiver of apprehension at admitting to his identity so freely after all the years of hiding. 'Though I am only their founder and teacher, not their leader,' he added.

Genza nodded once at the guide, who walked away. 'Please join me,' she said to him, gesturing to the couch.

He sat down beside her, aware that sharing her couch was probably a great honour. Genza introduced him to the other men and women. Most were patriarchs and matriarchs of Kave's wealthier families – Mirar had met a few during healing visits. Others included the local Dedicated Servants, war chiefs, and ambassadors from Avven and Mur.

'And here are our candidates.'

All turned to the front of the pavilion. Four men and one woman, all dressed in colourful clothing, stood before them. All traced a star in the air before Genza. The Voice rose and greeted each in turn, wishing them luck.

The first was a man in his late thirties, with a little grey showing in his hair. He gave an impression of maintained fitness and health, and his gaze was sharp.

Next came a younger man with broad shoulders and the muscular body of active youth. His eyes kept moving to someone behind Mirar and he appeared to be struggling not to grin.

Beside him stood another young man. This one was thin and serious. He did not have the fitness of the first two, but his face was prematurely marked with lines that suggested he spent a lot of time in thought – or worrying.

The fourth candidate was a woman in her thirties. She stood with a straight back and her expression was all suppressed defiance. The last was a man Mirar judged to be in his fifties, with a wiry body and a kind face. His clothing was as bright as the others' but at close inspection was clearly of low-quality cloth.

At a word from Genza, the five contestants turned to face the crowd. She stepped past them, into the rain. A quiet slowly fell over the city.

'Today each of these men and women will undergo physical and magical ordeals,' she said, her voice unnaturally loud. 'Their knowledge, intelligence and morality will be questioned, then their reputation examined and their popularity weighed. They must pass all these Trials, but only the one with the highest score shall win. Wish them luck!'

A cheer rose from the crowd. Genza lifted her arms and they quietened again.

'The first Trial is that of physical strength, stamina and agility. A path has been set out that they must follow.' She paused. 'Do not interfere with the candidates' progress,' she warned. 'Cheating or sabotage will be punished by death.'

She dropped her arms and turned to face the candidates.

'Are you ready?'

The five nodded.

A spark of light appeared above Genza's head.

The spark flared.

'The Chieftain Trials begin *now*!' she shouted.

The city erupted in cheering as the contestants hurried away, descending the pyramid. Genza returned to her seat. A moment later Mirar glimpsed a contestant running under the houses. He noticed coloured poles rammed into the ground, ribbons strung between them, and black-clad Servants standing beside them.

Genza turned to regard Mirar again. 'So, Mirar of the Dreamweavers, how long have you been in Dekkar?'

'A few months.'

'You didn't make your presence known for some time, then?'

'I was unsure if I would be safe here.' He paused, then raised an eyebrow at the woman. 'Am I?'

She smiled. 'That depends on your plans. If you decided to rule Dekkar for yourself we would ensure it was the shortest reign of a Chieftain in history. And there have been some *very* short ones.'

'I have no ambition to rule any country. That is a task better suited to people such as yourself.'

'And what am I?'

He looked at her, surprised by the question. 'Favoured by the gods. Smart. Beautiful. People like leaders with those qualities.'

Leaning back, she regarded him through half-closed eyes.

'You are charming – and not so bad-looking yourself. I must admit, I was expecting an old man.'

He smiled. 'I *am* an old man.'

She laughed. Then she leaned forward and touched his knee lightly. 'I'll tell you a secret. I am not as young as I look either.'

Again he felt surprise. Genza's gaze was dark and her smile was mischievous.

I'd think she was flirting with me, if she wasn't a . . .

A Voice? He'd heard nothing to suggest the Voices were celibate. He knew their Servants weren't, though he'd always suspected the rumours of ritual orgies were exaggerations.

Was she merely being friendly or was she offering him something more? If she did proposition him, what would he do? She was attractive, and something told him she was *very* experienced . . . but something else made him hesitate.

Maybe it was natural caution. He couldn't know what consequences might come out of bedding a woman in such a position of power. Then he remembered that Pentadrians in Jarime had arranged for Dreamweavers to be murdered a few months before. Genza may have had something to do with that, and the thought was more than enough to extinguish his interest.

She appeared to sense it and leaned back in her seat again.

'So what are your plans for the future, Dreamweaver Mirar?' she asked.

He shrugged. 'My people are everywhere in Southern Ithania. I would like to travel around the continent, learning about the languages and ways of the people, and teaching healing skills as I did in the past.'

She nodded. 'Then you must come to Glymma. Come to the Sanctuary and introduce yourself to my fellow Voices.' Her smile broadened and she lowered her chin and looked at him from under her brows. 'Even if they do not make a fuss of you, I will. I see the potential for a profitable alliance between us.'

He chuckled and regarded her thoughtfully. 'Ah, your gods choose well. Why am I unsure if you're trying to seduce me politically or physically?'

Her eyes sparkled and she grinned widely. 'Success is reaching a position where one's talents are best utilised.'

He nodded. 'That is true. I'm afraid I have proven to be a bad example for Dreamweavers at times. I try to avoid what

I don't have a talent for. My talents are those of a healer, teacher and guide, so I can only speak for Dreamweavers in a very limited way.'

'Yet as a teacher and guide, your actions could still affect the future of the Dreamweavers. You could still guide the Dreamweavers, say, away from a continuing friendship between Dreamweavers and Pentadrians.'

'I could, but I would not, of course.'

'Of course.'

'And I might seek a reassurance on their behalf that Pentadrians do not intend us any further harm.'

Her eyes narrowed, suggesting she had caught his reference to the Dreamweaver murders in Jarime.

'Be assured, then, that we do not regard Dreamweavers with any animosity,' she told him.

No animosity, he mused. *But you won't think twice about using individuals to further your own ends again.*

'What do you know of the candidates?' she asked him, changing the subject.

He shrugged. 'Very little. Only the gossip I've overheard from other Dreamweavers. I don't completely understand what the Trials are for. Why this physical test? Is it necessary? A ruler can be fit yet not fit to rule.'

Genza's shoulders lifted. 'It is a tradition. It increases the chances that a ruler will last a while. The physical trial isn't overly demanding, but it removes the weak and those inclined to laziness and excess.'

'They might put aside laziness and excess only for as long as it takes to win.'

'Yes,' she agreed. 'And there is always the chance that a candidate's youth will allow them to perform well now, only to be ruined by excess later. Ah, speaking of excess . . .'

Servants were entering the pavilion carrying platters of food and large pitchers. For the next hour or so Genza encouraged all her companions to eat and drink. From their constant thanks Mirar guessed she had paid for the feast.

From time to time a candidate would be seen and pointed out, and the conversation would turn to speculation and wagers increased. The two young men were the first to return to the pavilion, where they were set to the task of picking up heavy stone balls of increasing sizes. The woman arrived next, but struggled with the lifting task. The sharp-eyed man followed soon after and managed well, while the older man came last but surprised all with his strength.

Now a large frame of wood the size of a room was wheeled to the pavilion by several muscular men. It was covered in a fine netting. A simple but beautiful timing device of glass tubes was set in front of Genza. Mirar heard a low whine over the chatter around him. It grew louder as five large baskets were carried to the frame and set on the ground.

The city was buzzing with voices and Mirar sensed their rising excitement and curiosity. From the candidates he detected anxiety and a little dread. The muscular young man appeared to be the most frightened.

Genza inspected the frame, walking around it slowly. When she had circled it, she turned to the candidates.

'This is a test of your magical skills. As you have all guessed, each of these baskets contains zappers. A hundred in each, which I can assure you was no easy task to arrange. You will enter the cage and the net will be secured. The zappers will be released. You must protect yourself and kill the entire swarm as quickly as possible with magic.' She smiled. 'If any of you doubt your ability to complete this task please step aside now. We have a Dreamweaver here, but I'm sure he'd prefer not to spend the afternoon removing zapper larvae from your bodies.'

None of the candidates moved, though the muscular young man shuddered.

'Good. Who would like to go first?'

The candidates exchanged glances, then the sharp-eyed man stepped forward. There was a cheer from the crowd. Genza told him to pick up a basket and carry it inside. He set it in a corner, then backed to the far side of the cage. The netting was carefully fixed back into place.

Genza waited until all was silent, then she made the smallest gesture with one hand. The lid of the basket flew off and a black cloud rushed out.

The sharp-eyed man attacked with magic immediately, turning the zappers' attention to himself. It was hard to see the insects, they were moving so fast. Mirar caught glimpses of segmented tails and antennae. The buzz of their wings was deafening, but the stunning flashes of their magic were silent.

Mirar had heard of these jungle insects. The magical stun of one insect was painful although not fatal, but when struck by many stings at once an animal could be paralysed. Most of the time the insects stunned only to protect their nests. But at certain times, triggered by the full moon, the insects stunned in order to lay eggs in living flesh. A lamp hung over a basket of zappers triggered the same instinct.

Which was hardly needed for this Trial. The zappers would attack savagely enough without being induced to lay eggs, and the candidates were not being tested for their ability to fight them, but how long it took to kill them all.

The buzz had diminished now. As the sharp-faced man killed the last of the insects Genza glanced at the water timer.

'Five and a half measures. Well done.'

Mirar found himself caught up in the tension despite himself as the other contestants each had their turn in the cage. The sharp-faced man proved to be the fastest, though the older man was nearly as quick. The serious young man picked the zappers off slowly, which told Mirar that he probably wasn't Gifted enough to draw magic for multiple strikes.

The floor of the cage rattled with dead zappers as it was wheeled away. Now the candidates were given stools to sit on and some water and fruit to eat. Genza invited a patriarch in the pavilion to ask questions of them. The man described complicated trading scenarios that involved mathematics and an understanding of trading terms, and it soon became clear that the older man struggled with both.

As Genza chose another in the pavilion to ask a question, then another, Mirar began to wonder if all in the shelter would be required to quiz the candidates. The war chiefs and the Dedicated Servants seized the opportunity with enthusiasm, asking strategy and religion-related questions. The other patriarchs and matriarchs tested the candidates on law and moral dilemmas.

When all had had their turn Genza turned to him.

'I have not asked you to prepare a question, Dreamweaver Mirar, but you may ask one if you wish.'

He nodded. 'Thank you. I would be honoured.' He turned to face the candidates. 'This is a question for all of you. It does not involve calculations or recitation of laws. I am merely interested to know: what will you do for the people below during your rule?'

The woman smiled, the older man flushed red with pleasure and straightened with pride, but the three other candidates frowned. For the thin, serious young man it was a frown of thoughtfulness, however. The other two were scowling.

'Ask them what they need and want, and provide what can be affor—' the woman began.

'Build platforms,' the older man said. 'The city can afford

it. Once we're off the ground we'll have the same chances as everyone else, and the city will be healthier all in all.'

Mirar turned to the sharp-eyed man. The man looked at Genza, then shrugged.

'Nothing. There will always be people below. There's nothing we can do to help them if they won't help themselves.'

The older man turned to glare at him. His mouth opened, but as Genza cleared her throat he stilled and hunched sullenly on his stool.

Mirar looked at the two young men. The muscular one shrugged. 'Offer help only to those who'll work for it.'

'Yes,' the serious one said. 'Though we can't expect the truly feeble or the very young to work. Some help can be freely given, some should encourage improvement. We must accept that there will always be outcasts and those who cannot help themselves, but for the sake of the city and decency we should look for ways to improve their surroundings.'

'An interesting question to end with,' Genza said. She stood up and her voice echoed through the city. 'Now begins the Trial of Reputation.'

The candidates rose and moved to one side. Servants removed the stools. Mirar realised that the rain had stopped and the weak sunlight had brightened a little.

Genza rose. 'The Reputation of each candidate is now on trial,' she called out. 'Anyone may speak for or against them. We will listen and consider your words.'

For the next few hours people filed through the pavilion, stopping to tell of their encounters with one or more of the candidates. Some were there just to get a look at Genza or speak of minor wrongs like being short-changed.

Mirar began to see that the older man was a popular leader among the people below, while the woman was well-loved by those above. Few had anything ill to say of either of them.

The younger men proved to have fewer supporters and more detractors. The muscular, young man was inclined to foolish, drunken behaviour. The sharp-eyed man's most damning critic was a limping, battered merchant who claimed an assassin had been sent to kill him so he wouldn't reveal the illegal trading the man was involved in.

A bell rang out, marking the end of the Trial. Some of those who had not spoken yet were angered by this, but all were sent away. Once more Genza addressed the crowd.

'Now the Trial of Popularity begins. Leave your ribbons in the baskets provided. Tonight the baskets will be weighed, the points of each candidate tallied, and the new High Chieftain announced.'

Mirar watched as the citizens of Kave began to file across the bridge. They selected lengths of ribbon from a huge basket then placed them into one of five smaller baskets bedecked with the colours of the candidates. A Servant stood by each basket, watching closely.

Genza returned to her seat, then grimaced apologetically at Mirar. 'I'm afraid this is the least interesting part of the rites, but at least we have each other for company.'

'It has been more entertaining than I expected,' he told her. 'I am grateful for the invitation.'

She laughed quietly. 'That is good. So. One of those five will be High Chieftain of Dekkar at the end of the day,' she said. 'Who do you think will win?'

'The one you and the people of Dekkar find most suitable,' he replied.

'How diplomatic. Do you care to guess which that will be?'

He shrugged. 'I don't know enough about them.'

Her eyebrows rose. 'You truly haven't taken any interest in them, have you?'

'No.'

'I would have thought you'd be at least a little concerned about who the next High Chieftain is. He or she will be the one you will have to deal with.'

'I doubt I'll have any reason to. I prefer not to involve myself in politics.'

She smiled. 'But what if politics decides to involve itself in you?'

'I will endeavour to discourage it.'

'And me? Will you try to discourage me?'

Mirar's skin prickled in warning. He made himself smile. 'If I must, though I'll admit I would gain no pleasure from it.'

Her smile widened. 'Then don't. I will be returning to Glymma in a few days. I want you to accompany me. You should meet my fellow Voices.'

A chill ran down Mirar's spine. This was no invitation, though it wasn't a straight order. He regarded her seriously. 'Be assured I am honoured by the invitation. I do intend to visit Glymma and would like to meet the other Voices. I would prefer to have seen more of Southern Ithania first. Must my visit be so soon?'

She nodded. 'Your travels can wait. There can be nothing more important for you now than establishing a friendly acquaintance with us.' Her expression softened and she tilted her head. 'And I think you will provide entertaining company on my return journey.'

Mirar suppressed a sigh. He was not going to be able to refuse her.

'When do you leave?'

'In two days.'

A cheer gave him an excuse to shift his attention away. The muscular young man was performing acrobatics to entertain the voters. Genza snorted softly.

'Thank the gods the Chieftain is not chosen by popularity alone,' she murmured.

'Do the Trials have any effect on the decision?'

She gave him an affronted look that was clearly faked.

'Of course they do. If we didn't let the people think they had a part in it, they might not accept our decision.'

He nodded. 'I guessed as much.'

'You disapprove?'

'Not at all. I know you'll choose wisely.'

'How can you be sure?'

'While you and your fellow Voices are probably willing to sort out any troubles in Kave, I'm sure you'd rather not make the long journey here too often, especially not in summer.'

She chuckled. 'Kave isn't at its best this time of year. There's no better time to visit Glymma, actually. Will you come with me?'

He smothered a sigh and considered. *I have no pressing reason to refuse and risk offending her and the other Voices. Since I will most likely meet these Voices eventually, it may as well be at their invitation.* He nodded.

'Wonderful!' she exclaimed. 'I shall arrange a cabin for you on my barge.'

Another cheer came from the crowd. Looking out at the city, Mirar thought back to the battle between the Circlians and the Pentadrians. He remembered watching a black-robed woman, one of the Pentadrian leaders, slaughtering mortals with magic. He realised then that Genza was the Voice that had bred the black birds that had savaged the Siyee, clawing at wings and eyes and sending sky people falling to their deaths.

So? Auraya probably killed just as many Pentadrians, he reminded himself.

But somehow it was easier to imagine Auraya feeling bad about it than Genza.

Auraya had learned much about Nekaun, the First Voice of the Gods, since the previous day. After she had taken the food she had stolen to the two Siyee, she had carried Mischief to a new vantage point. From there she watched with both mind and eyes the activities below. Though she could not sense the mind of the First Voice, she could observe him through others.

He had been elected by his people, not by his gods. Prior to his election he had been in charge of a temple dedicated to one of the Pentadrian goddesses, Hrun. That goddess was a benign one concerned with love and family, and his role had been to arrange and lead the rituals of the Temple.

The Second Voice of the Gods, Imenja, was rumoured to dislike and disagree with Nekaun. This was attributed to the fact that Imenja's adviser, Companion Reivan, was known to be Nekaun's current lover. All expected this situation to improve when Nekaun, notoriously fickle, moved on to a new lover.

Good to see our enemies enjoy just as much scandal and gossip as we do, she thought.

Imenja and two of the other Voices were in Glymma. Ironically, it was Genza, the woman in charge of the fighting birds the Siyee had tried to attack, who was furthest from the city, attending to a ceremony in the south of the continent.

Auraya had also learned much about the Pentadrian religion. Information gathered by the White's spies had told her the names of the Voices and their gods, as well as a few Dedicated Servants, but no Circlian spies had been able to supply many details of their beliefs and hierarchy. All Servants could wield magic except, interestingly, this Companion Reivan, who had gained the position in return for a good deed during the war.

Reivan had been a member of a group of intellectuals known as the Thinkers. In Jarime there were social circles of academics and enthusiasts, but nothing like this organised society of men and women of learning.

Not long after dawn the town had begun to stir. Auraya had watched, Mischief curled up in her lap, as the inhabitants had risen and set about their daily tasks. Some of the Pentadrians, however, were occupied with less routine work: tending to and arranging for the transportation of their Siyee prisoners to Glymma.

Auraya watched as uncovered platten were hired in one part of the town and Siyee were given water and bread in another. She observed Nekaun through the eyes of his Servants. All the time she looked for flaws in their plans that might give her and the Siyee the opportunity for escape.

So far the Siyee had been securely imprisoned close to Nekaun inside a building. Once outside, the only person who could prevent her freeing them was Nekaun. Any attempt to free them would have to happen before they reached Glymma. She was sure escape would be much harder to arrange once they reached the city.

A line of platten now waited outside the building. The First Voice emerged and walked around the vehicles as if inspecting them. She tensed as she detected the Siyee's fear rising. They were being taken out of the room they had been imprisoned within. Pentadrians guided them firmly out of the building. She watched as, one by one, they were taken outside, lifted into the platten and bound to iron rings attached to the vehicles' sides.

If only Nekaun wasn't here, she thought.

But even if he hadn't been, how could she have freed the Siyee without fighting off the attacks of the Servants? She ground her teeth. Chaia's voice echoed in her memory.

. . . If this ambush of yours leads to Auraya turning from us . . .

She was determined to disappoint Huan. If she was going to fail a test of loyalty, it would be by doing something much less trivial than fighting when she had been ordered not to.

But what if not fighting leads to the Siyee's deaths? Auraya's jaw ached from grinding her teeth. She rubbed it, then sighed. *I'll only be able to decide that when – if – the time comes. But if they die I will make Huan pay for it. Somehow.*

She grimaced at her own thoughts then. How had she come to the point of wishing to take revenge on a god she had once loved?

Mirar would find this amusing.

The platten were full of Siyee and Pentadrians now. The last of the vehicles bore only Nekaun and a driver. They began to move.

People paused to stare as the procession wound through the town. The Siyee were a strange sight to them. A frightening one, too. Siyee had killed many Pentadrians during the war.

As the platten reached the edge of the town and set out along the road to Glymma, Auraya began to rise. Mischief gave a sleepy whine of protest as she lifted him into her pack.

'Pack bad,' he murmured.

'I'm sorry, Mischief,' she told him.

Stepping off the rock pinnacle she had been sitting on all night, she propelled herself after the Siyee and their captors.

CHAPTER 21

A familiar figure stood before the Sanctuary flame, head bowed. Reivan approached slowly and stopped several steps away, not wanting to interrupt Imenja's thoughts. She heard the Second Voice murmur a prayer, then saw her straighten.

'Ah, Reivan.' Imenja turned and smiled. 'What do we have to sort out today?'

Reivan walked to Imenja's side. The flame twisted and snapped like fine cloth in a wind. Its constant movement was hypnotic, and it was said the gods could steal one's sanity if one dared look at it too long. She forced her eyes away.

'Karneya has appealed to us again to release his son from slavery. You asked me to report whenever he did.'

Imenja grimaced. 'I pity him. It is hard to accept that one's own child has committed a terrible crime.'

'In any other land his son would have been executed.'

'Yes,' the Second Voice agreed. 'And we cannot grant his request, but I will write to him. What else?'

'Tiemel Steerer wants to become a Servant, but he believes his father will disapprove.'

'He's right. This will be a difficult one.'

'His father cannot prevent him.'

'He'll try. Even if it means having him kidnapped and sent to Jarime.'

'Does he disapprove of us that much?'

Imenja laughed. 'No, quite the opposite. But Tiemel is his only son. Who will run the ships when he is too old?'

Reivan didn't answer. Better that the business be sold than the son spend years doing what he hated, his magical Skills wasted.

Imenja turned suddenly, her gaze shifting to the distance. She frowned, then her face relaxed and she sighed.

'These matters will have to wait,' she said. 'Our wayward acquaintance has returned.'

Reivan felt a thrill of hope. 'Nekaun?'

Imenja nodded and smiled knowingly. 'Yes.'

The Second Voice's smile widened as Reivan felt herself blush. 'Come on then. Let's go together.'

She led Reivan away from the flame into the Sanctuary buildings. At first the Servants they saw were quiet, pausing to make the sign of the star as Imenja passed. Then a messenger raced past, his urgency making Imenja pause and frown. Closer to the entrance of the Sanctuary they encountered small groups of Servants whispering together.

'What's going on?' Reivan asked.

Imenja sighed. 'They've heard reports he's bringing prisoners with him. Not ordinary men either.'

Hearing the frustration in Imenja's voice, Reivan decided to keep her questions to herself. It was already clear her mistress hadn't approved of Nekaun's secrecy. If people realised the other Voices hadn't known the reason for his disappearance they might conclude that Nekaun didn't trust them, or value their opinions.

They reached the hall and crossed to the other side. Shar and Vervel waited within one of the arches. Imenja walked over to join them.

'Here he comes,' Shar murmured.

Following their gaze, Reivan saw that a crowd was emerging from one of the crossroads of the Parade. It spilled out into the main thoroughfare and split into two, allowing room for several open platten to approach the Sanctuary.

Inside the platten were Servants and several children, the latter tied by their wrists to the rails of the vehicles.

Reivan heard shocked gasps around her and found herself agreeing. Why had Nekaun taken all these children prisoner? What could they have done to deserve this treatment?

'Siyee,' Vervel said, his voice low and dark with hatred.

Siyee? Reivan looked closer. The faces of the prisoners were not those of children, but of adults. Memories of the war rushed into her mind. It had been hard to judge the size of the sky people when they were in the air. She had seen dead ones on the ground, however. Had even examined one of them, fascinated and repelled by the distortions of their limbs and the membrane that formed their wings. Some of her fellow Thinkers had wanted to take a few home to study, but the Voices had forbidden it.

The last platten had only one passenger, and her heart swelled to see Nekaun smiling broadly. As the platten stopped he leapt out and strode effortlessly up the stairs. He did not look at Reivan; his attention was fixed on his fellow Voices.

'How have you all been the last few days?' he asked. 'I hope everything ran smoothly in my absence.'

'Smoothly enough,' Vervel said calmly. 'I see you've been busy.'

'Yes.' Nekaun turned to look at the platten. The Servants had begun untying the prisoners from the rings. The Siyee were bound together at the ankle. 'The gods informed me that Siyee warriors were coming to attack Klaff and that I should deal with them and their sorceress.'

'Sorceress?' Shar repeated.

Nekaun looked up at the sky, his gaze roving about. 'The former White.'

Imenja drew in a sharp breath and looked up. 'Auraya?'

He looked at her and smiled. 'Yes. She followed us here so I have no doubt she is somewhere close.'

'Is she a danger?' Vervel asked.

'I don't think so. The Siyee believe her gods have forbidden her to fight us.' Nekaun smiled, then looked down at the sky people. 'I had better escort our prisoners to their cells.' He took a step away. Reivan felt a pang of disappointment. He hadn't looked at her. Not even a glance.

'There are no prison cells in Sanctuary,' Imenja pointed out.

Nekaun turned and smiled at her. 'Yes there are, they just haven't been used for a very long time.'

As he turned away, Imenja made a small stifled sound.

'The caves,' she said with obvious disgust. 'What are we becoming?'

'They are our enemy and they did try to attack us,' Shar reminded her.

'The Siyee belong in the prison complex,' she said. 'Outside the Sanctuary.'

'Nekaun needs to be close to prevent Auraya rescuing them,' Shar said, shrugging. 'We can't expect him to live in the prison complex.'

Imenja frowned at him, then sighed. Reivan hesitated as her mistress turned and stalked away. The Second Voice stopped and looked back. She smiled with obvious effort.

'Come, Companion Reivan,' she said quietly. 'We have work to do.'

Sreil hurt all over. His arms were sore from being held in one position for so long and his wrists were red and blistered from the ropes, but that was not all. The vehicles that had carried them to the city had shaken and jerked constantly until Sreil imagined all his bones would surely be loosened from their joints. His muscles were sore from bracing himself against the rocking, and his side was bruised from knocking against the railing.

It was only the beginning. There was sure to be worse to come. He had been certain of it from the moment the net pinned him down. The Pentadrians hadn't killed them, so they must have some other terrible plan.

The previous night, tied up in a large room covered with dried grass and in the company of the animals that pulled the vehicles, he had slept fitfully. Nightmares had taunted him, shaped from old stories of the early days of the Siyee. A time when their bodies had warped and changed. The older ones whispered these stories late at night. It was wise to remember the sacrifice and the cost of transformation, they whispered. The pain. The suffering of the failures. The deformed ones.

Those stories came back to haunt him, perhaps drawn out by the twisting of his arms. A single torch on a stand provided the only light in the enormous room they were in now, making the broad columns they had been chained to look like the trees of the Open. On a raised area to one side an enormous stone chair towered over them, crumbling with age. Perhaps one of the Pentadrian gods visited from time to time. At that thought, he could not help also imagining that the Siyee had been left here as sacrifices.

If he pushed his mind away from such dark places he only ended up thinking about his mother and the grief she would feel when she heard of their failure. He hoped the two Siyee that had escaped made it back home. If they didn't his mother might send more Siyee out to find out what had happened. It was clear he and his warriors had been betrayed, so it was likely that any others who came would also be ambushed and captured.

'Sreil.'

He jumped at the voice and turned to see that the Siyee chained to the other side of the column was peering around at him.

'Tiseel?'

'I've been thinking,' the warrior said. 'About who betrayed us.'

Sreil noticed that other Siyee had heard and were watching him.

'So have I,' he said.

'You don't think . . . you don't think Auraya could have?'

'No,' Sreil said firmly.

'But she didn't help us.'

'She isn't allowed to. The gods forbade her to fight, remember.'

Tiseel sighed. 'Why did they do that? It doesn't make sense. Or maybe she's just saying they have.'

'Teel said so, too. If she had betrayed us, she would have ridden with the Pentadrians, not followed us from the air,' Sreil reasoned. 'The Pentadrian leader kept watching her, as if he was worried she'd attack him.'

Other Siyee nodded in agreement.

'Then who?' Tiseel asked. 'Surely not a Siyee.'

Sreil shook his head. 'No. What would anyone have to gain?'

'Landwalkers did it,' someone hissed. 'A spy who heard about our plans from the White.'

'That's possible,' Sreil agreed.

'Or maybe the Elai,' another said.

Heads turned toward the speaker. He shrugged. 'I heard the Sand Tribe suspect the Elai are trading with Pentadrians.'

'They'd never betray us,' Tiseel said. 'How could they have heard of our plans, anyway?'

'Huan says the Pentadrian sorcerer is a mind-reader,' a new voice said. All eyes turned to Teel. 'He probably read our intentions from our minds when we flew over the city.'

Sreil felt his heart sink. *I led us over the city. It was all my fault. But how could I have known their leader could do that? Nobody told me. Not Auraya, or Teel . . .*

'Will the gods let Auraya rescue us, Teel?' someone asked.

'I don't know,' Teel admitted. 'Perhaps only if it doesn't involve fighting.'

'Was our capture part of some bigger plan?'

'I don't know,' the priest repeated. 'All we can do is stay faithful to them and pray.'

And then he began to do the latter. Though a few of the Siyee groaned in annoyance, Sreil felt the words soothe him. It was comforting to hope this was all part of a grander scheme.

That it wasn't my fault, he told himself.

Closing his eyes, he concentrated on the young priest's words in the hope they would keep darker thoughts at bay.

The walls inside the lower levels of Hannaya's Palace were so thick the rooms appeared to be connected by short passages. Niches had been carved into these and some were lined with fresh stone. Busts of important men and women peered out, their expressions uniformly dour.

Men and a few women hurried about. It was easy for Emerahl to imagine they were eager to be out of this oppressive place, but she sensed no fear from them. There was only the usual undercurrent of irritation, purpose and anxiety she had felt in a dozen other cities.

According to The Twins, the palace had been the home of the royal house that had once ruled Mur but which had long ago died out. The maze of rooms, both grand and crude, were still occupied by the same range of servants, courtiers and artisans, but the ruler was now a Pentadrian Dedicated Servant, known as the Guardian.

Two of the Thinkers searching for the Scrolls were from rich and influential families who lived in the palace. They were providing accommodation for the others. For most of the day, however, the five of them gathered in the library. It was there that Emerahl was heading now.

The boy she had paid to take her there turned toward another passage, leading her deeper into the cliff. Her pulse quickened as he stopped before two large carved wooden doors. The boy held his hand out to her. She dropped a coin into it and he raced away.

Emerahl paused to take a deep breath, then knocked.

A long silence followed. She concentrated on the space behind the door, picking up emotions of several people. Most were distracted and quiet, but one was purposeful and a little irritated.

Then the handle lifted and the door swung inward. An old man peered down his long nose at her.

'Yes?'

'I wish to see the Thinkers,' she told him. 'Are they here?'

His eyebrows rose, but he said nothing. Stepping back, he gestured at the room behind him.

And there was a lot of room to gesture at. The roof, like in most rooms in the palace, was disconcertingly low. The far wall, in contrast, was some distance away. The long side walls were lined with shelves piled with scrolls and other objects. Statues and tables covered with arrangements of curious and ancient objects divided the room into three sections.

The old man moved to a scroll-covered table next to a half-empty shelf. He lifted a piece of wet cloth from a clay tablet and put it aside, then picked up a scribing tool. As he turned his attention to his scrolls, Emerahl smiled wryly. Clearly she was to find the Thinkers herself.

She walked down the length of the library slowly, examining the objects on display. Several men of different ages were scattered about the room, some reading, some writing, and a few talking quietly together. At the far end five men of differing ages were relaxing on benches, talking. Fragrant smoke wreathed up from a smokewood burner set between them, most likely some kind of stimulant.

As Emerahl approached, the three men who were not talking looked up at her. The younger watched her curiously, while the others turned their attention back to the speakers. She stopped between the benches of the pair who were talking, and the conversation ended. A large man with thick eyebrows and a thin, lipless man looked up at her and frowned in annoyance.

'Greetings, Thinkers,' she said. Now all were watching her. She glanced from face to face and settled on meeting the stare of the larger man. 'Are you Barmonia Tithemaster?'

The eyebrows rose slightly. 'I am.'

'I am Emmea Startracker, daughter of Karo Startracker, a nobleman and mathematician of Toren.'

'You are far from home,' the youngest of the men remarked.

'Yes. My father and I have an interest in antiquities.' She lifted the box containing the fake scroll. 'Recently he bought this, but being unfit to travel he sent me here on his behalf to search out more information. My enquiries have led me to you. I think you will find it most interesting.'

The large man made a sceptical noise. 'I doubt it.'

'I did not mean the box,' she said dryly. 'I meant the contents.'

'I assumed so,' he said.

She met his eyes again. 'I was warned that the Thinkers had no manners, respect for women, or personal hygiene, but I did expect to find clever and enquiring minds.' This brought a smile to the younger Thinker's face, but the others looked indifferent.

'We're wise enough to know no foreign woman could ever bring anything of interest to us.'

She looked at the burner then smiled and nodded to herself. 'I see.'

Turning away, she strolled back down the length of the library. On a heavy table lay a slab of stone, carved with ancient glyphs. To her surprise it was a monument stone from a long-ago dismantled Temple of Jarime – or Raos, as it had once been known. She had probably walked past this very stone in its original resting place many times. How had it come to Mur?

Footsteps drew closer and she realised that someone was approaching. She kept her eyes on the stone, expecting the man to pass, but he didn't. He moved to her side and when she looked up she realised it was the younger of the Thinkers.

She resisted a smile. Of course it was.

'Bar's always been like that,' he said. 'He doesn't like women much. I hope that you are not too disappointed.'

'It is his loss, not mine. Tell me, how did this monument stone come to be here?'

He shrugged. 'It has always been here.'

She chuckled. 'Now I *am* disappointed. Are you Thinkers so befuddled by your smoking herbs that you don't even know the treasures you have here?'

'This is no treasure.'

'A monument stone from ancient Raos no treasure? Do you know how rare these are? The Circlians destroyed so much from the Age of the Many that our history is in fragments.' She pointed at a glyph. 'This priest, Gaomea, is one of the few whose names are still known.' She ran her finger down the line of symbols, translating to Murian. 'Are there any other stones like this here?'

He was staring at her now. 'I don't know, but I can ask the librarian for you. If there is anything here, he'll show you if I ask for it.'

She turned to regard him. 'It's that bad?'

'What?'

'I can't ask for them myself?'

He grimaced. 'No. Like Bar said, you're a woman *and* foreign.'

She sighed and rolled her eyes. 'Well, I suppose it's still better than home. The only way you can see old treasures is to buy them off a rich noble, and only if he or she is willing to sell.'

He led her away from the table toward the old man cataloguing his scrolls. 'All this belongs to the Pentadrians,' he said in a voice that indicated he didn't think much of that.

'At least they haven't destroyed it. The Circlians would have. I was lucky to save this.' She patted the box.

'So . . . what's in there?'

'Just a fragment of a scroll.'

'Why did you come here with it?'

She paused and regarded him carefully. 'It's in Sorl.'

He stared at her in disbelief. She continued on as if mistaking his silence for puzzlement.

'An ancient priest tongue of Mur. I would have thought you'd know that.' She shook her head as if exasperated. 'I was hoping it would make more sense to a local, who might know the places it refers to and what "breath offering" means.' She slipped the box into a bag at her waist. 'Could we ask about those treasures now? I think they're all that's going to make this trip worth the effort.'

The tension and excitement within the young man was palpable. With admirable self-control he kept silent. She was expecting this: the younger Thinkers rarely did anything without consulting their powerful peers first.

'Then I'll just have to make sure old Rikron shows you everything.'

CHAPTER 22

Auraya had tested a few limits to her abilities in the last few days. It was not possible for her to sleep and remain airborne at the same time, so she had remained awake as she hovered over Glymma. After a few sleepless days it became difficult to concentrate, so last night, at Juran's urging, she had retreated to the hills to rest.

Her willingness to obey the gods was constantly tested. She could hear the thoughts of the Siyee. She knew they were chained somewhere below the Sanctuary. She knew they were frightened and despairing.

But they had not been harmed physically. Nobody in the Sanctuary – nobody whose mind she could read – knew what Nekaun planned to do with his prisoners. Some thought he intended to ransom them. Others considered a possibility Auraya was glad the Siyee had not considered: that the sky people would be handed over to a group known as the Thinkers, who would probably study and experiment on them.

Returning to her position high above the Sanctuary, Auraya began to skim the minds of those below.

The first mind she found was that of a Servant given the task of alerting the Voices if Auraya approached the Temple.

The woman had already seen Auraya. She had informed Nekaun telepathically though her star pendant.

Auraya ignored the woman and skimmed over the minds of other Servants and the domestics that took care of mundane chores. Fragments of prayers, recipes, sums and songs came to her. Snatches of gossip, instruction and intrigue threatened to distract her. But her need to find the Siyee was all-consuming.

There. They're still there.

The impracticalities of being physically chained to the same place were beginning to have an effect. She sensed humiliation and revulsion as well as fear. Then she sensed their fear deepen. Looking closer, she saw that one of the Siyee was being taken away. She felt her stomach clench and realised she had let herself drop toward the Sanctuary. Pulling up, she watched and waited, dread growing.

She saw Nekaun through the Siyee's eyes. Nekaun said something, but the Siyee was too frightened to comprehend it. Something about leaving.

Then the chains were removed from the Siyee's wrists. Doors opened and the sky appeared. The Siyee took a step forward, but the man caught his shoulder in a firm grip.

'Tell her to meet me on top of the Sanctuary,' he said slowly.

The Siyee nodded. He was to be a messenger. That was the price of his freedom. The man holding the Siyee let go. The Siyee staggered forward toward the doors. There was a short drop outside. Was this a window, then? No matter. The wind was good. His legs were still stiff. He stretched his arms – he ought to warm his muscles up more before attempting to fly but he wasn't going to stay any longer than he had to.

Reaching the opening, he leapt out and felt his heart soar with joy as the wind lifted him up.

Free . . . but what of the others? He circled higher. *The man wants to speak to Auraya. Maybe she can work something out. But where is she?*

Auraya descended quickly. The Siyee saw her and rose to meet her. He flew in a tight circle around her.

'The leader freed me,' he told her. 'Gave me a message for you. He wants to meet you. On top of the buildings.'

She whistled that she understood.

'How are the others?'

He described what she had seen in the Siyee's minds: the hall, the lack of sanitation and his fears that they would soon lose the ability to fly.

'I took food and water for Zyee and Siti to leave at the places we camped,' she told him. 'Is your water skin empty?'

'Yes.'

'Swap it with mine.'

She flew alongside him to make the exchange. When she was done he circled around her, looking down anxiously.

'Can I help?'

'No. Go home.'

He whistled an acknowledgement.

'Then good luck. Be careful. Could be a trap.'

'I know.'

She watched him fly away. He was tired and hungry. How would he manage to return to Si, across the Sennon desert, with no food but the little she had stolen from Klaff and only one skin of water?

I should have stolen more and flown it back to some of our camps in Sennon. She frowned. *Maybe I should do that now, as well as catch up with him and . . .*

:*Auraya?*

She looked down. A mind was calling her name. Concentrating, she identified the Servant woman given the task of watching for her. The woman was uncertain that her call would be heard, but Nekaun had asked her to try.

Auraya searched for the woman. She found three figures standing on the roof of the topmost Sanctuary building. The woman, Nekaun and another, who was full of suppressed excitement and self-importance.

:Juran? Auraya called.

:Auraya. What is happening?

She told him that Nekaun had freed a Siyee in order to give her a message, and of his request.

:Should I meet with him? she asked.

:This could be a trap, Juran warned.

:I'm willing to take that risk. If I don't meet with Nekaun, he might retaliate by killing Siyee.

:Go then. See what he wants.

She looked up at the tiny speck that was the escaping Siyee.

:If Nekaun wants to ransom the Siyee, will you agree to it?

:That depends on the price.

Taking a deep breath she drew magic, created a barrier around herself and began to descend. She felt a movement in her pack and cursed under her breath. If only she'd thought to ask the Siyee to take Mischief with him. But the veez would have been an extra weight the Siyee didn't need.

Three upturned faces watched her. The woman looked at Nekaun abruptly, made a gesture with her hands, then walked away. She lifted a hatch in the roof of the building and descended into darkness.

Auraya landed several strides away from the two men.

Nekaun smiled. 'Welcome to Glymma, Auraya,' he said in heavily accented Hanian.

Looking at the man standing beside the Voice, Auraya read from his mind that he was Turaan, Nekaun's Companion, and was here to help translate. His master did not yet know any of the northern languages well and doubted Auraya had learned any of the southern ones.

I must be careful to avoid showing an understanding of anything said in the southern languages, she thought. *Nekaun might reason that I have learned them somehow, but the gods will know that isn't true and guess that I'm reading minds.*

'Welcome?' she replied in Hanian. 'I doubt I am.'

Nekaun's smile widened. He spoke in his own language and Turaan repeated his words in Hanian. 'Not to some, but they do not understand your reasons for being here.'

'And you do?'

'Perhaps. I must admit, I am guessing at a few matters. From the Siyee's minds I learned you are forbidden to fight. I guess from this that you are here only to protect them. I think maybe you mean my people no harm.'

'Only if you do no harm to mine.'

His eyebrows rose. 'Yet they came here to harm my people.'

She smiled thinly. 'That is not true.'

He frowned, then chuckled. 'Ah, that is right. They came here to harm the birds. So if a few people got in the way, the Siyee would not have hurt them?'

Auraya crossed her arms. 'I did not give them their orders.'

'It must be difficult to love a people yet watch others rule them badly.'

'It is not a unique position to be in.'

His gaze wavered, as if what she had said had caused him to think of something, then steadied again. 'I make you an offer. If you will stay here and let me show you my people and my city, I will free the Siyee. For every day you are here one will be freed.'

She narrowed her eyes at him. 'All I have to do is stay here?'

'And let me show you my people.'

'Why?'

His expression became serious. 'Your people do not under-stand mine. You think us cruel and depraved. I wish to show that this isn't so.' He grimaced. 'I do not want to harm the Siyee nor do I want to enslave them, as is allowable by our laws. I could ask for money in exchange for their freedom but I do not need it. What I want more is peace. You are not a White, but I doubt a White would ever come here no matter how humble our request. However, you are their ally. You can tell them what you see here.' He looked at her earnestly. 'Will you stay?'

Auraya regarded him suspiciously. It might still be a trap. There was no knowledge of one in Turaan's mind, but he might not have been told.

So? Some risks are worth taking, for the sake of the Siyee.

'One Siyee every day,' she repeated.

'Yes.'

'I must witness them leave.'

'Of course.'

'You will give them food and water for the journey home?'

'It will be arranged.'

'And sanitation for those that remain?'

'I have people already seeking a solution to that problem.'

'Will you swear it on your gods?'

He smiled. 'I swear, on Sheyr, Hrun, Alor, Ranah and Sraal, I will release one Siyee prisoner per day and night you remain here, and that you will not be harmed during that time.'

She looked away, as if considering.

:Juran?

:Yes?

She described the terms of the bargain.

:He will try to recruit or convert you.

:I expect so. He will fail.

:Yes. I believe he will. This is a dangerous game, Auraya, but if you're willing to play it, you have our approval. Good luck.

Meeting Nekaun's eyes, Auraya nodded once.

'I will stay.'

After reporting to Emerahl and The Twins, telling them of Genza's request that he travel with her to Glymma, Mirar had let himself drift into sleep. He dreamed Auraya was trying to tell him something, but a knock interrupted her. Then he realised his eyes were open and he was staring, awake, at the ceiling.

Something just woke me up. Sitting up, he frowned and listened. He looked toward the door . . .

. . . and sensed both hope and uncertainty. A familiar presence stood beyond the door, determination rapidly waning.

Dardel. She's finally got up the courage to approach me again.

For a moment he was caught between conflicting feelings. The memory of Auraya's presence in his dream lingered in his mind. Yet he knew this opportunity to reassure Dardel might not come again.

Auraya isn't here, he told himself. *She's not in love with you.*

Standing up, he walked to the door and opened it. Dardel stared up at him, eyes wide.

'What can I do for you?' he asked.

'I heard you were leaving. I came to . . . to say goodbye.'

Though she did not meet his eyes, he could feel her conflicting emotions. She was hoping they would do more than just *say* goodbye.

'I'm glad you did,' he told her. 'Dardel . . .'

She looked up. He raised an eyebrow. Her lips curled into a smile. 'I hope you don't mind the late hour. I couldn't sleep.'

'Not at all. These hot nights do make sleeping difficult. Would you like to come in and . . . talk?'

She slipped past him into the room. Shutting the door, he turned to find her shrugging out of her vest. 'This heat just makes me want to take off all my clothes.'

He laughed quietly. 'I thought I was the only one.'

Coming over to him, she took hold of his vest. 'Let me help you.'

Dreamweaver robes discarded, they moved to the bed. She smelled of sweat and jungle flowers; the moonlight caught the curve of a shoulder. Breast. Hip. Warm skin under his palms. Hands moving over his body. They drew ever nearer, teasing with fingers, exploring with lips, until they couldn't get any closer. He felt her heels press into his back and then they were rocking back and forth, the only sounds their breathing and the soft creak of the bed, taking him ever closer to that moment when pleasure overtook thought.

When thought returned she pulled away from him. He reached out to touch her, but she caught his hand. Surprised, he looked at her closely and sensed a thoughtfulness.

'Something is different,' she said. She looked at him. 'I thought it would be more exciting now I know who you are. But it isn't. It's . . .' She frowned and shook her head. 'I don't know.'

He leaned back against the wall.

'Sometimes a fantasy is more exciting than reality,' he said.

She nodded, then frowned and shook her head again. 'It's not that.' She looked at him and smiled. 'Well, it is a bit. But there's something about you that's always bothered me. You remind me of . . . have you . . . ?' She stopped and looked thoughtful. 'I get the feeling there's something distracting you, even when you're most, um, attentive.' She paused. 'I'd normally guess it was a woman. I hope that's not too presumptuous.'

She was perceptive, he mused. He also recognised her mood. A bit of conversational intimacy sometimes rounded off bedroom encounters nicely, though women liked it more than men. He had learned to appreciate this long ago. They could be frivolous, funny, outrageous or show depths of intelligence and insight. Sometimes they simply needed to talk about their problems. At times a little too much. That took a little patience.

Dardel was no complainer. He could have shrugged off her guess, but there was no reason to, so long as he kept Auraya's identity secret.

'There is a woman,' he told her.

She looked up at him. 'Then why aren't you with her? Is she in the north?' Her eyes widened. 'Are the Circlian gods keeping you apart?'

He smiled. 'No. Unfortunately she doesn't regard me in the same way I regard her.'

'Oh.' Dardel's shoulders dropped and she smiled at him sympathetically. 'Then she's a fool.'

He chuckled. 'The number of times I've said that to women in the opposite situation. Now I'm reassured that it helps – a little.'

But Dardel didn't appear to be listening. Suddenly she looked up and punched him lightly in the shoulder.

'And you just bedded me! How can you do that when you love another!'

He caught her wrist. 'Do you really expect me to be celibate for a woman who has no interest in me?'

She smiled. 'No. I suppose not.'

'I can think of a few ways you could show your support for my decision not to remain celibate.'

Her eyebrows rose. 'I'm sure you can.' She tilted her head thoughtfully. 'It's nice to know you're human enough to be a fool for love.'

'Is it?' He grimaced. 'Glad it's nice for someone.'

'Aw.' She grinned and patted his cheek. 'Then I guess I'll have to make sure it's extra-nice for you.' Leaning forward, she began to trace her fingers across his chest. He smiled, caught her hand, and pulled her closer.

CHAPTER 23

The Sanctuary, in contrast to the Temple, was a jumble of interconnected buildings on several levels. Auraya felt as if she was descending into a maze, yet every time she began to feel trapped and disorientated Nekaun would lead her into a corridor open to the air on one side, or out into a courtyard. She realised that this form of architecture allowed breezes to flow through the building, making the dry heat bearable.

Most of her thoughts circled around the situation she was now in. The Siyee were hostages. They were fortunate to be, as they had come here to attack Pentadrian property – or forces, depending how the Pentadrians regarded their birds – and could have been killed in retaliation.

Instead they were being used to blackmail her. The price appeared to be small. She must simply stay here a while. Meet Nekaun's people. That was all.

There has to be more to it than that. At best he will try to gain knowledge about the White from me. At the worst he is keeping me near while he works out if he can kill me.

So far Nekaun had led her about the Sanctuary, stopping here and there to point out decorations or explain the use or significance of features. He was playing the gracious host. She felt that while her body was keeping up, her mind was lagging far behind, not yet fully grasping everything that had happened in the last few days, and the full consequences of what she had agreed to.

Nekaun said something in a grand tone.

'And here', Turaan translated, 'are your rooms.'

A servant opened a large pair of double doors. Auraya drew her attention back to her surroundings and followed Nekaun inside. The first room was the size of a house and sparsely furnished. Nekaun gestured at a doorway. Stepping through, Auraya found herself in a broad room filled with an enormous bed. An archway to one side led to a room covered entirely with tiles, a sunken, empty pool in the centre.

'Domestics will bring you water when you wish to bathe,' Nekaun told her through Turaan. He pointed to glass and pottery bottles. 'A selection of perfumes and oils.'

So I am to live in luxury while the Siyee are chained beneath the ground.

'I want to speak to the Siyee,' she found herself saying. 'It is needlessly cruel for them to be ignorant of our agreement.'

Nekaun regarded her thoughtfully.

'I will take you to them,' Turaan translated. 'But only if you swear by your gods that you will not attempt to free them. I would have to stop you, and they might be hurt in the process. I do not wish to harm them.'

'I understand,' she replied. 'I swear on the Circle that I will not attempt to rescue the Siyee you hold captive while our bargain holds.'

He nodded. 'Follow me.'

To her relief he did not stroll along pointing out features of the Sanctuary as he had before. Nor did he set a swift pace, however.

'The Siyee regard you as their own personal White,' he said. 'They believe you consider them your own people. Is that true?'

'It is and it isn't. I am not Siyee. I will never be Siyee.'

'But you have much in common with them. Flying, for instance.'

'Yes.'

'Do you regard Si as your home, or Hania?'

She frowned. 'Si is my home for now, but I will always have a link with Hania.'

He smiled. 'Of course. Did you leave the White in order to live among the Siyee?'

'I am not going to tell you my reasons for leaving the White.'

He chuckled. 'I thought not. But I had to ask. It has been the source of much speculation here.'

They had descended into an underground corridor. The walls were bare and the floor dusty, suggesting this area was little used. The floor dipped slightly at the centre, implying wear over many centuries, perhaps millennia. Intrigued, Auraya looked for other signs that might indicate what this part of the Sanctuary had once been used for.

Nekaun led her through a gate into a passage. They passed a few alcoves, each holding a lamp. At the end they came to a small room. An iron gate filled a large archway, two Servants standing guard on either side. Beyond was a much larger hall filled with columns. At the far end was a chair of enormous size.

It's an old temple, she thought. *That is the throne of a god. A dead god, most likely.*

Then a movement drew her attention to the base of a column and she felt her heart sink.

Siyee were chained to the columns. They sat or crouched on the floor, their thoughts despondent and fearful. Wooden bowls had been set by each Siyee for their excrement, and she could smell the stench of it.

'You said your people would provide sanitation,' she said, turning to face Nekaun. 'This isn't healthy.'

Nekaun's eyebrows rose. 'They *are* prisoners. You can't expect me to treat them like honoured guests.'

She thought of the rooms he had presented to her. 'I don't,' she said. 'But I do expect them to be healthy enough to return home when they are freed. They will sicken like this. They must be allowed to exercise or their wing muscles will grow too weak for flying.'

He looked at the Siyee and nodded slowly. 'I understand. Once I am sure this hall is secure, I will have them unchained from the columns. An area will be set aside for the collection of excrement.' He spoke to the Servants. One drew a key from beneath his robes then moved to the gate and unlocked it.

Auraya strode inside. The Siyee looked up as she approached, their faces and thoughts full of hope. She searched for Sreil. Finding him, she walked over and crouched beside him.

'Are any of you hurt?'

The young man shook his head. 'Scratches, sprains, but nothing more.'

She looked around at the hopeful faces. 'I'm not here to free you,' she told them. 'At least not today. But I have come to an arrangement with Nekaun, the leader of the Pentadrians. Every day I remain here he will set one of you free.'

'There are over thirty of us,' one of the Siyee said. 'That's a whole month. We won't be able to fly if we stay like this for a week.'

'I have explained that to him,' she told him. 'He has agreed to unchain you.'

'Do you trust him?' Sreil asked.

She looked at him and sighed. 'I have to. He swore on his gods. If that doesn't keep him honest, nothing will.'

'What does he want from you?' the priest asked.

'I don't know,' she admitted. 'He says to stay here and meet his people.'

'He will try to corrupt you. Turn you from the gods,' Teel warned.

'No doubt,' she agreed. 'Tomorrow morning we will see if he keeps to his word. I will insist on watching him free one of you.'

Among their doubts and hopes was a concern for herself and gratitude for the risk she was taking for them. She could not help feeling a surge of affection for them. If Nekaun had not been watching and listening, she would have moved among them, talking to and reassuring each, but she did not want him to see how much she valued them or his demands in return for their safety might increase. Standing up, she managed a smile.

'Be strong and patient,' she told them. 'I'll be thinking of you all every moment.'

'And we of you,' Sreil said.

Turning away reluctantly, she forced herself to stride back to the gate. Stepping outside, she turned to face Nekaun.

'If any of them are unable to fly from the Sanctuary, our deal is finished.'

He smiled and nodded. 'Of course. I will see that they are made more comfortable.'

The Palace library closed in the evenings for all but the 'members', which usually gave the Thinkers all the privacy they needed while discussing their progress in the search for the Gods' Scroll.

Or lack of progress, Raynora thought. *I wonder how many other clues my companions have overlooked or dismissed because they didn't like the gender or the race of the one who supplied it? Has their jealousy of all with magical Skills driven them to ignore important information too?*

He felt a familiar twinge of envy and smiled wryly. All

Thinkers coveted magical power, even himself. You always wanted what you couldn't have. Knowing he couldn't become a Servant had made him all the more fascinated by them. He'd wanted to be one once, but when a Thinker was ordained in the aftermath of the war he found his interest waning. He couldn't hope for a role as prestigious as Companion, and the humble life of an ordinary Servant didn't appeal so much when there still wasn't magic involved.

Whereas being a Thinker does gain me some respect from others, and I don't have to give up my assets, small though they may be.

Having come to that conclusion, Ray had found his interest in the Scroll of the Gods diminishing as well. It had been part of his fascination with religion, but now that was gone he was finding the unpleasant personalities of the principal searchers wearing. Barmonia was the driving force of the group, but his arrogance irritated Ray. Mikmer's cynicism was no longer amusing, and gods help you if you got Kereon started on one of his favourite subjects. The only Thinker close to Ray's age was Yathyir, but Ray secretly suspected the Dekkan's parents had made a pact with the gods – to give their son a genius for remembering facts – however, to make room the gods had removed any ability to understand social norms, jokes and subtleties of conversation.

So why am I still here? Well, I was made an offer too good to refuse . . .

'What are you smiling about, Ray?'

He turned to find Mikmer regarding him suspiciously and felt a pang of guilt. To compensate, Ray grinned even wider. 'I was just calculating how much gold the Scroll will bring me when I sell it.'

The others turned to stare at him.

'We are *not* going to sell the Scroll!' Barmonia declared, his face beginning to turn red already.

'Oh, I don't imagine you would,' Ray agreed. 'But I'm sure you'll pay a lot to get it off me.'

Yathyir smiled. 'He means to find it himself.'

Barmonia's eyebrows rose. 'You think you can do so without our help, do you?'

'Maybe,' Ray replied, lounging in his chair with deliberate nonchalance. 'If I can persuade that woman to help me after you all treated her so rudely the other day.'

'That northerner woman!' Barmonia huffed. 'You're welcome to her. All you'll get from her is scabs.'

'Because all northern women are diseased, are they?'

The big man stared back at him. 'No moral woman travels on her own.'

'No moral unSkilled woman, anyway,' Mikmer said quietly.

'She's Skilled?' Yathyir asked, turning to look at Mikmer. 'How do you know?'

The older man's shoulders lifted slightly. 'An educated guess.'

'But you don't know for sure?' Yathyir asked.

Mikmer rolled his eyes, He was not the most patient of men, especially when it came to Yathyir's literal way of thinking. 'Of course not. Did she use magic while she was here? No. Is it likely I went out and found her and asked her to demonstrate, and she agreed to? *No.*'

'Oh,' Yathyir replied, looking thoughtful. Fortunately he never took exception to Mikmer's sarcasm. He accepted it as the normal behaviour of an older, more experienced Thinker.

'You think we should use this woman?' Kereon asked Ray.

All turned to regard the man. Kereon rarely spoke unless he felt he had something worthwhile to say, but when he did he could drone on for hours.

'I do,' Ray replied. 'She read the tablet as if it was her own language, and hinted that she can read ancient Sorl.'

'And if we bring her here and she can't?' Mikmer asked.

'No harm done.'

'Unless she learns something of the Scroll from us,' Yathyir warned.

'She won't learn anything we don't want her to. She only has to try to read the bones.'

'And if she understands them she'll know what we're after,' Barmonia said. 'We can't risk that.'

'Why not? What can she do with that information?'

'She might find it herself.'

'Not if we invite her to join us.'

'Join us!' Barmonia exclaimed. 'We're not working with some foreign flit.'

'She'll steal the credit from us,' Mikmer agreed.

'Don't be ridiculous,' Kereon said, gaining a look of surprise from Barmonia. 'Who would believe her? Nobody.' He leaned forward, mostly toward Barmonia. 'If she can help us, we invite her in. She'll accept because she won't get to see our other artefacts or learn what we know unless she does. When we find out where the Scroll is, her part in it ends.'

Barmonia's eyes had taken on a gleam of interest.

'She won't tell us what the bones say unless we take her with us.'

'If she's clever. Even so, once we have the Scroll we won't have to give her anything. Certainly not any credit.' Kereon smiled. 'Do you really think anyone will believe she had anything to do with finding it, except cooking for us?'

Barmonia sat back and shook his head. 'No. Very well. Bring her in.'

Kereon looked at Ray. 'She'll be suspicious if anyone but you approaches her.'

Ray nodded. 'I'll find her. I can't guarantee that I can persuade her to join us after the way you all treated her the other day, but I'll try.' He narrowed his eyes at Barmonia. 'You'll have the hardest challenge.'

'Putting up with her,' Yathyir said, nodding.

'No,' Ray replied. 'Remembering what manners are.'

As the others grimaced or rolled their eyes, Ray considered how he was going to persuade Emmea to cooperate. He had no illusions that the others would even attempt to be civil. If the woman was going to spend any length of time helping them, she'd need a friend who sympathised with her.

Or more than a friend, he thought. *I'm sure she was flirting with me the other day, though probably only in order to gain my help. She's not young, but she's still attractive despite her age. Besides, they say older women can be very 'educational'* . . .

The news had come like a chill wind, whipping its way through corridors and halls to every corner of the Sanctuary. Servants and domestics alike had been in a fervour of excitement and terror since.

Auraya is here! they whispered. *Nekaun has brought an ex-White into the Sanctuary! The one that can fly! The one that killed Kuar!*

Kikarn had told Reivan in the morning, between a trader protesting against the limitation to his imports and a cousin of the new Dekkan High Chieftain delivering a generous donation from his family. Reivan had thought of Imenja first. Her mistress had respected the former First Voice and had grieved his death. What would she think of Kuar's killer walking freely in the Sanctuary?

Reivan half expected to be summoned, but no mental call came through the pendant until the evening. As she continued to work, she found herself wondering if she might encounter Auraya on her way to meet Imenja. The idea didn't appeal to her. By the time she was free to leave she was dreading the walk up to the Upper Sanctuary. It seemed longer than usual, but all she encountered were other Servants from whom she heard tantalising snatches of conversation.

She found Imenja in a dark mood.

'So you've heard about our special guest,' her mistress said as soon as she saw Reivan, rising to look out of the window at the lights of the city. 'I suppose the news has spread through the city by now. Nekaun has decided to play host to the enemy.'

'She's not one of the White any more,' Reivan reminded her.

'No. But still a Circlian priestess.'

Moving to the other side of the window, Reivan watched Imenja's face closely. 'Does Nekaun hope to change that?'

Imenja scowled. 'I can see no other reason.'

Reivan frowned. 'How did he persuade her to . . . ah, the Siyee.'

'Yes. He has promised to release one every day she remains here.'

'Nothing more?'

'I suppose he could have threatened to torture or kill them,' Imenja muttered. 'But even he has enough sense to realise that would hardly persuade her to join us.'

'I meant: was staying here all he asked from her?'

Imenja's lips pressed into a thin smile. 'Yes. I doubt she would have agreed to join us in exchange for their release. No, he'll have to woo her, and she knows it. His greatest challenge. A seduction worthy of . . .' She paused and grimaced apologetically. 'I'm sorry. Those words were badly chosen.'

Looking away, Reivan tried to push aside the tight, uncomfortable feeling that had gripped her. She had hoped Nekaun would visit her last night, now that he had returned, but her bed had remained empty.

It's only one night, she told herself.

He was busy planning his seduction of Auraya, a dark voice in the back of her mind added.

'Tonight there will be a great feast for her. We're not invited. He doesn't want to surround her with powerful sorcerers in case she feels threatened.'

'I suppose you'll get to meet her eventually.'

Imenja nodded, then her eyes sharpened. She pointed out of the window. 'There she is now.'

Reivan turned and looked in the direction Imenja had indicated. A movement in a courtyard a few levels down caught her eye. Two people walked across the pavement and stopped in a pool of light cast by a lamp: one male in black robes, one female in the white clothes of a Circlian priestess. Underneath the strange overgarment, she was wearing a short tunic.

And trousers, Reivan noted. *How strange.*

The pair moved to the fountain. It was the one Imi, the Elai princess, had recovered in during her stay. As Auraya turned to look up at the statue Reivan had a good view of her face. She felt her heart sink.

Even from here she is beautiful and exotic. She reluctantly made herself read the messages in Nekaun's stance. It brought the word 'seduction' back to her mind. His appearance of intense interest in Auraya might simply be an act for the White's benefit, but it was a convincing one.

Too convincing?

She shook her head and turned her mind to more practical matters.

'What will happen if he succeeds in his seduction? Will we go to war again?'

Imenja made a low noise. 'I hope not.'

'It is possible,' Reivan said to herself. 'Or he might simply be removing an advantage the White have over us.'

'And gaining it for ourselves.' Imenja looked thoughtful.

'Just in case the White have ideas about invading.' She paused and looked at Imenja. 'Do they?'

'I'd have thought not, if not for the Siyee attacking Klaff. It would make sense to kill off the birds if they were planning to wage war against us.' Imenja crossed her arms. 'The Siyee believe their action was retribution.'

'For what?'

'A failed plot. Not mine.'

Reivan smiled at the wary tone in Imenja's voice. Obviously this plot was yet another one her mistress could not discuss. She looked down at the courtyard again. Auraya gestured toward the pool. Suddenly something jumped out of the woman's bag and onto the pool edge.

It was an animal of some sort, small and lithe. After drinking from the pool, it scampered around the fountain then, at a gesture from Auraya, slunk reluctantly back into her bag.

Reivan found herself thinking of something a Servant in the monastery she had grown up in had told her once. *'You can tell a lot about a person from how they treat animals, and how animals treat them.'*

Auraya and Nekaun moved out of sight. Reivan sighed. If Nekaun did manage to 'seduce' Auraya would she stay here in Glymma? If so, she would not be embraced by most Pentadrians. She had, after all, struck the blow that had killed Kuar and won the war for the Circlians. She would have no friends here.

Imenja abruptly moved away from the window. 'When I do meet with her, I want you with me to help translate.'

Reivan followed her mistress to the chairs.

'I'll be there. Not sure if I'm looking forward to being in her presence, but I'm sure it will be interesting.'

Imenja's mouth twisted into a half-smile.

'Yes, but interesting isn't always pleasant.'

CHAPTER 24

E merahl approached the library door slowly, concentrating her senses on what lay beyond. She sensed only a handful of minds. Some were dark with annoyance and scepticism, others curious. One was a little more familiar than the rest, and full of anticipation.

Ray, I'm guessing.

He had pounced on her in the market, seemingly oblivious to her embarrassment at being discovered selling cures, and invited her to meet with the Thinkers again as soon as she was able. They had arranged a time for that afternoon, and she had returned to her room to deposit her cure bag and collect the fake scrolls.

Taking hold of the handle, she twisted it and felt the latch slide free. The door swung inward easily. She stepped into the library and closed the door behind her.

The librarian regarded her suspiciously over the same pile of scrolls she had seen him cataloguing last time. She ignored him and walked to the end of the room. The same five men sat in the same positions.

Almost as if I hadn't left, she mused. *Except this time they're not ignoring me.*

Ray stood up and smiled. 'Greetings. Thank you for

returning. Here,' he gestured to an empty chair. 'Please sit down.'

She sat where he indicated and looked around at the faces.

'This is Emmea Startracker, in case you didn't catch the name last time,' Ray said to the other men. He gestured at each man in turn, beginning with the larger. 'This is Barmonia Tithemaster, our leader and expert in history and old languages. This is Mikmer Lawmaker, another historian. Kereon Cupman, finder and collector of artefacts, and Yathyir Gold, who has a flawless memory for facts.'

He then placed a hand on his chest. 'I am Raynora Vorn and I've spent too much time studying dead gods and their followers.'

She did her best to look impressed. 'With such qualifications I would be surprised if none of you could help me with this scroll.' She lifted the box.

'Well show us then,' Barmonia said, holding his hands out.

As she gave him the box her heart began to beat faster. Though The Twins had guided her in making the scroll, they hadn't actually seen them with their own eyes. They looked convincing enough to Emerahl, but these men were experts.

Barmonia opened the box and gently lifted out the roll of parchment. He unrolled it slightly and a fine dust wafted off. His eyebrows rose, then his eyes moved back and forth as he scanned the glyphs.

Abruptly he stood up and moved to a table. There he weighed down the corners of the scroll and carefully rolled it open further. As the other men rose and walked over to watch, Emerahl followed them.

'This means "priest",' Barmonia said, pointing to a glyph. 'And this "most favoured" or "special".' He paused.

'It says ". . . the goddess ordered her favourite priest to write her words on a scroll . . .",' Emerahl told him.

A tense silence followed, then Barmonia sighed heavily. 'You can read this?'

'Yes. I don't understand some of it. What does "breath offering" mean?'

Barmonia smiled. 'To offer your last breath to the goddess. Which is just another way to declare oneself a follower in the hope a god or goddess will take your soul when you die.'

Emerahl nodded. 'I see. I was a bit worried it meant voluntary strangulation or something similar.'

'When it comes to history it is all too easy for the imagination of the untrained to blur the truth. Especially with young women.'

Emerahl met his eyes and held them. The man's face began to redden. She felt a hand on her shoulder.

'We're all very impressed, Emmea,' Ray said. 'Would you read out the entire scroll for us?'

She turned her attention back to the roll of parchment, stepping closer to Barmonia. It was supposed to be a scrap of a record of the priests of the goddess Sorli, and the information was all accurate according to The Twins. When she had read it out the men were thoughtfully silent.

'Well then, what else can we get her to read?' Ray asked.

Barmonia sighed. 'Bring out the bones.'

'Bones?' Emerahl asked.

Ray smiled but did not answer. She watched as Kereon and Mikmer disappeared through a door and returned carefully carrying a long, heavy box between them. They placed it on the table and Barmonia lifted the lid.

Emerahl did not have to fake her surprise. Within was a skeleton. That was not surprising. The Twins had told her the Thinkers believed that there was significance in 'a lot of old bones'. But they didn't understand what it was because the Thinkers didn't.

They must have known why the bones were special, Emerahl mused. *They just left that bit for me to discover.*

The bones were covered in glyphs. As Ray picked one up and handed it to her she saw that the symbols had been carved into the surface, then painted black. She stared at them in wonder.

'Where did you find this?'

'Dug up in an old temple,' Kereon said lightly. 'This man must have been very important.'

She looked down into the box, read the rest of the glyphs and nodded.

'He was. This was the last favoured priest of the goddess Sorli.'

And the glyphs confirmed the Scroll's existence and location . . . but she wasn't going to tell them the latter.

'Read,' Barmonia said in a low voice.

'The glyphs on the skull say: "I am the favoured priest of the goddess Sorli." On the right arm it says: "To me are entrusted the secrets of the gods". Not "god"; it is the plural form. On the left it says: "Seek the truth in the sacred chamber when the gods are most . . ." Hmm, "occupied" is the closest translation.' She chuckled. 'A riddle. I so love it when there's a riddle. The legs say: "Sorli will direct the way. A mortal may enter and take the secrets."' She paused.

A mortal may enter and take the secrets? Does that mean not an immortal? Where can a mortal go that an immortal can't?

'Is that it?' Barmonia asked.

'No, there are glyphs on the ribs. Are they in the right order?'

The men exchanged looks of dismay. None were experts on anatomy, she knew.

'What do they say? Maybe we can work out their order.'

She gave them enough words to describe the place named

on the ribs, but not the directions. 'If arranged like this,' she changed the positions of a few ribs, 'it says "heart speaks more". I'm guessing that means there are further instructions in this "sacred chamber".'

Barmonia scowled, but she sensed that he was pleased.

'Then we'll just have to take you there,' he said.

She narrowed her eyes at him and pretended dismay and suspicion.

'Take me where?'

'The famous city of Sorlina.'

The platten driver and his assistant scurried about erecting the tents and setting a fire. The Dunwayans were as comfortable outdoors as in their fortresses and even the most powerful and rich clan leaders were happy to sleep in the open during long journeys. Camping areas were maintained along every road. If there was no river there was always a well. Fireplaces of various sizes could be found and piles of firewood, and in some places constructions had been built designed for exercise and the practice of fighting skills.

Another benefit of camping was that a traveller's identity was less likely to be noted than if he or she stayed at a fortress. Ella had found spies in the few forts they had visited in order to buy food. Though these spies hadn't identified her, they had heard of her arrival and departure from Chon and had been told to watch for her in case she had not returned to Jarime, as I-Portak claimed.

Danjin and Ella were sitting on wooden boxes near the fire, blankets folded several times as cushions. Gillen was still inside the platten; he had been asleep when they'd arrived and Ella had decided not to wake him. Yem was gathering together some of the cooking implements and supplies.

Cooking was one of the warrior's many unexpected talents,

and he said the easiest dish to make while camping was called 'coopa': various ingredients cooked in spices and water to which dry bread was added to help form a sauce. The previous night he had disappeared into a forest and returned with a large bird, an arrow protruding from its chest. He'd kept the feathers and stowed them away in the platten somewhere.

Now he was carrying a large pot, some root vegetables and a package to the newly made fire. Danjin watched as the warrior chopped ingredients and added them to the pot. From time to time he rose to collect water or leaves from plants in the camp site. The smell of the bubbling concoction became more and more appetising. Then Yem unwrapped the parcel.

At first Danjin caught his breath in horror. In the dark the contents looked like swollen fingers. But as Yem began to slice them Danjin realised they could not be. They were some kind of stuffed tube. Yem glanced up at Danjin and smiled.

'They're made of shem intestines,' Yem explained. 'Washed out and stuffed with meat and spices. These are made with a very rare spice. The one the spy in Chon sells.'

Danjin nodded and watched doubtfully as the warrior deposited the sliced tubes into the pot. The mixture was bubbling gently. A rich aroma wafted out and set Danjin's stomach growling.

'How long have we been here?' a muffled voice asked. All turned to see Gillen emerging from the platten. He looked at the tents, now fully erected, and his eyebrows rose. 'That long? You should have woken me.'

'You obviously needed the sleep,' Ella told him.

The man grimaced. 'Yes. Don't tell any Dunwayans or I'll never be able to negotiate a deal again, but I've never taken a liking to sleeping on the hard ground,' he said quietly in Hanian. He walked over to the fire and drew in a deep breath. 'I see we're in for a treat tonight,' he said in Dunwayan. 'Or rather, an extra-special leg of the superb culinary journey we are undertaking.'

Yem looked up and grinned. 'It would be a shame if our visitors left Dunway having only experienced sleeping on hard ground and chasing after vagrant servants.'

Gillen blushed. Danjin chuckled as the ambassador sat down and sighed. 'My secret's out. I'm unworthy,' he mourned. Yem smiled and said nothing as he stirred the pot.

Looking at Ella, Danjin noted the distant focus of her gaze. Her forehead was creased and her lips pressed into a thin line. Whatever – whoever – she was listening to was causing her both concern and anger.

The servant they were following was half a day's journey to their east, nearing the south-western coast of Dunway. He had no idea if he was close to his destination and those that had helped him along the way were no better informed. If he reached the coast he would have to turn east or west. Or leave Dunway. Ella was less concerned about the latter than the possibility there was a Pentadrian base in Dunway.

They were all used to her silences now. Danjin turned his attention back to the other two men, and they talked of places they'd seen and their experiences in the war. At some point Yem decided his 'coopa' was ready and scooped some into bowls for them. Even the servants received some, despite the expensive meat tubes it contained.

The spice from the meat had flavoured the whole dish, giving it a heat that set Danjin's mouth burning pleasantly. The meat itself was a little too spicy for his taste, however. And very salty.

After they had eaten, they drank a little fwa and talked some more. Ella roused herself and joined in. Eventually the yawns of Gillen prompted her to suggest they retire to bed.

Danjin rose to follow, but Ella placed a hand on his arm.

'Stay a while. I need to talk to you.'

He sat down again.

She smiled and looked up at the sky. 'Look at the stars. Are they brighter here than in Jarime?'

'I was told once that all the lamps and lights of Jarime make them seem dimmer.'

'I have never slept out of doors before this journey. It is pleasant, though I can imagine it wouldn't be if it were raining or cold.'

'No,' he agreed, thinking back to a few uncomfortable nights in his youth, and during the trek to the battle with the Pentadrians.

'The Siyee live in tents all the time, don't they?'

Danjin nodded. 'Larger and more resilient than these, of course. They call them bowers.'

'Bowers,' she repeated, glancing toward the tents of Yem, Gillen and the servants. 'Good,' she murmured. 'They're asleep.'

'That's quick,' Danjin said quietly. 'Gillen must not be feeling the hard ground as much as he claims.'

She smiled, but her expression quickly became serious again.

'I have bad news for you, Danjin. Auraya has joined the Pentadrians.'

He blinked, then stared at her in shock.

'No,' he found himself saying. 'She wouldn't have. Not willingly.'

'She has, though I do not know on what terms.'

Danjin looked away. Auraya and the Pentadrians. It wasn't possible. She resented them as much as any Circlian did for daring to invade and causing the death of so many – especially the Siyee.

There had to be a reason . . .

'The gods must have asked her to,' he concluded aloud. 'She would never turn against them.'

Ella smiled. 'Your loyalty is your strength and your weakness, Danjin Spear. Do you have the same faith in me?'

He met her eyes and nodded. 'Of course.'

'But in Auraya your trust is misplaced. She has already disobeyed the gods once.'

He looked away. 'I know you're referring to her resignation. I accept that there are details I don't know. That you cannot risk telling me.'

'Risk? No. I did not tell you because I did not want to disappoint you,' she said gently. 'I could see that you regarded her with a similar pride and affection that you feel for your daughters. Any ill doing of hers would hurt you.' She sighed and straightened. 'But it is time you knew the truth. If she has truly allied herself with the Pentadrians your loyalty is a trait she can exploit.'

He felt a stab of fear, then smiled at the irony. Now that he was going to learn what Auraya had done he didn't want to. Ella was not going to take pity on him, however.

'You know of her affair with the Dreamweaver Leiard,' she began. 'What you don't know is that he is not who he claimed to be.'

He frowned. 'Who is he?'

'Mirar.'

He stared at her for a long time, expecting her to smile and admit to a joke. But she didn't. She returned his stare with grim determination.

'But . . . that's not possible,' he finally said. 'Juran would have recognised him!'

She grimaced. 'Somehow he suppressed his true identity to the point that neither he nor the gods were aware of it. But when he regained it the gods were able to identify him. Juran says his memory of Mirar had faded, and Leiard looked very different.'

'I doubt the gods were happy about this.'

'No. They sent Auraya to kill him.'

Danjin drew in a sharp breath and stared at her, appalled. 'And she couldn't.'

'No.'

'So they threw her out of the White.'

'No. She resigned, having rightly concluded that an inability to obey the gods is a weakness a White should not have.'

He winced. 'They couldn't expect her to kill someone she loved. Couldn't someone else have done it?'

'He isn't the man she loved. He is Mirar. And he was in Si. No other White could get to him as quickly as she.'

'Oh.' *I bet she was cursing her flying ability that day*, he thought.

'Leiard was a temporary personality behind which Mirar hid. She would not have been killing her former lover. She knew that.'

Danjin sighed. 'I'm sure she did. Even so, I wouldn't find it easy to kill the *likeness* of someone I loved.'

'Being a White is not meant to be easy.'

He nodded at that. She was right, but he found her ruthless judgement hard to accept. Surely she was being too hard on Auraya. But how could she feel sympathy for Auraya when she hadn't yet faced such a dilemma herself?

Then how is it that I can sympathise with Auraya? Is Ella right? Am I too blindly loyal?

He sighed. 'So she returned to Si . . .' He frowned as he realised what that might have meant. 'Was Mirar still there?'

'No. He escaped to Southern Ithania, where the Pentadrians have welcomed him.'

The Pentadrians. And now Auraya was there. Danjin's heart sank. 'Is she now Mirar's lover?' he asked with difficulty.

'I don't believe so.'

'So her joining the Pentadrians has nothing to do with him?' he asked hopefully.

Ella looked away and frowned. 'I don't know. But there is something else you should know. Auraya met with a mysterious woman a few months ago. We believe she was a Wild, and taught Auraya forbidden Gifts. The ability to shield her mind from the gods . . . and perhaps the secret of immortality.'

'Auraya is a *Wild*?'

'Possibly.'

He shook his head. 'So that makes her an enemy of the gods?'

Ella glanced at him and looked away again. 'No.'

She didn't elaborate, and it was curious to see her looking so uncomfortable. Perhaps only because she didn't have the answer to this.

Danjin considered all he had learned. The gods hadn't rejected Auraya. Ella had said Auraya was *possibly* a Wild. Perhaps the gods' acceptance of her meant she wasn't.

Or perhaps the existence of immortal sorcerers doesn't bother them so long as those sorcerers worship them.

Ella turned to regard him again. 'So, as you will see once you get over the surprise of these revelations, if the Pentadrians have a Wild's strength to call upon they will be considerably stronger. Add to that the knowledge Auraya has of Circlian strengths and weaknesses and any thought of future conflicts is alarming.'

'Yes,' Danjin agreed.

'She knows us too well, but you know her better than anyone. I want you to consider all the ways she could use her knowledge of us against us, and how can we use our knowledge of her against her.'

He nodded. 'Very well. I could do with something to occupy my mind on this journey.'

She gave him an odd look. 'You are not distressed by the thought of plotting against Auraya?'

He smiled. 'Another advantage of my loyalty. I don't mind imagining her doing it because I don't believe she will.'

Ella shook her head. 'If that's what it takes, then I won't shatter any more of your illusions.' She rose. 'Good night, Danjin Spear.'

'Good night.'

CHAPTER 25

A soft mattress meant a bed, and a bed meant Auraya was in her room in the Tower . . . but that couldn't be true.

Auraya opened her eyes and groaned as she remembered everything: the failed Siyee attack on the Pentadrian birds, her agreement with Nekaun; that she was in the Sanctuary, the enemy's home. She was instantly awake, her mind going straight to the day ahead and what must happen soon.

I have been here nearly one night and day. If Nekaun keeps his word a Siyee will go free.

And if he doesn't?

Then she would leave – if she could – and try to find a way to free the Siyee.

As she got out of bed she heard a small, sleepy noise of protest. Looking down, she saw Mischief blinking up at her. He stretched, the end of his tail quivering.

'Fooaaawwwd,' he said at the same time as yawning.

'I'll see what I can arrange,' she told him.

Servants had brought her a mountain of clothing the day before. She had selected a simple shift to wear while sleeping, then cleaned and dried her circ and the trousers and sleeveless tunic she had arrived in. Changing into her priestess clothes again, she moved to the window.

It gave a splendid view of the city and the roofs and court-yards of the Sanctuary. The rooms she had been given were probably for important guests. *I wonder who has stayed here before. The rooms are large, but they're not highly adorned. There isn't much furniture. Kings and such would probably stay somewhere bigger and fancier.*

Mischief leapt up onto the sill, his ears pricked and his nose twitching.

'Stay here,' she warned. His ears dropped in disappointment, but he settled into a crouch with his tail wrapped around his body, his mind all acceptance.

A knocking came from the next room. She froze, then drew in a deep breath and let it out slowly. Walking away from the window, she moved to the double doors of the main room. When she opened them, Nekaun's Companion, Turaan, bowed his head to her, as did the crowd of servants behind him.

Not servants, she reminded herself. *Domestics*.

'Good morning, Priestess Auraya,' Turaan said. 'I bring food and water.'

She stepped aside. The domestics filed into the room, each carrying something. The man ordered them about. Several set their burdens on a table, then lifted woven covers to reveal elaborately prepared and arranged food, including fruit and bread. Two enormous pottery jugs were set on the floor, then a small crowd of men poured water from pitchers into them until they were close to overflowing.

Other domestics disappeared into the bedroom. Looking inside, she watched them tidy the bed with practised efficiency, gather up the clothes she had slept in and those she had ignored, then file out of the room again. They did not touch her pack, and didn't appear to notice Mischief sitting on the windowsill.

One, a young woman, turned to face Auraya, eyes downcast. She pointed to the tiled room, then at the jugs of water.

Auraya shook her head, though not without a twinge of regret. It had been a long time since she had enjoyed a hot bath, but she would not be able to relax knowing she would soon be playing guest to Nekaun.

'Priestess Auraya.'

She turned to face Turaan.

'The First Voice asked me to tell you he will be with you shortly. Please eat and be refreshed. You will accompany him to the roof to witness the release of a Siyee.'

She nodded and then watched the servants file out of the room again. Though they were quiet and reserved, their minds were full of curiosity, resentment and fear. She was the enemy. She was dangerous. Why was Nekaun treating her like a guest?

When the doors had closed behind them, she moved to the table and examined the food. Last night she had considered the possibility that Nekaun would try to poison her. She hadn't tested her healing Gift on poison yet, but when she had considered how she would deal with such a threat she felt her confidence rising.

Taking fruit and bread, she moved to the window to eat it. A small thump drew her attention back to the table. Mischief was sniffing at one of the plates. As he began to nibble at one of the morsels she felt a stab of apprehension. What if he ate something poisonous? She could probably heal him, but what if she wasn't there when it happened?

I'll just have to take him with me everywhere.

She finished eating, then retrieved her pack from the bedroom. There was little inside. Just an empty water skin, some cures, a spare tunic and pair of trousers.

Emptying it, she shook sand and dust from it and set it aside. Then she sat down to wait.

Not long after, another knock came from the door. This time Nekaun stood beyond, Turaan behind him.

'Greetings, Sorceress Auraya.'

'Priestess,' she corrected.

'*Priestess* Auraya. It is time I honoured my side of our bargain,' Nekaun said, smiling.

'Just a moment.' Picking up the pack, she called to Mischief. The veez bounded over to her and leapt up into her arms. Used to this routine, he dived straight into the pack. She hitched it over her shoulder and turned to face Nekaun.

'I'm ready.'

He nodded, then ushered her out into the corridor.

'What do you call that creature?'

'It is a veez,' she told him. 'From Somrey.'

'A pet?'

'Yes.'

'It speaks.'

'They learn the words they need to express their wants or concerns, such as food, warmth and danger – which doesn't make them stimulating conversationalists.'

He chuckled. 'I suppose it wouldn't. Did you sleep well?'

'No.'

'Did the heat bother you?'

'Partly.'

'You did choose the hottest part of the year to visit us,' he reminded her.

She decided not to respond to that. He led her up a flight of stairs.

'Was the food to your liking?' he asked.

'Yes.'

'Anything you would like to request?'

She felt Mischief stir inside the pack. He was uncomfortably warm inside, and a little stifled.

'Raw meat for Mischief,' she replied. 'And that all food be

removed from my room when I leave it. I do not want him eating anything unsuitable.'

He'll like the meat, she thought. *And if he is poisoned I will know the attack was directed at him in order to harm me, rather than him taking food meant for me.*

'That will be arranged,' Nekaun told her. 'Here we are.'

He led her up a narrow staircase through a hole in the ceiling. They emerged into bright sunlight, on the roof of a building. She had seen seats and potted trees on many of the Sanctuary rooftops, indicating that they were treated much like courtyards.

Four Servants stood near another hole in the roof. They looked at Nekaun expectantly. He spoke a word and they turned to look down into the hole.

Auraya's heart twisted as a Siyee climbed up onto the roof. He winced, then blinked rapidly as his eyes adjusted to the light. Rope bound his wrists together, which must have been uncomfortable as it pinched in the membrane of his wings. His head moved from side to side as he took in the rooftop he was standing on. When he saw Auraya beside Nekaun and Turaan he stilled.

I'm the first, he thought joyfully. Then he felt a wave of guilt. *The others . . . I don't want to leave them behind . . . but I must. If I don't, it might end this deal Auraya has made.*

A Servant cut his bonds and another held out a water skin and a parcel of food. The Siyee examined them suspiciously, then tucked them away in his vest.

He looked at her, his mind full of gratitude. She nodded to him.

Just go, she thought at him.

As the Servants stepped away the Siyee turned his back on them and broke into a run, leaping off the building and gliding away.

315

Auraya slowly let out the breath she had been holding. The winged figure arced away from the Sanctuary, circling the hill and heading south. She watched him until she could no longer see him.

Then Nekaun turned to her and smiled.

'Now you must keep your side of the bargain, Sorceress Auraya, and I have much to show you.'

Rain and heat assailed Kave in successive waves each day, so the air became thick with humidity. Washed clothes refused to dry and dry clothes were wet with perspiration as soon as they were worn. The stink of the refuse below the city rose to cover all in a layer of foulness. Biting insects swarmed in clouds, forcing the city's inhabitants to stay indoors, so Mirar and Tintel saw few people as they walked toward the river.

Tintel wiped her brow with a wet cloth and sighed.

'I so love this time of year,' she said dryly.

'How long does this last?' he asked.

'Up to four weeks. Once it went for six. Anyone who can afford to leaves Kave for the summer. Even if they can bear the heat, there is the summer fever to avoid.'

Mirar thought of the increasing number of sick people coming to the hospice. The other Dreamweavers had explained that this was a yearly occurrence, and soon the whole House would be filled with beds occupied by the sick. The fever was rarely fatal, however.

Ahead the houses ended abruptly a few hundred paces from the river's edge. Narrow wooden staircases descended to the muddy ground below, where a temporary road of planks led away to the water's edge.

Mirar and Tintel stopped. They could see a barge tied up to pylons, surrounded by Servants. Men dressed only in short trousers were carrying boxes and chests on board, their backs slick with sweat.

'I have a parting gift for you,' Tintel said.

Mirar turned to regard her.

'You don't have to—'

'Wait and see,' she told him sternly. 'You will need this gift.'

Opening the bag hanging from her shoulder, she lifted out a clay jug with a narrow neck. The top was sealed with a lump of wax from which a string protruded. Grabbing the string, she pulled the wax plug free.

'Hold out your hands.'

Mirar did as she asked. She tipped the bottle and a yellowish oil filled the hollow of one palm. It smelled pleasantly herbal and zesty.

'Rub this into all exposed skin,' Tintel instructed, tipping oil into her own hand. 'It helps keep the bugs and summer fever at bay.'

'So the bugs bring the sickness?' he asked as he rubbed the oil over his hands then onto his face.

'Maybe.' Tintel shrugged. 'Maybe it's just a convenient side effect of the oil. It does help to cool the fever.'

'It is surprisingly refreshing. Makes the heat a little more bearable.'

She stoppered the bottle and replaced it, then drew out a small wooden box. Opening it, she showed him that it was full of candles.

'They're scented with the same extracts. Use them sparingly and they should last you the journey to the escarpment. We sell both oil and candles each summer, for the cost of making them. We are the only ones who make it, even though we give the recipe away to anyone who wants it.'

'So anyone seeking a profit can't compete with you. Do you ever have a shortfall of oil and candles?'

'Yes.' She frowned. 'Would you have us make a profit on a cure?'

'If people are harmed by a lack of oil, then yes. The profits can go toward the House or the sick.'

'You have no idea what a relief it is to hear you say that.' She closed the box and returned it to the bag, then handed the bag to him.

He smiled. 'Are you testing me, Tintel?'

She chuckled. 'I might be. Intention and meaning can change over many years. Some Dreamweavers believe you forbade the selling of cures.'

'It's not adv—'

'Dreamweaver Mirar?'

The voice was full of confidence and power. He turned to face the owner, who was climbing the last few stairs up to the platform.

'Fourth Voice Genza,' he replied. He gestured to Tintel. 'This is Dreamweaver Tintel, who runs the Kave Dreamweaver House.'

Genza nodded at Tintel. 'I must apologise for taking your founder and guide from you. I know at this time of year his knowledge and powers would be of great benefit to the city.'

Tintel shrugged. 'We have been dealing with the fever every year for centuries. I'm sure we will cope well enough without him.'

Genza's eyes brightened with amusement. 'Indeed, you have. Kave owes you a great debt.' She turned her attention to Mirar. 'We are almost ready to leave.'

He nodded and turned to Tintel. 'Thank you for putting up with me. I hope the summer heat ends early in Kave.'

Tintel nodded. 'I hope all goes well in Glymma. I expect you'll continue to explore Southern Ithania afterwards. I look forward to seeing you in Kave again, though perhaps in a better season.'

'I would like to see it in full flood,' he told her.

'Perhaps next time.' She made the old Dreamweaver gesture – a touch to the heart, mouth and forehead. 'Goodbye.'

Surprised, he returned the gesture, then turned to Genza and she, taking that to indicate he was ready, led him toward the stairs.

As he followed her down to the plank road, then along it toward the barge, he thought of the news The Twins had delivered in a dream link last night.

:Auraya is in Glymma, they'd told him. As they'd described the Siyee mission and its failure Mirar had been stunned that the White would do something so foolish. He was not surprised that the attack had failed, though it was worrying that the Pentadrians had been forewarned. Was there a spy in the Siyee ranks? There couldn't be one among the White's most trusted, or they would have read the deceit from the spy's mind.

He hadn't been surprised to learn that Auraya had accepted Nekaun's offer, agreeing to stay in Glymma in exchange for the release of the Siyee. *I wonder how the White regard her striking a deal with the enemy. Or rather, allowing herself to be blackmailed into staying there in exchange for the Siyee's freedom.*

There were twenty-eight Siyee prisoners remaining. One would have been released today. From Tintel's description of the river journey to the escarpment, more than three quarters of the Siyee would be free before he'd travelled a third of the way to Glymma. At this time of year, the river moved so sluggishly that barges must be poled or rowed up and down.

So Tamun and Surim have nothing to worry about. The Twins had been concerned that Nekaun planned to use Auraya against Mirar, or vice versa.

:Everyone thinks you and Auraya are deadly enemies. Some believe that Nekaun will offer to kill you in exchange for Auraya's support. Or that he'll offer to kill Auraya in order to gain your support.

:*Auraya won't ally herself with the White's enemy*, Miràr had replied, though he wasn't completely sure that was true. She had sacrificed a great deal to save the Siyee before.

:*Good thing they don't know how you two really regarded each other, eh?* Surim had said. *They'd just have to decide which to imprison and which to blackmail.*

:*Blackmail wouldn't work on her*, Mirar reminded them.

:*Ah, but it would definitely work on you.*

Surim was right, but Mirar had reassured himself with two facts: he was never going to get to Glymma in time, and it took a lot of magic to imprison someone as powerful as Auraya. It would occupy one or more of the Voices night and day, in shifts. It would make them less able to defend themselves should the White attack.

He and Genza had reached the barge. She ushered him on board and showed him the cabin that had been prepared for him. It was tiny, but clean.

Ropes were untied from pylons and crew used poles to push the craft out into the river. Shallow-hulled, the barge rocked ponderously in the water. Genza moved to the prow then turned and said something to the crew, who withdrew their poles.

Then Mirar took an involuntary step backwards as the barge began to plough through the river, churning up waves on either side. He felt his stomach sink at the same time as his heart lightened.

Looks like there is a good chance I will make it to Glymma in time to see Auraya.

CHAPTER 26

Auraya had walked down corridors tiled in intricate patterns, entered rooms carpeted in rich colours and strolled through courtyards cooled by elegant fountains and exotic plants. She had been served meals of artfully prepared food from pottery and glassware of the highest quality with utensils fashioned of gold. She had heard strange and beautiful music and admired sculptures and artwork, the most amusing being a map of all Ithania made of tiny glass tiles in which the Elai were depicted as golden-haired maidens with fish tails and the Siyee as humans with feathered wings sprouting from their backs.

Nekaun was doing his best to impress her.

Though she couldn't be sure it was his true purpose, he was making it no secret that he intended to win her over. The possibility that he might believe she would turn from the Circlian gods and ally herself with the Pentadrians had been so ridiculous that she had discounted it at first. But she soon realised he had to consider the possibility that she might have left the White, perhaps even turned from her gods, due to a conflict. She might change sides if she wanted revenge, a return of power, or simply found the ideology of Pentadrians suited her better.

He would give up if she appeared incorruptible. Yet the sooner he felt he had won her over, the sooner he would stop trying. There were twenty-seven Siyee still imprisoned in the caves beneath the Sanctuary so she had to keep this game going for twenty-eight more days.

I have to seem impressed, but not too interested. Resistant, but not unpersuadable, she told herself. *I should pretend to have the occasional moment of weakness in order to keep him hoping he can win me over.*

Nekaun was leading her down a wide corridor that apparently connected the Lower Sanctuary with the Upper Sanctuary.

'Is it true that the White live in rooms as plain and small as those their priests occupy?' he asked, his ever-present Companion, Turaan, repeating the words in Hanian.

'Plain, yes,' she replied. 'Small, no.'

It took constant concentration to ensure she didn't reveal her mind-reading ability. The sooner she learned some of the local language the better. Someone had advised her of that. She heard a familiar voice in her memory.

'You never know when a bit of the local tongue might work to your advantage. Perhaps even save your life.'

Danjin had said that. She felt a pang of sadness. It had been so long since she'd seen him. She missed his sturdy presence.

'You lived in the White Tower, didn't you?' Nekaun asked.

'Yes.'

'Do all priests in the Temple live in the Tower?'

She looked at him sceptically. 'I only agreed to stay here, not to give you information about your enemy.'

His smile widened. 'Forgive me. I did not intend to take advantage of you. I am merely interested. Here,' he gestured to a narrow opening in a wall. 'Here is a place very precious to us. The Star Room.'

From Turaan came a sudden nervous excitement, and she read

from him that this was the Pentadrians' primary worshipping place. An altar of some kind. As Nekaun stepped through the gap Auraya hesitated. How dangerous could the altar of the enemy gods be? Could they do anything to her there that they couldn't outside of it?

Nekaun promised on those gods that I would remain unharmed, she reminded herself. *And I agreed to stay and be shown around. If either of us is going to break our word, I won't be the first.*

Taking a deep breath, she stepped through the gap into a large room. Black walls, floor and ceiling surrounded her. The walls were at strange angles. She realised there were five of them; the room was a pentagon. Nekaun was standing at the centre, between lines of silver set into the floor. A chill ran down her spine as she realised they formed a giant star.

She looked up at Nekaun.

'Am I to be introduced to your gods now?' she asked, pleased to hear that her voice was calm.

His smile, usually so charming, was wry.

'No. The gods choose when they appear, not I. They don't often speak to us, and rarely instruct us. We appreciate the freedom to govern ourselves and they trust us to do it well.'

'If they never appear, then some of your people must come to the conclusion they do not exist.'

He chuckled. 'I didn't say they *never* appear. You do not believe they are real, do you?'

'I know at least one is,' she told him, 'as I saw him during the war.'

He blinked in surprise. 'You saw one of our gods?'

'Sheyr, I believe.'

'He only appeared the once.' He narrowed his eyes. 'You were there?'

'Yes. When your people emerged from the mines. That is how we knew to return from the pass and meet you.'

He shook his head. 'What were you doing there?'

Moping over Leiard, she thought wryly. *Can't tell him that* . . . 'Exploring,' she told him. 'I was about to leave, but Chaia stopped me.' She smiled. 'Sometimes it is better when a god is willing to visit and instruct his followers.'

His eyebrows rose, giving him a thoughtful expression.

'Do you believe my gods are real?' she asked.

His shoulders lifted. 'I have not seen them, but I believe it is likely.'

'Are your gods survivors of the War of the Gods?'

'I don't know,' he replied frankly. 'They have never said they aren't.'

She shook her head. 'Either your gods are new, or my gods were not aware your gods had evaded them.'

He pursed his lips and considered her. 'Are you ever disturbed by the knowledge that your gods claim to have murdered so many other gods, and are proud of it?'

She frowned. 'No. The old gods were cruel and used mortals badly.'

'And your gods did not?'

Abruptly, Auraya thought of Emerahl's story of Chaia's seduction of women, and of the tales of deformities during the years of transformation by Huan that the Siyee told to each new generation.

'You hesitate,' he pointed out quietly.

I believe I've just given him one of those moments of weakness I was planning, she mused. *Except it wasn't planned and I wasn't pretending.*

'They may not be without fault,' she conceded. 'But beings as old as they, are likely to have made bad decisions from time to time. From what I have been taught, the dead gods were guilty of far worse. What matters more than past errors is that the Circle has brought peace, order and prosperity to Northern

Ithania since they united. In the last hundred years seven countries have become allies, and no wars had been fought – until your people invaded.'

His expression was unreadable now. Stepping out of the star shape, he walked over to face her, then gestured to the opening. 'Shall we move on? I would like to show you the Lower Sanctuary, where we meet and deal with the public. If you are committed to peace, order and prosperity I think you will find it interesting.'

She smiled and graciously let him usher her from the room.

The sky was streaked with clouds of bright orange deepening into pink, but a wall of darkness hid the source of the fading light. The escarpment looming over the dry land shortened the days by blocking out the sun in the afternoon.

I wouldn't like to live here, Emerahl thought. *There's something ominous about that cliff. I feel like it is going to tumble onto us at any moment.*

The speed at which the Thinkers had managed to bring together a caravan of platten to take them all to Sorlina was impressive. Two days after her reading of the bones, Emerahl paid her board and transferred her belongings to one of several covered platten heading out of the city. Barmonia told her that he was leading the expedition, as he had travelled to the ruined city so many times that he had lost count. She might have taken the jovial way he spoke to her now as an indication that he was warming to her, if she hadn't been able to sense his disdain whenever she was around.

Let him play at being friendly, she thought. *The journey will be less pleasant otherwise. I can't exactly tell him I know he and his colleagues are planning to dump me on a ship once they've found the Scroll.*

A faint vibration ran through the ground, strong enough

to set the tent ropes swinging. Emerahl looked up at the men sitting around the camp. Most had paused and wore alert, wary expressions, but these quickly disappeared as the vibration faded away.

'Tremor,' Yathyir murmured to himself before helping himself to another bowl of the overly spicy grain dish the servants had cooked up for them.

Ray looked up at Emerahl and smiled. 'Happens all the time,' he told her. 'The great Thinker Marmel believed that the escarpment is a sheet of the world sliding over another sheet – the one we're sitting on. Sometimes the earth shakes so hard you can't stand up. Sometimes it brings down houses.'

Emerahl looked up at the escarpment and frowned.

'I'm surprised that Hannaya still stands.'

'Oh, bits of it collapse from time to time, but it is strong enough to withstand most tremors. Carved out of solid rock by sorcerers, they say.'

'How far does the escarpment go?'

'All the way to the south-west coast. In some places it is higher, some lower. We're going to one of the few gaps, where it has split.' He held his hands out, palms down, and mimicked the sliding top sheet of land breaking apart and the two sides moving away from each other. 'The land between is a long, steep slope. It was one of the few inland crossings from Avven to Mur for thousands of years, so the people who controlled and tolled the transfer of goods from one land to another became wealthy. Then the War of the Gods happened and within a year power shifted from followers of dead gods to followers of the Five.'

'A year? How do you know that?'

'If you look at stories from the time you can piece together a certain order. Of course, some claimed their gods were alive when they weren't. Others claimed gods of their enemies were dead when they were still alive. But most were killed over a short space of time.'

Emerahl shook her head in wonder. She had never known how or when the deaths had occurred. The consequences had come slowly. 'It must have taken mortals some time to grasp what had happened.'

'Some never did. It is hard to prove the death of invisible beings. There are no corpses. No witnesses. Just silence.'

'Yet their loss affected the world dramatically.'

'Yes. Priests lost their powers. Gods no longer advised or controlled their followers. Some people took advantage of their enemy's weakness and uncertainty. But not for long. The Five united to bring order to chaos.'

'So the Pentadrian gods existed before the war?'

'I believe so. Sheyr was the God of Prosperity, Hrun the Goddess of Love, Alor the God of Warriors, Ranah the Goddess of Fire and Sraal the God of Wealth. They are still worshipped as such in some places.'

Emerahl considered the list of names and titles. The Circlian gods had once claimed their own titles. Chaia had been the God of Kings and Huan the Goddess of Fertility.

Fertility and Love. Not such a big difference. Both sides have their war god, too. I guess they are matters people are most likely to pray about. Give me a lover, protect my lover, give me children, make me wealthy, don't let me die . . .

As for the rest of the gods, the Pentadrians appeared to have the advantage, Emerahl mused. A God of Wealth had to be more useful than Saru, the former God of Gambling – or even a God of Kings. But the southern continent could do with a Goddess of Women, if the dislike for her gender was as strong in the general population as it was with these Thinkers.

Barmonia stood up and yawned loudly.

'We start early tomorrow,' he warned. 'So don't stay up too late.'

As he stalked off toward the tents the other men got to their feet like obedient but reluctant children. Emerahl found Ray smiling at her.

'Would you let me have the honour of escorting you to your tent?' he asked.

She laughed quietly. 'It is I who would be honoured,' she replied with equal mock formality.

Kereon glanced back at them and rolled his eyes, but said nothing. Yathyir stared, his suspicions about Ray's motives painfully clear from the avid gleam in his eyes and the adolescent jealousy she sensed.

From Raynora she discerned expectation. She wasn't surprised. Men were opportunistic and often assumed women living anything other than the life of a dutiful wife must be doing so in order to have their pick of lovers.

Not that Emerahl wasn't.

The tent was not far away, but getting to it required stepping over several ropes. Ray hovered close, ready to help if she tripped, and she sensed disappointment from him when she arrived without mishap. She turned to face him.

'You're very beautiful,' he said softly.

She nearly laughed out loud. He was gazing at her as if in awe, but she could sense he was mainly feeling desire.

Still, he was charming and good-looking. There might be advantages in taking him to bed. He was also the first man who had shown an interest since Mirar . . .

. . . *and that hadn't come to anything.*

She felt a pang of guilt at that thought. It was unfair. Leiard had been controlling him.

Then suddenly she remembered Leiard in the cave in Si, staring at her out of Mirar's eyes.

'. . . joining the brothel was necessity . . . but I also wonder if you unknowingly seek the same kind of assurance that Mirar seeks. You seek a reminder that you are a physical being, not a god . . .'

She took a step away from Ray. The thought of bedding him no longer appealed. The other Thinkers might take it as proof that their prejudices about foreign women were correct – not that they'd suddenly respect her for remaining chaste.

'Good night Ray,' she said. 'I'm tired. I'll see you in the morning.'

She backed into the tent and closed the flaps firmly. He was all surprise and disappointment, then amusement and determination. After a moment she heard him walk away and breathed a sigh of relief. She drew magic and put a barrier across the entrance.

I'll have to turn him down a few times before he gives up, she told herself. She regarded the narrow bench covered in a thin mattress that served as a bed and shrugged. *Well, it's better than the bottom of a boat, and I don't want to fall asleep too quickly anyway*.

Lying down, she closed her eyes and let herself relax. Slowly her thoughts began to drift. Soon she had completely lost track of time.

:Emerahl.

The Twins' dual voices were like an echoing whisper in her thoughts.

:Surim. Tamun.

:You were wise to reject your admirer, Tamun told her.

:Oh? Why?

:Surim would have found it much too interesting.

Emerahl felt a surge of relief. She hadn't considered that The Twins might end up watching her bedroom antics through the eyes of Raynora. The thought was disturbing.

:You wouldn't have watched me, would you, Surim?

:I'd have to, in case something happened to you. It would be entirely for your own protection.

:I see. And if something did happen, what could you do to protect me?

He didn't reply.

:We've discovered the true source of the money being offered to Raynora for the Scrolls, Tamun said. *It is coming from the Voices. They or their gods must have known the Thinkers are seeking the Scrolls, and don't like it.*

:Which supports our suspicion that the Scrolls contain something dangerous to the gods, Surim added.

:Could I bribe Ray to give them to me? Emerahl asked.

:No. You risk revealing your knowledge of his mission. His gods may be watching.

:If they are, they will be suspicious of me already since they can't read my mind.

:True. They probably tolerate your involvement only because your help enables Ray to steal the Scrolls sooner.

:How can I stop him?

:Easy. Steal them yourself.

:Steal the Scrolls from the Thinkers, the smartest people in Southern Ithania, while their gods watch? Emerahl felt a rush of amusement. *Now that is going to be satisfying.*

CHAPTER 27

As Ton reached the crest of the hill, panting and sweating, he paused to catch his breath. Looking up, he forgot his weariness and stared ahead in awe. The land before him undulated in gentle hills, then descended to an abrupt stop where a flat expanse, glowing with the light of a low-hanging sun, stretched to meet the sky.

The sea, he thought. *So that's what it looks like.*

The water glittered like expensive cloth or a great rippling sheet of gold. He suddenly understood that the strange tang in the air was salt.

I must be getting close to the haven . . . unless it's over the sea, He scanned the hills before him, his whole body trembling with anticipation and exhaustion. He felt as if he had been walking forever. The life he'd left behind seemed like a dream. A bad dream.

Near the coast were the tiny shapes of many, many houses. A fine thread wound past them: a river. He could make out smoke ascending in the dusky air. Was this the haven Chemalya had told him of?

Only one way to find out. He pushed himself on. *At least it's all downhill from here.*

As the hours passed he kept his mind occupied with thoughts

of his wife Gli and their two boys. They would love it here. His boys had never seen the sea. He must learn how to sail and take them out. Perhaps they would become fishermen. Or farmers. It would be hard work, but better than being treated like a slave. Not that Ton had suffered as much as Gli had in her youth. They both hated Gim and his clan. All that talk of honour and pride. He'd never met a warrior who had a decent thought in his head. The sooner Ton got his family away from there the better.

His mood turned gloomier as night descended. He rested beside the road until the moon rose and gave him some light to travel by, then he pressed on. Just when he began to wonder if the road had missed the village he saw lights in the distance. His stomach fluttered with excitement, stirring the hunger that had nagged at him for days.

But as he reached the first house a powerful reluctance to draw attention to himself or disturb the villagers came over him. He slowed and plodded quietly on. The houses were widely spaced at first, but soon they occurred more often until they sat side by side. A man emerged from a door ahead. As he drew closer to Ton he frowned and stared in an unfriendly fashion. But then a smile sprang to his face.

'Newcomer, eh? They'll be waiting for you. Big drinking house a few doors down on the right.'

Ton mumbled thanks and hurried on. He could not have missed the drinking house. Light and many voices spilled from the windows and door. A tall lanky man sitting on a bench outside smiled as he saw Ton, and stood up.

'I'm Warwel. Who would you be?' he asked.

'Ton.'

'Ah. Welcome to Dram. Come inside. You must be tired. And hungry.'

'Very,' Ton admitted.

The man placed a hand on Ton's shoulder and steered him through the door. It took a few moments for Ton's eyes to adjust to the bright lamplight, but he heard the pause in conversation. Looking around, he saw that the room was full of men and women. Some regarded him with welcoming smiles, others with curiosity, and a few with guarded expressions.

'This is Ton,' Warwel announced loudly. 'A newcomer from . . . ?' He looked at Ton.

'Chon,' Ton said quietly.

'From Chon,' Warwel boomed. 'Ton from Chon. He's come a long way.'

Murmurs of welcome filled the room. Warwel gestured to a woman. 'Kit, would you bring him something to eat?' Ton felt his heart lift at the polite request, and the dignified clothing of the woman. She must be a servant or Warwel wouldn't ask her to fetch anything, yet he hadn't treated her like a slave.

Maybe it's true what the spice seller said. Of course it's true. I wouldn't have left my family and come this far if I hadn't believed him.

Still, it was such a relief to know he hadn't been deceived.

Warwel guided Ton to a bench before a large table occupied by several other people. They were drinking, but none looked drunk.

'Chem told me about you,' Warwel said.

Ton blinked at him in confusion. 'He did? I thought he didn't know where you were?'

Warwel tapped his forehead. 'We talk with our minds. I don't have to tell him where I am.'

'Oh.' Magic. Ton looked around at the people. They looked a lot like Chem. Or rather, Chem looked like them.

As the truth dawned on him, a huge bowl of soup was placed in front of him and a plate of bread.

They're all Pentadrians, he thought. He looked down at

the soup and his stomach growled. *The enemy*. There was a utensil of some sort in the bowl. He lifted it. *If I join them I'll be a traitor to my country*. It was a small ladle, and there was a piece of meat in it. He stared at it in disbelief. Meat! *But the warriors will kill me and my family if they find out*. The meat sank out of sight as he let go of the ladle. He looked up at Warwel.

'My family . . .' he began, then sought the words to explain.

'We'll make every effort to bring them here,' Warwel assured him. 'Though I must be honest: it will be more difficult now that the clans are looking for spies.'

Ton nodded. 'Is Chem . . . ?'

'Alive? Yes, he appears to have escaped notice for now.'

Then there was a chance. Ton picked up the ladle and brought it to his mouth. The soup was hot and spicy. It smelled of Chem's shop. The meat was tender and as delicious as he had always suspected it would be. Why else did the warriors hoard it to themselves? He ate steadily until both bread and soup were gone, then he turned to Warwel.

'So how do I convert?'

The man blinked in surprise, then laughed.

'You don't have to, Ton. But if you want to we'll teach you about the Five.' He hesitated. 'You would so easily turn from the Circle?'

Ton shrugged. 'What has Lore ever done for me or my family? He only cares about warriors.'

'And the other gods?'

'Never did me any good either.' Ton yawned. Exhaustion, the warmth in the room and the food were making him sleepy. Gli had always accused him of making hasty decisions when he was tired. He frowned. 'I suppose I should wait until Gli gets here, but in the meantime it can't hurt to learn about your gods.'

Warwel smiled broadly. 'Then we'll teach you. But for now I think what you need the most is a good night's sleep. Come with me and I'll arrange a bed for you.'

The freed Siyee was now a speck in the hazy morning sky. In the corner of her eye, Auraya saw Nekaun uncross his arms and knew the game was about to begin again.

'I thought we might explore the city today,' he said lightly. 'I would like to introduce you to my people.'

His people, she mused. *As if he is the sole ruler of this continent. I wonder how the other Voices feel about that.*

'That would be interesting,' she replied. 'I'm sure I have seen everything and met everyone in the Sanctuary by now – except the other Voices, of course.'

'They are eager to meet you,' he told her.

She smiled thinly. 'I doubt that.'

He chuckled. 'You must remember that, unlike myself, they once faced you across a battlefield. They may be quite intimidated by you.'

Intimidated? She frowned. *More likely he's worried that they'll attack me and break his promise that I won't be harmed.*

He gestured toward the stairs. 'Shall we move on?'

She followed him into the building then through the Sanctuary. Turaan came after them silently. Servants paused to stare at her briefly before hurrying away. From their minds she read a now familiar mixture of curiosity and dislike for her. The Pentadrians knew her only from the battle. She was an enemy who had killed their former leader. They accepted Nekaun's judgement, however, and concluded that if he was treating her politely, they would do the same.

Their regard for Nekaun was high, but not quite the same as the affection they felt for the other Voices. She also picked up thoughts in which he was compared to his predecessor, and from these she guessed that while Nekaun was liked and respected, Kuar had been adored.

Nekaun wants that adoration, she guessed. *What will he do to earn it?* She shivered. *Invade Northern Ithania again?* Yet by introducing her to his people and showing her their ways he was making a small step toward encouraging understanding between Circlians and Pentadrians. Perhaps he hoped that *avoiding* a war would raise him in the eyes of his people.

They had arrived at the large hall that was the entrance to the Sanctuary. It was as busy with Servants and non-Servants as it had been when Nekaun had first shown it to her. They paused to watch as Nekaun led her to the arched facade at the front of the building. He stepped out and began descending the wide staircase.

At the edge of the road below, several muscular, bare-chested men and a Servant stood beside a litter. Looking closer, Auraya picked up thoughts of boredom and resentment as well as resignation. These were the first slaves she had seen. Nekaun had told her of the tradition of enslaving criminals. It was a novel idea – perhaps more merciful than execution – though only useful to the Servants since the system would work only if slave masters were Gifted enough to suppress rebellion.

Nekaun ushered her onto the litter, where she sat opposite him and his Companion. The Servant barked orders and the slaves bent to pick up the litter. It was a disconcerting sensation being lifted by the men. Though the worst they could do to her was drop the litter she could not help feeling uneasy.

At Nekaun's order they set off down the wide main street of the city. Her host began talking, and Turaan translated. He spoke about the houses that had been removed long ago to make this parade, and other changes that had been made a hundred years ago. Auraya barely heard. Her attention was being drawn away by the thoughts of the people around her.

As they noticed the litter they stopped to stare. Initially it was Nekaun that attracted their interest, as the sight of the First Voice was something that excited them. She caught glimpses of plans to boast to friends and family about sighting him.

But the excitement was short-lived. All around her, interest was changing to shock and anger, and she was the cause. Those that didn't recognise her from the war were informed by those who did. Rumours had circulated that she was in the Sanctuary. Few favoured her presence, but now they were outraged that she might show herself so openly to the kin of those she and her allies had killed.

Never mind that this was Nekaun's idea, she thought wryly.

As the anger of the crowd increased, Auraya's skin prickled with warning. She drew a little magic and surrounded herself with a light, invisible barrier. Nekaun's chatter had slowed. A slight crease appeared between his brows, but he kept talking. Auraya endeavoured to look unconcerned, hoping that if they kept moving the crowd would not have the chance to gather and confront them.

Not that I have anything to fear from them, she told herself. *But it would be embarrassing to Nekaun, and that's never good for a man in his position.*

People had begun to follow the litter. She felt her heart-beat quicken. As the crowd grew, the slaves noticed and began glancing around with worried expressions. Turaan was pale, but he kept translating doggedly. Nekaun ordered the litter into a side street.

They had travelled only a short way along this when people began to emerge from narrow streets on either side. A noisy crowd formed around the litter, forcing it to stop.

'Murderer!' someone shouted.

'Go home. You're not welcome here!'

Those and following shouts were spoken in the local tongue, but Auraya knew she could pretend she guessed their meaning from their tone. She looked around at the people. One man met her eyes, scowled, then spat at her face. The spittle splattered against her shield and dropped to the ground.

She realised her heart was racing. Though she did not fear these people, she could not help reacting to their threatening behaviour. Nekaun ordered the litter lowered. As it met the ground he stood up. The crowd drew back a few steps and quietened.

'People of Glymma, do not shame me,' he implored. 'I understand your anger. Here before you sits a sorceress who was once our enemy, and you see no reason to gain her favour. But there is a reason. A very good reason. She does not know or understand you. If she did, she would love you as I do. Like me, she would not bear to see you or your families harmed. I know you are honourable and loyal. Let her see *that*, not this pointless hatred.'

The people were not entirely convinced, but Nekaun's words had subdued them into a dissatisfied and begrudging obedience. They drew back, muttering. Nekaun sat down and nodded to the Servant controlling the slaves. The litter rose again, and the crowd parted to allow it to continue.

Though Nekaun appeared relaxed, there was a stiffness to the way he braced himself against the swaying of the litter. He did not meet her eyes. It was obvious he had miscalculated his people badly.

Her heart was still beating quickly, yet she felt only sadness. *They hate me*, she thought. *They hate me and I understand why. I represent their enemy. Nekaun will have a hard time convincing them to ally with Northern Ithania in the future. In fact, it may be impossible.*

As soon as the litter had turned down the next street Nekaun ordered the men to return to the Sanctuary. Auraya looked at him questioningly.

'We will return and change to a covered platten,' he told her. 'Not for your safety,' he assured her. 'You are in no danger, but it will be more convenient and prevent delays. I am sorry you had to see that.'

'Are you? Or was this to show me the effect of my apparent crimes?'

'No. I did not expect it,' he said. 'I forget sometimes that most people are less forgiving than I.'

'You were not in the war, then?'

'I was.' He turned back to meet her regard, all signs of weakness gone.

'Then surely you understand their anger,' she said. 'It is never easy to forgive the killing of family and friends, and they have no choice but to believe the invasion of Northern Ithania was justified or else they would lose faith in their gods and leaders. So they blame the people they invaded.'

'Your people are not innocent of that crime now,' he reminded her. 'It is amusing to hear you admonish us when you accompanied those who invaded us.'

'The Siyee attack on the birds?' She shook her head. 'That was no invasion, but a foolish act of vengeance for the actions of your people in Jarime.' *Arranged by Huan*, she added silently.

'Interesting that you think so,' he said.

'What else would it be? Your defences must be weak indeed if thirty or so Siyee could have threatened Southern Ithania.'

'Thirty-three Siyee and one sorceress,' he corrected. 'Ah, but you were forbidden by your gods to join in any fighting, weren't you? How strange.'

She shrugged.

He smiled. 'I suspect your gods have other reasons to send

you here. Trouble is, I cannot guess what. Except, perhaps, that you are a spy.'

'Then why are you giving me the tour of your city?'

'Because I know you will find no great secrets or weaknesses here. We are not planning another invasion of Northern Ithania. I am serious about forging peace between our peoples.'

She looked at Nekaun. 'But I *have* discovered a weakness here. You do not truly understand your own people. You may read their thoughts, but you won't accept that there is too much hatred between our peoples now for peace to come so easily. Either side will resist any attempt to ally with those that killed their kin. They crave revenge, and if they get it vengeance will be dealt out in kind. It may go on and on, year after year, century after century. Why? Because your gods urged your people to invade mine.'

He stared at her, then slowly smiled.

'Ah, but have you ever wondered why they did?' he asked. 'Because yours won't tolerate followers of any gods but the Circle. Don't the peoples of the world deserve the freedom to worship who they wish?'

The litter was coming alongside the Sanctuary steps. Auraya met Nekaun's eyes. 'Perhaps they do, but if your gods thought invading Northern Ithania would free mortals from Circlian intolerance they made a supremely grand mistake. All they did was kill a lot of people, Circlian and Pentadrian, and ensure many more would continue to die.'

The litter stopped. Nekaun gave no orders, instead considering her words.

'To that I can only make two replies. Firstly, that the decision was not the gods', as they leave such matters to us to decide. Secondly, that we will never find peace if we never look and strive for it. It may take time and much effort.' He smiled. 'Unlike you, I have all the time in the world.'

* * *

Since announcing that the servant had reached his destination and ordering Yem, Gillen and Danjin back into the platten, Ella's attention had been caught in some distant place. The men now spoke in hushed voices to avoid distracting her. When Gillen won a game of counters his comical choked noises and gestures of suppressed glee made Danjin's loss of coin less painful.

It helped that Danjin rarely lost to Gillen. Yem, on the other hand, was surprisingly adept at the game. Fortunately Yem was as scornful of wagers and gambling as Gillen was enchanted by them. Losing to him only cost Danjin a little pride.

Gillen had put away the set now and was sitting with his eyes closed. Slowly the man's head tilted sideways and his mouth opened. A soft snorting filled the cabin.

Yem didn't appear to notice. He was sitting with the relaxed ease of a younger man, his eyes almost closed and his gaze distant. He went into this meditative state whenever conversation lapsed, and Danjin would not have been surprised to find it was a skill all warriors were taught. Whenever there was a loud noise or someone spoke, Yem's eyes would open and he was instantly alert.

I could do with that skill, Danjin thought.

He turned to regard Ella, and was surprised to find her watching him. She smiled.

'Have you learned much?' he asked.

She nodded, then glanced at Yem, who was now regarding her expectantly.

'I will tell you,' she said. 'Then we must sleep as best we can. We will travel through the night to lessen the chances of the villagers learning we are coming. A platten passing at night might attract some curiosity, but if we travel during the day we are sure to be noticed.'

'The arem will not last,' Yem warned.

'Then we will purchase more.'

Yem's brow furrowed, but he said nothing. Danjin had seen the warrior helping the servants tend to the animals, and had even heard him murmuring into one of the arem's ears soothingly when a distant howling in the forest had spooked it. Few Dunwayan warriors owned reyna, but those that did all but worshipped the animals. Danjin had never seen a warrior show any regard for the slow, practical arem.

Danjin looked at Gillen, who was still snoring. He nudged the man's foot with the toe of his sandal. It took a few taps before he woke up.

'What? Are we stopping now?' Gillen asked, blinking at them.

'No. Ellareen is going to tell us what she has discovered,' Danjin replied.

Gillen rubbed his eyes. 'Oh.'

'Take a moment to wake up properly,' Ella said gently.

The ambassador slapped his cheeks. 'I'm fine. Go ahead.'

Ella smiled and shrugged. 'The story I've pieced together from the villagers' minds is this: almost a year ago a Pentadrian ship was wrecked near a village named Dram. The villagers rescued as many as they could and welcomed them into their homes. The survivors repaid them by working in the fields or with domestic chores. When they expressed a wish to stay, the villagers helped them build homes and find work, with the permission of the clan that owns this land.

'What they don't know was that the ship had been deliberately wrecked, and that those on board had not struggled to live in their infertile homeland, as they'd claimed. They were Pentadrian priests and their families, sent to befriend and then convert Dunwayans.'

She scowled. 'They've managed to convert half the village

so far. The rest accept the conversion of their fellow villagers, though a few resent the newcomers for various petty reasons.' She looked at Yem. 'Once settled, the Pentadrians began to arrange for discontented servants to be brought to Dram. I don't know why the local clan has allowed these Pentadrians to stay, but I intend to find out. The villagers believe the increase in produce from the extra workers ensures their leaders aren't looking too closely at matters.'

Yem shrugged. 'We don't often see the Correl clan in Chon. They pay their taxes and cast their votes, but otherwise keep to themselves.'

'I want to pay them a visit,' she said.

'We will pass the road to their fortress tomorrow,' he told her.

Ella looked thoughtful. 'Good. We'll need their help rounding up these Pentadrians.'

'You risk warning the Pentadrians of your arrival if you visit the fortress,' Gillen warned. 'What if there are spies there?'

'I will find and deal with them,' she said firmly.

Yem shifted in his seat. 'What will you do with the Pentadrians?'

Ella frowned. 'That will be up to Juran and I-Portak to decide.'

'Along with the fate of the villagers?'

'Yes.'

Yem's brow furrowed again, but he stayed silent. Gillen grimaced and sighed.

'The villagers were deceived,' Danjin pointed out. 'All they are guilty of is extending a helping hand to people they thought were in need. Surely they won't be punished for that.'

'The clans won't care,' Gillen said. 'They will want to make an example of them, to discourage servants from leaving their masters or hiding the enemy.'

'They will be given a chance to explain themselves,' Yem assured Danjin.

Will it do them any good? Danjin wondered. Dunwayan justice tended to be unforgiving and brutal.

'They turned from the gods,' Ella said darkly. 'They are not completely guiltless, Danjin.'

He stared at her, perturbed. Her eyes narrowed and he felt a chill run down his back. *Why do I feel like she is looking for signs of disloyalty?* He pushed the feeling aside. *My role is to advise. I'm supposed to ask uncomfortable questions.*

'What of those villagers who did not turn from the gods, who do not know they were deceived?'

'Who ought to have reported the presence of the enemy?' she asked in reply. 'Nobody is guiltless in this case, Danjin.'

'The lack of interference from the clan may have been taken as approval,' Danjin argued. 'They would have feared to speak against their masters.'

'You don't know that, Danjin,' she said, smiling, 'but we will find out soon enough. If it will ease your conscience, I will look for such thoughts among the villagers. I doubt, however, that the clans will be as sympathetic as you are.' She looked at Yem, who shrugged resignedly. 'Now let's get what sleep we can. Tomorrow will be a busy day.'

CHAPTER 28

The hall in which the Voices held formal dinners for guests echoed with Reivan's and Imenja's steps. Five places were set at the end of the long table. Just five people dining in this enormous room. It seemed ridiculous, but it was all part of Nekaun's efforts to impress Auraya.

As Reivan and Imenja neared the end of the table a door opened nearby. A woman entered and for a moment all Reivan saw was the white garb of a Circlian Priestess, and she felt a rush of fear.

Then she saw Nekaun following the woman, Turaan trailing behind. The black of his robes were a contrast to Auraya's white. An equally powerful statement. She felt fear subside to a nervous excitement.

With both Imenja and Nekaun present, Reivan was safe enough. Auraya could not hope to overcome Nekaun and Imenja in magical strength . . . though it was hard for Reivan to imagine the two Voices cooperating.

They would if they had to, she thought. Taking a deep breath, she hoped her fear hadn't shown on her face. Of course, that wouldn't help much if Auraya could still read minds. She glanced at Imenja.

:Can she?

:We are not sure.

'Priestess Auraya, this is the Second Voice, Imenja,' Nekaun said. Turaan translated the words into Hanian. 'Imenja, this is Priestess Auraya, formerly of the White,' Nekaun finished.

'Welcome to Glymma and the Sanctuary,' Imenja said in Avvenan. 'It is much better to be facing you over dinner rather than a battlefield.' Auraya's expression remained blank until Turaan translated, suggesting to Reivan that Auraya could not read minds.

The former White smiled faintly. 'It certainly is – for myself as well.'

Imenja turned her head slightly toward Reivan, as if reluctant to stop watching Auraya for even a moment.

'This is my Companion, Reivan.'

Auraya met Reivan's eyes. 'I am honoured to meet you, Companion Reivan. Nekaun has told me much about you, including how you led the Pentadrian army out of the mines.'

Reivan felt her face warm. 'I am honoured to meet you, too.' *How much did he tell her about me? Oh, don't be ridiculous, Reivan. He's not going to discuss matters of the heart with a former White.*

The former White looked amused, no doubt because of Reivan's blush. Reivan was relieved when the woman's attention shifted back to Imenja, who said something about Reivan knowing the Sennon language so perhaps they should all speak that, but Reivan barely heard because Nekaun had finally met her gaze. He smiled, making her heart skip, then looked away and gestured to the table.

'Please sit down,' he said. 'We shall talk in comfort.'

Imenja and Auraya moved to opposite sides of the table, while Nekaun took his customary place at the head. Reivan found herself sitting opposite Turaan. The man gave her a brief haughty look before turning his attention back to the others.

'It is an interesting idea, this position of Companion,' Auraya said. 'I had an adviser, but he was not required to become a priest.'

'Why was that?' Imenja asked.

'An adviser need only be smart, educated and well-connected. A priest or priestess must be Gifted. If we restricted our advisers to priests and priestesses, we'd bar potentially valuable people from our service.'

'That is true,' Imenja agreed. 'Which is why we no longer require all our Servants to have Skills.'

Please don't tell her I've got no magical ability, Reivan thought at Imenja. *That's something I'd rather a former White didn't know.*

'Most of our Servants are Skilled,' Nekaun added. 'The few that aren't have exceptional abilities that more than make up for their lack of magical talent.'

'Do you have a group similar to the Thinkers?' Imenja asked.

Auraya shook her head. 'There are wealthy, educated men and women who explore academic pursuits for the sake of entertainment, self-improvement or trade, but they have not united as a collective that I know of. What have your Thinkers discovered or developed recently?'

Nekaun began to describe several constructions the Thinkers had designed. Servants brought the first dish and conversation shifted to other subjects, slowed by the constant need for translation. Turaan drank a lot of water, but his voice grew hoarse as the evening lengthened. Reivan barely needed to speak at all. Instead she concentrated on absorbing and considering everything about Auraya.

After the last dish was eaten and the plates taken away, Imenja leaned forward.

'So what are your impressions of the Sanctuary and Glymma so far?'

Auraya smiled. 'The Sanctuary is as beautiful as a palace.

Glymma has obviously been planned and laid out with forethought and common sense. I'm particularly impressed by your aqueducts and uncluttered streets.'

'And its inhabitants?'

'No better or worse than those in the cities of the north.'

Imenja smiled. 'No worse?'

'No.'

'I would have thought we had one point in our favour.'

'What is that?'

'We do not mistreat or despise Dreamweavers or those who follow dead gods.'

Auraya nodded. 'That is true. But my people do not invade other lands. I think that is a point in our favour that far outweighs yours.' She paused to hold Imenja's gaze, then shrugged and looked at Nekaun. 'And attitudes toward Dreamweavers are changing for the better, with the encouragement of the White.'

Imenja's eyebrows rose. 'Encouragement? Didn't they recently drive Mirar out of Northern Ithania?'

Auraya's eyes widened, then narrowed. 'That wasn't their intention,' she said, a touch of irony in her tone.

'No? So he's welcome to return any time he wishes?'

'I doubt it. The Circle may be willing to encourage acceptance of Dreamweavers, but they haven't changed their minds about Mirar.'

'Why do they regard him so unfavourably?' Nekaun asked.

Auraya's mouth tightened as she paused to consider her answer. 'Their conflict began centuries ago, and I cannot tell you exactly why.'

'There must be more to it than Dreamweavers not worshipping gods,' Imenja said.

Auraya nodded. 'I believe he foolishly set himself against them. I don't think he'll make the same mistake twice.'

Or would he? Reivan wondered. *The Voices need to know if Mirar is dangerous. If he is so dangerous that the Circlian gods tried to kill him, is he dangerous to us? He survived being attacked by the most powerful White, so he must be magically strong . . . and Genza is bringing him here!*

Auraya's gaze snapped to Reivan, then away again.

'Would you like to know where he is?' Nekaun asked.

'I have no interest in Mirar,' Auraya said. 'If he's in Southern Ithania, you're welcome to him.'

'Am I?' Nekaun chuckled. 'How generous of you.' He leaned back and swept his gaze over them all. 'It is late. Tomorrow I have more of the city to show Auraya, and then we have dinner with Third Voice Vervel. I will escort Auraya to her rooms.'

Reivan barely heard him. She was sure something strange had just happened, but she wasn't sure what, and now Nekaun seemed almost eager to leave. As the others rose and pushed back their chairs Reivan followed suit. They spoke polite farewells then parted, Nekaun, Auraya and Turaan leaving by the door they had arrived through.

As Imenja started back down the hall, Reivan replayed the conversation about Mirar through her mind. *She gave me such a look, but I'd said nothing. Surely that means . . .*

'She probably read your mind,' Imenja said. 'I think we finally caught her out. However, we don't want her knowing that we have. Once she does we lose a small advantage.'

'So I won't be meeting her again?'

'Not until we reveal our knowledge of her ability.' Imenja smiled apologetically. They moved out of the hall and into the corridor. 'What did you make of her?'

Reivan considered. 'I can't say the chances of her allying with us are high.'

'Not even if Nekaun offered to hand over or kill Mirar?'

'No,' Reivan said slowly. 'If she is loyal to her gods, she will not turn from them no matter what Nekaun offers.'

'That depends on what will please her gods more. Would they sacrifice her in exchange for Mirar's death? She is no longer a White, so maybe her loss isn't important to them.'

'She is a powerful sorceress. They would not want to lose her – at least not to us.'

Imenja nodded. 'I agree. But we can't dismiss the possibility that she will pretend to join us in order to secure Mirar's death.'

'That would be a dangerous game to play. Would she risk discovery and death for the sake of killing Mirar?'

'It depends on how much her gods want Mirar dead.'

'And whether Nekaun does,' Reivan added. 'Mirar is a powerful, *immortal* sorcerer. If he allies with us it won't matter whether Auraya joins us or stays a Circlian ally.'

'That would be a much better arrangement for all, I think,' Imenja agreed. 'Genza likes him, and thinks we will, too.'

'There is one significant problem, however.'

'Oh?'

'Dreamweavers do not kill. He would not be much use as an ally to counter Auraya.'

'Ah. That is true.'

'Having them both on our side would be even better.' Reivan chuckled. 'Though that would be problematic, if they were at each other's throats all the time.'

Imenja laughed darkly. 'Yes, though it could be entertaining.'

Lifting the flap of the platten cover, Danjin saw the gates of an impressive structure ahead. The fortress of the Correl clan enveloped the crest of a hill with almost sinuous grace. All that could be seen of it were high walls, but those walls rose from the earth like natural outcrops of sheer rock. They looked as if they had been there for millennia and, despite or perhaps because of the subtle signs of repairs here and there, as if they would be forever.

Inside lived the small, reclusive Correl clan. Yem had told them the family's decline was due mostly to few male heirs being produced. The current leader was an old man whose only son had been killed in a training accident. He had nominated a child of one of his granddaughters to succeed him.

But there were nephews and cousins enough to provide a small force of warriors.

Yem had gone ahead to announce their arrival. Danjin could not help worrying about the young man's safety. If the warriors had been converted by the Pentadrians, too, who knew what could happen?

Danjin let the flap fall and looked at Ella. She smiled back at him.

'Don't worry, Danjin. Yem is safe, and has arranged everything.'

The platten slowed as it reached the hill. The arem were exhausted. The sound of their hoof beats suddenly echoed off close walls and the platten reached flat ground. It stopped and Ella drew the hood of her cloak over her head. Danjin followed her out and Gillen clambered after them.

They had arrived in a courtyard between two fortress walls. It was empty but for two warriors standing by a second gate and a pair of guards that Ella glanced at briefly. One of the warriors was Yem, the other a broad-shouldered man with grey in his hair.

'Greetings, Ellareen of the White. Welcome to my home,' the older warrior said quietly.

Ella smiled. 'Greetings, Gret, Talm of Correl. This is Danjin Spear, my adviser, and Gillen Shieldarm, Ambassador of Hania.'

'Welcome. Come inside where we may talk in comfort,' he invited.

Ella had asked Yem to arrange for this meeting to be held with as few witnesses as possible. They saw no others as they walked through the second gate, along a narrow corridor and into a hall. Ella's gaze was slightly distracted and Danjin guessed she was checking for the minds of unseen watchers.

Gret led them along the hall to a staircase and they ascended to a corridor. He stopped beside a door and ushered them into a cavernous room decorated with large wall hangings.

Ella took the seat Gret offered. The old warrior moved to a side table and poured fwa into five goblets, then handed them around.

'That is an impressive hanging,' Gillen murmured. He was gazing up at the largest. It depicted a grand view of hills divided into fields by low walls, with small villages glimpsed in the creases. The sea was a shimmering expanse beyond and huge clouds floated over all.

It's just coloured thread on cloth, Danjin thought. *How do they get the sea to shimmer and the clouds to look so real just with stitches?*

'My late wife made it,' Gret said. 'She was gifted at the art. It is of the view from the roof of this fortress.'

'She was indeed gifted,' Gillen said. 'It is an unusual subject for a Dunwayan hanging.'

'Unusual in such a large hanging,' Gret agreed. 'Women often make smaller hangings of their homes, and keep them in their private rooms – which is why you have not seen them before.' He smiled. 'Tia was more ambitious. I like them, so I had them moved in here after she died.'

He turned away and sat down opposite Ella. Gillen and Danjin took places on either side of the White. Looking up at the hanging again, Danjin wondered if one of the villages depicted on it was the one the Pentadrians had settled in.

'Yem said you were here on a matter of urgency and importance,' Gret said. 'How can I be of help to you?'

'I need the assistance of your warriors,' Ella began. As she told him of the Pentadrians who had settled in Dram, the old man's expression changed to dismay.

'Are you sure of this – that their intentions are ill?'

'I have read it from their minds,' Ella replied.

'I was told they were hard workers and kept their ways to themselves.'

'You did not investigate yourself?'

He shook his head. 'I trust Dram's leader. He would have reported any trouble. The Pentadrians pay their tithe. Some have even married locals.'

'You allowed marriages between Circlians and Pentadrians?'

He shrugged. 'Of course.'

Ella shook her head in disbelief. 'Tell me, was it a Pentadrian or Circlian rite?'

Gret shrugged. 'I didn't ask.'

'Did the Pentadrian of these couples convert to a Circlian, or the Circlian convert to a Pentadrian?'

He spread his hands.

'What will their children be, Pentadrian or Circlian?'

'I don't know.' He was frowning now. 'I prefer to leave them their privacy.'

'An admirably generous policy, if these newcomers were from Sennon or Hania. But these people are our enemy. They follow gods that would destroy us, if they could. We can't trust them – as has been demonstrated here.' She leaned forward to stare at Gret. 'I-Portak agrees with me. The Pentadrians and the people of Dram must be taken to Chon to be judged.'

Gret's mouth dropped open, but he quickly closed it again. His face reddened.

'To Chon? Is that necessary? We could hold trials here.'

Ella shook her head. 'It is impossible to hide something of this magnitude, Gret. People will find out.'

'But should the Pentadrians have the satisfaction of the world knowing of their success – no matter how brief?'

'People need to see what they have done in order to be alert for such deception in the future. And they need to see that rapid and appropriate punishment is dealt out to those who harbour Pentadrians.'

'But do *all* of the villagers have to go north? What of the old? Women? Children? It is a long way and a cruel hardship for the innocent.'

Ella grimaced. 'They must all go, or innocents will be targeted in the future. Will you assist me?'

Gret's shoulders drooped. 'Of course.'

As Ella began to discuss numbers of men and a strategy for approaching and dealing with the villagers, Danjin considered the old warrior. Clearly his pride would suffer if others knew he had been deceived by the enemy. His income would suffer, too. A village emptied of workers meant crops, animals and fishing boats left untended. Danjin had to wonder how much of Gret's dismay was due to loss of honour and profit, and how much at the journey and punishment his people were about to face.

Yet at the same time Danjin felt sympathy toward Gret's protestations, and a nagging dismay. Was Ella so eager to make an example of the village that she would punish all with equal harshness, whether convert or not, old or young, adult or child?

I guess we'll find out soon.

CHAPTER 29

As dawn crept through the jungle, Mirar wiped his brow and tried to ignore the sweat already running down his back. Soon Genza would emerge from her cabin and propel the barge up the river again, and the motion would bring the relief of a breeze.

Mirar could imagine how unpleasant a river journey through Dekkar would be without a Voice on board. Each night, when Genza stopped for a meal and sleep, the breeze died. There was little or no wind on the river, and the heat was relentless.

Mirar had found his cabin stifling, so he slipped out each night to sleep on the deck with the crew. The jungle was never quiet. The buzz of insects and calls of birds formed a constant background noise. Occasionally other calls echoed through the trees. Some of these attracted more attention than others. Once a deep rumble close to shore caused all dinner conversation to end abruptly. A crewman had told Mirar it had been the call of the legendary roro, a giant black-furred carnivore with enormous pointed teeth. Stories had been told of roro that had swum out to vessels at night and dragged away passengers or crew.

Which explained why they kept several lamps burning brightly at night, and why they moored in the middle of the river, away from overhanging branches, and looped ropes around the vessel strung with bells.

The crewman was a wiry middle-aged man named Kevain. Each night the man invited Mirar to sleep beside him on the crowded deck, under his bug net, in exchange for some of Tintel's oil. Kevain brought out a small skin of a potent liquor and they exchanged stories until the drink made them drowsy enough to sleep.

A sound nearby drew Mirar's attention to Kevain. The man was climbing to his feet, deftly rolling up the bug net and stowing it away. He grinned at Mirar.

'We reach Bottom today,' he said. Bottom was the name of the town they were heading for. 'You fear being up high?' he asked, pointing at the escarpment that loomed over them.

Mirar shook his head.

'Good. Good.' The man clenched a fist and waggled it – a gesture that Mirar had taken to be approval of courage. 'It's hard for those who do. If you feel bad, don't look down.'

'I'll remember that,' Mirar replied.

Kevain's grin widened. 'After that, you ride the winds. Lucky you. Ah, the Fourth Voice is awake and I best be getting to work.'

He hurried to join the crew, leaving Mirar to greet Genza. A quick morning meal was served then Genza took her position at the bow.

Finding a place to sit out of the way, Mirar watched as the jungle slid past and the cliff drew closer. After an hour or so the barge slowed. A small pier had appeared ahead of them. Genza left the job of steering the vessel to the pole men, who deftly brought it up to the pier and bound it securely.

A short but hurried interval of organisation followed as supplies were carried off by domestics. Mirar collected his bag from his cabin, nodded farewell to Kevain, then waited near

Genza until she gestured for him to join her. They stepped onto the pier together and started down it, Servants and domestics following.

At the end of the pier an equally narrow street passed between wooden houses built right up against each other. Walls were coloured with bright paint in various stages of deterioration. The street was covered with sand, which seemed odd. Mirar had seen no sand in the jungle so far. Signs bearing pictures illustrating the business within hung above each door. There was little variety. The locals sold food, wine and transportation and hired out beds and women.

The latter leaned out of doorways wearing unconvincing smiles and bright, revealing clothes. They looked sick and unhappy, and shrank indoors at the sight of Genza and the Servants. He felt a pang of sympathy, and resolved to return here one day and see if he could help them. Genza barely glanced at the women, striding on to the end of the street.

A large building stood there. Behind it was the escarpment wall. Genza stopped to watch as a wooden box began to rise from the roof. Mirar noted the thick ropes stretching upward. He looked up. The escarpment loomed over the village. A tiny object moved against the dark rock: another box.

'The supplies are already on the way up,' Genza said. 'We'll catch the one coming down.'

Mirar noted a small crowd gathered outside the building. He sensed annoyance already changing to begrudging respect as these men and women saw the reason their ascent had been delayed.

Genza led him inside the building. A large iron wheel filled most of the room. Ropes as thick as Mirar's arm stretched up through a gap in the roof.

'The lifters must hold close to the same weight,' Genza said, holding her hands out and raising one while dropping the other, then reversing. 'The weight of the load coming down is often less than that coming up, as Dekkar has more produce to sell than western Avven. The operators load bags of sand to balance it.'

Mirar nodded. That would explain the sandy streets of the village. There would be no use in sending it back up.

As the descending box slowly dropped through the roof, Genza led Mirar up a set of wooden stairs to a platform. A man waited there, and as he saw Genza he respectfully made the sign of the star.

The box stopped level with the platform. The top half of the box's side was open and Mirar could see several people within. He sensed fear and relief, but also exhilaration and boredom. Mirar recognised the smell of a root Dekkans used for its calming effect. Several of the passengers were chewing.

As the passengers saw Genza, their eyes widened. All made the sign of the star. The operator unlatched the bottom half of the box and opened it like a door. Once the people had left, descending from the platform using a different staircase, the man dragged out a few bags of sand. He stepped aside, and lowered his gaze as Genza entered. Mirar caught the man's quick, curious glance as he followed.

A bell rang. The box jerked into motion. As it emerged from the roof, Mirar looked out on a sea of trees.

The jungle stretched out before them, only broken by the river, which twisted and turned upon itself several times. The view improved as they rose. He realised he could see the sea in the distance. *This is what Auraya sees when she flies*, he thought suddenly. He felt an unexpected pang of envy. *Emerahl failed to learn to fly, but that doesn't mean I would. I wonder if I'll ever get a chance to ask Auraya to teach me. And if she'd agree to. I taught her to heal. She owes me something in return . . .*

'What do you think of this little contraption?' Genza asked.

Mirar turned to regard her. 'Impressive. Have there been many accidents?'

'A few.' She shrugged. 'Mostly due to the foolishness of passengers. The rope is replaced every year, and tested carefully for flaws.' Looking out at the view, she gave a little sigh. 'I never tire of this, no matter how many times I see it.'

Mirar gazed out at the view again. It truly was spectacular. Too soon the box slowed and then jerked to a halt. It had drawn level with a platform built out from the side of the cliff, surrounded by a railing. Mirar followed Genza out of the box and into another small village.

This place was as sprawling as Bottom had been compact. A broad street ran between widely spaced clay houses. Everything appeared to be the same bleached sand colour — even the clothes of the locals — though that might have been the effect of the bright sun. It was both hotter and drier and the relentless sound of insects and birdsong had been replaced by the constant whine of wind.

'This is Top,' Genza said. 'I know, not very imaginative names.'

The boxes and chests from the barge were being loaded onto a tarn, while two platten waited nearby to carry the Servants. Genza checked that all was arranged as she wished, then bade the Servants a good journey. Mirar looked at her questioningly. She smiled.

'We'll go on alone from here. It'll be much faster.'

'How?'

Her smile widened. 'By windboat. Follow me.'

She strode through the village. At the edge Mirar saw a flat, featureless desert extending to the horizon. Genza led him to one of several windowless, two-storey stone buildings at the village edge, and through a door. The interior was dark after the bright sunlight. As Mirar's eyes adjusted he realised there was no ceiling above him. The building was hollow. To one side there were several large wooden doors. One was open, allowing in enough light to reveal the strange contraptions within.

Boats. Strange narrow boats with oversized sails. Mirar gazed around the room at the different vessels. All had flat, narrow wooden hulls and pale sails bound tightly to graceful masts. Genza looked up at him and grinned.

'You'll like this.' She turned away as a middle-aged local man hurried toward her. He ushered them outside.

'The two windsailors over there are waiting for you,' he said, pointing at two figures in the distance standing beside two of the strange boats.

'I will not need a sailor,' she said, 'but my companion will. Are the winds favourable?'

The man nodded. 'If they keep up, they might take you all the way to Glymma.'

She thanked him and strode toward the distant figures. Mirar followed.

'Can they really take us all the way to Glymma?'

'So long as the wind holds,' she said. 'We should be there in four days.'

Four days? Mirar shook his head. *Now I know why she didn't bother sailing around the coast. A ship would never have made it to Dekkar and back as quickly.*

The figures were two young men. As Genza approached they smiled and made the sign of the star. She examined the windboats, then chose one. The sailor let go of it reluctantly. Mirar guessed that boats belonged to and were maintained by their sailors, and wondered how the young man would get his vessel back.

A gust of wind battered them, and the remaining windsailor was clearly straining to hold his boat still. When it had passed, Genza pointed to the front of the hull.

'You sit there, face forward,' she explained. 'Don't move. It takes balance as much as windsense and magic to sail these.'

Sitting down, Mirar placed his bag between his knees. He looked back to see that the windsailor had wound a scarf about his face and was now sitting at the stern. Genza settled in the same part of her adopted windboat and as another gust of wind rushed around them the sail unfurled and she shot forward.

As the boat beneath Mirar tilted, he grabbed hold of the edges. He heard the young man speak, his voice muffled. Glancing over his shoulder he saw the man pointing to the hull. He looked down and saw handholds. There were also two hollows for him to wedge his heels into. As he took advantage of both the young man made an undulating cry and the boat began to move.

It did not fly forward as Genza's had, but slowly gained momentum. Mirar looked up to see that the sailor was unfurling the sail slowly.

They gathered speed. The boat slid away from the village. Mirar felt the wind gust against him from one side. Another cry came from behind him and he heard a snap of fabric as the sail unfurled completely. The boat turned abruptly and shot across the sand.

It was exhilarating. Mirar found himself whooping along with the windsailor. They scooted toward an unchanging horizon. But soon the sailor quietened, though the speed of the vessel didn't diminish. The occasional crosswind blew dust into the side of Mirar's face. The air was dry, and the sun beating down on them was hot and relentless.

Hours passed. Eventually they reached a stretch of shallow dunes. Gusts of wind began to buffet them from the side. Mirar felt every movement of the sailor as he fought the crosswinds. He felt a growing respect for the skill of the young man.

Then he remembered Genza and searched the sands ahead of them. There was no sign of her. But her boat carried only one passenger, so it was bound to go faster than his. He probably wouldn't see her again for hours – probably not until they stopped for the night.

A spray of sand and a gleeful yell told him otherwise. Genza shot past them, laughing. Mirar could not help chuckling as she deftly sent her boat leaping off the crests of dunes and skimmed down their sides, showing skill probably gained over many more years than a mortal could ever hope to dedicate to the art.

If Genza is an example, these Voices are a lot better at having fun than the White, he thought.

Then he sobered. It was so easy to admire Genza in this place and at this moment. But this was the same woman who bred and trained birds to kill mortals, who waged war and ruled, along with her fellow Voices, an entire continent.

I will remember this side of her, he told himself, *but I will not be charmed out of good sense and caution*.

Though he pretended indifference, Barmonia never failed to be impressed by the ruins of Sorlina.

The high escarpment wall that had cast its shadow over them during the previous afternoons had collapsed here, and on the broken ruins of it a city had been built. The collapse had formed a natural, though steep, access point from the highlands of Avven to the lowlands of Mur, and while it was no surprise that a city had reaped the benefits of that in the past it was strange that none thrived here now.

The foreign woman had stared up at the city all the morning, stupefied by amazement. At one point, during a crossing of the river, she had said something to Raynora about there being too little water in it to sustain a city. Mikmer had put her in her place by pointing out it was the dry season, so of course there was little water.

She had looked at Mikmer with that amused, almost pitying way, but said nothing. Of course, if a city couldn't sustain itself all year round it was bound to diminish and die anyway, but Barmonia hadn't been about to shame Mikmer by pointing that out.

The old road zigzagged up the slope. It had once been smoothly paved, but the ground had shifted and the surface was broken in places. For this reason they had left the vehicles behind and now rode the arem that had pulled them, leading those carrying tents and supplies.

The road wound past rows of low stone walls, the remains of ancient houses. *Or not so ancient*, Barmonia amended. *The city only died a few hundred years ago. Not like old Jeryma in the north or Karn in the south.*

But the younger the ruin the less chance it had been plundered. In the past, Barmonia had opened tombs here still stuffed with treasures, and taken many statues and carvings back to Hannaya's library and to sell to collectors. They weren't as rare as the truly ancient pieces of other ruined cities, but they still attracted good prices. The statues often had remnants of paint on them, which buyers didn't like, and he alone had found a method of removing it that didn't harm the stone.

He smiled. If the directions written on the priest's bones were correct, he was going to discover not just a new tomb, but a whole new section of the Temple of Sorli.

They were passing the larger houses near the top of the city now. Barmonia could hear Raynora talking to the woman.

'. . . over there. Public latrines. Yes, that's right. They peed in front of their neighbours, and both men and women used them. Can you imagine the smell – oh, we dug up some of the dirt inside. No charcoal or dyes, but lots of the same straw-like stuff that we found in the latrines of private houses. Lots of coins, too . . .'

The road turned and they entered the first of the higher levels of the city in which public buildings had been constructed. Many walls still stood, as they had been made thicker and sturdier in order to support larger buildings. Ray named the buildings and described their uses.

Then the road turned again and they ascended into a large public square. The sight, as always, was both impressive and disturbing. It had been paved with enormous slabs of stone, and as the ground had shifted these had lifted and tilted. Few lay flat, so the whole space was an uneven jumble. Some of the slabs had even managed to shift into a vertical position, while others projected at such an angle that they looked as if they might fall over at any moment.

Ray fell silent as Barmonia dismounted and began to lead his mount and pack beast across the square. There had always been something eerie about this place. The wind made strange noises. The crossing took concentration and could not be done quickly. When heavily burdened, the arem could not deal with too great an incline.

When he reached the other side he breathed a sigh of relief. Sitting on a fallen column, he waited for the others to join him. The woman looked up at the structure behind him.

'The Temple of Sorli,' Raynora said quietly, leaning closer to her.

The others looked up and Barmonia watched as their faces fell.

'The dome is gone,' Yathyir said, pointing out the obvious.

'Yes.' Barmonia stood up and turned to regard the remains of the building. 'It collapsed in a recent tremor most likely. Let's hope it hasn't blocked anything or we'll have to get local help in.'

He handed the lead of the arem to a domestic then turned and walked inside.

Light and rubble now filled the large hall that had always been dimly lit. The former revealed the wall paintings in their full glory, as well as the damage that rain had caused. The latter had covered the floor with fragments from the size of pebbles to enormous slabs of stone. He made his way to the altar and paused to look up. The head of the massive stone goddess had broken off. He cast about and glimpsed an eye behind a large piece of the fallen dome.

Another piece rested between the back wall and the hips of the seated figure. He had to climb up into the wedge-shaped gap behind it to reach the doorway to the inner chamber. The magnificent carved doors had been removed centuries ago to become part of a collector's mansion in Glymma.

Better that than rotting here, he thought. *Or more likely the locals would have cut them up for firewood years ago.*

The chamber beyond was roofed and dark, so he sent Ray back for torches. Barmonia was amused when Ray returned with only five and handed them out to the Thinkers, leaving the foreign woman without a light.

Perhaps he's not as enchanted by her as he appears.

The inner chamber was a small room with an empty altar in the centre. Barmonia had no idea where the statue had gone and would willingly pay a good sum to find out, but he had seen sketches of it. He was satisfied to see the woman was frowning at the altar.

'The bones said "Sorli will direct",' she said. 'Sorli is no longer here.'

'Obviously not,' Mikmer replied dryly.

'There's a picture of her in the library,' Yathyir said gravely. 'I remember it.'

Barmonia smiled. This was why he put up with the strange

boy. He might be a freak, but his memory was impressively good.

'Describe her to us,' Barmonia ordered.

The youth considered the stone, then walked over to Raynora.

'Help me up,' he said.

Ray hoisted Yathyir up. The boy moved to the centre of the altar and paused to think.

'She holds a cup in one hand and is pointing at the ground with the other,' he said, mimicking the pose.

'So the entrance to the secret temple is below this stone?' Ray asked, regarding the huge block dubiously.

'Probably.' Barmonia moved behind the stone and rubbed his shoe on the floor. 'There are scratches here. Thinkers have always believed they were made when the stone was first moved here, but perhaps it was shifted more often than that.'

'How?' Yathyir asked, jumping down to examine the scratches.

'With magic,' Barmonia replied. 'Skill is always a requirement of priests.'

'How are we going to shift it, then?'

'With *our* skills.' Barmonia turned to the entrance. 'Which is why I brought so much equipment.'

'You didn't need to,' the woman said quietly.

Barmonia turned to regard her. She no doubt wanted to show off whatever Skill she had, but he had no intention of letting her. 'This should be moved gently and carefully or you—'

'Oh, spare me the lecture,' she interrupted. 'You obviously don't know anything about magic if you think it less subtle than levers and ropes.'

He felt anger flare at her arrogant tone, then bit back a curse as she turned her back on him to face the altar.

'Don't you . . .' Taking a step forward, he reached out to

grab her shoulders but his hands skittered over some invisible barrier. The others were moving backwards, their faces betraying curiosity and excitement.

'I'll lift it first,' she said to Ray. 'Take a look underneath and tell me what you see.'

Barmonia felt a chill run down his spine as the altar stone rose slowly upward. His stomach clenched. Magic always had that effect on him. A woman should not be able to lift a huge block of stone. It was unnatural.

Ray dropped to the ground and examined the gap between the stone and the floor. Incredibly, he ran his hands under it, trusting that she wouldn't drop the stone on him.

'There is a square hole beneath. Looks like you could slide the altar to the back of the room without breaking anything.'

The woman nodded and the stone began to move backward. A staircase descending into darkness was revealed. The stone settled onto the floor without a sound.

The bitch has control, Barmonia conceded. Then another thought occurred to him. *If she is this powerful, how are we going to get rid of her?*

They'd have to trick her, which shouldn't be hard. She was a lone woman in a land she didn't know, where people spoke a language she had admitted she had only recently learned. They might have to slip away from her rather than send her away. Whatever happened, he was not going to let some foreign sorceress take any of the credit for finding this tomb.

I can turn this to our advantage. If we tell people about her moving stones like some magical work beast, that's all she'll be remembered for.

He stepped forward. Suddenly respectful, she moved back and allowed him to lead the others down the stairs. At least she knew her place. She was the magical work beast. He was the leader of the expedition.

The walls were carved with religious scenes, but they were too coated in dust to make out. There would be time for that later. He gave up counting the stairs after one hundred. Their descent seemed to go on forever, so when he suddenly found himself at the bottom it was a surprise. He stopped.

A narrow corridor just wider than his shoulders continued into darkness. He started along it, moving slowly. The corridor was free of rubble at first, but soon became cluttered. At one point he stepped over a crack as wide as his hand that had severed the entire passage. Not long after he saw a faint light ahead, then several strides later he had reached the end of the passage.

'Halt!' he called, fearful that the others would blunder into him and push him over the precipice.

'What is it?' Mikmer asked, his voice close to Barmonia's shoulder.

'A crack,' Barmonia replied. 'An enormous crack. It must be two hundred paces to the other side.'

'Does the passage continue on the other side?'

'I don't know. I can barely see it.'

'Let me come forward and I will make a light,' the woman offered.

Barmonia was tempted to refuse out of spite, but he could think of no other way to know the size of the crevice.

'Come forward, then.'

There was a shuffling behind him as the men made room for her to pass them. A spark of light flared into existence and floated past his shoulder, moving slowly out into the void. The opposite wall brightened. There was no passage in it.

'No,' Barmonia said. 'The corridor ends here.'

As the light brightened he looked down. Not far below was a jumble of rocks, filling the crevice. Looking up, he felt his blood turn cold.

A massive slab of the wall beyond had fallen forward and now rested precariously against the opposite surface. A tremor of enough force would one day free it, and it would come crashing down on top of the rubble below.

He drew in a deep breath and let it out again. Looking down, he surveyed the floor of the crack. Some pieces of the rubble were larger than a house.

'Hopeless,' he muttered. 'If anything was there it is gone now.'

He turned and pushed past the woman. The others looked at him closely, reading the disappointment from his face. He began to move past them, to lead the way back.

'There are handholds in the rock.'

Barmonia turned to see Yathyir crouching by the edge.

Walking back, he peered over the edge and saw that the boy was right. Grooves had been carved into the wall below the passage. Looking closer, Barmonia realised that the outside edge of the passage had been carved with a decorative border. This was *meant* to be a precipice.

Leaning out further, he saw that the handholds continued down to the floor of rubble.

'If there is anything down there, it is well buried,' he amended.

'But it can be dug out,' the woman said.

'That will take months.'

'It doesn't have to.'

Barmonia turned to glare at her.

'Or maybe it does.' She shrugged. 'The choice is yours.'

'Let me see,' Kereon said.

The woman and Yathyir moved back into the passage to allow Mikmer and Kereon to look at the crevice. Mikmer turned back, allowing Raynora past.

'I don't like the look of that bit of wall above us,' Mikmer said. 'I think, whatever we do, we should do it quickly.'

Kereon nodded in agreement.

'I most definitely agree,' Raynora said from the end of the passage, still looking upward.

Barmonia managed to stop himself scowling at them. Local workers would have to be paid. And watched, which meant someone had to be in there with them. They could be clumsy. A loud noise might be enough to send the wall tumbling down on them. Then there'd be more rubble and rotting bodies to clear.

He turned to the woman. 'Then you had better get started.'

'I will,' she said, holding his gaze. 'Tomorrow. This will take concentration and I could do with a night's sleep.'

He shrugged. 'Tomorrow then.' The others looked relieved – happy to leave the work to another. Yet Barmonia did not like the thought of her uncovering anything without someone else around. She might pocket something. Someone must watch her. He considered his fellow Thinkers.

Not Raynora. He's too weak when it comes to women. Mikmer and Kereon will insist on shifts if I pick them. That leaves Yathyir. Yes, he'll do.

The boy was a useful freak, but still a freak. If the ceiling fell, it would hardly be a loss to the world.

Turning on his heel, Barmonia led the others back along the passage.

Auraya had settled into a routine in the evenings. First she and Nekaun would enter her rooms. He would draw her attention to a new gift and she would make the appropriate noises of gratitude and admiration. Then he would leave and she would pause a moment to look around and sigh with relief.

The tables and shelves of the room now bore many objects. Large stone statues of dancers, tiny blown glass warriors and carved wooden animals stood next to toy ships floating in pottery bowls. Bolts of fabric patterned with pictures of farmers and aqueducts were neatly draped across a bench. Reed chairs had been delivered the day she had visited the river where the source plant was harvested. After a walk in one of the city's lush gardens she had returned to find a cage containing two brightly coloured birds.

All this was hers to keep, or so Nekaun had said. Which meant nothing, because she couldn't fly back to Si carrying reed chairs and stone statues and she didn't intend to return in a Pentadrian ship.

Next she would look for Mischief, who always hid when Nekaun was about. Tonight it took only moments to find him. A familiar pointy nose emerged from behind one of the large pottery water vessels brought every day. She crouched beside it.

'There you are, Mischief.' She smiled as he hauled himself to his feet with obvious effort and let her scratch his head. The heat made the little veez sleepy and subdued. During the day he lay sprawled on the stone floor, rising only to eat or drink. The domestics seemed fascinated by him, brought him fish, and had taught him the Avvenan words for food and water.

Danjin would be amazed to see Mischief now. He'll be annoyed to hear the veez didn't give the Pentadrians any trouble.

Reassured that Mischief was alive and well, she sat down in one of the reed chairs for her next nightly task. Closing her eyes, she focused her mind on the ring around her finger.

:Juran.

:Auraya. How are you?

:I'm tired of this game. Heartily sick of the sight of Nekaun, too. But otherwise I'm fine.

:And the Siyee?

:Twenty-one free, twelve still imprisoned. What has Teel reported?

:That they are in good spirits, though staying fit enough to fly is increasingly hard in the close confines of their prison.

:Have any of them reached Si yet?

:I don't know. None have reached the Open yet. He paused. *I don't suppose the Voices have given away any useful information about themselves?*

:Nothing new.

:When is Mirar due to arrive?

Auraya felt her heart skip a beat.

:Any day now.

:We have discussed this at length. At first we felt it best that you ignore him. But if the Voices intend to recruit him, then you ought to do whatever you can to stop them. Or persuade him not to join them.

:How do you suggest I do that? Auraya could not help sounding a little resentful.

Juran was silent a moment.

:I am not suggesting you seduce him.

:No, but last time we met I was sent to kill him. He's hardly going to trust me now.

:He might. After all, you didn't kill him.

Neither of them said what was obvious: that Mirar would not have been a problem now if she *had* killed him.

:I won't know what is possible until he gets here, she told Juran. *In the meantime, my main priority is freeing the Siyee.*

:Yes. Of course. I will speak to you again tomorrow night.

Standing up, Auraya moved into the bedroom and lay down. She closed her eyes and tried to relax, but her mind kept moving from the Siyee's predicament to Mirar's impending arrival. Soon she was staring at the ceiling.

She had communicated with the priests in the Open, asking them to pass on to Speaker Sirri the bad news, then later to tell them of her bargain with Nekaun and suggest that Siyee fly food and water out into the Sennon desert for the freed Siyee. A few times she had skimmed minds looking for the Siyee returning home. She had only found a few, and they had been tired, thirsty and distressed. She could do nothing to help them.

The last thing she wanted to be worrying about was meeting Mirar. But they would be watching her and Mirar closely. They would expect her to treat Mirar as an enemy, or at least someone she considered dangerous and untrustworthy. They would expect him to treat her the same in return. The trouble was, their relationship wasn't that simple. She had no idea how she *would* react to him.

I'm going to have to pretend to hate him, she thought. *And he'll have to do the same to me. That will be an even greater challenge for him, if he still thinks he loves me.*

If the Voices thought she or Mirar had any fond feelings for each other, they would take advantage of it. Nekaun had already shown himself willing to use blackmail.

I'm already expecting him to offer to kill Mirar in exchange for some favour. More likely he'll offer to kill me in order to seal a bargain with Mirar.

I hope Mirar realises how badly timed his little visit is.

I hope he has seen the danger he'll be putting us both in.

I hope he knows he must behave as if he hates me.

I hope he isn't intending to take Nekaun up on his offer to kill me.

I hope ... bah! I should just dream link with him and ask.

Closing her eyes, she forced herself to breathe slowly. Though she tried to let her mind drift, it refused to settle into more than an anxious semi-conscious state.

A small, soft thump and vibration brought her back to full consciousness. Lifting her head she smiled wryly as she saw that Mischief had jumped onto the bed and was curling up nearby. Though it was cooler for him to sleep by the water vessels, he still preferred to be close by when she slept.

Somehow his presence made it easier to relax. She lost track of time. Her thoughts fragmented, then drew together again so that she was conscious, but also aware that she was not completely awake. Time to call Mirar.

His response was immediate.

:*Auraya!*

The feeling of surprise and pleasure that came with his response told her that she didn't need to worry that he planned to let Nekaun kill her. She only had to worry that his infatuation with her would get them both into trouble.

Still, it was nice that someone was glad to hear from her.

:*Mirar. I've heard you're coming to Glymma.*

:*Yes. I'm afraid I have no choice in the matter. Fourth Voice Genza made it clear her invitation was more of an order than a suggestion.*

:*How did they find out who you are and where you were?*

:*Did you expect me to hide my identity here?* he asked in reply.

She considered his question. Pentadrians tolerated Dreamweavers. Why would he hide? The only reason she could think of was so that he could avoid the Voices. Perhaps he didn't want to. Perhaps it had been his intention all along to ally himself with them.

I've been thinking that it was bad timing for him to be visiting Glymma now, but in truth there is nothing unexpected in him coming here. It's just bad timing that I happen to be here.

:*I suppose not*, she replied. *But us both being here at the same time is going to be awkward. The Voices will expect us to behave like sworn enemies.*

:*And we aren't?*

:*I have no intention of killing you.*

:*Even if the gods order it?*

374

:They know the limits to my obedience. Mind you, I'd reconsider if you gave me a reason to.

:Then I had better reassure you that I have no intention of killing you, or agreeing to any offer by the Voices to do it for me, he said.

:That is a relief. How good are your acting skills?

:I think I can convince them that I despise you. That is what you have in mind, isn't it?

:We could hardly pretend to be the best of friends. Nekaun has already blackmailed me. I don't think he'd hesitate to do so again. If he proposes to either or both of us that the other be killed, we can at least buy time while making up our minds. If he decides one of us might be manipulated by threatening the other, he will do so without hesitation.

:And by pretending to hate each other, we buy the Siyee more time.

:Yes. Auraya felt an unexpected gratitude and affection. Thank you for doing this. It won't endanger you or the southern Dreamweavers, will it?

:No. Once you are gone, I can claim I was bound by the Dreamweaver vow to never harm another – even my enemy.

:A vow which makes you less valuable as an ally.

:But hopefully reassures them that I am no threat to them. I'm sure the Voices and I can come to an understanding.

:I'm glad we sorted this out. When will you arrive?

:Tomorrow, or the next day. It depends on the wind.

:The wind?

:I'll explain when I get there.

:Just make sure you do it in an angry, accusing tone.

She felt a wave of amusement.

:I will explain in a dream link, he told her. We should link each night, to make sure we both know what the other has said or done – and what the Voices have said or done. I wonder which of us will get the best offer to join them. We should keep score.

:This isn't a game, Mirar.

:No, of course not. But we could have a little fun at their expense, so long as it doesn't do any harm.

The idea was tempting, but . . .

:I'd rather not take the risk. Not with Siyee lives at stake.

:No, you're right. Well, I best get some sleep. It could be a long ride tomorrow.

She bade him good night, then, as she sank toward sleep, could not help noticing how much better she felt. As if a burden had been eased. It was more than just relief that Mirar agreed with her on how they would act.

I won't be alone here any more, she thought sleepily. *I'll have a . . . an ally? No, perhaps just a friend.*

CHAPTER 30

Conversation around the balcony dwindled to silence as footsteps echoed in the corridor beyond. A Servant appeared in one of the archways and made the sign of the star.

'First Voice Nekaun sends his apologies. He will not be able to attend the meeting,' the man said.

The Voices and Companions exchanged glances.

'Thank you, Servant Ranrin,' Imenja replied.

The man inclined his head, then hurried away. Reivan felt a sinking disappointment. She hadn't seen Nekaun in weeks. Not since Auraya had arrived. She guessed he was catching up on the normal business of a First Voice after finishing with his guest for the evening. He was too busy to visit her. She could accept that . . . though the longer it had been the stronger the pangs of jealousy she felt.

But . . . tonight she had been looking forward to just *seeing* him. To hearing his voice. To the way he smiled at her as if she was his special secret . . .

When the Servant's footsteps had faded beyond hearing, the three, Voices shifted in their seats so they faced each other. Vervel grimaced as if he had just tasted something unpleasant.

'Shall we proceed?' he asked.

Imenja looked at Shar. 'I can't see why we shouldn't.'

The blond Voice nodded. 'Me neither. Where shall we begin?'

'With our own lands, as always,' Imenja decided.

Reivan listened as they discussed matters in Glymma, then moved on to a few domestic issues within Avven, Mur and then Dekkar.

'There is merit in the new High Chieftain's idea,' Imenja said. Vervel's eyebrows rose.

'Oh?'

'In other cities it is possible for lowly citizens to work their way to higher standing in society. From beggar to domestic, for example. But the physical limitation placed on the poor living below Kave makes ascending to a better position near impossible.'

'And how will the High Chieftain's idea solve this?' Shar asked.

'It creates a middle level which might act like a step on a ladder. A ladder leading to self-improvement.'

'A fanciful idea,' Vervel said. 'I doubt it is practical.'

'But worth a try.' Imenja's shoulders lifted. 'In a small area at first, perhaps.'

Vervel shrugged. 'Perhaps.'

The two Voices stared at each other, then Imenja smiled.

'Contact Genza and ask what she thinks. She has seen Kave only recently.'

Vervel gave a quiet snort and looked away. 'Why waste her time?'

Imenja frowned. 'Because we should at least try to serve the gods,' she said firmly.

An awkward but mercifully short silence followed. Reivan looked down at her glass of water. This was the closest the Voices had come to acknowledging the changes that Nekaun had brought. She knew what Vervel had wanted to ask. *Why waste Genza's time asking her opinion, when Nekaun might override all the other Voices when it came to the final decision?*

She drew in a deep breath, but resisted the urge to sigh. The way Nekaun treated the other Voices was unnecessary, surely. She could see that, but at the same time another part of her believed he must have a good reason, even if she could not see it at the time. The gods had chosen him. He was intelligent and clever.

How was it possible for her to see his flaws, but not believe what she was seeing? Or not feel alarmed?

'Genza says we should support the idea.' Vervel's gaze was distant. Imenja nodded.

'Now we should look beyond our lands,' Imenja said. 'Has Sennon shown any inclination to reject the White and join us again?'

Shar shook his head. 'No. The emperor refuses to see our messengers and returns our gifts.'

Imenja grimaced. 'I don't expect that to change.' The other Voices nodded in agreement. She sighed. 'Our people in Jarime have been executed.'

A shock went through Reivan. She did not know what had gone wrong with the mission the Servants had undertaken in Jarime, but she felt a pang of sympathy for those who had died.

'Has the new White been seen in Dunway recently?' Imenja asked.

'Not since she disappeared,' Vervel replied.

'Have our people there been warned?'

Vervel looked away. 'No. He thought they would panic and draw attention to themselves.' Reivan guessed 'he' was Nekaun.

Imenja's eyes narrowed for a moment. 'I see. Well, I have received strange news from Genria and Toren. The two lands abruptly gathered together their armies, had them camp outside their main cities, then with no explanation dismissed them again.'

'The two monarchs do not get along, and the nations were often at war in the past,' Shar pointed out.

'But since the battle they have been the best of friends.' Imenja shook her head. 'There were no reports of conflict between the two countries. In fact, both armies expected to join the other for some purpose, though none knew the reason.'

'Perhaps they were competing to see whose army was most efficient,' Shar's Companion, Bavalla, suggested.

Imenja smiled and spread her hands. 'Who knows? I find the Torens and Genrians the most inexplicable of northern peoples, sometimes.'

Vervel cleared his throat. 'I have some news of a less welcome kind. Our people have been ordered to leave Somrey.'

Imenja frowned. 'Why?'

'A decision of the Council of Elders. It's rumoured that the Dreamweaver and Circlian Elder votes were in agreement for the first time in history.'

'Of all northern lands but Sennon, Somrey has been the most accepting of different religions and cults,' Imenja said. 'Our people studied their laws. There was none that could be used to remove us once we were accepted there.'

'The council created a new law so that they could achieve their aim,' Vervel said.

Imenja's eyebrows rose. 'Oh. Our people should examine this law, to see if there are any ways around it.'

'I've already given them the task.'

'Good. Now for Genza.' The three Voices stared into space for a moment, then smiled and looked at each other again. 'All is well,' Imenja said for the benefit of the Companions. Is there any other strange and unfortunate news from the north? Or perhaps good news?'

The others shook their heads.

'Very well. I would rather discuss the next two subjects with

380

Nekaun present, but I would also prefer to tackle them now without him than not tackle them at all. Firstly, the Priestess Auraya's presence here. Secondly, the Dreamweaver Mirar's coming visit. Nekaun's intention with Auraya appears to be to recruit her,' Imenja continued. 'We should do nothing to jeopardise that aim.'

'Are you sure that is his aim?' Shar asked.

Imenja looked at him. 'Has he said or hinted otherwise?'

Shar shook his head. 'But we have to consider other possibilities. He might simply be delaying Auraya's departure in order to keep her from assisting the White, or so that she will be here when Mirar arrives.'

'Perhaps Genria and Toren dismissed their armies because Auraya staying here upset some greater plan,' Vervel suggested.

'Such as invading Southern Ithania?' Imenja asked.

'None of the other Northern Ithanian lands are preparing for war, as far as we know.'

'As far as we know,' Shar echoed, smiling. 'It is hard to tell, since they decided to start regular war training and recruitment, but haven't yet managed to settle into a routine.'

'If Nekaun wants to prevent her assisting the White, why doesn't he simply kill her?' she asked.

'He may not be sure an invasion is planned,' Vervel replied slowly. 'If one isn't, and he kills Auraya, that might be the insult that starts a war.'

'But surely he won't let her leave,' Shar said. 'He'll kill her when the last Siyee flies.' He turned to Imenja, eyebrows raised in question.

Imenja said nothing. Reivan looked at the Second Voice and saw a distracted frown on her mistress's face.

'What is it?' she murmured.

Imenja looked up at her, then at the other Voices and Companions.

'I have a suspicion. I've kept it to myself because there was no point in airing it after Kuar's death. It is hard to argue against what appeared to be obvious, and if I had, some might have thought I was trying to shift the blame to Kuar. That would have been petty.' She paused and her gaze slid away to some distant memory. 'During the battle with the Circlians we were drawing magic to the limit of our Skills. It is tempting at that point to take risks, and I foolishly relied on Servants to protect my back. A Siyee struck me with one of their poisoned darts.'

All nodded. Reivan remembered the moment vividly.

'I had to use magic to drive the poison out,' Imenja continued. 'It cost me some strength. And at that moment Auraya struck Kuar.'

And killed him, Reivan thought. Her chest tightened at the memory. She had seen the body. All his bones had been shattered by the blow.

Imenja shook her head. 'My power was diminished by the smallest amount. Not enough to cause Kuar to falter.'

'So . . . you suspect the White were stronger?' Vervel asked, frowning.

'I believe so,' Imenja said. 'But more importantly, it was Auraya who struck Kuar down. There was no lessening of strength in the others' attack. *She* must have been the one with extra strength in reserve.'

The others exchanged glances.

'Does that mean she is more powerful than a First Voice?' Shar asked.

'It's possible.'

'So maybe Nekaun can't kill Auraya.'

'Not without help.'

'And he doesn't realise this.'

Imenja shrugged. 'I have *tried* to tell him.'

Vervel sighed and rolled his eyes.

'So how does Mirar affect all this?'

Imenja smiled crookedly. 'It depends on how much Auraya wants him dead. I doubt she'd join us in exchange, but she might stay here longer if that meant he was killed.'

'You don't think Nekaun will try to recruit Mirar?' Shar asked.

'I think Mirar knows his future in Southern Ithania depends on coming to an understanding with us, but I doubt he would make an effective ally in war, since Dreamweavers do not kill. He will not balance the advantage the Circlians have over us with Auraya on their side.'

'Unless we kill Auraya,' Shar said.

Imenja smiled grimly. 'That is true.'

'Should we keep Auraya and Mirar apart?' Vervel asked.

Imenja considered. 'Not unless Nekaun decides we must. I would like to observe them when they first meet.'

Vervel chuckled. 'I think we all would. It should be *very* interesting.'

'Then we shall have to see what we can arrange.' Imenja straightened in her chair. 'Are there any other questions? Matters to discuss?'

As one of the Voices began talking about a feud between merchants in the city, Reivan let her mind drift away.

I wonder if Auraya knows Nekaun has no intention of letting her leave? I wonder if she knows she is stronger than Nekaun, and is gambling on him trying to kill her without the other Voices' help. Her heart started to race as a terrible possibility occurred to her.

She'll kill him! He won't listen to Imenja, so he has no idea of the danger he's in. I have to warn him!

It was a long time before her heart stopped pounding and she could hear the discussion again. Then she only wanted the

Voices to finish, even though she knew she could not rush to Nekaun and deliver her warning. Not while Auraya was with him, able to read Reivan's mind.

This is going to be a very long day.

It had taken several hours for Emerahl to move the rubble and dirt to the sides of the crevice. She could have worked faster, but she did not want to risk that the vibration of shifting large amounts of rubble might dislodge the slab of wall wedged so precariously above her. Though the barrier she kept above herself at all times should be strong enough to protect her, she did not relish the thought of being buried alive.

She was also wary of breaking anything she uncovered. Using magic, she first blew dirt and dust aside, then she lifted away the rubble and boulders she had uncovered until she had to stop and blow away more dirt.

A channel now stretched from where the handholds met the rubble to the far wall. Temples tended to be symmetrical in design so if anything lay buried here it was probably in line with the handholds and the passage above it.

The writing on the bones was never far from her thoughts. If only a mortal might take the Scroll, then something must prevent an immortal. Whatever that was, it must be powerful. And dangerous.

Pausing to rest earlier, she had lifted her light higher to examine the slab of wall above her and discovered something else. She could see beyond it in one corner. What remained of the roof was covered in cracks. Unlike the cracks in the passage that ran in the same direction as the crevice, these cracks formed radiating patterns. At the centre of one was a small crater.

Emerahl was sure they were impacts from some magical attack. There were none on the walls, however. Whoever had made them had attacked the roof specifically, perhaps in order to cause the collapse which had filled the crevice's floor.

As she blew aside more dirt a smooth stone surface appeared. She shifted away more rubble and uncovered what might be a domed roof.

'You've found it!' Yathyir exclaimed.

'Looks like it,' Emerahl agreed.

'I'll tell the others.'

She opened her mouth to tell him to wait, but decided against it. It wouldn't hurt for the Thinkers to watch her finish uncovering this and know the care she had taken. Not that Barmonia would ever acknowledge it.

As she continued lifting away rubble, more of the dome appeared. Soon footsteps echoed in the hall. She turned to watch as the five Thinkers climbed down the wall.

Barmonia picked his way over to her, looked down at the dome and scowled.

'Yathyir was probably a bit premature,' she said, shrugging.

He looked at her, eyebrows arching, then turned on his heel.

'Continue,' he ordered.

She rolled her eyes. Turning back to the hole she had made, she resumed shifting dirt and rubble. The dome was large, so she concentrated on removing the debris on one side. An edge appeared. She cleared more and uncovered a wall. Finally the top of an arch appeared. Remnants of a wooden door still hung from a hinge and rubble had tumbled into the structure.

'Halt!' Barmonia barked.

She stopped. He climbed down to the opening and thrust his torch inside. Interior walls were illuminated. He climbed back out again.

'Continue.'

Suppressing a sigh, she cleared the opening. When the

entrance was uncovered, Barmonia barked at her to stop again. He moved past her and looked inside, then turned back.

'We'll do the rest by hand.'

The other Thinkers followed him in. Ray paused beside her. He glanced up at the steep slope of rubble on either side.

'Your hard work is appreciated, Emmea,' he murmured.

She smiled. *By you or your secret benefactor?*

He looked up. 'It's unnerving. This crevice and the cracks in the passage run the same direction as the escarpment. I can't help thinking the city is slowly falling down into the lowlands.'

Emerahl looked at him in surprise, realising he was probably right. *If he's right, this is a silly place to hide a treasure. But to be fair, the priest of Sorli probably didn't know this was going to happen.*

Ray moved inside the building. Following him, Emerahl paused in the entrance as she saw that the Thinkers were clearing rubble away from a large stone box with their bare hands. Barmonia was grinning broadly and she could sense intense anticipation and excitement. She took a step inside . . .

. . . then stopped. A familiar feeling had come over her. Her skin prickled, but it took a few seconds for her to recognise why.

This room is a void!

A void. Here of all places. Was this part of the reason no immortal might take the scroll? With no magic, she could not protect or heal herself. But neither could a mortal.

Yathyir had paused to look at her. She forced herself to step over the fissure, all the while watchful for some trap that might spring from the walls, ceiling or floor. The thought of the slab of wall hanging above was suddenly much more discomforting.

Emerahl looked down at the box. It was the shape of a coffin. Barmonia leaned over and blew the dust from the surface, revealing glyphs.

'What does the script say, Emmea?' Ray asked.

She moved forward and traced her fingers over the carvings. 'It says: "Even that which has no flesh may die".'

'A tomb for a goddess,' Kereon said.

'Well at least this time we won't be disturbing a corpse,' Barmonia said lightly. Bracing his hands against the edge of the box, he pushed. Nothing happened. Ray joined him and the lid slowly slid aside with a dry, scraping sound.

The men drew in a collective breath of awe and greed.

The torchlight reflected from precious metals and gems. A tangle of chains, vessels, bangles and weapons filled the box, but it was the gold object in the centre that demanded attention.

A gold scroll, Emerahl thought. *I suppose parchment would have rotted away.*

It lay open, the 'parchment' artfully curved in a way real skin would not have. The rods at either end were a twisted mess of elaborate trimming, patterns and projections, studded with gems. The runes were also decorated, some so much that the shape of them was distorted.

'It's beautiful,' Kereon breathed.

No, it isn't, Emerahl thought. *It's garish and overdone.*

'What does it say, Emmea?' Yathyir asked.

Making herself ignore the sheer ugliness of the object, Emerahl focused on the script. She nearly groaned aloud.

'It rhymes. It's poetry. Very bad poetry.'

'But what does it say?'

Emerahl paused to read. 'It's a history. It tells how the goddess was grieved by the deaths of other gods and . . . that's interesting. It says she helped kill them, and felt a terrible guilt.' She paused to read more. 'She gave her priest all the secrets of the gods. Here it says she bade him record them in an indestructible form. Then . . . Well!'

'What?' Barmonia demanded.

Emerahl looked up at him and smiled. 'Then she killed herself. Here. In this very place. Do the gods become ghosts, I wonder.'

Yathyir looked around nervously and the others smiled.

'And the secrets?' Ray asked.

'The scroll doesn't describe them,' she told him, frowning as she realised it was true.

The Twins are going to be disappointed, she thought, feeling an unexpected bitterness. *And I've put up with the Thinkers for nothing. At least it won't matter if Ray destroys the scroll. It's worth only what money the gold would fetch if it were melted down.*

'Let's take all this out,' Barmonia said. Everyone fell silent as he bent to pick up the scroll. He grunted as he lifted it.

'It's heavy,' he said. 'Yathyir?'

The young man's eyes widened and he held out his hands for the scroll. 'Yes?'

'Not this, you idiot,' Barmonia growled. 'Climb back up and bring us something to carry it all in. Packs would be best. Empty packs.'

As Yathyir obediently hurried out of the building, Emerahl followed him. She stepped outside and breathed a sigh of relief as magic surrounded her. Nothing bad had happened to her. Perhaps whatever trap had been set for immortals had long ago deteriorated.

'Emmea?' Ray called.

She turned to see him staring at the remnants of the wooden door, still half buried.

'What is it?' she asked.

He pointed at the door. 'What does this say?'

Forcing herself to step back inside, she turned to the door and saw that large glyphs had been carved into the surface. She felt a chill.

'It says: "Beware, immortals",' she told him. 'There's more.'

He cleared away more of the rubble, revealing the rest of the message.

'Beware, immortals. No magic lies within. Enter and know your true age.'

She felt a smile tugging at her lips. No magic. A void. Whoever had carved this had believed immortals couldn't exist within voids. They probably imagined that, without magic to sustain them, immortals would revert to their true age.

That would be an impressive, though ghoulish, sight. She turned away so Ray would not see her smile. *It's nice to know gods and their priests don't always know everything.*

But still, she longed to get out of this place and into the sunlight, and away from these selfish, arrogant men. Tonight she would dictate as much of the poem as she could remember to The Twins. Tomorrow . . . tomorrow she would congratulate the Thinkers and start the long journey back to familiar lands.

CHAPTER 31

Danjin stared at the cover of the platten and slowly realised he was awake. The two men opposite him were conscious but their attention was elsewhere. Gillen looked more alert than he had for any of the journey so far, rubbing his hands together in excitement and anticipation, while Yem was even more subdued than usual. The warrior had worn a constant frown since they'd left the fort and Danjin suspected he was caught between sympathy for the servants that had escaped oppressive clan rule and outrage that the Pentadrians had subverted them.

Danjin looked at Ella. Her eyes were closed and her breathing was slow.

Ultimately I have to trust her and the wisdom of the gods. If this tough stance on associating with Pentadrians wasn't needed we wouldn't be ambushing a village with the help of the local warriors.

The platten slowed. Ella moved abruptly to open the flap of the cover.

'We're here.'

Danjin felt his stomach sink, but said nothing. He heard the sounds of doors slamming and distant shouts. Angry and frightened voices surrounded the platten as it slowed to a stop.

Ella smoothed her circ, then looked at Yem, Gillen and Danjin.

'Stay close,' she said, then pulled the flap wide and stepped out.

Danjin followed, then Yem and Gillen. Men and women milled around the platten. When they saw Ella their eyes widened and they quietened. A few faces betrayed dismay and alarm. Others showed amazement and curiosity.

Looking along the street, Danjin saw warriors ushering people toward the growing crowd. Men, women and children emerged from houses, some dressed in their nightclothes. From another direction came a large group of locals. From the sweat on their brows Danjin guessed they had been gathered from homes and farms further from the village centre.

As the crowd swelled, Danjin looked closely at the people. In the torchlight the physical characteristics that marked them as Dunwayan or Southern Ithanian were heightened. Pentadrians varied from pale to dark-skinned, and their builds could be as varied, so it was easier to identify them simply as those that didn't look Dunwayan. He judged the crowd to be a quarter Pentadrian.

A group of Dunwayan warriors, their faces almost black from tattooing, surrounded the villagers. The grey-haired clan leader, Gret, stepped forward. He made the sign of the circle.

'We have brought the occupants of all of the local farms and homes,' he told her. 'Some may have evaded us.'

Ella nodded. 'Who leads this community?' she asked, her voice ringing out above the noise of the crowd.

A discussion followed. Danjin made out enough to understand that an elder of the village spoke for the village when dealing with the local clan. The man came forward.

'Who leads the Pentadrian community?' she demanded of him.

He hesitated, but Ella had already turned away from him. 'Servant Warwel, come forward.'

Silence followed. People exchanged nervous glances. Ella's eyes moved over them and stopped.

'You can walk, Servant Warwel,' Ella said warningly, 'or be dragged. It is your choice.'

A man moved forward. He was tall and walked with dignity. His expression was grim and resigned. He stopped a few steps from Ella and returned her stare silently.

'People of Dram, you have been deceived. This man and those of his ship were sent here by the leader of the Pentadrians, Nekaun,' Ella said, turning to meet the eyes of the village elder. 'Their ship was not wrecked accidentally. It was wrecked deliberately so that they might gain the sympathy of Dunwayans. They were then to settle here and befriend as many Dunwayans as possible in order to convert them to their own religion.'

She looked out over the crowd. 'They have succeeded far too easily. I see many here who have been corrupted by their influence. I also see many who were then lured out of service to their clans with promises of freedom. Clans whose warriors had fought for them but a few years ago. Fought those who invaded our lands in order to enslave us.' A murmur of protest rose, but Ella raised her voice. 'They may have used gentler methods this time, but do not doubt that their intention is the same. This is – was – just another invasion. They came here to separate you from the Circle of Gods, abusing your generosity and preying upon your weaknesses in order to do so.'

She paused to scan the crowd silently for a moment. 'It is a pity you all allowed this to go as far as it has. I see some here who did not allow themselves to be corrupted, but who remained silent out of fear or greed. I see very few here who were powerless to protest or act and I will speak in their defence. As for the rest of you: it is up to I-Portak to decide what is to be done with you, Pentadrian and Dunwayan alike.'

Turning to Gret, Ella nodded. 'They are yours to deal with.'

The clan leader barked out orders and warriors began to move people along the road out of the village. Danjin noted that the old warrior was making a good show of following Ella's orders with distaste. Every time a crying child was herded past, Gret looked at Ella pointedly. She ignored him, her expression stern and disapproving.

'Where are you taking us?' someone called.

'To Chon,' a warrior replied.

'Let us go back to our homes for clothes,' one woman begged of a warrior. 'We'll freeze to death like this.'

'My cures,' an old man croaked. 'I won't make it without my cures.'

'What will we eat?'

'My mother is sick. She'll never make it to Chon.'

Gret turned to one of his companions. 'Get someone to take the woman and the old man back to their homes.'

At once several other voices rose pleading for the same opportunity.

'No,' Ella said. 'Take a few and the rest will demand the same. Keep the prisoners here and send a few warriors to the houses to gather blankets, food and clothing for all.'

Gret's eyebrows rose, then he nodded at his companion. 'Do it.'

Danjin felt a chill run down his spine. Surely a delay now would be better than deaths along the road . . .

Ella turned to Danjin. 'Find out what the old man needs and fetch it,' she murmured.

'Yes, Ellareen of the White,' he replied.

He hurried away and started looking for the old man.

Circling around the crowd, he looked back to where Ella stood. She held her head high and was staring loftily down her nose at her prisoners. He felt his stomach sink a little.

She's only doing that in order to intimidate them into obedience, he told himself.

But they will remember it. They will tell others how cold and uncaring Ellareen the White is. How cruel and inflexible the White's justice was.

He shook his head. *She has to do this. She can't override Dunwayan law. And if she was without pity she wouldn't have sent me to find the old man's cures.*

Then why did he feel as if he wasn't watching an act? Why did he suspect that Ellareen hadn't tried to persuade the Dunwayans to treat the village with some sympathy because she didn't want to?

Why did she disturb him sometimes?

Sighing, he turned away, found the old man and pulled him aside to question him.

The Sanctuary was not as impressive as the Temple in Jarime. There was no huge White Tower or Dome looming over all, just a wide stairway and a single-storey façade of welcoming arches, then a jumble of buildings rising up the hillside behind.

Perhaps that's the idea, Mirar mused. *They don't want to intimidate visitors; they want them to feel welcome.*

The winds had not taken them as far as Genza had hoped, so they had had to travel the rest of the way in a platten. The litter that he and Genza had ridden in from the ferry port stopped and the carriers lowered it to the ground. As Genza rose, Mirar followed suit. She smiled.

'Welcome to Sanctuary, Mirar of the Dreamweavers.'

'Thank you.'

Gesturing for him to follow, she started up the stairs. They passed through one of the archways into a wide, airy hall full of black-robed Servants and ordinary people.

'This is where we greet all visitors to the Sanctuary,' Genza told him. 'Servants listen to all, from the lowest beggar to the wealthy and powerful, and direct them to whoever can best meet their needs.'

Mirar noted that some of the visitors were talking boldly and confidently to the Servants. Others were tentative, waiting nervously to be approached or keeping their gaze lowered as they talked. Sensing distress, Mirar found a Servant patting the shoulder of a crying woman.

'Do you think you could find my daughter?' he heard the woman ask.

'We can only try,' the Servant replied. 'Are you sure her father took her?'

'Yes. No . . . I . . .'

A laugh drew his attention to a richly dressed man crossing the hall in the company of a male Servant.

'. . . like to present gifts to the Elai as well. After all, they sank the ships that were . . .'

Elai sinking ships? He resisted the urge to look back at the man.

'This is the main courtyard,' Genza said. 'From here passages lead to all areas of the Sanctuary.'

The courtyard was fringed by a veranda. He made appreciative comments as she pointed out the fountain and told him that it both helped cool the air and the noise made discussions more private. As they continued deeper into the Sanctuary he noted how the Servants paused to watch her, tracing a sign over their chest if she happened to look their way. He sensed admiration and respect – even adoration – from them.

He also sensed curiosity directed toward himself and

wondered how much they knew about him. Were they curious because Dreamweavers weren't often seen in the Sanctuary? Did they wonder if he was the legendary, immortal founder of the Dreamweavers, or did they already know who he was, having been told Genza was bringing him here?

Genza guided him along corridors and through courtyards, climbing ever upward. Occasionally he glimpsed the city from a window or balcony, and each time the view was more impressive. As they continued further into the Sanctuary Mirar felt a nagging uneasiness.

I'm completely at a disadvantage here, he mused. *The Voices may be more powerful than me. Even if not individually, they would be if united. They're surrounded by hundreds, maybe thousands, of mortal sorcerers willing to do their bidding.*

I expected that. What I didn't expect was that this place would be such a maze. Without Genza I'd be completely lost.

Yet he did not feel in danger here. The noises of the city were distant, he sensed no threatening emotions from the Servants he passed, and the sprawling design of the Sanctuary, with its many courtyards and corridors open to the air, suggested a place of relaxation and tranquillity. Still, this was also a place of political and magical strength, and he did not let the subtle magical barrier about himself fall.

At last Genza stepped out of a corridor onto a long, wide balcony occupied by several men and women sitting in reed chairs. All looked up at him, their gazes bright with interest.

'This is Mirar, leader of the Dreamweavers,' Genza told them. She glanced at him. 'Dreamweaver Mirar, this is Second Voice Imenja.'

The woman she gestured to was tall and slim. It was hard to guess her physical age.

This was the one who faltered during the last war, allowing Auraya to kill Kuar, he thought.

She smiled politely. 'I am pleased to meet you at last. Genza has found much to praise about you.'

Mirar inclined his head. 'A pleasure to meet you, too, Second Voice.'

'This is Third Voice Vervel,' Genza continued, waving at a man with a robust build.

I remember him from the war, but I know nothing about him. I'll have to fix that.

'This is Fifth Voice Shar.'

The slim, handsome young man with the blond hair smiled, and Mirar nodded in reply.

He's the one who breeds the vorn. The one the southern Dreamweavers say can be cruel.

Genza then introduced the others. They were 'Companions' and their roles were as assistants and advisers to the Voices. The Twins and Auraya had already told him about them.

'Join us, Dreamweaver Mirar,' Second Voice Imenja invited, gesturing to an empty chair.

Mirar sat down and accepted a glass of water from one of the Companions.

'We have been discussing, of all things, war,' Imenja told him.

'Any particular war?' he asked.

She shook her head. 'All wars. Warfare as a subject. Dreamweavers do not fight wars, do they?'

'No. We acknowledge the need for a person or country to defend themselves, but our vow to never do harm prevents us from fighting ourselves.'

'So you don't approve of our invasion of Northern Ithania, but would approve of us defending ourselves if we were invaded?' Imenja asked.

He nodded.

'Yet your people don't help in the defence of their country.'

'We do only by healing the wounded.'

'You heal the wounded of both sides.'

'Yes. My people honour their vows to heal all those in need as much as their loyalty to their homeland, knowing that Dreamweavers everywhere would do the same.'

'I see.'

'Surely this causes conflicts between Dreamweavers and the people of their land?' the woman's Companion asked. 'Don't people resent Dreamweavers for helping the enemy?'

'Of course.' Mirar smiled. 'As often as someone may be grateful to a Dreamweaver of their enemy's land for saving one of their own.'

'The White and Circlians have caused your people great harm,' Vervel said. 'Would your people fight them?'

Mirar shook his head. 'No.'

'Not to escape oppression? Not for the freedom to follow your own ways?'

'Not even if we thought either was possible. We might kill all of the White, but the gods would soon find replacements.'

'So you believe the Circlian gods are real?' Imenja asked.

Mirar smiled ruefully. 'I know it. A reliable source of mine assures me yours are too.'

The Voices looked at each other, each glance swift and meaningful.

'If we defeated the White,' Vervel said. 'If all Circlians became Pentadrians, the Circlian gods would not find anyone willing to take the place of the White.'

'Ah, if only that were true!' Mirar sighed. 'Unfortunately it would require every single Circlian to willingly reject their gods and convert to yours.'

'They might, in time,' Shar said. 'Of course, there would be followers of the Circle meeting in secret, rebels and such. We would have to hunt them down and—'

'The point is, with us in control, your people would be free to live as they pleased,' Vervel interrupted. 'Surely that is worth bending a few rules for?'

Mirar shook his head. 'The trouble is, it is not some minor rule, but our primary law and principle.'

'But they tried to kill you,' Genza reminded him.

Mirar met the woman's gaze. 'And your people arranged for Dreamweavers in Jarime to be murdered so that Priests would be blamed.'

Genza's eyes narrowed slightly, then she turned to look at Imenja.

'I guess we are lucky that your people don't take sides,' Imenja said quietly. 'Rest assured that not all of us were in favour of that sordid little scheme.' He noticed that the woman's Companion was staring at her mistress, radiating suspicion and horror. 'We do not intend to repeat that mistake. However, I'm sure the White would attempt to kill you again, if they could.'

Mirar laughed darkly. 'I know. They've already tried.'

Imenja's eyes brightened with interest. 'Recently? Is that why you came to Southern Ithania?'

'Yes. And now I find the very woman they sent to execute me is here, being treated as an honoured guest.'

He noted which faces betrayed surprise and which did not. Imenja was smiling.

'You know Auraya's here?' Genza asked. 'And you still came?'

Mirar shrugged. 'Of course I know. The city is full of gossip – and Dreamweavers.'

Imenja chuckled. 'And Nekaun has hardly kept her a secret.' She looked at Mirar and sobered. 'You're in no danger. We will not allow her to harm you. And it seems we need not fear you will harm her.' She watched him closely, probably looking for signs that he might make an exception to his rule against violence. 'In a week she will be gone.'

Mirar nodded.

'There is no need for you two to meet. Perhaps you would prefer to avoid her,' she continued. He sensed disappointment from the Companions and resisted a smile. Clearly they were curious to see what might happen if he and Auraya encountered one another.

As am I, he thought. *To know she is this close and not see her once* . . . Surely there would be no harm in meeting.

'I don't care,' he said. 'In fact, it would be satisfying to let her see me, alive and well treated by her enemy.'

Imenja chuckled again. 'That, too, can be arranged.'

CHAPTER 32

*D*reamweaver Mirar is a good-looking man, Reivan thought as she watched him and Imenja stroll toward the Sanctuary flame. *Not my type, though. He looks like a northerner, and there's something else . . .*

He reminded her of a Thinker she had once been infatuated with as a young woman. The Thinker he reminded her of had appeared at a meeting one day and charmed everybody. A few months later he vanished. In the following years he arrived and left unannounced numerous times. Every time he visited Glymma he found himself a different pretty girl, then discarded her. Reivan had felt jealous at first, then sympathy for the girls who had been promised so much but were left broken-hearted, sometimes burdened with an occupied womb.

Mirar had a confidence about him that drew people, and it was this that reminded her of the Thinker. He had the same restlessness in his gaze, as if he were always planning his next destination. Yet while the Thinker had moved whenever there was something to escape, she imagined Mirar simply drifted about, observing whatever he encountered, then drifted on.

He doesn't hurry, she thought suddenly. *That's the difference. And why would he, when he's immortal?*

That was what most fascinated her. The Voices were

immortal because the gods wanted them to be. Mirar had somehow achieved it without help. She itched to ask him how, even though she doubted she would understand the answer.

He and Imenja had been standing before the Sanctuary flame. Now they turned and walked back toward Reivan.

'. . . ever blown out?'

'A few times. We haven't hidden the fact. People can be superstitious about such matters. They might think that if the flame went out the world would end, or something equally ridiculous, if we didn't tell them it happens occasionally. As it is, they still try to find some significance to the few occurrences they know of.'

Mirar chuckled. 'I imagine they do.' He looked up. 'Is that a Siyee?'

Following his gaze, Reivan saw a winged figure circling upward.

'Yes,' Imenja said. 'One of the group we are holding prisoner. They attacked one of our villages. Nekaun is letting them go, one by one, in exchange for Auraya staying here.'

Mirar nodded. 'I heard about that. It is wise, letting them go separately. They can't easily band together and attack again.'

'Yes.'

'You must be treating them well,' he added. 'Or by now they would not be able to fly. Are you giving them supplies to get them home?'

'They can't carry enough to last all the way to Si, unfortunately, but what we give them should sustain them until they reach Sennon.'

Imenja ushered him to the staircase that led down from the Sanctuary flame into the buildings below. Following them, Reivan heard voices coming from somewhere ahead in the corridor. Mirar and Imenja turned a corner and stopped. As she reached them, Reivan recognised the voices and a shiver ran over her skin. She looked at Mirar. His mouth was set in a smile. His eyes were bright – perhaps with fear, perhaps amusement.

Reivan looked at the object of his attention. Auraya stared back at Mirar through narrowed eyes. She stood very still, as if frozen. Nekaun gave Imenja a very direct look, then turned to Auraya and opened his mouth to speak – but he did not get a chance.

'Mirar,' Auraya said, her voice full of contempt. 'I see you've arrived.'

'I have,' he replied, glancing at Imenja. 'And received a warm reception.'

'I would expect nothing less of our hosts.'

Auraya's gaze was intense, but Mirar did not flinch.

'I would have expected otherwise based on the rude reception I received in the north,' Mirar said airily. 'But then I thought "it has to be better in the south, because it could hardly be worse".'

Auraya smiled. 'They just haven't got to know you yet.'

Mirar's smile faded slightly, and a small crease appeared between his brows.

'How are the Siyee faring these days?'

'Well,' Auraya said shortly.

'The White finding them useful allies?'

'Of course.'

'I hear their latest mission failed.'

'I'm afraid that's old news here.'

'Yes,' Mirar agreed. 'I suppose I have the White to thank for this opportunity to meet you again – under much more enjoyable circumstances, too.' He looked at Imenja. 'I hope there will be time for us to converse again, before you leave. Perhaps over dinner?'

'It can be arranged,' Imenja replied mildly.

'Perhaps a quiet, private dinner,' Auraya said, her eyes gleaming. 'Just the two of us. We could resume our previous conversation. Pick up again from where we stopped.'

'I'm sure my new friends would like the opportunity to join in,' Mirar replied. 'Especially when you are leaving so soon. They have first claim on you, since your time here is finite and mine is not.'

Nekaun chuckled. 'Dreamweaver Mirar is right. We still have much to show you, and your time here is fast dwindling.' He looked at Imenja. 'Perhaps we can all meet at dinner tonight.'

'I'll see to it,' she replied.

'Now, I have another trip outside the city to take you on.' Nelsaun touched Auraya's shoulder lightly and she tore her eyes from Mirar's smug expression to look at the First Voice. 'It will take half of the day to get there, so we should leave without delay.'

Mirar watched Auraya leave, his eyes narrowed, but as Imenja turned to him he looked at her and smiled broadly. She nodded at a corridor leading in another direction. 'Would you like to see the Star Room, where we hold our ceremonies?'

He nodded. 'Sounds fascinating.'

As they set off at a leisurely stroll, Reivan analysed the conversation between Mirar and Auraya.

'I would have expected otherwise based on the rude reception I received in the north.'

'They just haven't got to know you yet.'

Auraya won that exchange, Reivan mused. The former White had insinuated that Mirar made himself unwelcome wherever he went. *She might have a point.*

Mirar had made a veiled jibe about the White sending the Siyee on a doomed mission, but Auraya hadn't appeared ruffled. Then Mirar had taunted her, pointing out that she could do nothing to him here.

'. . . Just the two of us. Pick up again from where we stopped.'

Reivan caught the chuckle that welled up inside her. *Auraya won that exchange, too*, she thought. *She all but pointed out that his safety depended on us, and that she was willing to kill him if the Voices gave her the chance. But Mirar had the last word, I think. What did he say again?*

'I'm sure my new friends would like the opportunity to join in . . . your time here is finite and mine is not.'

She frowned. Had Mirar guessed that the Voices didn't intend to let Auraya leave? Or was he merely pointing out that the Voices had more reason to protect him than her, since he was immortal and would be a more useful ally in the long term?

He's smart enough to have guessed the Voices' plans, Reivan decided. *Anyone who thought the situation through carefully could have.*

But had Auraya?

Mischief leapt up onto the mattress. He spent a few minutes roaming about, assessing the best position to sleep according to merits only he understood. When he found a satisfactory place, he curled up and sighed.

Staring at the ceiling, Auraya considered what she had reported to Juran that evening. Or rather, what she *hadn't* reported.

:*Mirar is here*, she had told him. *We encountered each other in one of those accidental crossing of paths that obviously wasn't accidental.*

:*What happened?*

:*Nothing. He pointed out that the Voices would protect him and that the Siyee mission was doomed.*

:*I fear he is right on both counts.*

She hadn't told Juran about her and Mirar's agreement to act as if they were enemies. It would make it obvious that she *didn't* consider Mirar an enemy, and that would hardly please Juran. She didn't want to give him any further reason to distrust her.

Now she had the last task of the evening left. Each night since she had first dream linked with Mirar they had communicated the same way. Tonight they would have much to discuss. Closing her eyes, she sought the state of mind she needed.

:*Auraya.*

It took her a moment to realise she must have fallen asleep straightaway.

:*Mirar?*

:*At last! How late do you turn in?*

She felt amusement at his impatience.

:*As late as I wish.*

:*Ah. It's like that, is it? Got all haughty since the Voices started treating you as an honoured guest?*

:*Only when I need to. Did we do well today?*

:*It was a start.*

:*Ha! I came up with the best snappy replies!*

:*I had the last word.*

:*You did,* she agreed.

:*So where were you tonight? I was looking forward to continuing over dinner.*

:*Didn't Imenja explain? We roamed so far from the city that we couldn't get back in time.*

:*Is that the truth, then?*

:*Yes. Of course, Nekaun and I might have spent a little longer than necessary inspecting the glassmakers' workshops.*

:*Well, I suppose the Voices expect you to avoid me.*

:*And I'm afraid I'll run out of snappy replies if we meet too often.*

:*You have a collection of them, then?*

:*A handful. All waiting for the right moment.*

:*Who'd have thought you'd have such a talent for bitchiness?*

:*Thanks. So have the Voices made you any offers yet?*

:No. They questioned me about the Dreamweaver law against violence the day I arrived. Maybe my answer put them off.

:Hmm. Remember, even if they don't offer to kill me for you, they might still offer to kill you for me.

:Then they're being remarkably good at hiding it. We've been talking a lot about the Dreamweavers and my place among them. Whether I am a leader or guide. Imenja said that whether I want to be their leader or not, Dreamweavers regard me with reverence. The trouble with being dead for a while is people have a gilded image of you in their minds. I assured her that I never let them worship me before, and I will not now. She said she believed me.

He had turned serious, and Auraya had a disturbing feeling she was talking to Leiard. She pushed it away.

:I suppose she read the minds of Dreamweavers in order to find out what they think of you.

:Yes. Oh, something she said . . . I think they know you can read minds.

Auraya felt a chill. Was there any danger in the Voices knowing she could read minds? Jade had thought it would be dangerous for the gods to know Auraya had regained the ability, but she had meant the Circlian gods.

Still, it was possible that the Circlian gods occasionally read the minds of Pentadrians. Unless . . .

:Do you think only the Voices know, or others?

:I don't know. I could search some dreams tonight and see if I can find out for you.

:Yes. I'll do a bit of mind-skimming, too. There might be someone still awake.

:When you do, look for any thoughts about the Elai. I overheard a comment when I arrived suggesting that they were sinking ships.

:Sinking ships? That is an alarming possibility.

:Yes. Now, we both have much to do, and the night isn't getting any longer.

:No. Good night.

:Good night.

:Mirar?

:Yes?

She paused, suddenly worried that what she had been about to say would give him a false impression. After a moment, she decided it wouldn't.

:Thank you for your help.

:Don't thank me yet. Not until the last Siyee is free and you escape this place. When the last Siyee flies be prepared for betrayal, Auraya, he warned. *I don't think the Voices intend to let you go.*

As he broke the link she floated in an uneasy dream state, thinking about his warning. *If I was in Nekaun's place, I wouldn't let me go either. I'm going to have to give him a reason to let me go.* She was too tired to consider that now, and she still had mind-skimming to do. Concentrating, she sent her mind out into the world.

Moving from mind to mind, she skimmed the thoughts of the Servants and domestics still awake in the Sanctuary. When she encountered the mind of a Voice's Companion she felt a thrill of satisfaction. The woman, Reivan, was restless and unable to sleep and her thoughts revolved around First Voice Nekaun.

It's been so long, Reivan thought. *Surely he could have found the time to visit me once. How am I going to warn him about Imenja's suspicions? I can't go near him in case Auraya reads my mind.*

Auraya's stomach sank. That confirmed what Mirar had told her. Her mind-reading ability had been detected.

But then, why would he listen to me if he won't listen to Imenja. No, I can only hope he doesn't underestimate Auraya. He'll come back to me once he's killed her, Reivan told herself.

Auraya felt a shock. Somehow it was more chilling to hear Nekaun's intentions stated so clearly in the woman's mind.

But she also sensed doubt. Companion Reivan knew the other Voices believed Nekaun would kill her, but they didn't know for sure. He was secretive. He kept his plans from them. Then Auraya saw the woman's greatest fear, lurking constantly at the edge of her mind. The other Voices believed Auraya was more powerful than Nekaun. Reivan worried that if he attempted to kill Auraya, he would do so alone. She feared he would fail.

Interesting, Auraya mused. *I wonder if they are right. And it is odd that Nekaun keeps himself separate from the other Voices. It's a weakness that could be exploited.*

The Companion was drifting off to sleep now. If she knew anything about the Elai, she wasn't going to be thinking about it any time soon. Her thoughts were full of Nekaun. Auraya moved on, seeking other minds.

She would not abandon the remaining Siyee imprisoned here, but when the last of them flew, she would be ready to defend herself against Nekaun.

CHAPTER 33

Have you made a copy of this scroll? Tamun asked Emerahl as soon as The Twins dream linked with her.

:I'm trying to, Emerahl replied. *The only reason Barmonia lets me see it is because I can translate for him. He won't let me write it down for him. He won't even let me take notes. I've had to memorise what I can and write it down secretly.*

:What form are you writing it down in? Tamun asked.

:I've burned it onto the inside of my water skin. They'll never find it there.

:In what language?

:Hanian, so they won't know what I wrote if they do find it.

:You must use the original glyphs! The smallest mistranslation can change the meaning of a phrase!

:She won't mistranslate, Surim injected.

:Thank you, Emerahl said, pleased at his defence of her.

:She might not realise she has, Tamun countered. *We can't take any risks. In the old priest tongue words often had two meanings.*

If Emerahl had been awake she would have sighed. Tamun hadn't taken well to the news that the scroll was useless. She refused to believe it, saying the poem must be a code.

:Very well. I'll copy the glyphs somehow. But what then? It's just a history. There are no directions to these secrets about the gods.

:No? Tamun's amusement rippled over Emerahl's mind. *What you have recited bears some obvious clues.*

:Obvious?

:The secrets were preserved in an indestructible form. What is indestructible?

:Nothing.

:Gold, Surim said. *Or so a smith once told me. It can be melted and mixed with other metals, but alone it never rusts or deteriorates.*

:If the secrets are recorded in gold, and gold can be melted, then the secrets can be destroyed, Tamun pointed out.

:Then it must be something so hard and solid it can't be broken.

:Diamond? Emerahl suggested. Her mind shifted to the treasures found in the coffin. There had been plenty of precious stones among the jewellery and trinkets.

:A diamond can be cut by another diamond, Tamun said. *That makes it as fragile as gold.*

:What else is there? Surim asked.

The Twins fell silent as they considered. Emerahl's mind kept returning to the jewellery and trinkets. If the secrets were preserved on a diamond it would be a clever trick to hide it among the treasure.

Though there couldn't be many secrets if they were carved into a diamond. Some of the gems in the collection were impressively large, but there was little room for more than a few words on them.

:It would be easier if you just stole it and brought it to us.

:I'm not stealing that great hunk of gold! Even if it wasn't a big ugly piece of dung too heavy to carry, we know Pentadrian Servants want it. I could have half the Servants of Southern Ithania on my tail all the way to the coast, and I might not be able to find a ship to—

:Emerahl. Wake up. Something has happened. The traitor has—

Suddenly Emerahl was aware of a voice. Barmonia's voice.

He was shouting. At once she slipped from the dream and into full consciousness.

'. . . stinking whore of a thief! I'll rip your guts out with my bare hands and feed them . . . !'

Getting up, she wrapped a blanket around her shoulders and hurried out of her tent. The shouting came from the direction of the arem and domestics. Barmonia's words echoed in the still night. Kereon and Yathyir stood beside the fire, Kereon scowling and Yathyir looking wide-eyed with fright. The older man looked at Emerahl, then nodded toward Barmonia's tent.

The front flap was open and they could see the mess inside. A battered, misshapen item lay on the floor: the Scroll.

'Smashed,' he said.

Emerahl did some silent cursing of her own. Barmonia had been so protective of the Scroll, insisting he be present whenever anyone studied it, she had assumed it would be safe enough.

I am a fool! she thought. *The Twins are going to be furious.*

The shouting stopped, then two figures emerged from the darkness. Mikmer and Barmonia were arguing.

'. . . miss him in the darkness. When the sun rises we can track him,' Mikmer said.

'He'll hide his tracks once he knows we're hot on his tail. I'm going after that slut-raised, traitorous . . .'

Barmonia froze as he noticed Emerahl, then closed his mouth. She tried not to show her amusement at this.

'What happened?' Yathyir asked in a small, frightened voice.

Barmonia scowled. 'Ray smashed the scroll. The domestics say he took an arem and left.'

'When?'

'Not long ago.'

Only minutes ago, Emerahl realised. *Ray must have decided to do this while The Twins and I were discussing the Scroll. If he'd planned it before now, they would have known.*

'Was he carrying anything?' Kereon asked.

'A pack and a large bag,' Mikmer replied. He frowned as Barmonia hurried into his tent. 'Why?'

A roar came from the leader's tent. Barmonia emerged, his face dark with anger. 'He took the treasure.'

A cold chill ran over Emerahl's skin. *If I'm right, and the secrets are on a diamond somewhere in the treasure . . .*

It did not surprise her that Ray had stolen the treasure. He'd need money, since his membership as a Thinker would end once the news got about that he'd betrayed them. What didn't make sense was that he had smashed the Scroll. He was supposed to steal it.

Had he worked out that the secret was in the treasure?

The Scroll wasn't going anywhere. If the Thinkers could restore it, they would. She didn't need to wait around for them to do it.

What matters is retrieving the treasure.

'We can't wait until morning,' Barmonia growled.

'We should split up, take a few domestics each, and go in different directions,' Kereon advised.

Mikmer sighed, then nodded. 'I'll go north. Someone should stay here and guard what's left of the Scroll.'

Barmonia looked thoughtful. 'No point in sending Yathyir. I had better stay.' He looked at Kereon and Mikmer. 'Bring him back here. I'll deal with him.'

The two men nodded, then hurried away. Emerahl heard them barking orders at the domestics.

'I could go too,' she offered.

Barmonia gave her a hard, suspicious stare.

'No. He could be dangerous.'

She smiled faintly. 'I doubt it.'

'No. I need you here.'

'I've translated the Scroll,' she argued. 'What else is there for me to do?'

'Stay where I can see you,' he snapped. 'To be honest, I don't trust you.'

She shrugged. 'Fair enough. I'll go back to bed, then.'

'Stay by the fire,' he ordered.

She hesitated, tempted to just leave. He couldn't stop her. But there might still be something significant about the Scroll. She might need to remain on good terms with him.

Out of the darkness came a domestic. He reported that a light had been seen moving down the road to the lowlands.

A light, eh? I don't think Ray would be so foolish as to use a lamp when there'll be plenty of light when the moon rises. More likely he tied a lamp to an arem, pointed it in the direction of the lowlands and gave it a good slap. He'll have gone in the other direction, towards Glymma and his reward.

A little mind-skimming would confirm it.

She gave a mock sigh of exasperation and walked to the nearly burnt-out fire, where she lay down on one of the mats and covered herself with her blanket.

Yathir and Barmonia returned to their tents. She heard Barmonia muttering about the Scroll and whether he could salvage it. Soon he would be too distracted to see her slip away.

Then she would collect her pack and an arem to ride and she would set off after the traitor and his stolen goods.

Auraya drifted, alone in the dream trance. Beneath the Sanctuary two Siyee waited to be freed. In less than two days she would escape Glymma and Nekaun.

In a room somewhere closer, Mirar's body rested while his mind skimmed the thoughts of others. She felt a wave of affection, and a wistful amusement. First, as Leiard, he had been a mentor then a lover. In Si he had been a teacher again, then an enemy. Now he was a welcome ally. A helper. A friend.

I like him, she thought, *and it's not because he reminds me of Leiard. I can't see him, so my eyes aren't telling me I'm talking to Leiard. Sometimes there's a hint of Leiard in what he says through the dream links, but mostly I am talking to someone else.*

Mirar. The enemy of the gods. Auraya gave a mental shrug. *So is Jade, but that didn't stop me liking her, once I got to know her. Must I hate whoever they hate in order to be considered loyal?*

They can't make me love someone. Is it the same for hate?

It was an interesting question, but she still had much to do. She had been skimming minds every night since Mirar first suggested it. Bit by bit they had put together enough information to confirm that Pentadrian Servants had been sent to all countries of Northern Ithania to establish themselves and start converting locals. The White had managed to find and put a stop to most of the attempts, including the most successful one, in Dunway.

Now, as she sent her mind out, she reached towards the closest mind, but then stopped in surprise.

Not far away, loud voices buzzed within the magic of the world.

: . . . happens when you don't consult others.

:I consulted.

:We talked about exercises and tests, not the full assembling of armies.

:Assembling a full army quickly takes practice.

The defensive voice belonged to Huan, whereas the accuser was Saru.

:It also raises expectations and—

I've stumbled into another of the gods' conversations, Auraya thought. *Chaia warned me that I could be detected. I should stop listening and . . .*

:Do you really think he'll believe such a feeble excuse? This was an older male voice. Lore. Auraya hesitated, amazed that gods

415

other than Chaia had confronted Huan. *The Circlians are now wondering if we know what we're doing.*

:Which is hardly my doing, Huan said. *I didn't give the order for the armies to stand down.*

:What were you intending them to do, if not finish their 'exercise' and go home?

The question was from Chaia. Auraya felt her heart warm at the sound of his voice.

:More exercises? Huan suggested. *Too bad you ordered them to stand down. They could do with a bit of training.*

:Which you knew the Pentadrians would hear about, Lore said. *You can't pretend to be ignorant of the consequences.*

:They would have killed Auraya, a quiet female voice said. This could only be Yranna. *The balance would have been regained.*

:No, it would have tipped in the favour of the Pentadrians, Lore said. *They have Mirar.*

:Who won't fight, Saru reminded them.

Huan ignored him. *We've never been in a better position to be rid of him, too*, she pointed out.

:If all that worries you is balance, we can order Auraya to stay out of any battles.

:And she would obey, if the Circlians were losing?

Though the gods now began arguing about whether she was to be trusted or not, Auraya found herself puzzling over Huan's claim that Mirar was in a good position for them to get rid of him. How could he be, when he was within the Pentadrians' centre of power? Perhaps there was an assassin here in the hire of the White. How had he or she managed to avoid detection by the Voices? Or were they unaware who their employer was?

:Auraya isn't the reason the Circlians will go to war, Huan boomed suddenly.

Go to war? Auraya suddenly regretted becoming distracted.

Were the Circlians actually going to attack the Pentadrians, or were the gods simply speaking in terms of possibilities?

:They won't go to war, Lore replied. *A few Pentadrian plots to convert Circlians aren't enough reason to invade another continent.*

Auraya felt relief.

:The White would only go to war if we ordered it, Saru agreed.

:So? Yranna said quietly.

:It's not right to interfere, Lore said firmly. *They must come to the decision themselves.*

:I don't see why we can't nudge them, Saru said. *Last time it was a mortal's decision, why not ours this time?*

:I will only agree to it if Auraya is not involved, Chaia said.

:You fool, Huan said, her voice seething with anger and contempt. *You would have us return to the old days, when the world was crowded with gods and none of us could do anything without others spying upon us.*

Spying . . . Remembering Chaia's warning, Auraya reluctantly moved away from the gods as they began to argue again.

: . . . going to tell her . . .

:Once you have, which . . . kill?

:I don't . . .

As their voices faded out of her hearing, she returned her awareness to her own self, and opened her eyes. Snatches of the gods' conversation repeated in her mind. There was much to puzzle over. She listed what she had learned.

The gods want a war, they're just not in agreement about the timing or who will be involved.

For beings that didn't mind breaking their own laws in order to kill Mirar, they're remarkably concerned that a war would be a fair fight between equals.

Chaia is still defending me. In fact, he seemed to offer his support for war in exchange for me being sent safely out of the way.

Mirar is not as safe here as he believes he is.

And if she warned him, would she be allying herself with the gods' enemy.

Did she care?

Lu hadn't felt so tired since . . . since after Ti had been born. Like that night, tonight she could not sleep despite her exhaustion. Back then it had been worry over Ti, who had been weak and sickly. Now she fretted for her whole family.

She turned to look at her husband, Dor. He was glowering at the night sky. His cheekbone was swollen and darkening into a bruise where he had received a blow from one of the warriors, tired of Dor's attempts to talk his way out of this.

Might as well try to talk the stars down from the sky, she thought. Warriors and servants alike, we all follow our rules and traditions blindly. That's what the Pentadrians said. She frowned. *They said they could change Dunway, but nothing changes if the clans don't want it to. They like things just as they are.*

'It's all their fault,' someone said nearby. Another voice murmured something in reply. Something defensive.

Whispered conversations had passed between the villagers and newcomers since the warriors had ordered them to lie down and sleep. She had listened to arguments and accusations, fears and hopes. All the while there had been the soft sound of weeping from all directions, and old Ger had begun coughing again.

'. . . do we believe? Her or them?' a voice said. Lu recognised it as Mez, the smith.

'She knows the truth. She's got powers. She can read minds,' another replied. Pol, a farmer.

'She could be lying.'

'Why would she?'

'Because she don't like outsiders interfering and making low

418

people stronger. She got a deal with I-Portak to keep him and his warriors in charge.'

'The gods chose her,' Pol said. '*I* still follow the Circle.'

'This'd never have happened if we'd had our own priest,' a different voice lamented. Roi, the baker's wife.

A short silence followed. Ger stopped coughing.

'Doesn't matter,' he said hoarsely. 'Nobody cares about us. Not the newcomers or the warriors or the White. If the newcomers cared about us they would have gone home, not got us all in trouble.'

'We were trying to make things better,' a different voice interjected. Lu recognised Noenei's voice. Lu had admired the woman's dignity and tranquil bearing. Now, on the road to Chon and judgement, such qualities didn't matter.

'You shouldn't have brought the servants here,' Roi said. 'That got their attention.'

'We . . . we just wanted to help them.'

'Well, you didn't. Look at us now. All of us are going to die because you didn't know when to stop.'

Another silence followed.

'Why couldn't you have put aside *your* gods for *ours*?' someone further away asked angrily. 'Not one of you became a Circlian, but lots of us became Pentadrians. Seems to me if you wanted to be Dunwayan like you said, you would have.'

The answer came from another newcomer too far away for Lu to hear.

'Your gods aren't helping you now, are they?' a woman said bitterly. 'They're not helping us, either. I wish you had never come here!'

Others voiced their agreement. Ger's coughing grew louder. More accusations rang out. Suddenly lots of people were shouting. The air vibrated with pent-up anger and fear. Someone leapt up and Lu flinched as she saw them deal out a

419

savage kick, though she could not see the victim. There was a cry of pain and several of protest, then people all over the field were scrambling to their feet — some to strike at the newcomers, some to get away.

Lu grabbed Ti as she rose and turned to Dor, but he was gone. She searched for him, heart racing with terror.

'STOP!'

A light flashed so bright Lu found she could not see properly. Ti began to wail.

'THERE WILL BE NO FIGHTING!'

The voice was the White's. Vision was slowly coming back. Lu blinked hard and held Ti close as she searched for her husband. Warriors marched across the field, snapping out orders.

'Pentadrians to the left, Circlians to the right,' one was saying.

They're separating us, she realised. *Where's . . . ?*

Out of the crowd came Dor, his face dark with suppressed anger. She hurried to him and saw his expression soften. As his arm came around her shoulder she sighed with relief. Then she noticed the blood on his knuckles. She looked at him questioningly.

He smiled grimly. 'A lucky hit,' he said. 'After that I couldn't get close. Nobody could. Most of them are sorcerers.'

'Sorcerers?' she repeated.

'Yes.' He sighed. 'I think the White must be right. Ordinary people might have a few Gifts, but nothing like these. We've been tricked, Lu.'

Lu looked down at Ti, her little face screwed up as she cried with all her being, then over at the crowd of newcomers — no, Pentadrians — now settling down on the other side of the field. She felt something she had never felt before.

Hate.

CHAPTER 34

Wrists were unbound. A water skin was handed over, and a parcel of food. Sreil turned to look at Auraya. His concern for her, and for the priest left alone below, was so strong she felt battered by it. She held his eyes and watched his thoughts shift to those who had gone before him, and home. He nodded once, then turned and leapt off the building.

She watched him fly away, relief washing over her. He still had to survive the long journey home, but the chances she could face Speaker Sirri again without terrible guilt and grief were better. She did not know how she would, if Sirri's son did not make it home.

One Siyee left to free, she thought, conscious of the man at her side. *If Nekaun is going to move against me he will do it soon.*

'What are you going to show me today?' she asked, turning to regard him.

His shoulders lifted. 'Nothing. I have shown you everything within reach of the city. Today . . . I thought we might relax and talk.'

Auraya smiled wryly. She could never allow herself to relax when talking to him. He led her down into the building and through corridors. Parts of the Sanctuary were familiar to her now. She rarely lost her sense of direction. As Nekaun took her a few levels higher than she had ventured before, she found her curiosity growing.

Reaching the end of a corridor, Nekaun led her through a set of double doors and led her into a large, airy room. Domestics waited.

'These are my private rooms,' he told her. A few words in Avvenan sent the domestics hurrying away. Nekaun opened a pair of wooden doors, revealing a balcony.

'Come outside,' he said. 'It is a pleasant place to sit and talk, especially on a day like this when cool breezes ease the summer heat. I have ordered drinks and food.'

Auraya followed him out. Elaborately woven reed chairs filled the space. A blown glass jug stood on a table next to two intricately decorated goblets. Nekaun poured water into the goblets and handed one to Auraya.

Sitting down, she sipped it cautiously. Nekaun settled into a chair facing hers.

Turaan sat further away. The Companion barely spoke these days and most of the time she forgot he was there. Whereas Nekaun used to speak in his own language and allow Turaan to translate, he spoke Hanian now. Yet the Companion remained. Nekaun still needed to consult Turaan on the less common words he did not know yet.

Auraya always waited until Hanian was spoken, despite knowing that her mind-reading abilities had been discovered. So long as the Voices pretended the fact was a secret, so would she.

'So what do you think of my home now you have seen more of it?' Nekaun asked.

'The Sanctuary is pleasant,' she replied.

He smiled. 'And the city?'

'Prosperous. Ordered. I wish Jarime had been planned with as much foresight.'

'One doesn't plan unless one needs to. Hania is not as dry as Avven. What of my people? How do you regard them now?'

'As I always have,' she told him. 'People are much the same everywhere. They love and hate. They follow good traditions and bad. They work, eat, sleep, raise families and grieve the dead.'

Nekaun's eyebrows rose. 'Yet you do not regard them in the same way you regard the Siyee?'

'The Siyee don't hate me. Your people do.'

'Hmm.' He nodded. 'But you did not know this until you came here.'

'No, but I reasoned that they would. I would have been deluded if I'd thought I'd be welcome. Your people have much to hate me for.'

His eyes brightened. 'You could redress that,' he said softly. 'If you stayed here. You have an opportunity to gain their favour.'

'And earn the hatred of my people?' she asked.

'Ah, but would you? If you brought about a lasting peace between our people you may be loved by all. It might not be easy at first, but if you succeeded . . .'

Auraya looked away, through the railing of the balcony to the city below. His vision was a powerful one. A tempting one. As a White, she had been known for her ability to unite people. Her naïve suggestions had brought about the freeing of her village from the Dunwayans who had taken it hostage. Her insight into the Dreamweavers had allowed her to achieve an alliance with the Somreyans, and to encourage tolerance and cooperation between the cult and Circlians. Her empathy and love for the Siyee had united the sky people with the Circlians. Making peace between the Circlians and Pentadrians almost seemed the next logical step.

But she was no longer a White. More importantly, she no

longer had their complete trust. A negotiator needed the trust of all parties he or she dealt with.

Then there were the gods. She could never succeed at making peace between Circlians and Pentadrians with Huan working against her. She could never succeed unless the gods wanted peace. *All* of the gods.

Until the Circle decide to accept their Pentadrian counterparts there can be no peace.

A chill ran through her as she realised the truth of that. Peace was not in her hands, nor in the hands of any mortal or immortal. Mortals were helpless so long as the gods fought each other.

And so long as the gods used mortals as their tools and weapons. *Why do they have to involve us?* she thought, feeling anger stirring. *Why can't they settle their differences and leave us be? They lose followers in wars. Surely it would be better to make peace with each other?*

From what she had overheard of Huan, she doubted the goddess could ever rise above petty hate and pride to negotiate with the Pentadrian gods. And what she had overheard of the gods' conversations told her their own alliance wasn't as solid as they liked mortals to believe.

Nekaun shifted in his seat, drawing her attention back to him. She felt an unexpected sympathy. He could not see that his ambition was impossible.

'I wish it were possible,' she told him. 'But I cannot be the peacemaker. Not unless all the gods wish it.'

'My gods may wish it. Do yours?'

She grimaced. 'I don't know.'

He looked into the room. She saw that domestics had arrived with platters of food. They brought them outside and set them on low tables. Nekaun took a handful of nuts and chewed as he waited for them to leave.

'Is there anything I can offer you to persuade you to stay,' he asked when they had.

Auraya hesitated to answer. Once she let him know there was nothing to keep her here he would have no reason to keep his promise to let the Siyee go. No reason but the vow he'd made.

'Perhaps just a little longer,' he said. 'A few months?'

She shook her head. 'If you do achieve the peace you seek I would consider visiting Glymma again.'

He smiled. 'There is something I could offer you, though it is too small a thing to offer in exchange for anything but a delay in your leaving.'

Turaan's mind was suddenly alive with expectation and a name. Auraya managed to stop herself smiling.

'Oh?'

'Mirar.' Nekaun waved a hand. 'His death could be arranged. It could even be arranged that you kill him yourself, if you wish.'

Auraya allowed herself a brief chuckle. 'Forgive me, but for a moment there I had to wonder if you were interested in converting to the Circlian religion.'

He looked bemused. 'Why?'

'This would please my gods greatly.'

'I see. And you remaining here would not.'

She shrugged. 'Until they indicate otherwise, I have to assume so.'

He nodded. 'Then all I can hope for is that they will indicate otherwise.' Taking another handful of nuts, he ate silently. Auraya took the opportunity to cautiously sample the dried fruit.

A door closed within the room. Nekaun looked up and frowned. A Servant stepped onto the balcony, radiating anxiety. He said something quickly. Reading the meaning from his mind, Auraya went cold.

Nekaun turned to regard her. 'I'm afraid the last Siyee has fallen ill. It is doubtful that he will be able to fly tomorrow morning.'

She rose. 'Take me to him.'

He nodded and stood up. 'Of course. We'll go there directly.'

Morning had confirmed what the night had hinted at: Avven was a near desert. Sunrise had painted the eroded landscape beautiful shades, but once the sun rose higher it leached everything of colour. The air was dry and full of dust. Vegetation either huddled about the occasional water source or spread thinly across the rocky land, stunted and tough.

Sorlina's one road led out of the city into a deep ravine, following the thin river that had once supplied the city. Emerahl had kept the arem walking at a steady pace all night. By morning the ravine and river were far behind and the road wound between fantastically eroded rock formations.

Ahead she had sensed a spark of triumph and gleefulness. Sometimes it drew away, sometimes she felt she was coming closer to it. Ray was pushing the arem hard, then stopping to rest when it tired. He wasn't foolish enough to kill his mount. Not only would pursuers catch him easily, but walking in this hot dry land would be unpleasant and possibly fatal.

Emerahl had grabbed her water skin as she had slipped away from the Thinkers' camp, but it held only enough to last her a day in this heat. She would have to hope there were sources of water along the road. If arem were common along this route there must be a well for them. But she wasn't sure if the road was still used by travellers. She had seen none passing through the city to the lowlands, and the city itself would only attract the occasional curious traveller.

Ray would not have come this way if he didn't think he could make it to Glymma, she told herself. *He's a greedy traitor, but he's not stupid.*

The long ride through the night had tired Ray and his emotions were not as loud to her senses as they had been. The footprints of his arem in the dusty road were easier to follow, however. She was tired and fighting off sleep was more difficult when she could sense the arem's weariness. She wanted to tell The Twins what had happened but she could not trust herself to wake up after a dream link.

I wonder if I could doze while riding. I could give it a try. I'll know that I've failed when I hit the ground . . . no, I must keep awake in case the tracks . . .

She pulled the arem to a halt. The road surface ahead was smooth. No tracks.

Turning in her saddle she looked back. Not far behind she could see tracks leading off the road. She turned the arem and sent it back to that point. The tracks led away toward a rock outcrop.

Searching with her mind, she sensed a vague relief. The faintness of what she could detect suggested the source was sleeping. She smiled.

Dismounting was painful. She smothered a groan and massaged her legs and rear, then stretched carefully. Pouring a little water into a bowl she wedged it between a few rocks and left it for the arem.

Stepping off the road, she walked slowly toward the rocks, trying to keep the crunch of her footsteps on the stony ground as quiet as possible. The outcrop was the size of a large house. She picked her way around into its shadow, then stopped and smiled.

Ray was lying on a blanket. His arem stood with its head hanging, its lead tied to Ray's wrist. It still carried packs and saddle.

A precaution, she thought. *In case he has to leave in a hurry. Poor thing. All that treasure must be heavy.*

She drew magic, created a basic protective shield and walked toward them. The arem took a few steps away, its lead jerking Ray's wrist. Emerahl smiled as Ray grimaced and sat up, rubbing his eyes. Being woken was not pleasant when one was that tired.

'Greetings, Raynora,' she said, stopping a few steps away.

He blinked at her, then crossed his legs and sighed. His dismay was palpable. She sensed frustration too. He knew she was a sorceress, and that he could do nothing to stop her.

'Emmea. I should have guessed. Barmonia was so eager to get rid of you. Are you here to kill me or drag me back?'

'Neither. Bar didn't send me,' she told him. 'He ordered me to stay put then sent Mikmer and Kereon after you. They fell for your trick, of course. Hurried after your decoy arem.'

His smile was strained. 'But you didn't.'

'Of course not.' She shrugged. 'I know where you're heading and I know why. I've known about your mission all along.'

'How? I didn't know I'd accept it until last night.'

She just smiled.

He frowned. 'Why didn't you tell the others?'

'Do you think they would have believed me?'

Ray shook his head. 'No. If you knew my mission, why didn't you stop me destroying the Scroll?' His eyes widened. 'You wanted it destroyed, just like the Servants did!'

She chuckled. 'No. I didn't care about the Scroll itself. Ugly thing, really. Not worth the gold it's made of. I would never have got it out of the country. No, I wanted what it led to.' She nodded to the pack.

He followed her gaze, then a smile spread across his face. 'Ah.'

'Yes. Exotic. Old. Relatively pretty.' She walked over to the arem and stroked its nose. 'And now I don't have to share any of it.'

'But—'

'But what? You have a reward to claim?' She moved to the packs and opened the bulky, heavy-looking one. Gold, silver and gemstones formed a tangle of chains and trinkets inside. Reaching in, she raked through, half-heartedly looking for something extraordinary, but unsure what it might be. Something containing a—

Diamond! The gem was impressively large and held in an odd silver setting. Plucking it out, she examined it closely. There were glyphs all over the setting. Looking at the gem itself, she felt her heart skip a beat as she saw tiny markings inside it.

This is it! she thought. *I know it!*

Pulling the chain free, she looped it over her neck. Ray was sitting with his head in his hands. As she went to close the pack she caught a glint of green: an enormous emerald on a thick gold chain. She freed it. Closing the pack, she lifted it from the arem and slung it over her shoulder.

'Ray.'

He looked up at her.

'Catch.'

She tossed the emerald to him. It landed neatly in his palm. 'What's this for?' he asked.

'Something to remember me by.'

He sighed. Weariness and resignation dulled his anger. Once he'd had a good night's sleep and time to think, that anger might put ideas of following her into his head, she realised. Unless she gave him reason not to. She walked away toward the road, then turned as if something had just occurred to her.

'Did the Pentadrians ask you to destroy the Scroll or the secrets contained in it?'

He shrugged.

'Oh, Ray,' she said, smiling. 'You were the only one who was nice to me. I really wish it wasn't you . . . I'd hate for you to not get your reward after all this. Did you know Barmonia sent a copy of the Scroll back to Hannaya?'

His eyes widened and she sensed a sudden anxiety from him.

'Good luck,' she said. Turning away, she shifted the heavy pack onto her other shoulder and headed back to her arem.

I had better be right about this diamond, she thought. *But I'd wager I'm right about the Scroll. Barmonia's no fool. He probably did send a copy to the city. More than one copy, most likely.*

She hoped so, since it was possible that the Scroll contained more important clues. The Twins would be furious if Ray did succeed in destroying all copies of it and Emerahl's hunch about the diamond was wrong.

CHAPTER 35

As she and Nekaun left the balcony Auraya sought the Siyee priest's mind. It took some time to find him, and when she did she realised why. Teel was barely conscious and in terrible pain.

Though Nekaun set a rapid pace, she wished he would walk faster. Run, even. Yet at the same time she could not help remembering that Teel was the only Siyee she had ever felt a dislike for. His self-righteous pride and fanaticism, encouraged by Huan, had grated on her nerves during the journey here. But she would never wish this pain and suffering on the young man.

They reached the old part of the Sanctuary and hurried into the corridor that led to the hall. The two Servants that guarded the gate opened it as she and Nekaun appeared. Two more Servants waited inside – a man and a woman. They hovered around a Siyee lying beside the huge throne. From their thoughts she read puzzlement and concern. They did not know what ailed him. As they saw her and Nekaun they stepped back. She drew magic in preparation, set a barrier about herself and dropped into a crouch beside the Siyee.

'What is wrong?' Nekaun asked.

The two Servants spoke at once, then the woman lapsed into silence. Auraya placed a hand on the Siyee's chest.

431

'He looked well enough this morning,' the male Servant confessed. 'It's strange. There is a—'

Nekaun raised a hand to silence the man. 'Auraya will want to make her own assessment,' he said. Looking at her, he nodded. 'Go on.'

She closed her eyes and quietened her mind as Mirar had taught her. It was not easy, but the distress of the body beneath her palm drew her in. She gasped at what she saw.

'He's dying,' she said.

'Can you do anything?' Nekaun asked.

She began to influence the body's processes, giving his heart strength, encouraging his lungs to work harder. Wherever she looked, organs were failing. Then she saw the cause. Something coursed through his veins. The source was his stomach.

Teel had been poisoned.

She reached for more magic . . . and was surprised and horrified when her efforts to heal the Siyee floundered. She reached out, trying to draw power to herself, but nothing came. In a rush, her awareness left the priest and flew outwards. She recognised the lack around her.

A void. I'm in a void. A big one, too. I should have detected it before but I was only concerned about Teel. He'll have to be moved. I wonder if Nekaun knows . . .

A chill ran through her body. Of course Nekaun knew about the void. How could he not? It was within the Sanctuary, the home of the Voices.

A trap. I fell right into it.

She was suddenly aware of him leaning over her. Moving away, she stood up and turned to face him.

'He has been poisoned,' she said.

Nekaun smiled. It was not the charming smile she had grown used to, but a smirk of satisfaction and menace. Her heart began to race.

He took a step toward her. 'Then I don't think we will be able to release your Siyee friend tomorrow.'

She backed away. *Maybe he doesn't know about the void. Maybe I'm misinterpreting his smile . . .*

'Did you order it?' she asked.

'Yes. How else was I going to get you down here?' He looked over her shoulder. Her stomach sank as she realised the two Servants were standing behind her. From their minds she read his orders.

Surround her. She cannot fight you. As you have noticed, there is no magic here.

They hadn't known of his plans, but recovered from their surprise quickly. She felt hands grasp her arms and tried to twist away, but both Servants were strong. Both were Servant-warriors, who prided themselves on their physical fitness as well as magical Skill.

'Let me go,' Auraya demanded.

They were amused by her order and had no intention of following it.

Nekaun was smiling broadly, enjoying the moment. As he stepped closer Auraya's heart lurched. *So is this how I'm going to die?* she found herself wondering. *Will Chaia take my soul?* She searched for some sign that the gods were close but found none. Nekaun looked beyond her to the Servants.

'Behind the throne you will find chains.'

Chains? Auraya felt her heart swell with desperate hope. *He doesn't mean to kill me! Unless he means to kill me slowly. What will it be? Starvation? A slow poison? Or something worse?*

Her mind shied away from that thought. She stared at Nekaun, wanting to say something to make him change his mind – a threat to frighten him, or an offer he would be tempted by. But her mind refused to think and she could not make herself speak. Her heart was pounding and she reflexively strained against the hands holding her, all the while uselessly reaching for magic. A Servant brought out the chains, which were firmly bolted to gaps in the arms of the chair.

'Put her back to the throne,' Nekaun instructed. 'Lock her wrists in the shackles.'

The Servant woman held Auraya's left arm outstretched, then her right, as the male Servant snapped the manacles around Auraya's wrists. When they were done Nekaun waved them away. He reached out and grasped Auraya's hand. She bit back a protest as he pulled off her priest ring.

But it doesn't work in voids, anyway, she remembered.

He stepped back to regard her.

'That was much too easy,' he said, shaking his head. 'Who would have thought a White – a former White – would be so easy to catch?'

She clenched her teeth. Did he want her to beg and plead? Make a bargain in exchange for her freedom?

So much for peace and alliances. So much for vows of safety.

'You swore by your gods that I would not be harmed while I stayed here,' she said in his language, so the Servants would understand. 'How can you, their First Voice, break a vow in their names?'

His smile vanished, but his eyes still gleamed.

'I can,' he told her, his voice hard and serious. 'But only at the orders of my gods. They told me to do this. Just as they told me to see if you could be persuaded to join us. Just as they told me your Siyee were coming to attack us.' He shrugged. 'Just as I will kill you if they ask me to. You had best hope they do not.' Then his smile returned. 'At last I can get back to some *interesting* work.'

Turning on his heel, he strode out of the hall, Turaan and the pair of Servants following.

*   *   *

It was a sad procession that made its way along the road to Chon. At the front the Pentadrians walked, flanked by warriors. Ella, Danjin, Yem, Gillen and Gret came next, riding in the covered platten. The villagers followed at the rear, surrounded by more warriors. A cart and arem had been found on one of the farms for small children, the old and the sick to ride on.

Those in the covered platten had talked little. Gillen had tried to strike up a conversation mere hours after the journey had begun, but the others had all but ignored him. Hurt, he had lapsed into a sullen, resigned silence.

Danjin looked at Yem. The young warrior was all quiet dignity now he was in the company of a clan leader. Gret seemed determined to sulk over the shame that one of his villages had welcomed Pentadrians, and the evidence was now being paraded through Dunway. Ella was as distant as she had been on the way to the village. Her attention was elsewhere. From time to time her expression changed subtly. She would frown, sigh or smile without obvious reason. He knew she was keeping an eye on the Pentadrians in case they tried to flee or attack the warriors. While the warriors were not lacking in Gifts, none were powerful sorcerers and would need assistance if their prisoners rebelled.

The door covers of the platten had been pinned back. Danjin would have appreciated the view if it wasn't spoiled by glimpses of the villagers following them, pricking his conscience. Now, to make things worse, he heard a faint patter and realised it was raining. How long would it be before the rain-soaked villagers became sick?

'The Scalar warriors have reached the village ahead of us,' Ella said suddenly. 'We will meet them there and stop to rest and gather food.'

All looked at her and nodded. Gret's brows managed to knit even closer together. He turned away and glowered at the rain outside.

They passed a house, then another several minutes later. The platten slowly descended into a valley, following a road that ran beside a swift-flowing river. Then suddenly they were in the midst of houses, all huddled in a bend in the river. Locals stood on the road or in doorways, watching.

Ella looked at Gret. 'Would you greet the Scalar for us?'

Gret's scowl eased at that. She was giving him the opportunity to appear in control of the group. He nodded once, then climbed out of the platten, jumping to the ground while it was still moving. Danjin heard orders being barked.

The platten rolled to a halt à short while later. Ella climbed out. Following her, Danjin examined his surroundings. The Pentadrians had been herded into what looked like a stock sorting yard. Gret and several Dunwayan sorcerers were standing nearby. The arrested villagers were huddled under the broad veranda of a storage house. A subordinate of Gret's hurried over to Ella, in the company of a broad-shouldered man with tufts of grey in his hair.

'This is the village leader, Wim,' the warrior said. 'He says he has plenty of food and suggested we take some for the journey.'

The man made the sign of the circle. Ella nodded in reply. 'We shall do so. Thank you.'

As the pair moved away, Ella walked over to greet the Scalar. The sorcerer warriors looked formidable in their blue clothes and radiating face tattoos. Gret introduced them to the leader, Wek.

After greetings had been exchanged, Ella turned to nod at the Pentadrian group.

'There are a few strongly Gifted ones,' she warned. 'So far they have been little trouble.'

Wek nodded. 'We have orders to execute them immediately.' He looked at her. 'Can you confirm that every man and woman in that group is a Pentadrian?'

'They are,' she said, nodding once. 'All but three of the

women and one of the men are from Southern Ithania. The four Dunwayans consider themselves fully converted Pentadrians.'

Wek's nose wrinkled in disgust. 'And the villagers?'

'Some are guilty of helping the Pentadrians, some only of neglecting to report their presence. Some may be excused, as they were too young or addled by age to act for themselves.'

Wek nodded. When he did not ask any further questions, Danjin felt his stomach sink. He looked at Ella intently, but she did not meet his gaze. Instead, she turned to Gret. 'I must talk to you privately.'

As she moved away, she paused and looked back at Danjin. 'You too, Danjin.' She almost seemed to smile, then her expression grew serious again as they drew out of the hearing of others. 'I am to go to Chon as quickly as possible,' she told Gret. 'Danjin, you are to go with me, but not the others. I must travel light for the sake of speed.' She paused. 'I am to give you both the bad news that we are going to war. The gods called the White to the Altar a short while ago. They have decided we must do what we should have done all along – rid the world of these Pentadrian sorcerers.'

So that's what she was doing while we were in the platten, Danjin found himself thinking. *Linked to Juran or one of the other White, she was actually talking to the gods!*

Gret's eyebrows rose in surprise, and an eager light came into his eyes. Danjin could see how this turn of events worked in the man's favour. He might have harboured Pentadrians unknowingly, but now he had the chance to redress the stain on his honour. And he wouldn't have to endure the shame of accompanying the villagers to Chon.

'I will come with you, Ellareen of the White,' he said. 'When will we leave?'

She smiled grimly. 'As soon as we can find a platten and fresh horses.'

'Then allow me to hunt you down a set.'

He walked away, his back straight and his steps jaunty. Danjin shook his head.

'Warriors,' he muttered.

Ella chuckled. 'Yes, they love a chance to show off their skills.'

He looked at her sideways. 'A war, then? And this time we are the invaders.'

She nodded. 'The gods' patience at these attempts to subvert Circlians has been stretched too far this time. We have found Pentadrian Servants in all lands except Si. In Somrey they have been appallingly successful at attracting converts. In Toren we've discovered a secret group recruiting the poor and the homeless in exchange for teaching them to use magic to rob the rich. In Genria they pose as healers who specialise in fertility. And in Sennon . . . well, they've always been in Sennon, along with every other madman who follows dead gods or invents new ones.' She grimaced in disgust. 'There's a new cult there that worships the Maker, who apparently created the gods themselves. Strange how the gods aren't aware of this.'

Danjin smiled. 'Strange indeed.'

She sighed. 'But they aren't concerned about this Wise Man and his ideas. It is the Pentadrians we must worry about. We cannot kill their gods, but if we kill the Voices we may weaken them enough that they do not threaten us for a time.'

He nodded, but could not help thinking how closely matched the previous battle had been. Until Auraya had killed the enemy leader, the Circlians had been losing.

Ella smiled. 'Yes, we have considered that, Danjin. But this time we have an advantage.'

'Auraya?'

She frowned. 'No. We can't rely upon her help, but the gods have assured us she will not hinder us. No, our advantage is not one individual but a nation: this time we have Sennon on our side.'

'So long as the emperor doesn't change his mind at the last moment.'

'He won't,' she assured him. 'Not this time. We are going to take this battle to the Pentadrians, and he knows that means it will be fought on his land, at the Isthmus.'

Danjin looked at the arrested villagers. 'What of these people? How will I-Portak know who is innocent if you are not there to read their minds?'

Ella shrugged. 'Their system of justice has operated well enough without my assistance in the past, as I'm sure it will now.'

'Do you really believe that?' he asked.

She looked at him, then sighed. 'I have to. What else can I do?'

'Write a list,' he suggested. 'Noting which villagers are guilty of which crimes.'

She considered him, then nodded. 'I can do that.'

'I don't suppose I can persuade you to excuse the children and the sick from this march at the same time?'

Ella shook her head. 'Who would look after them?'

'Surely someone would.'

'Even if someone did, would you like to be the one to take a child from their parent?'

He could not answer that. *I'd want to spend as much time with my child as possible if I thought I did not have much time left*, he found himself thinking.

She sighed and suddenly looked tired. 'I must admit, it's a relief to leave at last.'

Danjin felt a pang of sympathy. 'Watching other lands deal out such harsh punishment is never an easy task.'

She gave him an odd look. 'I meant to go to war. The gods

kept changing their minds. They had us prepare for war, then stand down our armies, then rouse them again. I think it was because of Auraya. When she decided to stay in Glymma it spoiled the gods' plans. Now perhaps she has left, and we are free to make our move.'

Danjin nodded. 'So will she be joining us soon?'

'I don't know.' Ella shrugged and turned to meet Gret, who was driving a platten pulled by two fresh arem.

CHAPTER 36

Footsteps were like hammers in Teel's head. He opened his eyes. Black-robed men were approaching. They crowded around. He felt hands under him, around him, gripping hard. Pain ripped through him. It crushed his thoughts.

Something cool touched his lips. Rousing again, he swallowed as water was poured down his throat. It tasted sour. He remembered a voice from earlier. A familiar voice.

'He has been poisoned.'

He spat out the water, but the hands and black robes crowded him. Cruel fingers pressed into his jaw. The foul water came again and he surrendered to it. The sooner he died, the sooner the pain would end. He would go to Huan. He was her favourite. She would take him in.

For a time he wallowed in blackness. The pain eased. He had no strength and he was very cold, but he felt better. Opening his eyes, he looked up at the high ceiling of the hall, and remembered his fellow Siyee flying carefully in the close quarters.

All gone, he thought. *I'm alone here.*

:No, Teel, you are not.

The voice in his mind startled him. It was not Huan. It had a maleness about it.

:I am Chaia.

Chaia!

:Yes. Look to your right, Teel.

He obeyed. The oversized throne loomed above him. He could remember being dragged there after the illness – poison – took hold. He also remembered being lifted and carried back.

A movement attracted his gaze and for a moment he couldn't believe what he was seeing. A woman stood before the throne. Chained.

Auraya!

:Yes. She has been betrayed.

Teel groaned.

:I'm never going to get out of here, am I?

:It is unlikely. I cannot free you. There is nobody here who will obey my orders.

Why doesn't Auraya use magic to break the chains?

:She is in a place of no magic.

Auraya's gaze was focused on some distant place. She looked dazed. Teel felt an unexpected sympathy for her. She was so used to being powerful and invulnerable. This must be hard to accept. And humiliating.

:I cannot reach her, Chaia repeated. *So you must. Will you speak to her for me?*

:Of course.

:Tell her this . . .

Teel listened carefully, then drew a breath and called out to her. It came out weaker than he'd intended, but her gaze sharpened and her eyes snapped to his.

'Teel!' She frowned in concern. 'How are you feeling? The Servants gave you something. I hoped it was an antidote to the poison.'

Suddenly he knew who he had heard speak of poison.

'Oh. I thought they were . . .' he paused, suddenly breathless

'. . . giving me more poison.' Talking was hard. It seemed to drain more energy from him.

She smiled faintly. 'No, but it was a logical conclusion to make. I would have.'

He would have shrugged if he could bother moving. 'Doesn't matter. Chaia . . . gave me . . . a message for you.'

'Chaia?' Her eyes widened and he saw hope in them.

'Yes. He said . . . he will try to keep . . . talking to you . . . through me.' It was *such* an effort to talk. 'If the enemy . . . takes me away . . . he'll find . . . someone else. You'll know . . . him from . . . a word . . . "shadow".'

He stopped, his head spinning. Closing his eyes, he felt himself drifting away.

'Teel!'

Dragging his eyes open, he smiled at her.

'Stay awake, Teel,' she said. 'Talk to me.'

He opened his mouth to speak, but it was too much effort. There was a rushing sound in his ears. The room brightened and grew hazy at the same time. It was a cold light. He could not feel his hands. Or his feet. Breathing was such an effort.

Too much. He gave it up and the light rushed in to burn his thoughts away.

Reivan sighed as she climbed into bed. The summer heat was relentless. She found it hard to remember what the other seasons were like, but easy to imagine this one had no end.

It had been more than a month since Nekaun had visited her. Lately she had begun telling herself that he wouldn't again. He'd seen all he'd wanted to see of her. His curiosity had been satisfied. He had moved on to more interesting challenges.

Like Auraya.

But Nekaun was no longer trying to charm Auraya. Imenja

had told Reivan, with obvious satisfaction, that Nekaun had imprisoned Auraya.

How that was possible was still not clear to Reivan. Or why Nekaun hadn't killed Auraya. When she had asked, Imenja had simply talked about something else.

The news had brought smiles to many Servants' faces, and the relief of all was heard in the voices of those gossiping in the Baths and corridors. Reivan had been surprised at her own pleasure at the news. *I should be worried about the advantage we are losing by not gaining Auraya's alliance, but all I can think of is that Nekaun won't be spending all his time with her now!*

A knock at the door interrupted her thoughts. She sighed. The news must have spread beyond the Sanctuary by now. Many of the people she dealt with on Imenja's behalf would want confirmation.

Reaching the door, she opened it and froze in disbelief.

'Good evening, Reivan.'

I'm dreaming, she thought. *I probably dreamed I got out of bed and in a moment I'll wake up.*

But she didn't. Nekaun really was standing there. She didn't know what to do. Or say.

Nekaun smiled. 'Aren't you going to let me in?'

Speechless, she stepped back. As he walked past her she caught his scent and felt a deep longing. Nekaun turned to regard her. 'It is too long since we talked, Reivan.'

She nodded and closed the door. Moving to the table she poured water into two glasses and handed one to him.

Just as she used to.

He drank, set aside the empty glass, then moved closer and took hers from her hand.

Just as he used to.

'You've heard the news?' he asked. 'Auraya is trapped, help-less, beneath the Sanctuary.'

Auraya. She frowned as the word woke her from her daze. 'Yes.'

He sighed. 'I don't know why the gods put me through all that. Were they testing me or her? I don't know. Right now I don't care.'

'So you weren't enjoying her company, then?' she found herself asking.

He grimaced. 'Tedious beyond description.' His eyes narrowed. 'Were you jealous of her?'

She looked away, knowing it was pointless denying it.

He laughed softly and drew her into his arms. 'Oh, Reivan. How silly of you. Who could be attracted to such a sour, suspicious woman? I'd rather woo an arem.'

His smell, his warmth, overwhelmed her. *He's back!* she thought.

How long for? a dark voice asked.

Be quiet, she told it.

'I've missed you,' he said.

Her heart flipped over. 'I've missed you, too.'

He drew closer. She knew what came next and felt her heart racing as he leaned down to kiss her.

Then he froze, his eyes widening in surprise. A fierce, intense look came into his eyes. Reivan pulled out of his rigid arms, a little frightened by his expression. His eyebrows lowered into a scowl, then he let out a sharp breath and his eyes met hers. They blazed with anger.

'I'm sorry, Reivan. I will not be able to stay.' His jaw clenched. 'The gods have just ordered me to ready our army. The Circlians are planning to invade us.'

She stared at him, shock almost overcoming her disappointment as he touched her gently on the cheek, then marched from the room.

*   *   *

Second Voice Imenja had kept Mirar occupied all day, taking him to see artisans on the outskirts of the city. They had eaten fish caught fresh from the river and talked about healing and magic. All day he had been aware that only one more Siyee remained to be freed. He expected Imenja to offer up Auraya's death at any moment, but she had said nothing.

Returning late to the Sanctuary, he had sensed a buzz of excitement and satisfaction in the air. As soon as he had reached his rooms he lay down and entered a dream trance, intending to skim the minds around him and find out what had stirred the Servants up. But before he could send his mind out, another called to him.

:*Mirar!*

:*Surim? Tamun?*

:*Yes*, Surim said. *I have news. Bad news.*

:*Oh?*

:*The Voices have imprisoned Auraya under the Sanctuary*, Tamun said.

Mirar jolted awake. He stared at the ceiling, then closed his eyes and forced his heartbeat and breathing to slow. It took a maddeningly long time to settle into a dream trance again.

:*Surim?*

:*Mirar. You woke up?*

:*Yes.*

:*Sorry. I should have broken the news more gently*, Tamun said.

:*Don't apologise. Just tell me how and why.*

:*It appears there is a void under the Sanctuary. It must have been a secret, known only to the Voices.*

:*A void. She will be completely vulnerable.*

:*As vulnerable as any mortal.*

:*Why didn't she sense it? Surely she wouldn't have entered it if she had.*

:*I don't know. A distraction, probably.*

:Why did they imprison her? Why not kill her? Mirar paused. *They haven't realised that she and I were once lovers, have they?*

:Not as far as any mortals there know, Surim assured him.

:You will know if they try to use her against you, Tamun pointed out.

:More likely they'll take you down there and offer to let you kill her in exchange for something, Surim warned.

:And what will they do when I refuse?

:I wouldn't, if I were you. I'd pretend to think about it.

:You can't be sure you are the only reason they've done this, too, Tamun said. *The Circlians have summoned their armies. They're coming to invade Southern Ithania. Keeping Auraya out of the way is a wise decision.*

:Wiser to kill her, Mirar disagreed grimly. *If the Pentadrians know war is coming, they'll try to recruit me and my Dreamweavers again.*

:What will you do?

Mirar did not answer. Would the Pentadrians make him choose between breaking the laws of his people and sacrificing Auraya?

They'll try, he thought.

:I'll rescue Auraya, he told The Twins.

:That would be extremely, foolish, Tamun said. *You would earn the enmity of the Pentadrians. All Dreamweavers will suffer.*

:Only if they know I did it.

Pulling out of the dream link, Mirar stared at the ceiling. Then he sent his mind out to skim those around him.

Sure enough, the news of Auraya's imprisonment had spread through the Sanctuary. He searched and found the minds of two Servant-warriors guarding an underground hall. Through their eyes he saw a lonely figure, arms chained to an oversized chair. His heart shrank, as if as appalled by the scene as his mind was.

447

In a void she had no access to magic. She was more vulnerable than the least Gifted beggar woman. Worse, even, for she wasn't used to physical hardship or humiliation.

He drew back, sank into the dream trance and sought her mind.

:Auraya?

She didn't reply. After several attempts he returned to the minds of the guards. The chained figure moved and he realised she was awake.

I couldn't sleep if I were in her position, he thought. Frustrated, all he could do was watch her through another's eyes. *I will free her*, he told himself. *I will find a way. And when I do, the Voices won't even know I had anything to do with it.*

Clever plans were easier hatched with two minds than one. Drawing away from the sight of Auraya and into the dream trance again, he sought the mind of an old friend.

PART THREE

CHAPTER 37

Despite a week spent resting at the edge of the Si forest with plenty of food and water provided by the local tribe, Tyziss still had to fight a deep, unshakable weariness in order to fly. He craved rest, but his longing to reach the Open and his family was more powerful. Though news that he had escaped the Pentadrians must have reached them, he knew they would not stop worrying about him until he was home.

Sreil flew a short distance ahead. Their leader hadn't rested more than one night in one place since being freed from the Sanctuary. He had refused to rest any longer, determined that he wouldn't be the one to delay the return of the warriors to the Open.

He must be exhausted, Tyziss thought. Only half of the freed Siyee had made it back to the Si border. The water and food the Pentadrians had provided them with had not been enough for the journey, but then the Siyee couldn't have carried more anyway.

Tyziss had decided to return home by a different route, following the coast of Sennon. He dropped into villages to ask for water and food, figuring that there was no longer any reason to fear that Sennonion Pentadrians would report the presence of Siyee in their land.

Only the warriors who had come to the same conclusion had survived the journey. It was a longer route, however. It had taken Tyziss four weeks to reach Si. Sreil had arrived a week later.

When the first Siyee made it to the edge of Si the local tribe had flown out into the desert with water for following escapees, but most of the Siyee who had died had probably perished of thirst within a few days of reaching Sennon. Some would have fainted and fallen from the sky, others were perhaps too weak to become airborne again after landing for the night, or might have lost their sense of direction. A few days before Tyziss had reached Si he had followed a trail of faint footprints in the desperate hope they'd been made by a landwalker who might help him. Instead he'd found a Siyee lying in the sand. He'd landed only to find the man was dead. It had taken so much energy to run himself into the air again he had nearly blacked out. Only a short distance later he'd seen a well in the distance.

Poor Tilyl. He didn't know how close he was.

He pushed that thought aside and tried to think of home, but his mind moved to darker places. Thirst had not been the only killer of Siyee. When Sreil had ordered them to leave for the Open the day after he arrived, someone had asked about the priest.

'Teel is dead, and Auraya has been imprisoned,' Sreil told them heavily. 'She spoke to me in a dream and told me of it.'

At least she managed to free all but one of us, Tyziss told himself. He could not imagine how the Pentadrians could keep her constrained. She was a powerful sorceress. But so were the Pentadrian leaders. And there were *five* of them.

The Siyee crested a ridge and a great scar of stone on a mountain slope appeared ahead. The Open. Tyziss felt a rush of emotion so powerful it left him weak and dizzy. His arm muscles began to tremble. Taking a deep breath, he forced himself to remain rigid and in control.

I'm not going to fail now, so close to home.

It seemed to take forever for them to reach that distant stretch of exposed rock. Siyee flew up to meet them, whistling greetings. Tyziss started to shake again as he saw his wife. He saw tears in her eyes. His own were quickly dried by the wind.

At last they were circling down to land. When Tyziss's feet met the ground he sighed with relief. Yissi embraced him tightly. He was home at last.

'The girls?' he asked.

Yissi smiled. 'Well enough. I've left them with my sister.' A crease appeared between her brows. 'Oh, Ty. Will you be leaving straightaway? You're so thin. You look worn out.'

'Leaving?' he asked.

He heard Sreil's voice growing louder.

'When did they go?' the young man demanded.

'At the last black moon,' an old man, who Tyziss recognised as Speaker Ryliss, replied.

Sreil glanced at the returned Siyee. 'We must join them.'

'No,' Ryliss said firmly. 'You and your warriors are exhausted. You haven't the strength to catch up with them.'

'A night's rest will do,' Sreil replied.

'No, Sreil. I forbid it. Too many have gone, leaving us vulnerable. We need some fighters to remain in case we are attacked.' The Speaker glanced at them and shook his head sadly. 'Though we were hoping more of you would return than this.'

'There are too few of us to turn back an invading army,' Sreil said. 'But we can help the Circlians fight the Pentadrians. There is no point in us staying—'

'Are you so keen to drag these men across the desert again?' the old man asked.

Sreil stared at him, then shook his head.

'They aren't fighting in green Hania, Sreil,' Ryliss explained. 'They are taking this battle to the Pentadrians. Crossing Sennon to the southern continent. You would not reach them in time. More likely you would never reach them at all. Stay here, where you are needed.'

Sreil's shoulders dropped. He nodded and the Siyee around him sighed in relief. Tyziss turned to Yissi.

'The Circlians are invading Southern Ithania?'

She nodded.

He straightened and shook his head. 'Another war so soon after the last?' He frowned as a suspicion dawned on him. 'Where are my parents?'

'Gone,' she said, sighing. 'They weren't the only ones too old or too young to be going to war, and yet our army was half the size of the last.' Her hand slipped around his waist. 'If I hadn't been so sure you were coming back I would have joined them myself.'

He looked at her closely and felt a pang of affection at her serious expression.

'You? A warrior?' he asked in mock disbelief.

She poked him in the ribs. 'A fine husband you are. I tell you I never lost hope and would have sought revenge for your death, and all you can do is laugh at me?'

He nodded. 'Yes. Let me laugh. I haven't had much reason to lately. Now, where are those girls of ours?'

She smiled and led him away.

The light of Emerahl's magic-fed spark revealed an empty room. She ducked through the small doorway and moved inside, relieved to see that nothing had been disturbed. Her accommodation was a dome made of woven reeds secured to the sandy riverbank. Everything here by the river was made of reeds, from boats to furniture to houses, including these little domes for hire.

The walls gave an illusion of privacy, but there were plenty of gaps in the weave through which someone could look. So far she hadn't caught anyone spying on her. The locals considered such an act a crime, but that would be no deterrent if anyone suspected she carried a fortune in treasure.

She opened the reed basket that held the freshly steamed fish and reed shoots she had bought. As she ate she eyed the patch of matting under which she had buried the bag of treasure.

It was proving to be more of a nuisance than a benefit. In the last two weeks she hadn't encountered a town large or wealthy enough to sell any of it in. Even the smallest piece was obviously worth a lot. Anyone she tried to sell it to would assume she had stolen it. Even if they didn't care about that, they might guess she had more and try to rob her. While she was confident she could stop them, she did not want to draw attention to herself.

According to The Twins, Raynora had been caught sneaking into Barmonia's tent a few days after Emerahl relieved him of the treasure. He had convinced Barmonia that Emerahl had tricked and robbed him. Barmonia had sent out a warning to Thinkers in Glymma, telling them to look out for a woman of Emerahl's description, who carried stolen artefacts.

That made selling the jewellery dangerous in Glymma. The Twins were searching for someone she might be able to sell it to in the city. She could take some of the uglier pieces of jewellery apart and sell gems and chains of gold separately, but she didn't like the idea of pawning any of it to some lowlife who didn't know its true value. They were more than just pieces of gold and gems; they were from another age, when there had been more gods than countries in Ithania.

It would be safer to sell the treasure in the northern continent, but that meant lugging the heavy bag around with her. She was tempted to hide it somewhere, but hadn't yet found a place she considered secure enough. In the meantime, she was running out of money. There was little profit to be gained as a healer here. Dreamweavers were as common as blacksmiths and cloth merchants. Days before, she had been forced to sell her arem. The money she'd received in exchange should last her until she reached Glymma.

If she could sell some of the gems, she would buy passage to Karienne on a ship. If not, she would have to walk across the Isthmus or see if she could work in exchange for passage on one of the small boats sailing across to Diamyane, the town at the Sennon end of the Isthmus. Either way, she would go up to the Red Caves and The Twins.

The Twins. She smiled. They had been alarmed when they heard of the chance she had taken, leaving the Thinkers on the hunch that the secrets of the gods were among the treasure Ray had stolen. Now they were anxious to see the diamond themselves. Perhaps they would have more success with it than Emerahl had.

She decided she would get no more flesh from the bones of the fish and wiped her hands. Drawing the chain out from beneath her clothes she examined the pendant hanging from it closely. The diamond was held within two intersecting bands of silver. On each band were glyphs. The first or second of each set were upside down:

One light / death
Two lights / one key
Three lights / two truths
Four lights / three secrets

456

She looked at the diamond closely. The bands framed the four largest facets. When she held it up to her spark the light cast shapes against the walls. If these were part of a language, it was either so old or obscure she had never encountered it before. The trouble was, neither had The Twins.

As the pendant revolved at the end of the chain, the glyph shadows moved, some to the left, some to the right. The ones turning to the right were blurred and she recognised reversed versions of the shapes turning left. A dark line of shadow crossed the wall as a silver band passed. Lines and glyphs followed.

Then she suddenly recognised a glyph. A full Sorli glyph representing 'light'. She turned to stare at the diamond. The facet facing her light was the one contained between the bands marked *one light / qıvəp* and *two lights/ʎɔʎ ɔuo*.

She turned the diamond between her fingers, keeping that facet facing toward her. If she read only those glyphs that were the right way up when positioned above the diamond the words were:

> *One light / one key*

Emerahl smiled. Using the same rule, the rest read:

> *Two lights / two truths*
> *Three lights / three secrets*
> *Four lights / death*

Taking hold of the chain, she let the pendant hang again. She moved her spark closer and watched as the lines and shapes on the wall grew larger. Finding the 'light' glyph, she felt a thrill as she realised that what she had assumed were more of the unfamiliar symbols were the simple glyphs for numbers.

But the thrill quickly faded. She still couldn't make sense of it. The unfamiliar glyphs on the reverse side overlapped and obscured the familiar ones. Moving her spark closer only made the effect worse.

If I could just get rid of these symbols from the reverse side . . . She blinked, then smiled. *Of course, I can. I just have to get the light past them.*

But that meant moving her light into the diamond. She wasn't sure if she could do that without damaging it.

Dropping the pendant into her lap, she considered the risk. Maybe she should wait until she reached The Twins. Or at least ask them if it was possible to move a light into a diamond without damaging it. Perhaps they had tried it before.

She looked at the matting where the treasure was buried.

Perhaps I can try it on another gem first.

First she checked for minds close by. None were closer than the next reed dome, several paces away. She uncovered the treasure quickly and carefully, making sure none of the moist soil spilled onto the matting to hint that something might be buried here. Searching through the jewellery and trinkets, she was pleased to find a diamond set in a thick gold ring tangled among the chains near the top.

Freeing it, she sat back and considered the stone. There were no markings in it. In the past several weeks she had carefully checked all of the treasure and found nothing marked with glyphs or with other significant features.

Bringing her light close, she made it as small and cold as she could. Slowly, she moved it to the surface of the diamond. There was no resistance as, with a push of her will, she shifted it inside.

The effect in the room was quite pretty. The facets of the

stone made patterns on the walls. They shifted, the slight movement of her hands magnified so that no matter how hard she tried to keep her hand steady the room looked like it was trembling.

Moving the light out of the gem, she put the ring down and picked up the pendant. Taking a deep breath, she held it as steady as she could and moved her light inside it.

The walls swirled with glyphs and lines, then steadied. She looked around and felt her stomach sink with disappointment. The glyphs still overlapped each other, forming a muddle of unrecognisable symbols. But as she turned to look behind her she felt a small thrill of relief and triumph. One section was clear. Lines and numbers surrounded the glyph she had recognised.

But now it was the curved dark weave of the dome wall that made it difficult for her to understand what she was seeing. She needed a flat wall. Or some other flat surface.

Looking around, she saw that the shawl she had draped over her pack hung relatively flat in places. Removing the light from the diamond, she put the pendant down and picked up her blanket. She hung the blanket from the roof using fishing hooks and twine.

She picked up the diamond and carefully introduced the spark again. Turning the pendant so the *one light / one key* side faced the blanket, she stared at the shape that appeared.

An octagon, marked with unbroken lines. At the centre of this was the glyph for light. Lines of dots crossed the octagon, each marked by a number. The whole diagram shook from the slight tremble of her hands.

She had no idea what it meant. The word 'light' within the octagon surely represented a light within the diamond. But what did the numbers and radiating lines mean?

I've never been much good with numbers and equations. This is

one for The Twins, she decided. She stared at it until she was
sure she had memorised everything, then drew her light from
the diamond. Hanging the chain around her neck, she replaced
the ring and buried the treasure again. Then, making sure the
dome was well protected by a barrier of magic, she lay down
to sleep.

*:At first I thought it was unlikely this Elai child they rescued was
a princess*, Mirar told Auraya. *Surely a princess would be too well-
guarded to fall into the hands of raiders. But everyone I've skimmed
believes it is true.*

:So does everyone I've encountered.

*:Then yesterday Nekaun told me of the treaty with the Elai. He
sounded quite proud of the fact, even though he had nothing to do
with it. It was all the doing of Second Voice Imenja and her Companion.*

*:I can't see the Elai king making a treaty with landwalkers for
anything less than the return of his daughter. It is quite a feat.*

*:And a surprise. I can't see any great benefit to the Pentadrians
in this treaty. The Elai are hardly a powerful or numerous people.
They might eventually keep raider numbers down, but that won't be
a huge boost to trade since few Pentadrian traders bother travelling
to Toren or Genria.*

*:But if they can sink ships, they may be a valuable ally in war.
The White need to know about this.* Auraya paused. *Would you
send them a message for me?*

Mirar felt his stomach sink.

:They wouldn't believe anything I told them.

*:They don't have to know who it came from. It would have to be
an anonymous warning.*

*:I'm not sure that would be wise. What will the White do to the
Elai? If they know the sea people have joined the Pentadrians they
may attack them before the battle, in order to keep them out of it.
This may be a matter best left concealed. I doubt the Elai will make*

much difference in the war, and if the White win at least there's a chance of peace later.

:The White won't attack them, Auraya assured him. *They need to know their ships are in danger.*

Mirar was beginning to wish he hadn't raised the subject. It seemed wrong to be disagreeing with Auraya when she was trussed up in an underground prison for weeks while he was still an honoured guest. And he hadn't yet found a way to rescue her without his involvement being obvious and ruining the good will between the Dreamweavers and Pentadrians. But he couldn't let guilt and pity stir him into doing something he didn't agree with.

:Have you been able to skim minds as far away as the Circlian army? he asked, changing the subject. *Have you overheard any of their plans?*

:Not yet. I expect I'll encounter the same problem I have with spying on Pentadrian war councils. Some of the gods will be there, and I'll have to stay away in case they detect me.

Mirar felt a twinge of apprehension. He could only assume that if he couldn't sense the gods when mind-skimming, as Auraya could, then they couldn't sense him. Unfortunately, he was usually busy being shown about the Sanctuary or Glymma by Dedicated Servants whenever a war council was in progress so he never got a chance to spy on them anyway.

:You'll just have to skim the minds of the Companions after the council, to see what they remember, he told her. *And do the same for the advisers of the White.*

:Yes, she agreed. *Though Companion Reivan's mind is nearly always on Nekaun.*

:She's completely infatuated, Mirar agreed. *Yet I don't think she actually likes him. I know her mistress doesn't . . . Listen to us, gossiping like old women!*

:It might be useful gossip, if we can bend the situation to our advantage.

:That's true. Trouble is, I have no idea how.

:You'll think of something. Or I will. Not much else to do right now.

Mirar's heart twisted.

:Are you sure you're all right?

:Yes. I'm fine. I can endure a bit of physical discomfort.

He did not point out that she was suffering more than that. Though she said nothing, he knew she must be living in constant fear. At any moment Nekaun might decide it was time to kill her. Mirar was not entirely sure why the Pentadrian leader hadn't yet.

A sound caught his attention and he felt himself drawn out of the dream trance.

:I have to go, Auraya, he said. *I will link with you tonight.*

:You'd better, she said. *Or I'll . . .*

But he didn't hear the rest. The knocking at the door of his rooms was loud. Rising from the bed, he looked around and sighed.

I was worried that I wouldn't be able to forge an understanding with these Voices, that they wouldn't want me in their lands. Now that I find I'm welcome, I can't enjoy the fact. If Auraya wasn't here, I'd be delighted. But because she is their prisoner, I find myself thinking of them as our enemy.

It was a strange and complicated situation, and with the Circlians coming to wage war on the Pentadrians, it wasn't about to get any simpler.

CHAPTER 38

The squeak of the gate opening jolted Auraya's attention back to her surroundings. She felt her stomach clench as she realised someone was entering the hall, then felt it sink as she saw that the visitor was Nekaun.

As always, questions crowded her mind. Would he free her? Would he kill her? Would he interrogate her, torture her, or ask for some terrible favour in exchange for her freedom?

She took a deep breath, pushed the questions and the fear they brought to the back of her mind, and straightened.

He stopped and regarded her silently, a faint smile curling his lips.

No, it looks like he'll do the same as last time, she thought in answer to her earlier questions.

She almost longed for the solitude of her first days, when she had been left alone and unattended and the only indication that her presence was remembered were the Servants guarding the gate.

Chained as she was, she could not lie down to sleep. Instead she had to sink into a half-kneeling, half-hanging position. Feeling would slowly leave her arms, and her shoulders and knees would start aching. The cold in the hall didn't help, but it was the least of her worries.

After a day the cycles of her body had begun to present unpleasant problems. First she grew thirsty, then hunger began to nag at her. Neither were pleasant to endure, but the consequences were less humiliating than the need to relieve herself. She could not remove her clothing or move far from her position. Eventually she had stretched her body as far to one side as she could so at least she would not be standing in her own urine and excrement.

Who'd have thought ordinary physical processes that one tended to every day and barely thought about could cause such distress? She had consoled herself that if they did not bring her food or drink these problems would not bother her for long.

When Nekaun returned after three days she was too weak to stand. He had said nothing but simply looked at her and the mess beside her, his nose wrinkling in disgust. Then his expression became thoughtful and a gleam entered his eyes. He turned to the Servants and spoke.

She nearly cried out a protest at his orders. Catching her tongue between her teeth, she told herself it would be more humiliating to beg and plead than to endure what he planned. And begging probably wouldn't stop him anyway.

Domestics were brought. They cut away her clothes and threw buckets of cold water over her and the floor. They brought water for her to drink and a thin sludge she guessed was made of some kind of grain. She could not feed herself, so she had to let them tip the water and sludge into her mouth.

By then Nekaun was smiling. The gleam in his eyes intensified when she had been stripped, but disappeared as she was fed. It was clear he was enjoying her humiliation. She was tempted to spit the sludge at him, but she was too hungry to waste it.

That day she discovered she wanted to live. She wasn't sure

how badly yet, but she dreaded finding out what she might be willing to do in order to . . . and beyond that. At what point would she change her mind and long to die?

If Nekaun was curious to know the answers to the same questions, he was in no hurry to find out. All he had done so far was taunt her.

'Greetings, Auraya,' he said. 'I trust you are finding your accommodation satisfactory?'

She ignored him. He asked something similar every time. *'Are you enjoying your stay?' 'Is there anything I can get for you?'*

Seeing movement beyond him, she turned her attention to the domestics that were hurrying into the room. They scuttled past him hesitantly. The first two held buckets of water. She gritted her teeth against the cold of her daily dousing. The second bucket was thrown over the floor then a broom used to sweep faeces off the dais.

A third domestic held a bowl of water to Auraya's mouth. She drank it all, knowing no more would be brought until tomorrow. The last domestic lifted the usual bowl of grainy sludge.

'Stop,' Nekaun said.

Auraya felt her heart sink as the domestic lowered the bowl. She hoped she was managing to keep her expression bland and devoid of fear as Nekaun came closer, sure that any sign of apprehension would only encourage him to find more ways to torment her.

He took the bowl from the domestic, then lifted it to her mouth.

She paused only momentarily. If she refused to eat from his hands he would starve her until she did. Better to pretend it didn't matter.

He watched her, smiling, as she ate. She did not meet his gaze, instead concentrating on a small scar on the side of his nose. She hadn't noticed it before. She wondered what had caused it.

The bowl tipped higher, forcing her to gulp to avoid the sludge spilling over the lip and being wasted. When it was empty Nekaun stepped back. He held the bowl out to one side and the domestic hurried over to take it.

'Go,' he told the domestics. They scurried away, relieved. One of them wondered why they feared the First Voice here when they didn't elsewhere. He concluded it was because he had no idea what to expect of the man in this situation. The sorceress was an enemy. Nekaun might order that something awful be done to her, and the domestic didn't want to be the one to do it.

If Nekaun heard the domestic's thoughts he gave no sign. He stared at Auraya. She fixed her gaze at the wall past his shoulder. Though she could not sense any thoughts from him she sometimes felt she knew what he was thinking. Like now, when his attention drifted below her face. She knew he was either pretending to be interested in her nakedness in order to intimidate her or . . . or he was excited by it.

He took a step toward her, then another. She felt her heart begin to race and breathed a little slower, willing herself to remain calm. A step away he paused, his nose wrinkling.

'Really, Auraya,' he said, shaking his head. 'You should take better care of yourself. You smell terrible.'

Turning on his heel, he stalked away.

She watched him leave. The Servant guards locked the gate behind him. Footsteps faded to silence.

She sighed with relief.

Just trying to intimidate me, she told herself.

Leaning back against the base of the throne, she closed her eyes and sent her mind out into the world. This was how she spent most of her waking hours. Several times a day she checked on Mischief. One of the domestics had adopted him as her pet. He stayed because Auraya encouraged him to through dream links and he was used to being left with a carer.

During the evenings she dream linked with Mirar. The rest of the time she skimmed minds. Being chained up in a cold, empty hall wasn't exactly stimulating for the mind. At least, not in a good way. Exploring the world kept her mind busy.

It was a secret source of pride to her that she was getting better and better at sensing other minds every day. Each time she reached out she managed to read minds further from her position than she had the previous time. In this way, she heard the rumours of war the day after her imprisonment. Nekaun's breaking of his vow had made sense then. If the Circlians were invading he would not risk that his attempts to charm her had failed. He knew if he let her go she would probably return to the White to fight with them.

Would I have? she asked herself. *Perhaps. I wouldn't have liked it, but if the gods ordered me to I would have fought for them.*

What didn't make sense was that Nekaun hadn't killed her. Why imprison her? Did he plan another bargain, with her as payment? Did he think he could persuade the White to go home in exchange for her return?

She smiled wryly. *Huan would never agree to that.*

But Chaia might. She thought of his message, sent through the dying Siyee priest. None of the domestics that tended her had spoken a word to her, let alone his 'key' word. She doubted any message from Chaia would come through Nekaun. Nobody else had visited her.

Gods had, however. Saru, Yranna and Lore had hovered around her briefly. Their conversation told her that they had come to confirm that she was imprisoned here, but had revealed little else.

Did Chaia have a plan in place to free her? Or was he too preoccupied with preparations for war? There was only so much he could do here, in a land where nobody worshipped or obeyed him.

Maybe he intends for me to be freed once the Circlians are victorious. But I expect Nekaun will ensure I die if the Pentadrians lose. He'll give my guards orders to kill me.

She opened one eye and looked at the Servants standing by the gate.

Unless someone stops them.

She thought of the hint the gods had given that they could get rid of Mirar, even though he had the Voices' protection. If there was an assassin here, perhaps they could help her.

But they wouldn't unless the White ordered them to, and she hadn't been able to tell the White about her situation. Even if Nekaun hadn't taken the priest ring, she could not have used it. The void would prevent it working. So instead she had tried to contact Juran via dream links. None of her attempts had succeeded. She had tried calling to Mairae, and even Dyara, but neither had answered. This morning Mirar had given her an idea.

'You'll just have to skim the minds of the Companions . . . And do the same for the advisers of the White.'

She couldn't dream link with the White, but perhaps she could reach Danjin.

Relaxing against the throne, Auraya slowed her breathing and sought the dream trance. Once there, she called out Danjin's name.

There was no response at first, but after several attempts she heard a familiar but confused mental voice.

:Auraya?
:Yes, Danjin. It's me.
:Auraya . . . I'm dreaming.

:You are and yet you are not. This is how the Dreamweavers communicate.

:A dream link?

:Yes.

He paused and she felt both concern and guilt.

:I'm not supposed to talk to you.

A chill ran down Auraya's spine.

:Why? Do the White believe I've changed sides?

:They . . . have to consider it a possibility. They haven't heard from you in weeks.

:I can't reach them. I was tricked. Nekaun has imprisoned me inside a . . . She paused as she realised Danjin didn't know what a void was. Did the White know what voids were? She hadn't until she'd met Jade.

:Auraya? Danjin asked, his tone full of concern.

:Nekaun took away my priest ring. I've tried to dream link with Juran and the others but it doesn't work. Maybe because they're never asleep when I try; maybe because they can't . . . or I'm being prevented. I need you to tell Juran I'm a prisoner.

Danjin didn't reply.

:Danjin?

:Yes. I'm . . . not near Juran. I'll tell Ella and she'll pass it on.

She sensed wariness.

:You are not sure if you can believe me, she stated.

:No, he admitted. *The White advised me to be careful.*

She felt a stab of hurt, then annoyance.

:Then tell them carefully. It's up to them to decide if they believe me or not.

:I want to believe you. I do believe you. He sounded tortured. *I will believe you until I have evidence otherwise, but I must behave as if I don't believe you until I have evidence otherwise.*

And he wasn't liking it much. *Ah, Danjin,* she thought. *I miss you.*

:I understand. Thank you, Danjin.

Breaking the link, she roused herself to full consciousness, looked around the hall and sighed.

Well, Chaia did warn me that Huan would use those I love against me.

The large, tiled room echoed with the chatter of Voices, Companions, Servants and Thinkers. Standing beside Imenja, Reivan looked down at the floor. The mosaic map glinted softly, reflecting the light of lamps brought in to supplement what daylight reached the room from the entrance. Pottery figurines of Pentadrians and Circlians had been placed on the floor. They looked like toys left behind by a child. A rich child, too, as the figurines were finely detailed. Reivan saw that there were little Siyee men among the Circlians. Unlike the winged people depicted in the mosaic, they were accurately represented right down to the bones visible within the membranes of their wings.

'Nekaun comes,' a voice murmured from the direction of the entrance.

All fell silent and turned to wait. As Nekaun stepped into the room many hands sketched the symbol of the star. A strange expression was on Nekaun's face, but it vanished at the greeting. He looked around the room, meeting gazes and nodding.

'Forgive me for my lateness,' he said. 'Another matter delayed me.' He moved to the edge of the map and looked down at the Circlian figurines. 'Is this where the enemy army is?'

'According to our spies,' Dedicated Servant Meroen replied. The man was only in his thirties, but had proven himself an intelligent strategist during the previous war.

Nekaun paced around the map. All eyes followed him. Reivan heard Imenja's barely audible snort and guessed what her mistress was thinking. The First Voice didn't need to circle the map – he just liked to be the focus of attention.

'Has the Sennon emperor responded to my message?' Nekaun asked, this time looking at Vervel.

The Third Voice shook his head. 'No.'

Nekaun must know this, Reivan thought, *but he had probably asked for the benefit of the others.* He nodded and looked around the room.

'Can anyone suggest a way we might change his mind?'

When no answer came, Nekaun frowned and his gaze returned to the white figurines.

'How large is the Circlian army?'

Now several people began to speak. Meroen spoke of thousands gathered so far, then others began to debate how many more might join them. The Dunwayans had yet to join the army. Then there was the question of whether the Sennons would, or if they would remain uninvolved except to allow passage of the Circlian army.

'There are fewer Siyee this time,' he added.

'How fast is the Circlian army travelling?' Nekaun asked. 'When will they reach the Isthmus?'

'At a steady pace; if no sandstorms delay them, one cycle of the moon,' Shar said. 'They travel through desert and will have to take water and food with them. The town of Diamyane will not be able to sustain them, so they will need to transport supplies from the north.'

'So we attack their supply caravans.'

'Or ships.'

Nekaun smiled. 'Our Elai friends may prove useful after all.' He looked at Imenja. 'Have they replied to our request?'

'I doubt it has reached them yet,' she answered.

Nekaun looked around the room. 'What are our strengths and weaknesses?'

'We have few weaknesses,' Vervel said. 'The Isthmus is an effective barrier. The Circlian army cannot cross in large numbers. We have plentiful supplies of food and water and fight on familiar ground. We should be able to raise an army to match theirs. Our fleets are equal and our crews are better trained.'

Dedicated Servant Meroen shook his head. 'Why do they attack us if they have no obvious advantage?'

'They must have been relying on Auraya's help,' Shar said.

Nekaun smiled. 'Perhaps. But they won't have it.'

'Will they turn back once they know she has been captured?' Genza asked.

Several spoke in response.

'Surely they already know.'

'If they don't we should make sure they know.'

'Send them her corpse.'

Nekaun was still smiling, but in a distracted way. It was the same strange expression he had been wearing when he had arrived. For some reason it sent a shiver up Reivan's spine. There was something unpleasant in that smile.

'When the Circlians reach the Isthmus they will be stalled,' Meroen said, pitching his voice loud enough to be heard. 'But remember: the Isthmus is a barrier to us as well. We may find ourselves caught in a protracted war. Crops will go unplanted, traders will be unable to dock, and Voices will not be able to leave the Isthmus lest the White take advantage of their absence.'

The room had quietened. Nekaun frowned at Meroen then his gaze shifted from face to face.

'So what do we do to avoid a stalemate?'

A murmuring began as the question was discussed.

'We could hide our army behind the Sennon mountains,' a Thinker suggested. 'When they arrive at Diamyane we attack them from all sides, and drive them into the sea.'

'Siyee scouts would see us.'

'And we lose our best advantage,' Nekaun said quietly. 'The Isthmus. No. Let them settle in Diamyane. We will cut off their supplies. Let them starve a little before we break them.'

He smiled again, his gaze shifting to some distant place for a moment. Reivan shivered and looked away. When she turned back she found him watching her. Suddenly she felt foolish. He was only anticipating victory. It was just disturbing to see a hint of bloodlust in the eyes of a man she had taken to bed. It ought to make him more exciting. Powerful. Dangerous.

But it didn't.

He turned away, an entirely different expression on his face. She felt her insides turn cold.

Unless she had imagined it . . . and she knew she hadn't . . . it had been an expression of unconcealed contempt.

CHAPTER 39

The Dunwayan army was an impressive sight.

Warriors marched ten abreast along the road. At the head of each clan walked a man bare of all clothing but a short leather skirt and carrying a brightly painted spear. Members of the tribe took turns at the position, each stripping to reveal the tattoo patterns of their clan. They shared the role not to avoid enduring long hours of bad weather, if it came, but because all members of a clan would fight for the honour otherwise.

Every other man in the army carried half or more of his body weight in weapons. Even the sorcerers carried them; having more than average Gifts did not excuse any warrior from proper war training. Two-wheeled war platten pulled by reyna bred and trained for battle followed behind the troops; warriors would not suffer the indignity of tramping through reyner manure – except that left by the beasts pulling the platten of their leader. Behind the cavalry were arem-drawn four-wheeled supply tarns and the clans' servants.

Danjin had a fine view of the column of fierceness. The platten he rode in had no cover. Ella and I-Portak sat facing the front, while Danjin and Dunwayan advisers rode facing the White and the Dunwayan leader.

They did not have to look behind to know the army followed;

the rhythmic pounding of boots was a constant background to their conversations. If Danjin looked past Ella and I-Portak he found himself easily hypnotised by the near-flawless rise and fall of heads and shoulders beyond.

Watching the army make camp was even more fascinating. Everyone knew their task and worked without need for consultation or orders. All was done with practised ease, a credit to their training. If any Dunwayans were anxious about the coming confrontation they didn't show it.

I wonder what happens to the failures. The boys who don't grow up strong. The men who suffer injuries, illness or melancholy. Are they hidden away, or cast out of the tribe to become servants?

He thought back to the day the army had left Chon. Women had lined the streets and thrown a tart-smelling herb onto the road for the warriors to march over. Some had looked stricken, others relieved.

I hope my letters make it home. He suppressed a sigh. *I wish I could have seen Silava and the girls. And even my father, though I'm sure he'll outlive me even if I survive this war.*

He had dreamed of his family every night since hearing of the villagers' fate. It had been bad enough witnessing the executions of the Pentadrians, though it was the reaction of the villagers that he would find hardest to forget. Some had cheered, some had cried, but most had huddled together silently, their faces white with fear. They'd had reason to fear. Dunwayan justice was harsh. Later, in Chon, those villagers who had been the most welcoming to the Pentadrians had been executed. Those who had simply not protested were sent to work in the mines. But to Danjin's relief, I-Portak had been more lenient on those Ella had listed as being powerless to object to the Pentadrian presence. They, the old and the children, had been sent back to their village. Danjin imagined the village was now a sad place, populated by so few people.

In his dreams of his own family, he had ridiculous conversations with his wife and daughters. Occasionally they were unaware that he was there, no matter how much he tried to get their attention. Thinking of those dreams now, he felt a familiar mix of fear and resignation. And sadness. If he didn't return . . .

Don't think it, he told himself. *If you think it, you'll make it happen.*

But at some point between leaving Chon and now, the thought that he would not survive this war had taken hold of him and he'd been unable to shake it. *Where is all the confidence I had during the previous war?* He grimaced. *It was not confidence, but ignorance.*

Or maybe Auraya had given him hope. To see her fly . . . it had been hard to imagine anything defeating her.

He shivered. Last night, in a dream, she had told him the Voices had imprisoned her in Glymma. There had been no vision of her, just her voice, but the dream had seemed so real he had been certain that she had truly spoken to him. The next day he had told Ella of the dream and asked if she thought Auraya might have been communicating with him. Ella had said it was possible, but she hadn't heard such news from the White or the gods.

After the dream Danjin lay awake thinking about Auraya. He worried what might happen if she was a prisoner. If the Voices were powerful enough to hold her captive they were powerful enough to harm her – even kill her.

But if they were, why hadn't they?

Now he worried that Auraya was, as Ella had warned, trying to trick him. He considered reasons why she might want him to believe she was a prisoner. *To make me, and the White, believe she's still on our side when she isn't. Why would she do that?* He sighed. *To trick us into a confrontation that we can't win.*

Sometimes he was sure it had been a dream, and he had nothing to worry about.

:*If it wasn't a dream, Auraya is a prisoner,* Ella's voice said in his mind. *If it was, we still have much to worry about. We haven't heard from Auraya in weeks.*

Startled by the voice in his head, Danjin looked up at Ella.

:*Careful,* she added. *One of the advantages of mental conversations is that others aren't aware of them. It kind of spoils things if you jump like that every time I speak to you.*

He looked away.

:*Do you have any idea where she is?* he asked.

:*No. And no, the gods do not either.*

:*What will happen if she has changed sides?*

:*The gods are confident that they can prevent her fighting us.*

:*Prevent her . . . they didn't arrange for her to be imprisoned, did they?*

Her amusement was like a tinkle of glass.

:*Maybe. It would be quite a feat, wouldn't it? Convince the enemy, without alerting their gods, to imprison someone who was willing to join them.*

She was right. It was a silly idea.

:*If she is a captive, then she hasn't turned on us.*

:*Not necessarily. She may have turned on the gods in her heart, but still was not willing to join the Pentadrians. And she may not be a prisoner at all.*

:*She might not even be in Southern Ithania,* he added, mostly to himself. *She could be anywhere.*

:*Then why doesn't she contact us, or the gods?* she asked.

He couldn't answer that. Glancing at Ella, he saw her lips twitch into a sympathetic smile. Then her expression suddenly grew serious. She stared into the distance and her face relaxed.

'Juran informs me he has passed the last town before the pass. We should meet them within the week.'

I-Portak turned to regard her. 'Or earlier, if the weather holds.'

She smiled. 'Your warriors never cease to impress me with their stamina, I-Portak. Leave them a little strength for the journey across the desert.'

His shoulders lifted slightly. 'I am. We are not unfamiliar with desert conditions. Don't tell the Sennon emperor this, but we have been sending small warrior groups into the desert to train for centuries.'

She laughed quietly. 'I'm sure the Sennon emperor is quite aware of that.'

Danjin suppressed a smile as I-Portak regarded her with barely concealed dismay.

'Do you mean all the secrecy we have practised has been for nothing?' he eventually said.

'Practice is the only route to perfection,' she said, quoting Dunwayan tradition.

He chuckled and turned away. 'And perfection only exists in the realm of the gods.' He shrugged. 'So long as the emperor pretends ignorance, we will pretend that our forays into his land remain unknown.'

Far out at the edges of the city was a training ground for warrior Servants. Auraya skimmed over the minds there, glimpsing practice bouts both physical and magical. When she found what she was looking for she smiled. Two Dedicated Servants were sharing a meal and discussing the size, strengths and weaknesses of the Pentadrian army.

A loud clang of iron interrupted their conversation. For a moment she wondered why the man and woman hadn't reacted. Then her stomach sank and dread clutched her heart as she realised her own ears were hearing the sound.

Her awareness snapped back to her surroundings. Opening

her eyes, she drew in a deep breath and let it out. The same four domestics hurried toward her. Nekaun strolled after them.

The smell of flowers came with them. It sent her pulse racing though she wasn't yet sure why this should bother her. Looking at the domestics, she realised they were all carrying buckets. Bags were slung over their shoulders. Obviously they were planning to do more than just wash and feed her.

She resisted the temptation to look at Nekaun.

The first domestic swung the bucket toward her. She braced herself for the chill water and nearly gasped as she was battered with warmth instead. Before she had recovered from the surprise the second domestic tipped more water over her head. This, too, was warm.

Setting aside their empty buckets, the domestics drew objects out of their bags. Pottery jugs were uncorked. Hands drew out fistfuls of something resembling very fine wet sand.

She flinched as the first spread the substance onto her arm and began to rub it against her skin. It *was* sand. This, she remembered, was how the locals preferred to clean themselves. The rich used a fine, rare sand from some distant place. The two domestics scrubbed her arms, neck and scalp then, to her embarrassment, worked ever lower. Their touch was efficient and their faces expressionless, but she gritted her teeth and tried not to show how much their touch unsettled her.

All the time she felt Nekaun watching.

Finally the domestics had scrubbed her all over. The other two approached with their buckets and carefully washed the sand off her skin. This rinse water held the perfume she had noticed earlier. It was cooler, but not cold.

When they had stepped away Auraya's skin tingled all over. It would have felt good to be clean, if Nekaun hadn't been there.

He hasn't asked me any of his stupid questions yet, she realised. The domestics swept the dais and then hurried from the hall. None had brought any food. *Perhaps because there's no point. Why bother feeding me if I'm about to die. But why clean me? Does he prefer to kill clean people?*

She nearly giggled at the silliness of that thought. But all humour vanished as he moved closer. Her skin felt too sensitive. Her body felt too exposed. She resisted the temptation to curl up as much as the chains would allow.

'That's better,' he said quietly. 'Don't misunderstand me. I like a bit of sweat and dirt. But not utter filth.'

He stopped a mere step away. *He's just trying to intimidate me,* she told herself. *And he's in the void now. He's vulnerable too.*

Now that she would have to go out of her way to avoid looking at him, she met his gaze with what she hoped was a blank stare.

He stared back.

That's different, she thought. *He usually smiles and says something snide and ridiculous to point out that he's in control.*

When he spoke next, it was in Avvenan. The two Servants guarding the door paused, then walked away.

That sent a shiver of pure terror through her. Why send away the guards unless he was about to do something he didn't even want his own people knowing about?

'There,' he said. 'A little privacy.' She resisted the urge to shrink away as he moved a hand toward her, then tried not to flinch as his fingers touched her throat. His hand curled around her neck, warm and firm.

'So thin. I could throttle you right now,' he murmured. 'But I don't gain any pleasure from killing.' His gaze shifted lower. 'Did I ever tell you that I was the Head Servant of the Temple of Hrun before I became First Voice?'

His hand slid downward to her breast. Her mouth went

dry. *Intimidation*, she repeated. *Don't react. Be boring. Give him nothing and he'll lose interest and go away.*

'Hmm. How tense you are.' His breath was sickeningly warm. She tried not to breathe it in. 'So am I. Here, I'll show you.'

He pressed his body against hers, pushing her against the stone wall. Smothered by black robes, revolted by his breath, she felt herself shudder in horror at the hardness of his groin beneath his robes.

He really means to do this . . .

No. Stay calm. He wouldn't dare. It's just intimidation.

His hand left her breast. Her relief was brief. She felt knuckles dig into her belly as he pulled at his robes. His breathing was fast. Despite herself she looked up. He bared his teeth.

'Yes. That's right. Where are your gods now, Auraya? They can't help you.'

Her mind spun in increasingly frantic circles, then abruptly she saw, with awful clarity, that he did mean to do what he threatened. *This is going to be revolting and humiliating and painful but I can bear it. I will have to . . .* But she had glimpsed the wounds and scars in the minds of women who had been used by men. *He has, too. He knows he'll leave me with more than his . . . oh, gods.* She had no magical means to prevent conception. *But he won't want to sire a child*, she reasoned. *But he's in the void too. His magic won't work either. Gods, no!* She bit back a scream as she saw herself, chained and bloated with his child, in this place. Imprisoned without and within. *But if he's in the void he's vulnerable too. I can hurt him. I can kill him.* She felt her jaw tense. *I will bite out his throat. I will . . .*

'Nekaun.'

The voice was unearthly. It echoed and whispered around

the room like wind. Nekaun whirled around. Looking over his shoulder, Auraya saw a being of light. She felt her mouth go dry. She had seen this god before.

'Sheyr!' Nekaun gasped.

'Come here.'

Nekaun hurried off the dais and threw himself to the floor before the feet of the glowing figure.

'Do not harm Auraya,' the god said. 'Revenge will come, but not in this way. What you wish to do may disadvantage us.'

'But . . .' The word was barely audible.

The being straightened. 'Do you dare to question me?' he boomed.

'No, Sheyr!' Nekaun shook his head, his whole body quivering at the movement.

'You would take unnecessary risks for a moment of gratification.' The god's head rose and he stared at Auraya. 'Be satisfied that she is alone and friendless, with only her shadow for company.' His head snapped back to Nekaun. 'Do you understand?'

'Yes.'

'Then go.'

Nekaun scrambled to his feet and fled. The glowing figure looked at Auraya again.

He winked, then faded away.

In his place stood a Servant. The man blinked and glanced around the hall, then backed away from her. She looked into his mind and realised that he had given his will over to the god. Otherwise Sheyr would not have been able to see her, or speak with a real voice.

He saved me. She shook her head. How could she feel such gratitude toward one of the Pentadrian gods when they had ordered Nekaun to break his vow and trap her here? '. . . *with only her shadow for company.*'

482

And the significance of his last words came to her. Shadow! She quietly began to laugh, not caring that there was a hysterical edge to her voice.

It was Chaia! And Nekaun fell for it!

CHAPTER 40

At the first opportunity, Reivan slid out of bed. Her legs were shaking and for a moment she didn't know what to do. Seeing her robes on the floor, she decided she would feel better dressed. Those were torn now. She moved to a chest and drew out another set.

'What's wrong?'

She looked back at Nekaun. Lounging naked on the bed he was so beautiful it was painful. It took her breath away, but she made herself straighten her back. *Stand up to him.*

'*That* was unpleasant,' she told him.

His eyebrows rose. 'Oh? You didn't like it?'

'No.'

'You usually like it. Aren't I welcome here any more?'

'Not if it's going to be like *that*. You . . . you nearly choked me.'

'Some women like that. They say a little fear makes it more thrilling.'

She turned away and drew the robe around herself. 'I don't.'

'Don't be angry. How could we know that until we tried it?'

She felt her anger weakening. 'You should have asked me first.'

'Then you would be expecting it. Surprise is part of the pleasure.'

'It wasn't. And the rest wasn't much fun either. It was like . . .' She grimaced. Her insides felt bruised.

'Like what?'

She frowned. There was something in his voice. Almost a smugness. Almost as if he liked seeing her discomforted.

Turning to face him, she held his gaze. 'It was like you were punching me with your . . . Surely, with your background in the arts of lovemaking, you would know that is not pleasant for a woman?'

He laughed. 'You're hardly the goddess of love. You've got a lot to learn. I think you could come to like a bit of rough play.'

'I don't think so.'

He grinned. 'Oh, I think you found what we just did more than a little exciting.'

She stared at him. 'You can't be serious. It was nice at first, but later . . . what part of "Stop, you're hurting me" didn't make sense to you?'

He laughed. 'You didn't mean it.'

'You *know* I did.' She shook her head. 'I think you enjoyed hurting me. You had that same look in your eye you've had since you chained Auraya up. I almost expected you to call out her name.'

His smile faded, then his eyes narrowed. Rolling to the edge of the bed, he stood up. She watched as his robes rose from the floor to his hands and he began to dress, his movements quick and angry.

She felt her anger ebb, leaving her numb. 'You're leaving.'

'Yes. If my efforts aren't appreciated,' he said, 'I'll go where they are.'

Stung, she felt tears spring into her eyes. *Stop it*, she told herself. *Stop being a fool. He meant to hurt you, so don't let him see he succeeded.*

He marched out of the bedroom. The sound of the door slamming echoed through her rooms. The silence afterwards thundered in her ears. His words repeated over and over in her head. *'You're hardly the goddess of love.'*

I'm not good enough for him. That's why he was rough. He got impatient with me.

She moved to the bed, thinking only to curl up and give in to her misery. Then she saw the bloodstains. Her blood. A few drops only, but enough to remind her of his body slamming against hers, the manic look in his eyes, the hand about her throat and the way he had laughed when she had protested. Anger flared again. She rose and stalked to the bathing room.

I will scrub every last bit of him away, she told herself. *He can bed every woman in Glymma. He can bed Auraya for all I care. If that's what it takes to satisfy him he can find it elsewhere. I'm done with him.*

If it weren't for the constant nagging thought that Auraya was suffering in her prison under the Sanctuary, Mirar would have considered the day to have been particularly satisfying and enjoyable.

He had met with over a hundred of Glymma's Dreamweavers to discuss their role as healers after the coming battle. Dreamweavers were travelling to the city from all over the continent, and Arleej had asked him to oversee all accommodation, food and travel arrangements. Though most of this work was organised by Dreamweaver House leaders, they all needed someone to make decisions where there was disagreement, and mediate with the Voices and Servants.

The Dreamweavers had joined together in one large mind link, and he had learned much from them. He let his mind shield slip only long enough to confirm his identity. He wanted to tell them of his 'death' and survival, but Auraya featured too much in the story and he couldn't afford chancing that the Voices would read their minds and discover that he didn't dislike her as much as they believed.

From the Dreamweavers he had learned that they had suspected that he wasn't really Mirar, that the Voices had recruited a Dreamweaver willing to pose as Mirar in order to influence Northern Ithania. Arleej had assured them this wasn't true, but some were still shocked to discover, through the link, that he was their legendary, immortal founder.

After dining with Glymma's Dreamweaver House leader, Mirar had returned to the Sanctuary late and immediately received an invitation to meet with Second Voice Imenja. A Servant escorted him to a balcony overlooking a courtyard, where a fountain glittered in the light of several lamps. Imenja was sitting in a reed chair and rose to greet him.

'Dreamweaver Mirar,' she said. 'How did your meeting with your people go?'

'Very well,' he told her. 'I still can't get used to seeing Dreamweavers living without the constant fear of persecution. I'm heartened to see that they can exist in harmony with a religion of dominant power.'

She smiled. 'Just like old times?'

He shook his head. 'Yes and no. In the past there were so many gods that few dominated as completely as yours do. A single god might rule in small nations like Dunway, but never an entire continent. And never united with other gods.'

'I would like to hear more about those times. What do the Circlians call them?'

'The Age of the Many.'

'Yes, and now we live in the Age of the Five. Or should that be the Age of the Ten?'

Mirar shrugged. 'At least when I tell you tales of the past, it won't be your gods' evil deeds I tell of.'

She chuckled. 'No. I gather Circlians aren't aware of their gods' past, then?'

'No. Only Dreamweavers know, passing down experiences and stories through mind links.'

'So perhaps that is the reason your people are badly treated there and well treated here. Our gods have no need to fear the stories Dreamweavers might tell.'

Mirar looked at her, impressed. It made sense, though he was sure he would have come to the same conclusion eventually.

Imenja looked out at the courtyard. 'I have to warn you, the closer war comes the more we will want you to commit to helping us in some way.'

As she turned to look at him he met her gaze steadily.

'Dreamweavers do not fight.'

'No, but there may be other ways you can assist us.'

'We heal the wounded. What else can we offer?'

She shifted in her seat to face him. 'If someone attacks a patient you are healing, what do you do? Allow them to be harmed, or protect them?'

'Protect them,' he answered.

'If someone attacks a friend – or a stranger – what do you do? Allow them to be harmed, or protect them?'

He frowned, suspecting he knew where this was leading. 'Protect them.'

She smiled and turned back to regard the courtyard. 'Nekaun might be satisfied with a compromise.' Her smile faded and she sighed. 'I can't promise that he won't punish you or your people if you don't offer him something. That something doesn't have to involve your people. He wants it to appear that we have you, the legendary Mirar, on our side.'

Mirar shook his head. 'That may endanger Dreamweavers in the north.'

She looked at him, her expression sad. 'I know. It is a choice I don't envy you for.' She stood up and smiled. 'But if you join us, there's a good chance we'll win, and that will probably be a better result for Dreamweavers than the alternative.'

He nodded. 'You have a point.'

'Consider what I've proposed,' she told him. 'But it is late, and even Voices need to sleep now and then.'

'And immortals,' he said, rising. 'Good night, Second Voice Imenja.'

'Good night.'

The Servant who had escorted him to the meeting appeared and guided him back to his rooms. Mirar stared out of the window for a while, thinking about what Imenja had suggested.

A compromise. One that doesn't involve my people, just me. I protect the Pentadrians with magic. That frees the Voices to put more of their magic into fighting. With Auraya locked up below the Sanctuary, surely the Pentadrians will win this time.

How would his people feel about that? Would they lose respect for him for choosing a side? They might, but the southern Dreamweavers would feel betrayed if they knew he could have prevented the Circlians conquering the southern continent and subjecting them to their habitual prejudice.

Sighing, he retired to bed. As soon as he reached a dream trance he sought Auraya's mind, but the only response he got was disjointed and reluctant, and he decided to let her sleep. He called another name.

:*Emerahl.*

:*Mirar*, she responded without hesitation. *I was just talking to The Twins. How is life in Glymma?*

:*Good for me; no different for Auraya.*

:*Poor woman. Have you found a way to free her?*

:No. She is too well guarded, as am I, but I am hoping that may change as the war begins to distract everyone. If I show any interest in her Nekaun starts asking if I want to be present when he kills her. When I ask why he's delaying he just says 'when the gods decide'. Imenja made a suggestion to me tonight. He told her what the Second Voice had proposed. *What do you think I should do?*

:Don't get involved. But since you're already involved then don't take sides. But since these Voices probably won't let you, then do what she suggests. But not straightaway. If you give in now they will start asking for more. Wait until the last moment. And if you can, make Auraya's fate part of the deal, even if it only means delaying her execution.

As always, she was a source of good advice.

:That sounds like a good plan. How is the Quest for the Scroll of the Gods progressing?

:We haven't figured out what the symbols mean yet. I haven't had much time to work on it. The Twins want me out of Southern Ithania, in case the Thinkers track me down. I'll be coming through Glymma. She paused. *Could we meet safely? I'd like you to look at the diamond.*

:I'd like to see it, but I think it would be too dangerous. Though I'm free to come and go from the Sanctuary, I don't know where we could meet safely and I'm certain they have someone following me when I do go out.

:The Twins probably wouldn't like it. Not only would we risk the Voices finding us, and then taking and destroying the diamond, but the last thing we need is the Pentadrians blackmailing me into joining them, too.

:No, Mirar agreed. *The Circlian gods would just love that. According to Auraya, they've been hanging around the Sanctuary quite a bit.*

:The Pentadrian gods don't chase them off?

:She hasn't said anything about sensing them.

:That's odd. Maybe they fear the Circlian gods.

:Maybe they are so different in nature that Auraya can't sense them, Mirar suggested.

:Maybe they know she can overhear gods, and are avoiding her. I guess we'll never know.

:Not unless they decide to tell us.

:I can't see that happening any time soon. Any other news?

:No.

:Good luck, then. I will let you know when I've reached Northern Ithania.

:Good luck.

Her mind faded from his senses. Fighting off a niggling weariness, he embarked on his last task for the night: sending his mind out to skim the thoughts of the people around him.

CHAPTER 41

Three days had passed and Nekaun had not returned. The domestics continued their routine of dousing Auraya with cold water and feeding her the grainy sludge. The cold water left her shivering and she almost wished they would leave her grimy. It was bad enough that she was cold all the time, but the chill that came after her dousing seemed to drain all strength from her.

She craved real food and sometimes found herself dreaming about it. When she skimmed the minds of people eating, her own body ached for sustenance. She longed to lie down. Her arms hurt. Her legs sometimes cramped painfully despite her efforts to flex and stretch them. Most of the time she was so tired she slumped against the wall.

Exploring the minds of the world kept her consciousness away from cold, hunger and pain. Through other people she saw the sun rise and set, felt happiness, love and contentment. She began to avoid the minds of those in pain or misery. The thoughts of those preparing for war no longer seemed so important to watch.

What difference does it make if I know what they're planning? I can't do anything to stop them. I can't even reach the White and tell them what I've learned. Danjin doesn't trust me. Chaia . . .

Chaia had saved her. But questions had been forming in the back of her mind. If Chaia could impersonate another god, then could other gods do so too? Could Pentadrian gods impersonate Circlian ones? That must be why he had given her the code word 'shadow'.

But thinking about Chaia's visit was too close to thinking about what Nekaun had been about to do to her, so she turned her mind away.

Which did not work all of the time. Sometimes something would jolt her back into a memory of smothering black robes and exploring, unwanted hands. Her skin crawled and her heart raced.

She hated that she had been so affected by the incident. *It's this weariness making me feel so weak*, she told herself. *If I were stronger I would feel less affected.* She grimaced. *If Chaia hadn't interrupted I'd be in an even worse state.*

'Auraya.'

For a moment she thought the voice was a memory, but when it repeated her name she opened her eyes and found herself staring at a glowing figure. The Pentadrian god, Sheyr, smiled at her.

'Come out of the shadows, Auraya,' he said.

'Chaia,' she breathed.

'Yes.'

Remembering the Servant that had been revealed when he had vanished last time, she looked closer.

'Who is . . . ?'

'Another loyal mortal,' he replied. 'He will not remember this conversation. He has put aside his will for me.'

'For Sheyr.'

He shrugged. 'Some mortals are easily deceived.'

She glanced at the Servant guards. The pair were watching intently, their expressions awed. They must have opened the gate to allow the god-possessed man into the room.

'But what of the Pentadrian gods?' she asked.

Chaia's smile widened. 'I have ensured their attention is elsewhere.'

'They must know you deceived Nekaun. Will they counter your orders?' *Will Nekaun come back to finish what he started?*

The god shook his head. 'To do so would reveal they can be impersonated.'

She let out a sigh of relief, then frowned. 'Are you here to release me?'

'I cannot. If this mortal enters the void I can no longer possess him.'

'But you could order him to release me.'

He shook his head again. 'I cannot interfere, and I cannot explain why I cannot interfere.' His lips twisted into a crooked smile. 'You already know we gods have agreements to keep.'

She felt a sudden flash of insight. 'Huan wants me to stay here.'

'Not exactly.'

Auraya narrowed her eyes at him. 'Ah. I see. She wants me dead. This is a compromise?'

'Leaving you here is, for the moment.'

'So you all want me out of the way.'

'Yes.'

'I'm surprised you don't want my help in this war.'

He frowned. 'How did you learn about the war?'

A chill ran over her skin. *He still doesn't know about my mind-reading.*

'I think Nekaun told me. You didn't want me to know about it?' she countered.

'I came here to tell you.' He looked away, his expression thoughtful, then took a step closer and smiled. 'I love you still, Auraya. I will do what I can to get you out of here. Then . . . in return I want you to promise me you will stay

494

out of the conflicts of this world – even those of the Siyee. Keep yourself apart from it, or Huan will find an excuse and a way to kill you. I . . .' His gaze slid from hers to a place to his left and he scowled. 'I must go.'

Auraya caught the presence of another god before it flashed away. The figure of Sheyr vanished. In his place stood a Servant barely past boyhood. The young man glanced around the room, then his eyes snapped to Auraya. His gaze dropped and he turned a bright red.

A voice called from the gate. The youth spun around and, seeing the Servants guarding it, hurried toward them. One of the guards patted him on the back. He stayed a short while, talking to them excitedly of his experience, then hurried away.

Auraya sighed and leaned against the throne base. *Chaia may love me*, she thought tiredly. *But not enough to defy Huan and free me*. How much of recent events had been arranged by the gods? Had they ordered for her to be imprisoned to keep her out of the way?

She thought of Nekaun's reaction to Chaia/Sheyr's orders: 'But . . .'

But what? Had he been ordered to rape her? By a god?

She shivered. It was impossible to know, and she was beginning to feel uneasy again. Closing her eyes, she sent her mind out in search of a distraction.

Standing at the stern of the boat, Emerahl watched as the city of Glymma slowly shrank to a line of lights in the distance. She felt relieved and disappointed. The last few days had been full of tedious delays. After buying a ride on a reed boat down the river to the city, and selling a bracelet to a collector The Twins had recommended, she had discovered Glymma's wharves were full of Servants anxious to know who was arriving and leaving their city. It took several bribes and a few veiled threats in order to find herself a captain willing to take her across the Gulf of Fire to Diamyane.

Now that she was leaving she felt a wry disappointment that she'd had no chance to explore the city. Looking back at the glittering lights, she also felt a niggling guilt. Somewhere under the sprawling Sanctuary was Auraya, trapped in a void.

If I could free her, Mirar wouldn't have to risk his life trying to. She shook her head. *But if he can't manage it, I doubt I could.*

She had come to respect Auraya during the weeks she'd spent teaching the former White. She had even liked her a little. *I hope the Pentadrians aren't treating her too badly.* She snorted quietly at the thought. Of course they were treating her badly. She was their enemy. She'd killed their former leader. *They'll be making her suffer in as many ways as they can make a woman suffer. This is a war, after all.*

She shook her head, sighed and turned away. *That doesn't stop me hoping she won't lose any of that spirit and optimism she had before. Or wishing I could help her – without putting myself at risk of ending up in her position, or dead.* The two lamps of the boat cast shadows of the masts across the deck. She, too, cast a pair of shadows, and where they crossed they formed a comically skinny silhouette of herself. She smiled at it, then at herself for noticing at all. Staring at the shapes the diamond cast for days had made her all too aware of shadows. At least the diamond needed only one light source to work . . .

She caught her breath. *Or did it?*

What would happen if she used two, or three, or several? Suddenly the glyphs on the sides of the pendant had a possible new meaning. And the diagram . . .

One light / one key

The diagram could be seen with one light, and it was the key to the rest.

Two lights / two truths

It was so simple! Two lights might make the shadows overlap in a way that created different shapes. Possibly even glyphs.

She cast about. The ship was a simple merchant vessel. Its wide hull was used to carry cargo, not passengers. All the crew were on deck. They didn't sleep at sea as the journey across the Gulf could be made in a night or a day. She doubted they went below except to check the cargo or take up food or fresh water.

There was a way she could go below and ensure she would not be disturbed. Moving to the captain's side, she waited until he turned to look at her.

'I need a little private time,' she said to him, smiling wryly. 'Is below decks suitable?'

He nodded once. 'I'll make sure no one goes below. There's a pot down there.'

'Thank you.'

He gestured to the hatch. A few of the crew nodded to her as she passed them. She nodded back, sensing that curiosity had replaced anxiety over her presence now that they had left Glymma. The story she had told the captain was that her husband had come to Glymma a few months before, hoping to find a trading partner. He had left her behind while he returned to settle business in Sennon. The war had prevented him returning for her so she had to flee on her own.

Reaching the hatch, she climbed down a ladder into the dark. She created a spark of light and looked for the pot. The captain might suspect she'd been stealing or snooping through their goods if she didn't use it. She found it not far from where they had stowed the travel chest she had bought for the treasure.

Taking a length of string from her pack, she tied it to hooks for securing goods on either side of the hull then folded her shawl over it. If someone did come below they would assume she had hung it up for privacy.

Checking that the pot was clean, she turned it upside down, sat on it and drew the pendant out from beneath her clothes.

It was not easy holding the diamond steady in a rocking ship. Eventually she used magic to suspend it in the air. Creating a spark, she moved it within the diamond and turned it so that the 'key' face cast shadows onto her shawl.

Examining the diagram she felt a thrill of excitement. One dotted line crossed one side of the octagon, two the next, three the following and four the last. The numbers might relate to angles. She wouldn't be sure until she tried.

Turning the pendant so the *two lights / two truths* side faced the shawl, she introduced another light. She moved the two lights around in the centre of the diamond. As they drew further apart she saw the shadows on the shawl passing each other. Suddenly she glimpsed recognisable glyphs. She halted the movement of the sparks and drew them a little closer again.

There! That's it!

Normal Sorli glyphs covered her shawl. Whispering a cheer of triumph, she began to read.

When Surim had first come to the swamp he had thought it an ugly, smelly place. After a few thousand years of living in luxury, the muddy, constantly damp, wild surroundings had seemed like a place out of his worst nightmare.

But as he had learned to live there he had grown to appreciate its beauty. *So much life*, he thought as he guided the boat through the water. *All this variety in plant, animal and insect, all in one unique place.* The local people appreciated this to a point. They adapted their lives to fit the swamp as much as they adapted the swamp to fit their lives. Outsiders did not understand it – did not try to understand it. They cut down the trees, dredged out deeper, wider rivers and tried to drain the waterlogged land.

The swamp was beautiful during the day, but eerie at night. Without his light to illuminate the way, Surim would have been lost in utter darkness. He ducked under a web stretched across the river, then turned back and saluted the enormous spider waiting in the middle.

'Have a care where you weave your webs or you will be my dinner,' he told the spider. Turning back, he looked up at the rock wall ahead. Guiding his boat along this, he listened to the sounds of the swamp. Each chirrup, buzz and cry brought its owner to his mind's eye. A rainbow flier buzzed past his ear. A distant honk of a randy swamp bogger was answered from somewhere close by.

Guiding the boat around a bend in the river, he steered it toward dark holes in the base of the rock wall. As it drifted inside, the shadows appeared to shrink away from his light.

'Flee, shadows!' he whispered. 'Flee as fast as you can!'

The boat emerged into a cavern. Another light and a figure drew him toward the far side. Tamun's arms were crossed.

'You're late.'

'Am I?' He smiled. 'I didn't know I was supposed to be anywhere at any particular time.'

She narrowed her eyes at him. 'You know what I mean. You usually return before dark.'

'I do,' he agreed. 'It was an unusual night. Or the usual unusual night.' He guided the boat up to the ledge and rose. 'How many times does it have to be unusual for it to be a usual unusual night?'

She sniffed. 'A lot less than the number of times you've asked such ridiculous questions. Hurry up. Emerahl has deciphered the secrets.' Turning away, she walked through the ledge into the caves.

A rush of excitement went through Surim. He leapt out of the boat and quickly tied it up, then hurried after her.

Gods were notoriously unwilling to discuss their own limitations, to mortals or immortals. When he and Tamun had seen hints that there might be a scroll full of secrets of a dead god somewhere in Southern Ithania the knowledge had been painfully tantalising. He had considered leaving the cave to seek it himself. It was almost worth the risk he might be discovered by the gods. Almost. What had stopped him wasn't the thought that the gods might notice him and arrange for him to be killed, but that Tamun would be left alone for so long. For the first time in two millennia. He liked to think he could survive without her. Of them both, he had changed the most in the last century. He didn't want to risk that she couldn't survive without him.

Our strength is our weakness. Our weakness our strength. Separating our bodies was hard enough to accept. Death is unimaginable.

Then Emerahl had come along and happily taken up the Quest for the Scroll of the Gods. Tamun thought she had taken too great a risk in leaving the Thinkers and gambling that the secrets were among the treasure. Surim didn't care. Only someone willing to take a few risks would have undertaken the search in the first place. And Emerahl had been right.

He followed Tamun up to their favourite cave. They both lay down in the nest of cushions Tamun had made. He heard her take a deep breath, then let it out slowly. Closing his eyes, he slipped effortlessly into the link trance and entwined his mind with Tamun's.

:Emerahl? they called.

:Tamun. Surim. At last.

:Greetings, Surim, another voice said.

Surim felt a mild surprise.

:Gull?

:Yes. It is I.

:I thought he might want to hear what she has to say, Tamun explained. *And The Gull agreed that it was time Mirar knew of his existence.*

:And I am still getting over the surprise, Mirar added.

:Save that for later, Emerahl said. *I have worked out how to see the glyphs within the pendant.*

As she described her discovery Surim felt a wry amusement.

:It is so simple, Emerahl finished. *I can't believe I didn't see it at first.*

:Most puzzles are simple once you know the answer, Surim told her. *So what do the glyphs say?*

:I started with the side marked 'two lights / two truths'. The glyphs read: 'All gods were born mortal. They learned to become immortal first. They learned how to become gods last'. There is a gap, then: 'All gods love/hate/need as mortals do. All gods need mortals to see/connect/change the world.'

The five immortals remained silent. As the silence lengthened Surim began to wonder if they were still linked.

:That explains a few things, he said, when he couldn't stand it any longer.

:Indeed it does, The Gull agreed.

:So the gods were immortals, Mirar mused. *Does that mean we could become gods? That would explain why they fear us so much.*

:They fear we will discover how to become gods, Surim agreed.

:Though would we want to? The Gull asked quietly. *It says the gods feel human emotions, yet need mortals in order to affect the world.*

:To feel desires, but not be able to satisfy them, Mirar said. *No wonder the gods have no sense of humour.*

:Does the pendant explain how to become a god, Emerahl? Tamun asked.

:No, she replied.

:So you have read the other sides?

:Yes.

:Tell us what it says.

:Three lights gives us three secrets, Emerahl told them. *They are: 'No god can be in two places at one time. No god can exist where there is no magic. No god collects and preserves souls of mortal dead.'*

The silence that followed the list lasted longer than before. This time Surim was too caught up in the implications to be bothered by it.

The gods don't take souls! The lie they had maintained for thousands upon thousands of years was so enormous Surim felt giddy. *They need mortals to affect the world*, he thought. *So they need mortals to believe they need gods.*

:Your Dreamweavers will be reassured by that, Mirar, Emerahl said.

:Reassured? I don't know. They know they give up any chance of their soul continuing after death when they become a Dreamweaver. But how will they feel knowing it is no special sacrifice?

:I think most of your people don't believe in souls anyway, Tamun said.

:What of the other two secrets? The Gull asked.

:We knew that gods couldn't exist in voids, and suspected they couldn't be in two places at once, Surim said. *What of the last side of the pendant, Emerahl?*

:I thought you'd never ask, she said smugly. *The fourth, if you recall, is death. Listen to this: 'All gods are equally powerful. None can affect the other but in position.' There is a gap, then: 'Six surround*

one results in immobilisation. Six surround one and take magic results in capture or death.'

:Six surround one? Surim repeated.

:One above, one below, one on all four sides, Mirar said. *The victim within. If the six draw away all magic the god within can't exist.*

:The voids! The Gull exclaimed. *I'd wager that is how the voids were created.*

:Of course, Emerahl said. *Hmm. I wonder how that will make me feel the next time I'm in one, knowing that a god died there.*

:Depends on the god, Mirar murmured. *If I knew where a few particular gods died, I'd be tempted to go there and have a little celebration.*

Something wasn't right. Surim repeated the secrets to himself a few times before he saw it. *So if six gods had to surround another to kill him/her . . .*

:There are only five gods, he pointed out. *Where is the sixth?*

:Sorli was the sixth. She killed herself, Emerahl reminded him. *Remember the story on the Scroll. She felt guilty about what they had done and killed herself.*

:How? Mirar asked. *Ah, of course. The voids. She must have entered one.*

:Thrown herself into oblivion, The Gull agreed. *She must have felt very guilty indeed.*

:Would you? Emerahl asked. *Would any of you?*

:Once again, it depends on the god, Mirar said. *I wouldn't feel a shred of guilt if I could get rid of the lot we have now.*

:But you're a Dreamweaver. You don't kill, Surim pointed out.

:I don't kill humans. I think I can make an exception for the gods, even if they were once human.

:Why do you ask, Emerahl? Tamun asked.

:I have been wondering, Emerahl said, her mental voice tense with excitement, *if immortals can create voids.*

Surim felt a chill run over his skin.

:We could give it a try, Tamun said.

:Perhaps between us, Mirar added.

:If there were six of us, The Gull finished. *We are only five.*

:Auraya might— Mirar began.

:She won't, Emerahl pointed out. *She still thinks she serves them.*

:She might have changed her mind about that recently, he countered.

:We can't take that risk, Tamun said firmly. *If she knows we can do it she might warn the gods. Unlike gods, we can't fly away to the other side of the world in an instant if it doesn't work.*

:She should be told the rest — all we have learned, apart from how the gods were killed, Emerahl said. *She needs to know the true nature of the gods she serves.*

The others murmured agreement.

:So what do we do without her? Mirar asked. *Wait until another immortal comes into his or her powers? That could take a thousand years.*

:If we have to, Tamun replied. *Or until the gods have hurt and offended Auraya so much that we are sure she hates them as much as we do.*

:Whichever comes first, The Gull agreed. *Though if Auraya's current situation ends badly, we may have no choice but the former.*

:Not if I can help it, Mirar said.

:Now, Mirar, Tamun began. *Don't take any foolish risks. We will have a long wait before us if we have to wait for* two *immortals to come into their p—*

:I have to go, Mirar said abruptly.

As Mirar's presence vanished from their link, Surim sighed.

:I do wish you'd stop encouraging him like that, sister.

504

CHAPTER 42

The ache in her shoulders had become a sharp pain, while her hands had lost feeling some time ago. Auraya opened her eyes and forced her legs to straighten. Her knees popped and her thigh muscles began to tremble.

This isn't good, she thought. *I'm getting weaker. I must exercise.* She flexed her muscles, moving her weight from leg to leg. As feeling came back to her hands it seemed as if a thousand needles were piercing her skin. *What I wouldn't do for a chair . . .*

Suddenly the pain increased tenfold as something touched her arm. She gasped and looked up, then gasped again in surprise as two round eyes stared into hers.

'Mischief!'

The veez was on the seat of the throne, leaning over to regard her. He dropped down and she winced as he landed on her sore shoulders.

'What are you doing here?' she whispered. 'I told you to stay with the nice servant.'

'Owaya,' he said, his whiskers tickling her ear. 'Bad man. Chase.'

He was radiating fear and agitation. Concentrating on his thoughts, she picked up flashes of memory. A man he

505

recognised. One who had been with her a lot. Shouting. Dodging magic. Fleeing.

'Nekaun,' Auraya hissed. 'He tried to kill you.' She sent the veez a feeling of sympathy and pride. *Clever Mischief.*

He nudged her ear. 'Scratch.'

'I can't,' she told him, demonstrating by pulling against the chains. 'Auraya caged.'

'Free Owaya,' he said decisively. Running up her arm, he sniffed the cuffs. She felt a thrill of hope and looked toward the Servant guards. They appeared to be absorbed in conversation. Mischief's whiskers quivered, then his ears suddenly lay flat. She sensed his confusion, and she suddenly understood.

'No magic,' she explained. 'No magic here. You use magic to undo locks.'

The veez did not understand. He leapt up onto the throne seat and crouched at the edge. His fur stood on end and she sensed he was deeply unhappy.

She could say nothing to reassure him, so she said nothing at all. Sighing, she closed her eyes and sent her mind out into the world.

By habit she brushed the minds of the two Servants guarding her. They were in the midst of discussing the two times Sheyr had possessed mortals and entered the hall. It hadn't occurred to them that the god might not have been the one he appeared to be. They didn't know that one of the men had gone mad, and that the other now woke several times each night screaming. She knew this from skimming their minds.

Moving beyond, she picked up the thoughts of other Servants. Their minds were full of their daily tasks, petty grievances, gossip, friends and family, and war. She skimmed through these looking for anything unusual. Nekaun's name caught her attention several times. A few women, Servant and domestic, contemplated with unease his visit to their bedchamber. Auraya shied away from these recollections, then stumbled upon the domestic who had been caring for Mischief. She was heartened to see that the woman was upset, both by Nekaun's attempt to kill the veez and that the creature hadn't come back.

Leaving the Sanctuary, Auraya flitted through the mind of Glymma's citizens. Their thoughts were on the usual concerns: work, family, love, hunger, food, ambition, pain and pleasure. War was on everyone's mind.

The previous day she had managed to reach beyond the city limits to some of the riverside villages. Today she stretched her senses out in a different direction. There were fewer minds, which was unsurprising since all appeared to be surrounded by desert sands. Most were focused on using magic and physical skill to control some kind of vehicle. Looking closer, she slowly came to understand these were boats driven by the wind that slid over the desert sand.

Looks like fun, she thought.

:*Auraya!*

At the call her mind shifted automatically into a dream trance.

:*Mirar?*

:*How are you?*

:*Tired. Sore. Nekaun tried to kill Mischief. He's here now.*

:*The bastard. It's a shame these people are ruled by such a man. The rest of them seem a lot nicer.*

:*Even Shar, the one who had his vorn kill innocent people in Toren?*

:*Well . . . I haven't spoken to him much so far. Anyway, I have to tell you something. The other immortals said you should know.*

:*The other Wilds?*

:*Yes. Emerahl, and a few others who managed to avoid being killed by the White.*

:*Emerahl?*

:*The woman who taught you to hide your mind.*

507

:Oh! Jade.

:Yes. Jade. Emerahl. The Hag. He paused. *They're very concerned about you and have been helping me try to find a way to free you.*

:*They have? Even though I'm a White?*

:*You're not a White any more, Auraya.*

:*Oh. That's right. But still. Me, an ally of gods and all that.*

:*Are you sure you're okay?*

:*Yes. Just tired. What did these Wilds want to tell me?*

:*I can only tell you what the others feel you can be trusted to know,* she said.

She forced herself to concentrate.

:*So there's more that they don't trust me to know?*

:*Yes.*

:*And you agree?*

:*Let's just say I know which secrets you can be burdened with, and which you can't.*

She considered his words and found herself liking him for them. *He wants to tell me something, but he doesn't want to put me in a difficult position.*

:*So what are these secrets you can trust me with?*

:*There's a story to it. I can't name all involved, but since you've met Emerahl I can safely describe her part in it.*

He explained briefly about the rumours of a Scroll containing secrets about the gods, and that Emerahl had found it.

:*This is the task she had to delay in order to teach me?*

:*Yes. Now, this Scroll was made by Sorli's last priest . . .* He went on to relate the story on the Scroll. *There were six gods at the end of the war,* he told her. *Sorli killed herself after having the secrets of the gods preserved for others to find.*

:*And you found the secrets?*

:*Emerahl did, and she deciphered them. This is what the others agreed I could tell you: all of the gods were born mortal, became immortals like us, then transformed themselves into gods.*

:They were Wilds first?

:Yes. And they were once ordinary mortals, with powerful Gifts. There's more. You're not going to like it. I don't think anyone's going to like it. The gods certainly aren't going to like anyone knowing. I could ch—

:Get on with it, Mirar.

:The gods can only exist in one place at any time and no god can exist where there is no magic.

:I knew that.

:But I'd wager you didn't know this: the gods don't take people's souls. It's a lie they've been using for millennia to give mortals a reason to obey them.

Auraya felt her curiosity turn to disbelief.

:That can't be true. I don't believe it.

:You don't want to believe it. These are the words of Sorli herself. The sixth god, who helped the Circle kill all the other gods. How did she put it? 'No god collects and preserves souls of mortal dead.'

:She was lying. She was probably mad. After all, she killed herself. She may not have even existed at all, and this is all some trick someone set up centuries ago in revenge against the gods.

:You don't believe it because you don't want to. And I can hardly blame you. I—

:No, you're believing it because you want to. It suits your view of the world very well, Mirar. Doesn't that sound suspicious to you? If I wanted to trick you, this would be how I'd do it. Feed you what you want to hear so you don't question what comes with it. She paused as an unpleasant possibility occurred to her. *What did come with it?*

:I can't tell you that.

:Then . . . just be careful. If it is a trick, that other part may be the trap.

He paused a long time before answering.

:I will keep that in mind. There is something else I think I can tell you.

509

:Oh?

:*Voids were created when a god was killed.*

She felt a thrill of mingled alarm and excitement.

:*Did this Scroll tell you how the gods killed each other?*

He paused.

:*Is there a god you'd like to kill?* he asked.

:*Maybe.*

:*Who? Ah! The Pentadrian ones, of course. What have they ever done to you?*

:*Had me chained up in a void.*

:*A reasonable, if personal, grudge*, he conceded.

:*And they encouraged their people to invade Northern Ithania*, she added.

:*Yes, that wasn't very polite.*

:*I suppose you're going to tell me the Circlian gods are guilty of worse?*

:*I could. But I won't. So you don't have any personal grudges against them?*

:*Just a small one. It seems fair that if Huan wants me dead then I can wish the same of her.*

:*Sound rea— . . . Wait. Huan wants you dead?*

:*Why are you surprised? You warned me the gods would try to kill me.*

:*But they didn't.*

:*Chaia keeps coming to my rescue. Well, as much as he can when there are 'rules' and such to make it difficult for him. He says he can't set me free.*

:*Does he? I had assumed none of the Circlian gods could venture into the Sanctuary without attracting the attention of the Pentadrian gods.*

:*So did I.* She briefly told him that Chaia had impersonated Sheyr twice, though she did not mention why. *He says Sheyr won't alert the Pentadrians to it because it means admitting it can happen.*

510

:And then nobody will know whether they can believe it is him or not when he appears. How frustrating for him. The others . . . Ah. I must go, Auraya.

:Whatever you do, don't endanger yourself or the Dreamweavers on my account.

But his mind had slipped from her perception and she heard no answer.

Sighing, she let herself drift for a while, but her mind returned to Mirar.

He's so much more confident than Leiard, she thought. *Though Leiard was like that when he was in the forest. He was only fearful in Jarime and around the White. Except . . . he wasn't fearful when we were lovers. He was more like . . .*

The recognition was like a jolt of energy. When Leiard was being her lover he had been more like Mirar. Mirar had been with her all the time she had been with Leiard, even if in a diminished, half-forgotten form.

Perhaps it was only her weakened, vulnerable state that was heightening her feelings, but she was overwhelmed by a longing to be with him. And it was followed by an equally powerful terror.

I must be careful, she told herself desperately. *I think I could fall in love with anyone who got me out of this place, and I would never know if it was real.*

For the last few days the Dunwayan army had marched between the Hollow Mountains on the right and the sea on the left. The road had been all gentle curves, the weather had been mild and the smell of the sea gave the air a clean, fresh tang. The forest of Dunway gave way to rocky land covered in tussocky grasses and wind-twisted bushes and trees.

The thinner vegetation allowed frequent glimpses of white sand and blue water. Danjin felt a wistful disappointment every time he saw another seemingly idyllic stretch of beach. He could hardly stop to enjoy the beauty of the area; he was part of an army, and that army was hurrying to meet another.

Traders taking goods to Dunway occasionally used this road, but for most of the year the weather favoured ship transportation. I-Portak scanned the horizon from time to time, no doubt looking for his own people's warships. After several hundred years of peace in Northern Ithania, only the Dunwayans kept a fleet of warships and trained their warriors in the art of sea warfare. According to spies, the Pentadrians had their own small fleet and some skill in using it. During the previous war, Danjin had asked Lanren Songmaker, the White's war adviser, why the Pentadrians hadn't sailed into Jarime instead of invading through the mountains. The man had explained that sailing the long way around the west side of the continent would be slow due to unfavourable winds, and the east side was guarded by the Dunwayan warships. The Dunwayans would have relished the chance to practise their skills on an enemy.

Nothing prevented the Dunwayans sailing south, however. Not when Sennon was supporting the Circlians. The Dunwayan warships were to meet the rest of the army in Karienne, the Sennon capital, then defend ships supplying the army as they travelled south to the Isthmus of Grya.

But we have to get to Karienne first, Danjin thought. *Across the Sennon desert. Relying on Sennon help to supply us with enough water to keep an army from dying of thirst.*

The land was growing steadily drier. Thinking back, Danjin realised it had been at least a day since he'd seen a tree bigger than a man. The tussocks of grass were smaller and thinner. The soil was so dry and dusty it may as well have been sand. Looking past Ella and I-Portak, Danjin noted the water carriers striding up and down the column of warriors, filling cups from large skins whenever a fighter called for a drink. Their services would be in high demand over the next few weeks.

I-Portak straightened in his seat. Looking at Ella, Danjin saw her expression become intent. They were both gazing over his head. He felt the platten tilt and realised it had just topped a ridge and was descending steeply.

'The desert begins,' I-Portak murmured.

Danjin turned around, as did the other advisers. A pale, flat land lay before them, its surface disturbed by the ripples of dunes. At the base of the ridge the road continued on to the horizon, as straight as a Dunwayan spear. At the horizon wisps of sand or dust curled into the sky. A windstorm, perhaps. Danjin had heard about desert storms so ferocious the sand in them flayed the skin from travellers, or buried them alive.

'That is the army,' he heard Ella say. 'They have made good time.'

Danjin felt a surge of excitement and relief. No storm. Just the Circlians.

'We should reach them tonight,' I-Portak replied. 'Or sooner, if you wish.'

Turning back, Danjin was relieved to see Ella shake her head.

'Tonight will be sufficient. Let's not tax ourselves until we need to.' Her shoulders rose and fell, betraying a sigh. Danjin suppressed a smile.

This was proving to be a boring journey. Though Ella had spent a good deal of the trip to the Pentadrian village with her attention on the fleeing servant's mind, she had 'surfaced' often enough to make conversation – or to watch Danjin and Gillen play counters. Even Yem had been a more interesting companion than I-Portak and his advisers.

Ella's gaze shifted to his and he saw a small smile curve her mouth. She leaned forward.

'Have you packed that little travel set of counters, Danjin?'

He nodded.

'Let's have a game to pass the time, then.'

Surprised, he pulled his pack out from under his seat and drew out the game box. Opening the drawer, he began to take the pieces out and slot them into their holes. I-Portak watched with interest.

So it was with some embarrassment that Danjin found he couldn't get to the last piece. The drawer, as always, wouldn't open fully. The piece was somewhere at the back, but he couldn't tilt the box or shake it without dislodging the pieces already set up. Digging inside with a finger, he found that the piece had wedged itself between the back of the drawer and the inside of the box.

Sighing, he tipped the pieces into his lap and began to work on the one wedged in the drawer. When he closed the drawer and shook the box he could hear something rattling inside.

No, he thought suddenly. *There are two things inside.*

Opening the drawer again, he found that the game piece had moved to the front. He removed it, then reached inside again.

Something was still there. Something just a little too wide to allow the drawer to open. Something smooth.

Taking hold of it, he gently prised the top of the box upward. The object slipped through and the drawer fell out completely. Opening his hand, Danjin stared down at a white ring.

Ella leaned forward and took it from him. 'That's a priest's ring.'

'Yes,' Danjin agreed. 'But how did it come to be inside my counters game?'

She shrugged, then frowned. 'Unless . . .' Her eyes narrowed and she looked at him suspiciously. 'What happened to Auraya's link ring?'

Danjin felt a rush of realisation followed by guilt. He felt his face warning.

'I, ah, well . . .'

'You didn't return it, did you?'

He spread his hands. 'Nobody asked for it. I put it aside and forgot about it.'

'You put it in here?' She pointed to the game box.

'No.' He looked at the box and frowned. 'Someone must have. Someone who wanted me to find it, perhaps.'

She looked at the ring again. 'Someone who wanted you to be able to contact Auraya?'

'I can hardly use it for any other purpose.'

To his surprise, she handed it back to him. 'Put it on.'

'Now?'

'Yes. I want to see if it works.'

To speak to Auraya . . . he felt mingled eagerness and doubt. He looked up at Ella.

'What if she . . . ?' He caught himself and managed not to look at I-Portak.

'You're also wearing my ring,' she pointed out. 'I should hear everything she says to you.'

Taking a deep breath, he slid the ring onto a finger. Nothing happened. Ella frowned.

'Call her,' she suggested.

He pictured Auraya in his mind.

:*Auraya!*

Silence followed. He called again and again, wondering if she was ignoring him, was asleep or – and he started to grow alarmed at the thought – was dead.

'Danjin.'

He looked up. Ella was staring at him, an unreadable expression on her face.

'Give it to me.'

He took off the ring and dropped it into her outstretched hand. She smiled, then slipped the ring under her circ.

'I had better keep this for now,' she said.

'Do you think . . . ?'

:*I don't know what to think*, she told him. *I won't speculate until Juran examines it.*

Leaning forward, she looked meaningfully at the tile game.

'It's been a while, but I used to play a mean game of counters.'

He managed a smile, then held up the box and started arranging the pieces again.

CHAPTER 43

Diamyane was still the same dry and ugly place Emerahl remembered from her previous visit, on the way to the Red Caves. Panic had set in since the news of the advancing Circlian army had arrived. The previous day, Pentadrians had taken control of every ship in the area in order to prevent the Circlians using them. Now people were fleeing the city by any means – mostly on foot and carrying their possessions.

In their place came Dreamweavers. Today it seemed as if every third or fourth person she walked past was a Dreamweaver. *Little wonder they were called harbingers of war*, Emerahl thought. *It was said when a battle was imminent Dreamweavers and carrion birds were sure to appear. The former healed the wounded, the latter dealt with the dead.*

She had always kept away from battlefields in the past, until the previous battle between the Circlians and Pentadrians. Battles were dangerous places to be. Now she felt a strange reluctance to leave. Was it curiosity that tempted her to stay and witness the battle?

No, she decided. *It is more than that. It is this nagging thought that an opportunity might present itself for us immortals to use the information in the diamond. No matter how unlikely that is, if we're not here to take advantage of it we will wait a long time for another chance.*

Where the Circlians and Pentadrians clashed, and the White and Voices fought, the gods were sure to be. All ten of them. In one place. That didn't happen very often. In fact, it would probably *only* ever happen during a war.

We need six immortals. It all hinges on Auraya. If she were free, do I think she would help us kill them?

She shook her head. *No, but if Mirar believes there is a chance maybe we should be here in case he is right.*

She turned to regard her room. The furniture was old and there were few comforts, but it had a view of the main road into the town. The occupants had departed hastily, leaving most of their belongings behind. She felt only a little guilt at taking them as her own, since she had chased off looters every night. With the markets closed she had little choice but to start eating the small store of food. *I suppose I could buy supplies from the Dreamweavers, but they'll need all they have and what's here will spoil if someone doesn't eat it.*

Looking back out of the window, she watched another pair of Dreamweavers passing. Her mind returned to the problem of how to kill the gods.

Six attackers, she thought. *One above. One below. One on each side. How are we to do that?*

Unlike gods, immortals were subject to gravity. They could take positions on all sides, but that relied upon the gods being near the ground. The places above and below still presented a problem.

Except to Auraya, she reminded herself. *She can fly. The place above is obviously hers, if she decides to take it. So what of the one below?*

Gods, as non-physical beings, could pass through solid objects. Immortals obviously couldn't. Whoever took the place below would have to hope there was a handy cave or tunnel in the right position.

And where is the right position likely to be? She pursed her lips. *The White and the Voices will probably face each other before the battle and exchange the usual threats and bluster.* She smiled as she realised where this meeting would probably take place. *On the Isthmus.*

Thinking back to her last visit to Diamyane, she considered the tunnel she had passed through with the family travelling north to hear the Wise Man of Karienne preach. It had been controlled by thieves, but that could be remedied.

They might have fled, along with the locals. Or more likely they're looting houses, which is probably a more lucrative activity now. Her smile broadened as she recalled them fleeing from her magic as she melted the gate they had used to control travellers passing through the tunnel.

The only trouble with this tunnel was that it cut through the Isthmus, not along it. And it was positioned close to the Diamyane shore. That meant she and her fellow immortals had to hope the meeting would take place right on top of the tunnel, which was unlikely. More likely it would happen in the centre.

Then she remembered what the father of the family had told her. He said there had been several tunnels through the Isthmus in the past, but they had been filled in. Perhaps some could be opened again.

But which ones? Ah, it's all a nice daydream, she thought wryly. *And it'll probably stay that way.* Standing up, she moved to the bed and lay down. *I had better find out what Mirar is up to.*

Closing her eyes, she slowed her breathing and steered her mind toward sleep. When she reached the right state she called Mirar's name. There was no answer, so she stretched out to skim the minds around her. Most were predictably involved in thoughts relating to the coming conflict. She reached toward the wharves and found a few Pentadrian spies. Then she followed the few traders, travellers and Pentadrians allowed on the Isthmus. Searching along it, she found no thoughts of men or women beneath the land bridge.

:*Emerahl!*

She let her awareness of the minds outside fade.

:*Mirar. How are things in Glymma?*

:*The same. Where are you?*

:*Diamyane.*

:*When are you leaving?*

:*I . . . I don't know*, she admitted. *I'm beginning to think we all ought to be here, just in case. If no opportunity comes to kill the gods we lose nothing, but if one does and we aren't here . . .*

:*We'll curse ourselves*, he finished.

:*Yes.* She told him of her ideas about the positioning of the immortals around the gods, and the tunnel.

:*It's worth investigating. But you do realise that if we are to attack while the White and Pentadrians are meeting, those of us not underground will be in full view.*

:*Yes. If you agree to protect the Pentadrians, you'll be there anyway. As for the rest of us, we'll have to hope the gods' attention will be on the meeting. I could disguise myself . . . actually, there's an idea. Would you mind if I pretended to be a Dreamweaver?*

She felt his amusement.

:*Why ask me? You didn't last time.*

:*I didn't know you were around to ask*, she retorted.

:*Fair enough. You're welcome to join my people. Perhaps if I can find some excuse for Dreamweavers to follow the White out onto the Isthmus, you could go out with them.*

:*Then Surim and Tamun will have to approach from the sides. In boats.*

:*Yes. I just have to free Auraya.*

She caught a hint of desperation.

:*No ideas yet?*

:*I've skimmed the minds of several Servants, but all I've learned is that it would be impossible to sneak in and free her. My plan so far was to insist that I get to tell Auraya of the White's defeat. That will keep her alive until after the battle. I'll slip back to Glymma while the Pentadrians celebrate their victory and free her then.*

:*A bold plan. She'll hate you for helping kill the White.*

:*And blame herself for it, too. Still, I'd choose for her to live over the White any day. And I get the feeling she already blames the Circlian gods for her predicament. She seems to hate Huan, who she says arranged for the Siyee to be captured and is intent on killing her. Chaia has admitted he could free her only if the other gods would agree to it.*

:*So she'd kill Huan, but not the others. I don't see how we can arrange that.*

:*No. And we still need to free her before the battle if your plan is to work.*

:*Yes. Hmm. Something just occurred to me. We need Auraya for more than just to be our sixth immortal. She's the only one of us who can sense if the gods are actually where we need them to be.*

:*You really are taking this seriously, aren't you?*

:*Just trying to work out how to make it work in case the opportunity comes.*

:*Then you ought to test the theory first. I want to be sure if I can draw enough magic to create a void before I put myself near both the White and the Voices and try to kill their gods.*

:*Yes, it would be sensible to confirm that it works. One of us needs to attempt to make a void. One of The Twins, maybe, since using that much magic would attract more attention than you or I need.*

:*Yes. So go chat to them. I'll talk to Arleej. And see if I can find a way to free Auraya before the battle.*

She felt a pang of concern.

:*Be careful.*

:*I'm always careful. After all this time I've become rather fond of being alive.*

After his presence had faded, Emerahl turned her thoughts to The Twins.

:*Surim. Tamun.*

They responded with their usual promptness.

:*Greetings, Emerahl.*

:*I have a few idea and suggestions for you.*

:*Oh?*

:*How long would it take for you two, and The Gull, to get to Diamyane?*

:*Now, Emerahl*, Tamun said sternly. *You agreed with us. You didn't think Auraya would ever turn against the gods.*

:*I did. But if there's a chance she will, I think you should be here. Listen, I have been thinking . . .*

Since being doused with cold water, Auraya hadn't been able to stop shivering. She longed for a blanket, or just a tiny bit of magic with which to heat the air around her. Mischief had curled himself around her neck. His breath smelled bad and she didn't like to imagine what he had caught and eaten for it to be so foul. She was grateful for the little warmth he gave her, but he was too small to make much difference. Her chest hurt and her shoulder ached . . .

Think of something else, she told herself.

It was hard to think. She was tired and her mind seemed to work slower every day. But she had plenty of time. Puzzling over the 'secrets' Mirar had told her kept her occupied from time to time. These secrets had apparently been told by a goddess who had killed herself. How did a god commit suicide? She frowned, sure the answer was important. It might be a clue as to how the gods had killed each other.

'*Voids were created when a god was killed.*'

That was another clue. A void was a place lacking in magic. The gods were beings of magic, which was why they couldn't venture into a void. What would happen if they tried? Would they die? If so, then perhaps that was how this goddess had killed herself.

Could a god be forced into a void by other gods? Perhaps. But Mirar had said voids were created *when* a god was killed. That meant voids were made deliberately. Perhaps in order to kill.

So how was a void made? How did a god create a lack of magic? *Well, that is obvious. Draw away all the magic in one place.*

She blinked. Was it *really* that simple? Did a god draw all the magic away from where another was in order to kill him or her? What prevented the other god from doing the same in return? Why wouldn't they simply dodge?

She shook her head. These questions made her head spin. She let her thoughts drift for a while, too tired to bother skimming minds. Her senses had become dull and she hadn't the energy to concentrate.

Some time later she heard footsteps, but couldn't be bothered opening her eyes to see who approached. Only when Mischief uncurled from her neck, letting cold air chill her, did she rouse herself.

'Auraya.'

A glowing figure stood at the edge of the dais. Sheyr.

'Chaia?' she croaked, surprised.

'Yes. I have come to offer you an escape, Auraya.'

'The other gods finally agreed, did they?' Speaking brought the need to cough. She resisted it. 'How did you convince Huan?'

He smiled. 'I didn't. They don't know and wouldn't approve of what I am about to offer you.'

She straightened and felt a surge of hope. Would he defy the others for her sake? Then a fit of coughing took hold of her. When it had passed she felt dizzy and her lungs burned.

'So what's the offer?' she whispered.

'I can't free you,' he said. 'The others will not allow it. But they said nothing about teaching you. I could teach you something that would allow you to free yourself.'

She stared at him. He smiled.

'Go on. I'm listening.'

'It has been clear to me for some time that your Gifts surpass those of any sorcerer. You are immortal, but you are more powerful than immortals. You can read minds. You can sense the presence of gods. You can hear us speak to each other. It would take but a little instruction from me for you to join us.'

'Join . . . you?'

'Yes. To become a god yourself.'

He must be kidding me, she thought. *But why would he? It would be a poor joke. Maybe this is Sheyr. He's come to torment me.*

From somewhere at the back of her mind she heard Mirar's voice. *'All of the gods were born mortal, became immortals like us, then transformed themselves into gods.'*

A thrill of excitement rushed through her, painful in its intensity. *I could be a god!*

But Mirar's voice continued in her memory. *'The gods still feel human emotions and yet they can't perceive or affect the physical world except through mortals.'*

Well, there had to be a price, she thought. *And it's got to be better than being dead.*

'The gods don't take people's souls.'

She frowned and shook her head. The movement made her dizzy. She drew a deep breath to steady herself but only ended up coughing again. When she had her breath back she looked up at Chaia.

'Why?'

He smiled.

'I don't want to lose you, Auraya. You're sick. Your body will die if you do not have a chance to heal it. If you were a god, you would never be sick again. We could be together always.'

'But if I died we would be anyway. You will have my soul.'

His smile vanished. 'It would not be the same, Auraya. The dead cannot touch the living. I want you to rule the world by my side.'

'And Huan's?'

'Not if you do not wish it.'

'If we were enemies, it would hardly be good for mortals.'

'You would let her frighten you out of fulfilling your full potential?'

She looked away. 'No.'

He held out a hand. 'Will you join me, Auraya?'

She sagged against her chains. *I don't know if I want to become a god.* To be separated from the physical world. To only know it and other people through their minds . . . and the other immortals would be invisible to me. Would Mirar consider me his enemy? The implications piled upon one another, too many for her exhausted mind to think about.

'I don't know,' she said. 'I'm too tired to think about it. I need time to consider.'

Chaia nodded. 'Very well. I will tell you what you must do. You are sick, and I fear by the time I return it will be too late.'

Auraya nodded. She closed her eyes and concentrated all her strength on listening to Chaia describe what she must do to become a god.

CHAPTER 44

Mirar had pieced together the route to the underground cavern from the memories and thoughts of the Servants and domestics that guarded or attended to Auraya. There were three gates blocking the route, each guarded by two magically powerful Servants.

As he approached the first gate, the two Servants guarding it watched him warily. Mirar smiled at them.

'So this is where the famous Auraya is being held?' he asked casually.

The two men exchanged glances, then one looked at Mirar and nodded.

'Can I go in?' Mirar asked.

'Only in the company of a Voice,' the other said.

Mirar looked beyond the gate, then shrugged. 'Maybe another time, then.' Turning away, he walked back up the corridor.

He had expected nothing different. The Voices must have a reason to keep her alive, so they wouldn't want him killing her. Yet.

The Voices would hear of his visit to the gates. That was deliberate, too. He wanted them to know he was thinking about Auraya, and that she might feature in any deal he made with them.

Turning a corner, he stopped and blinked in surprise. Nekaun was strolling toward him.

News certainly travels fast in the Sanctuary. He must have concealed people watching all the corridors approaching the underground area.

'First Voice Nekaun,' Mirar said. 'What a coincidence. I was just wondering who I should ask to take me to see Auraya.'

Nekaun's eyebrows rose. 'You would like to speak to her?'

Mirar grimaced. 'No. I just want to see her. Our conversations were amusing when she was free, but now I fear there'd be no fun in crossing mental swords with her.'

Stepping past him, Nekaun looked back. 'Come on then. Let's enjoy the view instead.'

The two guards did not appear surprised when Mirar and Nekaun appeared. They held the gate open in readiness. Beyond, the walls were unplastered stone. Dust covered all surfaces.

'I get the feeling this place hasn't been used in a long time.'

Nekaun smiled. 'No. This is the old Shrine.'

'Shrine?'

'This hill has been a sacred place for thousands of years. The Sanctuary was built over the ruins of an ancient place of worship: the Shrine of Iedda.'

'Iedda? One of the dead gods?' Mirar asked in surprise. 'I'd have thought your gods would choose a new site. Somewhere that wasn't associated with old gods.'

'Why? The evil of the old gods died when they did.'

Mirar looked up at the ceiling and nodded. 'I suppose building over the Shrine is like replacing the old ways. If it still existed, even in ruins, memories would last longer.'

'It still exists,' Nekaun assured him. 'Come in here.'

They passed through another gate. The corridor descended further, then turned abruptly. Two Servants stood before the third gate. Beyond was a large hall. The first thing that attracted Mirar's attention was an enormous, oversized throne.

Then he saw the figure chained to the throne. Naked, streaked with grime, and thinner than he remembered, Auraya sagged against the base. He could see her brow was shiny with sweat, and he could hear the faint sound of laboured breathing.

She did not appear to be awake.

'What's keeping her there?' he forced himself to ask.

'She is in a void. Do you know what a void is?'

Mirar nodded. 'I've encountered them before.' He could not tear his eyes from Auraya, though he knew Nekaun was watching him closely.

'You pity her,' the Pentadrian leader said.

Mirar sighed and nodded. 'I pity anyone the gods – the Circle – use and manipulate. I can't help wondering what she might have become, if she hadn't been raised by their priests and taught to hate. It is an unfortunate habit of mine to pity my enemy.'

'Do you think you could undo the damage?'

'No.' Mirar shook his head. 'She would never give me the chance. At the first opportunity, she would kill me.'

Nekaun made a satisfied sound. 'She won't get that opportunity. But, of course, if the White are victorious it won't be Auraya you have to fear.'

Mirar turned to meet Nekaun's gaze. 'I can't fight for you,' he told the First Voice frankly. 'Nor can my people. It would break a thousand-year-old law.' He looked down. 'But I can use my powers in defence. I can protect you, your fellow Voices or your army. I have only one small favour to ask in return.'

Nekaun's eyes narrowed. 'And that is?'

Mirar turned to look at Auraya. 'I want to be the one who tells Auraya that the White have been defeated.'

The corners of Nekaun's mouth twitched upward. 'Ah.'

When he said nothing more, Mirar turned to regard him.

'Will you accept my offer, and terms?' Mirar paused and frowned. 'I guess you must consult the others.'

The First Voice glanced at Auraya, then shook his head. 'No need. We have discussed all options and possibilities. This one is acceptable.'

He held out his hand, palm upward and fingers splayed. Mirar paused, then did the same. Nekaun grasped his hand.

'A deal, then.'

Mirar nodded. 'A deal.'

Letting go of Mirar's hand, Nekaun turned away and started back along the corridor. Mirar looked at Auraya one last time, then followed.

'I should also add that, in my expert opinion, your prisoner looks to have a fever,' he said quietly. 'And I don't much like the sound of her breathing. I'd rather she was alive and well enough to comprehend the news that her world has ended, when the time comes.'

Nekaun glanced at him and nodded. 'It would be a shame if she missed the end of the story. I will get some of my healers to look her over.'

Mirar nodded. 'If you need Dreamweaver advice, I'm sure one of my people would agree to help.'

'Thank you. I'll keep that in mind, if my Servants find it beyond their abilities.'

There was something about Chaia's offer that didn't make sense, but Auraya couldn't gather the strength to think about it closely enough.

So much for taking time to consider. Why am I bothering anyway? I might not like the idea of having no physical body, of having to perceive the world through mortals, but that's got to be better than being dead.

Especially if Mirar was right, and the gods had been lying about taking people's souls. But Chaia had denied that, hadn't he? He had said something about the souls of the dead not being able to interact with the world of the living. A god could, so wasn't that the better choice?

She thought about that for a while, but her mind wandered. Then suddenly a shock of cold jolted her awake. Water. She began shivering again. A domestic moved close and lifted a bowl of slush to her mouth. She took a sip then began coughing and couldn't stop . . .

Something slapped against her face. She realised she had fainted. She struggled to wake up. *I must eat. Open my eyes* . . .

The face before her was unfamiliar. A man. Frowning. There were others. *Why are they here?* Then she saw Nekaun standing at the edge of the dais and suddenly she was more alert than she had been in days.

From the minds of the Servants around her she read that they had been ordered to heal her. She read their assessment of her state: her lungs were clogged with infection, her body was dehydrated and weakened by lack of good food. She also read their distaste at having to treat her. They'd rather let her die.

The cures they rubbed her chest and arms with smelled painfully familiar. At least they were using the right ones. They produced a large shirt. One of the Servants approached Nekaun, who dropped a small object into the man's hand. The Servant returned and moved to Auraya's left arm. She felt her heart skip as she felt the chain loosen – Nekaun had given the man the key to the locks. She stared at it and could see nothing else. This one small object kept her immobile. Such a simple thing. Anyone could use it. No magic involved . . .

Then her arm fell to her side and pain ripped through her shoulder, and she forgot all else.

The Servants massaged her arm and shoulder until the pain eased, then dropped the shirt over her head and pushed her arm through the sleeve. Her arm was stretched out to be chained again, then they released her right arm and manipulated her into that side of the shirt. The cloth was rough and didn't warm her hands or feet, but she could still relieve herself without soiling her 'clothes'.

The Servant returned the key to Nekaun, then helped the others give her more water and feed her plain bread. When they were done she leaned back against the throne, exhausted but free of hunger and thirst for the first time in weeks. Through half-closed eyes she watched Nekaun and the Servants leave.

Let me out of the void, she thought at them. *All I need to get well again is magic.* She closed her eyes. *Or to become a god.*

Then she frowned. *How can I become a god if I'm in a void? Gods are beings of magic. They can't exist in a void. As soon as I become a god I'll cease to exist.*

She shook her head. Chaia must intend to free her first. But that wasn't what he'd said. He'd said she could do it herself, while he was away.

Suddenly she felt a chill rush over her, colder than the water that had set her shivering before.

Unless this is a trick.

Was Chaia trying to get rid of her?

But he loves me.

There was no way she could become a god and survive.

A soft chirrup brought her attention to the throne seat. Mischief was staring toward the entrance.

'Bad man,' he said quietly.

'Yes,' she agreed. 'Gone now.'

Slowly possibilities entered her mind. If she truly had the ability to become a god he might be trying to prevent it by encouraging her to make the change in the one place where doing so would kill her, rather than risking that it would happen somewhere else.

If he wanted her dead, then something had happened to change his mind about her. Huan claimed she was dangerous. Had something happened to convince Chaia?

Suddenly she remembered Mirar telling her that the other Wilds had important secrets. Ones he did not trust her to know. She thought of his question: '*Is there a god you'd like to kill?*' She had assumed he was being flippant, but what if he hadn't been? What if the Wilds *could* kill a god?

Then he is the threat, not me. Chaia should know that I'd never . . . But then again, I would if it was a choice between me dying or Huan . . .

She grimaced. Obviously he didn't feel the same. Or he just couldn't trust her not to kill the rest of the gods. He couldn't see into her mind any more, and she had become, as he'd said, more powerful than an immortal.

He didn't trust her. He had tried to kill her. For a long time she stared at nothing, feeling only a terrible loss and betrayal. She was too tired for anger, too tired to make up excuses. All she had energy left for was acceptance. She drew in a deep breath and let it out slowly, letting the last shred of her loyalty to the gods slip away.

CHAPTER 45

*D*anjin.
:   The voice was dreamy and sad. Danjin slowly became aware that he was no longer asleep, yet not fully awake either.

:*Daaaaanjinnnnn.*

He knew the voice. As recognition came, he felt a mild surprise.

:*Auraya?*

:*Yes, it's me. How are you?*

:*Asleep.*

:*Not quite. We're dream linking again.*

:*Are we?* He felt alarm and his thoughts sharpened. *Where are you?*

:*Still locked up. I feel better. I was sick. I think I nearly died. Obviously that's not part of Nekaun's plans. He had them bring me clothes and better food.*

Clothes? Danjin felt a pang of horror and concern as he realised what that meant.

:*I bet you didn't expect to march into another war again so soon,* she said.

A tingle of warning ran down his spine. How did she know about the war? Had the Voices told her? Of course they had.

533

:No, he said warily.

:I've been watching the army, she told him. *Watching you all marching across the desert. Watching the Pentadrians preparing to meet you. I wish I had something I could tell you.*

:Tell me . . . ?

:A secret about the Pentadrians. Something vital to help you win the battle. But the White's spies and advisers already know everything.

:How did you . . . ?

:Mind-skimming, Danjin. There's nothing much else for me to do – except talk to Mischief, and you know what a great conversationalist he is. I wish I could talk to you more often. We all know the Voices will kill me before they set off to meet the White. It would be nice to have someone to talk to during my last days who didn't constantly demand scratches or shower me with bits of whatever he's managed to catch and eat.

Danjin felt as if he were choking. How could she speak so casually of her death? Maybe that was because she was making it all up?

No, he thought. *There's something else. She's making light of it, but really she's desperate.* He felt a wave of grief and pity. *She's alone. She knows she's doomed. How can the amazing woman I knew end like this? I suppose the only alternative is to die in some spectacular magical battle.*

:Danjin?

:I'm here.

:In case you think this is a dream, I'll tell you this. There's a messenger from the Sennon emperor about to enter the camp.

And then the sense of her presence vanished. Danjin opened his eyes, sat up and looked around. Grabbing his blanket to protect himself from the chill night air of the desert, he rose and left his tent.

The thought that Auraya was watching them was both disturbing and reassuring. He had to know if it were true, and the best way to do that was to go to the White's tent and see if a messenger from the emperor arrived.

Under the light of the moon the tents of the Circlian camp looked like a great ghost army of myth. They spread in all directions, lit by lamps from within or fires from without. The army was no larger than the one that had met and defeated the Pentadrians a few years before – in fact it was smaller – but from where he stood it appeared to have no end.

The stretch of desert the army had settled onto for the night was relatively flat. With no features like rivers or hills to consider, the tents, supply carts and platten had been set down in a circular pattern: a wheel in which the White and leaders of their allies gathered at the hub and the gaps between the armies of each land formed spokes. Danjin didn't know if there was any tactical advantage in this. Perhaps only in that many would feel reassured by such a powerful use of the symbol of the gods.

Reaching the war-council tent, he asked the guard to request permission to enter.

Do we need reassuring? Danjin asked himself. *We won last time. But having gods on one's side does not make victory sure. The Pentadrians are proof of that. The Pentadrians know us better now. They won't make the same mistakes.*

'Here's my ever-doubtful Danjin,' a familiar voice said from inside.

The flap of the tent opened and Ella beckoned him in. He saw that Juran and Dyara were standing beside a table covered in a map Danjin recognised from the last war. Mairae and Rian were absent.

The Circlian leader met Danjin's eyes and nodded. Danjin made the sign of the circle.

'Now, Danjin. Why can't you stop worrying?' Ella asked.

'Somebody has to,' he replied. 'Consider me your personal worrier.'

Her eyebrows rose and she glanced at Juran, who returned her look with a half-smile.

'Did I say something wrong?' Danjin asked.

Ella laughed. 'No. Juran was saying something similar just a moment ago. He says you are my conscience and common sense.'

'Am I?' Danjin looked at Juran. He couldn't help wondering if that meant Juran thought Ella had too little conscience and common sense.

Juran chuckled. 'You do not blindly trust that events will turn out as the gods would have them,' he said. 'Ella cannot comprehend anything but victory.'

'Why send us to Southern Ithania if they can't ensure victory?' she asked.

'There is always the risk of failure,' Juran replied. 'Even if it is a small one.'

'Why do we bring an army with us if the gods' power, channelled through the White, is all that is needed?' Danjin asked.

Ella shook her head. 'We all know the army is only needed in order to control the land one takes. The real fight is magical. Magic is the province of the gods, so victory is sure.'

'Unless the Pentadrian gods are stronger,' Juran pointed out.

'If that were so, the Circle would not send us to war.'

Juran smiled and waved a hand in her direction. 'Enough of that. Danjin came here to discuss other matters.' Danjin felt his heart skip as the Circlian leader looked at him earnestly. 'I see you have spoken to Auraya again.'

Danjin nodded, then related what he could remember. When he had finished, the White silently exchanged glances, communicating in their unique way.

'She is alive; she has been sick but is better,' Dyara summed up. 'Can she really see us?'

Juran shrugged. 'We can only wait and see if this messenger

536

turns up.' He turned to Danjin. 'Ella has told me you found the link ring Auraya made for you among your possessions. Do you know why it was there?'

Danjin felt his face warm. 'I am not sure . . . but I have a suspicion my wife may have put it there.'

'Why would she hide it?'

'Oh, she wouldn't have meant to hide it,' Danjin explained hastily. 'When she packs for me she often puts things in odd places in order to fit more into my trunk. She probably intended for me to find the ring when I opened the game, and didn't realise it would get stuck in the drawer.'

Juran nodded. 'So why pack it at all?'

'A precaution, I suppose. I've found a lot of strange items in my trunk over the years, and when I ask her about them she usually says she put them there "just in case".'

'Just in case of what?' Juran said thoughtfully. He said it as if he were wondering aloud, not expecting an answer. Danjin shrugged. The Circlian leader took something from within his robe. A white ring. Danjin guessed it was the ring in question.

Juran held it out to him. 'Put it on.'

'But . . .' Ella stared at Juran, who returned her look with an unreadable expression. She bit her lip and watched as Danjin took the ring.

The small signs of concern her face betrayed negated any eagerness Danjin had felt at the chance to communicate with Auraya. He considered asking if using the ring was dangerous. But so what if it was? Juran had ordered him to, anyway, and he would not refuse.

'What should I say?' he asked.

Ella shrugged. 'Tell her we are relieved that she is alive.'

He nodded. Taking a deep breath, he slipped the ring onto his finger and closed his eyes.

:Auraya?

No answer came. He called several times more, then looked at the Voices and shrugged.

'Perhaps it isn't working any more.'

'Take off the ring, Danjin,' Ella said.

Juran held out his hand. Danjin removed the ring and handed it over. The three White were frowning.

'That's not it, is it?' he asked tentatively.

Juran looked at him thoughtfully. 'The ring may not be enabling us to speak with Auraya, but it has not lost another quality. While you wore it I could not read your mind. Ella could, as you are wearing her link ring, so I had to watch through her mind.'

'Is it the same ring, then?'

'Yes, it definitely is. We knew about the flaw, but had no time to make another at the time, as Auraya had to leave for Si.'

Juran regarded the ring speculatively, then looked at Ella. 'This could be to our advantage. So long as Danjin wears this ring, his mind will be hidden to all but us.'

'And Auraya,' she pointed out.

His lips thinned. 'I wish I knew she could be trusted.' Curling his fingers around the ring, he let his hand fall to his side.

The entrance to the tent opened and a guard stepped inside and made the sign of the circle. 'A messenger from the Sennon emperor requests an audience with the White.'

Juran looked at Danjin, but his smile was forced. 'Thank you for alerting us to this, Danjin. You had best get some sleep.'

As Danjin moved toward the tent flap Ella touched his arm gently. 'She is alive, at least,' she said quietly.

He sighed. 'Yes, but for how long?'

'That is in the hands of the gods,' she said.

Nodding, he stepped out into the desert night and headed for his tent.

The Gull felt the power of the wave gather behind him. As it reached him he stretched out and rode it forward. The rock wall of the stack rushed toward him. He twisted at the last moment, his body moving automatically to lessen the impact, his fingers catching familiar cracks and protrusions. As the wave retreated he began climbing.

He had done this so many times he didn't need to think about where the next handhold was. Reaching the cave, he hauled himself inside and stood up.

Looking back out, he regarded the dark waves that surged around the stack. He could see no sign of the shipwreck. Even had it been a bright, clear day he wouldn't have been able to see that far. But he stilled his mind and reached outward.

Silence.

The Gull shook his head and sighed. They had probably all drowned. The irony was, he had intended to sink the raider ship himself, but at the right time. Once he'd had time to get to know the crew, to sort the ill-fated from the ill-natured.

He hadn't had time. If he hadn't been asleep he might have sensed the approach of the Elai and been able to warn or help those of the crew who were worth saving. But he needed to sleep, just as any mortal did.

Yet he didn't waste effort in annoyance at the Elai. Their attacks on the raider ships were justified after all they had suffered. He did worry where their newfound confidence and taste for killing would take them, but he wouldn't try to steer it. Though he and the Elai were both famous for their relationship to the sea, they had no other connection. For millennia he had been a legendary figure of the folklore of landwalkers, whom the Elai hated. The Elai were a young race created by a goddess who hated immortals.

Huan, he thought darkly. He frowned as he remembered the strange distorted creatures, dead or barely alive, that he had chanced upon long ago. They kept appearing, for over a century. Only when the early ancestors of the Elai appeared toward the end of that century had he found an answer to the mystery. The twisted creatures had been the experiments and failures of the sorcerers fulfilling Huan's great ambition to create a people adapted to living in the sea. She and her followers didn't suffer as the animals and people did. *At least the people chose their fate, though I'm sure they didn't expect to be cast out to sea or left to die when the work failed.*

Eventually Huan had succeeded. Out of a goddess's vision and mortals' willingness to do her bidding had come two miraculous peoples, the Elai and the Siyee. Out of cruelty had come beauty. This was the way of the ocean, too. Sometimes the most beautiful creatures were the most deadly. Starfan fish were brightly coloured, but so venomous one prick of their spines could kill in a few breaths. The doi was a playful, intelligent creature, loyal and affectionate. Sailors believed that doi swimming in the prow wave of their ship was a sign of good luck. But The Gull had seen doi treat their own kind with a cruelty he had otherwise only observed in humans.

He shrugged. The gods had once been mortals. They were driven by the same emotions and needs. Therefore it was no surprise they could be as cruel as humans. The trouble was, while the occasional human was inclined to behave badly, all of the gods had dealt cruelly with humanity at some point.

No, not all, he corrected. *The old gods weren't all bad. Is it so strange that those remaining are cruel? They were the ones willing to murder the rest.*

His mind was beginning to wander in old and familiar

circles. He didn't mind that, but he had agreed to contact The Twins tonight. Moving to the back of the cave, he lay down on some old blankets. He closed his eyes and sent out a mental call.

:*Gull*, Tamun answered. *You're late.*

:*Ignore her*, Surim added. *She's grumpy.*

:*Oh? Why is that?*

:*Everything is happening too fast. It scares her.*

:*I am not scared!* Tamun protested.

:*Not a bit*, Surim agreed unconvincingly.

:*What is happening too fast?* The Gull asked.

:*Emerahl wants us to go to Diamyane*, Surim explained. *And you, too.*

:*She wants to attempt to kill the gods?*

:*Only if an opportunity arises. She has rightly pointed out that it would be a shame if one does and we are not there to take advantage of it.*

:*That is true.*

:*Are you willing to go to Diamyane, hang about in the middle of a battlefield with all the risks of being discovered that it entails, just in case Auraya somehow manages to escape and decides to help us kill her precious gods?*

The Gull considered. He could see the advantages of being in the place where the White and the Voices clashed. The gods were sure to be present. They might be able to kill several at once.

Yet he could also see that the chances that everything would fall into place were slim.

But if there was even a slim chance . . .

:*Yes*, he said. *If I remain hidden in the water, discovery is unlikely.*

Tamun cursed.

:*Sorry, sister*, Surim said. *Emerahl wins this time. We had better start packing.*

:And I have a long way to travel, The Gull added.

:Will you make it in time?

:Yes, if I leave tonight.

:Then travel well. We will speak to you again tomorrow night, Surim finished.

Opening his eyes, The Gull stared up at the roof of the cave. He rose and moved to the cave entrance. Closing his eyes again he sent out his mind, seeking a familiar pattern of thought.

It did not take him long to find it. Slow, male and calm, the mind roused at his familiar presence. He posed a query; it answered with an affirmative.

Pleased, The Gull waited.

Some time later he felt the same mind's anticipation of arrival. Looking down, he saw the great head of the roale, as large as a fishing boat, surge up out of the water, turn and crash down again. One eye glinted in the starlight.

:Thank you, he said to it. *We will swim south together, where the water is warm and full of fish.*

:Yes, the roale replied. *Food.*

Stretching out his arms, The Gull leapt from the stack and dived into the sea.

Every time the Voices gathered without Nekaun present Reivan felt uneasy, yet she no longer felt comfortable in his presence either.

The other Voices weren't conspiring against him, yet in his absence they were more likely to voice their opinions. It didn't help that they often discussed ways to lessen the impact of his mistakes, or verged on complaining about his methods.

Today they were discussing the Sanctuary's remaining honoured guest, the Dreamweaver Mirar. Though Reivan had seen him several times now, she found it hard to believe this

542

man was over a thousand years old. It wasn't that he looked no older than thirty – Imenja was far older than she appeared as well, but she had a bearing that suggested the confidence and wisdom of an older woman. Mirar lacked the aura of power Reivan had expected. He seemed too humble to be a great sorcerer of legend and the founder of a cult as old as the Dreamweavers.

The Voices were concerned with more important matters.

'So can Mirar read minds or can't he?' Shar asked.

'He can't,' Genza replied.

'But your test worked. He reacted.'

'He sensed a threat to himself, but not its nature,' Genza explained. 'If he had known what the threat was he would never have stepped into the alcove. That indicates he has an ability to sense the mood of those around him, not read minds.'

'If I'd been observing people for a thousand or so years I would be able to sense moods too,' Vervel said. 'Is it a magical ability or good observation?'

'The assassin was out of sight,' Genza reminded him. 'This isn't observation, it's a Skill.'

'There is one final test I'd like to make,' Imenja said. The others turned to regard her. 'A test that would surely betray his ability.'

'What is that?'

'Allow our Companions to know the true nature of the relationship between Mirar and Auraya.'

The other three Voices exchanged glances.

'If he can read minds, he will know we know,' Vervel pointed out.

'Yes. But he will also read that it only improves his position. That we have something to offer in exchange for his help in the battle. So long as he knows we are willing to make that offer, we will have his cooperation.'

'But we may lose it if Auraya dies,' Genza added.

'Most likely,' Imenja agreed. The Voices exchanged long looks, then she nodded. As she spoke her gaze moved from one Companion to the next.

'The gods have told us Mirar and Auraya were once lovers. It is more likely that he wishes to rescue her than kill her.'

Lovers? Reivan straightened in surprise. *Surely not!*

'She worships the gods who want him dead!' Vervel's Companion, Karkel, protested.

Reivan remembered something else. 'Mirar said Auraya tried to kill him. Was that a lie?'

'Probably,' Shar replied.

'Does this mean he is a spy for the White?' Vilvan, Genza's Companion, asked.

'The gods did not say so.' Imenja spread her hands. 'They just warned that he would try to rescue her.'

'By asking if he can deliver the news of the White's defeat to her, he ensures she lives a little longer,' Genza said.

'By suggesting we'll give her to him, we ensure he does help us during the battle,' Shar added.

Genza frowned. 'We're not actually going to give him Auraya in exchange for his help, are we?'

Imenja sighed. 'If we want to stay on good terms with Mirar, we must consider it. I don't like the idea, but once the White are gone Auraya would be of little threat to us. Nekaun does not agree. He'll keep her alive only so long as Mirar is useful.'

Vervel chuckled. 'I feel a bit sorry for Mirar. He seems a good man.'

'If Mirar is a good man, he will not want to endanger his people through his actions,' Shar added darkly.

Vervel grimaced. 'If he still loves Auraya, incredible as that may be, he has a difficult choice ahead of him. He may have to choose between his lover and his people. Now I feel even more sorry for him.'

Shar snorted. 'I can't feel sorry for anyone who has such bad taste in women,' he muttered.

Imenja's lips twitched into a smile, then her expression grew serious. 'I don't think we should force such a choice on Mirar. Dreamweavers are a people of great usefulness who are of little threat to us. We should not risk spoiling our friendship with them because of a personal dislike of Auraya or our desire for revenge. Then we would be no better than the Circlians.'

'I agree with you,' Vervel said. 'This may be why the gods want her alive.'

'For now. If Auraya proves a nuisance, we can get rid of her later. And she is, after all, only mortal,' Shar said.

'But what of Nekaun?' Genza asked. 'We all know how much he wants to kill her.'

Imenja paused, then lifted her head and looked at each of them in turn. 'If we are in agreement on this, we can persuade him otherwise.'

The room fell silent. Reivan's heart was racing. Imenja was suggesting they unite against Nekaun. Until now the others had never been willing to stand against the First Voice.

'I will at least try,' Vervel said.

'And I,' Genza added.

Shar shrugged. 'He would not defy the gods, but if he tries, I will give you my support.'

Silence followed. Imenja bowed her head.

'Thank you.' She drew in a deep breath, then stood up. 'Reivan and I will now test whether Mirar can read minds. If not, I should still be able to ensure Mirar doesn't attempt to rescue Auraya and spoil our plans.'

'How will you do that?' Genza asked.

Imenja smiled. 'I will merely let him know that if he helps

us win this war, we will give him Auraya to do with as he wishes afterward.'

Shar chuckled. 'He'll think we're playing right into his hands. Unless, of course, he can read minds.'

'I guess we're about to find out,' Genza concluded.

CHAPTER 46

As Auraya woke she recalled where she was, and groaned. The trouble with regaining some strength was that she was able to feel and think with more energy. Mostly she felt boredom and frustration. She had returned to her mind-skimming, but it seemed the only subject on the minds of people outside the hall was war.

War, war, war, she thought. *I can't blame them for being so caught up in it, but I so wish they could think about something else or at least get it over with. This waiting is unbearable.*

Yet every moment brought her death closer. Was she so keen to die?

It would be much more comfortable than this, she thought wryly. *And perhaps then Mischief would leave me and find his way to a safe place.* She felt a pang of anxiety. He hadn't appeared since Nekaun's last visit, when the Servants had first treated her with their cures. Reaching out with her mind, she called his name.

:*Mischief?*

A familiar mind touched her own, sending a formless re-assurance, and she sighed with relief. Wherever he was, he was not frightened or hurt.

:*Mischief doing what?*

:Hunting, he told her.

She smiled. He had become proficient at it, dragging birds and small creatures down into the hall. Sometimes he offered them to her, but even if she could have brought herself to eat them it would be almost impossible to do so without her hands. She might have managed to swallow the smaller of them whole, but the thought made her stomach turn.

Satisfied that the veez was well, she closed her eyes and sent her mind out. First she searched the minds in the Sanctuary for signs of Mirar. She saw news spreading among the domestics awake at this early hour. Mirar had agreed to join the Voices in the battle. He would lend his strength to their defence, but as Dreamweavers abhorred violence he would not join any attack on the enemy.

How clever of you, Mirar, she thought.

:Auraya?

Surprised, she slipped into a dream link.

:Mirar? Did you hear me thinking?

:No. What were you thinking about?

:You.

:Really? I hope they were good thoughts.

:I just heard the latest gossip. The legendary Mirar has agreed to help the Voices, but only in defence.

:Ah. Yes. A compromise. I'm . . . sorry. If I could do this without harming your former colleagues I would.

She paused as she realised what he was referring to. If he helped the Voices, the White would probably be defeated. Juran, Dyara, Mairae and Rian would die – and the new White, Ellareen.

I can't blame him for deciding to take this path, she thought. *He must stay on good terms with the Voices for the sake of his people. And if the White win, Dreamweavers in Southern Ithania will be treated as they are in the north. Even though the situation is improving* in the north, it will take years for people to come close to respecting Dreamweavers like the Pentadrians do. And they may never do so.

Yet she did not want the White to die. Or for Northern Ithania to be taken over by the Pentadrians. The thought of Nekaun ruling the north made her feel nauseous.

:We are leaving Glymma today, Mirar told her. *It will take less than a day to reach the Isthmus. Last night Second Voice Imenja promised me that they would give you to me in exchange for my help, after the battle. I have no idea how long this battle will last. The Isthmus will lessen the numbers of soldiers that can face each other at once. The Dunwayan fleet and Pentadrian warships don't have that problem, of course, so maybe it will be a sea battle. Then there's the White and the Voices. Will they fight at the same time on the ships or Isthmus, or wait until later?*

:If the Voices have the magical advantage, they will force the White to fight them from the start, Auraya said. *Fewer of their own people will die.*

:True.

:If your help brings about a quick conclusion, at least you will be saving mortal lives.

:I hope so. He hesitated. *I have sent out a message to my own people subtly suggesting they use their magic in defence of whichever side they wish to support, Pentadrian or Circlian.*

:How will the Voices react to this? They will suspect you ordered it!

:I will point out that while I can't give them orders, I also can't prevent my people emulating me. I could hardly forbid them to do something I am doing. And the advantage is still the Voices' because I and the Dreamweavers here are stronger than those of my people defending the Circlians.

:You are too clever for your own good, she told him.

:Am I? You must tell Emer— . . . wait. Someone is knocking on my door. I must go.

:*Good luck.*

:*You too.*

Then he was gone. Auraya stared at the floor and felt her heart twist.

I hope he knows what he's doing. If he dies . . . She swallowed hard. *I think I'd actually regret it. And not just because the last of Leiard dies with him. Or that I'll probably die, too. I think I'd actually regret knowing Mirar the Wild no longer existed.*

The wide Parade outside the Sanctuary was well-suited for assembling an army. Thousands filled the space. Servants dressed in black robes stood in neat, disciplined rows on one side, soldiers in black uniforms with shining armour stood in rigid formation on the other. Highly decorated litters for the Voices and their Companions and advisers waited before the stairs. Larger four-wheeled tarns laden with supplies were lined up at the distant rear of the assembly.

It was an impressive sight. If Mirar hadn't seen entire armies perish before handfuls of sorcerers, he would have thought the Pentadrians sure of victory.

If it weren't for a handful of sorcerers, urged on by their gods, would these people even be here? he asked himself. It was an impossible question to answer. The world had never been free of gods, so who could guess how mortals would behave without them? He had seen wars waged for reasons as flimsy as revenge for an insult, or simple greed. Mortals did not need gods to order them to kill each other. They were quite capable of finding reasons to do so themselves.

First Voice Nekaun stepped forward to address the crowd. Mirar stopped listening after a few sentences. He had heard it all before.

'What are you thinking about?' a voice said softly at his shoulder.

He turned to find the Second Voice regarding him.

'The futility of war,' he replied.

Imenja smiled. He found her likeable, but she had lived long enough to have refined her skill at putting others at their ease so well it was undetectable.

'You think this war is futile?' she asked.

He shrugged. 'Even if you kill the White and defeat the Circlians, the Circle of Gods will still exist.'

She nodded. 'That is true. What comes after this confrontation will be as important as the battle itself. We hope that, in time, the people of the north will see our ways are better and kinder, and will embrace the Five. There will always be those who continue to worship the Circle, but the Circle's power over Northern Ithania will be diminished.'

'So not entirely futile, in your view,' he finished.

She smiled again. 'No. But I would understand if you wished we could kill the Circlian gods as well. It would make the world much safer for you. What are you smiling at?'

Mirar chuckled. 'Just the thought of you killing the Circlian gods for me.' *And that if we immortals allowed the Voices and the White to 'discover' how to do it, we might only have to sit back and watch them both rid the world of our problems.*

Which might not be a bad fallback plan if no opportunity to free Auraya came, or she refused to help. He had not been able to find a way to free Auraya except forcing his way into her prison himself, which would certainly spoil the goodwill between the Voices and himself, and perhaps for his people too. The best option for Dreamweavers was to hope Imenja kept her promise.

However, if the Voices won the battle there might be no White left to attack the Pentadrian gods. Still, the Voices could kill the Circlian ones, and that might be all the Wilds needed. The Pentadrians ones didn't seem too bad so far.

Nekaun fell silent and the crowd cheered. Making an expansive gesture, he indicated that Imenja and the other Voices should follow him down to the litters. Imenja's smile altered slightly, and Mirar was sure it was now forced.

As the Voices descended he followed a few steps behind, among the Companions and advisers. A few steps from the vehicles Genza glanced back at him, her eyes narrow and thoughtful.

'Would you mind if the Dreamweaver travelled with me, First Voice?' she asked. 'You know I find long journeys tedious.'

Nekaun paused to regard her, his eyebrows high. 'It's hardly a long journey,' he said. Turning to Mirar, he smiled politely. 'Dreamweaver Mirar, would you honour me with your company as we set out?'

'The honour is mine,' Mirar replied smoothly.

Genza shrugged. 'Perhaps later, when all the talk of violence and strategy begins to bore him.'

They settled onto the litters, which were each lifted by several muscular slaves dressed in finery. The army could see their leaders clearly. *And me*, Mirar thought grimly. He had explored the dreams of Dreamweavers last night. Their reaction to his deal with the Voices was mixed. Some disliked it, some did not. All but a few believed he had been forced to make the deal, probably by circumstances, perhaps by a more direct threat.

'Don't let Genza make you feel . . . obligated,' Nekaun said to him as the litter moved forward.

'I won't,' Mirar replied, smiling. Genza had stopped flirting with him when they'd arrived at the Sanctuary; Nekaun must not know that.

'I feel I should warn you. She can be persistent. The more you resist her, the more interesting she will find you.'

'I know the type,' Mirar assured him dryly.

Nekaun chuckled. 'I'm sure you do. You would also know that she would leave you alone once her curiosity was satisfied. She only wishes to see if your reputation is deserved, as I'm sure many women do.'

'I am not a slave to my reputation,' Mirar replied.

'No, you are not. I respect that.' Nekaun's eyes glittered with satisfaction. 'You are a man who knows when to be flexible, and when to be unbending.'

Mirar stopped himself from grimacing at this reference to his agreement to help the Voices. He smiled slyly. 'I thought it was only women who spread such rumours about me.'

As the litter began to move between the columns of Servants and soldiers, the Parade echoed with Nekaun's laughter. Looking up at the prow of the boat, Tamun smiled. Her brother stood straight-shouldered, his hair whipping in the wind. The boat was speeding through the water, propelled by magic, guided by his will. Water sprayed out from either side of the prow and the hull shuddered every time it struck a wave.

She noted the muscles in his arms, earned by many hours of rowing and poling through the swamp. He had grown more masculine since they had taken up residence there. Her sister had become quite a handsome brother. Why hadn't she noticed that before?

Perhaps she spent so much time with him that she never stepped back and *looked* at him. But the changes were not only physical. And Surim had changed himself slowly to give her time to get used to it. He had become more adventurous, too.

I guess he couldn't before, she thought. They had been connected physically as well as mentally. She ran a hand over the scar on her side. As always, the memory of their separation brought pain and sadness, but it had been a relief as well. *More for him than me*, she admitted. *We may be twins, but we are different in many ways. I sit in our cave and resent him for leaving me alone, afraid that if anyone sees me the gods will find me. He explores the swamp, and mingles with the people there sure that the change prevents the gods from recognising him.*

And now she was far from the Red Caves, far from the swamp, speeding across the water to the very place where thousands of mortals, and perhaps a few immortals, would see her – and the gods were sure to gather. She shivered. It was madness. But it was also inarguably sensible. If they were ever going to kill the gods, they had to be close to them.

That the opportunity would arise in the next few days was doubtful. If she thought about that too much she felt unpleasantly giddy. Closing her eyes, she stretched out in search of other minds.

She found some fishermen first. They were returning late from their morning's work. Next she encountered the crew of a trader ship heading south to supply Diamyane. Several Sennon fighters and a Circlian priest were aboard and Dunwayan warships sailed close by. They were anticipating attempts by Pentadrians to stop supplies reaching the Circlian army.

Moving further away, she was drawn to the hum of many minds. The Circlian army now marched along the coast. They knew they were a day's journey from Diamyane. The more experienced priests, priestesses and soldiers looked ahead to the battle with both dread and determination.

Another shift brought her to their destination. Diamyane was populated by scavengers, Dreamweavers and Sennon troops sent ahead to prepare for the army's arrival. She sought the minds of the Dreamweavers, then searched for Emerahl in their thoughts. Or the woman Emerahl was pretending to be.

There she is.

Tamun smiled at the thoughts of the woman regarding the red-haired stranger. Arleej, official leader of the Dreamweavers, was not sure what to make of Emmea. Mirar had told her to include Emmea in all discussions and plans. The woman was likeable enough, if a bit impatient at times.

Arleej was relating to Emerahl what had happened when she told Juran of the White of Mirar's decision that he and all Dreamweavers could use their Gifts to protect whichever side they chose.

'He turned white,' Arleej said.

Emerahl chuckled. 'What did he say?'

'He accepted our offer of help. I suspect he wanted to refuse. He must have suspicions of treachery, but since the Circlians are weaker already with Mirar joining their enemy, he has to take that risk.'

'You aren't tempted to turn on the Circlians, are you?'

'No, of course not.' Arleej was amused by the question. 'Juran also agreed with my suggestion that some of us follow behind the White when they walk down the Isthmus to meet the Voices, as Mirar is sure to be with the enemy.'

'I'd like to be a part of that group,' Emerahl said. 'Mirar sent me to you because I am strong, and I can help redress the balance of power he's been forced to upset.'

Arleej considered, then nodded. 'You're welcome.'

The conversation turned to practical matters and Tamun wouldn't be able to dream link with Emerahl until the woman was asleep, so she moved southwards to another mass of minds. The Pentadrian army marched toward the Isthmus. They were half a day from the beginning of the land bridge, but didn't intend to cross it. It took her longer to find Mirar, as there was only one unshielded mind in his proximity. The woman's name was Reivan, and her role was as a Companion to the Second Voice, Imenja.

Reivan regarded Mirar with wary respect. She liked his ideals and dislike of violence, but didn't think they were practical.

Knowing she was in the presence of a man over a thousand years old had her more than a little awed. When she regarded the Pentadrian leader her mind filled with conflicting emotions and thoughts: the lingering remains of infatuation, worry, anger and a slowly but steadily growing hatred.

:Tamun? Surim?

Tamun recognised The Gull's mental voice. Drawing reluctantly away from the Companion, she focused on her fellow immortal.

:Greetings, Gull. Where are you?

:Nearing the Gulf of Sorrow. I shall reach the Isthmus tonight.

:Do you know of the tunnels Emerahl described?

:Yes. I used them often when they were open.

:We just have to hope there's one underneath the place the White meet the Voices.

:I have thought of a solution to this problem. If I were to collapse a small section of the Isthmus, they would be forced to stand on either side in order to face each other.

:Ah. Doubts crept in as she considered this. *But they will wonder who collapsed it and why. It might make the gods suspicious.*

:It might, he conceded. *I could make it look like a natural occurrence.*

:But it would still seem too much of a coincidence.

:Then I can think of only one other solution.

:Oh?

:I will have to carve out a tunnel along the centre of the Isthmus, underneath the road.

:That will take time.

:A day or so. I will begin at the centre, where the White and Voices are most likely to meet. There is only one drawback.

:What is that?

:It may cause the Isthmus to collapse anyway. Hopefully in a few years' time, not while I am inside it.

:Then you should be careful, Gull. We will find you if it does. We will dig you out, if we must.

:Then I had best seek lessons on surviving burial from Mirar, he said wryly. *I had better go. The roale will forget he is carrying me if I don't remind him from time to time. I won't arrive by tonight if he decides to dive.*

As his mind faded from hers, Tamun took a few deep breaths. What they were doing was dangerous in more ways than one. It might not even work. But she would try again and again if it meant freedom from the gods.

Some risks were worth taking.

CHAPTER 47

The sun had slipped beneath the horizon a short time ago, sinking with steady purpose as if it patiently went through its paces knowing that tomorrow's battle would come in good time. A glow filled the western sky, in parts strangely coloured. As Reivan walked toward it she wondered if a Thinker somewhere knew why the sky at these times could be such improbable colours like green and purple.

Then she reached Imenja and stopped. The Second Voice was staring at the Isthmus, which was bathed in the eerie light of the glowing sky. It stretched away into the gloom toward a barely visible shadow.

Sennon. Northern Ithania.

'They haven't arrived yet,' Imenja told her.

'Will we cross and take Diamyane?' Reivan asked. The possibility had been discussed in several meetings.

'No. Our advantage lies in remaining here. The Circlians can cross only a few at a time, so we can pick them off easily.'

'And if the White come at the front of the army?'

'Then we Voices will fight them.'

'Making the soldiers unnecessary,' Reivan observed.

Imenja smiled crookedly. 'Yes. Which is not a bad thing. War is not kind to unSkilled mortals.'

Reivan shivered. She was an unSkilled mortal. Imenja turned and placed a hand on Reivan's shoulder.

'Don't worry. You will be protected.'

'I know.' Reivan nodded, then sighed. 'But I will also be useless.'

The glowing sky had dimmed and Imenja's face was in shadow. Reivan could not see her expression.

'Not to me,' Imenja said, squeezing Reivan's shoulder. She looked back. 'The tent is up. We should join the others.'

They walked back into the camp. What had been a dry, dusty stretch of land was now covered in black pointed shapes, fires flickering like orange stars scattered between. Reivan had regarded the tents in dismay when she first saw them being erected. The five-sided design was an unnecessary complication that some of the domestics were finding hard to work out and the black cloth would trap the heat of the sun. Sometimes she wondered if the Pentadrians took their symbolism too far.

When the sun rose the army wouldn't be huddling in their overheated tents. They would be spilling blood. Or watching sorcerers throw deadly magic about and hoping they wouldn't happen to be in the wrong place when it went astray. She thought about what Imenja had said. A fight between only Voices and White sounded too good to be true. But the Servants and priests would not remain out of the battle. They would assist their side with extra magic. Once the Voices defeated the White, or, gods help them, the White defeated the Voices, there would be no point in the Servants or priests continuing the fight. But they might anyway. Just out of loyalty to their gods.

And what then? Reivan asked herself. *Once one side is defeated, what will happen to the armies?*

She doubted that the Voices would just let the Circlians go home, as the White had done with the Pentadrians after the last battle. She also knew that this would be a fight in which the Voices or White would not let their counterparts live.

Imenja checked her stride, then sighed. Looking up, Reivan saw that they were approaching a large tent. This one was not the plain five-sided shape of the rest, but a star shape. The entrance to the tent was a gap between two of the star's arms. As she followed Imenja inside she found herself in a five-sided room. In each wall was a door flap. They probably led to the private rooms of the Voices.

A huge carpet covered the floor and several woven reed chairs had been arranged upon it. On small, low tables were bowls of nuts and dried fruit and jugs of water. A Servant traced the symbol of the star as Imenja turned toward him. He lowered his eyes and gestured to a door flap.

Imenja pushed the flap aside, then held it open for Reivan to catch as she moved inside. Carpet covered the floor and trunks lay beside a large bed.

'Where will I sleep?' Reivan asked.

'There should be a tent for you nearby.'

Reivan nodded.

'Are your accommodations to your satisfaction?'

They turned to find Nekaun standing in the doorway, smiling. Reivan's skin crawled at the sight of him.

'I hardly know I've left the Sanctuary,' Imenja said dryly.

Nekaun's smile widened. 'You will tomorrow.' He glanced over his shoulder. 'Food has arrived. Come and eat.'

He retreated from the door. Reivan turned back to Imenja and found the woman smiling.

'Good to see he no longer has a hold on you,' she murmured. 'Though I wish that hadn't come about in such a painful way.'

Reivan blinked in surprise, then nodded as she realised Imenja was right. She no longer felt a thrill of admiration and weakness when she saw Nekaun. She no longer craved his attention. Ever since . . .

She shuddered as she remembered that last time. He had revealed a cruel, malicious side that she was both glad and a little worried that she would never forget. Now when she saw him she felt repulsed.

Imenja moved past, patting Reivan on the shoulder as she did.

'Let's eat.'

Following her mistress out, Reivan saw that the other Voices and their Companions had arrived. Domestics were carrying platters of steaming food into the room, filling the air with delicious smells. She sat down beside Imenja and began to eat. Dedicated Servants and even a few Thinkers entered. Nekaun made a small speech, telling them that while they feasted the Circlians were wearily making their final march of a long and exhausting journey, only to be defeated tomorrow.

Talk circulated around war. A Dedicated Servant reported that several Circlian supply ships had been sunk. During general chatter Reivan overheard the Thinkers discussing a giant sea creature that had been sighted swimming in the Gulf of Sorrow. They wanted to kill and examine it.

'If you do, we will withdraw our support in this war,' a loud, deep voice with a thick accent boomed.

All turned toward the entrance. Reivan's heart leapt with recognition. Looking around, she could see the effect the imposing figure of the Elai king was having on those who had never seen an Elai before.

Even if King Ais had been a landwalker, his height, the size of his chest and the gold jewellery he wore would have made him an intimidating figure. His blue-black skin, complete hairlessness, double-lidded eyes and webbed hands and feet just added a strangeness that some might find fascinating and others repellent. The king moved into the room, his eyes narrowing at the Thinkers.

'The ru-al is an ancient and benign creature of the sea, and though we would gain enough food from one creature to feed many, many families we Elai do not hunt them. To kill one for the sake of curiosity would be . . .' The Elai king shook his head. 'It would be both wasteful and cruel.'

'Nobody is going to kill the creature,' Nekaun assured him. He moved forward to meet the king. 'Welcome to Avven and the Pentadrian war camp, King Ais. I hope your journey was not difficult.'

As the two leaders continued with formal pleasantries Reivan looked away again. People were listening to and staring at the Elai king in fascination. Nekaun glanced away from the king and frowned, and those who were staring quickly turned away and struck up conversations.

'King Ais has learned Avvenan well,' Imenja noted. Reivan nodded. The Second Voice looked around the room, then turned to Vervel.

'Where is Mirar?' she asked quietly.

Vervel shrugged. 'He retired to his tent.'

'The trip wore him out?' Shar asked, smiling. 'Or was it Genza? He spent a long time with her.'

Genza regarded the Fifth Voice with one eyebrow raised in disdain. 'On a litter. In full view of the army.'

'Lucky for him.'

'Can an immortal get tired?' Vervel asked thoughtfully. Nobody answered.

'Maybe he's snuck back to the Sanctuary,' Genza said. She turned to face Nekaun as he left the king and moved over to join them. 'Is Auraya securely locked up?'

The First Voice smiled nastily. 'She is. Don't worry. Mirar is being watched. And her guards have orders to kill her if anyone tries to interfere.' Imenja looked at him sharply. He returned her gaze, his smile widening. 'I'm tempted to tell them to anyway, then bring her body back here to present to the White. That might make them pause.'

The other Voices exchanged glances, but said nothing.

'But you won't,' Imenja said quietly. 'Because she is the reason he is helping us.'

Nekaun shrugged. 'Mirar won't risk spoiling the pleasant relationship our people have with his.'

'And neither should we.'

The First Voice made a disparaging noise. 'We don't need the Dreamweavers.'

The room was quiet. All were listening and watching the two Voices intently. Reivan realised her heart was pounding. Imenja had never challenged him publicly before.

Imenja pursed her lips thoughtfully. 'Perhaps we should consult our people before we make such a broad-reaching decision for them. I wouldn't want us to cause an unnecessary division among them, or deny them access to the Dreamweavers' superior healing skills. Perhaps we could put it to a vote.'

She looked at the other Voices. They nodded and turned to regard Nekaun expectantly.

His eyebrows lowered and Reivan thought for a moment he would scowl. But he suddenly smiled and spread his hands. 'Of course we shall. After the war. For now, let's concentrate on the matter at hand. Come and meet the Elai king, Ais.'

As the Voices followed him, Reivan remained where she was. She watched Nekaun. Something nagged at her.

Then she saw it. After the war there would be no point in consulting the people about Dreamweavers. Nekaun would already have killed Auraya, or Mirar would have attempted to rescue her and forced Nekaun to carry out his threat.

The Second Voice looked across the room, met her eyes and

nodded. It was clear her mistress had read Reivan's mind, or come to the same conclusion independently. Nekaun knew about Imenja's promise to Mirar that Auraya would be given to him after the war. Was Nekaun teasing the other Voices with his talk of killing Auraya? Or would Nekaun kill Auraya in defiance of his fellow Voices' one attempt to interfere in his rule?

Reivan shivered. These days she couldn't say which was more likely.

Endless days of riding in a platten hadn't done anything to improve Danjin's fitness. Sweat ran down his face and soaked his tunic. The rings on his fingers dug into his hands as he gripped the oars. His shoulders ached and he longed to just lie down and pass out.

'Take your time,' Ella had said, patting him on the shoulder. 'Take all night if you need to. Just make sure you're well away by dawn.'

Then she had propelled him and the boat out as far as she could. He had estimated from the twinkle of lights on either side that she had driven him halfway across the Gulf. Once the boat had drifted to a halt he had taken up the oars and begun rowing.

Every hundred or so strokes he paused to catch his breath. Finally reaching the hundredth stroke again – he had lost track of how many hundreds long ago – he turned to look behind. To his relief he had managed to continue in the right direction. The lights of the Pentadrian camp were all to his left. Darkness spread to the right. Behind him he could just make out a thin, pale line: the beach.

And as he watched a tiny blue light appeared and died.

The signal at last! Turning away, he started rowing again, spurred by a dubious excitement. Part of him took some satisfaction that he had been chosen for a task more suited to a younger, more adventurous man.

'Why me?' he had asked Ella.

'You know Auraya well enough to resist if she contacts you through the ring and tries to lure you away. You're also smart enough to avoid heroics.'

'Like trying to rescue her?'

She had smiled. 'Yes. Even with your mind hidden, you'd never get into the Sanctuary or overcome her guards.'

Of course he had considered the possibility. Given the chance to free Auraya, he would have. Not just out of concern and loyalty to her, but for the sake of the Circlians. They needed her strength to tip the balance back in their favour.

But the White hadn't sent Danjin to free Auraya. They had sent him to meet the other cause of the imbalance of power.

The underneath of the boat scraped against sand. Danjin pulled in the oars and braced himself to stand, then nearly fell into the bottom of the boat as something began to pull it toward the shore. He grabbed the sides and twisted around, expecting to see someone hauling on the prow.

But there was nothing. He was heading toward a man-shaped shadow. The boat stopped a few strides away. Standing up, Danjin stepped over the side. Water chilled his feet and ankles. He looked down and frowned, but not at the soaking of his trousers and boots.

I had better leave on good terms. I'm not sure I could drag this boat back out into deeper water.

He looked up at the figure, took a deep breath and splashed toward it. That he had been betrayed and this was a Servant was the worst possibility, but not the only source of trepidation. Even if this was the right man, and although Danjin had worked with him before, there was much to fear and resent about him.

Stopping a few paces away, Danjin stared at the shadowed face.

'Welcome to Southern Ithania, Danjin Spear,' Mirar said dryly.

A chill ran over Danjin's skin. The voice was all too familiar, but the tone was something he had never heard before. Leiard had always been dignified and reticent. When he had said anything, it was in a quiet, almost apologetic way.

Though spoken quietly, these words boomed with confidence. But not arrogance, he realised. There was great age and experience in them. This was the voice of Mirar the immortal.

Or maybe I'm hearing what I expect to hear, he thought wryly.

'Thank you, Mirar,' Danjin replied. 'Though I have to wonder if you have permission to welcome me on the Pentadrians' behalf.'

'What they don't know won't bother them,' Mirar replied.

Was there a hint of contempt there? Danjin wondered.

'But the sooner I return the less chance my absence will be noticed and wondered about,' Mirar added after a pause. 'What have you come to tell me?'

Danjin straightened. 'The White have sent me to make you an offer. I am linked to them so if you have any question or request—'

'They want me out of the battle,' Mirar interrupted. 'I can't agree to that.'

Danjin swallowed. 'Not even in exchange for the freedom of your people?'

Mirar was silent for a moment. 'So are they making an offer or threatening me?'

'Not a threat,' Danjin said hastily. 'They will promise to allow your people to practise all their Gifts, including mind links, if you desist from helping the Pentadrians.'

'And in return for abandoning the Pentadrians my people

here will suffer. Which side is more likely to win this war if I take the White's offer, Danjin Spear?'

'It would be impossible to guess.'

'And which side if I remain with the Pentadrians?'

Danjin sighed. 'Yours.'

:Ask him if Auraya would forgive him for the deaths of her friends and people. Ella's voice was a whisper in Danjin's mind. He resisted the urge to touch her ring.

'How will Auraya regard you if you help bring about the deaths of her friends, family and her people?' he asked, keeping his voice gentle.

'Oh, she'll be in raptures of delight,' Mirar replied, his voice heavy with sarcasm. 'But at least there's a small chance that she won't be dead. If the White win, she *will* die.'

'Is that why you're doing this?' Danjin found himself whispering. *Why am I whispering? Do I think the White won't hear me?*

Mirar didn't reply. His silence might suggest he was unwilling to admit to something. *That he still feels something for Auraya?* Danjin considered Mirar's responses. He hadn't given away anything. *Perhaps he doesn't want to admit that his reasons are less than noble. That he's doing this out of revenge.*

'Is there anything the White can offer you?' Danjin asked.

He was surprised to hear Mirar sigh. 'No. But be assured that I will not compromise my people's stand on violence. It is a pity your people have not remained as consistent. Only a few years ago they were outraged at the Pentadrians' willingness to invade another land. Now they seek to invade in turn. Tell the White that if my assistance disadvantages the Circlians, perhaps they should abandon their plans of invasion. It would be better for all.'

Danjin felt a flare of anger. How dare this heathen sorcerer think he could change the course of a war as if he were a god. But then an idea came to calm his indignation.

'So if the White agreed to abandon the invasion, would you also withdraw your assistance to the Pentadrians?'

Mirar paused. 'I would consider it.' He turned abruptly to look behind him. 'A patrol is coming. You should go.'

A stab of fear went through Danjin. 'How far?'

'You have enough time to leave if you go now. I will push your boat out as far as I can.'

Danjin nodded in gratitude, then realised he was probably as hard to see in this darkness as Mirar.

'Thank you,' he said.

Turning away, he hurried to the boat and climbed aboard. Hearing splashes, he turned to see that Mirar had followed him.

'I will do what I can for Auraya,' Mirar said quietly. 'But be warned. If she returns you will find she is not the same woman you knew. The gods have betrayed her and used her like a piece in a game of petty revenge between themselves. One does not live through that and remain free of bitterness.'

Danjin shivered. This time there was definitely the sound of great age and experience in the man's voice. He gripped the sides of the boat as it jerked free of the sand and slid rapidly toward the water. Once it floated freely, it turned about. Danjin found himself facing the shore, just able to make out the figure standing there. Then the boat abruptly shot forward. It gathered speed, moving ever faster, until spray began to shoot up on either side. Danjin gripped the sides of the boat tighter, his heart racing. He began to worry that it would smash into something, but was too terrified to look around.

Relief washed over him when the boat finally began to slow. The lights from the Pentadrian shore were reassuringly distant. He turned and drew in a quick breath. The lights of Diamyane were unexpectedly close.

Mirar sent me much further than Ella did. He frowned. *Does this mean he is stronger?*

He sat there pondering this for a few minutes. Surely that wasn't possible. Ella had replaced Auraya, so they must be about equal in strength. The gods wouldn't have sent Auraya to kill Mirar if she was weaker than him.

A splash close to the boat brought his attention back to his surroundings. He peered over the edge, not expecting to see anything. Instead he found a pair of eyes staring back at him.

Paralysed by surprise, he stared back. Then two dark hands shot out of the water toward his throat.

He jerked back and shoved them away at the same time, getting an impression of cold and slippery skin. The hands grabbed hold of the side of the boat. They were extraordinarily large and there was webbing between the fingers. He heard a slap and turned to see another hand appear over the other side of the boat, holding a strange weapon.

:Ella!

:I see them! Give me a moment to find you!

Heads appeared. Black, bald heads with strange filmy eyes. Terror rushed through Danjin. Grabbing an oar, he swung it at one. It ducked. He reversed the swing and jabbed the paddle of the oar at the other. It connected with a satisfying crack.

The man dropped into the water, then the first disappeared. Danjin wondered if he had caused a fatal injury. If he had wounded the man, his companion might have to take him away. If he hadn't, or had killed the man, he'd have either one or two men coming back for revenge.

To his dismay, two heads appeared in the water nearby. One's nose was bleeding profusely, dribbling into a mouth caught in a snarl of hate. The blood was a livid red against the man's white teeth.

But a moment ago it was too dark for me to see this well . . .

The two men looked up and toward the shore, and their expressions changed to fear. They vanished underwater. Turning, Danjin saw a spark of light rushing toward him. He waved his arms, then tumbled into the bottom of the boat as it jerked into motion. Sighing with relief, he decided to stay there.

The journey to the shore was mercifully short. When he felt the boat slow he began to pull himself back onto the seat. Ella stood on the beach ahead, a white glowing figure of goodness. As the boat slid up onto the sand she strode forward, her dress and circ dipping into the water. He felt a sudden rush of affection for her.

'Are you all right, Danjin?'

He stepped out and looked himself over. 'Fine. A bit bruised in places, but otherwise happy to be alive.' He glanced behind. 'What were those creatures?'

'Elai,' she replied, frowning. 'Several of our supply ships and a Dunwayan warship have been sunk tonight. That wasn't a weapon you saw. It was a tool for drilling holes.'

Danjin nodded. Of course. Now that she had pointed it out, he recognised the tool as one used for ship repairs. In the hands of the creature it had taken on an exotic menace.

'We'll have to work out a way to fight them, or we'll never survive a protracted battle here,' Ella added.

'Well, I'm glad he didn't get a chance to drill any holes in me,' he said.

She smiled. 'And I am, too. I wish I hadn't needed to send you over there, but the only other way we could have talked to Mirar was through Arleej, and there may have been something he'd agree to so long as his people didn't know of it.'

'Did anything good come of it?' he asked.

She looked at him, then shrugged. 'Maybe. We will have to discuss it. You should get some sleep in these last few hours before the army arrives.'

'I don't think I will.'

'No, but you will try,' she said firmly. 'I'll need you alert and at your best tomorrow.'

Putting a hand on his shoulder, she steered him toward the town.

CHAPTER 48

As Auraya grew aware of her aching body again she nearly groaned aloud.

At least when I'm asleep I'm oblivious. I don't feel pain or frustration or boredom or worry or . . . What is that?

Something snuffled at her ear. She opened her eyes and turned her head. Round eyes and a pointed nose filled her vision. A narrow pink tongue licked her nose.

'Owaya,' Mischief said quietly.

'You're back.' She nearly sobbed with relief.

'Msstf hunt. Msstf find.'

He moved something from his hand to his mouth and scurried up her arm.

Shifting position, she went rigid with the pain that shot down her arms. Breathing steadily, she waited for circulation to return.

The weight of the veez and the prodding of his feet didn't help at all. As feeling returned his every movement sent shocks of agony along her arm.

'Ow! That hurts!'

He ignored her. Bending forward, she tried to see what he was doing.

And a wave of giddy, dizzy hope took her breath away.

Mischief was holding a key in his mouth. He was trying to insert it into the lock of the cuff around her wrist. Auraya gaped at him, but as she saw that he was trying to put the wrong end in the keyhole her wits returned in a rush. She glanced at the Servant guards. They were both leaning against the wall beside the gate, their heads lowered. Reaching out with her mind she saw that they were sulking about being left behind.

The strongest Dedicated Servant in Glymma and I end up a prison guard, one thought. *I must have done something wrong. What did I do wrong?*

Turning back to Mischief, Auraya touched his mind and sent the idea of turning the key around. He paused, then flipped it over, using both paws and his mouth.

It seemed to take forever for him to insert it in the keyhole. Once there she sensed he was unsure what to do next. Then he remembered how he normally undid locks with magic. There was usually something inside that turned. He tried to twist the key, but his paws weren't used to the action. Hearing a noise, Auraya glanced at the guards again. Her stomach lurched as she saw one was peering at her.

'You'd better hurry,' she told Mischief. 'Or they'll be eating veez stew tonight.'

As the guard reached toward the gate she felt a surge of desperation. Mischief must have sensed it, as he suddenly ran down her arm and licked her face.

'No, no, no!' she muttered.

He scurried back to the lock, to her relief. He paused to sniff at it. She heard the gate open and the voice of the second guard raised in query. Turning away she watched Mischief anxiously as he stared at the key. In the corner of her eye she saw the guards step into the hall.

Mischief took the key in his mouth and twisted.

The lock snapped open and Mischief leapt up onto the throne. Gritting her teeth against the pain of moving a wrist long held in one position, she slid her hand out of the cuff and twisted it around to take hold of the key.

The sound of footsteps grew louder, then more rapid as she pulled out the key and forced her arm around so she could insert it in the cuff around her other wrist. She twisted it. The lock opened.

She glimpsed a flash of light from the guard and threw herself to one side. Magic scorched the base of the throne. She darted behind the enormous chair, panting with exertion, her heart racing.

I have to get out of the void! She could hear two sets of footsteps drawing closer on either side. The Servants were coming around the throne.

She tentatively reached for magic and found it. The area behind the throne wasn't in the void! Drawing magic greedily, she created a shield around herself just as the Servants stepped around the throne and attacked. She knocked one down with a blast of power, then turned to face the other. He stared at her, eyes wide with surprise and horror.

Fixing him with what she expected was a look of utter fury, she took a step toward him.

He fled.

Smiling to herself, she straightened and drew more magic, sending it into her body to heal it. But even as she did she sensed the source diminishing. Moving further away from the throne, she felt a growing puzzlement as she entered magic-less space again.

Then she remembered that the void in the cave in Si had magic at its centre. A ring of void around a magic core. This was the same – or had been until she had used the remaining magic inside it.

The sooner she left the void the better. She strode out from behind the throne to the edge of the dais, then stepped off. Magic surrounded her again. She drew it in, feeling pain retreat as she healed herself.

'*Auraya.*'

Her heart froze as she recognised the voice. Turning, she felt her mouth go dry.

A glowing figure stood nearby, eyes blazing with anger and hatred.

Huan.

Auraya hastily strengthened the barrier around herself.

'Sorry to spoil your escape attempt,' the goddess said.

'No you're not,' Auraya found herself saying. Dismay had turned into a strange mix of defiance and resignation. 'You've been looking for an excuse to kill me and now you have it.'

'I don't want to kill you,' Huan told her. 'But I will, if I have to.' She took a step toward Auraya. 'I will make a deal with you.'

'A deal?'

'Yes. I ask for one small thing: that you open your mind to me. For that I will let you live.'

Auraya regarded the glowing figure. Behind the goddess's features the vacant expression of the Servant who had given over his will was just visible. It was the Dedicated Servant who had been sulking about guarding her. The most powerful Dedicated Servant in Glymma. His powers would be enhanced by the goddess, but by how much? Not as much as the Voices, surely.

At the same time she considered Huan's request. *What harm would there be in unveiling my mind?* Huan would know Auraya had become immortal, but she probably suspected that anyway. She would know Auraya had learned from Jade – Emerahl. She would know that other Wilds existed and knew how to kill a god.

I know how to kill a god. She'll kill me anyway, if she sees that.

She would also know that Auraya was strong enough to become a god, but then if Chaia knew that then Huan probably suspected it, too.

If I am, then I must be stronger than this Dedicated Servant.

The thought brought a smile to Auraya's face. 'I don't think you can stop me leaving.'

Huan's eyes flashed. 'You are wrong. But if you need convincing . . .'

The glowing figure opened a hand. White light flashed out and struck Auraya's barrier. Staggering backwards, Auraya drew more magic to her defence, then flung some back at the goddess.

Instantly they became locked in a deadly exchange of ferocious strength and speed. She felt the magic around her thinning as they both tapped into it. She felt the air vibrating between them. She deflected heat, lightning and crushing, hammering strikes.

She's matching me blow for blow. The realisation was worse than the crushing force of Huan's attack. *The Dedicated Servant must be more powerful than I thought. I guess if the Pentadrians vote to decide who become their Voices, it's possible that there are Dedicated Servants as powerful or even more powerful than the Voices were before the gods enhanced their powers.*

Huan moved closer, blocking her escape and forcing her to one side of the hall. Auraya could not get past her. Slowly the magic Auraya could reach dwindled, forcing her to back away to reach more. Huan watched, smiling.

I have lost. It is just a matter of time.

But Auraya fought on, refusing to give up. She used the columns of the hall to shield herself. Pieces of stone were blasted from them, and one after another they crumbled until Auraya feared the roof would collapse. When the magic in the hall had thinned to the point where Auraya could not sustain the attack, she felt herself faltering. Huan beat at her barrier and it finally collapsed.

A force enveloped Auraya. It drew her forward until she stood a few steps from the glowing figure.

'Now,' Huan sneered. 'Open your mind to me.'

A flash of stubborn defiance went through Auraya. *She'll kill me anyway, whether I do it or not.*

'No,' she replied.

Huan's eyes narrowed. 'You seem to think you have a choice. I shall convince you otherwise.'

Magic flowed from the goddess and wrapped around Auraya's body. *Into* her body. Pain ripped through her, pulsing up and down her limbs, tearing at her insides. She saw white and her eyes burned. Agony was all she knew.

Then it stopped. Vision returned. Auraya realised she was lying on the floor, but could not remember falling down. Her body felt bruised. She was gasping for breath and suspected she had stopped breathing during Huan's attack. Her mind began drawing in magic from the thin and depleted source around her to begin healing.

So, she thought. *It's going to be torture then.* She felt her determination waver. Then she thought of Mirar, and Jade. *I can't betray them.* From somewhere she drew up the resolve to stay silent.

'See?' Huan said. 'It doesn't take much magic. I can do it for years, if I want to. And I can do much, much worse. I can make you die of pain. Slowly. *Very* slowly.'

Once again Auraya considered what was in her mind that the goddess might want to see. Jade's identity came to mind. The secrets Mirar had told her. The realisation that the Wilds were up to something. They knew how to kill gods. Were they going to try it themselves?

I could let Huan see that and die quickly. All I gain from resisting is pain.

But the Wilds will lose any chance of killing the gods if I do.

And the gods deserve to die.

She thought of the stories Jade had told her, of the lies the gods had told, of Huan's manipulations and the Siyee's doomed mission. Anger suddenly boiled up inside her.

I can endure this. It won't be easy . . . and the Wilds had better succeed. She glared at Huan. *I don't want to die knowing I spoiled any chance of someone killing this bitch.*

At Auraya's glare, Huan straightened and magic flowed from her again. For a long time all Auraya was conscious of was the agony that moved through her body, the realisation that pain could be a burning, an intolerable cold, a crushing ache, a multitude of terrible sensations.

When it stopped, she found herself lying face down. Her nose was bleeding. Her forehead throbbed as if someone had kicked it repeatedly. She tried to move, then tried harder. Finally her body obeyed her desire and she rolled onto her back. A thousand hurts made themselves known and for a long moment she could not breathe.

Huan peered down at her from a few paces away.

'You're dying,' she told Auraya.

Gods I wish I could smack that smug expression from her face – or pluck out her eyes! But . . . Huan can only see me through the eyes of a mortal, Auraya found herself thinking. *If I can lure her out of that Servant at least she won't see me die. Ha! If I could get her out of the Servant she couldn't harm me at all!*

'Too bad,' Auraya said between gritted teeth. 'Even when Chaia takes my soul I won't tell you what I know.'

Huan laughed. 'Chaia isn't here. And I don't want your soul. You are going to cease to exist.'

Auraya laughed. 'If the gods have to be where a person dies

in order to take their soul, they can't possibly take all souls. They'd have to be in so many places at once . . .' She paused to catch her breath. 'But you don't take souls, do you? It's all a lie.'

Huan's glowing eyebrows rose. 'Oh? What makes you so sure of that?'

'Chaia told me,' Auraya lied.

'Did he?' Huan's eyes narrowed. 'I don't think he likes you as much as he claims. He's always giving me more excuses to kill you.'

'Then kill me.'

Huan shook her head. 'Hmm. Do you really think I'll let you die without seeing into your mind? I have to know what else he has revealed.'

Auraya had only a moment to enjoy the bitter triumph of knowing Mirar's 'secret' was true before the pain began again. This time it was worse, and when the attack stopped the pain continued. She felt a warm dampness behind her head, and when she moved her skull creaked disturbingly. Shooting pains in one of her arms told her a bone had broken. Her heels were afire. Her whole body was bruised. Her jaw ached and her teeth felt loose.

Huan smiled down at her.

'Open your mind, Auraya.'

If I do, she'll have to leave the Servant, Auraya thought. *That's my lure. When she comes to me I'll shut my mind again. But I can't stop her returning to the Servant . . .*

She groaned. The pain in her head was growing. She drew magic and began healing the damage, and the pain began to lessen. *It's lucky I'm not in the void.*

The void! If she could trick Huan into going inside the void . . . no, the goddess would never fall for that.

'Open your mind and the pain will end,' Huan crooned, bending closer.

I need a void. She remembered her guess at how they had been created. *Draw away all the magic in one place. If Huan senses it, she will move away. And then I'll have no magic to heal myself. Except the magic I draw in . . .*

'Just let me see, and it'll all be over.'

Lure her out . . . make a void . . . stop her returning to the Servant. Suddenly it all came together. Auraya opened her eyes and stared at Huan.

'All right,' she croaked. 'Look then. Look and see how much I hate you.'

Huan's eyes blazed with triumph. Her glowing features vanished and the Dedicated Servant's face appeared. He blinked with surprise.

Auraya reached out with her unbroken arm and grasped his ankle. At the same time she pulled into herself all the magic she could sense. All at once. Power flowed into her. Senses attuned to the magic of the world, she felt a presence forced away, then fleeing. She felt the magic around her part like torn fabric, leaving a sphere of nothingness.

It was a rent in the world, a terrible thing. She cried out in horror. Another voice joined hers and she felt hands around her arm. Pain snapped her back into an awareness of the world as the Dedicated Servant pulled her hand away from his ankle.

He will alert others, if Huan hasn't already, she thought, and felt a stab of panic. Magic burst from her. Still in the void, he had no chance to shield himself. She heard his bones crack as the blast hit him. He flew backwards and sprawled on the floor, twitching.

She spared him one small moment of pity, then the urgent call of her body drew her attention back. Using the magic she had drawn, she healed as much damage as she could before crawling out of the void and drawing more. Slowly bones mended, swelling eased and bruises faded. She got to her feet.

Pinpricks of pain assailed her all over, as nerves taxed by Huan's torture protested.

She walked toward the gate. Stronger magic surrounded her. A small surge of it broke the lock. Turning back, she looked around the hall. The thought came that she could destroy it easily. But then she remembered that there was someone in it that she wouldn't want to see harmed.

'Mischief,' she called softly. 'Mischief!'

A small furry shape leapt off the throne and bounded over to her. He shot up the bloodied sack she wore onto her shoulders. Auraya scratched him between the ears and walked out of the hall into the passage.

And came face to face with a handful of Servants. They formed a line across the passage. A moment later she sensed Huan join them.

Gods curse her! she thought. Then the irony of what she had just thought occurred to her and she choked out a crazy-sounding laugh.

She can only attack me when she has possessed a Servant, but these Servants probably aren't as powerful as the last one. The strong ones are at the battle.

As the Servants attacked, Auraya was relieved to find she was right. But more would join them as she tried to fight her way out of the building.

Do I even have to?

Once more she felt the itch to destroy this place. She knew that there was a thick layer of rock above the hall, then the buildings of the Lower Sanctuary. Backing away from the Servants, she retreated to the side of the hall she knew was not depleted of magic. They followed. When she was just within the gate she turned to face the room. Drawing in magic, she loosed it at the ceiling.

There was a deafening boom and the floor shook. Cracks

appeared where she had struck. Rubble piled into the hall. The Servants' attack faltered. Glancing behind, she saw that they were backing away, exchanging terrified glances.

It took three more blasts, each more powerful, to break through. Cracks crossed the roof of the hall. Faint sunlight filtered down, making curtains of light in the dust that veiled the piles of rubble that covered the floor below.

The Servants had fled.

Auraya paused to pat a trembling Mischief, who was now hiding down the back of her sacking shift. Then she straightened, drew magic greedily to herself and let it fly out. With a terrible crack, a great piece of the roof, thicker than a house was high, crashed down into the hall, crushing and burying the throne. Rubble flew past her and battered her barrier. Not waiting for the dust to settle, she strode forward, stepping over rocks and taking care not to enter either of the two voids.

White walls appeared above, part of the Sanctuary. At the sight of the sky beyond her heart soared. It was pink. Dawn.

'Owaya fly,' Mischief said into her ear.

'Yes,' she replied. 'Hold on tight.'

She felt the veez's feet grip her. Then she launched herself into the air, out of the hole, and up into the sky.

:The sun is rising, Tamun said. *Soon the armies will wake. Today the world will change yet again, whether we succeed or not.*

Emerahl hid her amusement. Sometimes The Twins spoke like storytellers, in dramatic tones and phrasing. Perhaps it was only because they had grown up in an older time that they spoke like characters in a historic epic.

No, I don't think people in the distant past spoke like that when doing the laundry or cooking a meal, she thought. *This is just The Twins' way of reminding us that what we are attempting is as risky as those feats of ancient heroes, and will change the world as dramatically.*

Then another voice joined the link.

:*I have finished*, The Gull announced. *I have created a tunnel along the length of the Isthmus, connecting it to the one Emerahl used. I have also created tunnels from the central one to the outside on both sides, so that Tamun and Surim will have a place to hide themselves and their boats.*

:*That must have taken you all night*, Emerahl said, impressed. *If we don't get our chance today, this will be an excellent place to lure the gods to another time.*

:*Only if we find a sixth immortal soon*, The Gull warned. *The Isthmus will not remain for long after what I have done.*

:*If an opportunity doesn't come — and it doesn't look like it will — we must keep watching for new immortals*, Emerahl said. *Since the Circlians and the Pentadrians are recruiting powerful sorcerers from a young age we'll have to expect to find one among their ranks. It'll be hard to find them and even harder to get them to join us.*

:*And once we have, we'll have to find a way to get the gods to gather somewhere we can surround them*, Surim added.

:*Surim? Tamun?* Mirar said as he joined them.

:*Mirar*, they replied.

:*The Pentadrians are stirring. This will be my last chance to link with you. Are you all in place?*

:*Not quite*, Surim replied. *We have arrived at Diamyane. The Gull has finished tunnelling so he, Surim and I should be in position soon. Emerahl must wait for the White. How is Auraya?*

:*I don't know. She wasn't asleep when I tried to contact her. I tried mind-skimming, but there's nobody there. Not even guards.*

:*I'll try*, Surim offered.

They waited in silence. Emerahl wondered if the others felt the same dread. The Voices could have left orders for Auraya to be killed, thinking that Mirar wouldn't know he'd been cheated until after the battle. That would explain the lack of guards. No point guarding a dead prisoner.

:She was the only flaw in our plan, Surim said quietly. *We have the perfect trap; we know we can create voids, since Tamun succeeded yesterday. All we needed was Auraya.*

:We had to be here in case, Emerahl repeated for the thousandth time. She felt her heart sink with disappointment. *If we had found the secrets of the gods earlier we could have all sought a way to free her.*

:AURAYA IS FREE!

Surim's voice was so loud in Emerahl's mind she nearly jolted out of the dream link.

:Alive? Free? How? Where is she? Why isn't she here? Mirar asked frantically.

:Ah! I see her. She is currently robbing a merchant, Tamun said wryly. *For food. Some cloth. Ah, she's promised the man she will return and pay him when she can. He doesn't believe her, of course, and I—*

:That's a fine piece of cloth, Surim added. *Who'd have thought she had such good taste. I guess she's been frustrated by those silly white robes for—*

:She hasn't much choice, Tamun reminded him. *She can't turn up wearing that dirty—*

:WHERE IS SHE? Mirar demanded.

The Twins paused.

:Near the mountains.

:That was fast, The Gull interjected. *They're a few days' ride from Glymma.*

:She can travel very fast if she wants to, Mirar said proudly.

:That's good, because if she's going to come back and help us she'll need to, Surim said.

:Why did she go to the mountains? Emerahl asked. *They're in the opposite direction to the battle.*

:She wants to be as far away from Voices and gods as she can get, Mirar guessed.

:Yet she hasn't joined the White, Tamun said. *You told her you were going to defend the Voices. She knows the White are doomed. Has she abandoned them, or is she biding her time?*

:I don't know. But you can be sure there's one option she doesn't know about, because you wouldn't let me tell her about our plans to kill the gods.

:We must tell her, Surim said.

:No, it's too risky, Tamun protested. *If she betrays us to the gods . . .*

:We came here in the hope that an opportunity would arise. If she doesn't know, that opportunity will never come.

:How can we tell her? Mirar asked. *She's awake and likely to stay that way until she has some distance between herself and the battle. Wait . . . I have an idea.*

The sense of his mind vanished.

:We can't tell her, Tamun began. *It's too much of a—*

:Sorry, sister, Surim interrupted. *But you're outnumbered. Am I right? Emerahl?*

:It's a risk, Emerahl replied. *But I don't think she'll tell the gods. Not once she knows we can't do it without her. She's gone out of her way to avoid bringing harm to us in the past.*

:Are you sure?

:I'm never completely sure about anything.

:Gull? Tamun asked.

:Emerahl and Mirar know her best. I agree.

:You're all fools. If she—

:Jade?

They all fell silent, surprised to hear Auraya's voice.

:Yes, it's me, Emerahl said hastily, when the silence began to lengthen.

:Or is it Emerahl?

:That's my oldest name.

:Mischief just started barking names in his sleep. There was Mirar and you, then 'Wins'.

:The Twins.

:So one of you was dream linking with Mischief?

:Yes, Mirar said. *I did.*

:Who are the rest of you?

:We are The Twins.

:The Twins, eh? I thought you were long dead.

:Not at all. I am Surim.

:And I am Tamun.

:Hello, Auraya said. *Not every day one meets a myth. There was another name. Sounded like 'Gill'.*

:That would be me, The Gull.

:Ah. Another living myth.

:You've escaped, I see, Tamun said.

:Yes. Partly due to Mischief. He brought me the key.

:What are you going to do now? Mirar asked.

:I don't know.

:We could use your help.

:Are you in trouble?

:Not exactly . . . and none of us would blame you if you refused.

:Tell me.

Emerahl explained about the voids being places where gods had died.

:I know. Mirar told me. The Circle killed the other gods by drawing away the magic, didn't they?

:Yes. Did he tell you that?

:No. I had an interesting experience with Huan earlier.

:Oh?

:She attacked me. I remembered what Mirar said about voids and decided to test a theory I came up with during those long hours chained up in one.

:Huan is dead? Surim asked excitedly.

:No. She dodged. But I guess that's why you need me. You need six in order to stop them escaping.

:Yes, Emerahl replied. *Will you help us?*

:Yes.

There was a long silence. Emerahl felt excitement growing as she realised what this meant. The chance had come. It was going to work.

:What about Chaia? Tamun asked.

:What did you have to go and ask that for! Surim exclaimed.

:Because we don't want her changing her mind at the last moment, Tamun replied.

:Chaia tried to kill me, Auraya told them. *He's the same as the rest. If I can't trust him, then I'm just like any other Wild . . . Not that that's bad . . .*

:We know what you mean, Surim assured her. *None of us like the prospect of hiding like criminals for millennia. That is why we're here.*

:Tell me your plan.

As Tamun began to explain, something – the sound of a horn – nearly dragged Emerahl from sleep.

:I must go, she began.

Then Emerahl started into consciousness to find Arleej leaning over her.

'I'm sorry if I interrupted something,' the woman said. 'But the White's messenger is at the door, asking why we haven't joined them yet.'

CHAPTER 49

Unable to stifle a yawn, Danjin covered his mouth. He hadn't slept well despite Ella's orders. Frustratingly, when the horn blew to rouse the army, his relief that the night was over had relaxed him just enough to fall asleep. By the time he woke again and reached Ella's tent, she had left. A servant told Danjin where she would be. That news had shaken off all lingering sleepiness.

She had gone to join the White at the Isthmus.

Leaving the tent, he had jogged to the start of the Isthmus. There he found, to his relief, that the White hadn't yet left. Ella smiled when she saw him, then beckoned.

'I didn't want to wake you,' she told him. 'You needed a rest after last night.'

'Hmph,' he replied. 'I know the truth. You were trying to sneak away without me.'

She grinned. 'Ha! You are too smart for me.' Then she sobered. 'Are you sure you want to come? We are taking only a small group of witnesses with us. There are powerfully Gifted priests and priestesses among them, and Dreamweavers, but they may not be able to protect you if the Voices attack at full strength.'

Danjin felt a stab of apprehension. He shrugged it off.

'War isn't without risks, and you may need me.'

He didn't say why. There was a small chance that, if Auraya had joined the enemy, his presence might make her change her mind. It was a very small chance, but it was worth being ready for.

Ella nodded. 'We might.' Her gaze shifted behind him. 'And here are our Dreamweavers. I doubt they have a reason for sleeping late as good as yours.'

Danjin turned to see several men and women in Dreamweaver vests approaching. He recognised Dreamweaver Elder Arleej and Dreamweaver Adviser Raeli. The pair left the rest and approached Juran. When their short exchange ended, Ella smiled.

'Time for us to meet our adversaries,' she said. 'Be careful, Danjin.'

'I will,' he assured her.

As she joined the White he moved to stand beside Lanren Songmaker. The military adviser smiled grimly, then they both started walking as the White set out along the Isthmus.

All were silent. Danjin alternately watched the white figures before him, their circs swaying as they walked, and squinted at the road beyond them, trying to see the enemy. Time dragged by. The sun rose higher, its rays delivering a heat that promised a hot day ahead. Water lapped at the sides of the isthmus in a gentle but relentless rhythm.

They must have been walking for over an hour when Lanren made a small noise of satisfaction. 'Here they come.'

Danjin stared into the distance, but saw nothing. Perhaps there were dark specks in the haze ahead.

'You have good eyesight, Lanren.'

The man shrugged.

Several more minutes passed before points of darkness in the distance became moving shapes. By the time these had resolved into figures Danjin was sure he had been walking for another an hour.

Slowly more details became clear. There were six figures. Five wore black. The other almost blended with the colour of the road.

Mirar, Danjin thought. He drew up memories of the man he had spoken to the previous night and felt a mingled sympathy and annoyance.

I wish Auraya had killed him. I understand why she didn't, but if she'd been a little tougher the odds today wouldn't be balanced against us.

Soon Danjin could make out which of the Voices was male and which female. He recognised four of them, but he was more interested in the one he didn't know. Nekaun, the new First Voice, was handsome in an exotic way. His bearing was arrogant. He was smiling as he strode toward the White.

When Danjin looked beyond at the small crowd of people that followed behind the Voices he felt a slight shock. A large, bald black-skinned man strode among them. He looked too much like the sea people who had attacked Danjin to not be of the same race. Gold jewellery glittered in the light. As Danjin watched the man dipped a cloth into a large bowl carried by a servant walking beside him then splashed and wiped himself with it.

This must be the Elai king, Danjin thought. The White hadn't brought the leaders of Somrey, Toren, Genria, Sennon or Si in case a magical fight began and they were unable to protect them. The Voices must be confident of their superior strength. *But they have Mirar, so they do have an advantage.*

Several strides from each other, the Voices and White slowed to a stop and regarded each other warily. From behind, Danjin heard a Dreamweaver speak quietly.

'Mirar is with the Voices. We can't hang behind like this and combat the advantage he gives them.'

'We will join them if they begin fighting,' Arleej replied.

'It may be too late by then,' the woman insisted.

He turned to see who was speaking, but stopped as he realised Lanren was staring up at the sky.

'Is that what I think it is?' the man said.

Danjin turned back just in time to see something blue flash across the sky. It came toward them. It took on form. Female form. As he realised who this was he felt himself go weak as relief and joy swept through him.

Auraya.

She was free at last. She had come to help them. No longer did the Pentadrians have the advantage. Now the Circlians did, if Mirar hadn't lied about not intending to fight and kill. Auraya would fight for the Circlians, and the gods.

The White had seen her now. The Voices followed their gaze and their leader's smile vanished. Auraya swooped downwards, the blue cloth of her dress rippling. As she drew closer he saw how thin and pale she was. Her clothing was not a dress, but a length of cloth wound about her wasted body.

He smiled to himself. From the looks on the faces of the Voices, her arrival wasn't part of their plan.

Auraya stopped abruptly, hovering above the White and the Voices. She wore an expression he had never seen before.

One of fury and hatred.

Watching from far above, the knots in Auraya's stomach tightened as the White and Voices moved closer together. She could see Mirar walking with the Voices. She could see Companions and Servants following a hundred paces behind their leaders. She could see advisers, priests, priestesses and Dreamweavers following.

Can I do what the other immortals want me to do? If they wanted to kill Huan, I would give them all the help they asked for. But Chaia . . .

What of Chaia? He had tried to kill her.

Yet he had been so good to her in the past.

I suppose that makes his betrayal all the worse. If I had taken his bait, I would have died not knowing that he had turned on me.

And the other gods? They had done nothing to her.

And nothing to help me, either. I've seen them shift their alliance from Chaia to Huan to suit their whims.

And the Pentadrian gods? She knew nothing of them. But they had sent their people to invade Northern Ithania. They had ordered Nekaun to break his vow and chain her up under the Sanctuary.

Then something occurred to her.

They must *die too. If the Circlian gods die, Northern Ithania will be vulnerable. The Pentadrians will invade again. There will be so much bloodshed.*

If all the gods were killed this day . . . there would be no reason for a battle. She could prevent many, many deaths.

Except the gods', of course. But that seems just. For so long they led us to believe they could provide life after death when in truth they just told us lies so we would obey them. Maybe it's time they faced the same fate.

But what would the world be like without gods? Would mortals descend into chaos and barbarism without their guidance? Without a priesthood to nurture and guide the Gifted, would sorcerers abuse their power?

And this war isn't barbaric? This isn't the gods abusing power?

Ahead, the White slowed. They were within a hundred paces of the Voices now. The two groups finally stopped a dozen paces away from each other.

Where are the gods? She felt a jolt as she realised she couldn't sense them, and stretched her senses out. Suddenly she did detect something – the Circle. They were flashing between the White and Voices so fast she would not have noticed unless she was watching for it. Puzzled by this behaviour, she descended to be closer, and concentrated harder. Though she could not read the minds of the White or the Voices, she could still hear the gods' voices.

Snatches of conversation reached her.

:... *we never agreed to this.*

She recognised Huan.

:*But we did. We knew there would be elements we could not control*, Chaia replied.

:*Small things. Weather or disease. Not these cursed interfering immortals. You've encouraged them—*

:*I have never encouraged any of them.*

:*You didn't get rid of him! You told Auraya we don't take souls!*

:*I did not.*

:*Will you stop arguing.* This was Lore. *The best part of the game is about to begin.*

A game? Auraya shook her head. *What game? And why are they in the minds of both sides? How can the gods even enter the minds of the Voices? Surely the Pentadrian gods would stop that. And where are the Pentadrian gods?*

The answer dawned on her then. It was so obvious she felt like a fool for not seeing it before.

The Circlian gods are the Pentadrian gods.

The truth set her body trembling with rage. They had *all* been duped. The White, the Voices, all mortals, everywhere. *Chaia wasn't pretending to be Sheyr when he appeared in the hall. He is Sheyr.*

The gods were still arguing. Still stunned by the revelation, Auraya had to drag her mind back to the gods' conversation.

:... *not interesting!* Huan spat. *It's not a fair match.*

:*The Wilds are a random element. That is exciting*, Lore disagreed.

:I'm with Huan, Yranna interjected. *We agreed on certain rules from the beginning. If one side wins because of the Wilds it won't be a proper contest.*

A suspicion was dawning on Auraya. She resisted it. The possibility was too appalling.

:We can't do anything about it now, Chaia said. *Let's just enjoy the battle.*

Auraya's heart froze.

Enjoy the battle.

If Chaia hadn't tried to kill her, she would never have believed he could say something like that. But he had, and she had overheard him. He hadn't realised she was close by and listening to him and his fellow gods. She could hear their argument continuing. The word 'game' repeated over and over. Each time her resistance to the truth broke down a little more. She looked at the Voices and the White. White-clad men and women. Black-clad men and women. Game pieces. The board was the whole world.

All we are to them is pieces of a game.

She propelled herself downward, aiming for a place just above the Voices and the White and the gods that buzzed around them like carrion birds.

When Auraya had descended from the sky, blue cloth swirling about her, Mirar's heart had stopped. For a moment he was full of doubt. She was going to join the White. She would betray the immortals.

Now they would face each other in battle. Unlike him, she was willing to kill.

Then she stopped and hovered above them. The White and the Voices stared up at her.

Someone gave him a small nudge. He turned to look at Second Voice Imenja. Her expression was grim.

'I guess our deal's off,' she murmured. 'Go, if you wish. I will ensure he doesn't stop you.'

He looked around. All of the Voices and the White seemed transfixed by Auraya. Catching a movement beyond the White, Mirar saw that Emerahl was striding forward, followed by a puzzled Arleej. Looking to one side, he saw Tamun peering over the edge of the road. He glanced to the other side and saw Surim duck out of sight.

Everyone is in place but me.

He backed away from the Voices. Nekaun turned to glare at him, but Imenja stepped forward to stand between them. Mirar hurried away, then turned. He looked up at Auraya.

She met his gaze and nodded.

'Now!' she cried.

Mirar drew in magic faster than he had ever needed to before.

Reivan gasped as a glowing sphere of light surrounded the White and the Voices. It was blindingly bright, too painful to look upon.

'What's going on?' someone shouted. She recognised the Elai king's deep voice.

'They're attacking each other!' a Servant exclaimed. 'Attack the enemy!'

'How? We can't see them!'

'And they can't see us,' Reivan found herself saying. 'All we can do is protect ourselves and wait.'

To her surprise, the men and women around her quietened. Heart pounding, she covered her eyes and mouthed a prayer to the gods that Imenja was alive and unhurt.

It surprised Emerahl how much magic she could draw and hold. There was a limit, however, and as she reached it she converted it to light. The others were doing the same, surrounding the Voices and the White with a great dazzling sphere.

Then, abruptly, the magic ran out and the glow vanished.

Emerahl found herself standing uncomfortably close to ten confused sorcerers. They were casting about, looking wary and uncertain. One of the Voices gave her a hard look.

Time to go, she told herself. But she didn't move. *We don't know if it worked or not.*

Then a glow began to form in the middle of the Isthmus. Emerahl felt her stomach sink to her knees as she recognised Chaia. He was not looking at her, but up at Auraya. Four more figures appeared.

Mouth dry and heart pounding, Emerahl took advantage of the distraction and walked to the edge of the road. Nobody moved to prevent her. They were all too stunned and confused. To her relief, Surim waited there in a narrow boat. She skidded down the steep side of the Isthmus and clambered aboard.

'Did it work?' he whispered.

She shook her head. 'Chaia appeared. He's still alive.'

'And trapped inside the void,' a new voice said quietly. She and Surim turned to see Tamun and The Gull emerge from a crack in the Isthmus wall, paddling in another narrow boat. 'Remember, there is often magic left in the middle of a void. We have only created a shell of magicless space about them.'

'Trapped for all eternity,' Surim said. He shrugged, then smiled evilly. 'Actually, I like that better.'

'I don't,' Emerahl growled. 'If they're alive, there's a chance they'll last in there until the magic seeps back.'

'Then we'll just have to sneak back and finish them off, when there are no White or Voices around to stop us,' Surim said, shrugging.

'They'll expect that. They'll make sure they're well guarded.'

'By who? Without the gods enhancing their powers, the White and Voices won't be as strong,' The Gull pointed out.

'They will be, inside the void,' Emerahl said.

'But the gods need that power to survive.'

'Where is Auraya?' The Gull peered up at the edge of the Isthmus wall.

Emerahl followed his gaze. 'She was still floating over them when I left.'

'She has issues to resolve,' Tamun said. 'And she can fly away when she's done. We can't. We should go.'

'What about Mirar?'

Tamun frowned up at the wall. 'He's probably stayed because Auraya did.'

They stared up at the wall in silence. Emerahl sighed.

'I'll wait,' she offered. 'You three get out of here.'

CHAPTER 50

The glowing figure of Chaia looked from Auraya to Juran. His lips moved, but she could not hear him.

Of course, she thought. *I can't hear him because there is a void between myself and him. He can only speak into minds – and he hasn't been able to speak into mine since I learned to shield it. He must either possess another or . . . I let my mind shield fall.*

Juran nodded and looked up.

'Chaia asks that you come down and talk to us,' he said. He frowned. 'He wants to know why you have done . . . whatever it is you've done.'

Auraya considered, conscious of the White and the Voices watching her. Seeing Nekaun, she shuddered. She wanted to get as far away from him as possible.

But the White needed to be told the truth. Even if they didn't believe it.

Can they, the Voices or the gods harm me? They could attack me, but only by using up the magic inside the void. The gods won't want any of it used. They're using up magic just to make themselves visible. Once it is gone they'll cease to exist.

Taking a deep breath, she drew magic to feed her barrier and so she wouldn't fall as she passed through the void, and descended to the ground.

Chaia turned to regard her. She would still be unable to hear him, unless she let the shield around her mind fall. There was nothing left to hide from them that they didn't already know. She looked at the White and Voices, and to her surprise she found she could read their minds. Which meant they no longer had the Gifts the god had given them. They could not read anyone's mind.

Still, it took a conscious effort to lower the veil. As soon as she did, Chaia spoke.

:*Once again, we have underestimated you, Auraya. You and your immortal friends have us well trapped. At least tell us why.*

'Why?' she repeated. 'You know why.' She felt a stab of anger. 'I suppose you thought you were putting me out of my misery when you told me I could escape the Sanctuary by becoming a god.'

He frowned.

:*I have never proposed that you become a god. I would not want to see you confined to this form. It would be a prison for you.*

'Then why would you tell me how . . .' She felt a twinge of doubt. Had he actually suggested she do it? She had been so sick that day. Surely she hadn't dreamed it . . . 'You said it was better that I become a god than die. That taking my soul isn't the same.' She gave a bitter laugh. 'Well, since Huan admitted you don't take souls I guess you were right.'

Chaia looked at Huan. The other gods turned to regard the goddess, who straightened and stared back defiantly.

:*You told her how to become a god?* Yranna accused. *You disguised yourself?*

Chaia turned back to Auraya.

:*Did I use our key word? Did I say 'shadow'?* he asked.

She frowned. Her memory was too hazy. 'I can't remember,' she admitted. 'I was so sick. It was hard to think.'

Huan laughed.

:Yes, it wasn't hard to fool you.

Looking up, Auraya shivered as she saw the goddess's gleeful expression.

:So you admit it? Chaia asked Huan. The goddess glared at him and said nothing.

:Who else would it have been? Lore said bitterly. *None of us broke the rules as often as Huan.*

:Rules! The rules applied to the game, not to threats to our existence! Huan roared. *If you'd listened to my warning about her*, she pointed at Auraya, *this wouldn't have happened.*

Chaia smiled grimly.

:We've all got into the habit of ignoring you whenever you spout foolish, paranoid nonsense. 'Immortals might become gods! If they do, they'll kill us all! Auraya is dangerous!'

:Huan was clearly right, Lore pointed out.

All fell silent. After a moment Juran made a strangled noise. 'I don't understand. What has happened?'

:The Wilds have done to us what we did to our fellow gods many centuries ago, Lore explained. *They have removed the magic from around us, trapping us in a small oasis in the centre. We cannot leave.*

:Not until the magic flows back in, Yranna added quietly. *Which will take thousands of years.*

Juran turned to stare at Auraya. 'You helped them do this?'

She forced herself to return his gaze. 'Yes.'

'Why?'

'Because they lied to us. They don't take souls. They play games with us like—'

Brash laughter drowned out her words. All turned to look at Nekaun.

'You've imprisoned your *own* gods?' He shook his head. 'What can I give you for doing me this service? Gold? Land? A place by my side?'

Auraya's skin crawled. It would, at least, be satisfying to deliver the bad news to *this* one.

'The Circlian and Pentadrian gods are the same,' she told him. 'They've been playing dual parts.' She looked at Chaia, then at each of the White and the Voices in turn. 'You see, this is all a game to them. And you are the pieces. The deaths in this war and the one before were nothing more than points scored, one side against the other. Points, not *real* people, with families and friends. Not—'

'They are *not* the same,' Nekaun snarled, his face dark with anger. 'My gods do not look the same. They do not even sound the same.'

:What Auraya says is true, Chaia said. His form shifted and suddenly he was Sheyr. The Voices stared at him in shock.

'Trickery!' Nekaun exclaimed.

Auraya turned to face him. 'You will know the truth soon enough. Without them to supplement your magical Gifts, you will be weaker. You can no longer read minds. You certainly aren't immortal.'

Nekaun's glare changed to a stare of uncertainty. Turning away, Auraya saw the same expression on the faces of the White.

'I'm . . . sorry,' she found herself saying. 'But with the gods constantly playing you and the Voices against each other, you weren't going to survive long anyway. Of course, if you continue with this war there's a good chance you still won't.' She grimaced. 'That's your choice. I will not help or hinder you.'

Juran looked from Auraya to Chaia. 'Is this true?'

:It is.

A wordless cry of rage broke from one of the White. All turned to look at the new White, Ellareen, who was staring at Auraya, her face white with fury.

'You,' she snarled. 'You *traitor*! You don't deserve to *live*!'

She made an abrupt gesture and a white pulse of light shot forward, scattering against Auraya's barrier.

:NO! STOP! the gods cried, their voices united. Yranna moved to stand in front of Ella.

:We need the magic you use to attack her to survive, Ellareen. Would you kill us in order to avenge us?

Ellareen stared at the goddess wildly, then shook her head. She took a step away, then looked up at Auraya, her eyes narrowed in hate.

Then another attack battered Auraya's barrier, followed by manic laughter. Shocked gasps and protests broke from both people and gods as they turned toward the source. Nekaun laughed again, then sent another blast at Juran.

'You fools,' he said. 'You just told me how to kill your own gods!'

Chaia shifted into Sheyr's form.

:STOP! he commanded. Nekaun laughed again.

'I'm not falling for that one again. I suppose it was you who stopped me having a bit of fun with Auraya. Well, I—'

Abruptly he staggered backwards, his eyes wide with surprise. The chill that had begun to crawl down Auraya's back at his words faded as she saw that the other Voices were dragging him away with their magic. He was resisting them, she saw, but with little effect. Then suddenly he jerked as if struck in the face, and dropped to the ground, unconscious.

As one, the Voices turned back to face the gods, all smiling with satisfaction. A short silence followed, then Juran turned to Chaia.

'If we are without your guidance, what will become of mortals? How are we to stop ourselves descending into lawless chaos?'

Auraya felt a pang of affection for him. 'So long as there are good leaders like you, Juran, mortals will do well enough.'

Chaia smiled.

:She is right.

'And when I die?' Juran asked, his voice tight.

:The worthy replacement you choose will take your place.

:We choose, Huan corrected, coming forward to stare at Chaia. She turned to regard the White and the Voices. *Your gods are not dead. We are alive! You will build a Temple here. You will come here to consult us on the governance of your lands.*

Chaia shook his head.

:The trouble with war is that the most powerful, ruthless and least scrupulous survive. They don't make for pleasant company.

Huan turned to sneer at him.

:You survived, too, she pointed out. She turned back to the White and the Voices. *A new era of cooperation must begin. You will build a Temple here and appoint priests to serve us. You will leave your strongest sorcerers here as guards while . . .*

Auraya stopped listening as Chaia turned to regard her.

:She is a fool, he said. *If one of your friends doesn't come back and finish us off, we will perish eventually anyway. It doesn't take much magic to maintain our existence. We might even live long enough to escape this place, but we would not be sane. Most of the gods we isolated within voids went mad, Auraya. We need mortals to provide a link to the physical world.*

She felt a pang of guilt. 'I'm sorry I distrusted you. I should have realised it wasn't you. But don't give up hope. Mortals will come here. They will build this Temple Huan demands. They will keep you from going insane.'

He nodded.

:Yes. They will. Will you?

She hesitated, then nodded. 'For you, I will.'

Chaia smiled.

:It is good to know that. If it weren't for Huan, I'd make you promise me that. But we both know Huan will continue to seek your

death, even from within the void. As for me, being a god with no physical body grew tiresome a thousand years ago. I would rather not exist at all than spend a thousand years trapped here in her company.

Auraya's heart skipped. A terrible suspicion was growing. 'Don't talk as though you're dying, Chaia. I'll find a way to heal the void. There must be a way.'

Chaia reached out and touched her cheek, his touch strange and familiar.

:Do that, Auraya. It would be a good thing. And don't ever use the knowledge Huan gave you. Being a god is not as glorious as we like mortals to think it is. I've done some terrible things, but I don't regret protecting and nurturing you. Goodbye, Auraya.

He stepped back from her. Confused, she focused on the magic around them, expecting to find it was dwindling to nothing. But what remained was plentiful enough to sustain Chaia, and the others.

Then she felt it all rush toward Chaia.

And finally she comprehended what he was doing.

'Chaia! Don't!'

Bright light blinded her. Though unable to see, she could still sense the gods. She sensed them vanish one after another, Huan in mid-sentence. Chaia vanished last, but not before she heard three final words.

:Don't forget me.

CHAPTER 51

Reivan had felt awe and then fear when the glowing figures appeared among the White, the Voices and Auraya. That they were gods she had no doubt, but *which* gods were they?

Mirar had moved to the edge of the road as if preparing to throw himself off it into the sea, but then he paused, listening. Reivan could not hear the conversation. Curious, she had edged forward, but before she could draw close enough Auraya shouted and there was a second flash of light.

Dazzled, it took a long moment before Reivan could see again. The White and the Voices were all looking at Auraya. The gods had vanished.

'They're gone!' Auraya exclaimed. 'Chaia killed them and himself!'

Though Reivan could not hear what was said, it was clear the White and the Voices were protesting and questioning what she claimed. Auraya's expression was terrible. Horror and grief twisted her features. She pressed her hands to her face, then shook her head and turned away.

As she began to walk off, the leader of the Circlians started after her. Reivan jumped as Mirar spoke.

'Leave her be,' he said, striding forward. They turned to

stare at him as he moved through them to Auraya's side and placed a hand around her shoulders. She leaned against him.

A touching scene, Reivan thought, smiling wryly. *The gods were right about them. Who'd have thought?*

Mirar drew Auraya to the side of the road. Looking over the edge, Reivan saw a woman guide a small boat toward them. Auraya paused, then let Mirar help her scramble down the bank and into the vessel.

'What now?' one of the White asked.

'We go home,' their leader said.

As they turned away, laughter rang out. Reivan felt a shiver run down her spine as she realised Nekaun was conscious and had got to his feet.

'Oh, what a fine trick! You knew you were going to lose, so your gods pretended to die so you could run away home without a dent to your pride. And you claim your gods are ours, so we won't chase you. Ah! I see your plan now. You think you can lure us over there and—'

'Shut up, Nekaun,' Imenja said.

Nekaun stared at her, his face darkening with anger. 'The gods won't let *your* betrayal go unpunished,' he began.

Imenja rolled her eyes and turned her back on him. She and the other Voices turned away from the retreating White, walked past Nekaun and started toward Reivan and her companions.

'Come back here *now*!' None even turned to look at him. 'I *order* you to come back.'

The Voices ignored him. Reivan flinched as he made a throwing motion at them, but nothing happened. He stared at his hand, frowned and cast about, puzzled by something.

Imenja looked at Reivan and smiled. 'He always was a bit slow.'

'What happened?'

'It's going to take some explaining.' Imenja glanced at the

other Voices as she stopped among the Servants, advisers and the Elai king. 'I felt something change after the first flash of light. A lessening of magic.' She looked at her pendant and frowned.

'That . . . that doesn't make much sense,' Reivan said.

'No, it doesn't.' Imenja sighed. 'Auraya says the gods are dead. All the gods. I believe she is right.'

Reivan stared at her in horror.

'But those glowing figures? What were they?' an adviser asked.

'They were the gods. Their gods. Our gods. The same, it turns out. They were trapped by something Auraya and Mirar did. But it didn't kill them. The gods did that. They did something and . . . it finished them off. At least, that's what Auraya believes.'

'And you believe her?' the Elai king asked.

'Yes.'

Reivan felt the implications slowly sink in as they all started to walk back toward Avven.

'Do you still have your Skills?' a Servant asked.

'I imagine I have those that were naturally mine before I became a Voice. That means I have lost immortality. I suspect I am no more powerful than our most powerful Dedicated Servants. Except . . . I can still read minds.'

Lost her *immortality*? Reivan felt her heart twist with sympathy.

'If you and the other Voices are not as powerful, will you continue to rule?' the Elai king asked.

'Without the gods, will we start fighting each other? Will the world fall into chaos?' a Servant added, his voice strained with a hint of hysteria.

Reivan couldn't help smiling. 'We were already fighting each other.'

Imenja chuckled. 'Yes. We were. But will we have reason to now? What do you think, Companion Reivan? Should we try to continue ruling our people, or should we find ourselves a quiet little hut on a mountain somewhere and wait for the world to end?'

Reivan looked at Imenja. The woman's eyes searched hers. She realised that this was not just her mistress asking her for advice, but a friend seeking reassurance.

'I think Southern Ithania will be fine so long as you are its ruler.'

Imenja smiled. 'I hope the rest of the south agrees with you, Reivan.'

Seeing a movement over Imenja's shoulder, Reivan looked up to see that Nekaun was striding toward them, his face rigid with anger.

'But I think you'll have a fight on your hands,' she murmured.

Imenja chuckled. 'Oh, I don't think Nekaun will be a problem. He's offended a remarkable number of people in the short time since he was elected.' Her shoulders straightened. 'And there's no way I'm going to let him get away with treating you so badly, or the other women he harmed that night.' She looked at her fellow Voices. 'What do you think?'

Reivan looked at Imenja, surprised and horrified to learn that she had not been the only Servant to experience Nekaun's idea of 'thrilling' lovemaking.

'I think we should apply the strictest of our laws,' Genza said. Vervel and Shar nodded.

Imenja spun around to face Nekaun.

'Nekaun, formerly First Voice of the Gods, I hereby charge you with the rape of a Servant, of which I know you are thrice guilty. What do you have to say in your defence?'

Nekaun had slowed to a stop, his expression incredulous.

608

Reivan glanced at all the Voices' faces, heart pounding with both dread and a dark hope. Surely they wouldn't . . . but they weren't going to tolerate Nekaun as their ruler now that they didn't have to.

Recovering from his surprise, he sneered at Imenja.

'You wouldn't dare.'

'I am daring,' she told him.

'The gods will never allow it.'

'The gods are dead, Nekaun.'

He rolled his eyes. 'You really are a fool if you believe that. Even if it were true, nobody is going to believe it – or this charge. They'll think it's nothing but a convenient lie invented to get rid of me. The people voted for me, remember. They won't like you defying their decision.'

Imenja looked at the Elai king. 'Your majesty, would you do me the favour of thinking of a word. Don't speak it aloud.'

He frowned, then shrugged.

'Rebellion,' Imenja said. 'Am I correct?'

The king nodded.

'Think of another.' She paused. 'Treaty,' she said. The king nodded again. After repeating the exercise three more times, Imenja looked around at the Voices, Servants and advisers. 'Are you all satisfied that I can still read minds?'

All nodded.

'Do you believe me when I say Nekaun is guilty as charged?'

All nodded.

'Will you testify to this, if this is ever contested?'

All nodded. Satisfied, Imenja turned to regard Nekaun.

'If I could charge you with incompetence and get the same result, I would,' she told him. 'But the charge of rape of a Servant is much more serious, and it would not be fair to the women you harmed to deny them justice.' She looked at her fellow Voices.

Vervel nodded. 'A single charge is punishable by ten years of slavery. A second earns a lifetime of slavery. A third—'

'—is punishable by death,' Nekaun finished. He crossed his arms. 'You don't stand a—'

Heat seared Reivan's face. She heard Imenja utter a cry of fury and the air filled with light and sound. Then all was quiet. Reivan stared at the scene around her. Several Servants lay on the ground, some groaning, some still. Imenja, Vervel, Genza and Shar stood over a charred body, still twitching.

Nekaun, she thought. *He's not going to recover from that.* The thought brought an unexpectedly powerful relief, but as she looked at the burned flesh her cheek began to hurt. A lot. Imenja looked up at her and her expression softened into sympathy.

'I'm sorry, Reivan,' she said, hurrying over. 'I didn't protect you in time. I expected him to strike at the Voices, not the Servants.'

Reivan shook her head. 'It's nothing.' She looked at Nekaun's body. It had stopped twitching. 'I guess you've made a fine example of him.'

Imenja gasped out a laugh. 'Oh, I think we have. You've got to make a few examples on the road to ruling the world. I can't think of a better one to start with than our former First Voice.'

Reivan looked closely at Imenja, but she couldn't decide if her mistress was serious or not. Imenja glanced at her. 'What is it?'

'You . . . you don't seem that upset about the death of the gods.'

'Oh, I'm upset,' Imenja said with feeling. 'And angry. Yes, and getting angrier. But I haven't decided what to do about that.'

'Hunt down Auraya and kill her?'

'I'm not angry with Auraya.'

Reivan lifted her eyebrows in surprise. It caused the skin on her cheek to stretch, and she winced.

Imenja frowned. 'I'll explain later. We have to get you to a Dreamweaver.' She looked at the Servants on the ground, then at those still standing. 'Go back and get help,' she told them. 'Don't rely on your pendants working.' Two of the Servants nodded and hurried away.

King Ais cleared his throat. 'If you do not need me, Second Voice, I will return to my people.'

She looked at him and nodded. 'Yes. Thank you for your assistance, King Ais. It was very much appreciated.'

He smiled faintly. 'I am guessing it is no longer required.'

'No. But we would be honoured to continue working with your people in the future.'

He bowed slightly. 'As we would be honoured to work with you and yours. Goodbye. And good luck.'

All watched him move to the edge of the road. He slid out of sight down the embankment, then a moment later they heard a faint splash. Imenja turned to Reivan and smiled.

'We have much to do, and I hope you'll help me do it.'

'Of course I will,' Reivan said. 'Whatever happens, I'm still your Companion.'

Smiling broadly, Imenja took her arm and they both started along the Isthmus, toward home and a new and unexpected future.

The White walked slowly and silently back to Diamyane, their heads bowed and their faces lined with grief and shock. None of the other advisers approached them, so Danjin did not either.

He did not understand what had happened. Questions crowded his mind. What had Auraya done? Were Mirar and the Dreamweaver woman who had run forward despite Arleej's protest a part of it? Why was Auraya so upset when she left?

He remembered how Mirar had comforted her, then guided her off the Isthmus to a boat, and he felt anger stirring. There was something between them still. That was obvious.

At last the White reached the end of the Isthmus. High priests and priestesses waited expectantly, ready for the battle to begin. The White stopped and exchanged glances. Juran looked back at the advisers and Dreamweavers who had followed them to the meeting with the enemy, then raised a hand to indicate the other White should wait.

When Danjin and the others arrived, Juran surveyed all who were watching.

'The gods are dead,' he said. 'Both the Circle and the Five are gone. There will be no battle. Pack up and prepare for the journey home.'

A stunned silence followed, then questions burst out. The White ignored them. They exchanged a few words, then parted, each heading in a different direction. Seeing Ella heading toward the docks, Danjin sprinted after her.

'Ellareen!' he called as he neared her. She paused and looked around at him. He stopped, shocked, as he realised that tears ran down her cheeks.

'Hello, Danjin,' she said, wiping her face.

'What happened?' he heard himself demand.

She looked away. 'Exactly what Juran said. The gods are dead.'

'How?'

'Auraya . . .' Ella's voice was tight with emotion. Her eyes were fixed on the Isthmus. 'The other Wilds. They trapped them. They killed them.'

Shocked, Danjin could say nothing. *Auraya did betray us*, he thought. *But not by joining the Pentadrians, as we feared. By joining the Wilds.*

Ella started down the dock toward a group of Dunwayans working on a ship they had hoisted up out of the water. She didn't turn to see if he followed. Looking beyond, he realised that every ship sat at an angle, their decks awash with water. Further from the shore a forest of masts had replaced the warships of the Dunwayans.

All sunk.

The Elai were the only people who got to practise their fighting skills in this war, he found himself thinking. The Dunwayans will be disappointed to hear the battle is not going to happen now.

The war had been abandoned. He ought to have been relieved at that, but instead he felt empty. Ella stopped and he managed to catch up with her.

'The Elai,' she muttered, staring out at the water. 'Must do something about them.'

Then she strode away again. Looking in the direction she had been staring, Danjin saw a distant shape. A tiny boat, three figures aboard. Something flashed a vivid blue.

Auraya, he thought. *The Wilds. The gods were right all along. They are dangerous. If they can kill gods, what else can they do?*

He shivered, suddenly cold. Thrusting his hands under his vest, he felt something hard in one of the internal pockets. Reaching inside, he pulled it out.

A smooth white ring lay in his palm. He felt a chill spread to his bones. It was Auraya's link ring. Ella hadn't asked for it back the previous night, so Danjin had pocketed it until he had a chance to give it to her.

Memories arose of the first time he had met Auraya. He had thought she would make a good White. Later he had come to love her like a daughter, and admire her for her compassion and intelligence. He had worked hard for her. He had worried about her while she was imprisoned in Glymma. He had never doubted her.

She betrayed us, he thought. *She turned on the gods. She killed them.*

Closing his fingers around the ring, he drew back his arm, moved to the water's edge, then threw it with all his strength. It disappeared into the murky water.

Then, turning away, he started back toward the town.

Neither Mirar, Emerahl or Auraya said anything during the journey to the Sennon shore. Mirar watched Auraya closely. She stared at the bottom of the boat, her expression closed and distant.

I will have to tell the others of Huan's trickery, and that Auraya learned too late that Chaia didn't try to kill her, he told himself. *And that he killed himself and the others. They won't understand why she grieves, otherwise.*

He couldn't feel the same sorrow. Chaia had done terrible things in his time. The world was better off without him. But Mirar knew he would not be able to express such an opinion to Auraya. Ever.

Finally the bottom of the boat scraped against sand. Auraya looked behind at the shore, then braced herself as Emerahl used magic to push the vessel high up out of the water, next to another.

The three of them rose and stepped out. They were in a small bay. Sand dunes hid them from the sight of all but passing boats. Three more figures waited, sitting on the beach. They had lit a small camp fire. Mirar caught the smell of cooking fish.

'This is a fine welcome,' he said.

'The Gull provided the fish,' Surim said. He handed Mirar a mug. 'I brought the kahr.'

Mirar drank a mouthful of the strong liquor. 'Ah!' he sighed. 'I needed that. I'm afraid I don't have anything to contribute.'

'You brought us Auraya,' Tamun said.

They all looked at Auraya, who remained silent, staring into the fire.

'So, what will we all do now?' Surim asked. He filled another mug with kahr and handed it to Emerahl. 'Any plans?'

Emerahl shrugged. 'I have always wanted to start a school of sorcery and healing.'

Mirar looked at her in surprise. 'I thought you decided you never wanted to be the centre of anything again, after being worshipped as The Hag?'

'I never meant that to happen, and I spent all my energy trying to escape it. Maybe if I start something myself, and put my energy into controlling it, it will work out differently. Besides,' she lifted her mug in salute to him, 'I've got an expert to consult on founding and controlling a group of sorcerers. What are you going to do?'

He shrugged. 'Help Dreamweavers recover from the last hundred or so years. This time I have two continents to roam. I always knew my people spread into the south; I don't know why I never visited them before.'

'Because the gods were doing worrying things in the north,' Surim answered.

'What about you two?' Emerahl asked, looking at Surim and Tamun. 'What will you do?'

Surim looked at his sister. 'Stop hiding, for a start. I'd like to travel.'

'I don't want to go back to being famous,' Tamun said. 'How can we give people advice, anyway? We don't know how the death of the gods will change things.' She looked at her brother. 'I don't want to travel yet, either. I think . . .' She paused to consider. 'I think I'd like to settle somewhere. A place where people make things. Craftspeople. Artists. That sort of thing.'

615

'And I will visit you — maybe I'll sell what your people make!' Surim exclaimed. 'I could become a merchant!'

The Gull chuckled. 'I guess I'll be seeing you on the water.'

'You're not going to change anything, are you?' Emerahl said.

The boy shook his head. 'The sea is my home. It took me a thousand years to find it, and I see no reason to change.'

They fell into a thoughtful silence. *A thousand years before he became The Gull*, Mirar thought. *And he was a legend before I became immortal. How old is he?*

'I'm going back to Si,' Auraya said. They all looked at her. Mirar felt his heart lift. *She'll be all right*, he thought. *In time she'll forget about the gods, and Chaia. And she has plenty of time to do so.*

Auraya frowned. 'After I retrieve Mischief,' she added. She touched the blue cloth wound around her body. 'And pay that merchant for this and the food I took.'

Emerahl chuckled. 'You'll need some money, then.'

Auraya looked up. 'Yes.'

'I have the next best thing. I buried it not far from here, actually.'

'The treasure,' Surim said.

Emerahl smiled. 'Yes. I think I can spare a little for Auraya. After all, she couldn't have turned up in rags – or with no clothes on. That just wouldn't have been right.'

'I don't know . . .' Mirar disagreed.

'Mischief,' Surim said. 'Didn't he free Auraya? Who is this man?'

'A veez,' Mirar said.

Surim looked at Mirar in surprise, then grinned. 'Do you mean that, after all you did – or failed to do – to free Auraya, it was a veez that managed it?'

'Yes,' Emerahl replied.

Surim laughed. 'I wonder if this poor creature realises it spoiled any chances you had that Auraya would fall into your arms in gratitude.'

Emerahl snorted. 'For the sake of women everywhere, tell me you wouldn't have done that, Auraya.'

The corner of Auraya's mouth twitched upward. 'I might have. I might not.' She looked at Mirar. 'I guess we'll never know.'

He shrugged. 'The past can't be changed. But the future looks good. Full of endless possibilities.'

Looking away, he saw that the others were exchanging smug grins before they quickly smoothed their expressions.

'And no gods,' Emerahl added.

'But still plenty of mortals,' The Gull said. 'Don't underestimate them. They can be as dangerous as gods. More dangerous, as the gods were limited by the need for willing followers to do their work.'

The others considered this silently.

'We should stay in contact,' Emerahl said, looking around. 'Visit each other – and perhaps meet once a year.'

'Yes,' Surim agreed. 'Perhaps at Tamun's new empire of artists.'

Mirar was pleased to see Auraya nodding.

'I'll visit you all, so long as you let me know where you are, as I travel around the continents,' he said. He looked at Auraya. 'Will I be welcome in Si?'

She almost smiled. 'Of course.'

Mirar felt his heart stir with hope. *Careful*, he told himself. *Don't jump to any conclusions. You mustn't rush her. She needs time to recover from everything that's happened.*

Emerahl rose to her feet. 'If we're going to get this treasure, we'd better do it before we drink too much.' She looked at Auraya. 'Would you help me carry it?'

Auraya shrugged, then rose and followed Emerahl into the sand dunes. Looking at her wasted body, Mirar felt a pang of concern. *Help her carry it? I don't think so.* He got to his feet and followed.

He caught up with Auraya soon after. She was out of breath, and had stopped. Emerahl's tracks led away, over the top of a dune. Auraya turned to smile ruefully at him.

'Your healing method does have its limitations,' she told him.

He nodded. 'You can only draw upon the resources you have. But a few meals should help fix that.'

Auraya nodded and looked at the ground, frowning. Concerned, he moved closer.

'Are you all right?'

She looked up, then smiled and, without warning, stepped close and kissed him on the mouth. It was more than a mere friendly kiss, but it was brief.

It left him frozen in surprise, heart pounding.

'What was that for?' he managed eventually.

'A thank you,' she said. 'All through my . . . my captivity you kept me company. You gave me hope and courage.' She paused. 'And as you said, the future is full of endless possibilities.'

She smiled and, not waiting for him to say anything in return, turned away to determinedly follow Emerahl's footsteps up the sand dune.

Mirar watched her disappear over the top, then followed, knowing he was grinning like a fool, and not caring.

EPILOGUE

The man that walked hesitantly through the door was thin and lean. His clothes were simple but the cloth was not poor quality, and his sandals were new. Despite his nervousness, he walked with the ease of a man confident of his place in the world. His hair was grey and his skin wrinkled, but his gaze was direct and sharp.

Propped up on pillows, the Emperor of Sennon assessed the man out of old habit and with skill learned over his long life. Though he saw intelligence and confidence in this man, he also noted with relief the absence of a certain hardness of demeanour he had come to recognise in men who were ambitious, greedy or cruel.

But the man is a fanatic, he decided. *I can spot them a hundred paces off.*

The man took in the bed, the emperor and his companion in one quick glance, then dropped to his knees and pressed his forehead to the floor.

Not too proud, the emperor noted. *Those god-cursed priests and Servants hate bowing to me. This man is smart.*

'Rise.' The visitor obeyed, but kept his eyes downcast. 'So you are the Wise Man of Karienne,' the emperor stated. 'Do you have a name as well as a title?'

The Wise Man nodded. 'My name is Eralayo Scribe. Or Ero.'

'You've been preaching for some time. If I was not so . . .' the emperor gestured at the bed '. . . so indisposed I would come to listen to you.'

'I am honoured you say so.'

'Which is why I have brought you here. Tell me about this Maker you speak of.'

The Wise Man looked up in surprise. He glanced at the emperor's companion, then met the emperor's eyes again. His shoulders rose and fell as he gathered his courage. Then he straightened.

'We are all creations of the Maker,' he said. 'Everything was made by him. Every animal, every plant, every man and woman. Even the dust beneath your feet. Even the gods.'

He paused and swallowed audibly. 'The Maker made the world, and his purpose is a mystery to us. We wonder why he made such a flawed world. The Maker made creatures that we consider evil. But why do we consider them evil? Because they kill?' He spread his hands. 'A reyna eats plants. Plants are living things as well. The reyna kills the plant it eats. We fear the leramars and the vorns because they can kill us, but they do not do so out of malice, but hunger. We dislike them because they eat our stock. That is not evil, just costly.'

The emperor smiled at that.

'We wonder why the Maker made mortals capable of evil,' the Wise Man continued. 'There is much about the Maker that we do not understand. We have only just begun to perceive him. Perhaps in time he will allow us to understand more.'

The Wise Man fell silent, but his expression was expectant. *He has preached so many times, he knows how to spur people into asking the right questions*, the emperor thought.

'How do you know this Maker is not some figment of your imagination?'

'For some, they only need look inside themselves. To close their eyes and search. The knowledge is there. It has always been there. We have simply never stopped to look for it before, because the evidence for the existence of the old gods was so obvious we never looked beyond it. The Maker does not make his existence known through magic. As the gods were beings of magic, the Maker is a being of all. Of everything. Of the world.'

'You say the Maker created the gods. How is it that they were destroyed, then?'

The Wise Man shrugged. 'He has given all things a weakness, perhaps to ensure that nothing can dominate forever. Eventually the gods' weaknesses had led to their destruction.'

'And will the weaknesses of mortals lead to their destruction?'

'Perhaps. But not for a long time, I'd guess. We are a resilient creation, despite our weaknesses.'

The emperor smiled. He paused as his breathing became more difficult. His companion brought the burner of cleansing herbs closer. When his lungs had cleared a little, the emperor looked at the Wise Man again. 'Does the Maker preserve souls?'

Again, the Wise Man shrugged. 'I do not know. But the Maker does not waste anything. When we reap the ograsi, we kill the plant, but the stalk rots and feeds the soil, and the seeds feed and nourish us. Our bodies may return to the world in the same way, enriching it and becoming new life. It may be that our souls are the same.'

The emperor considered this. He nodded. 'That is all for now,' he croaked, feeling constriction returning. 'Leave me.'

The Wise Man abased himself again, then, wearing a thoughtful expression, left the room. Sagging against the pillows, the emperor breathed the fumes of the herbs once more, then looked up at his one remaining son.

'I like this man and his Maker,' he said. 'What did you think?'

Herayla nodded. 'I can see no threat in it and plenty of potential.'

'So you approve?'

'Yes.' Herayla's brow furrowed. 'We have had fifty years of lies and disorder since the gods died. We need something to unite the people. This idea of a Maker, who created all, has many appealing qualities. Especially the idea that we all have a few weaknesses. It can't hurt for the people to expect and forgive a few bad traits.'

'Don't push them too far,' the emperor warned.

Herayla smiled. 'You know I won't.'

'No, you are too clever for that,' the emperor agreed. 'I have to admit, I'm glad it's over. I just have to live long enough to declare that I, the Emperor of Sennon, who has traditionally never favoured one religion over another, have converted to the cult of the Maker. It will be a powerful gesture. After that, the world is yours to rule.' He drew in a shallow breath and sighed. 'I hope, for your sake, it works.'

Herayla smiled. 'Don't worry, Father. Whether this Maker exists or not, he can't possibly make as great a mess as the gods did.'

The emperor chuckled. 'I hope you are right, my son. I hope you are right.'

GLOSSARY

VEHICLES

platten – two-wheeled vehicle

tarn – four-wheeled vehicle

windboat – a boat that uses windpower to travel across the desert

windsailers – the boat's operator

PLANTS

dembar – tree with magic sensitive sap

drimma – fruit of Southern Ithania

felfea – tree of Si

florrim – tranquillising drug

formtane – soporific drug

fronden – fern/bracken-like plants

garpa – tree; seeds are a stimulant

heybrin – cure believed to protect against sexually transmitted diseases

hroomya – coral that produces a blue dye

kwee bulbs – the edible fruit of a seaweed

mallin – herb that promotes circulation

mytten – tree with wood that burns slowly

ograssi – grain crop of Sennon

rebi – fruit found in Si
saltwood – wood that is resistant to decay
sea tube – ink-producing coral
shendle – plant on forest floor
sleepvine – uses telepathic compulsion to trap prey
smokewood – bark with stimulating qualities
velweed – cure for haemorrhoids
wemmin – fleshy flower
winnet – tree that grows along rivers
yan – tubers on forest floor

ANIMALS
aggen – mythical monster that lives in mines
amma – believed to be giantfish tears
arem – domestic, for pulling plattens and tarns
ark – predatory bird
breem – small animal hunted by Siyee for food
bulfish – shellfish that lives on rocky outcrops
carmook – small pet native to Sennon
dartfly – stinging insect of north-east mountains
doi – playful sea creature
fanrin – predator that hunts gowts
flarke – sea predator
garr – giant sea creature
giantfish – enormous sea creature
girri – wingless birds, domesticated by Siyee
glitterworm – insect that glows in the dark
gowt – domestic animal bred for meat and milk, resides in
    mountains
kiri – large predatory bird
leramar – predator with telepathic ability
lightfish – fish that glows in dark waters
lyrim – domestic herd animals

moohook – small pet
ner – domesticated animal bred for meat
reyna – animal for riding and pulling plattens
roale – large sea creature
roro – carnivore of the Dekkan jungle
shem – domestic animal bred for milk
shrimmi – freshwater shellfish
spikemat – spiney creature of reefs
spinerake – landwalker name for flarke
starfan – fish with deadly spines
takker – large snake
tiwi – insects that make a hive
veez – cute, telepathic pet that can speak
vorn – wolf-like animals
woodfish – tasteless fish
yern – deer-like, limited telepathy
yeryer – venomous sea creature
zapper – stinging insect

CLOTHING
circ – circular overgarment worn by Circlian priests and
    priestesses
octavestim – garb of the Priests of Gareilem
tawl – overgarment worn draped over shoulders fastened at
    throat
tunic – dress for women, shirt for men
undershift – undergarment for women

FOOD
coopa – Dunwayan drink
firespice – spice from Toren
flatloaf – dense bread
nutmeal – paste made from nuts, Si

rootcakes – patties of boiled and fried roots
wafercakes – fried, flaky pastry

DRINK

ahm – drink of Somrey, usually warmed and spiced
drai – Elai drink
fwa – Dunwayan drink
jamya – ceremonial drink of Pentadrians
kahr – Sennon drink
maita – stimulating non-alcoholic drink
teepi – Siyee drink
teho – drink of Sennon
tintra – Hanian drink
tipli – Toren drink

DISEASES

hearteater – disease that attacks lungs
lungrot – disease that, funnily enough, rots the lungs
woundrot – the festering of a wound

BUILDINGS

blackstone – stone that is dark-coloured
safehouse – place where Dreamweavers can stay
wayhouse – place for travellers to stay in
whitestone – stone that is pale-coloured

OTHER

canar – Sennon coin
sleepease – sleeping drug
smokewood – recreational drug

EXTRAS

www.orbitbooks.net

About the Author

Trudi Canavan lives in Melbourne, Australia. Her first published story received an Aurealis Award for Best Fantasy Short Story in 1999. She has since published the bestselling Black Magician Trilogy and is now a bestselling author in the UK, Australia and the US. For more information about Trudi and her writing go to www.trudicanavan.com

Find out more about other Orbit authors by registering for the free monthly newsletter at www.orbitbooks.net

An interview with

TRUDI CANAVAN

The publication *Voice of the Gods* will mark the completion of your second trilogy. How do you think your life and your writing have changed between when The Black Magician trilogy was published and now?

Aside from moving house three times, and going from different levels of broke to having financial security, there's a structure to the future that I'm not used to having. Having been self-employed for over a decade, I was used to not knowing what I'd be doing in a year or two. Now I plan my future in book series. Right now I know what I'll be working on for the next four years. It's strange, but reassuring.

The biggest change in my writing has been the introduction of deadlines. Because the Black Magician Trilogy was my first 'book' I had no contract, and writing wasn't my only income earner, so I could take as long as I wanted to rewrite and improve it. Having a deadline gives you less time to fiddle and tweak. Yet I've also noticed that I write slower now but my first drafts need less rewriting and polishing. Experience has taught me better plotting and how to avoid common structural mistakes. Not that I don't still make mistakes or don't still polish obsessively.

The world you created for the Age of the Five is more expansive, both in geographical scope and range of characters and peoples, than your previous trilogy. Did that bring any new challenges to your writing?

From the start I expected that having a larger world to set the story in would mean more world building. It did, but double the countries only meant double the work. Having a greater cast of characters, however, increased the work considerably. Each main character added a greater dimension to the plots and subplots of the other characters, so it creates work on top of work.

I hadn't created fantasy races before, so that was also a new challenge. The magical system was different to the Black Magician Trilogy in that it was applied to more than just special humans, but to all living things. This was new territory, and a lot of fun.

Both the human and non-human worlds in the Age of the Five are incredibly detailed and realistic. Did you draw from any real world examples or was it purely an imaginative process?

Nothing is ever a purely imaginative process. If there wasn't some familiar element to stories and worlds there's be nothing the reader could relate to or understand. It's more a matter of how close to this world you want your story and world to be. How much strangeness you can get away with.

There are plenty of books based on peoples and places of this world, both current, past and mythological. I prefer to draw more general ideas from these, mixing up elements of 'this world' cultures to get something new, but believable.

It's always interesting to see the reaction some readers have to these invented peoples. I saw one reader's comment where he or she assumed that just because I had a dark-skinned race living in a hot, dry climate they must be based on an Islamic race, but they could just as easily have been based on people from any dry country in Africa, or even some in South America! Another once claimed the war in Age of the Five was based on the Iraq War. Of course, there have been a lot more wars in this world, recently and in the distant past, than just the Iraq War. I could have based it on any of them, but I didn't need to. The story dictated how the war in Age of the Five should proceed.

All your books have a glossary of terms in the back. How important do you think creating a new language or new parts of a language are to establishing different world? And how do you come up with it all?

The most valuable lesson I've learned from reader feedback is how to tell what is a criticism and what is personal taste. One of the issues of personal taste is whether an author uses made-up names or not, particularly in relation to animals.

If I'm reading about a fantasy world and come across an animal from this world – say, a sheep – it shatters any feeling I have of being in a different place. So I prefer to invent a new creature to fit that role.

Now, naturally if I'm creating a domestic animal it's going to have to comply with the requirements humans have of them. Humans use animals for milk, meat and fibre, and those animals have to be docile enough in nature to handle with minimum effort, and it helps if they are social animals that tend to stay in groups. It's doesn't make much sense to have fancy lizard-like beasts that breathe fire and tend to fight each other on sight when all you need is some wool to spin and weave into cloth, and the occasional bit of meat in your stew.

So the animal sounds a lot like a sheep. I get the occasional reader asking me why I don't just call it a sheep. My answer to that is "why aren't you asking me why I don't just call it a llama?". In fantasy, most readers have a prejudice for the European style landscape and mythology. I don't want to have to invent

ludicrous animals just to make it obvious that mine aren't, so I make the differences subtle. And there are plenty of readers who like that about my worlds.

Of course, then it's a matter of courtesy to include a glossary in the back, so people can check what sort of animal/plant/object they're reading about if they happen to be interested to know.

You've gone from a non-religious world in the Black Magician trilogy to one in the Age of the Five where gods play an active, and not necessarily benevolent, role. Can you tell us a bit about that?

Not being a religious person, I wasn't confident about including religion in the Black Magician Trilogy. I also wondered if it would be refreshing to create a world without it. Bits of religion did seep in eventually, but mostly in distant countries.

I could hardly avoid religion in Age of the Five, since the idea sprang from wondering what it would have been like if the classical era gods had been real. They had a habit of interfering with mortals, which was usually to the detriment of the mortals. You had to wonder if praying was a wise thing to do, because if the gods did notice you it was all just as likely to end badly as it was to end well. Writing about a pantheon of gods was much easier because the scenario was so different to most of the religions practised today.

Both your trilogies feature very strong, very likable female protagonists. Have you always wanted to write characters like this?

Of course! And they couldn't be warriors, either. In so many of the fantasy books I grew up reading women had one of three roles: the princess, the warrior or the chaste priestess. I wanted to write of women who were strong because of their determination, integrity and courage. Of course, by the time I did write of one those sorts of characters were no longer hard to find. Which means there are lots of fabulous strong female characters for me to read about, too.

Some authors talk of their characters 'surprising' them by their actions; is this something that has happened to you?

It has occasionally. I didn't intend for Cery to have a crush on Sonea, for instance. And while Emerahl was supposed to be feisty, she came out much more feisty than I first expected. The biggest surprise was Ellareen, who changed considerably over the course of writing Voice of the Gods – but I can't tell you how without spoiling the plot!

On a bit of a related note, do you have any favourites among your characters? Who would they be?

I don't tend to have favourites, but some I enjoyed writing more than others. Cery was always fun, with his personal ideas of morality and ambition. Dannyl had a sense of humour I enjoyed. Emerahl was delightfully practical in her sense of self-preservation. Mirar was lovably flawed.

On the other hand, I could relish Regin's ruthlessness and Rian's bloodthirsty fanaticism. A character doesn't have to be wholly benevolent for me to like them.

Both The Black Magician and Age of the Five series have been immensely popular. Why do you think people connect with your writing as strongly as they have?

I'm not sure. I suspect it's a side-effect of my short attention span. I figure if I'm bored, the reader will be too, so I'm constantly trying to keep up the tension, mystery and pace.

On a more general note, do you have a personal theory on why Fantasy is so popular?

Perhaps because it is so varied. There are so many different kinds of fantasy: dark, humorous, epic, urban, futuristic, historic, mythic, fairy tale, animal, political, military, uplifting, depressing, magic realism… you can always find something to suit your mood or taste.

In the Age of the Five you created the characteristics and culture for at least five separate groups of people, including the non-human Elai and Siyee. Do you have any particular strategies for keeping track of it all?

I write lots of lists!

It's interesting to see how you manage your worlds; do you also have a method of managing you time? For example, do you have a set writing routine and if so, what is it?

Since I've been writing full time I try to write during normal work hours, though because it can be a bit rough on my back I take plenty of breaks. I probably spent at least one day a week on non-writing tasks, like accounting, reading fanmail, updating the website, blogging and publicity. If I have a looming deadline I'll slip back into an old routine of working four days then resting for one, which is a good compromise between resting my back, and retaining more in my head than I do over a two or three day break.

As an author and artist, what do you think of the packaging given to your books? Do you have any strong feelings on cover art?

I've been fortunate in that I've liked most of my covers. I do have strong feeling about cover art, because I have a graphic design, visual merchandising and illustration background. But it actually bothers me more if the title of the book is hard to read at a distance than if the illustration doesn't quite fit the story. I'd rather a reader wrote to tell me the cover is 'wrong' than to say they walked into a shop and didn't buy the book because they couldn't find it!

Do you read mainly fantasy fiction yourself, or do you like to take a rest after a hard day creating? What are you currently reading?

I don't read as much as I used to. Initially this was because I was self employed and didn't have a long journey on the train to work and back each day. Then it was because I moved into a house that didn't have a bath to relax and read in each couple of nights. Once I started writing full time I read even less, because I found the writing style of the book I was reading started to affect the tone of my own writing – great when the book you're reading is good, not so great when it isn't!

Now I find I'll read a lot of non-fiction when I'm writing. Partly as research and partly because it gives me ideas for new stories. I'm currently reading *Clay: The History and Evolution of Humankind's Relationship with Earth's Most Primal Element*, which is fascinating and has already given me an idea for a short story.

A lot of the fiction I read is fellow Aussie author's manuscripts. I get to read their latest work in exchange for giving feedback – and hopefully get the same favour in return.

Do you have any particular favourite authors who have influenced your work?

Too many to list here! Tolkein's work inspired me to write, Raymond Feist's *Magician* showed me fantasy didn't have to be *all* European-based, Tanith Lee's books showed me fantasy could be rich, exotic and come in different moods and styles, Guy Gavriel Kay's writing style blew me away, Jennifer Fallon's dialogue and humour is something to aspire to,

Glenda Larke's characters encourage me to break the mould, and Russell Kirkpatrick's work reminds me that landscape can be a character, too.

Your next project is going to be a return to the world of the Black Magician. Can you tell us a bit about that?

I was adamant up until the rewrite and polish of the end of The High Lord that I would not write a sequel to the Black Magician Trilogy. After all, at that time I'd been slogging away at that trilogy for seven years and needed something new to work on. But then an idea for a sequel suddenly wormed into my head. What would Kyralia and the Guild be like in 20 years? What would Sonea be like as a middle-aged mother? Without the Purge to unify them, what would happen to the Thieves? For that matter, how would the Guild deal with the possibility of future threats from Sachaka?

Well, I still needed a break and Age of the Five was stomping around demanding to be written. In the meantime an idea for a prequel set around the Sachakan War came to me as well, which would link to the sequel. What I especially liked about the prequel was the idea of taking Kyralian society back to a less developed state, where black magic was still used and the old apprenticeship system was in place.

Where do you think your writing will take you after *The Magicians' Apprentice*? Are there any characters or peoples from Age of the Five you'd like to return to at some point in time?

I have no plans to write more books set in the world of the Age of the Five, but if ideas for more Black Magician Trilogy books can pop into my head then it's possible more Age of the Five ones can too. But first there is a series of books, about sorcerers who travel and trade between worlds, that I have had waiting in the wings for some time. The first book, *Angel of Storms* has been written, though I suspect by the time I finish the Traitor Spy Trilogy I'll want to make quite a few changes.

And, lastly, for those writers who have yet to see their books appearing in the shops, how did it feel to see your first novel in print?

Wonderful, but also strange. A small bundle of paper and card turned up in the post, and though the words in them were mine it seemed like too small a thing to be containing so many years of work and a whole other world populated by characters I knew so well. It was definitely an example of something being worth more than the sum of its parts!

If you haven't read Trudi's debut novel,
here is an extract from

THE MAGICIANS'
GUILD

Several hundred people had gathered in the square. While many continued on through the Northern Gates, others lingered inside in the hope of meeting their loved ones before entering the confusion of the slums, and some always refused to move until they were forced to.

Cery and Harrin stopped at the base of the pool in the centre of the square. A statue of King Kalpol rose from the water. The long-dead monarch had been almost forty when he routed the mountain bandits, yet here he was portrayed as a young man, his right hand brandishing a likeness of his famous, jewel-encrusted sword, and his left gripping an equally ornate goblet.

A different statue had once stood in its place, but it had been torn down thirty years before. Though several statues had been erected of King Terrel over the years, all but one had been destroyed, and it was rumoured that even the surviving statue, protected within the Palace walls, had been defaced. Despite all else he had done, the citizens of Imardin would always remember King Terrel as the man who had started the yearly Purges.

Her uncle had told her the story many times. Thirty years before, after influential members of the Houses had complained that the streets were not safe, the King had ordered the guard to drive all beggars, homeless vagrants and suspected criminals out of the city. Angered by this, the strongest of the expelled gathered together and, with weapons provided by the wealthier smugglers and thieves, fought back. Faced with street battles and riots, the King turned to the Magicians' Guild for assistance.

The rebels had no weapon to use against magic. They were captured or driven out into the slums. The King was so pleased by the festivities the Houses had held to celebrate that he declared the city would be purged of vagrants every winter.

When the old King had died five years past, many had hoped that the Purges would stop, but Terrel's son, King Merin, had continued the tradition. Looking around, it was hard to imagine that the frail, sick-looking people about her could ever be a threat. Then she noticed that several youths had gathered around Harrin, all watching their leader expectantly. She felt her stomach clench with sudden apprehension.

'I have to go,' she said.

'No, don't go,' Cery protested. 'We've only just found each other again.'

She shook her head. 'I've been too long. Jonna and Ranel might be in the slums already.'

'Then you're already in trouble.' Cery shrugged. 'You still 'fraid of a scolding, eh?'

She gave him a reproachful look. Undeterred, he smiled back.

'Here.' He pressed something into her hand. Looking down, she examined the little packet of paper.

'This is the stuff you guys were throwing at the guards?'

Cery nodded. 'Papea dust,' he said. 'Makes their eyes sting and gives 'em a rash.'

'No good against magicians, though.'

He grinned. 'I got one once. He didn't see me coming.'

Sonea started to hand back the packet, but Cery waved his hand.

'Keep it,' he said. 'It's no use here. The magicians always make a wall.'

She shook her head. 'So you throw stones instead? Why do you bother?'

'It feels good.' Cery looked back towards the road, his eyes a steely grey. 'If we didn't, it would be like we don't mind the Purge. We can't let them drive us out of the city without some kind of show, can we?'

Shrugging, she looked at the youths. Their eyes were bright with anticipation. She had always felt that throwing anything at the magicians was pointless and foolish.

'But you and Harrin hardly ever come into the city,' she said.

'No, but we ought to be able to if we want.' Cery grinned. 'And this is the only time we get to make trouble without the Thieves sticking their noses in.'

Sonea rolled her eyes. 'So that's it.'

'Hai! Let's go!' Harrin bellowed over the noise of the crowd.

As the youths cheered and began to move away, Cery looked at her expectantly.

'Come on,' he urged. 'It'll be fun.'

Sonea shook her head.

'You don't have to join in. Just watch,' he said. 'After, I'll come with you and see you get a place to stay.'

'But—'

'Here.' He reached out and undid her scarf. Folding it into a triangle, he draped it over her head and tied it at her throat. 'You look more like a girl now. Even if the guards decide to chase us – which they never do – they won't think you're a troublemaker. There,' he patted her cheek, 'much better. Now come on. I'm not letting you disappear again.'

She sighed. 'All right.'

The crowd had grown, and the gang began to push forward through the crush of people. To Sonea's surprise, they received no protest or retaliation in return for their elbowing. Instead, the men and women she passed reached out to press rocks and over-ripe fruit into her hands, and to whisper encouragement. As she followed Cery past the eager faces, she felt a stirring of excitement. Sensible people like her aunt and uncle had already left the North Square. Those who remained wanted to see a show of defiance – and it didn't matter how pointless it was.

The crowd thinned as the gang reached its edge. At one side Sonea could see people still entering the square from a side street. On the other, the distant gates rose above the crowd. In front . . .

Sonea stopped and felt all her confidence drain away. As Cery moved on, she took a few steps back and stopped behind an elderly woman. Less than twenty paces away stood a row of magicians.

Taking a deep breath, she let it out slowly. She knew they would not move from their places. They would ignore the crowd until they were ready to drive it out of the square. There was no reason to be frightened.

Swallowing, she forced herself to look away and seek out the youths. Harrin, Cery and the others were moving further forward, strolling amongst the dwindling stream of latecomers joining the edge of the crowd.

Looking up at the magicians again, she shivered. She had never been this close to them before, or had an opportunity to take a good look at them.

They wore a uniform: wide-sleeved robes bound by a sash at the waist. According to her uncle Ranel, clothes like these had been fashionable many hundreds of years ago but now it was a crime for ordinary people to dress like magicians.

They were all men. From her position she could see nine of them, standing alone or in pairs, forming part of a line that she knew would encompass the square. Some were no older than twenty, while others looked ancient. One of the closest, a fair-haired man of about thirty, was handsome in a sleek, well-groomed way. The rest were surprisingly ordinary-looking.

In the corner of her eye she saw an abrupt movement, and turned in time to see Harrin swing his arm forward. A rock flew though the air toward the magicians. Despite knowing what would happen, she held her breath.

The stone smacked against something hard and invisible and dropped to the ground. Sonea let out her breath as more of the youths began hurling stones. A few of the robed figures looked up to watch the missiles pattering against the air in front of them. Others regarded the youths briefly, then turned back to their conversations.

Sonea stared at the place where the magicians' barrier hung. She could see nothing. Moving forward, she took out one of the lumps in her pockets, drew her arm back and hurled it with all her strength. It disintegrated as it hit the invisible wall, and for a moment, a cloud of dust hung in the air, flat on one side.

She heard a low chuckle nearby and turned to see the old woman grinning at her.

'That's a good 'un,' the woman cackled. 'You show 'em. Go on.'

Sonea slipped a hand into a pocket and felt her fingers close on a larger rock. She took a few steps closer to the magicians and smiled. She had seen annoyance in some of their faces. Obviously they did not like to be defied, but something prevented them from confronting the youths.

Beyond the haze of dust came the sound of voices. The well-groomed magician glanced up, then turned back to his companion, an older man with grey in his hair.

'Pathetic vermin,' he sneered. 'How long until we can get rid of them?'

Something flipped over in Sonea's belly, and she tightened her grip on the rock. She pulled it free and gauged its weight. A heavy one. Turning to face the magicians, she gathered the anger she felt at being thrown out of her home, all her inbred hate of the magicians, and hurled the stone at the speaker. She traced its path through the air, and as it neared the magicians' barrier, she willed it to pass through and reach its mark.

A ripple of blue light flashed outward, then the rock slammed into the magician's temple with a dull thud. He stood motionless, staring at nothing, then his knees buckled and his companion stepped forward to catch him.

Sonea stared, her mouth agape, as the older magician lowered his companion to the ground. The jeers of the youths died away. Stillness spread outward like smoke through the crowd.

Then exclamations rang out as two more magicians

sprang forward to crouch beside their fallen companion. Harrin's friends, and others in the crowd, began to cheer. Noise returned to the square as people murmured and shouted out what had happened.

Sonea looked down at her hands. *It worked. I broke the barrier, but that's not possible, unless . . .*

Unless I used magic.

Cold rushed through her as she remembered how she had focused all her anger and hate on the stone, how she had followed its path with her mind and willed it to break through the barrier. Something in her stirred, as if it were eager for her to repeat those actions.

Looking up, she saw that several magicians had gathered around their fallen companion. Some crouched beside him, but most had turned to stare out at the people in the square, their eyes searching. *Looking for me*, she thought suddenly. As if hearing her thought, one turned to stare at her. She froze in terror, but his eyes slid away and roved on through the crowd.

They don't know who it was. She gasped with relief. Glancing around, she saw that the crowd was several paces behind her. The youths were backing away. Heart pounding, she followed suit.

Then the older magician rose. Unlike the others, his eyes snapped to hers without hesitation. He pointed at her and the rest of the magicians turned to stare again. As their hands rose, she felt a surge of terror. Spinning around, she bolted towards the crowd. In the corner of her eye, she saw the rest of the youths fleeing. Her vision wavered as several quick flashes of light lit the faces before her, then screams tore through the air. Heat rushed over her and she fell to her knees, gasping.

'STOP!'

She felt no pain. Looking down, she gasped in relief to find her body whole. She looked up; people were still running away, ignoring the strangely amplified command that still echoed through the square.

A smell of burning drifted to her nose. Sonea turned to see a figure sprawled face-down on the pavement a few steps away. Though flames ate at the clothing hungrily, the figure lay still. Then she saw the blackened mess that had once been an arm, and her stomach twisted with nausea.

'DO NOT HARM HER!'

Staggering to her feet, she reeled away from the corpse. Figures passed her on either side as the youths fled. With an effort, she forced herself into a staggering run.

She caught up with the crowd at the Northern Gate and pushed her way into it. Fighting her way forward, clawing past those in her way, she forced herself deep within the crowd of bodies. Feeling the stones still weighing down her pockets, she clawed them out. Something caught her legs, tripping her over, but she dragged herself to her feet and pushed on.

Hands grabbed her roughly from behind. She struggled and drew a breath to scream, but the hands turned her around and she found herself staring up at the familiar blue eyes of Harrin.

If you enjoy Trudi Canavan's books,
you might like to read Jennifer Fallon.

Here is an extract from

WOLFBLADE

It was always messy, cleaning up after a murder. There was more than just blood to be washed off the tiles. There were all those awkward loose ends to be taken care of – alibis to be established, traitors to be paid off, witnesses to be silenced . . .

And that, Elezaar knew, was the problem. He'd just witnessed a murder.

A slight, humid breeze ruffled the curtain in the alcove where the dwarf was hiding, the tiled floors of the mansion echoing to the sound of booted feet. The faint, fishy smell of the harbour lingered on the wind, rank and uninviting. Or perhaps it wasn't the nearby bay Elezaar could smell. Maybe the decay he smelled was here. Maybe the swords of his master's killers had opened a vein some-where and the stench came from the moral decay that seeped from the very walls of this house and permeated everything it touched.

Still trembling at the narrowness of his escape, Elezaar moved the curtain a fraction and looked into the room. His master's corpse lay across the blood-soaked silken sheets, his head almost severed by the savage blow which had ended his life. On the floor at his feet lay another body. A slave. She was so new to the household Elezaar hadn't even had time to learn her name. She was only twelve or thirteen; her slender, broken body in the first bloom of womanhood. Or it had been. The master liked them like that – young, nubile and terrified. Elezaar had lost count of the number of girls like her he had seen led into this opulently decorated chamber of horrors. He'd listened to their screams, night after night, playing his lyre with desperate determination; he provided the background music to their torment, shutting out their cries for mercy . . .

This was no subtle assassination, the dwarf decided in a conscious effort to block the memories. This was blatant. Done in broad daylight. An open challenge to the High Prince.

Not that the attack was entirely unexpected. Elezaar's master, Ronan Dell, was one of the High Prince's closest friends – assuming you could call their bizarre, often volatile relationship 'friendship'. In Elezaar's opinion, his master and the High Prince shared a passion for perversion and for other people's pain rather than any great affection for each other. There were few in Greenharbour who would lament the death of Ronan Dell. No slave in his household would miss him, Elezaar could well attest to that. But even if the slaves of Lord Ronan's house stood by and cheered the men who had stormed the mansion – was it only an hour ago? – their change of allegiance would do them little good. Slaves, even expensive, exotic creatures like Elezaar, were too dangerous to keep alive.

Particularly when they could bear witness to an assassination.

Wiping his sweaty palms on his trousers, Elezaar stepped out of the alcove and made his way cautiously through the chaos of shredded bedding and broken glass to the door. He opened it a fraction and peered out. But for a toppled pedestal and a shattered vase, the hall was deserted, but there were still soldiers in the house. He could hear their distant shouts as they hunted down the last of the household staff.

Elezaar waited in the doorway, torn with indecision. Should he stay here, out of sight? Out of harm's way? Or should he venture out into the halls? Should he see if he could find anybody left alive? Perhaps the assassins had orders to spare the innocent. The dwarf smiled sourly. He might as well imagine the killers had orders to set them all free, as imagine there was any chance the slaves of the house would be spared.

Perhaps, Elezaar thought, *I should stay here, after all. Maybe the soldiers won't torch the place when they're done.* Maybe he could escape. Maybe Crys had found somewhere to hide. With their master dead, perhaps there was a chance to be truly free? If everyone thought Crysander the *court'esa* and Elezaar the dwarf had perished in the slaughter . . .

I have to get out of here. I have to find Crys.

Elezaar froze at the sound of footsteps in the hall, hurried yet fearless. He shrank back against the wall, holding his breath, his view of the hall beyond shrinking to a slit as he waited for the danger to pass. A figure moved in his limited field of vision. His heart clenched . . .

And then he almost cried with relief when he realised who it was.

'Crys!'

The tall *court'esa* turned as the dwarf called out to him in a loud hiss.

'Elezaar?'

'Thank the gods you're still alive!' Elezaar cried, looking up and down the hall furtively as he emerged from behind the door.

'It's a miracle *you're* still alive,' Crys replied, apparently unconcerned about the danger he might be in. 'How did you get away?'

'I'm small and ugly, Crys. People either don't see me or they think I'm stupid. How come you were spared?'

For a moment, Crys didn't reply. Elezaar looked up at him curiously. The brothers had always been close, even though their status as slaves had seen them separated more often than not since childhood. In fact, this was the first household they had ever served in together. Both played down the relationship, however. It didn't do to give a master any more leverage over you than he already had; particularly a master like Ronan Dell. Crysander was such a handsome young man, with his dark eyes and long dark hair. He was also blessed (or cursed) with the slender type of physique that so appealed to masters who wanted their slaves to have all the skills of a well-trained *court'esa* and yet still manage to give the impression they were an adolescent boy. Crys had suffered much in Ronan Dell's service; almost as much as Elezaar. But in different ways. And for different reasons.

The young man glanced down at Elezaar, smiling apologetically as he saw the dawning light of comprehension on the dwarf's face. Elezaar stifled a gasp. *No wonder Crys looks so unafraid. He wasn't in any danger from the assassins. He's one of them.*

'You betrayed my master.' It wasn't a question, or even an accusation. It was a statement. A simple fact.

'Not at all,' Crys said. 'I've been faithful to our master all along.'

Elezaar suddenly remembered the breastplates of the soldiers who burst into Ronan Dell's bedroom. The eagle crest of Dregian Province. He'd not had time in all the excitement to think about it before.

'We belonged to Ronan Dell, Crys.'

'*You* belonged to the House of Dell, Elezaar. I have always belonged to the House of Eaglespike.'

'And how does the old saying go? Beware an Eaglespike

bearing gifts?' Elezaar stopped abruptly as the sound of footsteps grew louder. 'We must find a better place to hide!'

'There's really no need—' Crys began, but before he could finish, a troop of soldiers rounded the corner. Elezaar began to panic, wondering if there was any point trying to make a run for it. There wasn't, he realised quickly. Crys might escape but with his short, stumpy legs, the soldiers would run him down in a few steps. The dwarf glanced up at Crys again, but the young man seemed unafraid. He simply shoved Elezaar back into the room, out of sight, then turned to the captain of the troop as the invaders approached. His heart pounding, Elezaar leaned against the wall, wondering how long it would be before he was caught. Crys might betray him in some misguided attempt to prove his loyalty to Lady Alija. Crys might betray him to save his own neck.

Or he might not. He was, after all, Elezaar's brother.

'Did you find them all?' Crys asked as the soldiers stopped in front of him.

Elezaar's heart was hammering so hard, he was sure they must be able to hear it in the hall. Through the slit in the doorway, he watched the officer in the lead sheathing his sword as he neared Crys.

'Thirty-seven slaves,' the man confirmed. 'All dead. There should be thirty-eight, counting the dwarf. We didn't find him.'

'And you won't,' Crys told them. 'He's long gone.'

'My lady wanted nobody left alive,' the captain reminded him.

'No credible witnesses,' Crys corrected. 'The Fool could stand on a table at the ball tonight in the High Prince's palace, shouting out what he'd seen here, and nobody would believe him. You needn't worry about the dwarf.'

The soldier looked doubtful, but Elezaar guessed they

were running out of time. And it was easy to believe some strange-looking, half-witted dwarf was too stupid to bear witness to their crimes. Assuming he even survived long on the streets of the city.

'I suppose,' the captain agreed doubtfully. 'What about you?'

Crys shrugged. 'My fate has been arranged for days. I've been sold. With the Feast of Kaelarn Ball going on at the palace tonight, by the time your handiwork has been discovered, I will have been safely under lock and key at Venira's Emporium for hours.'

'Then we're done here,' the captain agreed, his hand moving from the hilt of his sword to the dagger at his belt. Elezaar saw the movement – he was eye-level with the captain's waist – and opened his mouth to cry out a warning . . .

Then he clamped it shut again. To utter a sound would cost him his life. If Crys was in danger; if he couldn't see that Lady Alija would never allow a *court'esa* to live when he could testify to her direct involvement in the assassination of Ronan Dell – well, brother or not, Elezaar had no intention of sharing that danger with him. Besides, the man may simply have been moving his hand to a more comfortable position . . .

The captain's blade took Crys without warning. Elezaar's brother didn't even have time to cry out. The soldier drove the dagger up under the slave's rib cage and into his heart with businesslike efficiency. Elezaar bit down on his lip so hard it bled and turned his face to the wall, unable to watch something he had known was coming and had been powerless to prevent. He heard, rather than saw, Crys fall. Heard the creak of leather as the captain bent over to check that Crys was dead; heard the fading stamp of booted feet and the scrape of sandals against the polished floors as the soldiers retreated, dragging Crysander's body behind them.

Elezaar stayed facing the wall for a long, long time.

It was dusk before Elezaar found the courage to move. In that time, the room full of death where he waited had filled with the buzz of hungry flies, attracted to the feast laid out for them.

Immobilised by fear though he was, Elezaar had not wasted his time. His body was still but his mind had been racing, formulating and then discarding one plan after another.

The first thing he had to do was find somewhere safe, and for a *court'esa* bonded to a house that had just been wiped out, that was not going to be easy. The slave collar he wore would betray him if he tried to flee into the city. Even if Elezaar could find refuge among the homeless and the unwanted on Greenharbour's streets, they were too hungry and too desperate to shelter him for long. Particularly if there was a profit to be made by turning him in.

No. If he wanted to survive this, he needed protection. And Elezaar intended to survive this. He had a score to settle. His brother may have been a misguided fool, thinking he could betray one master for another, but his life had been worth more than a swift knife to the belly, just to keep him quiet.

Protection. That was what Elezaar needed. But who would protect a slave? More to the point, who would protect a Loronged *court'esa*? A dwarf *court'esa* at that?

Someone who will profit from it, Elezaar realised. What had Crys told the captain? *My fate has been arranged for days. I've been sold. With the Feast of Kaelarn Ball going on at the palace tonight, by the time your handiwork has been discovered, I will have been safely under lock and key at Venira's Emporium for hours.*

Elezaar finally found the courage to move.

Venira. The slave trader, he thought, as he opened the door. He stopped and looked down at Crys's blood pooled on the floor. Tears misted his vision for a moment. Elezaar wiped them away impatiently. He was too hardened to grieve for his brother. There was too much pain down that road. The dwarf looked away and forced himself to keep moving. It was almost dark. If he was caught on the streets alone after the slave curfew, he'd be in serious trouble. Or someone might come looking for Ronan Dell. He was expected at the ball tonight. The High Prince might send someone to fetch him if he didn't show.

And Venira's slave emporium closed at sunset. If Elezaar couldn't get to the slave quarter before the slaver left for the night, he ran the risk of a night in the streets, one he was quite certain he wouldn't survive.

Safety lay, Elezaar knew, with the slave trader. He'd already bought and paid for a Loronged *court'esa* from Ronan Dell. Elezaar would see that Venira got his merchandise. As arranged.

Just not the *court'esa* he was expecting, that's all.

FOR THE LATEST NEWS AND THE HOTTEST EXCLUSIVES ON ALL
YOUR FAVOURITE SF AND FANTASY STARS, SIGN UP FOR:

ORBIT'S <u>FREE</u> MONTHLY E-ZINE

PACKED WITH

BREAKING NEWS
THE LATEST REVIEWS
EXCLUSIVE INTERVIEWS
STUNNING EXTRACTS
SPECIAL OFFERS
BRILLIANT COMPETITIONS

AND A GALAXY OF
NEW AND ESTABLISHED SFF STARS!

TO GET A DELICIOUS SLICE OF SFF IN <u>YOUR</u> INBOX EVERY MONTH, SEND YOUR
DETAILS BY EMAIL TO: <u>ORBIT@LITTLEBROWN.CO.UK</u> OR VISIT:

 WWW.ORBITBOOKS.NET
THE HOME OF SFF ONLINE